LISA JACKSON

"Why did you come here, Max?"

"I'd like to lie to you, Skye, and tell you that
I stopped by to check on the lease.... But the truth
of the matter is, after I found the letter and saw you
again, I couldn't stay away."

—*A Is for Always*

"Where is he, Beth?"

"Where is who?"

"The kid who's supposed to be my son,"
Jenner growled.

—*B Is for Baby*

"I thought we should get to know each other."

"Why?" Sloan demanded.

"Because...because..."

"Because we made love," he said, finishing for Casey.

—*C Is for Cowboy*

Love Letters—Sometimes all it takes
is a letter of love to rebuild dreams of the past.

Books by Lisa Jackson

Silhouette Special Edition

A Twist of Fate #118
The Shadow of Time #180
Tears of Pride #194
Pirate's Gold #215
A Dangerous Precedent #233
Innocent by Association #244
Midnight Sun #264
Devil's Gambit #282
Zachary's Law #296
Yesterday's Lies #315
One Man's Love #358
Renegade Son #376
Snowbound #394
Summer Rain #419
Hurricane Force #467
In Honor's Shadow #495
Aftermath #525
Tender Trap #569
With No Regrets #611
Double Exposure #636
Mystery Man #653
Obsession #691
Sail Away #720
Million Dollar Baby #743
*He's a Bad Boy #787
*He's Just a Cowboy #799
*He's the Rich Boy #811
A Husband To Remember #835
*He's My Soldier Boy #866
†A Is for Always #914
†B Is for Baby #920
†C Is for Cowboy #926
†D Is for Dani's Baby #985
New Year's Daddy #1004
‡A Family Kind of Guy #1191
‡A Family Kind of Gal #1207
‡A Family Kind of Wedding #1219

Silhouette Intimate Moments

Dark Side of the Moon #39
Gypsy Wind #79
Mystic #158

Silhouette Romance

His Bride To Be #717

Silhouette Books

Silhouette Christmas Stories 1993
"The Man from Pine Mountain"

Fortune's Children
The Millionaire and the Cowgirl

Montana Mavericks: Wed in
    Whitehorn
Lone Stallion's Lady

*Mavericks
†Love Letters
‡Forever Family

LISA JACKSON

Love Letters

Silhouette® Books

Published by Silhouette Books
America's Publisher of Contemporary Romance

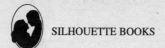 SILHOUETTE BOOKS

ISBN 0-373-20177-X

by Request

LOVE LETTERS

Copyright © 2000 by Harlequin Books S.A.

The publisher acknowledges the copyright holders of the individual works as follows:

A IS FOR ALWAYS
Copyright © 1994 by Susan Crose

B IS FOR BABY
Copyright © 1994 by Susan Crose

C IS FOR COWBOY
Copyright © 1994 by Susan Crose

Printed in U.S.A.

CONTENTS

A IS FOR ALWAYS   9

B IS FOR BABY   253

C IS FOR COWBOY   501

Dear Reader,

How exciting that Silhouette decided to reprint the LOVE LETTERS series! Many of you wrote to me requesting one or more of the books that you had missed when the series was first published. Now you have the first three books all in one volume!

When I first started thinking about writing the LOVE LETTERS stories for Silhouette, I began envisioning a unique and very rugged ranching family, headed by an iron-fisted patriarch. I had been vacationing with my parents in eastern Oregon and was taken with the beauty of the vast countryside, even going so far as to name my fictitious town after the breathtaking outcropping of rimrock that topped some of the mountains.

I wanted all the books to be tied together not just by location or family members, but by a series of letters between the characters in the books. And so the love stories for Max and Skye in *A Is for Always*, Beth and Jenner in *B Is for Baby* and Casey and Sloan in *C Is for Cowboy* evolved.

On a personal note, I named some of the characters in the books after beloved pets in my neighborhood. That's right. Kiki, Kimo and, yes, even Casey, Jenner, Max and Skye, have four-footed namesakes with unique characteristics. As you can see, I had a lot of fun writing this series.

The LOVE LETTERS stories are some of my favorites, and judging from the abundance of mail I received about them, they were yours, as well. So, whether you're a first-time visitor to Rimrock, Oregon, or returning to catch up on old friends in a unique Western town, welcome!

Lisa Jackson

A IS FOR ALWAYS

Prologue

Rimrock, Oregon
Summer—1991

Max,

If you're reading this, then I'm already gone and all my plans have been for nothing. I've made a lot of mistakes in my life, but I won't apologize for doing what I thought was right for you...for all of my children.

You know, son, I always favored you over your brother. Because you were my first, I suppose. Whether this be right or wrong, only God can decide.

I want you to know that I loved you and only wanted the best for you. That's why Skye Donahue left town. I forced her to go and I stand by my decision. She was the wrong woman for you, Max. She was too hot tempered, too much trouble.

But I thought you should know that when she left she

wasn't really running from you. She was running from me and what I threatened to do to her and her family if she ever came back looking for you. And I expect she will.

I don't regret what I did. She wasn't the right woman for you then and she probably isn't the right woman for you now.

But I thought you should know.

I've enclosed a letter that she left for you.

Your father,
Jonah P. McKee

July—1987

Dearest Max,

As I write this I'm telling myself that I'm doing the right thing—the best thing for both of us. Though I'll never love a man as I love you, I can't live here any longer.

So I hope you'll forgive me for leaving. I really don't have a choice.

I've been wrestling with this decision for two days. Should I stay and tell you all the reasons I had for leaving? Should I take a chance on our love and damn the consequences?

It's a painful decision, but I know that it's best that I go, Max. You have your life here in Rimrock and I have mine somewhere far away.

I know you'd say that I'm running away and maybe I am, but this is something I must do. For you. For me.

Believe that I cherish the moments we had together and that, no matter what happens, a part of me will love you forever.

Always,
Skye

Chapter One

Rimrock, Oregon
1994

Curling the yellowed pages in his fist, Max McKee swore beneath his breath and kicked a dirt clod across the pasture. The dry piece of earth landed with a thunk on the side of the stables and shattered into dust. Barn swallows, disturbed from their nests, squawked and dive-bombed the intruder, but he didn't give a damn.

He hadn't for a long time.

But the letters changed things.

He'd discovered the aged pages earlier while going through the old man's business papers, and there, in a thin file labeled MAX, were two handwritten notes that could have changed the course of his life. Max had read the damning words in his father's den, then heard his mother's soft crying whispering through the hallways of the old ranch house. Rather than disturb her grief, he'd walked outside, read each letter again and felt as if a vise had been clamped over his lungs and was slowly being tightened, ensuring that each one of his breaths was more difficult than the last.

"Bastard," he snarled, disregarding the fact that deep down he'd felt a kinship with the crusty old man who'd been his father—Jonah Phineas McKee. The great manipulator.

But it wasn't Jonah's letter that disturbed him most. It was the other single sheet with the flowing script signed by a woman he detested, a woman who had betrayed him, a woman for whom, at one time, he would have walked through the gates of hell just to see her smile.

His back teeth ground together as he remembered her as clearly as if she were standing beside him. Her loose blond curls caught in the summer wind, and wide eyes the color of a morning mist sparkled with an impish light whenever she teased him. Her laughter seemed to roll off the surrounding hills. Her chin stubborn, her mouth wide and sensuous, she stood nearly five foot eight, with a slim and athletic body honed by years of hard work.

She'd left him seven years before, and he'd never really understood why.

"Face it, son, she just wasn't the right woman for you. Too serious about that damned career of hers, too proud to admit when she'd made a mistake."

His father's sentiments had always been spoken brashly, without hesitation.

"She reminded me of one of them wolf dogs, you know the kind they've got down at the Purcell place," Jonah had continued, his dark brows inching up to his shock of thick, snow-white hair. "Them dogs are deceptive—all cuddly and soft as puppies, cute as all get-out. But watch out. Those damned pups turn into killers, like as not. Remember Amy Purcell nearly lost half her face to one of them she-wolves. Yep, you're better off without the likes of Skye Donahue.''

Max, after his initial denial, had finally decided his father was right about Skye. He'd told himself that Jonah had pegged Skye from the start, though, more often than not in recent years, Max had found himself at odds with his father and had started second-guessing his own loyalties. For years, Max, firstborn and groomed to inherit most of Jonah's estate, had believed that his father walked on water, a veritable god on earth. But as the years passed and he grew more independent, Max began to see Jonah with new eyes. He realized his cantankerous father wasn't as innocent as he would have everyone believe. Sure, Jonah had been a colorful character, as rugged and rough as the outcrop of rimrock that topped the hills surrounding this valley, but Jonah had also possessed a darker side, one Max had begun to discover and one he'd steadfastly ignored. Or been too blind to see.

Maybe Skye had been right all along.

Hell!

He brushed off his dust-covered hat and rammed it onto his head. The sun was beginning to set, the heat that had shimmered across the dry grass was letting up a little, and shadows stretched over the fields. Max decided he had to quit thinking of his father, of Skye, of the letters.

The damned letters.

He should burn them both and let the wind carry the ashes away, but he didn't. Instead he took the wadded-up pages and tossed them through the open window of his pickup where they floated onto the worn seat. He'd think about the letters later. Much later.

The screen door banged open and Max's sister Casey careened from the house. "There's just no talking to her!" Casey declared, blowing her bangs from her eyes. Petite, with shoulder-length brown hair and a temper that wouldn't quit, Casey stormed across the porch, stomped down the two steps, and landed on a lawn chair. She crossed her legs and bounced her foot up and down in frustration. "Idiot!"

"You're talking about Mom."

"Damn it, Max, do you know what she's trying to get me to believe now? *Do you?*"

"I hate to ask."

"She thinks Dad was murdered!" Casey looked up at the dusky sky, as if hoping God would send a lightning bolt straight from heaven and knock some sense into their mother. "Murdered! Like *anyone* has ever been killed in Rimrock!"

"There was Indian Joe."

Casey rolled her eyes. "He was ninety-five years old, blind, and he walked in front of a logging truck! Elvin Green didn't mean to run him over."

"I was just trying to calm you down."

"Well, you can't!" She shot out of her chair and marched up to her brother. Jabbing the air emphatically, she said, "Mom's gone 'round the bend on this one."

"She's still upset. It's only been a week."

Casey shook her head furiously. "She's beyond upset and plans on calling Myrna Cassidy, the reporter for *The Rimrock Review.* Oh, I can see it now. Inch-high letters screaming that Dad was killed by some unknown murderer. You know that Myrna's always looking for something more exciting to write about besides the school-bond measures and the county fair! She'll print this…this ridiculous theory of Mom's in a heartbeat—"

"Hold on a minute! Give Mom a break, will you?" Max closed his eyes against a sudden headache. "She's not going to go spouting off to the papers—"

"You'd better stop her! She won't listen to me." Casey tossed her hair out of her eyes and headed toward the barn. "I'm goin' for a ride. Tell Kiki not to hold supper."

"I don't think she'll worry about it."

Kiki, the gray-haired housekeeper who'd been with the McKees for as long as Max could remember, wasn't likely to keep anything warming. Long ago, Kiki had made it clear she thought all the McKee children—Max, his brother, Jenner, and Casey—were spoiled, and she wasn't about to take part in their pampering.

Max stalked into the house and found Kiki fussing over some peach dumplings bubbling on the stove. The aromas of cinnamon, cloves and nutmeg mingled and wafted through the old ranch-house walls, reminding Max of happier, simpler times, when he'd been a kid. Life then had been working in the fields, skinny-dipping in the swimming hole, fishing until dark, sneaking a smoke, and constantly wrestling with his brother. Later, as the years had piled up, he'd spent more time wondering about the mysteries of all females and Skye Donahue in particular.

"You'd better go see after your ma. She's carryin' on somethin' fierce!" Kiki didn't bother looking up from her kettle. "Damned peaches, trying to turn to mush on me. And don't you wear your boots on my clean floor. Curse it all, anyway."

Leaving his hat on a peg by the back door, Max walked swiftly down the hall of the rambling ranch house he'd lived in for twenty of his thirty-five years. Virginia McKee's sobs coaxed him around the corner and past the den to the master bedroom. Bracing himself, he rapped his knuckles on the double doors. He didn't wait for a response but slipped into the room where his mother and father had laughed, cried, made love, and argued loudly enough to shake the rafters of the sprawling old house.

Virginia McKee was sitting on the edge of the bed she'd shared with Jonah for only six months before Max had been born. She'd been pregnant when she'd gotten married, a secret she'd have preferred to have kept hidden, but her husband hadn't given a rat's hind leg who'd known the truth. He'd been proud of his virility, prouder still when he'd fathered a son.

Virginia was a small woman with fine bones and a slight figure. She was huddled into a little ball, her arms wrapped around her middle. "Why?" she asked in a whisper that cut straight to Max's heart.

"I don't know, Mom. It just happened."

"I don't think so. He wouldn't have been so careless. He was murdered, Max. I know it. I...just know it." Staring sightlessly down at her wedding ring, she gnawed on her lower lip. Tears began to rain from her eyes.

"Have you taken a tranquilizer? Doc Fletcher—"

"I'm not taking any drugs! Besides, that old sawbones thinks a pill will solve everything. A pill to sleep, another one to wake up, one to quiet a fast-beating heart, one to keep you from running to the bathroom every ten minutes... Oh, Lord, I'm prattling on about useless things when there's so much to do."

"The funeral's over, Mom. You can relax." He sat on the bed beside her and the mattress creaked with his weight. "You should rest. Get your strength back."

"He was killed, Max."

"No—"

"Someone murdered him."

Max rubbed a hand over his forehead. "He was drunk. He'd had five or six stiff drinks down at the Black Anvil. Jake, the bartender, thought about taking his keys, but didn't. Dad left, driving too fast. He lost control, couldn't make the corner, and the Jeep wound up at the bottom of Stardust Canyon. End of story."

Virginia shook her head. Her lips pulled together as if drawn by invisible strings. "I tell you, he was killed, Max."

Max closed his eyes and pinched the bridge of his nose. "Okay, Mom, just for the sake of argument, let's say someone tried to murder him. Okay?"

"They did!"

"How? Did they wrestle the wheel away from him and somehow make the Jeep leap the guardrail? Did they force him off the road? How?"

"I...I don't know," she said stubbornly.

"The sheriff's department—"

"Hasn't found anything, I know. But they just haven't looked hard enough!" She stood, maintaining her balance by holding on to one of the carved bedposts. "I know your father. He could hold his liquor. He'd driven that road a thousand times."

"Mom, his luck just plain ran out."

"So you won't help me on this."

"It doesn't serve any purpose."

Her eyes blinked rapidly. "I can't believe that you won't do something. Casey, well, there's no talking to her. She's such a…well, so stubborn, and Jenner, God knows he doesn't much care about the family. Never did. Always had to play the part of the rebel. But you…you were your father's pride and joy, the son who always did what was right—"

"I'm no saint, Mom," Max cut in, feeling the old, hard-edged emotions beginning to tear at him. "And I gave up being one of Dad's yes-men years ago."

"Still, you believed in him, and damn it, he believed in you. The least you could do is talk to Sheriff Polk, find out what really happened out on Elkhorn Ridge."

"Nothing happened, Mom. Dad just misjudged the corner."

She cut him a glance that silently called him a fool, and he stood to turn down the bed. "Come on, Mom." Patting the crisp percale sheets, he said softly, "Take your shoes off. Try to get some rest."

"I will not be coddled, son! And I'll go to bed when I'm good and ready and not a minute before." Sniffing back her tears, she angled up her thin face, glaring at her firstborn. "You do what you have to, Max, and so will I."

"Mom—"

"Don't you worry about me—I can take care of myself. And bring Hillary around more often. Just because Jonah is gone doesn't mean that I won't want to see my granddaughter.'' She dropped into an antique rocker positioned near the bay window.

"I'll have her this weekend."

His mother snorted. "A weekend father. I always thought more of you than that, Max."

He wasn't going to get into this no-win argument. If he'd had his way, Hillary would live with him, but Colleen had fought him in court and won joint custody, which meant she kept Hillary five days out of the week and Max got the leftovers. The important thing was that his daughter seemed to be doing fine. He'd heard somewhere that kids were resilient. He hoped so. If a child was loved, Max believed the rest would take care of itself. Both he and Colleen loved their daughter; they just didn't love each other. Probably never had.

Guilt was razor sharp as it cut through his heart.

He'd been at fault—the one to blame when the marriage had crumbled. He'd never really gotten over Skye, no matter how much he'd told himself that he had. She'd betrayed him, and he, wounded to the depths of his soul, had turned to Colleen to survive.

His father had been pleased.

But the marriage had been doomed from the start.

And now there were the letters...the damned letters. He felt as if acid had been poured into his gut because, until he found out the truth about Skye and why she'd left him, he'd never be satisfied.

He kissed his mother goodbye and left her sitting in the rocker staring sightlessly out the window to the dry, rolling fields dotted with white-faced Herefords. Somehow the ranch would survive. He wasn't so sure about his mother.

Avoiding further conversation with Kiki, he snatched his hat from its hook and strode outside to his pickup. He climbed in and saw the wadded-up letters on the seat. Growling an oath under his breath, he switched on the ignition and tromped on the accelerator. Within seconds, he was tearing down the lane at a breakneck pace, dust and gravel spewing behind him, pine trees and fence line flashing by in a blur.

He didn't want to think about Skye. Not now. Not ever. Thoughts heading in her direction invariably led to dangerous territory. Besides, what was done was done. If he'd wanted her—*really* wanted her—back then, he would have gone after her, wouldn't he have?

Frowning darkly, he switched on the radio, looking for sports scores. Instead, a Bruce Springsteen song of love gone bad drifted out of the speakers. *Tell me about it, Bruce,* Max thought grimly as he squinted through the dusty, bug-spattered windshield.

The asphalt road he barreled along on stretched for miles in either direction, a straight, paved line that cut through this valley where the John Day River flowed swiftly between the rolling hills of dry grass and sparse juniper trees.

When he finally reached town, he stopped at the feed store, bought several sacks of grain and loaded them into his truck before walking the short distance to the Black Anvil. Where his father, just the week before, had consumed too much liquor before ending up at the bottom of Stardust Canyon, the nose of his Jeep plunged deep into the swift waters of Wildcat Creek. Jonah's blood alcohol level had been near the stratosphere, he'd cracked his head on the windshield and died of heart failure, according to the county medical examiner. Jonah Phineas McKee, a Rimrock legend, had died, and the town had mourned.

Max would miss him, though for the past few years they hadn't gotten along.

Ever since Skye.

Shoving open the swinging doors to the bar, Max strode past the cigarette machine to the interior where smoke hung in a hazy cloud near the ceiling and the air-conditioning system clattered and coughed. Men, just off work, clustered at the bar where they eyed a television suspended from the ceiling, sipped from frosted mugs of beer, picked at complimentary pretzels, and complained about the game, the weather and their wives.

Max ordered a beer and slid into a booth near the window. He stared outside, past a flickering neon sign advertising beer, to the street where heat waves rose like ghosts, though the sun was beginning to dip below the mountains.

"Didn't expect to find you here."

Max lifted one side of his mouth at the sound of his brother's voice. "Can't say the same for you."

Jenner, a half-filled mug of beer in hand, slipped onto the opposite bench. Two years younger than Max, Jenner had always been the rebel, never doing one damned thing that was expected of him. Didn't even finish high school—just up and left to join the rodeo circuit. A cowboy's cowboy, he had only come home to roost a few years ago when his body, barely thirty, had been broken and taped together too many times from tumbling off wild broncs and Brahma bulls or crashing into the fists of indignant husbands. "Yeah, well, someone's got to keep this place in business," Jenner drawled with his go-to-hell smile stretching from one side of his face to the other.

Max and Jenner had been oil and water. Max, for years, had always tried to please their old man, while Jenner had done his best to thwart Jonah at every turn. If Jonah said white, then Max would say ivory, and Jenner was sure to bring up black.

"Mom thinks Dad was murdered," Max said, then, watching the foamy head of his beer sink into the amber depths, took a long swallow. The liquor was cool and malty and settled deep in his gut.

Jenner lifted a shoulder. "He had enough enemies."

"No one killed him, Jenner."

"Probably not."

"Probably?" Max couldn't believe his ears.

"Contrary to what you'd like to believe, the old man

was, well, borderline honest, would be the best way to put it. We both know it.''

Max didn't want to be reminded of his father's less-than-aboveboard dealings. "I know, but murder—''

"I'm not saying it happened. I'm just saying it's possible." He finished his beer and signaled for another round by lifting a finger. The waitress, a buxom woman named Wanda Tulley, winked at him. She was poured into a red-checked blouse and tight denim miniskirt. Her black boots reached midcalf on tanned legs that seemed to go on forever. A couple of years younger than Jenner, Wanda had been through two bad marriages and had been cursed with a crush on the younger McKee brother for as long as Max could remember. Max only hoped Jenner wasn't taking advantage of her affections—he seemed to have no sense of responsibility when it came to women.

"Here ya go, sugar," Wanda said, flipping her straight silver blond hair over her shoulder.

"Thanks. Put 'em both on my tab."

"You got it."

She slid the fresh mugs onto the table, then picked up the empties, allowing Jenner and Max a quick glimpse of the top of her breasts as she bent over, the red gingham of her blouse parting slightly.

As she left, Jenner ignored his beer. "I thought you should know…" he said, pausing as if something weighty was on his mind.

"Know what?"

"I ran into Doc Fletcher a little while ago. Seems he's taking on a new partner. Maybe even selling his practice."

"About time." Fletcher had to be pushing seventy and had been looking for a younger general practitioner to eventually take over his business. However, in today's world, most of the medical profession was specialized, and nearly all of the newly graduated doctors preferred to practice in the cities and suburbs where the money was better and the services of hospitals were close at hand.

Few were interested in a small clinic hundreds of miles from a major city.

"He said he wanted to go over some details on his lease with you. The estate owns the clinic building, doesn't it?"

"Yep, but Fletcher can link up with anyone he likes. Long as he pays the lease, I don't have anything to say about it."

Jenner's grin was downright evil. The first premonition of disaster skittered down Max's spine.

"Okay, so tell me. Who's the guy?"

"Not a guy," Jenner said, his gaze steady on his brother. "A woman. Not long out of medical school."

Max felt as if some great hand had wrapped around his chest and was slowly squeezing, because before the words were out of Jenner's mouth, he knew what they would be.

"Yep," Jenner drawled, little lines of worry forming between his dark eyebrows, "word has it that Skye Donahue's finally coming back to Rimrock."

Chapter Two

Skye rolled down the window of her '67 Ford Mustang, then scowled as the handle snapped off in her hand. "Some classic," she muttered, tossing the broken piece of metal onto the passenger seat already filled with her medical textbooks, notes and a bag of half-eaten French fries from the McDonald's she'd driven through before leaving Portland.

She'd been in the car five hours and her muscles were beginning to cramp, but she wasn't tired. No, as the miles leading to Rimrock disappeared beneath the balding tires of her little car, she felt a growing edge of anticipation. Adrenaline clamped her fingers around the wheel while she tried to ignore the feeling that she was making the biggest mistake of her life—second biggest, she reminded herself. The first was falling in love with Max McKee. Clenching her teeth together, she shoved aside the little tug on her heart at the thought of him. She didn't have time for second thoughts about Max. She'd been young and foolish. She was lucky she'd forced herself to forgo listening to her heart and refused to marry him.

Max McKee may well have been her first love, but he certainly wasn't going to be her last! Not that she needed a man. Being an independent woman had its advantages. She never had to worry about disappointing anyone else in her life, and if there was a void—an emptiness that sometimes seemed impossible to fill—well, that was all part of the choices she'd made. She wasn't the type of woman to moan and cry about lost loves or missed opportunities.

From the carrier in the back seat, her cat, Kildare, let out an impatient cry.

"Not much farther," Skye called over her shoulder. The cat, named for the doctor in Skye's mother's favorite medical show of all time, sent up another plaintive wail, but Skye ignored him and stared through her grimy windshield to the gorgeous Ochoco Mountains. The road edged the river as it cut a severe canyon through the towering hills topped with the stony red outcrop that had given the town of Rimrock its name.

The wind teased her hair and she rarely saw another car. She'd missed this—the solitude, the majestic stillness of the mountains, the peaceful quiet of the countryside—while she'd spent the past few years of her life in the frenetic pace of the city. Portland wasn't a large town compared with New York, Chicago or Seattle, but for a girl who had grown up in a community with a population of less than a thousand people corralled within the city limits, Portland had seemed immense, charged with an invisible current of electricity. The streets were a madhouse where drivers surged from one red light to the next, anxiously drumming fingers on steering wheels, smoking or chewing gum or growling under their breath about the traffic. Where the smell of exhaust fumes mingled with rainwater. Where night was as bright as day.

At first, she'd loved the city, the change of pace, the

demands of medical school. In her few precious hours of free time, she'd explored every nook and cranny of the restless town, indulging in the nightlife, the theaters, the museums, the concerts in Waterfront Park. She'd learned, as a matter of self-preservation, to be suspicious of nearly everyone in the city, and yet she'd met some of the most honest and true friends of her life while studying to become a doctor.

And yet she was drawn back home.

"Home." She mouthed the word and it felt good.

She hadn't been forced to return to the hills of eastern Oregon. She'd had options when she'd graduated and could have joined the staff of several hospitals in the Pacific Northwest, and another in Denver. Instead, after a year with Columbia Memorial, she'd decided to nose her little car due east and accept Doc Fletcher's offer to buy out his practice in Rimrock.

Because of Max. Because there's unfinished business between you.

Her fingers began to sweat over the steering wheel and she snapped her mind closed to that particular thought. Max was married, and she, perhaps romantic to the point of being an idiot, believed in the sanctity of marriage. Although her father was no longer alive, her parents had shown her love, laughter, trust and commitment.

So Max McKee was off-limits. Good. Even if he was still single, she wouldn't have wanted him. She'd never met a more stubborn, arrogant man in all her life. A man just like his father. Her stomach turned over at the thought of Jonah McKee and she shoved his image out of her mind. She would have preferred a practice somewhere in eastern Oregon farther away from Max, but Doc Fletcher's unexpected visit to Portland and his offer had been too tempting to turn down.

"We need young, dedicated, talented people, Skye," he'd said in his slow-moving drawl, his words punctuated by snowy white eyebrows that dipped and rose above the gold rims of his glasses. "But most young doctors aren't interested in a Podunk town so small you can drive through without blinking. So I thought you might want to come back home, be near your mother. I can offer you pretty good terms. Hell, I've made my money there, so I won't need a down payment on the business—and you're really just buying the practice. I lease the building, but there's an option to buy in a couple of years. We'll work out the contract so that you can pay me a balloon payment in five years...." He'd gone on and on, and though Skye had thought she'd turn him down flat, the deal had been too sweet to refuse. Fletcher had been right when he'd mentioned her mother. Irene Donahue, not yet sixty, wasn't in the best of health, and Skye did want to be close to her. In the end, Skye had agreed. She didn't regret her decision. The only hitch was Max.

As the road curved to accommodate the river and the mountains, she caught her first glimpse of Rimrock, little more than several blocks of buildings clustered around a single stoplight. She drove past the turnoff for the old copper mine and headed straight through the heart of town, past the small buildings, some ancient, some new, where afternoon shadows were slinking across the dusty asphalt streets.

On an impulse, she stopped at the Shady Grove Café, parked beneath an old oak tree and cracked open her windows before stepping onto the pockmarked asphalt of the lot. She set Kildare in his carrier in the shade of the tree, then walked to the twin glass doors of the old restaurant. An A-frame building with wings, the café had been through owners and names too numerous to remember.

Inside, the air conditioner rattled a noisy welcome. Several booths were occupied, but Skye didn't recognize anyone. The place smelled of stale coffee and cigarette smoke, while the deep fryer added its own special aroma. She slid into a booth near the window, and despite all the efforts of the air conditioner, the heat seeped through the glass and the clear, black plastic curtain that had been drawn to offer some shade.

A short waitress with a frizz of brown curls took Skye's order for a cola, then hustled, order pad and pencil in hand, to the next table. As it was the middle of the afternoon, the lunch crowd had dispersed and the dinner crowd hadn't yet arrived.

Within minutes, the waitress left a sweating glass of soda and a bill on the table before passing through swinging doors to the kitchen. Skye took a long swallow as she studied the menu that hadn't changed much in the past seven years. A bell tinkled and a gust of hot air whooshed into the room.

"I want chocolate and vanilla swirled together," an impish voice commanded.

"Then that's what you'll have."

Max! She'd know his voice anywhere—it still haunted her dreams and played with those memories that she'd sworn to tuck away forever. She froze for a second, then quietly took a breath and glanced up. Their gazes collided, and if she hadn't known better, she would have sworn there was a tremor in the earth. Her heart kicked into double time as she looked at him, tall and lean as ever, wide shoulders hidden by a time-softened work shirt, his brown hair still streaked by the sun. Raw as the wind that swept through this part of the valley and rugged as the hills that surrounded the river, Max McKee generated a kind of sexual energy that should have been reserved for movie stars and professional athletes. His lips were thin, nearly cruel, and the spark in his eyes was as cold as a Blue Norther.

Skye could barely breathe. She reached for her drink, nearly toppling it over onto the table.

His large, work-roughened hand was clasped around the chubby fingers of a springy-haired girl of five or six. *His daughter.* An ageless pain ripped through Skye's soul as she stared, speechless, at man and child.

She was vaguely aware that the other patrons had turned their heads, drawn to the silent scene unfolding in front of the counter.

Max, as if suddenly aware that he was causing a stir, pulled on the little girl's hand and guided her toward the booth where Skye sat frozen. His features, already hard angles and planes, seemed to turn more grim, and his eyes, shaded by thick gold-brown brows, were the same piercing, angry sea green that she remembered.

He slid onto the bench of her booth and glared at her without a speck of joy. "I heard you were coming back," he said without so much as a hello.

"Bad news travels fast."

He snorted. "The big city lose its attraction?"

"Something like that."

"Max, what'll it be?" The heavyset waitress appeared, pad and pencil ready, smile wide for the son of one of the richest men in the county.

"Coffee for me. A swirl cone for—"

"In a dish!" the child insisted.

"In a dish," he repeated, "for Hillary."

Hillary. A beautiful name for a pretty little girl.

"That's it?" the waitress—her name tag read Sarah—asked, smiling broadly, almost flirting with Max.

"That's it."

Sarah scooted away, leaving a yawning silence. Skye fiddled with her glass but managed what she hoped seemed like a genuine smile. "So, you're Hillary," she said, turning her attention to the curly-haired sprite who was playing with the salt-and-pepper shakers.

"Who're you?" the imp asked.

"This is Skye…Donahue?" he asked, then glanced pointedly at her ringless left hand. "*Dr.* Donahue."

Skye lifted a shoulder. "You can call me—"

"Dr. Donahue," Max cut in.

"You can't be a doctor," Hillary said, her little brow puckering in concentration.

"Why not?"

"You're a girl."

"A woman," her father corrected as his eyes locked with Skye's for an instant. Skye felt her pulse pounding in her throat. A tickle of a memory, of a dewy field and wild flowers, of sunshine and laughter, of kisses and cold wine, touched at her mind, but she shoved it steadfastly away. She would not, *would not,* remember all those rose-colored memories of her first love with the man bold enough to seat himself squarely across from her. The man who had turned out to be as ruthless as his father.

"That's right," Skye said, forcing herself to concentrate on the conversation, "but just because I'm a woman—or you're a girl—doesn't mean you can't do anything you want to."

"I don't want to be a doctor." Hillary wrinkled her nose at the prospect and grabbed her spoon. "I *hate* shots!"

Skye couldn't help but smile. "What do you want to be?"

"A bride!"

Skye's throat turned to sand. "A...a bride. Well, I suppose you can do that, but—"

"But you might want to have a backup plan, just in case things don't go the way you think they will," Max said to his daughter, though the words, spoken so coldly, could only have been meant for Skye.

Sarah brought Max his coffee and his daughter a towering dish of already-melting soft ice cream. Hillary, rather than accept a booster chair, knelt instead and, half-bouncing on the plastic-covered seat of the booth, dug into the sweet confection.

Stretching a jean-clad leg out to the side of the booth, Max said, "It surprises me—you coming back here. I thought you couldn't stand the sight of this place."

"It was time."

"Why?"

She bristled a little, then decided not to let her temper get the better of her. "Family. And Doc Fletcher's offer. It was hard to pass up."

He looked about to say something, but changed his mind and picked up his cup. "Not as much money as you could make in the city."

"There are some trade-offs."

"Are there?" He took a long swallow from his cup, and Skye tried not to stare at the movement in his throat. But she couldn't help feel the weight of his gaze and was suddenly more nervous than she had been in years. "You know, Skye, there are lots of small towns all along the west coast, towns that need medical professionals. You didn't have to come back to Rimrock."

Her temper started to rise. "I chose to, Max."

"And why's that?"

"My family's here."

"They've been here for the past seven years."

"Doc Fletcher offered to sell out."

Max smiled slightly as if he knew something she didn't. "He's been lookin' for a partner for a long time."

"But I wasn't ready."

"There must be more of a reason, Skye," he said, and for the first time she saw a spark of amusement in his eyes. He was baiting her and she knew it.

"Don't make more of it than it is, Max." She finished her drink, left a bill on the table, and when he began to protest, she cut him with a quick, scathing look that had kept more than one randy resident at bay. "Look, Max, I heard about your dad...I'm sorry."

"Are you?" His eyes narrowed up at her, challenging her.

Standing, she bit back the hot retort on her tongue. "Goodbye, Hillary, it was nice meeting you," she said, managing a tight smile for Max's daughter.

"Are you mad?" Hillary asked before Skye could escape the booth. Chocolate and vanilla were smeared over her lips and chin.

"Of course not."

"You look mad. Just like Mommy every time—"

"Enough, Hillary," Max snapped, his face flushed with a silent rage.

"You hate Mommy," Hillary said, and her little face crumpled. Tears rose in the corners of her eyes and she dropped her spoon.

"No, honey, I don't—"

Skye felt immediately contrite. What was she doing, letting herself be pulled into some infantile argument with a man who meant nothing, *nothing* to her? "I—I'm sorry, Max. I didn't mean—"

"It's not your fault," he retorted, snatching a napkin from the dispenser and tending to the ice cream and tears on Hillary's face.

"I..." She felt suddenly useless. She was a mature woman, a doctor, for crying out loud. She'd worked in emergency rooms, helped save lives, lost a few, told patients when their diseases were life threatening, and even consoled the grieving. Yet this one man, this one damnably arrogant man, and his imp of a daughter had reduced her to fumbling and stumbling and muttering apologies that she didn't mean. "I didn't expect to run into you this soon—"

"Just leave, Skye," he said coldly, his jaw suddenly as hard as granite. "It's what you do best."

She didn't need to hear anything else. Already a few eyebrows had risen behind the plastic-coated menus, and she felt more than one curious glance cast in her direction. She wasn't making a good impression. As the new doctor in town, she couldn't appear rash or quick-tempered or tongue-tied, or anything but a levelheaded professional. These people would have to trust her, depend upon her decisions when they were injured or when one of their loved ones was dying. She stiffened and managed what she hoped was a clinical smile. "I'll see you," she said to Max, though the words had a hollow and familiar ring to them.

"Sure."

She walked out the door and into the blasting heat. Grinding her teeth together, she marched to the patch of shade where she'd parked and flung open the car door. She wedged the cat carrier on the back seat and wished to high heaven that she'd never set eyes on Max McKee. Inside the sweltering interior of the Mustang, she turned on the ignition, praying under her breath as the engine coughed and sputtered then finally, with a wheeze, turned over.

"Thank you, God," Skye said as Kildare mewed loudly. Backing out of the parking space, she caught a glimpse of Max's rough-hewn profile through the window of the café. Just her luck to have run into him the first five minutes she was in town.

She drove through the familiar tree-lined streets, drumming her fingers on the hot steering wheel and half listening to the radio while she calmed down. It was inevitable that she would see Max again, and probably better to have gotten it over with. This was a small town and now the ice had been broken.

But her hands were still sweating as she turned down the familiar little avenue with its vintage cottages that were all, aside from the differing, peeling paint, nearly identical. She stopped at the curb in front of her mother's little bungalow—the house where she'd grown up. Covered in yellow aluminum siding, compliments of Jonah P. McKee, the house had never needed painting, though the porch sagged and the gutters had rusted. The old covered swing had grown dusty beside the living-room window and the hedge separating the side yard from the neighbor's property was in desperate need of a trim.

Her chest tightened as she snagged her purse and cat carrier and hurried up the cracked concrete path where dandelions, now gone to seed, grew tenaciously. After rapping softly on the door, she opened it and stepped into the darkened room. "Mom?"

"Skye!" Irene Donahue's voice drifted from the kitchen. "You here already?"

"Couldn't stay away." She followed the sound of her mother's voice to the small kitchen tucked in a back corner of the house.

Her mother was stirring sugar and lemon slices into a glass pitcher of iced tea. Balancing a hip against the cupboards, she dropped her wooden spoon and wiped her hands on her apron. Her cane was propped under the windowsill. "Dr. Donahue, I presume," she said with a proud smile.

"Sometimes I still find it hard to believe."

"Not me. Never had a moment's doubt." Frail arms surrounded Skye. "And you'll be the best damned doctor this town's ever seen."

Hot tears stung the back of Skye's eyes. "I hope so."

"I know it. I told old Ralph Fletcher so, too. Now, who's in here—Kildare, is that you?" she asked, peeking through the screen of the cat carrier.

A loud meow erupted and Skye set the plastic carrier on the floor. She opened the door and Kildare, a sleek gray tabby, streaked across the kitchen. "He's not very happy," Skye said as she found a small dish and filled it with water. "Abused, aren't you, boy?" Kildare rubbed against her legs, nearly tripping her while she made her way to the screened-in back porch and left the water dish near the door. She scratched the old tomcat behind the ears. Kildare had been her sole constant friend during the long years of medical school.

Two tall glasses of iced tea were already beginning to sweat on the tiny table wedged between the stove and back door. Irene settled into one chair and waved her older daughter into the empty seat. "Tell me all about your deal with Doc Fletcher," her mother insisted. "And if that old skinflint ripped you off, I'll personally drive down to the clinic and—''

"Hey, slow down.'' Once her mother got going, she was like a freight train gathering steam. ''Believe me, he didn't rip me off.'' Picking up her glass, she leaned against the windowsill and felt the slight breeze creep past the old gingham curtains as she sipped. The tea was cool as it slid down her throat. ''Actually, I think he was relieved I was interested. It's a good deal.''

''I'm just glad you're back.'' But her smile gave way. ''I hope you didn't feel obligated—'' she motioned to the hated cane ''—because of the stroke.''

''Of course not.'' Skye shook her head. ''I came back because I wanted to. I was tired of the city.''

Her mother's graying brows lifted suspiciously. ''What about all your declarations about never living here again?''

''I was a kid. And I was wrong.''

Her mother glanced nervously at her hands. ''You heard about Jonah?''

Blowing a stray strand of hair off her face, Skye nodded, though she didn't want to think about Max's manipulative father and the role Jonah P. McKee had played in her life. His had been much too large a role.

''Virginia's stirring up trouble. Claims he was murdered.''

''Murdered?'' Skye repeated.

''I know it sounds crazy, but she's hired a private investigator and insists that Sheriff Polk's involved in some cover-up or conspiracy or the like.''

''That's insane.''

''Tell it to Virginia.''

''All her kids think she's gone off her rocker, but she's standing firm, even called a reporter for *The Rimrock Review*. Oh, Lordy, poor old Jonah will never rest in peace.''

Skye bit the words that seemed destined to roll off her tongue. Jonah was dead. She was sorry that Max had lost his father, Virginia had lost her husband, and Hillary had lost her grandfather, but if she was honest with herself, she didn't feel a speck of grief for a man who had manipulated people and played with their lives, all for the love of the almighty buck.

It was ironic, she supposed, that she was back in town so soon after his death. It looked as if she'd been waiting for him to find a way to escape Rimrock. But the truth of the matter was that now was the most convenient time for her to return.

"He was a good man," Irene said, apparently reading her mind.

Skye couldn't let it rest. "He wasn't good, Mom. Not by any stretch of the imagination."

Irene's jaw tightened and her chin set stubbornly. "And where would we all be without him, hmm? When your father died and left us without a dime—no insurance whatsoever—what would we have done without Jonah's help? He gave me a job, a damned good job, and I was able to raise you and your sister decently. We never went hungry, now did we?"

"No, Mom, we didn't. Maybe we shouldn't discuss this right now—"

"And when I had to go to the hospital for that operation, didn't he see that all my bills were paid and the payments on the house kept up?"

"Yes, Mom—"

"So don't you go bad-mouthing him, Skye. You may be some fancy doctor nowadays, but you're still my daughter, and I won't have you or anyone else spreading bad words about the dead. Especially about a man who did us nothing but favors!"

Skye settled back against her chair and drained her glass. She thought about telling her mother the truth about all the reasons she'd left Rimrock so suddenly, but she hated to disillusion a woman who had done nothing but struggle to survive, who had given up her own youth so that her daughters could live better lives than she. For years, Skye had suspected that her mother had been secretly in love with Jonah McKee. In Irene's opinion, the man was nearly a god, saving her from ruin. He'd been upstanding in the community, an elder in the church, a faithful husband, loving father and honest businessman. Irene, as his secretary, had worshiped the ground he'd walked on and had continually compared him to the man she'd married, who had never had much ambition and had died in a logging accident when Skye was five and her sister, Dani, was only three. Though Irene had loved her husband, and Skye had faint, but warm memories of her father, Tom Donahue had made the mistake of dying suddenly and leaving his small family penniless.

Jonah McKee had stepped in and saved the day. Not only had he given Tom's widow a job, but he'd helped her move into this little house, a rental he'd owned. Eventually he'd written up a contract and sold the cottage to her.

Irene Donahue believed Jonah P. McKee was her personal savior.

And he was dead. It would serve no purpose to expose him now.

"I expect you're staying here?" Irene asked.

"Probably just tonight, and only if you want me."

Her mother smiled as if their argument about Jonah McKee had never been aired. "Of course I want you. Don't be silly. Dani will be over as soon as she's off work."

Skye nodded and put down her glass. Her younger sister seemed to have straightened out over the years, but she'd given their mother nothing but grief as a hell-raising teenager. "Tomorrow I have to go to the clinic. As part of the deal, Ralph offered to let me buy his old apartment house, too."

Irene's lips curved downward. "Isn't that a lot of debt? The practice and clinic building and house—"

"I'm only renting the clinic and I could live in one of the apartments while I rent out the rest of the building. It's half-filled already. Two more tenants and I could make money on the deal."

"Have you seen the place?" Irene asked, her brows knitting in concentration. "It needs a lot of work."

"Then I'll hire someone—offer an apartment rent-free for him to keep up the yard and house and manage the building."

Irene worried her lower lip. "I just don't want to see you biting off more than you can chew. You've already got college debts."

"I'll be all right, Mom. Really."

"Jonah always said you were ambitious. I guess he was right."

Skye didn't utter a word as she carried her glass to the sink. The subject of Jonah McKee wasn't comfortable. She knew too much. Way too much...

"I ran into Max today," she said instead. Her mother's back stiffened slightly. "He was with his daughter at the Shady Grove Café."

"He thinks the world of that child." Irene slowly rose from her chair to run hot water in the sink.

"I could see that."

"Too bad about him and his wife," Irene said, washing a glass. She wiped it dry with the corner of her terry-cloth apron and cast a worried glance at her older daughter. "They're divorced, you know. Have been for three...no, it's closer to four years now."

Skye's head snapped up. "He's divorced and you didn't tell me?"

"You never asked," her mother replied and went on polishing the rim of the glass until it sparkled. "The way you felt about Jonah and what you said about Max when you left town, I thought it best to keep my big mouth shut."

Skye felt as if the rug had been pulled out from beneath her feet. Max wasn't married? Her stomach clenched, but she lifted a shoulder. "Doesn't matter," she said, trying to convince herself. Kildare slid like a shadow into the room and rubbed up against her leg. "Max and I are history."

Chapter Three

Driving Hillary back to Colleen's place in Dawson City, Max ardently refused to think about Skye. He had enough problems as it was. His father had just died, his mother was losing her mind, Jenner's bad attitude was in the way, and Casey seemed about ready to explode. Then there was his continuing struggle with Colleen about Hillary. He glanced at his little daughter, strapped into her seat belt and half dozing, her head resting against the window. No, he didn't need any more complications in his life—especially a complication like Skye Donahue.

Max had convinced himself that he was over Skye, that when she'd driven away from Rimrock and left him in her dust, he was over her. But he'd been wrong. Seeing her again had only proved that point all too well.

Interrupting his troubled thoughts, Hillary stretched and yawned. As if she was able to read his mind, she said, "You liked that lady."

"What lady?"

"The one in the restaurant."

Max's teeth ground together. "I knew her a long time ago."

"Did you like her then?"

He didn't believe in lying to children. "I used to like her a lot."

"More than Mommy?"

"I knew her before I met your mommy." That was stretching the truth a bit, but not much.

"So why were you so mad?"

"I wasn't."

"You looked mad," Hillary accused.

"Did I? Well, I'll have to work on that, won't I?" he said as the truck rolled past the sign welcoming one and all to Dawson City.

Hillary turned her head, stared out the window and saw the familiar landmarks of the town where she now lived. A dark cloud seemed to settle over her small shoulders. She caught her father's eye and pouted, crossing her chubby arms defiantly. "I don't want to go back to Mommy's house."

"It won't be for long. I'll pick you up on Friday," he said, hoping to keep the conversation light but knowing that it would deteriorate as it always did. It wasn't that Hillary didn't love Colleen and vice versa, but Colleen, with two-year-old twins and a demanding husband had more than she could handle already. "I hate Mommy's house."

Max swallowed. He despised this separation every Sunday night. "You don't hate—"

"I do! I want to live on the ranch with you and Aunt Casey," she insisted as she did every time he took her home. "I hate Frank!"

"Frank's all right."

"He hates you."

"Enough with the hating, okay?" Max said tightly. Truth to tell, he didn't much like Colleen's second husband, either. Frank Smith was a blowhard with a quick temper, which hadn't improved with the birth of his twin girls. He'd been hoping for a boy and hadn't bothered to hide his disappointment when Mary and Carey had come along. According to Hillary, he was talking about having another baby.

What Colleen did with her life was her business. When it affected Hillary, it was Max's.

He pulled up in front of a two-story frame house located just within the city limits. The yard was overgrown and toys littered the sun-bleached grass.

"Please don't leave me, Daddy," Hillary said, her little chin trembling and tears filling her eyes.

His guts twisted painfully. "I'll be back."

"But not for five days."

"I know, but you know how to count, don't you?" He reached into the pocket of his work shirt for his weekly bribe and inwardly cringed that he was reduced to playing this silly game. She held out her hand expectantly and her tears dried surprisingly quickly. Max wondered, as he did every Sunday night, if he was being conned by one of the masters. "Okay, here you go—five candy sticks. You can have one each afternoon, and by the time the last one is gone—"

"The peppermint one," she said, her eyes suddenly dancing.

"What happens?"

"You'll come get me!"

"That's right, dumplin'."

She flung her soft little arms around his neck and encased him in the scents of baby shampoo and dirt. Though he always made her bathe before they returned to Colleen's house, the grit of the ranch seemed to stick to her. His heart seemed to rip into a thousand pieces, as it always did when he dropped her off.

He carried her through the gate and up two steps to the front porch, where she leaned over and rang the bell—

their Sunday night ritual. There was a loud crash and a baby started screaming loudly.

"Shut up!" Frank yelled from somewhere in the back of the house.

"The twins are dweebs," Hillary said.

"They're just little."

The door swung open quickly. Colleen's usually neat hair was rumpled, her lipstick long since faded. She was carrying one crying two-year-old while the other clung to the back of her legs, peeking up at Max and wailing, "Mommy, Mommy, Mommy."

"Well, come on, Hillary, hurry up," Colleen said. "Can't you see I'm busy?"

The baby on her hip let out a whimper of protest and Max felt Hillary's legs clamp more tightly around him.

"It's okay," Max said to his daughter, and Colleen blew her bangs out of her eyes.

"Of course it's okay," she said a little harshly, then seemed to melt. "Just let me put Mary in the playpen—she bumped her head, but she's fine now."

"Noooo!" Mary screamed as Colleen deposited her into a playpen pushed into a corner of the living room. The second little girl, Carey, Max presumed, still clung to one of Colleen's legs. "Now there, did you have fun at Daddy's?" Colleen asked as she took Hillary from Max's arms and set her on the floor.

Hillary was still clutching her candy sticks in a death grip. She sent a pained look to her father, then answered, "Lots of fun. I rode Cambridge and played with Reuben and—"

"Good, good, well, come along. Supper's almost on the table." Colleen raised her eyes to meet Max's worried gaze. "Goodbye," she said without a trace of a smile. "Next time, forget the candy, okay? I don't need trips to the dentist." She shut the door quickly, cutting him off from his daughter. Max's fingers curled into angry fists of frustration.

Not that he blamed Colleen. She'd tried to make him happy, he supposed, but he'd never loved her. Not as much as he'd loved Skye, and Colleen had sensed it. Their marriage had foundered, not so much from dissatisfaction as apathy, and Max had always felt that he'd failed Colleen, Hillary and himself.

Jaw clenched so tightly it hurt, he strode back to the pickup and drove away from the shaded sidewalk. Storm clouds were gathering in the Blue Mountains, and as he crested the hill just outside of town, the first fat drops of rain hit the dusty windshield and thirsty ground.

He flipped on his wipers. Just then an old love song, which had been popular years ago when he and Skye were dating, drifted plaintively from the radio. Old, nearly forgotten memories surfaced. Despite all his efforts, he couldn't keep his thoughts off Skye. With intelligent, hazel eyes that seemed to cut right to his soul, and tousled blond hair that framed a flawless face, she was, and always had been, the most interesting and frustrating woman he'd ever met. He'd fallen in love with her completely, without guarding his heart.

And though it had turned out his father was right about her temperament, seven years ago Max had loved her with a passion that scared the bejesus out of him. She'd meant everything to him, but she hadn't felt the same. She'd left Rimrock suddenly, never once glancing back over her shoulder.

Well, maybe she had, he thought sullenly as the wipers slapped the drizzling rain from the gritty windshield. The letter he'd just found the other day seemed to indicate that she'd had a few doubts of her own.

Damn the old man for lying to him. His back teeth gnashed together when he considered all the years gone by that his father hadn't said a word about Skye's letter. Not one goddamned word.

A prince among men, Jonah McKee.

Skye was back, Hillary was unhappy, and his mother was convinced that the old man had been murdered.

It had been one helluva week.

And it was only Sunday night.

The clinic had changed in the past seven years. It had originally been housed in the basement of Doc Fletcher's home, but after Skye had moved from Rimrock, Fletcher had leased the renovated single-storied complex on the adjoining property. Carpeting now covered the old linoleum hallways and new Formica cabinets replaced the metal cupboards that Skye remembered from the old house.

Doc Fletcher gave her the guided tour, showing off the four examining rooms, reception area and finally his office. He shepherded her inside and closed the door behind them without missing a beat.

"—and of course some of the equipment needs to be replaced," he was saying, "but everything's still operational and should last a few more years. We send all our lab work to Bend and any injury we can't handle goes to the hospital in Dawson City. There's the local ambulance service in town, all volunteer, and then we have life-flight capabilities thanks to a local helicopter service." Shedding his white jacket and hanging it on a peg near the door, he kept talking. "So we're not as backward as you might think—or as isolated." He used his fingers to comb his white hair while he ambled to his worn leather chair.

His desk was littered with open medical books, mail, patient charts, notes to himself, and folders. "I trust my accountant sent you all the records you need, including the information on the apartment house, right?"

She nodded. "I looked them over, then had a C.P.A. and my lawyer go over everything."

"Good, good." He seemed vastly relieved. "Let's take a look around the house and then we'll set up a meeting with my lawyer tomorrow. You can move in whenever you like. The main-floor apartment is vacant.'' He extended his hand and Skye clasped it firmly, though she felt as if she was sealing her fate in a town where she would never be wanted, might never belong.

Fletcher punched a button on his intercom, explained to his receptionist-secretary that he'd be gone for about twenty minutes, then led Skye out the rear door. A concrete pathway parted overgrown laurel hedges and ended up at the back porch of a three-storied home built sometime in the early part of the 1900s. The broad back porch was enclosed by windows and sagged a little on one side.

He opened the door and stepped into a kitchen that hadn't been updated in thirty years. The linoleum was cracked but clean, and the appliances looked as if they'd been new in the early sixties. ''Like I said, it needs a little work.'' Fletcher guided her through an arch to a dining room with a bay window and a view of an overgrown grape arbor. The living room, adjacent to the dining room, was graced with a fireplace surrounded by tile and carved wood. He led her through French doors to a sun porch and then on to the bedroom and a bath with a claw-footed tub.

''As you know, two of the units on the second floor are occupied, the third is vacant and needs work, and the unit in the basement—well, I won't lie to you. It needs to be gutted and reconstructed. I worked a deal with Jenner McKee. He's already signed a lease, and for free rent he'll do all the labor involved. He's kind of a jack-of-all-trades now that his rodeo career has— ''

Jenner McKee? As in Max's brother? ''I thought you said it was unoccupied.''

''It was, but Jenner needs a place to rest his boots for a few months, though he hasn't moved in yet. This isn't a fact, of course, but rumor has it that old Jonah cut the kid completely out of his will. They had a falling out a few years back and...oh, hell, here I am spreading town gossip and I don't know what I'm talking about.'' He offered a sheepish smile. "For all I know, Jenner could be loaded. Anyway, I thought since the basement needed fixing and he was looking for a place…is there a problem?"

What could she say? That she didn't trust anyone by the name of McKee? That she needed to keep the entire family at a distance? In this town? Who was she kidding? She'd only met Jenner a few times, but knew his reputation. A bad apple. The black sheep. Trouble from the get-go. But what was done was done and she'd rather deal with Jenner than his brother. "I'm sure there'll be no problem," she lied.

Fletcher clapped his hands together. "That's fine then. The McKees, they're all good people," Fletcher continued as they walked down a concrete stairwell to the lower unit. "Besides, I thought you might like an able-bodied man around, you know, to—" He stopped short, obviously seeing the censure in her eyes.

"Look, I appreciate everything you're doing for me, Dr. Fletcher, but since we're going to be working together, I think you should know a few things about me. The first is I *don't* need a man."

He shuffled his feet and had the decency to color behind his ears. "I didn't mean to imply that you did. Hell, you've been through medical school. In my time, few women dared even apply, but…oh, well. Didn't mean to offend you."

"No offense taken," she lied again.

He twisted a key in the lock and held the door open for Skye. He hadn't been kidding. The place was a mess. Most of the floor tiles were cracked or missing, exposing the dingy concrete below. The place smelled musty, the low ceiling sagged in several spots, and the old paneled walls were filthy and scratched. Some of the panels had fallen from the framework, revealing the dirty pink insulation. Ancient pieces of furniture and cabinets from the days when Fletcher's medical practice had been housed down here were stacked in a corner, and probably the homes of several nests of mice. The windows looked as if they hadn't seen any glass cleaner or a sponge for years. The smell was awful, a blend of mildew and dust and oil, and a bucket had been set in the middle of the floor to collect drips from an old pipe that drizzled rust and water.

"I have an inspector's report on this place," Fletcher said, suddenly embarrassed by the mess. "I'm replacing the roof and some of the porch beams where he found dry rot. I'll put up new gutters, as well, and install two new water heaters." He pointed to the ceiling. "These pipes will go. New ones will be installed and the insulation replaced where it's coming away from the walls. Other than that, it's up to you. I've already moved over to Hanover Meadows, so you can move into my old apartment tomorrow if you like. If the deal falls through, well, we'll work out something for your rent."

"It won't fall through," she said with a streak of conviction that surprised her. Suddenly she wanted very much to own this old house.

He cleared his throat. "I know there's lots of work to be done, but I think the price is fair."

Walking through the dingy basement unit, Skye didn't argue. He was willing to sell the house below market value in order that she take over his lease for the clinic. She'd hired her own inspector to check out both buildings, so she knew that Fletcher was being honest with her.

But she hadn't expected to have to deal with a McKee on a daily basis. Thank God it was Jenner and not Max.

Lugging two baskets of fruit, coffee and cookies up the stairs, Skye told herself that she was making the right move. Fletcher hadn't bothered to introduce her to any of her tenants and she wanted to meet each one on friendly terms.

There were three units on the second floor, each with one bedroom; one unit was unoccupied. She rapped softly on the door to the left. Through the door she could hear the sound of rock music, which was immediately switched off.

She saw an eyeball in the peephole, and then the door opened as far as the chain would let it. A girl about thirteen looked through the crack. "Yeah?"

"I'm Skye Donahue and I wanted to meet you. I'm going to be your new landlord."

"Mom's not here." The girl, whose face was covered with freckles, didn't bother to smile.

"Oh, well…"

"You probably won't want to talk to her, anyway. All she does is bitch about this place."

"All the more reason to meet her. I'd like to find out all about your apartment—what you like and what you don't like."

The girl's eyes narrowed. "She don't like anything about it. Neither do I."

"What's your name?"

Hesitation. Finally she said, "Paula."

The teenager's attitude grated on Skye's nerves, but she managed the cool smile she'd learned in medical school. "Well, Paula, maybe you could give her this basket and ask her to come down to the first floor and meet me. We could have coffee or something."

"Great." The girl rolled her eyes, reluctantly opened the door and held out her hand. Skye handed her the basket and the door was promptly slammed in her face. A few seconds later, the sound of heavy metal music seeped through the door.

"Great is right," Skye muttered under her breath. She turned and knocked on the door across the hallway. It was opened immediately as if the tenant had been lurking near the door, waiting.

A woman barely five feet tall, with gray hair tinged a soft apricot shade, stood on the other side of the threshold.

"You're the new landlord," she guessed, blinking through thick, rimless eyeglasses.

"Yes, Skye Donahue." Skye extended her hand, and the seventyish woman pumped it enthusiastically.

"Ruth Newby, and boy am I glad you've bought this building. Now maybe something will be done about my hot water heater, if that's what you call it. Why, it barely keeps the water tepid, and I've got a window that rattles something fierce when the wind kicks up, not to mention that there are rats...huge rats in the cellar. Some of them have climbed up the drainpipe and burrowed into my furniture, I'm just sure of it!"

"Well, Mrs. Newby, I'll try to fix anything that's broken."

"Good, because the oven thermostat is off by twenty-five degrees! Try to bake your grandson's birthday cake in that! It's a nightmare! Come in, come in, and I'll show you everything. I've already prepared a list." Mrs. Newby guided her through the small rooms decorated in green and gold, past a velvet sofa, fringed lamp shades and a gateleg table in the kitchen. "Here you go." Mrs. Newby pulled a typewritten list from a bulletin board in the kitchen and gave it to Skye. "I certainly hope you do something about these problems. I'd hate to think that we'd have to organize a tenant grievance committee as I threatened to do with Dr. Fletcher."

"But there are only two tenants."

"Oh, that doesn't matter." Her lips pulled together and she wagged a finger in front of Skye's nose. "It's not the size that matters, it's the voice!"

"I see. Well, I brought you this basket—"

"Oh, well. Oh, my. How lovely!" Mrs. Newby beamed as she took the basket from Skye. "Cookies and crackers and fruit and coffee. Why, aren't you a dear? Here, sit down, sit down, and I'll make us some of this coffee right now." She wouldn't take no for an answer, and Skye perched on one of the chairs while Mrs. Newby bustled around the room, setting out a plate of the cookies and perking coffee. "Isn't this just grand," she said as she finally lighted on one of the chairs and held up her bone china coffee cup. "Cheers." She clinked the rim of her cup to Skye's. "Here's to a long and mutually beneficial relationship."

"Cheers," Skye replied.

"Now, dear, let me tell you about the other tenants." Her gray eyebrows rose above her glasses. "The mother, Tina, is a divorcée and she's a good woman, but that daughter of hers is a wild one. Run away once already. Plays that darned music every minute she's not in school. I'm afraid you're going to have trouble with those two, if you're not careful...."

Less than a week.

Skye had been in town less than a week, and in that same amount of time, Max hadn't gotten a lick of work accomplished. It wasn't that he'd bumped into her, which he'd half expected to in a town the size of Rimrock, but he'd *felt* her presence, *sensed* that she was around.

He glanced in the mirror, frowned at his image and yanked off his tie. He wasn't a big-city lawyer, for God's sake. Skye had gotten to him, and the fact that he had to meet with her today was unnerving. It was more than unnerving. It was damn irritating.

He stripped off the white shirt, slid his arms into the sleeves of a faded blue chambray and told himself he was being a fool. He had a helluva lot better things to do than worry about running into Skye Donahue. His father had left him in charge of all the McKee holdings, which included a two-thousand-acre ranch, an old hotel on the north edge of town, three apartment houses, the mobile-home park near the river and on and on. McKee Enterprises, or companies owned by McKee subsidiaries, held the leases on most of the buildings in town as well as a few in Dawson City and a couple as far away as Bend. Including Doc Fletcher's clinic.

Then there were the problems at the ranch with his mother. He tended to agree with Casey. Virginia McKee seemed to be losing her grip on reality. She was pushing this murder idea too far. Instead of losing interest, she seemed to be gathering steam. Not only was the local paper interested, but a few reporters in neighboring cities had called.

Hell, what a mess!

Stuffing the tail of his shirt into the waistband of his worn jeans, he ignored his reflection in the mirror over his bureau. He buttoned his fly, then yanked on his boots.

The meeting would last less than twenty minutes. That was all. Not even a half hour. Then he wouldn't have to deal with her again.

Cursing under his breath, he thundered down the stairs and hurried outside. Atlas, his Border collie, jumped a greeting, and Max scratched the half-grown pup behind his black ears. "You stay," he said, but the dog, tail wagging wildly, leapt off the porch and dashed to the pickup.

Another truck roared up the gravel drive and shuddered to a stop near the garage. Chester, the ranch foreman, hopped from the cab and left the old Ford idling. Chester's hands were covered with black grease and he was sweating hard enough for the drips to be visible as they slid from beneath his old Oakland A's cap.

"Problems?" Max asked, not wanting to hear them.

"The tractor gave out."

The old vehicle had been threatening to fail for several seasons. "Great. Can it be fixed?"

Chester reached into his breast pocket for a pack of cigarettes. "Hope so. But it's old. Twenty-five years or better. I've been over to the dealer in Dawson City. You might want to think about investing in some new equipment." He lit up, sending a jet of smoke from the side of his mouth as he waved out his match.

"Okay, I'll check it out." Max reached the door of his pickup.

"There's more," Chester admitted, the lines of his face deepening into grooves. "Some of Cyrus Kellogg's calves have up and died. Four or five in the past three days. He thinks it's blackleg."

"Hell." Max frowned. Blackleg was contagious and deadly. The Kellogg place was just north of McKee property, bordering a stretch of timber and fields. "Didn't we inoculate?"

"Last year. This year I didn't bother. Hasn't been a case of blackleg in the county in—"

"Doesn't matter. Go to the vet and get the vaccine."

"Already done. We started giving shots this morning to the calves that have never been treated. Half the herd has already been taken care of. Got all the hands working on it. Should be done by tomorrow night."

"Good."

"I should have gotten more vaccine—"

"Don't worry about it," Max said. He climbed into the cab and leaned out the window. "From now on, we'll inoculate against everything. Anything else?"

"No," Chester said, but wouldn't meet his eye.

"What is it?"

Chester shoved the toe of his boot through the gravel and took a long drag on his cigarette. "It's Jenner."

"Giving you trouble?" Max didn't need this. Jenner was and always had been a hothead.

"Naw. He does more than his share of work, but he puts some of the men off, what with him being an old rodeo star and all."

"That was a long time ago."

"The men…well, they're so impressed they fall all over themselves whenever he's around."

"Does Jenner promote it?"

"Nope. Hell, I probably shouldn't have even mentioned it. Forget it. I'll handle the men." He patted the fender of Max's truck. "You know, I read in the paper that some people think your pa was murdered." He dropped the butt of his cigarette into the gravel and stomped it out. "Now, don't that beat all?"

Max couldn't even think about his father's death—not right now. Not when he had to face Skye again.

Chapter Four

The last person Skye expected to see when she entered the lawyer's office was Max McKee, but there he was, big as life, seated in a leather wing chair, one booted ankle resting on the worn denim covering his opposite knee. Two other men were seated around the desk, but Skye barely noticed Ralph Fletcher or his attorney, Alan Granger.

Max, looking as if he'd just come in from the range, didn't bother smiling. His jaw was clenched, his eyes cold and shuttered, his attitude I-don't-give-a-damn. Why was he here? What business did he have with Granger?

It took all of her willpower to manage a smile and force her gaze away from Max. The man she'd sworn to avoid, the man to whom she'd given her heart so recklessly as a girl, the man who had nearly destroyed all her dreams.

Her stomach knotted as she walked across the room in the company of Granger's petite secretary, Ramona Something-or-other. Though Skye managed a smile for the rangy man rising on the other side of an immense rose-wood desk, she was all too aware of Max.

Settled comfortably in his chair, Max stared at her with a look that could have cut through steel. His lips twitched slightly and his brows drew together in a grimace before he forced all emotion from his face again.

"Welcome," Granger said. "Ralph told us all about you."

"Did he?" she said woodenly. Why the devil was Max still seated in the room as if he belonged? He must've been here for an earlier meeting....

"Uh-huh. Now, I think you know everyone else."

"Dr. Donahue," Max drawled, saying her name like a filthy word.

The hackles rose on the back of her neck. "What are you doing here?" Just because his last name was McKee gave him no right, *no right whatsoever* to sit in on this meeting.

"I have a business interest." He shoved his sleeves up forearms tanned bronze from hours in the summer sun, and didn't budge.

Her nerves began to unravel. What did he mean? "A business interest? What kind of—?"

"Dr. Donahue, please, have a seat." Granger had straightened to the length of his six-feet-five-inch frame. His smile was a little on the plastic side and his mustache was clipped with military precision, but he waved her over to a side chair with the familiarity of one accustomed to dealing with touchy situations.

"Glad you could make it," Granger said. "Ralph, here—" he pointed to Doc Fletcher who was perched on the edge of a tufted couch beneath the windows "—he's been telling us all about you. How you graduated near the top of your class, worked awhile in the city and how lucky all of us in Rimrock are to have you back home."

"Oh, well...thanks." This wasn't the way she'd hoped to start the meeting. First of all, she hadn't expected to find Max in some kind of position to know anything about her, talking about her behind her back, for crying out loud, and she'd hoped to keep all conversation on an entirely professional level.

"Yep, Ralph here seems to think you're Rimrock's answer to Mother Teresa."

"Hardly," Skye said.

Doc Fletcher chuckled, Granger grinned widely, and Max stared at her grimly as if he were wishing the whole ordeal was over. She slid into the chair and decided to take the bull by the horns. Gazing pointedly at Max, she asked, "What do you have to do with this?"

Granger grinned. "Why, Mr. McKee is the president of J.P. Limited which holds the lease on the clinic building."

"The lease was signed by Carol Larkin." Skye had gone over the legalese with a fine-tooth comb.

"She's a vice president of one of my father's companies—J.P. Limited," Max said, his voice without a trace of emotion.

"Your father," she repeated, remembering the big bear of a man who had taken it upon himself to run her out of town.

"Good old J.P.," Max restated.

Skye felt the floor dropping from under her feet. *J.P. Limited as in Jonah Phineas McKee?* How had she been so blind? Of course the McKees would own an interest in the clinic. They owned nearly every piece of real estate in Rimrock. She'd read the lease a dozen times over and noticed Carol Larkin's signature, but she'd just assumed that Carol was the president and...big mistake. "I didn't realize," she managed to say, feeling the weight of Max's stare and wondering if she imagined the smirk in his blue-green eyes.

"Well, let's get started, shall we?" Granger fingered a flat file lying open on his desk just as his secretary, laden with a tray of cups and an insulated carafe of coffee, swept into the room. "Ah, Ramona, just in time."

Granger poured them each a cup, then got down to business. The lease and the option to buy the clinic building was first on the agenda, and Skye held firm. Max seemed to think that she didn't need to take on the obligation to buy the clinic, and she made damned sure she set him straight. If there was anything she'd learned from good ol' Jonah it was that you wanted to own everything possible.

Besides, the sooner she was out from under the broad McKee thumb, in this case under the guise of J.P. Limited, the better for everyone involved.

During the discussion, she managed to keep her equilibrium, though Max's gaze was unsettling. They discussed the terms of the lease first, hammered out the details, and eventually, after nearly two hours of heated debate, everyone signed.

As he scrawled his name across the appropriate line, Max looked straight at her. "Seems you got your way again, Dr. Donahue."

She bit back a hot retort, took the pen from his hand, and scribbled her name across the bottom of the lease. It seemed strange to see her signature so close to Max's. Long ago, she'd fantasized about signing a marriage license, a mortgage on a house, a release from the hospital for their new baby...but those had all been foolish fantasies. She'd known it at the time. Her stomach clenched painfully, and she shoved the paper back across the desk to the lawyer.

"Okay, that's one of the hurdles," Granger said, handing everyone a copy.

"You don't need me for anything else, do you?" Max asked, obviously anxious to leave.

"That's it."

"Good." Max rolled onto his feet. "So we're business partners, you and I, Doctor," he said, staring down at Skye. "Who would've guessed?"

"Not me," she replied, inching her chin up a fraction.

"Not in a million years." For a brief instant, she felt as if she'd signed her name in blood, contracted with the very devil himself. Who knew better than she how the McKees did business?

He strode out of the room without so much as a backward glance and she should have felt relieved. It was humiliating enough that he had a copy of her financial statement, that he knew how much money she owed and to whom, so she was thankful that he wouldn't be taking part in the rest of the negotiations.

But, like it or not, he was back in her life.

"I can't deal with Mom anymore. I'm telling you, Max, the woman needs help!" Casey was pacing from one end of the front porch to the other while Atlas chased after her, barking and jumping and hoping to be noticed.

"What do you want me to do? Haul her bodily to a doctor? Or have her arrested? Because short of that I can't do much," Max said. "She's a grown, rational woman."

"That's just it—she's not! She's taking this murder thing way too far. Not only has she got the press snooping around, she's also talking about hiring a private investigator—some guy from Dawson City." Casey flopped onto the old porch swing and scratched Atlas behind his ears. "Worst part of it is, she's got Grandma on her side. Those women haven't agreed on anything from the day Mom married Dad. Until now." Casey crossed her arms and glared up at her brother. "I said I'd stay with Mom until she pulled herself together, but I don't know if I can, Max. I have my own life to live."

"I thought you were through with L.A."

She worried her lip and her eyes clouded over. "It's not so easy to give up your dreams."

He knew. Probably better than anyone else. He had only to look at Skye to remember his own fantasies. "Maybe it's time to face reality, Case. You gave Hollywood a shot, it didn't pan out, now you go to backup plan B.''

''Which is what? Get a job as a P.E. teacher in Dawson City?''

''Would that be so bad?''

Her eyes darkened with a secret pain and she looked away. Something had happened in L.A., something she kept locked inside her and wouldn't share with anyone. Especially not her older brother.

''There are plenty of jobs with the company—''

She scowled her pretty face at him. ''Not interested.''

He didn't bother arguing. Casey would never be satisfied doing office work. Years before, their father had tried to steer her toward law. ''We could always use another smart lawyer,'' he'd told his youngest child. It was the same line he'd delivered to his firstborn and his second, but only Max had listened. Jenner had told the old man to quit meddling in his life. Casey had gone further than that; she'd actually had the audacity to laugh in his face.

''Me? In a three-piece suit? Carrying an eelskin brief-case? Talking about taxes and corporate mergers and God only knows what else? Get real, Dad,'' she'd said, rolling her eyes to the heavens. ''I'd die first.''

''Well, at least finish college,'' Jonah had insisted. ''All this talk about the movies—''

''Film industry, Dad. That's what it's called. And it's not like I'm talking about being an actress.''

''Doesn't matter. It's not solid. I don't trust those people in Tinseltown. Now you go back to school and earn yourself a degree.''

She had. In education. She'd graduated from the University of Oregon, turned south and never stopped until she'd reached L.A., where she'd worked as an assistant for a production company until she'd returned to Rimrock.

''Look, just try to talk some sense into Mom, okay?'' Casey climbed to her feet and dusted her hands. ''I can't stick around forever.''

She tried to breeze past him, but he grabbed the crook of her arm, stopping her cold in her tracks. "Whatever happened in L.A.—"

"Nothing happened, okay?" She tugged her arm away from him and frowned. "Nothing."

"You're lying."

"And your big-brother sensors are working overtime. I'm fine," she said firmly. "You're the one with the problem."

"Me?" Damn, he hated it when she turned the tables on him.

"Yeah, you. Because of Skye Donahue."

He felt every muscle in his body grow rigid. His jaw clamped together so hard it ached, and Casey lifted a knowing brow. "Ever since she waltzed back into town, you've been hell to get along with."

"I haven't—"

"Save it, Max. For Skye." With that she dashed down the steps and marched across the gravel drive to the shade of a gnarly barked oak where her favorite horse, a swift little mare named Murphy, was nipping at the dry blades of grass. She swung into the saddle, yanked on the reins and dug her heels into the horse's sides. With a holler, she leaned forward as the game mare took off across the parched fields.

Max watched his volatile sister disappear over the first hill and he told himself Casey didn't know what she was talking about. He was fine. Just because Skye was back, because he was her landlord, because he couldn't stop thinking about her, didn't mean there was a problem. Hell, no. He walked into the house, strode to the kitchen and yanked open the refrigerator door. Cool air wafted from the barren interior as he grabbed a long-necked bottle from a half-empty six-pack.

So Skye was in Rimrock. So what?

Twisting the cap from the bottle, he headed upstairs and down a short, dark hallway to the large room where he slept. King-size bed, single bureau, one lamp and a solitary mirror. This room...so long ago...before the house was finished. He took a long pull from his beer to quench his suddenly thick throat. He'd brought Skye here. He closed his eyes, squeezing them shut, blocking out the familiar memory of her lying naked beneath him on the hard, unfinished floor. "Jeez," he growled and turned to the room next door, a smaller room. He braced himself on the doorjamb, flipped on the lights and took another swallow from the bottle.

The room was austere. Just a single brass bed, the quilt his grandmother had pieced, an oval mirror, a small dresser and bookshelves filled with toys. Hillary's room. Every weekend. Two nights out of seven. What did that add up to in a year—about a hundred days, not quite a third of her young life. And then there were the weekends when she stayed with Colleen. Max had never fought his ex-wife when she'd planned something special or a family gathering and wanted Hillary included. He'd always thought it was best to lie back, give Hillary a broad base, let her know that he still respected her mother's wishes, though, truth to tell, sometimes it bugged the hell out of him. Maybe he'd been too accommodating. Maybe it was time to make a few more fatherly demands. After all, Hillary was his only child while Colleen already had the twins and was probably planning to have even more children.

In frustration, he snapped off the lights and finished his beer in the dark hall. Everything was so messed up. First his father's death and now Skye's arrival back in town.

He walked downstairs, left his empty on the kitchen counter and snatched his keys from a hook near the back door. Outside, the sun was just beginning to set, the sky streaked pink and gold, but he hardly noticed because, for the first time in his life, he'd decided to take his sister's advice. It was time to clear the air.

He climbed into his pickup, opened the glove compartment and pulled out the letters—the damned letters that had been nagging at the back of his mind for the better part of a week. He scanned his father's note quickly, then studied the letter from Skye. Why hadn't she told him she was leaving? Why had they argued so bitterly?

Because she's a lying witch!

But he didn't believe it, and even as the ugly thought entered his mind, he tossed it aside.

He started the truck, threw the gearshift into reverse and cranked hard on the wheel, making a police U-turn and spraying gravel from beneath his tires.

Seven years was a long time…too long. But his memory was sharp. Skye had been working that summer. Her mother, Irene, was recuperating from some kind of female surgery, and Skye had agreed to fill in for her, working long hours on a word processor in the offices of McKee Enterprises.

Max had been struck by her the first time he'd seen her at her desk. She'd glanced up at him and she'd smiled and his world had tilted. They'd begun to date and he'd fallen hopelessly in love with her. One look from her gorgeous smoky green eyes and he was lost.

Cursing under his breath, he rolled down the window, resting his elbow on the ledge. Warm air swept into the cab and the first few stars dared to wink in the thickening twilight. How many evenings such as this one had he been with her, kissing her, laughing with her, touching her and making love to her? He just couldn't seem to get enough of her. He remembered wrestling her to the ground one dew-drenched morning and kissing her so recklessly that he got aroused now just thinking of it.

"Hell," he muttered as Rimrock came into view. A small grid of lights guided him into the center of town, and within minutes he'd parked near a dilapidated old garage on the Fletcher grounds. The lights in her apartment weren't on and he noticed that the clinic was bustling with activity. Several cars were still scattered in the parking lot and the fluorescent lights glowed an eerie white-blue through the windows.

He cut the engine and sat in the dark.

Yep, it was time to have it out with Skye.

Once and for all.

Skye rotated the kinks from the back of her neck before she stuffed her stethoscope in a pocket of her lab coat and hung it on a coat tree in her office. Nearly dead on her feet, she was reminded of her endless hours as a resident. She felt that same fuzzy bone weariness. During the past week, she'd slept little, intent on establishing herself in the practice as well as moving into her apartment. Sighing, she snapped off the lights to the clinic. It was past eight, two hours after the small medical facility had officially closed. Her stomach rumbled noisily from having missed lunch. Aside from the usual sore throats, ear infections, jammed toes and physicals, she'd seen a fifty-five-year-old woman with a lump in her breast, a pregnant woman in the beginning of her third trimester who was spotting, twins who had broken arms and ribs in a biking accident and an elderly farmer who had nearly torn off his hand in a threshing machine.

Things weren't all that rosy in the office, either. The secretary, Madge, didn't make any bones about the fact that she considered Ralph Fletcher her boss and felt that Skye was an interloper. The bookkeeper was a sullen young woman with three kids who kept her on the phone all day, and one of the nurses had called in sick.

"What did you expect?" she chided herself as she walked past the laurel hedge and smelled the sweet scent of honeysuckle wafting from a hidden vine. Crickets chirped and somewhere off in the distance a dog barked. The thudding bass notes of rock music drifted through an open window on the second floor. The night was warm, the temperature still hovering in the eighties without a breath of wind.

Sweat beaded on the back of her neck and she imagined taking a long, cool shower, scrounging up some dinner and then unpacking some more boxes before falling into bed in an exhausted heap.

She rounded the corner, glanced at the back porch and stopped dead in her tracks when she saw the shadowy figure of a man lurking near the door. At the sight of her, the intruder shifted, still partially hidden and keeping away from the dull light of the single low-wattage bulb over the door.

"Keepin' kind of late hours, aren't you, Doc?" a familiar male voice said in a low tone that had once turned her knees to water.

Max.

Her throat turned to dust and her legs threatened to give way, but she forced herself to move forward and climb the sagging steps. Resting a hip against the porch rail, his arms crossed over his chest as if he had some kind of accusation to sling in her direction, he glared at her. In the shadowy light, the contours of his face seemed more angular, his expression even more grim than she remembered.

She didn't need this. Not now. "Was there something you wanted?" she asked, spying Kildare stalking beneath the laurel hedge. "Unless my memory fails me, the rent isn't due until the first of next month."

"I'm not here to collect the rent, Doctor."

"I'd have thought that the president of McKee Enterprises would have better things to do than prowl around in the dark."

"Is that what I'm doing?"

She shrugged a shoulder. "Looks that way."

"I was waiting for you."

Her heart seemed to stop and she swallowed with sudden difficulty. Why was it always this way with him?

Why? She had told herself, promised herself, that she was over him, that she'd never again think of him with that blind passion she'd felt seven years ago, and yet here she was barely able to breathe, lost in long-ago memories that should have been long forgotten.

"I don't see that we have any business to discuss—"

"Not business. It's personal."

"Personal," she repeated, and her heart began to thunder. "We don't have anything personal. Not anymore."

"Did we ever?"

"It's been a long time, Max, and I—"

"Why'd you leave?"

The question seemed to ricochet off the surrounding hills. "That's ancient history."

Even in the gathering darkness, she saw his face muscles tighten as he repeated, "Why'd you leave?"

She'd never been one to back away from a fight, never considered herself unwilling to tackle any challenge, and yet there seemed no point in dredging up all the old memories, all the old pain, all the old problems again. Around the light bulb a moth was fluttering, bouncing against the hot glass, drawn irresistibly to the incandescence and certain death. "It doesn't matter, Max," she said, refusing to see herself in the futile actions of the flying creature. "I left and that was it. End of story."

"I don't think so." He approached her with the determination of a predator, and though she shuddered inside, she stood her ground, refusing to give even an inch. "A lot happened before you left that I didn't know about."

Did he know about his father—all the underhanded deals?

Max stopped when he was close enough for her to smell the scents of soap and leather, musk and beer. His eyes had darkened to the color of a storm-tossed sea, his dark brows drawn into a single line. He looked ranch tough and there wasn't a trace of the younger man she'd known. With a face all angles and blades and an I-don't-give-a-damn attitude that seemed to radiate from him, he was purely business.

"What was this all about?" he whispered as he drew a faded sheet of paper from the inner pocket of his jacket.

"What—?"

"Don't you remember?"

Her heart caught as she recognized her own handwriting on the page, and a small sound of protest formed deep in her throat. Why was he bringing all this up now?

"The letter."

His smile was as cold as death. "Ah, so you do remember."

"It's been seven years."

"This," he said, crumpling the sheet of paper in his fist and holding it under her nose, "doesn't explain much."

He wasn't making any sense. "I said all I could."

"And then ran away."

"I didn't run. You knew where I was. If you wanted—"

"I wanted, Doctor," he cut in. "I wanted very much. That was the problem. I thought you wanted, too."

Something was wrong here. Very, very wrong. Aside from the fact that his angry breath was a hot stream against the base of her throat and that his eyes were flashing with the fury of a lightning bolt, something far deeper than simple irritation was being expressed.

"I don't know what you're getting at."

"Don't you?" One side of his mouth curled up into a cruel little smile.

"Max—"

He moved closer and she couldn't resist. She backed up a step and her rear brushed up against the door. Over her head, the moth battered helplessly against the bulb.

"You're a liar, Dr. Donahue," he said, placing a hand on either side of her head. "A beautiful, manipulative liar."

"I never lied."

"Didn't you?"

Oh, God, she could barely breathe. She was a doctor, for crying out loud, an independent woman—she didn't want or need a man, especially a man named McKee, messing with her mind. "Why'd you come here, Max?"

His jaw clenched tightly and a muscle worked frantically near his temple. "I'd like to lie to you and tell you that I stopped by to check on the lease, or look for my brother, or some other lamebrain excuse. But the truth of the matter, after I found the letter and saw you again, is that I couldn't stay away."

"You don't expect me to believe that after seven years—"

"Believe what you want, Doctor. I don't really give a damn." He stared deep into her eyes, and in that instant she knew with a certainty that what she feared would soon prove her undoing. He was going to kiss her.

Again she stepped back, but her shoulders only pressed against the unmoving siding of the porch. As his head lowered to hers, she swore she'd put up a fight, that she'd slap him across his arrogant McKee cheek, that she'd kick his shin or knee him in the groin to avoid letting his lips touch hers again.

But she didn't. When his mouth found hers, she remained still and lifeless, refusing to respond even though the long-banked embers of desire ignited in her blood. His lips were warm and inviting, and when he took her face between his callused hands, as he'd done a hundred times before, her heart seemed to crack.

He pressed up against her, his body straining beneath his clothes, the bulge in his jeans giving evidence to the passion singing through his blood.

Still, she closed her mind to the delicious sensations swirling deep within her, refused to accept the fact that her body was a traitor. When he finally lifted his head, she gritted her teeth and forced her bones not to sag.

"Got your jollies, Max?" she said caustically, though her voice was more breathless than usual.

His eyes narrowed. "Is that what you learned in medical school—how to be an ice princess?"

"Maybe I learned it from you."

"Oh, no, darlin'. If memory serves, you were one hot little number. You couldn't wait to get out of your panties and into my bed. I remember—"

Furious, she slapped him. The sound echoed through the night and Skye's hand stung. "Don't you ever talk to me like some cheap tramp," she said, enraged. Who was he to come here and insult her? She felt the heat climb up her face. "Get this, and get it straight, Max. I'm not some little simpering thing who'll run back to you just because you kissed me. Nor am I a woman who will stand by and be degraded and talked to as if I were a slut. I'm not impressed with you or your money and I won't tolerate your insults. What happened between us seven years ago is over, Max, and I would think—no, I would hope—that you would have the decency to leave it alone. I'm the town doctor now, whether you like it or not, and I won't let you treat me like some woman without an ounce of self-esteem who chases after the McKee men and the McKee money. If you don't have the decency to respect me, then just get the hell out!"

Eyeing her, he rubbed his stinging cheek. "That was some speech."

"I meant every word of it."

"You can't just ignore what happened between us."

"As if you haven't. For the past seven years neither one of us has talked with, written or called the other. I think we're doing a damned good job of ignoring it."

"So why are you back, Skye?"

"Not for you, Max," she said, though her voice nearly caught. "What we had once was special and I'll always have a soft spot in my heart for you, I suppose. You were my first love—but it's over. It ended a long time ago."

"Because you left."

"Because I couldn't stay."

"I always wondered about that."

"But not for too long," she noted, wanting to wound him for his crass remarks. "It didn't take you long to marry someone else." The color seemed to drain from his face and his lips flattened over his teeth. "Don't make it any more than it was, Max." She reached into a pocket and extracted her key ring.

Max placed a hand against the door. His smile was as cold as the bottom of a well at midnight. "I take it you're not going to invite me in."

"You take it right." She lifted her chin a notch, then slipped the old key into the lock. "Don't mess with me, Max. Let's just pretend that we never cared about each other."

"You think you can?"

"Of course," she lied, her heart still hammering crazily as she twisted the key until the lock clicked. She had been trained to sound cool and professional, even in the most stressful and emotional times, but no amount of practice could have prepared her for the emotions raging in Max's eyes. "Look, I think you should leave."

"I will," he agreed, holding the crumpled letter under her nose. "Just as soon as you explain this."

Oh, God. How could she begin to tell him all the reasons she'd left Rimrock with no intention of ever returning? The truth whispered through her heart, begging to be let out, but she wouldn't listen to that persistent little voice.

"I'm tired, Max." She opened the door to her apartment and slipped through the narrow opening. "And it's late."

"It's barely nine."

"I don't want to talk about it, okay?"

He studied her through the slit in the door and his expression was anything but friendly. "I won't give up, Skye," he said, "and I can be pretty stubborn."

"So can I."

"I remember," he said, and his face seemed to lose some of its harsh angles. He reminded her of the younger man, the kinder man, the man for whom she'd nearly thrown away all her dreams. Her throat tightened at the memory, but she shut the door and turned the dead bolt.

She wouldn't, *couldn't* let him into her life again. She'd never let herself be caught in that emotional tug-of-war. Waiting at the window, she heard the engine of his truck catch and listened to the whine of gears as he drove away. Only when the sound had disappeared did she relax, sagging against the wall and closing her eyes.

She was a fool. An overeducated, silly fool. She'd thought, actually believed, that she and Max McKee could live in this tiny community, come into contact on a regular basis, and still keep everything that happened in the past buried deep.

She'd been very wrong.

Whether she wanted to admit it or not, she'd never forget the love they'd shared together, the plans they'd made, the bitter disappointment of finding out he wasn't the man she'd thought he was. Nor would she ever truly forget her deepest secret—the reason she couldn't let Max, elder son of Jonah McKee and heir apparent to the McKee fortune, know the truth.

Chapter Five

Rimrock, Oregon
Summer—the Past

The noon whistle screeched from the fire station in town as Skye sprayed lemon juice onto her wet hair and flopped into a chaise lounge in the backyard.

"What's wrong with you?" Dani, hands on her slim hips, stared openly at her usually reserved older sister. "For the past two weeks you've run around here humming and smiling like you've got the biggest secret of all time."

Skye laughed as she finger combed her hair and closed her eyes. When she did, she saw Max McKee's handsome face behind her lids, and a tiny shiver of anticipation, unlike any she'd ever experienced before, swept through her.

She felt the warmth of the sun's midday rays caress her

skin and she experienced only a little jab of guilt that she was taking a break from picking corn and beans from the garden.

"You know, I have better things to do than this," Dani complained as Skye sprayed the lemon juice over her hair again in the hope that she could streak her blond curls to an even paler shade.

"Life is good," Skye said. "Slow down and smell the roses."

"This...from you?" Skye opened one eye and saw her sister registering mock horror. "You, the honor student with the scholarship to college, the girl who plans to be Rimrock's first woman doctor? Slow down? When you've been on the straight-and-narrow fast track for years?"

"Maybe it's time to take it easy," Skye said, stretching lazily.

"Something's up. Something I don't know about because life isn't good. You and I both know it." Dani wiped off a bead of sweat that had dripped below her rolled-up handkerchief, her answer to a headband. She was muscular and tanned from hours working with horses on the ranches bordering town, and she detested being trapped into doing anything the least bit domestic. Such as picking, husking and freezing corn.

"Has anyone ever told you you're a pessimist?" Skye rolled off the chaise, picked up her empty sack and started back to the garden.

Dani marched along at her heels. "Not a pessimist. A realist. Face it, Skye, we haven't had a ton of breaks. Dad died in a logging accident working for old Jonah McKee so long ago, I can barely remember him, but Mom gets lucky because Jonah feels some sort of guilt and he gives her a job. She works for him for years and she's still not earning enough to make ends meet and then she needs a hysterectomy—major surgery that will keep her off her feet for a couple of months at the least—so you, who should already be hot-trotting to medical school have to wait until she recovers. In the meantime, you get to wait on her and fill in for her at work. Doesn't seem right.''

"It's okay."

"I don't know why."

"What about you, Dani?" Skye asked as she stood in the shade of the cornrows and started searching for ripe ears. The fat leaves were scratchy against her bare arms and legs, but she didn't mind. Not today.

"I wasn't talking about me," Dani said from somewhere on the other side of the rows. "I don't have any big plans to leave Rimrock, and God knows I'd never be a doctor. But I'm not silly enough to think that life is good. Not by a long shot. It's hard work and it's long hours and it's bad news around every corner, and it's damn sure not good—at least not for us. Now, if I were Casey McKee, maybe I'd think differently."

There was a bitterness to Dani's words, but Skye held her tongue. Her sister had a right to her own pain, to her belief that life never turned out right unless you were privileged, and in this town that privilege meant being blessed with the McKee name.

She cracked several ears from the tall stalks as she made her way down the row. Dani had her own bone to pick with the McKees, so Skye couldn't very well explain that the reason she was on cloud nine was because of Jonah's older son, Max.

She'd just met him for the first time. She'd known who he was, of course. Who didn't? But he was five years older than she was, so they were never in high school together. He'd been to college in Seattle and law school somewhere in California and she and the rest of the town had expected him to join up with some big firm on the West Coast. However, after interning at a prestigious firm in San Francisco, he'd come home to Rimrock, and instead of hanging out his shingle for his own private practice, he'd started working for his father.

That's how he'd met Skye. He'd sauntered into the office on the first afternoon that Skye had filled in for her mother. Skye, with Dictaphone plugs in her ears, hadn't heard him, and suddenly there he was, an insolent hip propped against the table holding her word processor, a smile as crooked as the John Day River curving over his jaw, and aquamarine eyes that sparked with more than the hint of a devil.

"Who're you?" he'd said as Skye noticed the way a clump of brown hair had tumbled over his brow. "What happened to the old lady who usually stands guard here?"

"That 'old lady' is my mother, so watch your tongue," she'd said, irritated that he'd interrupted her. She'd never been impressed by rich men, especially rich, cocky men, and she was set to dislike him on the spot. Spoiled. Pampered. Born with a silver spoon wedged firmly between his gums, Max McKee represented everything she detested in men. The fact that he was handsome only added up to another strike against him. Rich, cocky, good-looking men were usually the worst.

Max held up his hands in surrender. "Didn't mean to step on any toes."

"She's recovering from surgery." Skye turned back to her work, but he snapped his fingers as if the light had suddenly dawned in his feeble brain. "That's right. I remember now. I've been out of town for a few days and forgot." His smile broadened. "No offense to your mom, but I like you better already."

"I don't type as well as she does."

He lifted a shoulder and gave her the once-over with those warm blue-green eyes. "I think you'll do fine. Just fine."

Seething, she said, "You don't know a thing about me, Mr. McKee."

"Not yet. But I'm working on it. And it's Max—"

"Max? Is that you?" Jonah bellowed from the other side of the door. "Where the hell have you been?"

The corners of Max's mouth tightened, and Skye realized that the firstborn son of Jonah McKee didn't like taking orders, not even from his father. "I swear the old man's got radar," Max muttered as he rapped his knuckles twice on the desk and reached for the door. But he hesitated and looked over his shoulder. "You're...?"

"Skye."

All at once everything came together in his mind, and the look of shock on his face warmed the cockles of Skye's heart. No doubt he remembered her as a gawky twelve-year-old. All legs and arms, no chest, unruly hair and thick glasses. She'd been a tomboy then, tall and lanky, more interested in scaling trees and playing sandlot baseball than in boys.

He rubbed his chin. "Saying the years have been kind would be an understatement, but I suppose you know that."

"Max?" Jonah's voice rumbled with irritation.

Max's jaw tightened. "Duty calls," he said and shouldered open the door to his father's inner sanctum.

"About time," Jonah growled as Max slid into the older man's office and Skye turned back to her word processor. She tried to type the agreements of sale and leases, but she found herself unable to concentrate. Her gaze kept wandering to the office door as she thought about Max McKee. Not that she was interested in him. He was everything she despised in a man. And yet...

Skye was still at her desk typing a water-rights agreement between McKee Enterprises and Fred Donner, a neighboring rancher, when Max and his father walked out of the office. Lines of strain showed on Max's rough-hewn features, but Jonah seemed pleased as he slapped a couple of files on the corner of her desk. "I'll need two copies of everything in these." He thumped the top file with an impatient finger. "By tomorrow at nine. And don't forget the Donner agreement. I'll need that, too." Without waiting for Skye's reply, he headed out the door of the reception area while Max lingered.

"He could have said please, but that's not his style," Max said gruffly.

"Is it yours?"

His brows lifted slightly. "You don't like me much, do you?"

"I don't know you well enough not to like you."

"But you disapprove of me." He glanced at the doors that closed behind his father. "Don't take too much guff from him."

Skye yanked off her earphones. "I won't. I don't believe women, no matter who they work for, should be treated as doormats. If he gets too offensive, I'll let him know."

"Will you?" Max seemed disturbed and stared at her long and hard, his eyes narrowing slightly. "Not many people have the guts to stand up to him."

"Then they're foolish," she replied.

"Or value their lives."

"Does he scare you?"

Max's grin was downright brazen. "I'm shaking in my boots. Can't you tell?"

"Better leave then—don't want Daddy to get angry."

"Anger is a way of life with him."

"Sounds like you don't like him much."

"I can just see his faults, that's all."

"So there are some? According to my mother, Jonah McKee walks on water."

That thought brought an irreverent grin to his face. "Next time he takes me fishing, I'll check," he said, and though he smiled there was an undercurrent of strain in his voice.

That had been their first meeting, and Skye hadn't been able to get him out of her mind since. Now, as the sun began to lower in the summer sky, she heard the cornstalks rustle, and Dani, her bucket filled with ears of corn, slipped between the heavy leaves. "You know, I just figured it out." Reaching into her jeans pocket, she withdrew a slightly squashed cigarette and a book of matches. "You met someone, didn't you? That's why you're not pulling at the bit to leave town." She lit up, inhaled deeply and spewed a stream of smoke from the side of her mouth.

"Those will kill you," Skye said, avoiding the topic of her love life.

But Dani, if nothing else, was dogged. "I'm not worried about lung cancer in fifty years—"

"It could be sooner, or it could be throat cancer, emphysema or heart disease. If I were you—"

"Spare me the lecture, okay? I'm a big girl. If I want to smoke, I'm damned well going to smoke." She drew in on her cigarette again. "And quit sidestepping the subject."

"Which was?"

"A guy. You're involved with a guy, aren't you?"

Skye decided there was no reason to hide the truth. Dani was bound to find out, anyway. "It's not that big of a deal," she equivocated, not wanting anyone to know, least of all Dani, how her heart hammered whenever she was with Max, how she listened for the sound of his voice all day long, how she felt warm inside when he smiled at her. They hadn't even dated, though he'd made a habit of meeting her for coffee and had brought in hamburgers when Jonah had insisted she work through lunch one day.

Once, while they'd been walking through the park after work, she'd thought he might kiss her. He hadn't, and she'd felt vastly disappointed.

"Whoever he is, he's not worth giving up your dreams for," Dani said, her eyes darkening through the curl of smoke that rose into the cloudless blue sky. "So, come on. Give. Who is he?"

"Max," she said, yanking off another ear of corn and brushing past Dani as she headed down the row.

"Max? As in McKee?" Dani's cigarette nearly dropped from her mouth. "Are you crazy?"

"I knew I shouldn't have said anything to you. It's not like we're even dating."

"I should hope not! Don't you know about him? All the McKees are trouble, every last one of them. But Max, he might be the worst."

"No one's worse than Jenner," Skye said. "He's been in jail and always seems to be on the wrong side of the law."

Dani bristled slightly. "At least Jenner's up-front. Max is as slick as a two-faced snake."

"What do you know about him?"

"Remember I was still hanging around here when you went away to school," Dani said. "He's gone with about every girl in town, broken more than his share of hearts. Then he was involved with some girl in Seattle, nearly married her, but something happened." She tossed her cigarette into the dirt and squashed it with the toe of her scuffed boot. "Rumor had it she was pregnant, but who knows?" Dani swallowed hard, and her eyes shifted to the middle distance as if she was pondering her own private thoughts. "If she was, no doubt his father found a way to convince the girl to get rid of the baby. Anyway, Max came out of it unscathed, of course, went off to law school in California and eventually landed here. Take my advice. Stay away from him—the guy's poison.'' She picked up her bucket and headed for the house.

Skye didn't argue with her. Dani had her own reasons for hating everyone with the last name of McKee. Ripping off the rest of the ripe ears, she followed her sister onto the back porch and decided to ignore Dani's well-intended advice. After all, she wasn't a silly little schoolgirl; she was twenty-three, a college graduate, and she knew her own mind. She'd dated lots of boys in her life, and though she'd never been involved with anyone as wealthy or as city polished as Max McKee, she felt she could handle him.

From the way he stalked out the door, it was obvious that Jonah McKee was furious. As he always did when he was in a particularly foul mood, he grabbed his favorite rifle, one his father had given him as a boy, and stormed out of the house. His face was a mottled red, his lips compressed into a tight, angry frown, and his eyes, two blue coals glowing with a savage light, were trained on the far end of a barn in an empty field where he'd set targets against bales of hay. His fingers clenched over the polished barrel of the gun as Max approached. ''What're you doing, getting involved with that Donahue girl?'' he demanded.

Max's first reaction was to tell him it wasn't any of his business, but he decided to keep his temper under rein. ''I just asked her for a date. I don't think that's getting involved.'' Max wished he'd kept his big mouth shut about seeing Skye, but he detested sneaking around and surely his father could already see that he was interested in her.

''She's not the right woman for you!'' Jonah shoved open a gate and spied Chester, one of the hands who worked the fields. "Saddle up Duke," he barked, and Chester nodded before heading off to the stables.

"Skye and I are just going to dinner, not that it's any of your business."

"You have a history with women."

"So do you."

Jonah spun on his older son and grabbed Max by the front of his shirt. Though no taller than his son, Jonah carried an extra seventy pounds on his large frame. "Who the hell do you think you are?" he growled, his lips barely moving, his breath smelling of expensive whiskey. "What I do is my business."

"And what I do is mine." Max shoved away from his father. "I may have to live here until my house is built, and I work for you, but don't think for an instant that you own me!"

"Don't I?" Jonah hoisted the butt of the rifle to his shoulder and fired. The bullet ripped through the center of the target. "Just remember," he said, sighting down the barrel, "I made you what you are. It was my money that sent you to college and law school, my money that bailed you out of that mess in Seattle, and my land where you're building your house. Think again before you say I don't own you, 'cause I do, son—lock, stock, and barrel."

"No way. I could've taken the job in San Francisco."

"Yeah, but you didn't, did you? Why? Because you didn't want to sweat your butt off in the city when you knew that you could come back home and have everything handed to you."

"If that's the way you feel," Max said, his voice as low as the wind rolling off the hills, "then you can take your job, your property, even your damned house and shove them all to a very dark spot where—"

"Strong words."

"And I mean every one of them. We had a deal, Dad.

I'd come back and help you with the business and you'd let me live my life the way I want to.''

Jonah's jaw tightened and he squeezed off another round. The target ripped near the center. "You're making a mistake with the Donahue girl.''

"I don't think so.''

"Damn it all.'' He reloaded, then sighted the rifle again. "You're as bad as your sister and brother. I thought, hell, I prayed, that you'd be different.''

"You mean you prayed that I could be manipulated? That I'd do whatever you wanted with no questions asked? You'd better understand something right now—if I don't agree with what you're doing, I'm going to call you on it. If I think you've made a mistake, I'll let you know. And if you start meddling in my personal life, I'll walk. Got it?''

Closing one eye, Jonah fired and missed the target entirely. "Son of a bitch,'' he growled, glaring at the bull's-eye. "You're a fool, Max. It can all be yours, you know. This whole damned ranch, the business, everything.''

"What about Jenner and Casey?''

"Jenner's made his bed, and as for Casey... she's...well, she's a woman.''

"A bright woman.''

"But she can't give me grandsons with the McKee name, now can she?''

"She can if she doesn't get married.''

Jonah turned away from the scope of his rifle and glared with pure malice at his elder son. "There will be no bastards in this family, Max, at least none that anyone ever learns about. You understand?''

"You can't control people.''

"I can damned well try.'' Jonah's grin was wide. "I bought you, didn't I?''

Before Max could answer, bootsteps and hooves

crunched in the gravel yard, and Chester, leading Jonah's favorite gray gelding, unlatched the gate. The nervous horse was already sweating as if he smelled the hostility simmering in the air and knew he was going to be ridden hard over punishing terrain. He pulled at the bridle, but Chester held him in check.

Swinging into the saddle, Jonah shoved his rifle into the scabbard.

"Goin' huntin'?" Chester asked as he rolled a blade of dry grass from one side of his mouth to the other.

"Be back at nightfall."

"It's not quite hunting season," Max said, and Jonah favored his son with a hard glance.

"I don't give a damn. In town, I play by the rules, but out here I make my own. This is my property and I own everything on it including you, my boy." With that, he shoved his heels into Duke's sides and took off at a dead gallop, heading toward the timber-laden foothills.

"Mean old cuss, ain't he?" Chester observed.

"Stupid, if you ask me. Bullheaded, proud and just plain stupid. Thinks he can bend the world to his way instead of the other way around."

"He'll git his," Chester predicted as his eyes narrowed on the distant speck that was Jonah McKee. "They always do."

The observation was disturbing. Chester was and always had been a loyal employee.

"Yep, they always do." Chester turned and headed back to the barn with his slow, purposeful gait. Max decided he wasn't going to let the fight with his father ruin his night. After all, wasn't that what the old man wanted? Brushing the dust from his shirt, he jogged back to the garage.

It was true that everything he'd earned had been paid for with McKee money, but he wasn't owned, nor could

he be manipulated or bought. Max's life was his own—
to do with as he pleased—whether Jonah knew it or not.
He'd see whomever he wanted. And right now all he
could think about was Skye. During the day, with her in
the office, he found it difficult to concentrate. Her perfume
lingered in the air, her musical voice swept over the hum
of computers and ringing of phones, and her eyes sparkled
with a special light, which made him want her all the
more. He couldn't seem to get away from her. Even at
night, visions of her crept after him and stole into bed
with him, making sleep impossible. He was hot and hard
and knew he wouldn't be satisfied until he'd made love
to her. Even then, he doubted he'd be sated. No, Skye
Donahue was the kind of woman that you just kept lusting
after. The more you had of her, the more you wanted.

Max wasn't inexperienced as far as women were concerned. For as long as he could remember, they'd been
chasing him. He wasn't stupid enough to kid himself and
knew the reasons that most of the girls found him irresist-
ible. Coupled with his rugged, ranch-tough looks was the
general knowledge that he had money. Lots of it. That he
stood to inherit a fortune. And that alone made girls and
women alike seek out his company.

As he slid into the soft leather seats of his BMW con-
vertible, he frowned. The car had been a graduation gift
from his father, and though Max loved the sporty silver
machine that hugged the mountain roads as he drove hell-
bent for leather, then roared down the straightaways while
the speedometer hovered around a hundred miles an hour,
he suddenly felt as if the sleek car was a rich boy's toy,
that it had been offered as a gift but had come with a
subtle price tag.

He eyed the expensive dash and grimaced. No wonder
his father thought he could be bought. If not money, then
a fast car, or a powerboat, or some other high-priced toy.

He squeezed his eyes shut and knew that above all else he had to be independent and respected within the company before he could ever hope to run the family business.

And it started with this car.

Glancing at his watch, he felt a sudden surge of power. There was still time, but not much. He fired up the powerful engine, let out the clutch and took off. Gravel spun beneath the tires and he left a plume of dust in his wake.

Jonah McKee was in for a big surprise. A surprise that would knock that smug, knowing grin clean from his face. Max felt a glow of satisfaction at shaking off some of the shackles of his father's wealth. It was high time he proved himself to be his own man, and he'd start tonight, first with the car and then with Skye.

Skye. His blood pounded though his veins a little faster as he thought of her. His fingers tightened over the steering wheel. As he drove through the heat of late afternoon, his thoughts spun ahead to the night stretching out before him. A night with Skye. He slipped a pair of aviator sunglasses over the bridge of his nose and smiled to himself.

Tonight he was going to take Skye to the most expensive restaurant in Dawson City and after that... His blood heated at the prospect because, though he'd tried for the better part of two weeks, he couldn't wipe the image of making love to her from his mind.

Skye was a nervous wreck. She tried on three outfits before settling on a denim skirt, white blouse and a wide black belt.

"This is crazy, you know," Dani said as she leaned against the doorway of their cramped bedroom, the same one they'd shared before Skye had gone away to school. "Going out with a McKee is about as sensible as drinking strychnine."

"Very funny."

"I'm not trying to be."

"Don't worry about me," Skye said, brushing her hair. "I can take care of myself."

"I always thought so. Until now." Dani shoved herself away from the doorframe and Skye let out her breath. She didn't need her sister giving her any advice. She'd opened her ears to the gossip surrounding Rimrock's most eligible bachelor. Most of the single women in town would gladly give their eyeteeth for a date with handsome, successful and incredibly wealthy Max McKee, but beneath the speculation about his money and sexual prowess, there had been an undercurrent of something darker, something dangerous. There were stories of women, none substantiated as far as Skye could tell, and hearts broken. She'd heard whispers about illegitimate children and Max's callous disregard for anything but his own pleasure.

The stories sounded more like rumor than fact, but her mother had always warned her that where there was smoke, there was surely going to be fire.

"Skye?" her mother called from the living-room couch. "You about ready?"

"Almost." She frowned at her reflection in the oval mirror over a long bureau, then took a few last strokes through her hair.

"Good. 'Cause you don't want to keep Max waiting." Irene Donahue was the only person in Rimrock who seemed pleased she was dating Max. "Come on out and let me see how you look!"

Feeling like a fourteen-year-old primping to get ready to go to her first dance instead of a twenty-three-year-old woman who had been accepted into medical school, she walked into the living room for inspection.

Her mother, propped by pillows and sucking juice through a straw, grinned at the sight of her. "Well, well, don't you look pretty?"

Dani snorted. Dressed in tight jeans, a tank top, her bare feet curled beneath her as she sat in their mother's favorite dilapidated rocker, Dani scowled darkly. "Like a lamb to the slaughter."

"Don't you go ruinin' Skye's good time."

"She won't," Skye said, shooting her sister a glance.

Dani shoved herself upright and stalked through the house to the back porch. Skye heard the hiss of a match being struck and knew that Dani was lighting up away from their mother's watchful eyes. Irene Donahue knew that Dani smoked, gave weekly sermons on lung cancer and heart disease, but in the end gave up and only insisted that Dani enjoy her cigarettes outside the house.

"She's always been a handful," Irene said. Just then the sound of an engine came in through the open window and the glow of headlights splashed against the wall. The older woman visibly brightened. "Looks like he's here," she said eagerly, as if it were she, not her daughter, who was going out. "You two have a good time, won't you?"

"The best."

"And never mind Dani."

"Believe me, I won't," Skye said and hurried to the little entry hall just as the doorbell chimed. She pressed her palms on her skirt, then threw open the door. At the sight of him, her throat tightened and her already-hammering heart clicked into double time. His gold-streaked hair had been combed, but was beginning to fall forward over his eyes, and his features, still all angles and planes, were more relaxed than they were in the office.

"Would you like to come in?"

He shrugged. "For a second, I guess."

She stepped out of the doorway and he passed by, only to be confronted by Skye's sister. Dani's eyes were at half-mast and her lips were twisted into a funny little pout. "Well, if it isn't his highness, Prince Maximilian."

He snorted a laugh. "It's Maxwell, but don't tell anyone. You can just call me Master."

Dani lifted an eyebrow. "I didn't know anyone named McKee had a sense of humor."

"It's a family trait we try to keep hidden."

"You don't have to try to be so rude just to impress him," Skye said, tired of her sister's antics.

Irene was waving from the couch. "Max, come on in. Ignore the girls. They're always bickering. Would you like some juice, or maybe some tea?"

Max shook his head. "Another time. We've got reservations."

"Well, go on then," Irene said with an easy smile she reserved for anyone with the McKee name. "Have a good time."

As they left, Max wrapped his fingers possessively around the crook of Skye's arm and held the door for her. Dani was still lurking in the hall, taking in the scene with angry eyes.

"What was that all about?" Max asked before opening the door of an old pickup painted with a flat gray primer.

"Dani works hard at being a rebel."

"Don't we all?" He slammed the door shut and jogged around to the driver's side of the truck.

The night was perfect. Shooting stars blazed across the sky and a quarter moon hung low over the hills.

Skye rolled down her window and felt the summer wind tug at her hair. Dust and the scent of freshly cut hay wafted into the cab of the truck and the soft notes of a country and western love song swelled from the single speaker in the dash.

"Is your car in the shop?" she asked as they rounded a curve and the lights of Dawson City glowed in the dark valley.

"Nope." He smiled, looking satisfied with himself. Patting the steering wheel, his lips twisting into a hard grin, he said, "This is my new set of wheels. What do you think?"

"Sporty," she said dryly.

"Zero to sixty in seventeen point six minutes." His smile disappeared. "Actually, I sold the BMW and bought this to make a point."

"With whom?"

"Jonah."

"Oh." Though she'd grown up hearing that Jonah McKee was the finest man to ever walk the face of the earth, she was beginning to think her mother's viewpoint of the man was skewed. Jonah was secretive and brash and there was a presence about him that made her uneasy. She'd told herself over and over again that she was being foolish, but she'd noticed the way his eyes could shift quickly, scanning a room without moving too much. He saw everything, it seemed, and he made it his business to know everything there was to know about Rimrock and its citizens. The men striding through the doors to his office were prominent citizens—Judge Rayburn, Dr. Fletcher, the mayor and several men on the city council—who came and went as if they were part of an exclusive men's club, a club that Skye guessed shaped the future of the little town of Rimrock.

"You don't like him, do you?"

Skye gave a little shrug. She didn't want to talk about Jonah. "I don't really know him."

"You work for him."

Smiling, she said, "It's only temporary, and if you want to know the truth, I'm not very good at taking orders. My mother thinks I have a problem with authority. My guess is she's right."

"Medical school might be rough."

"I'll manage," she said, her fingers curling into fists in her lap. No matter what it took, she'd get through the necessary training and the inevitable razzing from some of the guys and professors who didn't want a woman invading their turf. Most of the old prejudices had melted away over the years, but some remained, and there were always those who liked to see a woman fail. Well, this was one woman who wouldn't. "What was the point you were trying to make?" she asked when the silence had stretched too long.

He snorted. "Sounds silly."

"Come on."

"Okay. I think it's time my father knew that I'm my own man."

"He doubts that?"

"No. He *fights* it," Max said, the lines around the corners of his mouth becoming more visible. "But what else is new? Jonah P. McKee sees things only one way."

"So why didn't you stay in one of those big law firms in the city? Why'd you come back?"

Max's jaw grew hard and his eyes glittered with an intense fire. "Something I had to do." As if the conversation had suddenly become too personal, he changed the station on the radio and Rod Stewart's voice crackled from the speaker. Skye tried to recapture the carefree mood she'd felt only moments before but just the mention of Jonah McKee's name had changed the atmosphere in the truck, creating an invisible current of strain that weighed heavy in the darkness. She'd always assumed that Max and his father were similar; maybe she'd been wrong. She hoped so, because the more she knew of Jonah McKee, the less she liked the man.

Just the opposite was true with Max. The more she saw of him, the more she wanted to see. She had to keep telling herself that she might end up disappointed. He was, after all, a McKee, and as her sister Dani had been so quick to point out, McKees took what they wanted without regard for anyone else.

They drove into town, through the aging business section and toward the river. A cabin converted to a family-owned restaurant huddled on the banks of the John Day. Strings of light bulbs suspended from the roof to poles lining the walk swung in the breeze.

Inside, the restaurant was cut into small rooms angling from a small foyer. A smiling waitress guided them to a table with a view of the dark water. After they sat, she rattled off the specials of the day, then scribbled down their drink orders and promised to return soon.

The quivering flame from a fat white candle encased in glass was reflected on the glossy surface of the table, and soft music—an instrumental of an old Olivia Newton-John recording—was being piped to the rooms.

Max looked thoughtful and suddenly there was an uncomfortable silence between them.

''Why'd you ask me out?'' Skye asked. The question had been hovering in the back of her mind.

''You were surprised?''

''A little.''

A crooked smile caught hold of one side of his lips. ''I thought it was the next step.''

''To where?''

He shrugged. ''Who knows?''

''I don't think your father would approve.'' She'd recognized the looks Jonah had cast in her direction whenever Max stopped at her desk to talk. Mild disapproval beneath a benign facade. And there were other, darker glances she'd caught out of the corner of her eye when he thought she wasn't looking.

''Why wouldn't he approve?''

''He told me that you were dating Colleen Wheeler.''

Max snorted. "I took her out a couple of times. Before I met you. Jonah's idea."

"You always date the women he chooses for you?"

"Never. Except in the case of Colleen." The waitress brought their drinks and a basket of warm bread before taking their orders. When she moved to the next table, Max's eyes focused on Skye's with such an intensity her throat turned to sand. "Let's get something straight, right here, right now. I *don't* do everything my father tells me to. It may look that way because I work for him, and once in a while, I admit, I'll even humor him outside of the office, but my personal life is just that. Personal."

"He's a hard man to say no to," she observed.

"Believe me, I've had a lot of practice." He took a long swallow from his bottle of imported beer.

"So you're a rebel."

"Nope. I leave that title to Jenner." Max winked. "He works hard for it. I just question the old man a lot, that's all. It's good for him."

Skye wondered. From what she'd seen of Jonah P. McKee, she knew the man didn't like his authority challenged by anyone. That included his firstborn son.

The waitress brought their meals. Max cut into a peppered steak smothered in grilled onions while Skye, though hardly tasting the food, did reasonable damage to her salad and halibut in butter sauce. She tried not to stare at Max, was determined not to compare him to his father, but she couldn't help glancing up at him and finding him watching her with seductive turquoise eyes.

They lingered over cups of coffee and Skye listened as Max told her a little about growing up as a McKee. "It was both good and bad," he admitted. "The good was that I was given everything I wanted. The bad was that I was given everything I wanted." He set his empty cup on the table. "I can't lie. I liked the easy life, and when I finally figured out that I had to work for a living, it came as a big shock. I don't think Jenner ever got over it.''

Skye laughed. "So why do I think you're ambitious?"

He thought a minute while the waitress poured more coffee then moved to the next table. "Everyone grows up eventually. Especially when Jonah McKee gives you a swift kick in the butt. I guess he got tired of his kids being lazy, so one summer he told us that we had to learn to work if we expected to inherit anything. Jenner told him to go to hell, but I decided it was time to prove myself.''

Skye didn't comment. She'd been born with ambition. Growing up poor had only added incentive and given her the drive she'd needed to excel in school, to earn scholarships, to work as a receptionist at the clinic and put the money in the bank. While she was going to high school and clocking in more hours than the child labor laws would allow, Dani had tried to convince her to buy a car.

"We could use the wheels," Dani had said over and over again like a broken record.

Skye had been tempted, but she'd kept depositing her paychecks in the bank, looking toward a future that would help her leave Rimrock. She hadn't been able to wait to head for the city. Only now, since she'd met Max, did she question the driving force behind her need to succeed, a force that had been with her for as long as she could remember.

He drove her home in the old pickup. The summer evening drifted through the open windows. Crickets chirped in a soft chorus and the smells of dust and cut hay mingled in the warm night. He pulled up to the curb in front of her house, and as she reached for the door handle, he grabbed her hand.

"Skye..." he said softly.

She turned to face him and stared into eyes that had darkened to the color of midnight. Warm lips found hers and his arms surrounded her, drawing her close as her blood began to heat and her body began to respond. Somewhere in the back of her mind, she knew that kissing him was as dangerous as stepping over the edge of a cliff and not knowing where she would land, but she couldn't stop herself.

Her heart raced when his tongue prodded open her lips and touched the roof of her mouth. His hands splayed against her back, pressing her still closer until her breasts were crushed against his chest and her breath caught in her throat.

She felt his hands move, spanning her waist, inching forward to feel the weight of her breasts. Her insides quivered, wanting more, and his kiss deepened, turning hard and demanding.

Skye's mind began to whirl as he reached for the buttons of her blouse. The tiny pearls glided all too easily from their bonds and her breasts ached and filled her bra. Fingertips brushed her swollen flesh and sparkles of delight skipped through her blood.

"Skye," he whispered into her open mouth. He found the front clasp and her bra fell open, allowing her breasts to spill into his waiting palms. "Oh, Skye," he groaned as her nipples stood erect in the darkness, anxious and proud little points aching for more of his touch. "Please…" He lowered his head to taste her, and she, through the thin shutters of her eyelids, saw headlights flash as a car rounded the corner at the far end of the street.

At that moment, she realized what she was doing, what she was about to do, and she fought the urges that pounded through her blood. "No," she said, pushing away from him. "No, Max, I can't…not here, not now." She started fumbling with the buttons of her blouse and shook her head again and again. "I can't do this."

To her surprise, he released her. Jaw hard, he plowed both hands through his hair and let out a long, ragged breath.

"I'm sorry—"

"Don't apologize!" he snapped.

"But—"

"Just don't say anything. I rushed things. I didn't mean to, but I did." The car roared up the street, illuminating the cab with its bright lights for an instant, before passing quickly by. "Come on." He flung open the door. "I'll walk you to the house."

"You don't have to."

"Get out of the damned truck, Skye," he ordered. After she'd hopped to the ground, he slung an arm over her shoulders and guided her along the cracked walk and up the steps to the front porch where a single bulb glowed over the door. He rubbed his jaw and bit his lip. "We have to decide what we're going to do about this, you know."

"About what?"

"Don't play dumb with me, Skye. It doesn't suit you."

"I don't understand—"

"About *this!*" he hissed, kissing her again. His mouth was hard, the length of his body pressing intimately against hers even harder. Her body responded instantly, her blood heating, her knees beginning to weaken.

A wild heat began to uncoil within her and she kissed him back. This time it was her own tongue that plunged past his lips and discovered its mate. He groaned low in his throat and pushed against her, his body straining, her back flat against the screen door. Her heart thundered as he lifted his head and stared at her with glazed eyes. "Now do you understand?"

She nodded mutely and licked her lips. His eyes caught the motion and he kissed her again, more tenderly this time, but with the same undercurrent of urgency. When he lifted his head, he stared down at her and swore beneath his breath. "What you do to a man should be illegal. Hell, maybe it is." With that he pushed himself away from her and turned on his heel. Within seconds, the pickup disappeared around the corner and Skye was finally able to draw in a long, calming breath.

As she turned to open the door, she saw a movement of the blinds and realized that the window next to the old porch swing was partially open, letting in the breeze.

Great, she thought, opening the door. Dani was standing in the archway to the living room, near the window. "Have a good time?" she asked, obviously unconcerned that she was caught eavesdropping.

"It was fine."

"More than fine, I'll bet." Dani motioned toward Skye's blouse, the tail of which was pulled out of her skirt, the buttons half-undone.

"It's none of your business, Dani," Skye said, and the cockiness in Dani's stance disappeared.

"You're right," she said, biting the corner of her lip. "But just don't mess yourself up over Mr. Hotshot McKee. He's not worth it."

"You don't even know him."

"I don't have to," Dani said darkly. "I know his kind."

Chapter Six

"I won't have it, y'hear!" Jonah McKee glared out the window of his den into the black night, his fingers curling into fists of frustration. Slowly he turned and his voice was much lower, but still harsh with steely determination. "You're not to see her and that's that. How many times do I have to tell you that Skye Donahue isn't the woman for you?"

Max wasn't buying it. The old man's theatrics were beginning to wear thin. "Why?"

"What?"

"I asked why," Max repeated as calmly as he could, considering that he wanted to wring his father's neck. It was all he could do to stay sprawled upon the tufted leather couch in the den, cradling a beer and watching Jonah's jaw set into a hard line of resolve. "Why is she wrong for me?"

"A million reasons!" Jonah barked.

"One will do."

"First, she's not the same social station as you are, boy."

"No one is," Max replied, unable to hide the sarcasm in his tone. He sipped from the long-necked bottle and told himself to be patient.

"Next, she's too damned arrogant, won't do what you tell her to do."

"Doesn't she do a good job at the company?"

"Damned good," Jonah admitted. "But she doesn't like taking orders. I can see it in her eyes."

"I don't plan on ordering her around."

"Don't you? You're smitten, boy, and my guess is you're thinking about marriage." Jonah poured himself a stout three fingers of Scotch and tossed it back in one swallow. He stared at his son in the mirror over the bar. "You're getting yourself in too deep with that one."

"I just took her out once," Max said, though he cringed at the words. Jonah was right. If he had his way he'd spend every waking minute with her as well as sleep with her. And he *had* thought about marriage, for the first time in his life.

"But you sniff around her at the office, get in early, stay late. Mark my words, she's got her claws into you, boy."

Max laughed. "You've got it all wrong. I practically had to beg her to go out with me. I'm the one doing the chasing."

"Bah!" Jonah splashed more Scotch into his glass. "You're so blind you don't know when you're being manipulated."

"Good thing I've got you around to set me straight."

"Damn right," his father replied, ignoring Max's derision. "Now, you start paying attention to Colleen again. At least she's not after you for your money. The Wheelers are people like us. They belong to the country club in Dawson City, own a big spread *and* a chain of hardware stores. They travel in the same circles we do. And Colleen—'' Jonah waggled a finger at his son ''—she's a pretty thing, smart enough, but knows when to keep her opinions to herself. And she's no gold digger.''

"And Skye is?"

"She's always been after something more than she's got."

"I thought you admired ambition," Max said, tired of the conversation.

"I do. In my sons. But not in a woman. Gets their heads all turned around. Women need to do what their husbands say, make babies and keep their mouths shut."

"If I were you, I wouldn't be spouting that philosophy too loudly. Rimrock has its share of feminists, Dad, and they'd love to draw and quarter you for those kinds of sentiments."

"Like to see them try." Jonah rested a hip against his desk. "Don't get me wrong. I don't hate women. Truth to tell, I think they're the most important thing God ever gave a man. But it's not natural for them to go out and get jobs and send their kids packin' off to baby-sitters and such. It's just not the way God planned things to work, Max."

"According to you." Max finished his beer and tossed the bottle into the trash can. "Last I heard, you weren't sitting on a throne on the other side of the pearly gates."

"I'm just telling you what's best."

"And I'm just telling you that you've got to let me live my life the way I see fit, Dad."

"Not as long as you work for me."

Max's mouth twitched. "Is that a challenge? You want to see if I'll quit?" He waited a beat and saw a flicker of doubt in the old man's blue eyes. "Well, I will." Palms flat on the desk, he leaned forward so that his nose was close to his father's. "Not only that, Dad, I'll stay right here in Rimrock, start from scratch and beat you at your own game."

"You couldn't."

Max straightened and the light of challenge flared in his eyes. "Watch me."

"For God's sake, don't dig yourself into a hole you can't possibly crawl out of." He ran a tired hand around his neck. "Forget all this nonsense about Skye Donahue and quitting the company and just ask Colleen out."

"Go to hell, Dad." Without looking over his shoulder, Max strode out the door and headed toward the foyer. Voices raised in argument—his mother and Kiki debating how to dress a chicken from the sounds of it—drifted down the hallway.

Max didn't stop to listen, just left the house and climbed into his old pickup. He switched on the radio and shoved the truck into reverse.

He'd see Skye any time he damned well pleased.

Skye's shoulders ached from hours at the keyboard. She rubbed a kink out of her neck, then grabbed her purse and decided to call it a day. Though there were still a few more contracts to type, they would have to wait until the morning.

As she snapped out the lights, she heard the jangle of keys and quick, steady footsteps in the reception area. No one was supposed to be here. The hairs on the back of her neck rose as the door opened and Max strode into the suite of offices reserved for his father. Her heart was already knocking, but the sight of him caused it to beat a little faster. "I thought you went home," she said.

"I did."

"Forget something?"

His eyes found hers and her throat constricted. "Yeah." He grabbed her hand and started pulling her through the offices so fast that she had to run to keep up with him. "I forgot you."

"Wait a minute. What are you doing?" she asked, laughing and trying to catch her breath as they hurried down the stairs and out the front doors. Max paused to lock the building then hustled her toward his truck, which he'd left in a no-parking zone near the curb.

"I think it's time we got to know each other better," he said, casting her a glance she couldn't begin to understand. He seemed angry, but not with her.

"What's that supposed to mean?"

"You'll see."

"But I have to—"

"I already called your mother and told her I was taking you out. She didn't seem to mind."

"Don't you think you should have called *me?*" Skye asked, a little irritated. She wasn't a thirteen-year-old girl staying out after curfew.

"Maybe." He opened the door for her and she climbed onto the cracked seat. Once he was inside, he pumped the gas, switched on the ignition and joined the slow thread of traffic winding through town.

"I could have had plans," Skye commented.

His head whipped around and his gaze bored into hers. "Do you?" His tone was hard, demanding the truth, and yet she saw deeper emotions swirling beneath the surface of his eyes.

"No, but—"

"Then don't play silly games, Skye. It doesn't suit you." A tic developed under his eye as he squinted through the windshield.

"What is it with you?" she asked. "Have I done something to make you think that I need some good old caveman tactics?" She was flattered that he'd come and gotten her—good Lord, her heart was still racing—but part of her, the I'm-my-own-woman part, was a little incensed that he thought he could strong-arm her. So like a McKee.

"I just wanted to see you."

"You could have asked."

His fingers tightened on the steering wheel and a muscle worked in his jaw as if he was waging an inner struggle. "Would it have made a difference?"

"Yes!"

He slammed on the brakes, jerked the wheel around and skidded to a stop near the park. "Do you want to be with me?" he demanded over the noise of the idling engine.

"I meant you could have asked me to go out—"

"Do you want to be with me?" He grabbed her by the shoulders as if he intended to shake the truth from her. "Do you?" His face was a mask of determination and she could see the fine sheen of sweat on his brow, the tight lips, the anger simmering in his eyes.

"Yes, but—"

"Good!" He released her quickly, let out the clutch, ignored the speed limit and drove through town. The streetlights gave way as they slipped out of the business district and then closer to the outskirts of town, passed houses with picket fences and empty swing sets, sprinklers spraying water over parched lawns.

The road curved away from town into the surrounding hills and past the gravel drive leading to the old copper mine that had been a landmark in Rimrock for as long as Skye could remember.

"What's going on, Max?" she finally asked, when the lights of town glimmered in the distance.

"I just wanted to be with you. Alone."

He sounded sincere and she sensed a need in his voice she couldn't begin to understand. He stopped the truck at the side of the road, near a bend in the river. "Come on," he cajoled. He climbed out and reached into the back for a white paper sack.

"Where are we going?"

"You'll see."

With the aid of a flashlight, he led her down an overgrown path. Berry vines crept across the dusty trail and cobwebs stretched out in the brush and lower limbs of trees near the edge of the pathway. The smell of water filled the dry air and the rush of the river flowing swiftly on its course mingled with the hoot of a solitary owl.

"I'm not dressed for this," she said when her heel caught on a stone in the trail and she had to cling to his arm to keep from falling to her knees.

"Your mistake."

"What? I didn't even know— Hey, what do you think you're doing?" she demanded when he swung her into his arms and carried her along the treacherous path.

"Saving you and your precious shoes."

"My precious shoes are threatening to fall off," she told him as her high heels dangled precariously from her toes.

Max thought for a minute, then grabbed one of the damned shoes and slid the heel into his back pocket. He did the same with the second shoe and Skye tossed back her head and laughed. Golden hair spilled over his shoulder and the scent of her perfume teased his nostrils. Her breasts were crushed to him, and as he walked along the familiar path, he knew why he'd had to see her. It hadn't been his father's order to avoid her, though that was the impetus, but the truth of the matter was that ever since he'd kissed her, nearly a week before, he couldn't stop thinking about her and what it would be like to make love to her.

Working in the same office with her had been hell. Somehow he'd managed to joke and talk with her and they'd met for lunch one day, but the more he saw of her, the more he wanted her.

He'd had more than his share of women. Including Colleen Wheeler. It wasn't so much that he was always on the make, but women were drawn to him because of who he was. He didn't kid himself. He knew half the girls who had chased him in high school had crushes on him because he was a McKee. Later, the women in college and in San Francisco had seemed to smell his wealth—no, his *father's* wealth—and had been interested. He'd only brought three home to meet his parents and each and every one had tried to cozy up to the old man.

But Skye was different. She didn't fawn over Jonah, didn't seem to care that he was one of the most powerful men in all of eastern Oregon.

Now, with her arms around his neck and her face pressed close to his, he couldn't think beyond this night. The trees gave way to a stretch of sandy beach that hugged the river. Moonlight shimmered on the ripples of the current, and on the far shore, cliffs rose forty feet into the air.

"I used to come here as a kid," he said as he let her slide through his arms until her toes touched the ground. "Jenner and I would meet here, smoke cigarettes, drink beer and do all those grown-up things we weren't allowed to do at home."

She stood at his side, her arm brushing his sleeve. "I didn't think you got along with your brother."

"Sometimes he can be tolerable."

"And you?"

"Never," he admitted. "I'm always a pain in the backside. Just ask my old man."

She tilted her face up to his. "I don't think he'd let you work for him unless he had a pretty high opinion of you."

Max snorted. "He likes me as long as I do what he says."

"And when you don't?"

"Trouble. Big trouble." He dropped the sack he'd hauled from the truck onto the ground, then watched as the wind caught in her hair and moonlight painted the golden strands a pale shade of silver. "That's why I came looking for you tonight," he admitted, touching her silken tresses with one finger.

"Because of some kind of trouble?"

"Jonah, in all his wisdom, doesn't think I should see you."

"Why not?"

"He thinks I should date, and no doubt marry, someone he's picked out for me."

"Who?"

"Doesn't matter," he said and watched her brows draw together in frustration.

"Of course it does." He heard the hurt in her voice.

"It's you I want to be with, Skye," he whispered as if finally daring to bare his soul. "Only you." He brushed his lips across her cheek and she shuddered against him. "I've never felt this way in my entire life." She inched up her chin as if to argue with him but he captured her lips with his. The kiss shook him deep inside. When he forced her lips apart, she eagerly opened her mouth to him, and as he drew her to the ground, she offered no resistance.

She couldn't. Winding her arms around his neck, feeling the weight of his body, she fell to the soft bed of grass and sand. She didn't stop him when she felt his hand find the zipper of her dress. The fabric parted to allow the cool breath of the wind to touch her back. His fingers skimmed her spine and she wriggled closer to him.

This night there was no holding back.

He pulled the dress over her shoulders and slipped her arms from the long sleeves. The warm summer breeze brushed across her bare skin and caught in the lace of her slip.

He looked down at her, and with one hand on each shoulder, he slid off the silky straps of her bra and slip. "I want you, Skye," he said, his voice as husky as dry leaves turning in the wind. "I've wanted you from the first time I saw you in the office."

The straps fell down her arms, exposing more of her white skin to the moonlit night. She licked her lips and he groaned. The ache in his groin pounded, and hot, wet lust ran through his blood as he kissed her, and her lips seemed to melt against his. He pressed his tongue between her teeth, touching and flicking, wanting to taste every inch of her.

Skye couldn't think, could only feel as she kissed him and felt the magic of his fingers. His breathing was shallow, like her own, his hands molding over that filmy lace and kneading her breasts. Heat flooded through her body, and desire, primal and hot, exploded within her. Her breasts engorged as he touched them and her nipples strained against her bra, becoming hard, insistent buttons that needed to be stroked.

He kissed her eyes, her cheeks, her neck, leaving a slick trail of moisture to be dried by the wind. His hands, hard and demanding, delved deep within the cups of her bra, finding those hot little nubs and causing her to convulse deep inside.

"Max!" she cried, her voice caught on the breeze that crept through the canyon. "Oh, Max, please..."

He found the clasp of her bra and let her breasts spill into his hands. Stroking the nipples with hard thumbs, he buried his face between the soft mounds, kissing and breathing on her, stoking a fire so hot it was already consuming. She bucked upward, her spine arching off the ground, and he finally took one waiting nipple in his mouth.

She cried out, feeling as if he was drawing nectar from the very center of her, for with each pull of his lips, the void within her grew hotter and wetter and dark with lust. Her thoughts whirling, she found the buttons of his shirt, stripped him of the soft denim and felt his chest, rock hard with a dusting of springy hair.

He lifted his head to kiss her again, his mouth molding over hers and becoming one with her lips. She gazed up at him, his skin dewy with sweat, his hair tousled, the muscles of his shoulders straining.

"Make love to me," she said in a voice she didn't recognize as her own.

"You're sure?"

"That's why you brought me here, isn't it?" she asked, barely able to think, though the words tumbled heedlessly off her tongue. "To prove to your father that he couldn't tell you what to do, that you could take whatever you damned well pleased. Including me."

"I came up here because you're all I've been able to think about every day, every night." He swallowed and the lines of strain deepened around his mouth. "But if you don't want this—"

"I do."

"Why?"

"For the same reasons as you. I haven't been able to think about anything but you for the past two weeks," she admitted before his lips crashed down on hers and he kissed her with hungry abandon.

He stripped off her dress, kicked the garment free and then guided her hand to his jeans. "Prove it," he said gruffly.

"Prove what?"

"That you want me."

"Wh-what do you want me to do?" she whispered, her throat as dry as a desert.

"Take off my jeans."

She found his belt with trembling fingers and slipped it through the loops. Then slowly, gazing up at him and watching his every expression, she found the top button of his fly and yanked hard. The buttons, already straining from the bulge at his crotch, popped open like muted firecrackers on the Fourth of July.

"Oh, God," he whispered as she eased his jeans over his hips. He could wait no longer. He impatiently kicked away the hated clothes and suddenly lay atop her, his erection visible, his eyes as dark as the night. "I won't be able to stop," he said as if some latent nobility had risen to the surface.

"I won't ask you to." She drew his head to hers and kissed him. She didn't doubt that she was making a mistake, but she didn't care. She was too old to be a virgin any longer and Max was the only man she'd ever cared about. She didn't delude herself into thinking he loved her, or that she loved him, but she did care about him, did want to be with him and did want to make love with him.

She only hoped that when she told him her secret, he would understand.

He prodded her knees gently apart and then, with his lips still fastened to hers, thrust deep inside her, claiming her and making her a woman at last.

"You're sleeping with Max McKee, aren't you?" Dani drew deeply on her cigarette and the tip glowed bloodred in the night. She was sitting cross-legged on the old porch swing. Two weeks had passed since Skye and Max had first made love and in that time their affair had blossomed. They spent as much time together as they could.

"I don't see that it's any of your business," Skye said.

"You just don't understand about the McKees, do you? They're bad news, Skye. Real bad news. And if you've deluded yourself into thinking Max isn't a chip off the old block, you're wrong."

"Mom seems to think the McKees are the most upstanding people in the valley."

"Yeah, well, Mom's got a screw loose and we both know it. She idolizes old Jonah 'cause he came in and waved his magic golden wand when Dad died, but I don't see that he's done us all that many favors. He's a bastard," she said with such icy bitterness that Skye rubbed her bare arms.

"What did he ever do to you?"

Dani's eyes slid away and she jabbed her cigarette out in a jar lid she was using as an ashtray. "What hasn't he done to everyone in this damned town?"

"I'm not going out with Jonah."

"Max is just like him."

"You don't know what you're talking about."

"I know that he gave up a great life in San Francisco. He could have been his own man there, but instead he came running back here—to Daddy."

"You make it sound like a crime."

"Not criminal—just mercenary."

"Why do you hate them so much?"

Dani's lips tightened, then she sighed. "Personal grudge." She reached over to the windowsill and grabbed her pack of cigarettes. "You were off at college when it happened."

Skye saw the pain in her sister's eyes. "The baby," she said, her own throat working. The subject of Dani's child was never discussed; this was an unwritten law that Skye had never broken, a law that Dani had insisted upon when she'd turned up pregnant at seventeen. Dani had never named the father of her child, and with a chill as bitter cold as a November storm, Skye wondered if her younger sister had been involved with Max. Could he have been the father of her child? Oh, God. Her world turned inside out.

"Yeah. The baby." Dani nodded miserably and Skye leaned against the doorway for support.

"Wh-what happened?" she hardly dared ask. Her mind was spinning with questions and denials.

"I wanted to keep it—you know I did."

"That's all I know about it," Skye said, her heart knocking with dread.

"But Mom was worried, thought she'd end up raising it." Dani struck a match, lit her cigarette and sighed a cloud of smoke. She dropped the match in the makeshift ashtray. "Maybe she would have. I don't know."

"The baby's father—?"

Dani looked up sharply. "It wasn't Max, if that's what worries you."

Relief ran like a river through Skye's worried soul. "Then why all the hatred?"

"Because Jonah got involved. Mom was real upset and you weren't around. She didn't want to worry you, what with you being the first Donahue woman to ever set foot in a college. Anyway, she turned to McKee and he found a way for me to get rid of the baby."

"An abortion?" Skye asked, her fingers curling into the windowsill.

"No! That was his idea, but I refused and...he had a sister with a daughter who couldn't have any kids and so...well, he made all the arrangements." Tears filled her eyes and the cigarette shook in her hand. "I have a son, Skye. Somewhere...God, I don't have any idea where...there's a boy who'll be three on his next birthday, a boy I call Monty."

"You've never seen him?"

"Not since the delivery room and that was just a glimpse." Still holding her cigarette, Dani wrapped her arms around her middle as if to protect herself. "I'll probably never meet him, but I swear to God, Skye, I think about him every day of my life." She swallowed hard and blinked against the tears starring her lashes. "I never thought I wanted a kid, not like you do, but giving up my baby was the biggest mistake of my life."

"Why'd you do it?"

"For him," Dani said simply. "I didn't want him to grow up without a daddy, not knowing who he was, having people talk and gossip about him behind his back. Hell, I was still in high school, hadn't quite graduated yet. I didn't even have a job. What could I do for a kid?"

Skye dropped down on the swing. She wrapped her arms around her sister and felt tears build behind her eyes. "I'm sorry, Dani," she said. "You should have told me."

"Why?"

"Maybe I could have helped."

"It was my problem, not yours."

"But—"

"I figured the way things were, you wouldn't want to

think about my having a baby and not being able to keep it.'' Dani took a long drag on her cigarette, shrugged off Skye's arms and squashed the butt in the lid. "I'm goin' inside now, but just think hard before you get involved with a McKee. They're bad news—every last one of 'em.''

She climbed to her feet and slipped into the house before Skye could say anything else. Tucking her feet beneath her on the swing, smelling the lingering traces of smoke, Skye closed her eyes. Dani was wrong about Max. He wasn't like his father or the rest of his family. And she wouldn't get pregnant. No worry there. A sad little tug on her heart brought back the tears, but she wasn't one to feel sorry for herself. So she couldn't have children, so what? It wasn't the end of the world. Lots of people got by childless. Someday, she could adopt. She didn't even have to be married. Yet...to have a child with Max...oh, God, she shouldn't even think like this.

She was going to be a doctor.

She was going to be an independent woman.

And, whether she liked it or not, she knew deep in her soul, that she was falling in love with Max McKee.

Chapter Seven

Skye looked over the documents she'd typed—the deed and title for the old copper mine formerly owned by Ned Jansen, once a wealthy man who had fallen on bad times. Jonah McKee had been quick to buy the old mine and had convinced Jansen that the deal was sweet, that Jonah's team of geologists had found little copper ore in the mountains surrounding the mine, and only traces of anything else of value—oil, zinc, silver and gold. The team of experts had concluded that the hills around the old mine were put to better use as rangeland or as a quarry for gravel.

Jansen, a rotund man of forty-five going through his second divorce, had looked upon the McKee offer to buy the useless mine as a godsend. Not only would he be able to pay his alimony, child support, the IRS and his creditors, but he'd be able to pay the back property taxes to keep his ranch…at least for a little while. Skye had watched Ned sign the papers, stuff a check into the inner pocket of his jacket, pump Jonah's hand and thank him profusely.

"You won't be sorry you're doing this," Ned had prophesied, sweat beading near his temples. A ring of gray hair failed to hide the bald spot at his crown. "Great rangeland, a little timber and hell, who knows what can happen with the price of gravel?"

Jonah clasped the shorter man's hand warmly. "Who knows?" he said with a smile that appeared friendly and satisfied as if all parties to the deal truly were happy.

Jansen scurried out of the offices apparently glad to get away before Jonah changed his mind. The door closed and Skye realized that she and Max's father were alone. Everyone else had gone home for the day and the phones had been turned off a half an hour earlier. She felt a little edgy, but told herself she was overreacting. She'd been in the office with Jonah McKee often enough in the past, but not since his older son had defied him by openly dating her. At first they'd been discreet, but now everyone in the office knew that she and Max were seeing each other.

Jonah reached for his jacket on the brass coat tree near the door to his office, then hesitated, his hand dropping slowly. As if he was noticing Skye for the first time in weeks, he actually offered her a smile. "How's that mother of yours? She gettin' any better?"

"Every day, but it's slow and she's frustrated." Skye felt a few drops of sweat collect at the base of her neck. She shouldn't be nervous; he was just her boss, just Max's father, just the man her mother worshiped.

"I was hopin' she'd be back to work by now." He rubbed the back of his head thoughtfully, avoiding her eyes.

"The doctor said two or three more weeks, depending upon how she recovers."

He frowned for a second, then waved impatiently as if whatever he'd been thinking wasn't important. "Doesn't matter, really. Just as long as she gets well. She's a helluva woman, you know.''

"Yes."

"Worked hard to raise you girls right."

"I know."

"A shame about your daddy."

He paused, but Skye didn't respond, didn't understand where the conversation was leading. She was aware of the humming of her word processor and the tick of an old clock in the outer hall. The piped-in music was soft, a song she didn't recognize.

"I know that you've been seeing Max," he said slowly, every word measured. His blue gaze didn't move from her face even while he picked up a crystal paperweight in the shape of a ladybug and tested its weight.

"That's true."

He seemed to think things over, then said, "And you're probably sleeping with him."

"That's none of your business."

"Oh, I think it is." He tossed the paperweight into the air and caught it deftly. "He's not just my son, you know. He's the one who's gonna run this company one day. All of it—including the ranch. It's a lot of work, a lot of property to oversee, a lot of people to keep employed. Max will need a wife who can stand by him, support him without expect-ing too much for herself, a wife willing to let him be the boss—" his dark eyebrows rose over the tops of his glasses "—and most importantly, he'll need a wife who can give him sons. Strong sons."

Skye drew in a quick breath. *How did he know? How could he get the information—privileged information between a doctor and patient?* She swallowed hard but kept her gaze level, refusing to back down. "What is it you're trying to tell me, Mr. McKee?"

His eyes were suddenly opaque, without depth. "I'm just warning you that you're not the woman for my son."

Skye's insides began to shred. "Don't you think he should be the judge of that?"

"Not when he's in the throes of lust." He dropped the paperweight back onto the desk. "I just thought you should know how I feel. I won't change my mind."

"Neither will I," Skye assured him. Her fingers had curled into tight fists and she thought about the night ahead, how Max had asked her to meet him at the ranch. Would Jonah be there? Her stomach roiled slightly as he reached for his jacket again.

He didn't bother smiling when he said, "Don't forget to lock up."

By the time she got home, Skye's shock had given way to a raging fury. Who did Jonah McKee think he was—checking into her background, finding out her deepest secrets and then...and then trying to blackmail her with them?

She half ran across the dry lawn, sending grasshoppers flying out of her path, then slammed through the screen door of her mother's cottage and threw her purse on the table. Her face was hot, her fists clenched tightly, and it was all she could do to keep from screaming before she splashed cold water from the kitchen faucet on her face.

"Skye?" Irene's voice called to her from the living room. "Is that you? Are you all right?"

"No, I'm not all right," Skye said, wiping the water from her face with her hands as she strode into the living room.

Irene, in her favorite housedress, was stretched out on the couch, a glass of water on the table next to her, an old afghan tossed over her legs.

"Mr. McKee wants to know when you'll be back at work," Skye announced.

"I told him I'd return just as soon as Doc Fletcher gives me the okay. Oh, dear—"

"Don't worry, I said you'd take over when you could, and good ol' Jonah seems to be handling it."

"Are you so backed up with paperwork? Is it that busy?"

Skye shook her head. "Everything's fine as far as work goes. It's busy, but nothing I can't handle. The problem is," she said, unable to keep from blurting out the truth, "that your boss doesn't think I'm good enough to date his son."

"What? Oh, no, Skye, I can't believe—"

"Believe it, Mom. He's already talked to Max, then had the nerve to tell me to stop seeing Max—that I was the wrong woman for him."

"Oh, no!" Irene's bony hand flew to her mouth. "But why—"

"Seems he's interested in a grandson and he's already got me and Max waltzing down the aisle, saying I dos and planning a family, which of course is out of the question."

"You don't know that—"

"I heard what the doctors said after the appendicitis and P.I.D., Mom. Pelvic inflammatory disease. You remember. Because of what everyone said—that I must've gotten it from being sexually active or as a result of some sexually transmitted disease—when the truth was, it was from the appendicitis." She felt a rush of the old fury that had consumed her years before when Doc Fletcher had asked her all kinds of embarrassing questions about her sex life, which, at fourteen, didn't exist. She had been too embarrassed to talk and her mother had stood up for her. Only after discarding any of the other reasons for her infection, did Doc Fletcher decide the P.I.D. had probably been caused by her acute case of appendicitis two years before. "I'm on my way to medical school, and I know that my chances of ever having children of my own are slim."

"You don't know—"

"I do, Mom. That's the problem. Let's face it, my periods have been irregular from the beginning, and then there's the P.I.D."

"You have no reason to give up hope."

"I haven't, not really. I don't even think about it. Unless it's thrown in my face by someone like Jonah McKee." She threw herself into an old recliner by the window. "How does he know?"

Her mother had the decency to look down at her hands. She pretended interest in a nonexistent hangnail, then nervously licked her lips. "That's my fault," she admitted in a hesitant whisper.

Skye felt immediately contrite for putting her mother through this ordeal, but she wasn't going to let the subject drop. Some topics were personal—her infertility being at the top of the list. "You told him?" she demanded, trying and failing to keep her tone from being accusing.

"I had to."

"No one has to."

"All your doctor bills weren't paid by the insurance and Jonah knew about the appendectomy and offered to help out with the bills. He needed copies, of course, and well…he saw that you were having gynecological problems."

"Wonderful," Skye said with more than a trace of sarcasm. "Who else knows?"

"No one. Jonah would never tell a soul."

"How do you know that? The guy's a wild card. He plays by his own rules and damns the consequences."

Irene's back stiffened. She struggled to a sitting position. "He's been a godsend to us, Skye, and don't you ever forget it. Without Jonah's help after your father died, we would have been on the street."

"Dad died while working for him," Skye countered. "He probably just feels guilty."

"A lesser man wouldn't."

"What we're talking about is my personal life, Mom.

My female organs, for God's sake! He has no right, *no damned right* to know that kind of thing about me—''

"That couldn't be helped."

"And now he's using it against me. To get me to stop seeing Max."

"I don't believe it," Irene said firmly. "Jonah McKee is a good man. The best."

"Then God save us, 'cause we're all in a world of hurt."

"It'd be worse if he hadn't been around."

There was no talking to her mother when she was in this mood. Skye shoved herself from the chair and left her mother watching the news. In the bathroom, she stripped off her clothes and stepped into the shower. The hot water calmed her nerves, but as she lathered her body, her fingers brushed the scar left from her appendectomy, and she felt a chill as deep as the sea. Jonah McKee knew too much about her and now he was using that knowledge to manipulate her. As well as Max.

Thinking about Max, she smiled. She hadn't planned to fall in love with him; in fact had fought that silly notion. But as the days and nights had passed, she realized she'd fallen deeply, head over heels in love. Not that anything would ever come of it. Hadn't Jonah made it perfectly clear that Max was the McKee heir, that it was his lot in life to spawn children and inherit the family fortune? Leaning against the old metal shower stall, she closed her eyes and let the hot water run down her back. Children. She'd always wanted children. Or just a child. One would be enough, and the thought of never being able to bear Max's children was pure torture. Nothing would make her happier than to give Max a child.

But she'd learned long ago that children would probably never be a part of her life, not as a parent, anyway. So she'd chosen to become a pediatrician or at least a G.P. so that she could be around kids.

She hadn't wanted an emotional commitment—especially not with Max McKee. Maybe she shouldn't risk going to the McKee ranch later; maybe she was only borrowing trouble. But Max had invited her and she wasn't going to let some scare tactics from his father ruin her life. She'd meet Max as she'd promised, and if Jonah threw her off the place, so be it.

"Stupid girl," she muttered, the water running down her face.

Someone pounded furiously on the bathroom door. "Hey, leave me a little hot water, would you?" Dani yelled from the hall.

"Be right out!" Skye turned off the shower and the old pipes groaned in protest. She yanked at a towel hanging over the shower curtain rail, dried herself off and wrapped the thick terry cloth around her middle.

She shouldn't have fought with her mother. Irene was struggling to do her best for both Skye and Dani. Irene had only made the mistake of trusting the wrong man. Because he'd been kind to her. Because he'd cared for her small and very dependent family.

As she combed the tangles from her hair, she padded barefoot into the bedroom where she found Dani peeling off clothes that reeked of horses, sweat and smoke. "I thought maybe you'd up and died in there," Dani said. "I was about to dial 911."

"Very funny."

Wincing, Dani slid her arms from the sleeves of a dusty red blouse.

"Jeez, what happened?" Skye asked, staring at the bruise that had formed on Dani's upper arm.

"I got into a fight with a particularly stubborn yearling." Dani glowered at the purple welt.

"Looks like you lost."

"Yeah, but it's just round one. Unfortunately this one's bite is worse than his bark—or neigh."

Gently, Skye touched the tender area and Dani sucked

in her breath through her teeth. "What're you tryin' to do, kill me?"

"You should put some ice on it."

"Thank you, Dr. Donahue," Dani said sarcastically, then shrugged. "I'll get some from the freezer as soon as I clean up. She slid out of her smelly jeans. "Oh, guess who owns the colt? You'll love this."

Skye raised a shoulder. She didn't share her sister's love of horses—especially mean-tempered ones—and had no idea who Dani was working for this week. "I don't have a clue."

"Casey McKee. Can you believe it? She wants me to help train the mean bastard, and he decided rather than accept the bit to take a bite out of my arm."

Dani was working for Max's younger sister? "I thought she did all her own horse training."

"Too busy right now, I guess."

"Didn't you tell me once that Casey McKee was a spoiled brat?" Skye towel dried her hair and grabbed clean underwear from her drawer.

"That's right."

"But you're working for her? I thought you wanted nothing to do with the McKees."

Dani, standing in her bra and panties, grinned. "That's right, but I'm not going to turn down their money. Somehow taking money from those bastards seems like the right thing to do." She kicked her dirty clothes toward a hamper and rummaged around until she found her bathrobe. Slinging it over her shoulders, she said, "You know what the latest McKee scam is, don't you?"

"Scam?"

"Come on, Skye, you type all the papers. You've got to know that he and some of his bigwig partners—Judge Rayburn's one of them—have cooked up a deal to weasel Fred Donner out of his water rights."

"I don't believe—"

"Why not? Wildcat Creek runs through the Rayburn

spread and the Rocking M as well as the Donner homestead.'' Dani shot Skye a look over her shoulder. ''Your
boyfriend, Max, has his fingerprints all over that deal, and
it looks like Fred Donner and his family might have to
move even though his family's lived there for over a hundred years.''

Skye pulled on a plain cotton sweater and a pair of
jeans. ''I don't believe it. I typed a document for the company....'' What had it said? It was clearly about water
rights, but what was it?

''Read the fine print,'' Dani advised. ''I talked to Fred's
wife, Vickie, and she's sick over what happened. Trouble
is, she and Fred can't afford a big-city lawyer like Daddy
McKee's got in Max.'' Dani clucked her tongue. ''If you
ask me, it's criminal.''

''I don't believe it.''

''Believe what you want to believe, but old Jonah
McKee is an A1 bastard. Haven't you figured that out yet?
As for your precious Max,'' Dani said, throwing on her
robe and heading across the hall to the bathroom, ''you
know what they say. The apple doesn't fall far from the
tree.''

Dani didn't stay for supper. She had a date, didn't say
with whom, and ran out to the front of the house the
minute a huge black pickup pulled into the drive. ''Whose
rig is that?'' Irene asked, lifting herself up from the couch
and staring out the window as the truck pulled away.

''I don't know.'' Skye placed a plate of chicken and
dumplings on a TV tray and positioned it, along with the
remote control, near the couch. She felt a little guilty leaving her mother again, but she and Max were supposed to
have dinner together—just the two of them. The way
things were going, if Jonah had his way, this might be
their last time together.

''Dani doesn't confide in you?'' Irene struggled into a
sitting position and muted the television with the remote.

Skye shook her head. "She stopped doing that a long time ago. What would you like to drink. Soda? Milk? Iced tea?"

"Just water. I worry about her, you know," Irene said on a sigh. "I worry about both you girls."

"Just look after yourself, Mom. We're old enough to take care of ourselves."

"Are you?" She picked up her fork as Skye poured her some water from the pitcher on the table. "Sometimes I wonder."

By the time she'd reached the lane leading to the McKee ranch, Skye's stomach was in knots. Hands clamped on the wheel, she drove through an open gate emblazoned with the brand of the Rocking M and along a paved drive lined with hundred-year-old oak trees and a split-rail fence. "Give me strength," she prayed as a single-story ranch house came into view. Stained a warm brown, with white shutters and trimmed in river rock, the McKee home had originally been a single room, which had been added onto and remodeled until there were now two wings angling off the entrance. A wide porch faced west, shading the house from the afternoon heat.

Skye parked her car near the garage and breathed a sigh of relief when she noticed that Jonah's Jeep was nowhere in sight. She was hopeful she could avoid another confrontation with him.

She rang the bell and stiffened her spine, certain that Jonah would throw open the door and fly into a rage. Instead, when the door opened, she stood face-to-face with his wife, Virginia. She was a tall blonde, with warm brown eyes and an easy smile. "Come on in," she offered, waving Skye inside the rambling ranch house. "Max, Skye's here," she called over her shoulder.

Skye heard footsteps, but they were light and quick, unlike Max's heavier tread. Within seconds, Max's sister, Casey, rounded the corner. Shorter than Skye, with dark brown hair banded away from her face and a quick smile, she grabbed a worn jean jacket from a peg near the front door. Her face lost color at the sight of Skye. "Oh, God, is Dani okay?"

"She'll live," Skye said.

"You're not here because she was hurt?"

"Max invited Skye over," Virginia said, her brows pulling together. "Now what's this about Dani?"

Casey blew her bangs out of her eyes with a sigh of relief. "Thank God. I asked Dani to help me with Buckshot. She was here a little while ago and he tried to take a nip out of her."

"I told you that colt was too mean to keep around," Virginia said in a sudden flash of anger. "He's vicious."

"He just needs to know who's boss. That's why I called Dani."

"A lot of good it did." Some of Virginia's cordiality was wearing thin. "Where's your brother, anyway?"

"Last I saw him he was outside with Jenner."

At that moment, there were footsteps on the front porch and Max came striding in through the open door. Wearing faded jeans, a work shirt with the sleeves shoved over his forearms, he graced them all with a crooked grin before his gaze landed on Skye. "Didn't mean to keep you waiting."

"I just got here."

Virginia said, "I was just going to ask her to have dinner with us."

"Another time. We've already got plans."

"Yes, I know. Kiki told me," Virginia responded, then touched Skye on the arm. "But the invitation stands. You'll have to come out here, maybe with your family."

"I'd like that," Skye replied, though she knew it wouldn't happen. Jonah was the ruler in this family and there was no way he'd want her to sit at his table like his or Max's equal.

"We'll see you later." Max shepherded Skye into the

kitchen where the sounds of country music battled with the rumble of the dishwasher. The air was thick with the fragrances of cinnamon, coffee and fried chicken.

A thin woman with steel-colored hair was placing plastic containers into a picnic hamper while chicken sizzled in a frying pan on the stove. "I don't know why he needs all this," she said, fussing. "Easier to eat at the table, if ya ask me." Spying Max out of the corner of her eye, her pinched lips twitched a little. "Everything's done, but I can't be blamed if it gets cold by the time you sit down."

"It's fine, Kiki, really. Thanks," Max said, sweeping the hamper from the kitchen counter. "Much appreciated."

"Just see that all my things get back here."

"No problem."

He ushered Skye out the back door and helped her into his truck. "Your father's not here?" she questioned as he drove through the opened gates of one of the pastures near the house. A pair of ruts cut through the dry grass, and cattle and horses, locked away by an intricate set of gates and fences, grazed in adjacent fields. The truck bounced through the dry grass and over a small knoll.

"My father's working."

"In the office?" Skye asked, remembering Jonah as he'd left.

Max shook his head. "Meeting in Dawson City, I think."

"And you didn't have to go along?"

"I couldn't," Max said with a widening grin. "I had a date with a beautiful woman and no one, not even Jonah P. McKee, could convince me to break it."

Oh, Max! Jonah's words spun through her thoughts. *You're not the woman for him. You can't give him what he wants. He needs children—a son.* Her throat grew thick and hot tears threatened her eyes. He settled a hand over her knee and smiled at her and she melted inside. Could she deny him a child? Why not adopt? If an adopted baby wasn't a good enough grandchild for Jonah, well, to hell with the old man. But she was getting ahead of herself. Max hadn't asked her to marry him, hadn't even hinted they could have a future together.

And yet his hand was warm against her thigh, the glance he sent her confident and secure. He grabbed a pair of sunglasses from the dash and slid them onto his nose as the sun lowered over the western hills. "You take over," he said, braking for a gate.

He climbed out of the truck, slid the latch on the aluminum gate, and standing on the bottom rail, let the gate swing open. Skye put the pickup in gear and drove through, watching in the dusty sideview mirror while Max closed the gate. Tall and lean, with jeans that rode low on his hips and skin as burnished as tanned leather, he was handsome and ranch tough. No big-city lawyer, but a man weathered by the elements who could brand a bawling steer or draw up a legal contract with the same amount of ease, a man who was comfortable in faded jeans, or button-down collars and three-piece suits, a man at home on the wide open range or in the glass-and-steel towers of the city.

"Weren't you afraid I might leave you?" she asked after he climbed behind the wheel.

His smile was crookedly seductive in the hot interior of the truck. "Never."

"Never?"

He leaned over, the tip of his nose touching hers, his lips hovering just above her own. "Never," he whispered again and she felt her diaphragm slam up against her lungs. She thought he would kiss her, but instead he shoved the truck into first and drove through the pastures of bent grass and wildflowers.

"Aren't you going to tell me where you're taking me?"

"It's a surprise."

"I don't like surprises."

"Sure you do. Everybody does."

The ruts were less visible now and long blades of dry grass and weeds brushed the underbelly of the truck. They drove along the bank of Wildcat Creek until the water widened at the shallows.

Max turned into the creek.

"Hey, what're you doing?" she cried out, wondering if he'd lost his mind.

"Trust me. It's not very deep."

"Don't you people believe in bridges?"

"Not when we don't need 'em." The truck sloshed through the creek and climbed the bank on the far side where the road seemed almost nonexistent and a forest of pine and scrub oak grew on a low ridge of foothills. Finally they connected with a more defined gravel road and turned onto it. The stony drive curved through a stand of pine trees and emptied into a clearing. A house, as yet just concrete foundation, wood frame and plywood floors stood backdropped by the forest.

"What's this?"

"Home," Max said proudly. "Or it will be someday." He cut the engine and helped her out of the truck.

"I didn't know you were building a house," she said in amazement. The smell of milled wood and sawdust mingled with the dry scents of the forest.

"You thought I'd live with my family forever?" He laughed. "No way." Taking her hand, he guided her up a ramp leading to the front door, or the opening where a door would eventually be hung. "Come on in and I'll show you the place."

He guided her through the living room, den, kitchen and dining area, then helped her up a wide flight of stairs to the second floor where the rooms were marked with studs.

The sun dipped below the horizon, leaving gold shadows throughout the forest. The sky, visible through the open rafters which were waiting for a roof, turned a deep shade of lavender.

"This is the master bedroom," he said, scooping her into his arms and carrying her inside. The room was large, with a bay window overlooking what would someday be the backyard and a bathroom as big as the bedroom she shared with Dani. He set her on her feet and gazed into her eyes. "I wanted you to see it."

"Why?"

"Because I love you."

The words hung in the dusky summer air.

Her heart squeezed and she wanted to protest, but his lips found hers and he kissed her. Her breath was caught in her throat and those words, those magical, wonderful words, spun in her mind. He wound his fingers through her hair as she kissed him back, and when she finally lifted her head, her heart was pounding wildly, her insides beginning to melt.

"I love you, too, Max," she whispered, and they tumbled to the floor.

He kissed her neck and eyes while his hands delved under the hem of her cotton sweater to scale her ribs and stroke her breasts. He slipped the sweater over her head, made short work of her bra and guided her hand to the waistband of his jeans. "Make love to me, Skye," he whispered roughly against her ear.

She smiled up at him. "Always," she replied before his lips crashed over hers again. She meant it. She would love him now and always.

She clung to him as they made love and nestled her head against his shoulder afterward. Staring up at the stars through the open beams of the unfinished roof, Max held her against him and she felt the caress of a breeze wafting through windows without any glass. "I could stay here forever," she sighed contentedly and he squeezed her arm.

"I'm counting on it."

Her heart nearly stopped. "What?"

Levering himself up on an elbow, his muscular naked body pressed intimately against hers, he gazed down at her. "Marry me, Skye," he said, brushing a stray strand of hair from her cheek.

"Marry you?" The words echoed through her mind and it was all she could do not to fling her arms around him and swear that she'd be his wife forever. But she couldn't be rash and had to think about the future...about Jonah McKee...about the fact that she was barren. Her throat grew thick. She swallowed hard. "You're sure?"

"More sure than I have been of anything in a long time."

"But your father—"

"Has no say in this."

"I'd love to," she said, and triumph flashed in his eyes. He kissed her quickly and she pulled away. "Oh, Max, it's just not that easy."

"Of course it is."

"There's so much to think about." Dragging herself into a sitting position, she placed both her hands on his shoulders. "I'm not done with going to school."

"To be a doctor?" Max's brows drew together in the slightest of frowns.

"Yes."

"Are you sure that's what you want?"

"It's what I've wanted forever." Her heart nearly stopped as he stared at her, and for a second she thought he was going to tell her to give up her dreams, to be the kind of woman that Jonah thought Max needed for a wife. Instead, he grinned devilishly. "I won't stop you," he said, tracing the line of her cheek with one long finger. "If it's really what you want. But I want you to know that I believe children come first."

"Children—" *Oh, God!*

"For both of us. You and me. I mean, I don't expect you to give up your career for children. I'm not giving up mine, but we both have to agree that the kids come first. Before anything else.''

"Yes, but—''

He grinned wickedly. "We could start on a baby now,'' he said, drawing her close, letting her skin feel the hardness of his flesh, "before the wedding.''

"Wait a minute.''

He was leaning over her, his breath warm against her face. "You do want a baby, don't you?''

"Yes!''

"Then let's make one. Right here and now. In our house.''

"Whoa, Max. Can't we slow down a little? Your father—he doesn't like me. He warned me to stay away from you.''

"Did he?'' His eyes squeezed shut and rage tightened every muscle in his body. "The old bastard!'' With a string of oaths aimed at his father, he shook his head, then sighed. "He can't tell me or you what to do. He'll try, damn it, but it just won't work!''

"He'll never approve.''

"Who gives a rip?'' He hesitated, his eyes darkening and a knowing smile curving on his face. "You know nothing would make my dad turn around quicker than to become a grandfather. He talks about it constantly—grousing that there's no McKee heir, no new generation to take up the reins when Jenner and I get old. And he's hell-bent to have a grandson, not that he wouldn't love a little girl, but it's a boy he really wants.''

"That's so sexist,'' she said, feeling numb inside.

"Well, Jonah isn't exactly known for his belief in equal rights. Calls it militant feminist rhetoric. I'm not going to change his mind. Unless I give him a granddaughter.''

Skye's insides turned to ice. A child was the one thing she couldn't give anyone.

"We could be married next month,'' he said, still staring at her with those damnably erotic blue-green eyes.

"Next month? But—but I'll be at school!"

"Can't it wait?"

"No...I mean, I've been accepted...."

His jaw hardened a fraction. "So you don't want to get married?"

"Of course I do—"

"It's settled then."

"But can't we take it slower?"

Max's gaze centered on her lips. "When I'm with you, I can't think in terms of slow. I just know that I want you. Now and forever. Always."

"Always," she repeated, trying to think clearly as he kissed her.

Tell him. Tell him now! a horrid, rational little voice inside her head advised her. *Don't dig yourself into a deeper grave. He deserves to know that you can't have children, that you need your career to survive, that even though you love him with all your heart, you can't live a lie and be something other than what you are.*

Somehow she stilled that painful little voice, closed her eyes and lost herself in the wonder of Max's touch. She pushed aside all her problems and swore to herself that she'd deal with them later. When she could think clearly, when she could work her way out of this sticky situation.

She'd never been one to walk away from a challenge and she wasn't about to do it now. But she had to wait. Until the timing was right. Then, she promised herself, as she felt the weight of his body straining against hers and she gave herself to him, then she'd tell him the truth.

Chapter Eight

"**Y**ou're *what?*" Jonah roared, his eyes nearly bulging out of his head as he stared at his firstborn son. They were standing in the den, squaring off for the fight of the century, when Virginia, blast her, walked into the room. "Tell me I'm not hearing this."

Max stood firm, his damned McKee chin thrust forward in determination, the way it had all his life, his gaze rock steady. Like a stallion protecting his herd, the boy wouldn't back down an inch. "You heard me. Skye and I are getting married. Probably next month."

"That's wonderful news," Virginia said in that thin, reedy voice Jonah had begun to hate over the years.

"Bull! It's a pile of horse manure!"

Max's smile was cold. "What're you going to do, Dad? Cut me off?"

"Maybe. And wipe that stupid smirk off your face!" Jonah walked to the bar and poured himself a stiff shot, tossed the Scotch back and poured a second glass. "What about her going to medical school? I thought she wanted to be a doctor or some such nonsense.''

"It's not nonsense and she still will. Later." Max shifted slightly and Jonah smirked as if he knew he'd hit a nerve.

"You don't even know her."

"I love her. That's all that matters."

"Hell, love doesn't even enter into marriage—not a good one!" Jonah snorted. Max saw his mother get that wounded look in her eyes as she let out a soft whimper. Max suspected that Jonah didn't want to hurt her, but if she was going to go poking her nose in where it didn't belong, then he couldn't help the fact that she was upset. She should have grown a tougher skin after all these years. She was a fool if she believed that they'd ever really loved each other. As far as Max could see, love between his parents just plain didn't exist. There was lust, and his father seemed to have experienced that more than a few times, and then there was affection. But Max knew his father believed that love was an emotion created only by weak, simpering fools.

Max planted himself in front of the battle-scarred desk that had been handed from one firstborn male McKee to the next, the desk he was supposed to inherit. Jaw set, neck muscles taut, eyes glittering in determination, Max felt like a panther ready to strike. But obviously his father wasn't going to take this news lying down. Max realized that Jonah had a few tricks of his own. "You don't know all that much about her," Jonah said, watching Max's reaction. From the corner of his eye, he must have caught his wife's warning glare but ignored it.

"I know enough."

Jonah grinned. It was apparent he would love to whip the tar out of his insolent pup of a son. Unfortunately he probably couldn't anymore. Max was lean and tough and had the shoulders of an ox. "Just keep her as a mistress," Jonah suggested.

"Jonah!" Virginia stiffened in shock.

"It's the only sensible thing. Obviously he wants to get into her pants, so let him. But for God's sake—" he was staring at Max again "—don't make the mistake of marrying her! She'll make your life a living hell."

"How would you know?" Max's voice was low and full of menace.

"I know more that goes on in this town than anyone, especially you. I remember when Skye Donahue was born, when her sister came into the world and when her daddy was killed setting chokers. Hell, I owned the damned logging company where it happened." He finished his drink and wiped the back of his hand over his mouth. "I was there, saw the cable snap, saw him crushed." He gritted his teeth as if in frustration and pain. No matter what everyone in town thought, Jonah hated when one of his men was crippled or killed, and though he put up a good front, Max knew he felt a little guilty about sitting back and making money while good men risked their lives for him. He'd told Max so enough times. "Ever since Tom was killed, I've felt responsible, I guess. There wasn't much insurance money, so I helped Irene out, saw that those girls got through school, even stepped in when the younger one got into trouble." He eyed his empty glass thoughtfully and scowled. "Skye's a beautiful woman, I'll give her that, and she's smart as a whip, but she'll give you nothing but heartache, son. She's too bullheaded for her own good, wants a man-size job and won't have time for my grandkids. In fact, I'll bet she doesn't even want a family."

Max couldn't believe the old man's attitude. It wasn't as if he'd come in here expecting Jonah P. McKee's blessing. He'd just thought the family should know. After kissing Skye goodbye and watching her drive away from the ranch, he'd spied his father's Jeep in the garage and decided that it was time to tell his family how he felt.

"I don't know what you've got against Skye," he said,

every muscle in his body straining as he set his palms on the desk and glowered at the man who had sired him, "but she's going to be my wife and you, goddamn it, had better well accept her and treat her with the respect she deserves."

Virginia said, "There's no need to swear—"

"Is she giving up medical school for you?" Jonah demanded.

"No, but—"

"Did she say she'd have your kids and stay home and take care of them like she ought to?"

"Not exactly, but we talked—"

"Will she be willing to step back and let you run the business...be the breadwinner?"

"It doesn't matter."

Jonah's fist crashed down on the top of the bar. "Of course it matters, damn it! You don't need some modern woman whose head is full of all sorts of silly notions about having a career and—"

"I think Skye's a lovely girl," Virginia cut in, and her usually downcast eyes were hot with fury. "She's honest and good to her mother and ambitious and has enough spunk to stand up to you McKee men. I, for one, think this is wonderful news, and if you had any brains in that head of yours, Jonah, you'd be shaking Max's hand instead of trying to force him to make a choice between us and her."

Jonah's nostrils flared. "If she won't do what you want, and put your needs before any of her own ambitions, she's not worth it, son. You're making one helluva mistake!"

"Mine to make," Max said. Deciding there was no reason to prolong the discussion, he turned on his heel and strode out of the room, his mother's voice continuing to ring faintly in his ears.

"You had no right," Virginia said to her husband, "to talk that way to Max. Can't you see he's in love?"

"Oh, hell! *Love?* Take off your rose-colored glasses,

will you? Why am I the only one around here with enough sense to know that he's making a mistake that will ruin his life!''

Max stormed down the hall and onto the porch, letting the screen door bang shut behind him. The night was warm, with just the hint of autumn in the air, and insects battered their wings at the windows. Light glowed from the open doors to the machinery shed where he spied Jenner's long, jean-clad legs splattered with grease and extending from beneath the engine of a tractor. At the sound of footsteps on the gravel, Jenner pushed himself out from beneath the rig and stared at his older brother. ''Trouble in paradise?''

''You call this paradise?''

Jenner glanced around the night-darkened ranch. ''Heaven or hell. Sometimes you can't tell which.''

''Tonight it's hell. Believe me.''

An arrogant smile drifted lazily across Jenner's face as he stood and wiped his hands on a faded red rag he pulled from his back pocket. ''Let me guess. You had a run-in with the old man.''

''More than a run-in. I wanted to punch him out and he felt the same.''

''Great family, huh?'' Jenner snapped out the lights in the shed. ''Let's go into town, find ourselves a pint of whiskey and some good-lookin' women.''

Max didn't respond. He didn't need a drink and he didn't want any woman but Skye. Only Skye. Now and always. ''I'll pass.''

Shrugging, Jenner said, ''Suit yourself, but you look mean enough to spit nails.'' He walked to his truck, tossed the rag inside and opened a cooler he usually kept on the front seat. Grabbing a can of beer, he held it up in offering, but Max shook his head and leaned a hip against the battered truck's fender. Far in the distance, a train whistled and a coyote howled at the rising moon.

Jenner pulled the tab and took a long swallow. ''I always told you it's big trouble trying to kiss up to the old man. Following in his footsteps is a mistake.''

"I don't kiss up."

"Yeah, but you put on the 'good son' skin and sometimes it gets a little tight, doesn't it?" Jenner pulled hard on his beer.

"It fits better than the 'bad son' would."

"Does it?" Jenner barked a laugh. "I wouldn't know."

"Don't you get tired of being a rebel?"

"Don't you get tired of being a yes-man?"

"I'm not."

"Sure. You went to law school because you wanted to, right? And you came back here because you'd rather do business as a flunky for Jonah McKee than have your own practice in the big city or in some other town." He leaned closer and Max smelled oil and leather and beer. "You know that I believe in calling 'em as I see 'em, Max, and it looks to me like you're back here because of the old man's money. Old Jonah wanted you back and he reminded you that you wouldn't want to give up your inheritance—even if it cost you your freedom."

"That's not the way it is," Max growled, but Jenner's words stung like the bite of a whip.

"Isn't it? Then what're you so mad about?" Jenner drained his can of beer and crumpled it in his fist.

"We just had an argument."

"About?"

"A woman."

"The Donahue gal. I wondered when that would happen." Jenner stared off into the distance as if he could read the damned future.

"What's he got against her?"

"She's too smart. Knows her own mind. Doesn't keep her opinions to herself." Jenner swept his Stetson from the fender of his truck. Squaring his hat on his head, he said, "Don't you know that you don't have a choice about who you marry? Hell, man, you're the firstborn McKee son—the crown prince, so to speak. The old man will handpick your bride. Probably a local gal, good bloodlines, someone who has a little money. She'll have to be a good breeder. You know, someone who'll give the old man what he really wants—the next generation of McKees.''

''You make it sound like he's picking out a brood mare.''

Jenner shrugged. ''Same thing. He wants grandsons. Legitimate McKee heirs. No bastards. You've heard the speech.''

''This time he's gone too far,'' Max said. ''He doesn't know it yet, but he can't run my life.''

Laughing without a speck of mirth, Jenner climbed into his truck. ''Oh, yeah? Just watch him.''

For the first time in her life, Skye felt like a hypocrite. After making love with Max, she'd intended to tell him that she couldn't marry him, that she could never give him the children he and the rest of his family wanted. She was also going to let him know that she would never give up her career. She couldn't see herself in Virginia McKee's role, that of a housewife whose sole purpose was to stand beside her husband, be he right or wrong, never doubting him, always smiling, content to raise his children and maintain his house and, if push came to shove, blindly defending him against the world and keeping her mouth shut when she knew he was wrong.

She thought of Max and her insides warmed. He was strong and handsome and he loved her. So everything should be perfect.

As she drove home, she decided she had no choice but to tell him the truth and let the chips fall where they may. He needed to know how she felt about her career and the painful fact that she could never bear him a child. Oh, there was a chance, she supposed, but a slim one. She'd seen several doctors about her irregular menstrual cycle, and after giving each of them her history of pelvic inflammatory disease, it was generally concluded that she would have trouble conceiving. Then, even if she did, there would likely be problems in carrying the baby to term.

Maybe Max wouldn't care.

"Don't be a fool," she said aloud. "You saw how his eyes shone when he talked about children." She wouldn't deny him the right to be a father. She loved him too much.

She had trouble sleeping that night and was on pins and needles the next day at work. Max wasn't around. He and his father and some business partners had flown to Spokane, Washington, to discuss some real estate deal. He might be gone for several days and that thought was depressing.

Her in-basket was overflowing, and by the time five o'clock rolled around, she was barely half finished. She drove home and helped her mother and Dani with dinner. Dani had spent half the day at the McKee ranch, working with Casey's stubborn colt.

"Heard you caused quite a scene last night," Dani said as she fried strips of bacon for sandwiches. Irene was in the living room trying to watch the news, and the two sisters were alone.

"A scene?" Skye said, her insides tying into tense knots. "Mmm. Casey was in her room when all hell broke loose between Max and his old man." She swallowed hard. "Seems Max wants to marry you." Dani's eyes lifted to meet Skye's. The bacon sizzled, unattended, in the cast-iron skillet.

No reason to lie. "We've talked about it."

"And…" Dani prodded, her expression unreadable.

"And I left it up in the air."

"Why? Either you want to marry him or you don't," she said.

"Without any advice from you?"

"You know how I feel about the McKees. They're as thick as thieves. All of 'em."

"Seems you're there enough."

Grease spattered from the frying pan and Dani forked the bacon, flipping the strips over. "Look, I don't really like Casey. She's a spoiled brat, but—" she shrugged a shoulder "—she's not as bad as I thought she was."

"Maybe Max isn't, either."

"He's just like his father," Dani said, looking suddenly wise beyond her years.

Irene's voice rose above the chatter of the television. "What're you girls talking about?"

"Nothing, Mom," Skye said, sending Dani a pleading look as their mother shuffled her way into the kitchen. Irene was able to be on her feet for a few hours these days, but allowed her daughters to baby her by making dinner and cleaning the kitchen.

"Hey, watch that skillet," Irene said sharply to Dani. "Crispy is one thing. Burned black is another."

"Don't worry," Dani said as she started pronging the bacon out of the pan and dropping the greasy strips onto paper towels spread over a large, chipped plate.

"What's this about you and Max?" Irene stared at her elder daughter, and Skye suddenly wished she could just drop through the floor.

Though she knew she was begging for trouble, she couldn't lie.

"He asked me to marry him."

"Did he?" Irene's eyes suddenly glistened and she hugged Skye fiercely. "How wonderful!"

"I don't know if I can, Mom."

"Why not?" Irene asked, holding Skye at arm's length and staring at her as if she were crazy. "He's a wonderful man. Educated. Handsome. Sexy."

"Wealthy," Dani said with more than a touch of sarcasm.

"Well, yes, that never hurts," Irene said, still blinking from her sudden onslaught of tears.

"And he can be bought," Dani said.

"Hush! You don't know what you're talking about!"

"Don't do it, Skye. Max would only make you miserable." Dani picked up the skillet, burned her hand and let the pan drop back onto the stove. "Damn it!"

"I don't know what you've got against Max, but you're wrong. He's decent and fair—"

"Check with Vickie Donner or Steve Jansen." Dani turned on the faucet and stuck her burned fingers under the cold stream of water. "Vickie's husband and Steve's father were both swindled by Jonah McKee, and guess who drew up the legal papers? Good old Max. He's probably up in Spokane right now screwing someone over."

Irene caught her younger daughter's arm and squeezed with all the strength she could muster. "I won't have you talking like this, Dani!"

"I'm just tellin' it like it is."

"You won't bad-mouth the McKees! Not in this house."

"What if I do?" Dani asked, her eyes narrowing to small slits.

"Wait a minute." Skye tried to intervene as she dug out ice cubes from a tray and dropped them into a plastic bag. "Here, use this." She hoped the subject of the McKees would be forgotten, but Irene wasn't about to give up.

"I won't have all this rough talk in my house, you hear me? While you're living in this house—"

"Fine! Then I'll leave!" Dani jerked her arm away from her mother's grip. Her hand smashed into Skye's, sending the plastic bag flying across the room. Ice cubes skittered across the cracked linoleum of the kitchen floor. Dani, red-blond hair flying behind her like a banner, stomped to the little bedroom she shared with Skye. The door slammed with a thud that shook the house to its foundation.

"Oh, for God's sake!" Irene cried. "I don't know what will become of her!" Running a trembling hand through her permed hair, she sighed loudly. "I can't control her. Never have been able to. Oh, Lordy…"

"She'll cool off." Skye was already hurrying down the short hallway. She threw open the door and found Dani bending over the dresser as she ripped clothes from the drawers and flung them into the suitcase lying open on the bed. "What do you think you're doing?"

"What does it look like?"

"Dani, come on—" She tried to reach for her sister's arm, but Dani shoved her hand away and sent her a look of pure hatred.

"Don't, Skye, okay? This is something that's been coming for a long time!"

"You just can't walk out."

"Sure I can." She threw jeans, underwear, socks and sweatshirts into the suitcase, swept the bureau top clean of her earrings and makeup and tossed the whole lot into a zippered pouch, which she pitched into the open case.

"Dani, calm down. For God's sake—"

Dani snapped the case shut with a resolute click. "Leave it alone, Skye. You have no idea what I'm going through."

"Mom's still not on her feet."

"You take care of her."

"This will kill her."

Dani's smile was cold. "I don't think so." She threw her jean jacket over her shoulder, grabbed the bag from the bed and stormed out the door, nearly plowing into her mother. "She's only got another week, anyway, then she'll be back at work. Doc Fletcher told her so today. Not that I really give a damn."

"You're not leaving," Irene said, her spine stiff, though her lips quivered slightly.

"Sure I am."

"You can't—"

"I'm twenty-one, Mom. Last I heard I was considered an adult at eighteen. You can't stop me."

"But—oh, God, Dani," Irene whispered as if she finally understood that her daughter was truly leaving. "Where—where will you go?"

"Don't worry about it."

"And how?"

"I'll hitch."

"You can't! Danielle, don't be stupid. It's dangerous. You can't accept a ride with just any—"

"I can handle myself," Dani said and shoved her way past her mother to the front porch. "I always have." Her footsteps thundered down the steps.

"Don't let her do this," Irene begged weakly, clutching Skye's arm.

"I won't. Dani—" Skye ran after her sister, but Dani was already halfway down the block. "I'll be back later, Mom," she said, racing outside and leaving her mother sitting in the living room, her head cradled in her hands.

Skye ran to the Mustang and jumped into the familiar interior. The old engine coughed, then caught, and she let out the clutch and took off. Dust and gravel spun from beneath the tires.

She caught up with Dani at the first stoplight.

Leaning against a lamppost, smoking a cigarette, her thumb sticking up in the air, Dani in faded blue jeans looked like a cross between a hooker and a rodeo queen. Skye ignored the green light and leaned over, pushing open the passenger door. "Get in."

"No way."

"For God's sake—"

A horn blasted behind Skye, and a man in a red sedan shouted, "Hey, lady, it's not gonna get any greener!"

Skye ignored the taunt and the red car zoomed past her, leaving a cloud of blue exhaust fumes.

"Dani, please—"

"Oh, for cryin' out loud." Dani ground the butt of her cigarette under the toe of her boot. "Okay, I'll get in, but I'm not going back home. Not tonight."

"You sure?"

"Unless you promise to take me down to the Lucky Star, I'm not going anywhere."

"Okay, fair enough," Skye agreed. The Lucky Star was a dive of a motel located on Lee Street, but the units were clean and cheap. Dani would be safe for the night. Maybe by morning, she'd cool off, but the glower on her face didn't give Skye much hope.

Dani, muttering something under her breath, tossed her suitcase onto the back seat and slid into the front as another car, horn blaring loudly, squealed past. "I don't even know how we got into this fight."

"It was about Max."

"Oh, right." Dani fidgeted with the door handle, then said, "Do me and yourself a favor. Before you do anything as stupid as marrying Max, check out some of those deals his old man cooked up." She tossed her hair out of her face and slid low in the seat. "Maybe Max is clean. Maybe he found a way to keep from sticking his hands into his father's dirty business, but I'd bet against it."

Skye guided the Mustang through the narrow streets of Rimrock as Dani stared sightlessly out the window.

"Why do you hate Max so much?"

"Not Max. Jonah." She spat out his name as if it tasted foul. Hazarding a glance at her sister, she added, "I can't help it. I feel that he took away the only thing that ever mattered to me." Her mouth pinched hard at the corners. "He'd stomp on his own mother if it would make him a few more dollars. Believe me, Jonah's sold his soul to the devil—time and time again." They pulled into the parking lot of the Lucky Star and Dani's face drained of color. Her bravado seemed to fade. "You know," she said nervously, her fingers fumbling with the strap of her purse, "Jonah cheats on his wife."

"That's just gossip," Skye said quickly. "He's been married for years."

"And he's had one fling after another." Dani's face appeared gaunt in the harsh lights of the parking lot.

"Look, I don't like the man, but I don't believe every rumor I hear about him."

Dani studied her hands, and for a moment, Skye thought her hard-as-nails sister might break down and cry. "I think Max is a lot like his old man."

"You don't know that."

"Then prove me wrong." All the defiance had left her features and she simply looked tired. "You know, I hope you're right about Max. Because you love him too much. You've got him up on a pedestal and no man can handle that. He's human. And he does have faults. You're just afraid to look long enough to see them." She grabbed her suitcase and climbed out of the car. Kicking the door shut, she never looked back as she walked into the office of the motel.

Emotionally drained, Skye sighed. Her shoulders sagged and she leaned heavily on the wheel. Was it true? Was she seeing Max as she wanted to see him and not as the man he really was? She let the Mustang idle and watched the small motel office through the glass. A black cat was wandering over the counter, and the manager, a short man with strings of red-brown hair combed carefully over his thinning crown, appeared through a doorway when Dani slapped a bell. Displaying crooked teeth, he smiled at her as she registered. Then, with a wink, he handed her a key and pointed to an upper unit facing the street.

Skye waited until Dani had climbed the stairs and disappeared into unit 19 before she slammed the little car into gear and pulled out of the lot.

Dani was wrong. She had to be. Max was good. Fair.

Loving. And it didn't matter, anyway, because Skye couldn't marry him. But not because of any fault in him. Only because she was determined to have a career of her own, to carve out a niche for herself, and to accept the fact that she would never bear a child. Someday, after she'd graduated and established a practice of her own, she would marry. She and her husband would adopt children, or maybe he would have a son or daughter from a previous marriage. It didn't matter. She'd love those babies as if she'd carried them in her body. And she'd love the man…even if he wasn't Max.

Her heart caught at that thought and she drove without seeing the streets or paying attention to the traffic. Her motions were automatic, her mind wandering restlessly over disturbing territory. Her future. A future without Max McKee.

She felt the tears drip from her chin before she realized that she'd been crying. "Fool," she muttered, swiping at her eyes. She needed to get home, but Dani's words kept pounding in her brain, and she drove away from Irene Donahue's little cottage and farther into town. Her throat tight, she pulled into the city parking lot one block away from McKee Enterprises. She didn't even know what she was hoping to find out, didn't even have a plan. She parked in the lot as she did every day from habit, she told herself, not because she didn't want her car seen in the vacant company lot, not because she was going on a search for something incriminating against the man she loved.

Heart in her throat, she walked quickly along the darkened sidewalk to the back door of the building. With shaking fingers, she dug through her purse and found her mother's set of keys and unlocked the door, careful to bolt it again behind her. Jonah's office was on the second floor.

The building looked creepy at night. Cast in shadows, with only a few security lights glowing in a blue fluorescent haze, the rooms were a far cry from the bustling, noisy offices she was used to. As she took the back stairs to the suite of offices where she worked, she could hear herself breathe. No computers hummed, the air-conditioning wasn't rattling, no phones jangled, no co-workers laughed or talked, and no piped-in music played instrumental renditions of old rock-and-roll songs. The rooms were as silent as the grave.

Heart thudding, she switched on one bank of lights on the second floor and started going through the files. Starting with the Donner water-rights contract, she scanned all the documents, signed by Fred Donner, Ralph Fletcher, Jonah P. McKee and Judge Ted Rayburn. The agreement was straightforward. Donner would be compensated for his loss of water. Nothing wrong with that.

Skye worried her lip between her teeth. The last few years had been extremely dry, a drought of unheard-of proportions, and the money offered Donner couldn't possibly compensate for the loss of a means to irrigate. He was allowed some water, true, and she really didn't understand how much or how little that was. Enough for the house? The cattle? Did he have a well?

Her throat turned to sand as she picked through the documents and saw an old loan ledger for a note between Donner and McKee Enterprises for ten thousand dollars. Checking the schedule of payments, it was obvious Fred hadn't been able to pay back his loan and had defaulted. However, the note had been forgiven, marked paid in full upon the signing of the water-rights document. So Fred, probably desperate for cash, had made the mistake of borrowing money from Jonah McKee, and when he couldn't make the payments, Jonah had accepted compensation in the form of water rights.

Skye felt sick.

She told herself the agreement had been drawn up and signed while Max was still in college. The new agreement was just an extension of the old one. If Max was involved,

surely he wouldn't have suspected that his father had re-
sorted to some sort of legal extortion.

She shoved the file back in the drawer and found another, heavier sheaf of papers for the Jansen copper mine.
Sitting at her desk, she perused all the legalese, studied
Ned Jansen's financial statements and decided he, too, had
been in desperate economic straits. His house and ranch
were mortgaged to the hilt, he was paying two wives child
support, and the copper mine needed new equipment. His
geological surveys demonstrated that the land was valuable, while Jonah's had found the land worthless for mining. Either way, Jansen couldn't make the old mine prof-
itable. He'd sold the land and mineral rights to Jonah for
enough money to pay off the IRS, his ex-wives and the
back taxes on his ranch. Nothing illegal. Not really. It was
all just slightly unethical—like a vulture circling a
wounded sheep, waiting for it to die.

Her stomach was queasy as she read the final page of
the contract. She was about to stuff it into the file, but
froze. "Oh, God," she whispered, staring at the very bottom of the document. It was signed by none other than
Maxwell McKee.

Chapter Nine

No! She dropped the file onto her desk and thought she might be sick. A cold sweat broke out across her forehead. So he'd signed a few documents. Big deal. That didn't make him a criminal—just an opportunist. Oh, God. Insides churning, she pulled out a few more of the files she'd worked on recently. When she'd typed some of the leases for properties in town, she wondered why she hadn't looked deeper into the thick sheaves of paper in the document files. In several cases, there was proof that the person who had originally owned the building had gotten himself into financial trouble, and good old Jonah McKee had bailed him out by lending him money, which was inevitably defaulted on. The owner had no choice but to turn over the property used as collateral.

Jonah was as bad as Dani had said he was—maybe worse. And Max was following in his footsteps.

Max's signature wasn't on any of the older documents,

but in the past few months that he'd worked for his father, he'd signed several of the leases.

How could she have been such a fool? She dropped her head into her hands and barely heard the sound of footsteps in the outer hallway. Her heart jumped when she realized she wasn't alone, and she'd started to return the documents to the file drawers when the door to the suite swung open.

Jonah McKee loomed in the doorway. His blue eyes burned with rage and his color was high. He smelled of alcohol and his usually crisp western-cut suit was rumpled. "What're you doin' here?" he demanded.

"Just looking through the files."

"I can see that. Why?"

"I had to check some things out. Things that were beginning to bother me," she said, refusing to back down, though deep inside she was scared. It was time to get to the bottom of this. "The Donner water rights for one thing and the Jansen copper mine."

His jaw tightened. "None of your business. You're just paid to type an' file."

"You forced Donner off his land."

"Donner's a fool. Always has been." He waved away her arguments. "I didn't force anyone to do anythin'."

"What you did—"

"Was perfectly legal. Within the law." His eyes narrowed. "What do you care? How do you even know 'bout it? Ah, don't tell me. Donner's always been a crybaby. He's probably whinin' all over town about what a raw deal he got. But he came to me when he was in trouble and the bank wouldn't lend him another dime."

"So you stole his water rights."

"Bought 'em," Jonah clarified. "It was the only thing he had that I wanted."

"That's extortion!"

"Nope. That's good business. And all within the law. Now, let's get down to what we really need to discuss."

He sat on the edge of her desk and folded his hands in his lap. Though he seemed calm, a quiet rage still simmered in his eyes and a tic near his forehead gave away his impatience. "Max tells me he's asked you to marry him."

She felt her spine stiffen. She slammed the file drawer shut and leaned against the cold metal. "That's right."

"And what have you got to say about it?" He stared at her, unblinking, like a snake raising its head to test the wind.

She was cornered. "I love your son."

"You're not the first."

"I want to marry him."

"Again, you'll have to stand in line." He picked up a pen from her desk and studied the instrument's smooth plastic lines. "I told him I didn't think you were the right woman for him, that he'd have trouble keeping you in line, but he seems to think that no one else is good enough."

She didn't respond. Just waited for the bomb she felt sure was about to drop.

"I couldn't talk any sense into him. So I guess it's up to you."

"To do what?"

"Turn him down, of course." He reached into his pocket, found his checkbook and clicked the pen. "How much will it cost me?"

"What?"

"Everyone has a price. What's yours?"

She couldn't believe her ears. "You're out of your mind."

"Medical school's expensive."

"I can handle it."

"On what your mother makes?" He snorted and shook his great head. "I don't think so."

"There are loans and grants and scholarships—"

"Twenty-five thousand?"

She gasped. "You've got me all wrong."

"Thirty."

She pushed herself upright and walked over to where he was sitting on the edge of her desk. Then, to make sure he understood, she leaned forward and glared into those cold, unblinking eyes. The smell of Scotch and smoke clung to him. "*No* amount of money will convince me," she said.

His mouth twitched a little and he stuck a finger against her abdomen. "I know about you, Skye. You won't be able to give Max any sons. No grandkids for me and Virginia."

She wanted to die, but stood her ground. "It's not for certain."

"But you don't really think you can conceive, do you?"

"This is none of your business," she hissed, shaken by his sudden attack on her womanhood.

"It is when it involves my boy! I want grandkids. Lots of 'em. And not bastards. Good, strong, legitimate McKees. Now listen here, missy. I'm offerin' you good money to turn my boy down. All you have to do is take a check, tell Max no, and walk out of town. Easy as pie."

"I don't want anything from you," she said in a tone that could cut through steel.

"I'd be careful, if I was you. You know, your mama works for me and I make sure her bills get paid. Who do you think took care of the deductible for that last operation?"

"But—"

His features became even harsher. "And when your sister was knocked up, I found a way to get her out of town without doin' too much damage to her reputation. Found a family—a good, decent, God-fearin' family—to adopt her bastard without any questions asked."

"She hates you for it."

Something unreadable flickered in his cold, cold eyes.

"She might, but your mama, she was mighty glad I stepped in and played the role of the caring father. Your mama, she thinks a lot of me. Likes her job. Enjoys livin' in the cottage."

Skye sucked in her breath as she finally figured out what he was getting at. "You're *threatening* me?" she asked, disgusted at his tactics. "You'd actually threaten my mother and my sister just so I wouldn't marry Max?"

"Just showin' you all the considerations. Your mama's not in the best of health, and your sister, she's a stubborn one, a regular hellcat, who might land on her feet…and then again maybe she won't."

Skye couldn't give up without a fight. It wasn't in her nature. "I won't be intimidated into doing something I don't believe in, Mr. McKee."

She started to turn away from him, but his hand came out and captured her, hard, strong fingers wrapping around her slim wrist. "Just hear me out."

She yanked her arm away and took a step back. "I'll go to the press. Tell the newspapers what you've been doing, how you tried to bribe me, and when that didn't work, how you threatened my family."

"That wouldn't help Max."

"Max doesn't need help."

"Doesn't he?" One dark brow cocked insolently upward. "You should know that if I go down, he goes down…and I mean it. His reputation will be ruined and I wouldn't be surprised if he was disbarred. That's right, little lady, I won't take any fall alone. Max goes down with me in one bright, blazing ball of hellish fury."

"You'd do that?" she asked, horrified.

"In a heartbeat."

"To your own son?"

"He's in this with me."

"No—"

"Don't underestimate me," he warned. "Others have tried and they've lived to regret it." He motioned toward the file cabinets. "You've been snoopin' around, missy, and you're not dumb. Max has been hammering out quite a few deals lately."

"No!"

"I'm not gonna cover up for him." The set of his jaw and the determination in his eyes convinced her that he would do whatever it took to get what he wanted.

Dani's warnings clanged inside her head as she fumbled for the door. "I don't believe you."

"You'd better, Skye. Because I think you care about your mother and your sister, and if you leave my boy alone, I swear to you that they'll never have to worry. For the rest of their lives. You and I both know that you'll end up on top, go to school, earn your degree, come out a doctor. But that sister of yours has always been trouble. Never had a lick of responsibility. And your mama, well, she's gettin' up in years and her health's not that great to begin with. If she stays on here at the company, she's got a good job and a nice little retirement, but if I have to do some layin' off—"

"You're a bastard!"

"And you're pushin' me too hard. If you're gonna play hardball, Skye, be sure your bat's big enough. If not, get off the field."

A small sound of protest escaped from Skye's throat.

"I'll take care of 'em both," he promised. "Your mother and sister. They won't have to worry. I promise." His eyes suddenly turned warm, as if he enjoyed the thought of playing God, as if he couldn't wait to take Irene and Dani under his wing.

"Oh my God!" she whispered, and it sounded like a prayer. Her scrabbling fingers found the knob and she yanked the door open.

"You forgot something," he called out. He finished writing the check and ripped it out of his checkbook.

She didn't bother to answer, just slammed the door behind her and ran as fast as her legs would carry her down the stairs, stumbling blindly, just wanting to get away— far away.

How could she love someone as much as she loved Max when his father, the man he worked for, the man he would someday become, was such a self-important cheat? She couldn't imagine herself going to family dinners, or spending Christmas with the McKees at the Rocking M ranch, or traveling on business trips with her husband, knowing that he lived in Jonah's shadow and would someday become the president of such a morally corrupt business as McKee Enterprises.

Visibly shaking, she jumped into her car and pumped the gas, flooding the engine. "Come on, come on," she yelled hysterically as she pounded the steering wheel. This was no time for the car to be obstinate. With a roar, the engine caught, and she threw the car into reverse. Blinking against hot tears, she shifted again and tore out of the lot. The tires groaned and the engine whined as she shifted quickly through the gears.

The rest of the traffic went by in a blur. She drove without paying any attention to road signs or traffic lights, but somehow she made it home. Oh, Lord. Emotionally drained, she wiped her face and climbed out of the car.

Max was waiting for her on the front porch. Leaning against the back of the swing, one booted foot propped on his knee, he glanced at his watch, then studied her face.

"Something's wrong." His voice was like a caress. He was on his feet in an instant and she tumbled into his arms.

"Max," she whispered brokenly, knowing that this might be the last time she ever touched him. "Oh, God, Max!" She was kissing his face, his neck, his shoulders.

His strength seemed to bleed into her and she died a little inside knowing that she'd never again love anyone as passionately as she loved Max McKee.

"Skye. Baby, what is it?"

Everything! Me! You! The fact that I love you too much!
He was warm and solid. The truth lodged in her throat
and before she could say a word, the screen door creaked
open.

"Thank God you're home," Irene said, and with the
pale light from the living room at her back, she looked
older and more frail than her years. "Did you find Dani?"

"She's all right. At the Lucky Star." Reluctantly Skye
pulled out of Max's embrace. *Could it be true? Could he
be as ruthless as his father?*

"That's no place for a young girl!" Irene's hand flew
to her chest. "I'd better call down there—"

"Mom, don't!" Skye said in a voice sounding far too
husky to be her own. "She needs time to cool off."

"But alone in that fleabag? No way. I'll call the police—"

"Mom! No! Just listen. Dani's trying to make some
sense out of her life. She's been pushed around and
messed up for years. Give her the chance to find herself."

"But it's not safe!"

"It's a damned sight safer than hitchhiking, don't you
think? Who knows? In the morning, she may come back."

Irene's lower lip trembled. "Oh, Lordy," she whispered, "that girl will be the death of me yet." She stared
at her elder daughter in resignation. "All right, I won't
push her this time, but if anything happens to her, I'll
never forgive myself."

"She'll be fine."

"Well, come on in, both of you. I offered to make Max
some coffee when he came lookin' for you, but he wanted
to wait on the porch, but now—"

"Coffee'll be fine," Max said, his brows knit as he
gazed at Skye. He linked his fingers through hers and
offered her a smile she would treasure for the rest of her
life.

Something was wrong. Seriously wrong. Max could
feel it in his bones. Skye was hiding something from him

and it didn't have a damned thing to do with her sister taking a hike. No, it was a deeper trouble—he could see it in her eyes.

Gritting his teeth, he sat through coffee, managed small talk with Irene, then watched gratefully as Skye finally helped her mother to bed. The older woman was distraught, worried sick about Dani. But Max didn't give a rip about the girl; his only concern was Skye.

"What is it?" he asked when they were finally alone outside near the garden. "Something happened."

She wouldn't meet his eyes. "It's just Dani—"

"Don't lie to me!" His voice was a harsh whisper, and he grabbed her roughly, cupping her chin and forcing her to look into his eyes.

What he saw there tore at his soul. Desperation darkened his gaze. "You're not going to marry me, are you?"

"I..." She looked away and tears starred her lashes. "I...can't."

"Why?"

"So many reasons," she said heavily as if her heart was truly breaking.

"Name one." His fingers dug deep into her arms, and though he was afraid he might bruise her, he couldn't let go.

"Oh, God, Max, don't make me."

"Do you love me?" he demanded, his world beginning to crack. This couldn't be happening! He had so many plans for the future, plans that would quickly turn to dust if he had to do them alone. Without Skye, he had no reason to go on.

"It's not about love—"

"Do you?"

"Yes!" She sniffed loudly and stared up at him with glistening eyes. "I love you."

"Then there's no reason on earth, no reason good enough, to keep us apart." He felt a pressure building in his chest, then thundering and pulsing through his body. "What is it, Skye?"

She looked away and he shook her roughly.

"What?" he demanded.

"I can't be the kind of wife you need."

"Bull!"

"Believe me, if I could, I would."

Then it hit him. She was lying. About everything. She didn't love him, not the way he'd thought, not the way he loved her. Not with the blind, lust-filled need that had eclipsed everything else in his shallow life. Not more than her career, not more than her ambitions. She'd been lying all along. Oh, she cared for him, he knew that much, but she didn't love him.

Slowly he released her, his fingers uncurling as he let go. "Then I guess there's nothing left to say," he muttered, shoving down the pain, refusing to give in to the rage that threatened to burst inside him. He wasn't used to losing, to not having anything he wanted, and he wanted Skye. More than any man had a right to want a woman.

The earth seemed to buckle beneath his feet and he blindly turned and started for the front of the house where his pickup was parked.

"Max—"

"Forget it, Skye," he growled, wanting to hit, to scream, to drink himself into oblivion.

"But—"

He whirled, fists clenched, his skin tight from the anger that coiled all his muscles. She looked up at him with those incredible hazel eyes and he thought about making love to her again and again until she realized that she belonged with him. But he stood his ground and leveled her with a look of pure disgust. "Don't play with me, Skye. It's over!"

"Oh, God," she moaned, leaning against the gnarled bark of a solitary pine tree. The tracks of tears glistened on her cheeks, but Max wouldn't let himself be moved by her display. She was acting. It was so obvious now. And damn it, his father, curse the old man's thick hide, had been right about her. "Please, just listen—"

"What? To more lies?" he snapped. "I'm not that much of a fool."

"I do love you."

"You don't know the meaning of the word, lady," he snarled, wanting to wound her as badly as she'd hurt him. "And don't bother playing the part of the victim, Skye. It doesn't suit you." He turned and headed back up the overgrown path leading to the front of the house.

He had to get away, far from her, but over the pounding of his heart and the fury that thudded through his brain, he thought he heard her whisper, "I do love you, Max. I do. And I always will. Always."

It had been a lie, of course; he'd learned the truth later. But despite all the years that had gone by, he'd never forgotten the desperation in her tone.

Chapter Ten

Max was still caught up in memories of Skye and all her lies as he sat parked in his truck in the yard of the ranch house—his father's house. Though Jonah was dead, his spirit seemed to linger somehow, and as Max gazed into the night sky, he wished he'd known the truth about Skye before he'd gotten so involved with her.

Even after that last argument at her mother's house all those years ago, he'd wanted to believe her, to trust her. A part of him had been obsessed with her and he'd thought about talking to her again. But she'd left, and before he could chase her down and demand answers, his father had intervened. Max could hear the old man's words as if he'd spoken them just yesterday rather than seven years ago.

"Don't tell me," Jonah had said, a smile stretching across his face as he climbed out of the saddle. Duke sidestepped and Jonah slapped his reins into Chester's outstretched hands. "You think I had something to do with Skye Donahue taking a hike."

Max had been livid and ready to land a right cross on his father's jaw. "Did you?"

"Hell, yes," Jonah said, pausing to light a cigar. He puffed quickly until a cloud of blue smoke ringed his head. "It was easy, too. That little filly was ready to sprint. All she needed was a little incentive."

"What the hell does that mean?"

"Prize money."

"You *paid* her to leave?" Max was incredulous.

"Only gave her what she asked for."

"She wouldn't have."

"Okay, I asked her how much and she came up with a figure. Twenty-five grand. I wrote out a check and she left. End of story." The old man paused and studied his son. Smoke drifted upward to mingle with the diaphanous layer of clouds hanging lazily in the air high above. "I'm sorry, son, but that's the way it was. She didn't even barter."

He walked through the gate, leaving Max in the middle of the paddock feeling like a fool.

Later, almost reluctantly, Jonah had shown Max the canceled check—a check for twenty-five thousand dollars made payable to Skye Donahue.

"It was easy," Jonah had told him. "Too easy. I was willing to pay more if I had to, just to show you what kind of a woman she really is, but she couldn't wait to get her hands on this." He'd held up the check and sighed.

Max had felt as if he'd been kicked in the gut and every last shred of love he'd hung on to had been destroyed. Or so he'd told himself. But now she was back, and he was still thinking about her every waking moment, dreaming about her late at night, fighting to keep himself from falling for her all over again.

"Son of a bitch," he growled, thinking of the money.

A payoff. Twenty-five thousand dollars to leave town, and she'd taken it. He was better off without her. And yet he couldn't leave her alone.

"Hell." Angrily he climbed out of the truck and wished he could just take off. He didn't want to be involved in this family discussion, but he had no choice. He was late and all the members of his family had already gathered in the den. His mother ushered him inside and he took a seat on the old leather sofa. Sitting back, boots crossed at the ankles and propped on the oak coffee table, arms folded, he was introduced to Rex Stone, private investigator, the man Virginia had hired to find Jonah's killer.

Would this insanity never end?

Rex, smiling coldly, was holding court behind Jonah's desk, and even though the lamps were lit, the room seemed as dark as a tomb. And Rex looked like an interloper. The den would never be the same without Jonah.

Jenner appeared bored. He stared out at the still night from his perch on the windowsill. Casey, acting as if she was about to bolt, fidgeted in a chair near the door. Virginia, dry-eyed and tight-lipped, her chin thrust forward in determination, sat on the far end of the couch, with Max occupying the other end.

The detective was rambling on. "...so I agree with your mother," Rex said amicably, his pudgy face flushed as if he'd just run a marathon or imbibed a few too many drinks. From the webbing of veins visible on his nose, Max suspected the latter, even though Stone was rumored to be the best P.I. in all of eastern Oregon. "I think your father was killed, run off the road, from the looks of his skid marks. Though there were no other visible traces of tire marks, I'd be willing to bet he was forced through the guardrail.''

"The sheriff's department doesn't think that—''

"They might be changing their tune,'' Stone said with a smug little gleam in his eye. Max hated the guy on sight. The detective was too cocksure, ready to believe the worst in anyone. In Max's estimation, Stone was preying upon Virginia's vulnerability.

"New evidence?'' Jenner asked.

"I've just made them review the existing evidence— look at it from a different angle.''

Max wasn't convinced. "This better not be some shot in the dark,'' he warned. "Either you've got proof or this is a waste of our time.''

"I assure you, I mean business.'' Stone flipped through a few notes he'd taken, probably in previous conversations with Virginia.

Max, as he had all week, tried to quiet the restlessness that stole through his blood. Ever since kissing Skye on her porch the other night, he hadn't been able to put her out of his mind. True, she hadn't responded to him, in fact had told him to go to hell in so many words, but Max wasn't one to give up easily. Not when he wanted something, and damn it, he wanted Skye Donahue. He wanted her so badly he felt as if he'd turned into a randy teenager, resorting to cold showers, long hours of hard labor, even drink, to wash her out of his mind. Nothing had worked. Probably nothing would. Even reminding himself of her betrayal, telling himself that she'd taken money to leave him, hadn't cooled his blood.

Grinding his teeth together in frustration, he tried to turn his attention back to the short, opinionated private investigator. Stone was staring at Max and that damned insufferable grin hadn't gone away. "...usually someone close to the victim, who would gain from his death. Now, according to my notes, the ranch house and a few acres were left to Virginia, and there was a provision for Jonah's mother…let's see." He made a big production of shuffling his papers. "Here it is. Mavis McKee is to be taken care of for the rest of her life."

"That's right," Virginia said cautiously, some of her earlier enthusiasm waning.

"The rest of the estate is to be split up between the children." He looked over the tops of reading glasses for confirmation, and Virginia, glancing quickly from Max to the P.I., nodded slowly.

"The lion's share went to Maxwell, a smaller portion to Jenner and an even smaller one to Casey."

Casey's eyes narrowed on the man. "What're you getting at?"

"I'm just pointing out that the people in this room had the most to gain from Jonah's death."

"Oh, my God! You're not suggesting—" Virginia bit her tongue and cut off the rest of her thoughts.

"I'm just letting you know how I work, Mrs. McKee. I don't pull any punches, okay? And I don't bend the truth. Not for anyone." He was suddenly serious, the tiny smile having fallen off his face. "If I find out one of you did it, I'll tell Sheriff Polk and still expect to be paid."

"I didn't hire you to harass my family!" Virginia lifted her chin a notch. "No one here killed Jonah. It was someone else, someone bitter over a bad investment or something. Maybe someone with a personal grudge, but I assure you, Mr. Stone, it was not anyone here tonight."

Stone pulled at his tie and seemed to be considering her vehement speech. "Don't worry. I've only got a few questions." His gaze landed on Max and his eyebrows rose slightly. "I believe you found some letters after Jonah died. Letters that proved he manipulated your love life.''

Hell! Max tented his hands under his chin. ''That's right. But as you said, I found them *after* the funeral.''

''True. At least that's the way it appeared.''

''It's the way it was,'' Max said evenly.

''You could have seen them earlier.''

''I didn't.'' Max was firm. It was all he could do to sit still and not leap over the desk and strangle the fat little man with his own ugly tie.

Stone's gaze swept over his notes. ''You and your father were at loggerheads over the business, weren't you?''

''Often as not,'' Max said, meeting the smaller man's glare with his own. ''We didn't always get along.''

''No one did,'' Casey said, jumping to her feet and pacing to the blackened fireplace. ''Jenner was always rebelling and I...well, I didn't do what Dad wanted, either. He was a great manipulator, Mr. Stone. That doesn't mean we didn't love and respect him—''

''I didn't.'' Jenner's eyes had turned to ice. ''If you're lookin' for a prime suspect in the family, maybe you'd better start with me.''

''Jenner, no!'' Virginia gasped, her hand flying over her mouth. ''There's no reason to say those things. Your father is dead and—''

''Don't do this,'' Max warned, climbing to his feet and facing Jenner. ''Jonah's dead. Now, let the man—'' he cocked his head toward Stone ''—do his job.'' Turning, he leaned over the desk, so that he was nearly eyeball-to-eyeball with the short detective. ''I don't think my mother is paying your exorbitant fee just so you can dig up the skeletons in our closets, 'cause if she is, it will take you years to sort through 'em all. So you can take my word on the fact that none of us would have been stupid enough to kill Jonah. The way I see it, you're just milkin' this for as much money as you can squeeze out of it.''

Stone's already ruddy face turned a deep shade of purple and he rose to his full height of five foot six. ''I was hired to do a job, Mr. McKee, and I'll do it. I didn't mean to threaten anyone. I just like to put my cards on the table up-front. That way there are no big surprises.''

''Fine with me,'' Max said evenly. ''Just let me put my cards up there with yours. You're welcome to dig through all the company files and talk to anyone you please, just as long as you don't get in my way. But if I hear that you've started harassing my family, you'll have to deal with me.''

Stone's eyes narrowed and he looked angry enough to spit. Instead, he tapped his papers together, slid them into an expandable file and promised results. ''Expect a deputy from the sheriff's department to come on by and start asking questions again.''

''Great,'' Jenner muttered, closing his eyes. ''More B.S.''

''Thank you for your time, Mr. Stone.'' Virginia led the man out of the den and to the front door. Her heels tapped on the wood floors, but his footsteps were muffled by his crepe soles.

''Creepy bastard,'' Jenner remarked, frowning into the night.

''Maybe he will find something.'' Casey grabbed her hair and wound it into a ponytail. ''What do you think?''

Max shrugged. ''I don't think so, but he seems damned sure of himself.''

''Cocky and creepy bastard,'' Jenner clarified. ''Wonder how he found out about the letters.''

''I told him.'' Virginia walked back into the room. She seemed nervous. She rubbed her arms as if she'd caught a chill, even though it had to be over eighty in the room.

Avoiding Max's eyes, she admitted, "I knew about them...not in the beginning, of course. I didn't know that Skye had even tried to contact you after you broke up, but later I caught Jonah struggling with the right words to explain what he'd done. I had a fit, of course, but he told me it was water under the bridge and I wasn't to breathe a word to you. He pointed out that you were married and had a child to consider, although, at the time, I think you and Colleen had separated." She glanced up at Max who couldn't believe what he was hearing. It was one thing to think the old man had sabotaged him, but he'd always believed that his mother had been on his side "We, um, we all hoped that you and Colleen would patch things up. Your father, well, he thought the world of Colleen, you know, and I...I believed that it would be best for Hillary if you and Colleen worked things out. I...I guess I should have told you."

"Hell, yes, you should have told me!" Max roared, her betrayal burning a fresh wound in his soul. "This was my life! Mine!" He couldn't stand to look at her. His own mother. She'd known! Furious, he stormed out of the room. Virginia rushed after him, reaching for his arm, but he threw off her cloying fingers and flung himself out the door. A sour taste rose in his throat and he felt the urge to spit.

All the deception!

All the lies!

He climbed into his truck and roared down the lane. He'd get drunk. Rip-roaring, fall-on-your-face, staggering drunk, and then maybe he could blot out the pain of betrayal. First Skye. Then Jonah. Now his mother.

His fingers gripped the wheel so tightly that his hands began to sweat. He shifted through the gears, mindless of his speed, knowing that he just had to get away.

He drove flat out and didn't even realize where he was

going until he sped through town and stopped at the Black
Anvil saloon. *Fitting,* he thought, remembering that this
was the last place Jonah had frequented on the night of
his death. The regulars were huddled over the bar. He
waved to Slim Purcell and Jimmy Rickert who were nursing a couple of tall ones. Slim managed a hard-edged
smile, while Rickert, who spent every night on the same
stool, barely glanced at Max. Barry White and his half
brother, Steve Jansen, were playing pool in the corner.

As Max slid onto a stool, Wanda appeared, her plati-
num hair piled high on her head, her smile steadfastly in
place. "What can I getcha?"

"Beer. Anything you've got on tap."

She rattled off a list. He chose one and soon she returned carrying a sweating mug with a full head.

"Jenner's not with you?" she asked, trying not to look
disappointed.

"Not tonight."

"Tell him not to be a stranger."

"I will."

Wanda moved away and Max took a long swallow from
his mug. He just wanted to forget. But try as he might,
he couldn't shake the image of Skye from his mind. He
concentrated on the music, an old Waylon Jennings song,
but he couldn't help thinking of Skye and how she'd matured into the most beautiful woman he'd ever met. A
doctor. Despite the bad taste in his mouth when he
thought of her decision to leave him, he couldn't help
feeling a grudging respect that she'd gone after what she'd
wanted. Yep, she was a woman like no other.

He glanced up at the mirror over the bar and caught
Jimmy Rickert's gaze. The guy was short and thin, with
eyes that darted quickly from one spot to another. If it
wasn't for the fact that Jimmy loved beer so much, Max
would have believed him to be on coke or speed or some

other drug. Their gazes clashed and Jimmy turned quickly away with a guilty look. Which was no surprise. Jimmy Rickert, a known snitch, was guilty of all sorts of crimes. He'd been thrown into jail for being drunk and disorderly more times than Max would want to count. It was no wonder there was something unnerving about the little weasel.

Max took another swallow of his drink, decided he couldn't stand the smoky atmosphere and loud music another minute and threw some bills on the counter. He walked outside and felt the warmth of the summer night clear his senses.

Skye.

Why couldn't he stop thinking about her?

Maybe because things had never been cleared up between them. Maybe because there were too many things left unsaid. Maybe it was time to clear the air.

He slid into his pickup and drove with a singular purpose in mind—to have it out with her.

He drove straight to Doc Fletcher's old apartment house. Her Mustang was parked in the driveway and the windows on the ground floor of the building were warm patches of lamplight, softly beckoning. Max cut the engine and didn't wait until reason overcame his irrational need to see Skye again.

This was crazy.

But he couldn't drive her out of his mind.

She'd used him, betrayed him, taken a payoff and left town. And he needed to find out why.

"Hell," he grunted. His jaw clenched so hard it hurt, he jumped out of the pickup. His long legs made short work of the parched lawn. It was time to end this. Once and for all. One way or another.

He took the porch steps two at a time, nearly tripped

over a slinking gray cat, then pounded on her door. *Come on, come on!*

Within seconds, the porch light blinked on and she was staring at him through one of the narrow windows flanking the door. The beveled glass distorted her image a little, but she was still the most beautiful woman he'd ever met.

The door opened a crack, as much as the chain lock would allow. "What are you doing here?" she asked, her eyes suspicious.

"I need to see you."

"Forget it." She tried to shove the door shut, but he wedged his toe into the small opening.

"It's important."

"It didn't work out the last time, remember?"

"Let's try again."

"Just like that?" she said, shaking her head, her blond ponytail whipping back and forth. "No way."

"What're you afraid of?"

"Afraid?" she repeated. "Believe me, Max, you don't scare me."

"I need to talk to you."

She hesitated and for the first time she let her gaze lock with his. "Are you in some kind of trouble?"

"Probably."

"That's not an answer."

His fingers curled into fists of frustration. "Look, this isn't easy for me."

"Then don't keep coming back."

"I just want to clear the air. Is that too much to ask?"

He heard her breath sweep into her lungs and saw her bite down on her lip. For a heartbeat, she didn't say a word. The sounds of the night—traffic flowing sluggishly through the town, muffled music from the restaurant down the street, a dog barking from somewhere in the neighborhood, crickets chirping noisily from their hiding places—thrummed through his mind.

"I don't know if I want to."

"Sure you do," he insisted as if he could read her mind. "Come on, Skye. Let's just do this and get it over with."

Again she looked into his eyes and this time she threw up her hands. "Call me a fool." She unlocked the chain and stepped aside. He followed her into the kitchen where the smells of floor wax, disinfectant and pine cleaner greeted him. Wallpaper had been stripped from the walls and several different trial colors of paint had been brushed near the windows.

She stood near the sink and waited, one foot tapping impatiently, her heart pounding, her mind racing into dangerous territory. What was he doing here? She'd been certain that after the last time—after she'd slapped him and bruised his sensitive male ego—he'd never be back again. It had been over a week ago, but here he was, saying he wanted to talk, when he looked ready to explode. He radiated a tension, that same innate sexuality and restlessness that had attracted her years ago.

He'd aged well, the weathering of his skin and honing of his features adding to his masculinity. He was harder around the edges—tougher. And he was standing in the middle of her kitchen. "What did you want, Max?"

"Answers."

"Okay, but first I'll need questions."

He didn't miss a beat and his eyes narrowed on her. "Why did you leave?"

She wrapped her arms around herself as if to protect her middle. Or was it her heart? "Why do you care now? It's been seven years."

He grabbed a kitchen chair, swung it around and straddled it. Resting his arms on the back, he stared up at her with those sea green eyes she'd always found so erotic. "I didn't get the letters until a few weeks ago."

"Letters?" she repeated. "Plural?" Something wasn't right. "But I only wrote one. What do you mean you didn't get it?"

"I found them both—the one from you and one from my father—in a file."

"But—" If Max hadn't received the note she'd written him, if he hadn't known that she still cared about him when she'd left town, if…but all that was crazy. Of course he'd known! He had to have. As for the letter from Jonah, what did that have to do with her? "Look, Max, I don't understand. I wrote you a letter before I left town. I think it explained everything pretty well. And now, after seven years—"

"Why did you leave the letter with my father?" Max demanded, not moving from his chair but looking as if he might spring from it at any moment.

"I didn't…" Her throat worked soundlessly for a second as she remembered handing over the letter, sealed in an off-white envelope. She felt her legs might suddenly give way. "I—I gave it to my mom to pass on to you."

The lines around Max's mouth grew white. "Seems it got detoured. She must've given it to Jonah."

"No, she wouldn't…" But the words died in her throat. Irene Donahue had always trusted Jonah McKee. He was her employer, her friend, her benefactor and, Skye suspected, the secret love of her life. *Oh, God!* Skye felt the hot blade of betrayal turn in her gut. Irene should have known better. Oh, Lord, this explained so much. "I wondered why you never called…" She shook her head, not daring to trust him. "Then I heard that less than a year later you were marrying Colleen Wheeler."

"She was pregnant."

Pain ripped a hole in Skye's heart. *Pregnant with Max's*

child! Colleen had given him what she would never be able to offer—the greatest gift of all.

The skin of his face grew taut over his cheekbones. "I went a little crazy when you left, Skye," he admitted, standing and kicking the chair out of his path as he crossed the room. The chair banged into the wall. "I didn't understand how you could just walk away, and one night I went into town and got myself rip-roaring drunk. Colleen was at the Black Anvil. She offered to drive me home. We didn't make it. I spent the weekend with her, trying to forget you. It didn't work, of course." He was close enough to her that she saw the striations of green mixed with the blue of his eyes. "I still thought about you all the time, half the time missing you, the rest of the time cursing the day I'd met you. It didn't matter, though. Colleen told me she was pregnant and I married her. I thought a child would make things right." His eyes were dark and desperate, his breath warm as it fanned her face. "Hillary was born about eleven months later."

Skye could barely breathe. "Eleven, but—"

"Colleen lied." He snorted at his own foolishness. "It seems I have this problem of trusting women. Believing them. By the time I figured out that she'd tricked me, we were already married and then she really was pregnant."

Skye stared up at him and her fingers tightened over the hard edge of the counter. Sick inside that anyone would use a precious baby as a ploy, a trap, Skye saw the agony etched on Max's face, knew that she was responsible for some of that pain. "I—I'm sorry."

"So am I," he vowed.

She swallowed hard as he leaned closer, his face looming above hers, the streaks of gold in his brown hair gleaming in the lamplight.

"I've missed you, Skye. I tried not to. Hell, I fought it, but the bald-faced truth of the matter is that I've missed you.'' Strong arms slipped familiarly around her waist. He drew her close, pressing his lean body against hers, and his lips, full of promise and tenderness, found hers. The kiss was slow and sensual and awakened old emotions in Skye—emotions she'd locked behind closed doors, emotions so intense they frightened her. She knew that kissing him was dangerous, but she couldn't stop herself.

For so many years she'd dreamed of the day when his lips would find hers again, and though she'd shoved those dreams deep into her subconscious, they had lingered. His body was hard and lean, his muscles straining beneath his jeans and shirt. She closed her eyes and let go.... The world beyond them seemed to mute and blur.

When he lifted his head, she swallowed back a lump in her throat. ''I've missed you, too,'' she said, wishing she could lie to him, throw him out, tell him that she didn't want him. But she couldn't. Passion, dark and unwanted, sped through her blood, and though she knew wanting him was crazy, her traitorous body responded, tamping down the warnings screaming through her mind.

His lips crashed down upon hers again, and in one swift movement he lifted her into his arms. He didn't ask for her acquiescence, just carried her through the living room and beyond the sun porch to the small Victorian bedroom she'd lived in for less than two weeks.

Sweeping in through the open window, a breeze stirred the curtains and starlight gave the room a hazy glow.

Max stopped at the bed and they tumbled together onto the old hand-pieced quilt. Skye let herself go, closing her mind to the doubts and worries that plagued her. The night surrounded them in the darkened bedroom, and as he kissed her eyes, her cheeks and her neck, she felt her skin heat. Tiny impulses of desire swept through her blood, clouding her judgment, making her moan. She felt her shirt being slipped over her head and the magic of his fingers as he caressed her flesh.

His breath was warm, his hands rough and callused as they reached beneath her bra, bringing her breasts over the cups, rubbing hard thumbs over the nipples.

"I wanted to forget you," he whispered across the proud dark points. Warm, moist air swirled around her nipples and she arched upward, her fingers winding through his hair as she guided his head down toward a straining peak. "But I couldn't."

Sensations, hot and wild, streamed through her bloodstream as he unhooked her bra and hungrily suckled her ripe breasts, holding each soft globe between his hands. "I need you, I want you," he whispered.

His hands slid down her ribs to her waist and lower still. With maddening deliberation, he delved deep beneath the waistband of her jeans. She bucked up to meet him as his fingertips grazed the elastic of her panties and the suddenly damp curls at the apex of her legs.

He pulled off her jeans and stripped her of bra and panties, his hands everywhere, tracing her spine, caressing her buttocks, searching deep in the darkest of warm places. Sweat beaded on her forehead and glimmered on her breasts. Still he suckled, drinking from her, teasing her, while hot hands explored every inch of her.

Skye's mind was spinning wildly, her breath coming in short gasps. She writhed beneath him as he touched her, and she wanted more of this man who had haunted her dreams and shadowed her days, this man she had loved above all others, the only man to whom she'd given herself body and soul.

She felt a heat building within her, a hot fire, stoked by his deft fingers. She arched upward at the moment of release, the heavens seeming to rain shooting stars behind her eyes as she cried out his name.

Only then, after she lay sweating on the coverlet, her breathing still rapid, did he guide her hands to the bulge beneath his jeans. Only then did he seek his own release.

Her gaze locked to his, she opened his fly and slid his jeans and shorts off his long, down-covered legs. He wasted no time, but pinned her back on the bedding. Sudden worry shadowed his gaze. "You're sure about this?" he asked.

"I—I'm not sure about anything anymore," she admitted, staring up at him, his masculine body all muscle and sinew and tanned skin. She felt a void, hot and dusky, deep within her, a void only he could fill.

"Neither am I." He gently prodded her knees apart, thrust into her and fused with her body in a sensual rhythm that stole the breath from her lungs. She clung to him as he moved, his tempo quickening with each stroke. Her blood pounded in her temples, the heat within her building until she cried out in final release. She felt as if her soul had fled her body. Again the heavens shattered.

"Skye!" he yelled hoarsely, as if afraid of losing her. "Skye! Skye! Skye!" He collapsed against her, his weight crushing her breasts, his muscles gleaming with sweat.

She curled up against him as he held her close. Shutting her eyes, she felt safer and more secure than she had in a long, long while. He tossed the coverlet over their bodies and wound her in his arms. Skye sighed happily, drinking in the musky scent of him.

She didn't think about right or wrong or the consequences the morning would bring. For now, she was content to be held by the only man she'd ever loved and the only man who had broken her heart.

He awoke to the smell of baking bread and perking coffee. Opening one eye, he glanced around Skye's bedroom and sighed contentedly. It hadn't been a dream.

She'd been here and willing and warm and they'd made love long into the night before Max had drifted into a sleep more sound than he'd experienced in years.

Rubbing a hand over his beard-roughened chin, he climbed out of bed and stepped into his jeans. He found his shirt, wrinkled from being tossed recklessly into a corner, and slipped his arms through the sleeves. Shoving stiff fingers through his unruly hair, he walked through the tangle of rooms until he found her in the kitchen, humming softly, her hair piled on top of her head, though damp tendrils from her recent shower curled around her face and nape. She'd put on a red skirt and oatmeal-colored top. A black jacket was hanging at the ready over the back of a chair, and a cat, green eyes watching him suspiciously, was lurking over a saucer of milk near the back door.

Sensing him watching her, Skye slid him a sexy glance that couldn't help but arouse him. "So Sleeping Beauty finally awakens."

He ran a hand around his neck, stretched and listened as his spine popped. "What time is it?"

"A little after seven." She poured a cup of coffee from the glass carafe warming on the stove.

"I suppose you've been up for hours," he drawled, crossing the room and drawing her into the circle of his arms. After last night he thought he'd be sated, but already, just being around her, he felt as excited as a damned high school kid.

She smiled up at him. "Long enough to run for twenty minutes and shower."

"Sorry I missed that," he drawled, his gaze lowering to the collar of her blouse and those gorgeous breasts hidden by the silky fabric. He raised his hand and cupped one soft globe. Skye sucked in her breath.

"I don't think this is a good idea."

"You've been wrong before."

"But I've got to be at the clinic by eight—" He lifted her into his arms once again and carried her back to bed. The blouse and skirt were discarded quickly to collect in a pool by the bed.

"You've got a short commute. Besides, I'll be quick," he promised. She closed her eyes as her slip slid to the floor.

Later, she had to hurry to get to the clinic on time. She offered him a cup of coffee and a couple of slices of warm bread from the breadmaker she'd inherited from a college roommate who'd insisted the damn machine was responsible for her ten-pound weight gain. Then she ran out the door, coffee cup in hand.

"Didn't you forget something?" he asked, and when she turned to ask him what, he folded her into his arms again and kissed her full on the lips. The kiss was warm and sensual and filled with memories of making love. Her heart beat a crazy tattoo and her legs nearly gave way. Coffee sloshed onto the porch as she stumbled backward.

"You're dangerous to have around, McKee," she said, drawing in a deep breath.

"So are you, Doc."

"Don't forget to lock up when you leave." She knew her face was flushed with color as she hurried between the laurel hedges on her way to the clinic. Surely the heat would leave her cheeks by the time the rest of the staff showed up. She forced herself to concentrate on the day ahead of her as she unlocked the clinic to be greeted by the familiar smells of antiseptic and perking coffee. The coffee had been on a timer and she refilled her cup in the small room designated as the employee lounge before exchanging her jacket for a white lab coat and settling in at her desk.

She didn't think about the fact that she was involved

with Max again, didn't dwell on the consequences of falling in love with him. She was older now and wiser; she wouldn't give her heart so recklessly this time. She couldn't.

Chapter Eleven

"Looks like Stone means business." Jenner slapped a copy of *The Rimrock Review* onto the surface of Max's desk—his father's old desk—in the corner office of the McKee Enterprises office building. Bold black headlines announced that the sheriff's department was looking into the death of Jonah McKee as a possible homicide.

Suddenly cold inside, Max skimmed the article. The sheriff, Hammond Polk, was quoted as saying that the investigation was taking a new direction in light of new evidence. A five-year-old picture of Jonah, retrieved from the archives of *The Rimrock Review,* accompanied the piece. Max stared at the grainy black-and-white photo and frowned. His father was looking straight into the camera, his snowy hair combed, his smile as phony as a three-dollar bill. "Son of a bitch."

"My sentiments exactly," Jenner said, tossing the offending paper into a trash can near the credenza. "But as mean a bastard as the old man was, he didn't deserve to die. If someone actually did kill him, I think the culprit should be strung up.''

"You don't believe it, do you?'' Max asked, surprised at his younger brother's attitude.

"Looks like we don't have much choice.''

That much was true. Hammond Polk wasn't perhaps overly zealous, but he knew his duty. He wouldn't have reopened the investigation without evidence. Max glanced at the files stacked on the corner of his desk—files of deals that weren't exactly on the up-and-up and files Max was going over because, in many cases, he wanted to renegotiate the deals into fairer terms for the other parties. "Dad sure made his share of enemies,'' he observed.

"Yeah, but who hated the old man enough to run him off the road?'' Jenner rubbed his jaw.

"That won't be easy to find out,'' Max allowed. "A lot of people borrowed from him during the recession, hoping to get back on their feet. When things didn't turn around right away and they defaulted, McKee Enterprises had the right to demand their assets.''

Jenner's eyes darkened a shade and the corners of his mouth twisted into an unhappy smile. "So you finally figured out he wasn't a saint.''

"I've known it for a long time,'' Max admitted as he leaned back in the old molded-oak chair, making it creak. His father's chair. "Not when I was first hired. Hell, I trusted him completely. But it didn't take long to discover that everything wasn't exactly on the up-and-up. Some of the deals didn't smell so good.''

"But you went along with them.''

Max shook his head and remembered the furious argument he'd had with his father. Jonah had been in a rage that his son, an "upstart'' in the business, would dare question his authority. "Not once I found out what was going on. I raised holy hell and Jonah, believe it or not, agreed to change his tactics. He didn't, of course, but as far as I can tell, Dad never did anything illegal. Although

there were a few cases that weren't ethical. At least not
in my book.''

"Such as?''

"The Donner water rights.'' Max's guts twisted a little
as he remembered Fred Donner's ashen face when the
wiry rancher had come to Max, explaining the circumstances, calling Jonah every name in the book because
he'd been forced to sell the family homestead at a fraction
of its value. Without significant amounts of water, the arid
land had become useless. But Donner was only one. "Ned
Jansen's copper mine. Slim Purcell's racehorse. Betty
Landsburg's rooming house. The town's full of buildings
that Dad bought for a song when the owners hit upon hard
times. Usually Dad—well, McKee Enterprises—would
lend them enough money to fix up the place or pay the
back taxes, but then, soon as they were delinquent in their
payments, he'd snap up the property and lease it back to
the original owners, making a profit for the company.

"In some cases—Len Marchant's old bakery is a good
example—the land and buildings were close to being condemned and the owners were glad to get out from under
heavy mortgages, but more often than not, the owners
thought that McKee Enterprises, and Jonah in particular,
had fleeced them.''

"That's only the half of it.'' Restless, Jenner walked to
the window and stared through the glass, past the slow-
paced traffic on the streets of Rimrock to the Blue Mountains in the distance. "No tellin' how many husbands and
fathers would have liked to strangle him for foolin' around
with their wives and daughters.'' He rubbed the back of
his neck as if he was trying to erase a particularly painful
memory. "It's a wonder to me why Ma even cares. He
stepped out on her so often I bet she lost track.'' Squinting
against the glare of the afternoon sun, he added, "You
know, I don't blame Stone with startin' with the family.
We all had a bone to pick with Jonah.''

Max, conjuring up Skye's image, couldn't argue with that.

"He screwed you over royal," Jenner said, then picked up his hat from the couch. As he shoved it over his forehead, he admitted, "Did the same to me, you know."

"Beth," Max said, remembering the one time Jenner had been rumored to have fallen for a woman. Max had been in San Francisco at the time, but he'd heard from Casey that Jenner had finally fallen in love. Soon thereafter, Beth, like Skye, had disappeared. To this day, Jenner rarely spoke of her.

"I can't prove it, but I think he found a way to get her out of town. Not that it matters." Jenner's eyes flashed with malice and a deeper, more difficult to define emotion. "Face it, Max, the old man was a first-class bastard. No two ways about it. He did things his way and to hell with anyone else."

Max didn't argue. Ever since taking over the business and reviewing files that prior to Jonah's death had been off-limits to him, Max had found case after case of his father's larceny.

"I think I'll head over to the Black Anvil," Jenner said. "Want to join me?"

"Another time."

As his brother closed the door of the office behind him, Max was left with a bad taste in his mouth. True, Jonah had manipulated people and, in many cases, shown no empathy for anyone who didn't see things the way he did. But murder? In this sleepy little farming community? It seemed like blasphemy.

He spent the rest of the afternoon in meetings with lawyers and accountants and specialists who assured him that the company, McKee Enterprises, was doing well despite the loss of its figurehead and president. Cattle prices were on the upswing, and most of the rents were more than enough to cover the mortgages and maintenance on the buildings that were leased by McKee Enterprises.

More copper had been found in the old Jansen mine, timber sales were up and the Wagner sawmill that Jonah had acquired two months before his death in a desperation sale, was already breaking even. With the layoffs Jonah had insisted upon, the old mill would be turning a profit by the end of the year.

"What about the men who lost their jobs?" Max asked the skinny accountant with gold-rimmed reading glasses. Bill Renfield had been a few years ahead of Max in school—a scrawny, pimply-faced kid who was a math whiz. Now he was a number cruncher for the company.

"What about them?"

"Will they be rehired?" Max paced nervously between the window and his desk. All hell seemed to have broken out. The murder investigation, his ongoing battle with Colleen over Hillary and all the problems surrounding the business. The only bright spot was his one night with Skye. But even that little bit of heaven was complicated. Too complicated.

"I don't see how we can put anyone back on the payroll. At least not yet. Most of the men are collecting unemployment and Wagner had some kind of retirement setup for a couple of the guys who'd worked for him for thirty years or so, but the rest...well, they'll just have to retrain or find jobs in another mill."

"What other mill?" Max asked.

"Peterkin was hiring in Dawson City and over in the valley."

"These men don't live in the Willamette Valley," Max growled. "They live here."

"I know, Mr. McKee, but there are lots of changes all over the timber industry. What with the government ban on old growth, imported lumber taking away jobs from our mills and the trend to other kinds of building materials, times are tough for everyone. People—workers and executives both—will have to be a little more flexible."

"Except McKee Enterprises." Max's voice was laced with sarcasm. "Our mill is going to make a profit."

"And if things turn around, then we'll rehire." Renfield gathered up his notes. "That's the bottom line."

He left and Max kicked a metal trash can so hard it went reeling across the room to bang against the wall. His muscles were tight, his fists clenched in frustration. He wasn't a bleeding-heart liberal. Hell, he'd gone to law school and knew the score. Men and women were thrown out of work every day. He'd grown up with the dim realization that his father had power over other people's lives. But he didn't like being in command; he couldn't stomach hardworking people becoming desperate.

Just before five, Louise, his father's secretary whom Max had inherited when Jonah had died, brought in the old accounting printouts and checking-account statements that he'd asked for—statements that were seven years old. Louise Jones was a pleasant woman with a sharp mind. She had always liked Max and, despite being distraught over his father's death, had helped him ease into his new-found role as head of the company.

"Here you go," she said, blowing at the dust on the old ledgers. "Is there anything else?"

Max thumbed through the statements and old checks. "This should do it."

"Would you like me to stay?" she asked.

"Naw. I'll just be here a little while," he said with a forced smile. He couldn't tell her that his future rested upon what he found in the old records.

"All right then. I'll see you tomorrow." Her eyes clouded a little. "I hope that Sheriff Polk is wrong. I can't believe that anyone would want to kill your father."

"I guess we'll find out."

She made a quick sign of the cross over her frail chest and said a hasty goodbye.

Once he was completely alone, Max found a glass and an old bottle of Scotch in the bar, poured himself a stiff drink and began going through the old ledgers. As the smoky flavor of the liquor warmed the pit of his stomach, he began to read through the old pages and he hoped to high heaven that his father had been lying. Max hadn't believed that Skye would take money to leave and he didn't believe it now, seven years later.

He took another swallow of liquor when he saw the notation, made the day before she left, of a payment of twenty-five thousand dollars made payable to Skye Donahue. His jaw clenched and he felt a tic developing beneath his eye as he made a mental note of the check number, then began going through the old boxes of canceled checks.

It didn't take long. His heart nearly stopped when he found it—a check issued in Jonah's harsh script. The payee was Skye Donahue; the amount twenty-five thousand dollars. So Jonah hadn't been bluffing, hadn't shown him a fake check all those years ago. A part of him had wanted to believe that the old manipulator had taken advantage of Max's emotional state and shown him a fake payoff. "Hell." Max, his guts twisting at her deceit, flipped the damned piece of paper over. Oddly enough, Skye's signature didn't appear, but a stamp indicating she'd put the funds into her checking account convinced him that, as his father had so calmly attested, she'd sold out for twenty-five grand.

He felt like he might throw up. Bile rose in his throat and something deep inside him—faith, he supposed—seemed to wither and die. Hell, what kind of a fool was he to get involved with her all over again?

And involved he was. He hardly spent a waking moment without her image flitting through his mind. Closing his eyes, he silently condemned himself for being a fool of the highest order.

"Damn it all," he muttered, stuffing the check in his pocket, then finishing his drink in one quick swallow. The liquor burned a hot, angry trail down his throat and his fingers clenched hard over the glass. In a sudden burst of fury, he flung the glass against the wall and watched it shatter into a thousand pieces.

On his feet and striding to the door, he decided he'd give her a chance to explain, but this time, damn it, she'd better tell the truth. All of it.

"I can't believe you didn't give the letter to Max," Skye said as she rushed through the front door of Irene's little bungalow.

"What letter?"

"The one you gave to Jonah McKee. The one addressed to his son. The one Max never saw until his father died."

Irene, adding water to a vase of wilting flowers, stiffened and some of the water dripped onto the table. "Oh, Lordy," she whispered nervously and wiped up the spill with the cuff of her sleeve. "I had no idea—"

"Mom," Skye insisted, standing in the doorway and trying to quiet the rage that had been with her ever since she'd found out the truth. "Why didn't you see that Max got it?"

"I worked for Jonah, remember?" Irene said stubbornly, though her eyes had darkened with a private pain. "I never did anything behind his back."

Skye tried to hold on to her temper. Her fists tightened and she stuffed them into the pockets of her skirt. "You didn't have to tell him about the letter. It was personal and had nothing to do with the company."

"He would've found out and then what would I have said?"

"That it was none of his damned business!"

Irene bit down on her lip. "I honestly believed that he'd give the letter to Max. He said he would and then later when I asked him about it, he told me Max had torn the envelope up without even reading the contents. I was shattered and thought I should call you, but Jonah told me it was out of my hands. That I should let things run their natural course." Irene sighed loudly. "You don't remember him, do you? How he was always in charge? How he made every decision and never once changed his mind? How the world seemed to revolve around him?"

Skye couldn't stomach the lies. "I remember him for the manipulating bastard he was, Mom, while you remember him as some kind of god on earth. He was a man, Mom, and he made mistakes. A lot of mistakes. Bad ones."

Irene opened her mouth, shut it again, then carried the empty water pitcher back to the kitchen. Setting it on the counter, she paused, her back still turned to Skye. "I guess you should know how I felt about him."

"I think I already do."

"Oh, no. You think I just loved him from afar, that I never told him how I felt, but you're wrong." Staring out the window over the sink, her shoulders stiff, Irene blinked rapidly. "I guess I was a fool, too, because I did tell him how I felt."

"Oh, Mom, no." Skye's heart was hammering and she wanted to close her ears to her mother's confession. She didn't want to hear any of the sordid details and believed that her mother's private love life was none of her business. "You don't have to do this."

"It's time," Irene said, her voice trembling slightly. Skye leaned against the archway for support. "It was a mistake, I know. We were both working late, all alone in the office, and there was a rainstorm like none I've ever seen before or since. In minutes, the streets were running with water and the wind was lashing at the windows." Irene's voice had grown soft and her shoulders sagged a little as she reminisced. "Jonah helped me to my car, carrying an umbrella for me. It got caught in the wind and turned inside out, and there we were, alone in the night, rain washing down our faces. We just stared at each other and it was like…like we were the only two people in the world.''

Skye felt a chill as cold as an arctic sea settle in her heart.

''In a second I knew he would kiss me.''

''Mom, please—''

''He did, you know. Kiss me like I've never been kissed.'' Her throat clogged and she touched her lips as if she could still feel the heat of his mouth.

''Oh, God, Mom, don't—''

''I told myself that it was wrong, that he was married, but damn it, Skye, I loved him. So when he quit kissing me, I blurted it out. 'Jonah,' I said, 'I love you. I've loved you for years…I just can't help myself.''''

Skye wanted to drop through the floor. She could feel her mother's pain and embarrassment—hot and pulsing. It seemed to throb through the small kitchen.

''I suppose that sounds silly, but we were much younger then…you girls were still in grade school.'' She swallowed hard and pressed fingertips to the corners of her eyes. ''Well, Jonah told me he was flattered and kissed me again, then he helped me into my car and slammed the door. Through the open window, he told me that he'd always take care of me, that he'd provide for me, but that he respected me too much to sleep with me. I—I guess he needed me more in the office than…oh, well… Besides, he had lots of other women. Anyway, he never mentioned it again, but I got a raise and he kept good on his word, never letting me want for anything. You and I, we owe him a huge debt.'' Her throat caught on the pain of being a woman rejected.

''He tried to ruin my life,'' Skye said woodenly. More than ever, she viewed Jonah McKee as a fiend, allowing her mother to worship him and love him when he would never return any of that ardor.

''I know,'' Irene said, turning to face her daughter and sniffing back her tears. ''But you were strong, and Max, well, he seemed to survive. It didn't take him long to marry someone that his father approved of." Irene looked up at the ceiling. "You know, when you started dating Max, I thought my prayers had been answered. I'd always liked him and I wanted the best for you. I really thought it was a match made in heaven."

"Too bad Jonah didn't agree."

"You were the one who wasn't going to marry Max," Irene observed sharply. "You'd already decided. It really didn't matter what happened with Jonah. And now he's dead." Her throat worked and again tears shimmered in her eyes. "Maybe even murdered! Some private investigator Virginia hired, a man named Stone, was here today asking questions about the business. I wonder if Jonah will ever rest in peace."

There was a quick rap on the back door. Before Skye could answer it, the screen opened, and Dani, dressed in jeans, a work shirt, cowboy boots and matching tooled leather belt, let herself in. "So the rumor's true," she said, slanting a grin at her older sister, then hugging her fiercely. "You did come back. I wondered when you were going to land here in Rimrock. Jeff and I had a bet. Looks like I won. I'm sorry I didn't show up sooner. We've been busy this year." Dani smelled of horses and smoke, just as she had years before. She'd managed to build a reputable business training horses and leased a ranch near Dawson City with her husband, Jeff Stewart. They owned several prize quarter horses as well as some rodeo stock. "Oh, jeez," she added, apparently noticing Skye's pallor and her mother's glistening eyes. "What's going on here?"

"It's nothing…old business," Irene said and turned back to the counter to dry the pitcher. Dani's eyes met Skye's beseeching her silently for the truth, but Skye shook her head. There was no reason to prolong this conversation any longer. It would only add to the pain and there seemed to be enough of that around to last a lifetime…probably several lifetimes.

"Why did you think I'd be back?" Skye asked Dani, as their mother cleared her throat. "Didn't you know I had offers from some of the most famous medical centers all over the world?"

"Sure you did." Dani opened the refrigerator, spied a can of cola and yanked it out. She held up the can as an offering. "Anyone else?"

"Not for me," Skye said and Irene shook her head.

"God, I'm thirsty." Dani popped the top, then took a long swallow. Her brow was furrowed, and Skye knew that once they were alone, Dani would demand answers, but for now she dropped the subject. "I always figured it was inevitable that you'd come back here or somewhere close by," Dani said. "You don't strike me as a big-city girl."

"I lived in a city for seven years—all through school and residency. I liked it."

"But you wouldn't want to settle down there, raise a family…" Dani's voice trailed off when she realized what she'd said. "I just meant—"

"I know." Skye refused to give in to the old pain. At one time, she'd been jealous of Dani who'd been fertile and borne a child she couldn't care for—a baby she'd had to give up. But that had been years ago, before Skye had realized her own dreams of practicing medicine.

Dani, coloring, reached into her purse, pulled out a pack of cigarettes, and catching the warning glare from her mother, frowned and shoved the pack back into her fringed bag. "So what's it like being a doctor? Big bucks, a country club membership and dozens of handsome, rich, eligible bachelors all wanting to take you out, right?"

"Exactly," Skye agreed. "But you forgot about school debt, the mortgage, long hours and sick patients."

"Give me horses any day of the week. They're easier to deal with."

"Amen," Skye agreed and together she and her sister jollied Irene out of her bad mood. Skye tried to ignore her anger with her mother over the old letters. Too much time had passed to give in to the fury and hot injustice that had taken hold inside her. Despite everything, Skye believed that her mother had always done what she thought best for her daughters. And now, years later, Irene Donahue wasn't in the best of health. It would do no one any good to hang on to her anger. Forcing herself, she let it go.

By unspoken agreement, the name of Jonah McKee was left out of the rest of the conversation, though Dani did bring up a related topic. "Guess who I'm giving riding lessons to?" she asked with a cynical smile.

"I couldn't."

"No?" Dani rolled her eyes. "Hillary McKee. Can you believe it?"

Skye felt a tiny jab of pain in her stomach. "Hillary?"

"Mmm. Imagine that. Me working for a McKee again. It's the first time since I tried to break that stubborn colt for Casey years ago."

"I, uh, I thought you and Casey were friends."

Dani shrugged. "She's okay. But I'm still not crazy about her brothers."

"They're good people," Irene said. "Every one of them."

"Well, you know me, I never could pass up a chance at getting some of the McKee money. Besides, now that the old man's gone, it's easier to work over there."

"Dani!" Irene exclaimed.

"It's true."

"So…how's it going with Hillary?" Skye asked, eager for any bit of information on Max and his imp of a daughter.

Dani snorted. "That kid's a pistol. She wants to start with a flat-out gallop, and then maybe she'll consider letting the horse walk or trot." She hesitated a minute, then added, "You know I've never been a fan of Max McKee, but I'll say this about him—he loves that kid. Would spoil her rotten if he could." She looked away suddenly and her throat worked. "It's refreshing to see a man who cares for his children."

Skye knew Dani was thinking of her own child, the one she'd given up years before. To this day, Dani had never told a soul the name of the baby's father. She hadn't had a boyfriend at the time she'd gotten pregnant, and any time she was asked about the man, she clammed up, refusing to talk for hours. The subject was better left alone. "What does Colleen think about the lessons?" Skye asked, her heart wrenching a little to think that another woman had become Max's wife.

"She's busy with those twins of hers. Talk about brats! Jeez, they're a handful. And she's not crazy about Hillary taking up the reins. Even though she grew up on a ranch, Colleen's avoided horses, and anything to do with them, like the plague. Her brother nearly broke his neck in a bad fall when he was about twelve and she's always worried that something will happen to Hillary." Dani finger combed her reddish curls. "It's Max who just can't say no to his daughter, and right now that kid's determined to become a trick rider."

"Trick rider?"

"That's what she says. She knows I did some of that kind of stuff a long time ago and she's heard that Jenner was in the rodeo, so she's decided to be either a rodeo queen or a bride when she grows up."

Skye inwardly groaned. She'd heard about Hillary's ambitions before. Somehow she turned the conversation away from Max and his daughter.

Hours later, when Skye left her mother's cottage, she was completely wrung out. Thoughts of Max, Hillary, Colleen and Jonah jumbled in her mind and her emotions ranged from rage to worry. Could she blame her mother for trusting Jonah, the man she loved? Whether Skye wanted to believe it or not, Irene was right; Skye couldn't have married Max seven years ago. And if she had, there would be no Hillary. So why did she feel so betrayed?

She nosed her Mustang into the street and passed by her apartment house. It looked cold and gloomy and Max's truck was nowhere in sight. She turned the wheel and headed into the driveway, when she started having second thoughts. What better time to deal with Max than right now? After last night, they were involved in a relationship whether or not either of them wanted to be. It was time to set some ground rules.

Max slammed the receiver back onto the phone and swore roundly. Where the hell was she? He'd stopped by the clinic earlier, but it was already closed. Impatiently he'd waited at Skye's house for half an hour and felt like an intruder while that damned cat of hers had skulked in the bushes, glaring at him with unblinking green eyes. When Skye hadn't appeared, Max had driven to the Rocking M, checked in with Chester who was still arguing the merits of a new tractor and had finally wound up here, in his own house. Alone.

So what was she doing? Jealousy took a stranglehold on his heart and he laughed at himself. God, he was a fool.

The canceled check burned a hole in his pocket. Twenty-five thousand dollars. Payoff money. He ground his teeth in frustration and wanted to kick at something—anything. Judas that she was, she'd taken the money and turned her back on him.

When he thought of how much he'd loved her, how he'd planned to live the rest of his life with her, how he'd hoped to marry her and father her children, he burned deep inside with a rage that demanded to be unleashed.

So what are you going to do now? his nagging mind taunted. All day long, memories of making love to her had crept through his brain, weaving through his thoughts and bringing a smile to his lips. She'd been so vibrant and willing and warm. Then he'd found the check, and by all rights she should disgust him. The thought of making love to her should be repulsive. He should never want to see her again.

But his foolish heart wouldn't listen. Even now he could picture her lying beneath him, her hazel eyes dark with desire, her chest rising and falling in rapid tempo, her skin covered with a sheen of perspiration.

"Damn it all to hell," he growled, dialing her number again and waiting, only to hear her machine answer. "Damn it all to goddamned hell!"

Atlas, lying on the braided rug under the kitchen table, thumped his tail against the floor just as the sound of a car's engine roared through the open window. Tires crunched on the gravel of his private lane. Atlas bounced to his feet and began sending up an alarm as headlights flashed in the night.

Max's teeth ground as he saw the Mustang roll up the driveway. Atlas was barking out of his mind.

"Quiet!" Max ordered as he opened the door. The dog streaked through. "Well, speak of the devil," he said, walking onto the porch and watching Skye stretch out of her old car.

Her pale hair shone in the moonlight and she strode quickly up the walk and steps. A radiant smile tugged at her lips and her eyes seemed to dance in the moonlight. If she noticed his rage, she hid it well. She motioned toward the house with a sweep of her arms. "So this is what it looks like finished. You know, I always wondered."

"Did you?" Sarcasm edged his voice as he held the door open for her and followed her inside. "I'll bet you didn't lose too many nights' sleep over it."

Skye stopped dead in her tracks, then slowly turned to face him. The laughter in her eyes had vanished. "Am I missing something here?" she asked with a quiet authority she must've practiced in medical school. "Near as I recall, when I left you this morning, I thought everything was fine."

"Not quite."

"If you're still angry because of the letter, I can explain. I talked to my mom. She admitted that—"

"It's not the letter, Skye," he said harshly and saw confusion gather in her gaze like storm clouds. "In fact, I think your mother did me a favor by giving the letter to the old man."

"A favor? Why?" Was it his imagination or did she appear wounded?

He drew the check out of his pocket and slapped it into her palm. "Look what I found in the company records. It's funny, don't you think? My dad told me he'd paid you to get the hell out of Rimrock, but I never believed him. Looks like I was wrong. Again."

The color draining from her face, she stared down at the damning piece of paper and curled it in her fingers. "I didn't take a dime, Max."

"The check was deposited in your account."

"I swear, I never knew about it."

"Oh, hell, Skye, don't act like you don't know what I'm talking about. The money went out of the company account and into yours."

"No way." She carried the check into the kitchen and smoothed it over the counter, then flipped it over. Though she hadn't signed it, the check had been deposited to her account. She recognized the account number and her heart sank. So it was true.

"Don't lie to me."

"I'm not lying." She cleared her throat and sighed, dying a little inside. "I—I think maybe my mother used the money. This account is one we had together. It was set up so, in case of either party's death, the other could get the funds in the account. When I left for Portland, the account was still active, but the statements went to Mom, here in Rimrock. I never used it. I started a new account in a bank in the city. Mom signed on it, as well, but she never deposited anything or wrote a check from it. She used the account here in Rimrock—this one—'' she held up the check and shook it under his nose ''—and I used the one in Portland.''

''So you're trying to tell me that your *mother* took the payoff,'' he said with a sneer of disbelief.

Skye shook her head slowly. ''No. I don't think she would do that—''

''Well, someone did. It's gone, okay? And the last time it was seen, it was in your account.''

''Look, Max, I don't know what happened.'' She left the check on the counter and felt a chill deep in the middle of her bones. How could her mother have betrayed her so? ''You may as well know the rest of it,'' she said, dropping into one of the kitchen chairs and staring sightlessly out the window to the moon-drenched night.

''What rest of it?'' he said and trepidation entered his voice. It was obvious he didn't believe her, but Skye didn't back down. It was time everything was out in the open. Everything.

Cold as death, she said, ''Before I left town, I had it out with your father. He offered me money, even wrote out a check, but I wouldn't take it. Then he threatened my mother and Dani—told me that if I didn't get out of your life, he'd make theirs hell.''

''This is crazy. My old man would never…'' His voice trailed off and he leaned against the refrigerator, arms crossed over his chest, eyes narrowed on her like a judge ready to pass sentence.

''He would and he did,'' Skye said, explaining about her emotional conversation with Jonah. All the angry words, the threats and accusations rushed back into her mind and she didn't pull any punches. ''He was up-front about it all,'' she admitted as Max's skin paled. ''He didn't like me and thought I wouldn't be the kind of wife you wanted.''

"And you let him bully you?" Max said with a snort of disbelief. "I don't think anyone's ever coerced you in your life, Skye. You've always stood up for what you believed in, fought for what you thought was right. I can't imagine that one old man could make you turn tail and run."

"That wasn't the only reason, no," she admitted, wondering if she had the guts to tell him her darkest secret. Linking her fingers together, she silently prayed for strength.

His jaw tightened into an uncompromising line, and in that moment he looked so much like his father that Skye wondered how she could love one man so deeply while hating the other. "What was the other?" he demanded.

The seconds ticked by on the clock mounted over the stove. The dog whined to be let in. A soft summer breeze sifted through the screen, carrying the scents of mown hay and pine into the room. "I knew you wanted a family."

"So did you, if I remember correctly."

If you only knew how desperately! "I know, but it was different because…because—" *Oh, God, help me!* "—because I can't have children." She told herself she wouldn't cry, that she'd accepted her fate, that she could compensate for her childlessness, that her career meant everything to her, that someday she could adopt. But she couldn't fight the old pain she'd kept locked in a forgotten corner of her heart and she had to blink quickly to keep hot tears of regret from splashing down her cheeks.

"You can't—"

"I'm barren, okay? Infertile. I couldn't give you that all-important McKee son."

"So?" he asked, dumbfounded.

"So?" she repeated. Her chin wobbled slightly. "I know how much you love kids, Max. I've seen you with your daughter and your father told me that—"

"*My father* knew about this?"

"Yes." She sniffed loudly, then lifted her chin. "He found out because of the insurance and the payments to the doctors. I had a bad case of appendicitis, and later, P.I.D., pelvic inflammatory disease. It often renders women infertile."

Max's face twisted with silent rage. "Why didn't you tell me?" he said, his voice a low whisper.

"I couldn't."

"Why not? Didn't you trust me?"

"Yes, but—"

"Did you think I'd really care?" He crossed the room, reached around the chair and drew her to her feet. All traces of anger had disappeared from his face. "It wouldn't have mattered."

"Oh, Max, of course it did. You talked about kids. Our kids. When this house was just floorboards and studs, you showed me the bedrooms that you wanted to fill."

"And I still do. But we could have adopted. Maybe it made a difference to my father, but it didn't to me. I just wanted to be with you, Skye," he vowed, his voice suddenly husky. "I didn't care about all the rest of the B.S."

A huge lump formed in her throat as his arms surrounded her. Those tears she'd fought so valiantly spilled from the corners of her eyes.

"Did you really think I was like Jonah?"

"I didn't know. I didn't want to believe it, but you were following in his footsteps, being groomed to be the next president of the company. You went with him everywhere, did what he told you to do and even put together a few deals that weren't entirely ethical."

He stiffened, but his arms didn't abandon their possessive circle around her. "You know about those, do you?"

"Some of them. Jonah threatened to take you down with him if I were to turn him in. So…"

"Oh, God, Skye." He buried his head against her

shoulder and kissed her nape. She felt the tension and anger constricting his muscles. "I didn't realize what Jonah was pulling at first and I blame myself for being so blind. I should have looked at all the files on separate projects instead of just the current information. I was working hard, but not smart. I didn't understand until much later, after you'd gone, that good ol' Jonah P. McKee had coerced some of the people he worked with. When I found out, I hit the roof, and Jonah changed his tactics a little."

"Just a little?"

"There are a lot of people in Rimrock who had reason to hate him, who probably wanted to see him dead. I don't really blame them, but I've got someone going through all the old files. McKee Enterprises will make restitution, if possible. In some cases, it's too late. The people have moved on or died, but in others, we'll be able to make a difference."

Skye felt her heart soar. Did she dare believe him? She gazed into his eyes—eyes tortured by the mistakes of his youth—and her doubts fled. When he leaned over to kiss her, she wound her arms around his neck.

The kiss was warm and filled with promise.

He lifted his head and she sighed as their gazes met.

"Maybe I should show you the rest of the house," he suggested, his lips curving into a crooked and decidedly illicit smile.

"Maybe," she agreed.

He kissed her softly on the lips, leaving her trembling for more. "Come on," he urged, threading his fingers through hers and leading her toward the stairs. "You won't believe what I've done with the master bedroom since the last time you were here."

Chapter Twelve

"That should do it." Skye finished taking out the final stitch, leaving a clean little scar just behind Robby Mason's left ear. "Next time your brother comes after you with a slingshot, duck!"

"That won't happen again, Dr. Donahue," Robby's mother, Amy promised. Amy and Skye had gone to high school together before Amy dropped out to get married. "The slingshot's long gone—hauled away with last week's garbage. I can't thank you enough."

"No thanks necessary," Skye said, though she glowed under the other woman's appreciation. Most of the patients accepted her, but a few still insisted upon seeing Dr. Fletcher and resisted the idea of a young woman as their family physician. "Robby's going to be just fine."

"Good. Now, Robby, run along and wait for me out front," Amy said softly. She was a small, soft-looking woman with ample hips, a large bust and worried brown eyes. Her face was pretty but scarred, the result of being bitten by a wolf pup when she was just a girl.

"Ask Nurse Tagmier for a balloon," Skye suggested to the boy.

"A red one?" Robby asked, his eyes round.

"Any color you want."

He raced out the door, the sound of his sneakers muffled by the carpet. Once he'd disappeared, Amy, wringing her hands nervously, turned back to face Skye. "There's something I want to talk to you about."

"Something to do with Robby?"

"No." Amy colored and it was obvious that the subject was difficult for her. "It's about me." She cleared her throat and kept her eyes downcast in embarrassment. "About my scars. I think you probably know the story. My pa used to raise wolf pups. Well, most of the animals were tame and wouldn't hurt a flea, or at least they wouldn't take a nip out of anyone they knew. But years ago, when I was only five, I got to playing too hard with one of the fiercest little pups in a litter and ended up being bitten pretty badly. Doc Fletcher tried to fix me up, but I've always had scars."

Skye had heard the story more than once and, as a child, had been horrified by Amy Purcell's disfiguring scars—the result of her father, Otis's fascination with breeding wolves. Eventually she'd gotten used to her classmates, their personality quirks as well as their physical flaws, and she'd become blind to Amy's disfiguration just as she had to the fact that Eddie King had been born with webbed feet.

Now, since Amy had brought up the subject, she realized how devastating the scars must be, both physically and emotionally. One cheek was more hollowed than the other, and several scars, faded with time and half-hidden under a thick layer of makeup, webbed jaggedly across the right half of her face. Behind her glasses, her right eye drooped slightly.

"I was wondering if you had the name of a plastic surgeon, someone who might be able to fix all this." She forced a smile, but couldn't hide the desperate pleading in her eyes.

"I know just the right person," Skye said, giving Amy a confident smile. "When I was an intern in Portland, one of the best people on the West Coast worked out of Columbia Memorial Hospital." She searched in the pockets of her lab coat, came up with one of her freshly printed business cards and wrote the name and telephone number of Dr. Jason Phelps.

Amy took the card, biting her lower lip and trying to hide the hope that was already evident in her expression. "You think he'll take me as a patient?"

"I'm sure of it. Sometimes his bedside manner is a little gruff, but he knows what he's doing. You can have him call me if there are any problems."

Amy clutched the card as if it were the Bible. "Thank-you, Dr. Donahue."

"It's Skye, Amy. Okay? We've known each other too long to be so formal."

"All right, Skye."

"Take care of those boys now."

"I will." Still blushing, Amy hurried down the hall toward the waiting room and reception area.

Skye made a note on Robby's chart as her newly hired nurse, Belinda Tagmier, a petite brunette with a smattering of freckles over an upturned nose, poked her head into the examining room. "Believe it or not, that was the last one," she said with a grin. "We can go home."

"What, no emergencies?" Skye said, clicking her pen closed and tucking the file under her arm. "No scrapes, bruises, fevers, turned ankles?"

"None so far."

"Good. How about I buy you a drink?" Skye asked as they walked out of the room. She dropped the file on the desk in her office on the way to the employee lounge.

"Let's see—there's cola, diet cola, the uncola or orange. Go ahead. Live it up. It's on me."

"I'll have to take a rain check," Belinda said with a grin. "Dale's due home tonight after being three weeks on the road. I'm going to cook him a candlelight dinner, open a bottle of wine and wear his favorite dress...."

"Another time," Skye agreed as Belinda grabbed her purse, sweater and keys.

"Oh, I almost forgot." Belinda searched one of the large pockets in her white nurse's uniform. "Let's see. Here it is." She extracted a business card and handed it to Skye. "Some guy left it at the reception desk. He showed up, demanded to speak with you, and when we finally convinced him that your schedule was loaded, handed me this. Asked that you call him."

Skye read the card. Rex Stone, Private Investigator. Several phone numbers, including home, office and mobile, were listed. "A private detective?" she said, and then she knew. Somehow the man was linked to the investigation surrounding Jonah McKee's death. Her heart seemed to drop to the floor. She didn't want to think about Jonah or the fact that he may have been murdered.

"Look, I'll see you tomorrow." Belinda slipped through the front doors and locked them behind her. Skye was alone in the clinic. Ralph Fletcher only worked until two each day now and the office staff left promptly at five, after switching the phones to the answering service. The cleaning crew arrived around midnight. Skye checked her watch. Six-fifteen. "Not bad." It was the first night since she'd landed in Rimrock that she'd been able to lock up before dark.

Turning the bothersome card over several times, she walked back to her office. She tried to catch the investigator at home and left a brief message on his machine. That accomplished, she slid his card into the top drawer of her desk, then took the time to go through the files of the final three cases she'd seen and dictate memos that the secretary would type and file in the morning.

All in all, the second week had gone more smoothly than her first few days in town. Except for her relationship with Max. That was still complex. It was too easy imagining herself in love with him just as she had been before. But was it wise? They were older now; their dreams and lives had changed. She had her career; he had his. And he had a child and a business enterprise to run, while she had her ailing mother and the clinic to worry about.

With a sad smile, she realized that she really didn't have time to fall in love.

"Somethin's buggin' the hell out of you," Jenner said as he tossed the last bag into the bed of his truck and took a look around the Rocking M. "And don't try to tell me you're worried about the fact that Stone's got Sheriff Polk believing that Dad was murdered. It's more than that." His mouth quirked up at the corners. "If you ask me, you've got woman trouble. You want to talk about it?"

Irritated by the way Jenner had of always seeing though him, Max glared into the back of his brother's old truck. Two duffel bags, a bedroll and one box of shaving gear and cooking utensils. All Jenner owned in the world—well, almost. There were still three quarter horses, a few saddle blankets and various pieces of tack, but Jenner believed in traveling light. "Nothin' to say."

"Let me guess. You don't like me movin' in with the lady doc," Jenner said, his eyes glinting in the moonlight.

"I couldn't care less."

"And you're the worst liar in the county. You've been seein' her again and she's got your head all turned around and that ticks you off." Jenner yanked open the door of the truck. "I'm glad you don't mind me takin' the apartment over there 'cause that Skye, she's one fine-lookin' woman. Got herself a good job and a body on her that won't quit and—"

Before he could finish, the door was slammed shut and Max had his brother pinned against the cab. Max's reaction had been instinctive and fierce. The thought of another man with Skye, even his own brother, was too much to bear. "You leave her alone," he growled, his hands tightening in the folds of Jenner's shirt.

"Just as I suspected. You're still carryin' a torch." Jenner's crooked grin was downright insolent. Max knew there was nothing his brother liked better than a fight. They'd wrestled and boxed and tried to beat each other up for years before Max had gone away to school. Jenner's muscles flexed beneath his clothes and his nostrils flared as if he smelled a fight in the air.

"She's just not the kind of woman you're used to," Max said, backing up and silently cursing himself for letting his emotions take over.

Jenner's eyes darkened perceptibly. "You don't know what kind of woman I'm used to," he said, and there was something in the way he said the words, a quiet tone of emotion, that Max didn't understand.

Jenner had always been a love-'em-and-leave-'em kind of guy. Except for that one time with Beth Crandall, when Jenner had been the one left. What was it he'd told Max once? That the old man had screwed them both over when it came to women? Had Jonah intervened in Jenner's love life the way he had in Max's? Didn't seem possible. Jenner was too much a lone wolf to lose his heart to anyone or anything. Even Beth Crandall.

"Just back off," Max warned.

"If you're so interested in the lady doctor, why don't you take her out?"

"It's not that easy," Max admitted. Yes, he'd been with her twice, made love to her each time until dawn, but he'd rationalized his actions as pure lust and the love of a challenge. She'd left him years ago and now he was getting a little of his own back.

The trouble was that Jenner was right. All those old

feelings he'd denied for so long were back full force. He couldn't look into Skye's warm hazel eyes without seeing the future. His future. "Nothing's easy."

"Isn't it? Hell, the old man's dead. He can't do anything to you. It's over, man. All that old garbage. You can do whatever you damned well please. With Skye Donahue or not." Jenner climbed into his truck, slammed the door shut, pumped the gas and twisted the key in the ignition. Backfiring like a rifle shot, the old pickup took off, leaving a plume of blue smoke and the stench of burning oil. And he was going to Skye's house. A knot twisted in Max's gut. He'd told himself he wasn't going to go chasing after Skye again, that he needed time to think things through, to cool off, but it was impossible to keep cool with that woman.

"Damn it all," he growled as he crossed the lot, jumped into his old rig and headed into town. He'd rather forget about her, but he couldn't. Ever since making love to her, he'd been tormented by thoughts of her, erotic memories that would bubble to the surface of his mind at the most inopportune times.

Like now.

Skye read Mrs. Newby's list of complaints and repairs for the fourth time. The woman was crazy, expecting Skye to replace everything from light bulbs to the carpet as well as buy new appliances and repaint every wall. She wanted her rooms soundproofed and a security system installed on the doors and windows. She thought built-in shelves and a satellite dish to receive broadcasts from Louisiana, her home state, would be nice. How about security lights around the perimeter of the building? And about that cat, the gray tabby that hissed at her every time she walked up the stairs, well, he would have to go. Mrs. Newby was allergic to cats and didn't welcome the prospect of having her stockings snagged or her legs scratched by the beast.

"Dream on," Skye muttered, and wondered how she would get through to the sweet little lady.

There was a knock on the door and Skye found a petite, red-haired woman in her early thirties standing in the hallway. "I'm Tina Evans," she said with a sincere smile. "I just wanted to come down and introduce myself and thank you for the basket of goodies that you left with Paula the other day."

Skye liked the woman instantly. "You're welcome."

"I hope that Paula's music doesn't bother you. Because of my hours, I sometimes have to leave her alone. More than I'd really like to."

"She's been fine. Really," Skye said, cocking her head toward the living room. "Come on in. I've got a pitcher of iced tea in the refrigerator if you're thirsty."

Tina's grin widened. "It sounds like heaven! I've been working a double shift over at Oakley's Diner in Dawson City. One of the other gals called in sick, so I got elected to fill in. I sure can use the money, but as I said, I hate to leave Paula alone so much. She was okay, wasn't she?" Tina asked nervously, glancing up at the ceiling as if she could see through the floorboards into her apartment.

"I've only been home a little while, but I'm sure that if she was in any trouble, Mrs. Newby would have let me know about it. Pronto."

They sat at the table and chatted. Skye learned that Tina, originally from Des Moines, had been divorced for two years. Her ex-husband had disappeared with another woman and he hadn't paid a dime of child support. Ever since her parents' separation, Paula had become belligerent and confused. She was having trouble in school and seeing a counselor every other week. Her only interest seemed to be music. "She's a handful," Tina admitted. "Don't let anyone tell you the teenage years are easy. If they do, they're either liars or they've never raised any kids, let me tell you!"

She'd just about finished her tea when she noticed the

newspaper lying open on the table. "Doesn't that beat all?" she said, pointing to the headlines about Jonah McKee's death. "The man's been dead over a month, everyone around here thinking it an accident, and now, lo and behold, the sheriff and some private investigator think maybe he was murdered." She clucked her tongue and rolled her eyes. "I moved Paula here, away from Des Moines, to get away from all the violence that goes with a big city."

Skye's stomach seemed to drop. She didn't want to think that anyone would actually kill Jonah. Much as she hadn't liked the man, he certainly didn't deserve to be murdered. She thought of the investigator, Rex Stone, and wondered what he wanted from her.

"They think he was either run off the road or that he might have been drugged. Can you believe it—in a little town like Rimrock?" She shook her head and sighed. "Seems like they could've figured out all this before the family had the old guy cremated."

"Seems like," Skye said, unwilling to dwell on such a morbid topic.

"I never did meet the man, but I heard he was pretty powerful around here. You can't go a block without seeing McKee Enterprises on one building or another. You know, some people have all the luck."

"Don't they though?"

A loud knock sounded on the door.

"Oops. I bet that's Paula. I'd better get going." Tina drained her glass quickly and set it on the table. "Thanks for the tea and sympathy."

"Company," Skye corrected as she walked her through the living room. She opened the door and found Jenner McKee standing in the hallway, one hand raised as if he planned to knock again. "Why, Jenner," Skye said, surprised to find him in the hallway even though Dr. Fletcher had warned her that the younger McKee brother was looking for a place to stay.

"Doc Fletcher told me you could use a handyman around here," he said, ignoring the fact that Tina was looking him up one side and down the other. A Stetson was shoved back on his head, faded jeans were tight over his hips and a rawhide jacket was tossed over a sun-bleached plaid shirt. His skin was tanned and weathered, his body trim and tough as leather. He looked very much like the rodeo rider he'd been not so many years before. "He told me to stop by."

"He said the same thing to me," Skye said. "But the basement isn't fit to live in."

"Let me be the judge of that."

"And have the Department of Health after me? I don't think so." She shook her head and Tina stared at her as if she'd lost her mind. "There's a room up on two and an attic loft on three, each with working indoor plumbing, insulation and heat."

"The deal was for the basement," he said stubbornly.

"The deal just changed. Either you take a decent room or you don't take a room at all. Oh, and by the way, this is Tina Evans. She's one of the tenants. Jenner McKee."

Tina's mouth nearly dropped open. "McKee? We were just…oh."

"Pleased to meet you," Jenner said, charm evident in his sky blue eyes.

"Me, too." Tina, now that she'd quit staring, actually blushed.

Smothering a smile, Skye led them both up the flight of stairs to the second floor where she fitted the proper key into an ancient lock. The door creaked open and she hit the lights. This room was the smallest on the floor and needed work, but it was warm and weatherproofed and had working kitchen appliances as well as a hot shower, sink and toilet. "I'll offer you the same rate as Fletcher quoted. You can work off the rent by fixing up the basement and taking care of some of the problems in the other units. I've got a list downstairs for Mrs. Newby's apartment. The list needs to be trimmed a little, but at least it's a place to start.''

"Same amount of rent?"

"Exactly."

He eyed her for an instant before nodding curtly and extending his hand. "It's a deal."

Tina smiled widely, so pleased she looked about ready to burst. "So we're going to be neighbors."

"Appears as such," Jenner said just as the front door to the vestibule swung open and Max strode inside. He paused under the chandelier in the hallway and glanced up, his sea-colored eyes stormy.

Skye couldn't help the little flip her heart did at the sight of him. Where Jenner was range tough and handsome, Max was more polished and finer-featured. Yet he had the same underlying thread of steel in his stance. He took the stairs two at a time and stopped on the landing just as Mrs. Newby opened her door the width of the security chain, peered out, then shut the door quickly again, as if expecting the two newcomers to try to break into her apartment.

"I wondered when you'd show up," Jenner drawled with a knowing smile. "Just in time to help me move in."

"Right," Max replied sarcastically.

Skye introduced Tina to the second McKee brother to appear within ten minutes, then Jenner announced he was going to settle in. Tina reluctantly let herself into her own apartment, giving Skye a glimpse of old furniture and clothes strewed over an ironing board set up in the middle of her little living room. Heavy-metal music filtered into the hallway as Max and Skye headed downstairs.

Once they were back in her apartment, Max kicked the door shut. "I don't like him being here."

"Who?" she asked, then laughed at the jealousy evident in his features. "Jenner? Why not?"

"He's irresponsible and spends too much time at the Black Anvil."

Skye rolled her eyes and laughed again. "I'm not going to marry him, Max." He shot her a look that made her regret her careless reply. The subject of marriage cut too deep. For both of them. She cleared her throat. "What I'm trying to say is that as long as he does what I ask, I don't care where he hangs out."

Jaw clenched, Max didn't argue. He looked uncomfortable, as if his brother's presence upstairs was bothering him. "Let's go out," he finally said.

"Where?"

"Anywhere." He grabbed hold of her hand and the gleam in his eyes was unmistakable.

"Anywhere? That sounds dangerous."

"It could be," he allowed, his voice low and seductive.

"You're on." She locked the door behind her and followed him out to his truck. They drove out of town and far up into the foothills of the Blue Mountains.

Max pulled into a lane barred by a gate and posted with No Trespassing signs. "You own this?" she asked when he unlocked the gate.

"The company does." His expression grew dark as the pickup rumbled through the forest. "It was owned by Ned Jansen. Dad got this piece along with the copper mine." They stopped in a clearing, and through the trees the twinkling lights of Rimrock winked in the valley like diamonds.

"Come on," he said, taking her hand and helping her out of the truck. Together, hand in hand, they walked through the tall, dry grass of the clearing. Max folded her into his arms and his lips found hers in a kiss that was as warm as morning sunshine.

With a sigh, Skye melted into his arms and they fell onto a bed of sun-bleached grass and wildflowers. Max's fingers tangled in the curling blond strands of Skye's hair. "I never forgot you," he admitted as the wind whispered through the surrounding trees. "All the time we were apart, as hard as I tried, I never forgot you."

She smiled up at him, her eyes as dark as the night. "And I never forgot you," she said before dragging his head down to hers again.

Rex Stone was a disagreeable man. He seemed to think that Skye knew something about Jonah McKee's death and he didn't bother to hide the fact.

"He broke you and Max up, didn't he?" Rex was seated in one of the old club chairs Skye had inherited from Ralph Fletcher. Dressed in a cotton shirt and brown polyester slacks, he crossed one leg over the other and studied Skye with a look as hard as nails.

"I don't see that this is any of your business."

"I'm just trying to solve this murder investigation, Dr. Donahue, and in the process I'll need to know everything I can about Jonah McKee. You didn't like him much, did you?"

"That's true." Skye held the short man's gaze. "As you probably already know, I wasn't the only one and I certainly didn't want to see him dead."

"But you came back here and picked up with Max before the old man was cold in his grave. Don't you think that's a little convenient?"

"Coincidental is the word. I came back when I did because I'd finished my residency and I was offered a practice here by Dr. Fletcher. If you don't believe me, you can ask him."

"Why would I doubt you, Doctor?"

It was all Skye could do not to jump out of the old rocker in which she was seated and shake some sense into the foul little man. She'd returned his call, agreed to meet him and braced herself for the confrontation, but she hadn't expected him to suggest that she'd had something to do with murdering Jonah McKee. "Is there anything else you'd like to know?" she asked, glancing pointedly at her watch.

"A couple of things."

Skye inwardly groaned. They'd been talking for nearly an hour and her nerves were stretched as tightly as guitar strings.

"Who else would you classify as Jonah's enemies?"

"I don't classify myself as one."

His lower lip protruded and he shrugged. "Give me names."

"A lot of people who did business with him."

He didn't bother making a note. "Already checking on that."

"Neighbors, maybe. Women he might have been involved with."

"Such as?"

"I don't know," she said, and Stone's mouth twitched as if he was enjoying a private joke.

"No?"

"No."

"How about your sister? As I understand it, Jonah convinced her to give up her baby."

Skye's mouth turned to cotton. "I can't comment on that."

"And your mother. Worked for him for years. Everyone in the office suspected that she was in love with the old coot, but he never gave her a second glance."

Skye shot to her feet. Her insides had turned to jelly. "My mother would never have done anything to hurt Jonah McKee."

The doorbell chimed softly.

"You're in pretty tight with the McKee clan, aren't you? Seeing Max. Renting space to his younger brother. Working for the old man once."

"What are you getting at?"

"Nothing," he said as the doorbell pealed again.

"Good. Then I think we've finished, Mr. Stone," she said as she crossed the room quickly and threw open the door to find Max standing in the foyer. Relief flooded through her.

"Hi! I thought—" His gaze, which had centered on her lips for an instant, moved to a spot past her shoulder and turned instantly cold. "Stone," he said without a trace of inflection. "He bothering you?"

"Just asking a few questions, Max," Rex countered.

"It's okay," Skye interjected. "Mr. Stone was just leaving."

Rather than argue the issue, the detective slipped out the door and through the foyer, leaving Max still seething in his wake.

"He's a slimy bastard." Max peered through one of the narrow windows near the front door as Stone's Chrysler pulled away from the curb.

"Just doing his job," Skye remarked with a smile. Just the sight of Max seemed to make the gloom disappear.

The tension in Max's shoulders eased. "I have to go over to Dawson City to pick up Hillary," he said. "I thought you could come along and we'd all go out to dinner."

Skye hesitated. "I don't know. I wouldn't want to intrude."

"You won't," Max assured her as he linked his fingers through hers and pulled her close. As she turned up her face, he pressed warm lips to hers. "Come on," he whispered and she tingled inside. "It'll be fun."

"Promise?" she said, not daring to believe him.

He lifted one hand, palm out. "Promise."

Skye's stomach was in knots by the time they reached the two-story frame house where Hillary lived with her mother and stepfather. Max's face had grown tense, his knuckles white, as he gripped the steering wheel so hard Skye thought it might bend. He pulled close to the curb and swore under his breath. "God, I hate this."

"I'll wait here," Skye said. Even though she'd been invited, she felt out of place, as if she had no right to intrude in this part of Max's life.

She watched as he jogged up the path, took the porch steps in one stride and knocked rapidly on the door. Within minutes, the door opened and Hillary, dressed in shorts and a matching T-shirt, shot through, scrambling into her father's open arms.

Colleen, looking tired, stood inside with one crying toddler on her hip. She didn't smile at Max; in fact, her lips were pulled into a tight scowl of disapproval. She handed him a small suitcase seemingly relieved to let her daughter go.

As she turned in the doorway, her gaze moved to the pickup, and in an instant she caught sight of Skye. Her face drained of color and she cast Max a final glare before slamming the door so hard the house seemed to shake.

"Boy, was she mad!" Hillary announced as Max opened the door to the cab and she started to climb in. "Hey, wait a minute." Curious eyes met Skye's. "You're the lady at the ice-cream place."

"That's right."

Hillary's nose wrinkled. "I 'member. You're a doctor," she said with distaste in her tone.

"See how smart you are," Skye said to the precocious child.

Max said, "Her name is Dr. Donahue."

"You can call me Skye."

"Skye?" Hillary repeated, looking through the windshield to the heavens. "That's a weird name."

"Hillary!" Max's tone was harsh, but Skye laughed and shushed him with her gaze.

"Well, it's not nearly as pretty as Hillary."

"I hate my name," Hillary announced. "Kelsy Craig says it sounds snotty!"

"What does Kelsy know? It's a beautiful name," Skye said, still laughing as Hillary crawled across her lap and plopped herself down next to the driver's seat, wedging her little body between Skye's and Max's, and buckling her seat belt. "Know who else I am—besides a doctor?"

Hillary scowled and thought hard, as if Skye had asked her a trick question. "Who?"

"Dani's sister."

"The horse lady?" Hillary's eyes rounded in awe.

"The very same."

Hillary glanced up at her father for confirmation. "It's the truth," he said.

"Do you do tricks on horses, too?"

"To tell you the truth, Hillary, I avoid them as much as possible."

"Are you afraid of 'em?"

"Just careful," Skye said, and it was apparent from Hillary's reaction that being a doctor just didn't measure up to being an honest-to-goodness trick rider.

They planned to have dinner in one of Hillary's favorite restaurants, which was located in a shopping mall that had been made out of a converted theater and Quonset hut. In the middle of the mall a carousel with bright colors and lights was spinning and filling the little mall with organ music.

"I wanna ride!" Hillary enthused.

"After dinner." Max guided his daughter into the restaurant. It was painted in primary colors and offered slides, a small maze and differently shaped mirrors to amuse the children while their specialty pizzas were being prepared.

They ate in a booth painted with circus monkeys and smiling tigers. The pizza was hot, even if it wasn't the best Skye had ever tasted, and Hillary was anxious to eat her food quickly and join a group of noisy children running gleefully through the maze.

"So this is how you spend your Friday nights," Skye teased.

Hillary squealed in joy as she barely recognized her reflection in a wavy mirror that distorted her image.

"Most of the time." He stared at her across the table. "Sometimes we get really wild and see a Disney flick."

She caught the gleam in his eyes and her throat turned to dust. What was it about him that captivated her so? That made her think with her heart rather than her head?

Curls streaming behind her, Hillary ran up and threw herself into her father's arms. She climbed onto his lap and stole a slice of pepperoni from his forgotten piece of pizza.

"You're a thief, Hillary McKee," he accused as she chewed the morsel in front of him.

"You didn't clean your plate. Mommy says we gots to always clean our plates, but Mary and Carey they just make a big mess when they eat."

"Not like their big sister, eh?" Max said, beaming down at his daughter.

Skye felt a tug on her heartstrings. For years she'd been jealous of Colleen for giving Max what she couldn't and now she felt foolish. Hillary, spoiled though she was, was an adorable child, and if Max hadn't married Colleen, he never would have experienced the joy of becoming a father.

At that moment, her pager beeped and Skye excused herself to go find a telephone. She called her exchange, found out that one of the Donner kids had swallowed a half bottle of aspirin and was en route to the clinic here in Dawson City.

She made her way back to the table where Max and Hillary were just gathering up the remains of the pizza in aluminum foil.

"Something wrong?"

"Lenny Donner got into the medicine cabinet. Somehow he pried off the childproof cap and downed a few more aspirin than he should have. I'm meeting them at the Urgent Care Clinic here."

"Let's go." Max drove through the streets of Dawson City with Hillary babbling on and on about riding horses with Dani. He let Skye off at the emergency doors, then parked the truck. By the time he walked into the clinic, she'd already disappeared into one of the examining rooms. He felt a mild irritation at having his evening ruined. Though he realized that her patients had to come first, he couldn't help feeling jealous that her chosen profession could take her away from him at a moment's notice.

He read to Hillary from a children's book, then when she got restless, they wandered down the hallways and outside, only to circle back to the reception area where patients were waiting to be admitted.

"Let's go!" Hillary demanded finally.

"We will, soon."

"Where's Skye?"

"Helping someone," Max explained, glowering at the closed doors.

"Who?"

"A patient—a little boy who accidentally poisoned himself." Suddenly Max was ashamed of himself. What if he had discovered Hillary with a half-filled bottle of pills, or on the floor unconscious, or in the middle of a seizure? Wouldn't he want the best medical personnel available for his little girl? Swearing under his breath, he felt like a selfish fool. He picked up Hillary and held her close, silently thanking God that she was well and whole.

As Skye finally emerged from the back of the building, she was talking to Vickie Donner who was carrying her young son. The boy would be fine now that his stomach had been pumped, but Vickie was still shaken by the incident. They passed Max in the waiting room and Vickie shot him a hateful glance before scurrying outside.

Once Vickie had driven away, Skye turned to Max and found him holding onto his child as if fearing for her life.

"Sorry about the interruption," she said, offering a smile.

"Goes with the territory, I guess." But there wasn't any spark in Max's eyes.

Hillary yawned widely. "Can we go home now?"

"Sure we can, pumpkin." Max pressed a kiss to Hillary's crown of curls and once again Skye witnessed the incredible bond between father and daughter. She knew how much it pained him that Hillary didn't live with him, realized that he hated being what he described as a part-time father, only allowed to be with his child on weekends or whenever Colleen needed a break.

"How's the boy?" Max asked, once they were back in his truck.

"Fine now, but it was a good thing his mother knew what he'd been into."

Hillary snuggled next to her father as they drove away from Dawson City, and by the time Max turned into the driveway of the old house, she was snoring softly, her little lips moving as the breath rushed in and out of her lungs.

"She's precious," Skye said, touching Hillary's soft curls.

"The one thing I did right with my miserable life." Tenderly he brushed a stray wisp off Hillary's cheek and Skye felt the same old longing, the desire to have a child of her own. Her throat clogged with yearning and she blinked rapidly against a sudden rush of tears.

"I'll see you later," she whispered, and he leaned over to brush his lips with hers.

"You could come home with me."

She glanced at Hillary, sleeping so peacefully against her father. "Not tonight."

"She'll have to know sometime."

"Will she?"

The question hung between them in the soft summer-night air.

Max reached up and lifted a handful of Skye's thick hair. "She will if you're going to become her step-mother."

"Her what?" Skye asked, astounded.

"I want you to marry me, Skye." His eyes held hers

in the darkness. "And this time I won't take no for an answer."

Skye swallowed hard, joy leaping in her heart, love burning through her blood. She wanted to say yes and to hell with everything else, but Hillary, asleep between them, was a consideration. Could Skye be a part of this little girl's life, share her with her natural mother, keep her mouth shut when Colleen insisted upon something she disagreed with? And surely Max would want more children as did she. But not at this point in time. Now that she was committed to the clinic, could she become a full-time mother? Could she juggle the responsibilities of career and motherhood and do either justice?

"I don't know, Max," she said. "My first impulse is to say yes and let the chips fall where they may, but there are so many other people to think about, other responsibilities."

"Your job."

"My *career*. I have the clinic—"

"I own it. Don't worry about that."

"Patients—"

"There are other doctors."

"You...you want me to give it up?" she whispered, torn inside.

"Not completely, but can't you do it part-time?"

"I'm a doctor, for crying out loud, not a waitress! This is my profession!" And there it was, the old double standard, rearing its ugly head. He'd been raised to be in command, to be the boss, and he'd never want a wife whose career would threaten his control or be treated in equal terms as his. She stared into his eyes, dark with anger, and knew that it would never work. She'd been a fool to believe that love—their special love—could conquer all.

"I guess you've given me your answer," he said, throwing the pickup into gear.

She swallowed back the tears that rose in her throat and

the angry fear that she'd never find love again. "I guess I have." Before she broke down completely, she threw open the door, stepped onto the gravel and slammed the door shut.

He tromped on the gas pedal and took off, the taillights of his truck becoming red blurs as she watched him leave through the sheen of her tears.

"Fool," she said, dashing the damning tears away. How could she ever expect him to love her with that deep, soul-jarring love that she felt for him. To Max, love was one-sided. His way or no way. There wasn't room for compromise.

"Goodbye," she whispered brokenly. Clearing her throat, she squared her shoulders and refused to be one of those sobbing, pitiful women who clung to desperate dreams that would never come true.

But as she walked up the steps to the porch, the night closed around her, and she knew, deep in the darkest recesses of her heart, that her life would never be the same.

Chapter Thirteen

"I hate to say it, but it looks like that private detective your mama hired knows his stuff." Sheriff Hammond Polk reached into the back pocket of his uniform, drew out a tin and found a pinch of chewing tobacco which he stuffed behind his lower lip. He looked a little sheepish for a big man who was used to intimidating people by one hard look cast their way. An outdoorsman, he seemed out of place in the offices of McKee Enterprises. "Yep, makin' us look like buffoons, reopening the investigation and all, but I guess it had to be done."

In frustration, Max ran stiff fingers through his hair. "No one believed that Dad was murdered."

"I know." Polk settled into one of the chairs near the corner of the desk. "Damn it all, I didn't want to believe it myself. Murder? In Rimrock? The world's gone to hell in a hand basket, if you ask me."

"What do you want us to do?"

"Not much. Just cooperate. Answer the deputies' questions, let 'em have access to all your files. I'd rather not work with Rex Stone—always considered him an arrogant SOB—but since he caught us with our pants down, so to speak, I'd rather work with him than against him. That way the department won't suffer any more embarrassment." He shifted uneasily in his chair and rubbed his heavy jaw.

"Do you have any suspects?" Max asked as the enormity of the situation settled on his shoulders. This was *murder* they were discussing. Someone had intentionally edged his father's car off the road. Doom settled in his already-battered heart.

"We got a couple of leads, nothin' substantial, but we're questioning anyone who was at the Black Anvil the night your father didn't make it home. Some of the regulars were there, of course, but there were a couple of other fellas, as well, out-of-towners and the like. We've talked to them before, but we're gonna do it again, just in case we missed somethin'. Wouldn't want Stone to beat us to the punch." He placed his meaty hands on the arms of the chair and pushed himself upright. "I'll be talkin' to your ma about this." Squaring his hat on his head, he sketched a salute and left.

Murdered. The word kept echoing through Max's head and he wondered how it could have happened. The thought was unfathomable. True, his father had manipulated people and created more than his share of enemies. But murder? What had Jonah done that would make anyone want to kill him?

Max finished the dregs of his cold coffee, scowled at the bitter taste and set the cup aside. He tried to concentrate on some of the problems at the company. Two of the buildings in town needed to be renovated, but the tenants didn't want to deal with the inconvenience and noise of construction. They'd put together a petition claiming that they liked the aging Taylor Building and the three-storied old hotel just the way they were. The tenants were unhappy about the prospect of improvements that would mean an increase in their monthly rents. It didn't matter that the buildings were all but condemned, with the electrical wiring as well as the plumbing in both buildings needing to be completely redone.

There was a problem at the ranch, as well. A buyer for the cattle had backed out of the deal.

And then there was Skye. His jaw tightened and his mood turned even blacker.

It had been nearly a week since he'd last seen her at her house and those days had crept by at an agonizingly slow pace. He'd spent the weekend with Hillary, taking her fishing, playing catch with her, even participating reluctantly in a tea party. He'd watched as she'd tried to ride one of the older horses at the ranch with Dani Donahue Stewart as her instructor. He'd managed to speak civilly to Dani, though the two of them had never really gotten along. Throughout their short conversation, Max had tried to ignore the fact that Dani was Skye's sister, but it had proved impossible.

Eventually he'd taken an unwilling Hillary back to Colleen's house and left with the same heart-wrenching sense of loneliness that was with him every time he turned his back on his little girl. Hillary's tears tore at his soul, her trembling lower lip causing him the worst kind of mental anguish, and her outstretched arms were an invitation he was unable to ignore. Colleen and he would always be at odds, fighting for his only child.

A chill as cold as January settled over him.

Hillary and Skye—the only two things that made his miserable life worth living. The only two things that he never could have.

He gave himself a swift mental kick. How could he have been so stupid to have proposed to Skye, for God's sake, and why would he dare think that she would give up her life, a life she'd carved out for herself, for him and his daughter? He swatted at a fly buzzing lazily near the window and felt the urge to stretch his legs, get out of the office, run away from all the hassles at the company.

His father, curse the old man, had been right. Skye was not the right kind of woman for him. Too stubborn. Too independent. Too...too much like him. "Son of a bitch," he growled under his breath as he grabbed his jacket and headed for the door. He needed to get out of here; the walls were closing in on him. In just a few hours he could pick up his daughter. Together they'd have the best weekend in the world and he wouldn't dwell for an instant on Dr. Skye Donahue.

Skye lost five pounds in one week. Her appetite was nonexistent and she worked herself around the clock, from the minute she arose in the morning at 5:00 a.m. until she finally tumbled into bed near midnight.

After her usual morning run, she spent a full day at the clinic, and following a quick dinner, she tore into her work at the old apartment house. She spent her evenings cleaning, spackling, painting and wallpapering until her arms ached and her mind spun in weary circles. With every ounce of strength in her body, she forced herself to keep busy, to work until she dropped, so that she wouldn't second-guess herself about Max.

She wouldn't allow herself to fall in love with him. It would be too easy and only bring her heartache. But avoiding him proved impossible. Rimrock was a small community. Everyone knew everyone else's business and the fact that Max's brother lived upstairs didn't help. If that wasn't enough, the clinic was leased through one of the companies that Max owned.

No matter how much she tried to deny it, she was entangled with the McKees and would be as long as she stayed in Rimrock.

Maybe coming back home had been a mistake, she thought as she emptied the pockets of her lab coat and dropped it in the hamper near the back door of the clinic.

She'd never been a second-guesser, but dealing with Max was more than a challenge. It was a downright impossible task.

As she locked the clinic on Friday night, she rubbed the tension from the muscles of her neck. A dry wind blowing in from the east blew her hair over her face as she walked back home. It was time to treat herself. She considered all her options before settling for a hot bubble bath, a glass of cold Chablis and a good book. She'd go to bed at a decent hour for a change and will herself to keep thoughts of Max and all she'd given up at bay.

Or she'd confront him. Clear the air and tell him what she thought. If she was going to spend the next twenty years or so in Rimrock, she and one Maxwell McKee needed to get a few things straight.

Max swung the ax with such force that it split the knotty piece of oak clean through. He kicked the halves aside and grabbed another short log before hoisting the ax over his head and breathing hard. Again the sharp blade sliced through the air and cleaved the mossy chunk into two pieces.

"Looks to me like a bad case of sexual frustration." Jenner's voice carried on the stiff breeze and Max grimaced. The last thing he needed was some advice from his hellion of a brother.

"Yeah, and what would you know about it?"

"Plenty." Jenner swaggered toward the woodshed where Max was making kindling. "If this doesn't work, you can take up long-distance running or maybe shadowboxing."

"Thanks for the advice," Max snarled.

"Well, there's always cold showers, but they only work for so long."

Max tossed down the ax. Already spoiling for a fight, he would've liked nothing better than to knock Jenner on his denim-clad, know-it-all butt. He flexed his fists and Jenner had the irreverence to laugh.

"Man, you've got it bad."

"What?"

"Woman fever." Jenner leaned his shoulders against the unpainted siding of the old shed and propped the heel of one boot on the rough, weathered boards.

"I don't know what you're talking about."

"Then I'll make it simple. Dr. Skye Donahue."

"That's finished."

"Sure." Jenner's eyes silently accused him of being a first-class idiot.

Max wasn't in the mood for his brother's unspoken insults. He wiped the sweat from his brow on his shirt, which he'd hung from a nail, and picked up the ax.

"You know, you've been hell to get along with."

"Good thing you don't live with me."

"Yeah, good for me, but what about Hillary?"

Max stopped short. "What's that supposed to mean?"

"It means that for the first time in your life you've been so caught up in your own problems that you've ignored her. You weren't this bad during the divorce."

"I haven't—"

"Where is she now?"

"In the house with Mom."

Jenner's mouth compressed. "She's in the corral with Dani Stewart, trying to learn how to be a damned trick rider."

"Hell!" Max glanced at his watch and realized that for the first time since Hillary started taking lessons, he wasn't standing at the fence rail, watching and encouraging his daughter.

"Face it, Max. Right now you're no damned use to any of us."

Max didn't listen, just shoved his arms through the sleeves of his shirt and ran, shirttail flapping in the breeze, past the stables toward the corral. Night was settling in, shadows stretching long on the dusty ground, leaves turning in the wind. He thought he saw someone crouching behind a horse trailer parked near the brood-mare barn, but when he looked again, the person had disappeared. Probably just Chester or one of the hands finishing up. It bothered him a little, but he didn't have time to figure out who was trying to duck out of last-minute chores.

As he rounded the corner of the barn, he saw Hillary seated high in the saddle, her chubby little fingers tight on the reins, while Dani, lead rope in hand, commanded the mare to walk in a wide circle. Max's frozen heart melted at the sight of his daughter.

Skye was right about one thing. He loved kids, and if he had his choice, he would have half a dozen of them running around the ranch, yelling, fighting, playing and raising hell as he and his sister and brother had done. The tire swing in the backyard had never been taken down, the sandbox was still intact, and the trails that ran through the woods and along the banks of Wildcat Creek might be overgrown but still existed, as did the rope that hung from a branch of an old oak tree near the swimming hole. All waiting for his children. He gritted his teeth as he realized he'd have no more. Hillary was his one and only, and just a part-time daughter at that.

Damn, what a mess.

"Daddy, Daddy!" Hillary called out upon spying him. Perched atop an aging palomino mare, she grinned widely. "Watch me!"

"You got it, pumpkin."

Dani clucked her tongue, and the mare moved into a slow trot around the circle. Hillary's curls bounced around her face and she laughed in delight. "Faster, faster," she yelled, kicking at the mare's sides.

"First you have to learn to handle her at this pace," Dani said, her smile never faltering.

"But I want to go faster!"

"We'll get there," Dani promised. She smiled up at

Hillary before she spied Max and her grin faltered slightly.

Max didn't really understand her animosity. He knew that she hated all things McKee, except Casey, whom she'd come to trust, and Hillary. Dani seemed to have mellowed over the years, though her marriage to Jeff Stewart was rumored to be stormy. Several times in the past year, they'd separated, only to get back together again. Max didn't know the details; he figured it was none of his business. All he knew was that, in the past few months, she seemed to have thawed somewhat where the McKees were concerned.

"You look great," Max called from the fence.

"I'm gonna be a rodeo rider."

He laughed. "And I thought you wanted to be a bride."

"A bride *and* a rodeo rider."

Skye's heart knocked as she drove through the gates of the Rocking M. Twilight had turned the sky a deep, slumberous purple shade and the first twinkling lights of stars were visible in the heavens.

A stiff breeze played in the trees that lined the drive, causing the leaves to rustle in quiet whispers. Skye's palms were damp on the steering wheel of the Mustang as the sprawling ranch house and stables came into view.

Beneath the anticipation singing through her blood was a nameless fear. What if Max refused to listen to her? What if he threw her off the ranch? What, oh, God, what if he hated her?

She saw him the second she pulled into the parking area. He was standing at the fence, his tanned arms folded over the top rail, jean-covered hips thrust out, boots crossed at the ankle, his eyes trained on the paddock. His hair ruffled in the evening wind.

Skye's breath caught for a second, as it always seemed to do when she first caught sight of him. She had never really stopped loving him, probably never would, and yet their paths, which seemed to cross so often, didn't lead in the same direction. Tears burned at the back of her eyes, but she told herself to stop moping.

Hillary, chubby fingers tight around the reins, was riding a small mare. Dani was in the paddock with her, instructing the little girl in keeping her balance and using the leather straps attached to the bridle to communicate with the horse. Though Dani had the horse on a lead, Hillary was issuing commands, trying to make the mare move more quickly.

Max, hearing the Mustang's engine, turned to glance over his shoulder, and his pleasant expression turned instantly hard and menacing.

Skye's stomach turned over. This wasn't going to be easy. From his harsh expression, it was obvious it was going to be hell making any attempts at conversation.

Great.

Refusing to lose her nerve, she walked up and took a position near him, her eyes focused on horse and rider, her heart thudding so loudly she wondered if he could hear it. He smelled of sweat and musk, the scents lingering in the air tinged with the faint smell of smoke.

"Dr. Donahue," he drawled. "Well, surprise, surprise. What is this, a house call?"

Her temper simmered but she held her tongue. "I thought we needed to talk."

"Oh, so this isn't a professional visit."

"Knock it off, Max." She saw Dani staring at her, and Skye, forcing a smile she didn't feel, waved to her sister.

"Didn't we say everything we had to?"

You knew he wouldn't let you off easy, she reminded herself, but she hadn't expected the glacial coldness in his eyes, the angry set of his jaw, the stern censure of his stance. "You don't have to make this harder than it already is."

"I'm busy."

She touched his sleeve and he jerked away, the lines around the corners of his mouth deepening.

"Fine. You want to talk," he said, as the wind seemed to rise and tug at Skye's hair, "I'm listening."

It's now or never. The moment you've been waiting for. "It would be better done in private."

Eyes narrowing at her, he hesitated. "In private," he said suspiciously, an impatient tic developing near his jawline. "Well, why not? How about in the barn? That private enough?"

"It'll have to be."

With a wave to Hillary, he started across the yard, his boots crunching on the gravel. "I don't have much time," he said, checking his watch. "The lesson's over in less than ten minutes. Hillary and I always go out to dinner—"

"You don't have to be a bastard, you know."

He whirled to face her, and for the first time she saw beneath his anger to a glimmer of other, harder-to-define emotions hidden deep in his eyes. He grabbed her forearms, his fingers digging deep into the soft flesh. "I'm just not ready for you to start playing your mind games with me, Skye."

Jenner walked out of the house at that moment. His lips curled into a smug smile and Max didn't waste any time. He propelled Skye to the barn and kicked open the door, strode through and yanked it shut with one hand.

They were alone.

The barn was dark and warm. The smells of dry hay and dust, oil and leather permeated the air. As strong as a manacle, one of Max's hands still clenched her arm in anger. "What is it you want, Skye?" he asked, his voice low.

"I want us to be civil to each other."

"Civil? After what we've been through?" He glared at her as if she'd lost her mind. "What is this, Skye, some kind of game?"

"You should know by now that I don't play games."

"Is that so?" His eyes had turned dark in the half light of the barn. "Funny. I'd say that's all you've ever done. Say one thing, do another."

"I didn't come here to be insulted."

"Then why are you here, huh? Just wanted to see if I was still holding up? Well, I'm doing great, Skye, and believe it or not, I think I'll manage to live without you just fine."

She nearly gasped at the asperity in his words.

He hooked a thumb at his chest and growled, "Hillary and I did okay for a long time without you. It won't be such a loss."

She felt as if she'd been slapped, but then what had she expected? "We can't do this to each other."

"Do what?"

"Keep trying to hurt each other."

"Listen to me, *Doctor*," he snarled, grabbing her shoulders roughly. His skin stretched taut across his cheekbones and his eyes blazed with fury. "We aren't doing anything to each other anymore." The words were harsh, but she noticed the torment in his gaze as he glared down at her.

The barn seemed to grow hot, and inside that forbidden part of her heart, she felt an unlikely jab of hope, like a faint ray of sunlight piercing through the fog. "Aren't we?" she whispered.

"What do you want from me?"

Desperation tore at her soul. "I just don't want you to hate me," she said, and her throat was suddenly clogged with tears and something else, something choking.

Smoke.

The terrified scream of a horse cut through the silence.

"What the hell?" Max's head snapped up, and that's when Skye felt the searing heat, heard the ominous roar of fire. "My God," Max whispered, released her and started running. On the windows of the barn, she saw the reflections of flames, bloodred and shooting upward. "Hillary!" He was out of the barn in an instant, and Skye ran after him, her heart thudding in fear, panic streaming through her blood.

Men shouted. Horses squealed.

"Fire!" a ranch hand yelled, rushing toward the stables. Horses in the pastures were neighing and galloping toward the hills, their eyes crazed in terror.

Windows cracked in the stables and black smoke billowed into the sky. Flames, fanned by the hot dry wind, crackled upward, licking greedily at the roof and siding, causing the paint to peel. And the heat—such intense, lung-scorching heat.

Heart in her throat, Skye scanned the paddock where, only a few minutes before, Dani and Hillary had been working with the little mare.

"Hillary!" Max yelled just as the foreman caught up with him.

"I think she and the trainer are in the stables," Chester gasped, racing to the stables and throwing open one of the doors. Panicked horses, whinnying, hooves flaying, sweat lathering their hides, raced into the paddock.

"Oh, God, no," Skye moaned, but Max didn't break stride, just rushed at the inferno. "Max, don't—" But she cut herself off, for she, too, would fight the flames of hell to save his daughter and her sister.

A wail went up from the front porch as Virginia looked on the scene with horror. Kiki and Casey were with her. Max glanced over his shoulder and hesitated for a second. "For the love of God," he pleaded, then screamed at his mother, "call 911! Now! Get the fire department."

"Oh, dear Lord," Virginia cried, wringing her hands. "Where's—"

"Just do it!"

Skye, from the corner of her eye, saw Casey dash back into the house.

Horses screamed in terror.

Ranch hands began to battle the blaze with pitchforks and hoses.

"They can't be inside," Skye said, searching the surrounding fields, but there was no sign of Hillary or Dani or the mare. "Oh, God, they can't be." She watched in horror as the first ghastly flames tore through the roof, spraying hellish sparks into the black sky.

The fire roared, a huge, hungry beast. Max raced toward the open door of the stables. Skye was dogging his heels, trying to keep up with him.

"Stay back!" he yelled at her.

"You can't tell me what to do."

"For God's sake, woman, use your head!"

"Your daughter and my sister are inside. Now let's go!"

Black smoke billowed through the open door. A few more horses escaped, neighing in sheer terror, running wild-eyed through the paddock, trying to flee the deadly flames.

Max threw himself inside the inferno, his eyes watering from the thickening smoke, the roar of the flames deafening. "Hillary!" he yelled. "Hillary!"

"Dani!" Skye shouted, coughing against the searing smoke, her eyes blurring, the heat blasting her.

"Get the hell out of here!" Max growled at her, then again screamed, "Hillary!"

Please, God, keep them safe. Keep that precious little girl and Dani safe! Skye silently prayed as she squinted against the intense heat and ducked away from flames that reached out for her with hungry fingers.

Skye started coughing and couldn't quit. Max's arm was suddenly around her and jerked her back against him as the floor of the haymow gave way and burning boards tumbled downward.

"Over here!" Jenner's voice thundered from the direction of the stalls. "Max! For God's sake, get over here!"

Blinded, Max plunged through the smell of death. "I'm

coming!'' *God, help me!* He tripped on a water bucket and stumbled, his one hand on Skye. Fear clutched his throat, fear for Hillary and Skye.

With a roar from the flames, the roof started to give way.

''Max!'' Jenner called.

''Over here!'' Skye was leading him now.

He nearly stumbled into Jenner who was carrying Hillary in his arms. His grim face was black, fear etched in his features.

''Daddy!'' The little girl was sobbing and choking, coughing against the smoke. Max grabbed for his daughter, tucking her trembling body against his. ''Let's get out of here!'' He turned toward the door, but Jenner and Skye didn't follow. ''Come on,'' he yelled, the stench and acrid taste of smoke unbearable. His lungs screamed at the lack of air.

''I can't. Dani's trying to save the damned horses!'' Jenner yelled.

''We have to save her!'' Skye started forward, but Max caught her arm.

''You can't go back there.''

''But Dani—''

''I'll get her!'' Jenner rushed back into the heart of the blaze as Max carried his daughter and pulled the woman he loved back to the safety of the yard. Sirens screamed and people scurried around wildly as the first fire truck, lights flashing eerily, roared up the driveway. Men jumped from the truck before it stopped moving and long hoses were dragged toward the flames.

''Don't let it spread,'' the fire chief yelled. ''Hook up to the pump and use the lake if we have to!''

Choking, lungs burning, Max, Skye and Hillary escaped, but the beast raged on, and huge embers, swept by the wind, landed on the roof of the barn and the house.

''Oh, baby!'' Virginia rushed off the porch and took a

whimpering Hillary from Max's arms. Casey, hair billowing, ran after her.

"Watch the house! Kiki!" But the housekeeper, too, had started running away from the buildings.

"We're gonna have to evacuate!" the chief yelled. "Get these people out of here. Move it. Now!"

"Jenner and Dani are still inside," Max said, and turned back to the stables.

"I'm going with you!" Skye was chasing him again.

Max swept down on her like an avenging angel. "Like hell you are! The best thing for you to do, *Doctor,* is to stay out here until the ambulance arrives and take care of the injured. His face was black with soot and sweat and he glared at her, begging her to listen. "I'll find Dani and Jenner. You take care of my daughter."

Skye clutched him. "No," she cried, afraid that she would lose him forever, afraid that he was racing to a certain death. God, how she loved him and he'd never know. She'd never be able to tell him how much she cared. A horrible ache filled her heart and she tried to chase after him but the ranch foreman held her back. "No, no, no!" Skye knew the horror of watching the man she loved plunge toward an agonizing death.

"You have to help out here," Chester said, and as she saw Max disappear into the maw of the burning beast, she knew he was right. No matter what her own personal tragedy encompassed, she had to help those injured, if necessary, save lives. *Oh, please, God, be with him. Don't let him die. Don't let any of them die.* In her mind's eye, she saw Max, as well as Dani and Jenner, fighting the flames, fighting the heat, the deadly smoke. She'd been in enough burn wards to know the pain and suffering, the pure agony of trying to heal after the ravages of a fire. But she would help them. Each and every one. In her heart, it didn't matter if Max was burned beyond recognition. She would always love him.

"Come here," she said to Hillary, holding the trembling, crying child close to her breast.

"Daddy!"

"Shh, honey. Daddy will be fine," Skye said, her worried gaze finding Virginia's. No matter what were her own private fears, she would be strong for Max's daughter. Cradling his baby close, she silently sent up a prayer just as the first huge jets of water were pumped against the rising flames and charred shingles of the stables.

A second fire truck ground to a stop. Gravel sprayed and more volunteers began working, connecting hoses and listening to instructions from the fire chief.

Time seemed to drag on forever and the flames still reached for the heavens.

"Damn it, the toolshed's going!" Chester said. He was right. The wind had caught a spark and dropped it on the tinder-dry shingles of the toolshed.

Several hoses began pumping water on the house and barn and remaining buildings. A third truck screeched to a halt in front of an ambulance as the powerful streams of water continued cascading over the burning stables.

"Daddy," Hillary whimpered as Skye met with the fire chief.

"There are people inside. Three at least, maybe more," she said. "Three that we know of…and the horses…"

"Okay, men, we've got some people inside. Let's go."

Heart in her throat, Skye blinked back tears. She had to be strong. For Max. For Hillary. For Dani. For the wounded.

Heat seared through Max's body and smoke choked his lungs and burned his eyes and throat. "Jenner!" he screamed, but his voice couldn't compete with the roar of the fire. Fed by the hot summer breeze, flames crackled and whooshed, and terrified horses shrieked. "Jenner!"

"We're coming!" He saw them then, two blackened figures huddling together. Dani's arm was thrown over

Jenner's shoulders as they staggered to the door. Max stepped toward them.

Like a clap of thunder, a blast rocked the building. Max's feet shot out from under him and he hit the floor. Sparks showered from the roof, and the rafters, black from the flames, creaked loudly before giving way. Max curled into the corner, protecting his head with his arms, as a beam, like a flaming spear thrown from above, plunged to the floor and splintered, raining sparks.

His shirt ignited and he rolled quickly, trying to smother the flames.

A scream that sounded as if it was wrought from the very depths of hell pierced the dull roar of the fire, and suddenly water, gallons of it, was flooding over him.

Steam rose and still the flames crackled, but the roar of the fire had turned into a deafening hiss.

"Over here!" a man shouted. "Oh, God, look at this. Damn it, he's pinned."

"Help! Oh, God, please, please help us," came Dani's voice, small and frightened. She was coughing and crying hysterically.

"We've got you, lady. Someone get the man."

Max rolled onto his feet, ducking his head and running blindly toward the sound of the voices.

"The horses—" Dani said.

"No time, lady. Now, come on!"

Max stumbled forward and was caught by a fireman.

"Come on, let's get you out of here," the fireman insisted.

Then Max saw Jenner, his body crushed by the beam, his face twisted in agony, his hair singed away. Max didn't move. Couldn't. Life, as he'd known it, suddenly stopped. "Oh, God, is he—?"

"Don't worry about that one—we'll get him out of here."

"No way!" Max said, staring at Jenner. He stepped toward his brother's broken body and a million images flashed behind his eyes. Jenner with his cocky smile. Jenner trying to tame an ornery colt. Jenner sporting a cast from a rodeo contest. Jenner wrestling with him as a kid. Jenner the irreverent. Jenner the rebel. Jenner the bad son. Jenner his only brother. "No!" Max screamed. "No!"

"It's all right. I'll take care of him," the fireman said. "Now you just get the hell out of here!"

Max's soul seemed to rip from his flesh. Ignoring the fireman, he stumbled forward. "We've got to help him." His brother might be dying and he wasn't going anywhere. "We've got to get him out of here."

"I said we'll handle it. You take her—" Suddenly Dani was thrown into his arms and another fireman shoved them roughly toward the door. Max nearly tripped. Dani was crying and running. He couldn't breathe. The ground seemed to tip. Black water swirled around their feet. Dani was coughing so hard she nearly retched.

Together they staggered through the open door.

Men were everywhere, firemen and paramedics, neighboring ranchers and a reporter for the damned *Review.*

A paramedic grabbed Dani, while from the crowd, Skye broke free. "Max! Oh, God!" She was in his arms then, kissing his face and clinging to him. He gathered her in his arms, unaware that his shirt was black from the smoke and drenched with water. "I thought...oh, God!" Tears filled her eyes and streamed down her cheeks as she clung to him, seemingly afraid that he would disappear before her eyes. "I...I can't believe it. Oh, Max." She blinked hard and stared up at him. "I love you," she vowed. "I've always loved you."

Max felt her sag against him and he stroked her hair, leaving more black streaks in the fine golden strands. "And I love you, Skye," he said, his throat clogged, but no longer from the smoke. Raw emotion tightened his vocal cords. "I've never stopped." He held on to her fiercely, and when she tilted her face up to his, he kissed her with a passion that couldn't be denied. How long he'd been a fool. How blind he'd been to everything but the singular fact that he loved this woman with all of his heart.

Slowly he lifted his eyes and gazed back at the inferno. The flames were dying down, the charred ruins were more visible in the sheen of water and somewhere Jenner was inside. Alive or dead. Despair clawed at his heart. Jenner…the hellion. He couldn't be dead. He couldn't! Max's hands curled into fists of frustration.

Skye kissed his cheek and Max watched her transform into a professional. Her focus sharpened. "Are you all right?" Her hands were running over his body as she watched his face for any sign of pain. "Can you feel any burns?"

"I'll be fine," he said, closing his eyes and thinking of his brother. Jenner was tough, but how could anyone survive what he'd been through? Fresh pain slashed through him.

"But you inhaled a lot of smoke—"

"I said I'll be fine. Check on Dani and Jenner when they bring him out."

"Jenner?" she said, as if suddenly remembering that he was missing. "He's still in there?"

Max's throat worked. "He's in bad shape."

"Then we'll have to fix him, won't we?" Suddenly Skye was again all business—the doctor in charge of a medical emergency. She went over to Dani and started by asking her questions, then examined her quickly and insisted she be taken to the hospital.

"Hey, mister, come over here. Let's check you out," a paramedic yelled at him, but Max ignored him and kept his eyes trained on the door of the stables. Waiting. Jenner couldn't be dead! But how long could he survive in there?

"Daddy!"

Somehow Hillary was in his arms, and Max's eyes, already burning, began to tear. He clung to his little girl and gave thanks that she'd survived. "I love you, pumpkin," he said.

"I know." She burrowed her head into his neck and he swallowed against a hard lump in his throat.

"Come on, come on," he muttered as he watched the walls of the stables begin to crumble. Flames still leapt from the roof, only to sizzle and sputter as water drenched them.

Hillary wiggled to get down and Max reluctantly let her run to her grandmother. Then he started for the building, his legs carrying him faster and faster toward the open door. Where the devil was Jenner?

Fear gripped him hard in the gut and propelled him forward.

"Hey, you! Hey, you can't go in there! It's suicide!"

"Stop him!" the chief shouted, and he was restrained by two burly men who meant business. He tried to struggle free, but then saw a staggering fireman carrying Jenner over his shoulders. Several other men rushed over to help. They placed Jenner on a stretcher, and before Max could reach his brother's inert form, he was carried into a waiting ambulance.

"Let me go to him."

"Forget it, man. Leave it to the doc." Max watched as Skye slipped into the ambulance just before the doors were slammed shut.

"Wait!" Max cried.

"We can't, not if you want him to live."

"He's alive?" Max felt an instant of hope.

"Barely."

For the first time in a long, long while, Max McKee began to pray.

The hospital was a madhouse. Max was frustrated while Skye went right to work. She took only a few minutes to tell him Jenner's prognosis. Though Jenner would survive, several vertebrae in his back were broken, the result of the beam from the roof hitting him in the small of his back and crushing his thigh. No one seemed certain whether he would walk again.

"It depends on whether his spinal cord is severed or bruised and how bad the damage was," Skye explained hours later, as they stood on the roof of the hospital. The night was clear, the wind still strong, as a helicopter, blades rotating, stood ready. "Just because vertebrae are cracked doesn't necessarily mean that the spinal cord won't function."

"He won't want to live if he can't walk."

"We don't know that."

"I do."

"But he may walk again."

"He'd better," Max growled, feeling impotent as he watched his brother being lifted onto a life-flight helicopter that would take him to Columbia Memorial Hospital in Portland, where specialists would work with him. Colleen had come for Hillary, Dani was staying in the hospital overnight for observation and he and Skye were alone. His arm was draped possessively around her shoulders; her arm had slipped around his waist.

"I could go with him," Skye said as the pilot strapped himself into the chopper.

"What could you do?"

"Provide moral support."

"You're dead on your feet."

"It comes with the territory." She turned to look up into his night-darkened eyes and saw his pain. "Then again, maybe I should stay here and provide moral support."

"And Dani?"

Skye sighed. "She'll be okay. Smoke inhalation mainly. She's just staying overnight for observation."

Max squeezed her shoulders as the helicopter lifted off and the sound of his voice was nearly drowned by the engine and powerful, whirring blades. "Let me take you home. We'll drive to Portland tomorrow."

"I don't want to go home," Skye said, inching up her chin. "I want to stay with you."

"With me?" he asked as the helicopter became only lights in the sky.

"Forever." She licked her lips nervously, and while the wind blew her hair over her face, she said, "Those few minutes you were in the stables were hell, Max. I thought…God, I thought I'd never see you again and…and I knew I couldn't stand it." She drew in a deep breath and plunged on though tears seemed to fill her throat. "I want you to know that I love you, I've always loved you and I…I've dreamed about being your wife."

Something inside Max broke. The pressure of his emotions was too great and the dam of indifference he'd built in his heart cracked wide open. Skye's words were like wondrous music to his ears and yet he hardly dared believe her. "What about everything we talked about? Your job? Kids? The future—"

"It'll all work out," she said. "It's just the details. I just want to be with you. And Hillary." Her eyes were luminous in the darkness, her hair a pale shade of gold. Max trembled inside and he knew that this woman, this one woman was the only female on earth he would ever truly love. The only one who could satisfy him. In a heartbeat, his anger had disappeared.

He grabbed her so fiercely, he thought she might break. "God, I love you."

"Then, Max McKee, will you marry me?"

He couldn't fight the grin that curved his lips. "I'd marry you tonight if we could find a preacher." He drew her into the circle of his arms and felt her breasts, warm and supple, crush against his chest. Lowering his head, he kissed her as his heart took flight.

At last, after all these years, they would be married.

Nothing else mattered. Just Skye and Hillary and the fact that he would finally have the family he wanted.

There was work to be done. Though the livestock had miraculously been spared, the stables were a total loss as was the machinery shed. The only good news was that Chester would get his new tractor; the old one had burned in the fire.

Jenner was still in Portland, where specialists were observing him. His spinal cord wasn't severed, but he still couldn't walk or move his legs. The doctors said he probably would be transferred back to the local hospital by the end of the month.

Dani was still riddled with guilt. "I would never have taken Hillary into the stables if I'd known," she told Skye for the dozenth time. Sitting in the living room of Max's house, a neglected cigarette dangling from her fingers, she looked like hell. Though she'd only suffered slight smoke inhalation and a few burns where sparks had eaten through her clothes, she was wasting away.

"You couldn't have known. You were just putting the mare back in her stall."

"But I should have seen something or heard something," Dani said, sighing loudly. "If only I'd been more aware."

"It's not your fault!"

Dani closed her eyes. "I should have smelled the smoke, seen the flames. The fire chief thinks the fire broke out in the tack room and we were there just minutes before." She hung her head and jabbed out her cigarette. "I never liked Jenner McKee, but I never wished this on him." Biting her lips, she fought back tears. "And Hillary... When I think how close she came to being seriously hurt..."

Skye sat down in the chair next to hers. "You've got to quit beating yourself up over this, Dani. It was *not* your fault."

"But it was someone's," Dani said, staring blankly out the window.

True, the fire had been intentionally set. Arson. At least it appeared that way. And now Sheriff Polk thought that Jonah McKee's murder and the fire at the stables were tied together somehow, that some sick mind was trying its best to harm the McKees. Max had seen someone by the stables, someone he didn't recognize, just minutes before the blaze. The sheriff's department and the private investigator, Rex Stone, were looking into new leads, and soon, Hammond Polk hoped, they'd find the culprit. Skye didn't mention any of this to Dani; her state of mind was too frail as it was. Instead, she tried to cheer her up.

"Hillary's fine and Jenner's going to pull through. His prognosis is good. It looks as if his spinal cord wasn't severely damaged. Dr. Bradshaw thinks that someday he'll walk again. Maybe even ride a horse or two."

"It's not for certain," Dani whispered.

"Nothing in life is. At least everyone survived. Even the horses. You rescued the herd." It had been Dani's and Jenner's efforts that had saved the animals. "You almost lost your life doing it. I think the McKees owe you."

"That's a switch." She let her gaze slide guiltily away. "I guess I should admit something," she said, clearing her throat. "Something that's been bothering me for a long time. Remember that twenty-five thousand dollars—the check Jonah wrote to you? I convinced Mom to take it. She did it for me, and...well, I figured the McKees owed it to us, but now..."

"Shh." Skye took Dani's hand in her own and decided it was time to break the news. She and Max had kept their secret to themselves because of all the trauma in their lives. "Don't worry about it. That was a long time ago and now...now it doesn't matter because I'm going to marry Max."

Dani looked up at her sister and tears starred her lashes. "You are?"

"You bet. And nothing will stop me."

"That's right," Max's voice boomed as he walked through the open back door. Skye turned and found him carrying Hillary and smiling broadly. "This time I'm not going to let her wiggle out of it."

Hillary grinned at Skye. "See. You're gonna be a bride," she said, her eyes bright at the prospect of a wedding. "Daddy says I can be the petal girl."

"Flower girl," Max corrected.

Skye grinned and winked at her sister. "And I'm hoping you'll be my matron of honor."

"I couldn't—"

"Of course you could."

"But what about Jenner?" Dani asked.

Max kissed his bride-to-be on her forehead. "Jenner will be best man, if I have to push his wheelchair down the aisle myself." Max finally seemed relieved. Just that afternoon the doctors had told him that Jenner would walk again. It would take time and effort and lots of grit, but eventually he'd have full use of his legs. "It looks like, in time, he'll be back on his feet."

"Thank God," Dani said, blinking against her tears.

Skye helped her sister to her feet. "Go home. Spend some time with Jeff. Things are gonna work out."

"Since when are you such an optimist?"

Skye glanced at the man she loved and her heart seemed full enough to burst. "Since I decided to marry Max."

Hours later, Skye helped tuck an exhausted Hillary into bed. The little girl cuddled up to her teddy bear and didn't even fight the need to sleep that forced her eyelids down. Max kissed the soft curls on the top of her head and snapped out the light. Taking Skye's hand, he led her through the master bedroom and through French doors to the balcony.

The moon was full, casting a silvery light through the

forest. Max stood behind her, his arms around her waist, her head pressed against the base of his throat. "I have something for you."

"What?" Skye looked up at him.

He reached into his back pocket and handed her a rolled piece of paper held together with a slim gold band. A solitary sapphire glimmered in the soft summer evening.

"What's this?" she asked.

"Something for you to treasure the rest of your life." He slipped the ring from the paper and over her finger.

"I already have something," she said. "I have you."

"Always?" he asked, drawing her closer. She unrolled the paper and began to read the letter he'd written to her.

Tears of happiness filled her eyes. "Always."

Dearest Skye,

From the first moment I laid eyes on you seven years ago, I knew I wanted you for my wife. You touched me as no other woman has ever touched me and I was bewitched by you.

We lost something seven years ago and now we have a chance to get it back, sweeter now than ever.

I've made mistakes, probably more than my share, but I've never been guilty of not loving you. It has been my blessing as well as my curse, and I will gladly carry it with me to the grave.

From this day forward I vow that I will never leave you. No circumstance is great enough to keep me from you. We will raise our family and grow old together.

No other woman could ever take your place.

I love you with all my heart and I will never stop. You are the greatest gift in my life and I will cherish you forever.

Always,
Max

* * * * *

A Note from the Author

Fall—1994

In the summer of 1993, I was lucky enough to vacation for a few days with my parents in eastern Oregon. Though I've lived in the Willamette Valley all of my life and spent much time on the Pacific Coast, the Cascade Mountains or the high desert of central Oregon, I'd never been to the far eastern portion of the state.

While driving, the idea for the series came to me. I wanted to set the stories in this breathtaking portion of Oregon and name my fictitious town for the outcropping of rimrock that topped some of the mountains. I planned that the three books would be tied together with a common thread, not just the countryside, or a family, but a problem that carries through all the love stories—in this case, the murder of Jonah McKee.

I also hoped to start each book with a letter that would propel the characters into the story and force an immediate confrontation between them, then end the book with another letter—a love letter—from the hero to the heroine.

Max and Skye's story which you just read starts the ball rolling.

In the second book, *B Is for Baby,* Beth Crandall thinks she's long over Jenner McKee, the rebel son of Jonah McKee. She believes that Jenner, a rugged, lonesome cowboy, has no use for her or her son. *His* son. However, Beth receives a letter from Jenner's grandmother insisting that she return to Rimrock with her two-year-old son. If Beth doesn't comply, the old woman threatens to do everything in her power to take Beth's child, a McKee by blood, away from her. Beth has no choice but to return to the town she's sworn to hate and face a man who doesn't even remember her name, much less know he fathered a child.

Casey McKee, only daughter to Jonah, is the heroine of *C Is for Cowboy.* The story opens with a ransom letter demanding money for her safety. Casey's been kidnapped and the man who will be sent to rescue her, Sloan Redhawk, a half-breed Native American rodeo cowboy, is the wrong kind of man for Casey, but a man she finds impossible to resist. Sloan acts as Casey's bodyguard and though he swears that she's nothing more than a spoiled rich girl looking for trouble, he can't help mixing business with pleasure and ends up fighting his attraction to her.

I hope you enjoy all of the books in the Love Letters series and if you'd like to write me, I'd love to hear from you.

Lisa Jackson
333 S. State Street
Suite 308
Lake Oswego, OR 97034

B IS FOR BABY

Prologue

Dear Miss Crandall,

I know you probably didn't expect this letter and I must admit that I never thought I'd be writing to you, but I feel as if I have no choice because my grandson's future—his very life—may depend upon it.

Before you disregard me as an old, overly melodramatic woman, please read the enclosed article and know that Jenner McKee, my late son's boy, needs your help. Six weeks ago he was injured while trying to save my granddaughter and the livestock from a horrible fire at the Rocking M Ranch. He was pinned beneath a ceiling rafter that had fallen, his leg was crushed, and now the doctors aren't sure if he'll ever walk on his own again. I assure you I'm not stretching the truth. By all accounts, Jenner should be dead, as his father is, God rest his soul. I fear that if he finds no reason to look toward his future, his will to live may shrivel up altogether.

But there is hope. You see, I know your secret. Before his death, my son, Jonah, confided in me that you bore Jenner a son, but that you kept the secret of your pregnancy to yourself, never letting Jenner know that he was to be a father.

I believe with all my heart that if Jenner knew he had a boy of his own, he would find the will to live that he seems to have lost. I beg you, please, come home to Rimrock. Tell Jenner the truth. Let him see his son with his own eyes.

I'm afraid that if you don't comply, I will simply have to take matters into my own hands, and I vow to you, as God is my witness, I will see to it that my grandson is told that he's a father.

Please return. I'm afraid meeting his boy is Jenner's only chance.

Sincerely,
Mavis McKee

FIRE DESTROYS MCKEE STABLES

An explosion and three-alarm fire ripped though the stables of the Rocking M Ranch owned by McKee Enterprises. Several firemen were injured in the blaze along with Dani Stewart, 28, Hillary McKee, 5, and Jenner McKee, 33. Stewart and the McKee girl were treated for smoke inhalation and released from the hospital. Jenner McKee is in critical condition at Dawson City Hospital, where he is being treated for smoke inhalation, second degree burns and injuries to his spine and one leg.

Due to McKee's efforts, no horses were killed in the blaze, which destroyed the stables, a building housing machinery, as well as a pump house and part of a barn.

The cause of the blaze is under investigation, but Fire Chief Fred Swaggart hasn't ruled out arson....

Chapter One

Sometimes you just plain run out of luck. Especially with a man like Jenner McKee.

Angrily, Beth Crandall stuffed the rest of her mail into the pocket of her jacket and kicked at a stone in the parking lot, sending it skittering across the wet asphalt to land near the row of dripping rhododendrons that was the barrier between one sixplex and the next.

As if she hadn't tried to tell Jenner he had a son! A vision of Jenner, rugged and leather tough, flitted through her mind. Roguishly handsome, tall and lean, he'd used her as he'd used a dozen women before her, and she'd been foolish enough trust him.

She couldn't imagine him injured...crippled. He'd been so vital, so alive, so strong.

She stared down at the embossed letterhead and wished she'd never seen the letter from Mavis McKee, never ripped open the envelope, never scanned the words that were bound to control her destiny.

For nearly three years she'd convinced herself that she'd never have to deal with anyone named McKee again, but she'd been wrong. So very wrong. "Fool," Beth muttered as she climbed the steps to her second-story apartment in Oregon City.

The building was situated on a bluff overlooking Willamette Falls where the river tumbled over rocks and spillways to move steadily northward. On either bank were industrial buildings—factories and mills of different sorts with tall smokestacks that billowed steam into the gray sky. Highway 99 sliced along the shoreline, running parallel to the river and the railroad tracks that followed the Willamette's path.

Yes, she was far away from the sleepy little town of Rimrock, Oregon where she'd grown up and spent a lot of her adolescent years adoring a lonesome cowboy rodeo star, the rebellious second son of the richest man in the county.

Jenner McKee. Her heart squeezed at the thought of him. Beth had told herself she'd gotten over her schoolgirl crush long ago, that in the past three years she'd matured and given up the silly dreams she'd built around a man who probably didn't even remember her name.

And now he could find out about Cody.

Her insides turned as cold as ice. Numbly she walked to the edge of the cliff and looked over the railing to the sluggish gray waters of the Willamette. How had Mavis found her? Probably through Jonah McKee. Beth suspected that while he was alive, Jonah had kept track of her and her son.

Whether she liked it or not, she had no choice but to return, to come clean and admit to Jenner they had a son.

Otherwise, should she try to run, to hide Cody, she might lose her little boy forever. If Jenner decided he wanted custody, he could afford the most expensive lawyers in the state, he could buy witnesses and line the pockets of crooked judges, and Beth could lose her only son.

Her throat turned as dry as dust at the prospect.

How would it look to the judge?

In her mind's eye, Beth conjured up her worst nightmare. She stood alone on one side of the courtroom; Jenner and his team of lawyers swarmed together on the other. Gone were his faded, worn Levi's. Instead, he wore an expensive three-piece suit with a white shirt and solid-colored tie. His days' growth of beard had been neatly trimmed away and he was solemn and serious, no longer the rough-and-tumble rodeo rider who had never spent more than two weeks in any one spot. He'd inherited part of the vast McKee fortune and owned property, a huge house, acres of ranch land, timber and mineral rights, as well. Along with ranch hands, he had a maid and nanny on his payroll.

The judge's voice was stern. "Ms. Crandall, you're the daughter of Harriet Forrester, correct?"

"Yes."

"Let's see...Crandall...that makes you her daughter from her second husband...."

"Her first husband," Beth corrected.

"Winward was her maiden name?"

"Yes."

"Humph." The grim-faced judge leafed through a thick sheaf of documents and scowled, clucking his tongue sanctimoniously. "Harriet Winward Crandall Lambert Jones Forrester. My God, she's gone through enough husbands, hasn't she?"

In Beth's mind's eye, the judge smiled down at her, exposing yellowed teeth.

"I don't see what my mother has to do with this hearing," she countered, once again feeling the pain, the embarrassment she'd lived with all those years in elementary and high school. She'd heard the whispers, endured the taunts, knew that most of her classmates thought her mother was nothing more than a cheap hussy, a whore who went through husbands as quickly as some people went through toilet paper. At least that's what Dale Bateman had said to her when they were in the fifth grade.

"It's simple. You're the daughter of a...well, a very colorful woman. Why, she's practically legendary here in Rimrock, the way she's slept with just about every single man in town, and Mr. McKee, here, is the son of one of the most revered men in three counties." He leaned even closer, his judicial robes settling around his broad shoulders as he folded his hands and smiled. "Now, isn't it true you didn't tell Mr. McKee he had fathered a son?"

"Yes, judge," she imagined herself saying in a strangled voice.

"And is it also true that you took money from Mr. McKee's father—kind of a bribe to stay away from Jenner McKee?"

"Well, it wasn't really a bribe—"

"But it helped you pay off your education debts, allowed you to make ends meet while you had the baby and started looking for a nursing job, didn't it?"

"Yes, but—"

"Hold on a minute." In her painful vision, she could see him adjusting his reading glasses to peruse thick stacks of depositions. "While you work during the day, Mr. McKee's son is being cared for by an elderly woman who you only met once you moved into your apartment in the city."

"Mrs. Taylor is far from elderly! She's very active and has more energy than I do on some days. Besides, she loves Cody."

The judge sighed loudly. "And did you, or did you not, keep your son hidden from his natural father?"

"Yes, but—"

The courtroom was suddenly as silent as the tomb. Only the paddle fans whirring softly overhead made any sound. Shaking his head, the judge picked up his gavel. "I hereby grant custody to Jenner McKee! Ms. Crandall will have visitation rights, of course—" The imaginary gavel pounded down with a bang. Beth jumped, her heart drumming in fear, and her fingers tightened around the rain-slicked railing of the overlook.

Losing Cody was her worst nightmare. One she'd had over and over again. In the past couple of years, she'd convinced herself that it was only that—a worrisome dream. She'd never been to a custody hearing, and certainly they were much more fair than the horrible one she'd envisioned. And yet... She shivered inside.

Don't let Jenner get away with it! He never wanted Cody and he didn't want you! Fight him, Beth! Don't give up!

Hunching her shoulders against the rain, she headed back to her apartment. There was no reason to panic. Just because she'd received a letter from Jenner's grandmother was no reason to believe that he'd changed. He might not care that he had a son.

Except now he's injured—unable to walk on his own. That would change a man; make him realize what was important in life.

She stopped dead in her tracks as she reached the stairs to her second-floor apartment. What would Jenner do without the use of his legs? How would he function? She tried to imagine him behind a desk, pushing papers for McKee Enterprises, and she failed. He'd never be happy confined to a wheelchair, never be able to accept the fact that he couldn't ride a wild rodeo bronco, or rope a calf, or best a man in a barroom brawl...or make love.

Beth's throat caught and she took in a short, swift breath. She'd given up thinking about her one night with Jenner long ago, tried to forget how it felt to have him hold her, kiss her, touch her anxious nipples with his callused thumbs. Theirs had been a night of lovemaking, a single, special night that Jenner probably didn't even remember, one that she had treasured for months.

But that was all in the past now. Before she had her new life here in the Willamette Valley. With Cody. At the thought of her son, she raced up the stairs, her heels ringing on the metal steps. Suddenly she had to see his smiling face, hold his small body close to hers, convince herself that he wasn't going to be taken away from her.

She unlocked the bolt and threw open the door.

"Cody!" she called, sensing the apartment was empty. Panic swept through her. Maybe Mavis had already made good on her threat. "Cody!" She ran to her son's small bedroom, but the crib was empty. "Lela?" *Get a grip, Beth. They're just out. They'll be back in a minute.*

Fingers trembling, she slid out of her jacket and flung it onto the corner of her bed. Forcing herself to remain calm, she splashed water on her face in the bathroom, then kicked off her high heels and changed from her skirt, blouse and jacket into a soft pair of jeans and her favorite sweater.

Today had been her last day at the clinic. She'd been granted severance pay, of course, but not much because the clinic, run by government funds, was closing. The entire staff had been discharged, and there had been tears and laughter and worried goodbyes this afternoon.

Beth was certain she'd get another job; she'd applied at three hospitals, but she just didn't know when she'd be hired. Her life was falling apart at the seams, and now here was this letter with the horrid news that Jenner was hurt, maybe permanently.

It looked like his luck had run out, as well.

Beth felt a jab of guilt. Ever since opening the damned letter, she'd worried about Cody and herself and hardly given a thought to Jenner and his plight. Despite the way he'd treated her, he didn't deserve the injuries he'd received while trying to save the others.

Jenner McKee. Noble. Who would have thought?

She heard the door open and she raced into the living room, where Lela Taylor was busy unbuttoning Cody's jacket. Beth's heartbeat slowed a little and she forced a smile as Cody's blue eyes focused on hers and his face broke into a happy smile.

"Mommy!" he yelled, holding up his arms despite the fact that Lela was trying to shuck off his jacket. "Mommy! Mommy!"

Eagerly Beth plucked him out of Lela's arms. "Where've you been, big boy?" she asked. Planting a kiss on his soft cheek, she smelled the traces of baby shampoo in his hair.

"Oh, we took a big walk today, didn't we?" Lela chuckled. "We went over to the park and what did we see there, hmm?"

"Dog. Big dog!" Cody said, his eyes, so like his father's, shining brightly. "And puppies."

The two women exchanged glances.

"They were giving them away for free," Lela said a little sheepishly.

"Lela, you didn't!"

"Well…"

"I want!" Cody said excitedly.

"I couldn't resist."

"But we can't have a puppy here. Not in the apartment."

Lela lifted her hands in silent surrender. "Oh, I know, honey, and I respect that. But there's no reason Al and I can't keep the dog until you get a bigger place."

"Oh, no…" Beth felt as if her world was collapsing.

"If you don't want the dog, Al and I will just add him to our litter. One more won't hurt anything."

"As long as Cody understands," Beth said, but she was beginning to feel manipulated by a two-year-old imp and the woman who adored him.

"He can come over and see Barney any time he wants."

"Barney? You already named him?"

"Not me." Lela winked at Cody. "Your son did." Reaching into her pocket for her keys, she added, "Oh, I locked the stroller downstairs in the bicycle closet.'' She checked her watch. "Better be running along. Al will be home in half an hour and he doesn't take kindly to waiting for dinner. Turns into a bear if he has to watch the news before he eats.''

"You should make him cook his own,'' Beth said, thinking of the giant of a man who had been married to Lela for over forty years. A quiet man who rarely voiced his opinions, Al Taylor was the most unlikely person she knew of becoming a "bear.''

"I do. Every Friday night. We usually go out for pizza.''

As Lela reached for the door, Beth hugged her son and decided she had to start making arrangements to return to Rimrock. "You know, since I don't have to go into work next week, I think Cody and I might be taking a few days off to visit my mother.''

"Next week?''

"Who knows when I'll get some free time again?''

Lela's gray eyebrows rose over the tops of her tortoise-shell glasses. She had never pried, but she knew that Beth had left Rimrock for reasons involving Cody. Though Harriet Forrester had visited her daughter in Oregon City a few times, Beth had never gone back home in the few years that Lela had been Beth's neighbor and friend.

"Not bad news, I hope.''

Only the worst! "No, I, uh, just think it's time.'' Beth hated not confiding in the friendly older woman, but she had reasons to keep her secrets to herself. She'd never divulged the name of Cody's father to anyone other than her mother.

Until a few minutes ago, she'd thought her secret was safe; the only people who knew that Jenner McKee had fathered a son were Beth, her mother, Harriet, and Jenner's bastard of a father, Jonah P. McKee. Beth had heard that Jonah had died, of course. Her mother had informed her of the news, and now there was speculation that he might have been murdered. Mistakenly Beth had assumed he'd taken the secret of Cody's birth to the grave with him, but apparently he'd confided to Mavis that she had a grandson.

A grandson who no one was supposed to know about.

Lela promised to pick up the mail and water the plants, then left Beth clinging to her son. How many other people knew about Cody? Who else knew that Jenner McKee was a father? She'd hoped that once Jonah was dead, she'd be free of the McKees forever, but the damned letter had only proved that there would always be an invisible cord, as strong as steel, binding her to the richest family in Rimrock.

Beth felt the urge to run, to flee to some distant spot where no one would ever find her. But that was impossible. With the McKee wealth, influence and connections, she would never truly be safe. No, she had no choice. She had to go back to Rimrock, face Jenner, and tell him he had a two-year-old son.

"Just leave me the hell alone!" Jenner roared, his voice thundering through the halls of the old ranch house.

"Why should we?" Casey, his younger sister, snapped back. "So you can pour yourself into a bottle?"

Growling obscenities that would make a sailor blush, Jenner gave the damned wheelchair a kick and watched the useless contraption roll across the wood floor to land with a thud against the couch. "Good riddance." Grabbing his crutches, he stumbled to his feet. His left leg dragged, refusing to move on its own. "What I do is my business," Jenner said as he swayed, his weight shifting precariously. Gritting his teeth, he managed to balance on the crutches. He, who had once had the ability to stay astride a thousand pounds of ripsnorting, mean horseflesh, reduced to this. Hell. The doctors had predicted he might never walk again and he'd proved them wrong. He could walk, damn it, but he had to use the stupid crutches. And he limped. Badly.

He tried to turn his back on his muleheaded little sister, but she was having none of his stubborn streak. She stormed up to him, her hazel eyes sparking with fury, her chin thrust forward. A little thing, she had a temper that matched his own. A McKee trait. "Mom, Max, and Grandma and me—we're only trying to help," she said, poking him in the chest. "Why do you think Max is working like crazy getting that apartment fixed up for you? And Mom, with what she's going through since Dad died, it's a wonder she can put up with your mood swings. Then there's Grandma. She's as fit to be tied as I've ever seen her. The least you can do is smile once in a while."

"Did I ask for any of your help? Huh? Did I beg you to try to cheer me up, bring me food on trays, offer to push me around in *that?*" he sneered, raising up one crutch and pointing at the wheelchair. "Hell, no!" The crutch landed on the floor again, rubber tip sliding slightly on the polished wood. "I didn't ask you or Mom or Mavis for anything."

"You're an ingrate, that's what you are!"

"And that's the way I like it!" Jenner hobbled across the room to the window where he could stare out at the blackened remains of the stable. His skin crawled when he thought about the damned fire where he should have died. Even in the growing dusk, he saw the charred rubble and ash that had once been shelter for the McKee horses. Two other buildings—the machine shed and a pump house—had also been engulfed in the hideous flames that had devoured the stables. His head suddenly pounded with the shrill sound of neighs of terrified horses, the thunder of steel-shod hooves kicking in panic, the wail of his own screams....

Damn it all. He turned quickly, nearly fell over, and moved toward the bar, his father's bar, where a bottle of opened whiskey beckoned.

"Oh, great. Just what you need."

"What I *don't* need is a lecture." Propped upright with the crutches, Jenner poured himself a short glass from a bottle his father had barely tapped before he died.

"I just want you to pull yourself together!"

"Like you have? Hell, you don't even know why you're still in Rimrock. You're always spoutin' off about leaving but you never quite make it to the door, do ya?"

Jenner caught Casey's gaze in the mirror mounted above the brass sink and liquor cabinet. Concern engraved her skin with little lines around the corners of her mouth, and he suddenly felt like a heel. But he didn't want her worries. Nor her pity. He just wanted everyone to go away and leave him alone. Managing a hard smile, devoid of even the tiniest hint of humor, he lifted his glass. "Cheers."

"Jenner—"

"I don't need a mother, all right? I've already got one. And you don't have to nag like a wife—*that* I'll never need." He tossed back his drink and poured a second. Dark clouds gathered in his sister's usually clear eyes. "Keeping count?" he mocked.

"You're impossible."

"Damned straight!" He downed half of the second drink, savoring the smoky flavor that hit the back of his throat and burned a welcome path down to his stomach. His blood began to warm and his muscles relax. He caught a glimpse of himself in the mirror, unshaven, hair too long, except in the places it was growing in again in fuzzy patches where it had been singed by the flames. There was a scar near his right ear. His skin had been seared by an ember, but he'd been lucky. Or so the doctors had tried to convince him. With a snort, he eyed the whiskey bottle again.

"Have you ever wondered what you're going to do with the rest of your life?" Casey asked.

No doubt about it, she as a pest. "Have *you*?" he countered.

"Every day."

"And you get nowhere. Face it, Casey, you're spinning your wheels."

Even the insult didn't fend her off. She bristled a little and said, "I'm taking care of you. And Mom. Besides, we're not discussing me. You're the one who has to think about the future—to come up with some kind of game plan for the rest of your life."

Turning slowly to face her, he felt his fingers tense around the glass. "If you want to know the truth, Casey, I don't really give a damn."

She clenched her teeth. "You know, I believe you. I was going to offer to stay with you since Mom and Grandma have gone into town to meet Rex Stone, but—"

"What, my company's no good?" he mocked. "Gee, Casey, you make the popcorn and I'll turn on the TV. If we're lucky, we might not miss the final round of 'Jeopardy' and after that we could have us a rousing game of checkers." He drained his glass. "Well, no, that sounds a little too strenuous. I think I'll just have another drink instead."

"Do what you want. I'm tired of baby-sitting!"

He laughed then cringed a little at the hollow sound it made ricocheting through the hallways of the house where he'd grown up.

Muttering something under her breath about hard-headed, good-for-nothing men, Casey stalked out of the room.

Jenner snagged the bottle, settled into his father's favorite oxblood leather chair, and relaxed a little. He clutched his empty glass. Though the whiskey beckoned, he ignored the temptation. Instead, he laid his head against the back of the seat and closed his eyes. Why did she have to bring up the rest of his life?

The damned thing was he couldn't even think about tomorrow.

Beth's old Chevy Nova wheezed a little as she pulled into the driveway of the little bungalow she'd called home for most of her life. The house hadn't changed much and was still painted white with green shutters complemented by a black shingled roof. The lawn needed mowing, but the flower beds, her mother's pride and joy, were a virtual rainbow of pansies and petunias that flanked the sidewalk and peeked from low-growing shrubs next to the house.

"Come on, Cody," she said, sneaking a glance at her son as she cut the engine. "Let's stretch our legs."

"Stretch legs!" Cody said, his blue eyes shining as he held out his chubby little arms to her. A rambunctious toddler, he smiled easily, ran full tilt most of the day, and repeated everything that was said to him.

Slinging her purse over her shoulder, Beth climbed out of the car. Cody impatiently started work on the buckles to his car seat. "Out! Out!"

"Hold on a minute, peanut."

"Not peanut."

"Okay, okay." She unstrapped Cody from his car seat and hugged him close. "So where are we?"

He turned sparkling eyes up at her. "Where are we?"

"Grandma's house." Balancing him on her hip, Beth walked up the cement path to the front porch. The screen door opened before she could reach for the doorbell, and Harriet Forrester, beaming at her only grandchild, stepped onto the front porch.

"I was wonderin' when you'd show up," she said as she pried Cody out of Beth's arms. "How are you, big fella?" Nuzzling her grandson, Harriet sighed happily. "Oh my, how Grandma's missed you."

Just forty-nine, Harriet looked a decade younger. Her brown hair was devoid of gray and cut into a pageboy that feathered softly around her chin. Her eyes were still

clear and green with only a trace of webbing near the
corners. She'd always been a beautiful woman, a woman
men noticed. Not shy of the altar, Harriet had been married more times than Beth could imagine. Her current husband of the past six years was Zeke Forrester, who had
three ex-wives himself and was a foreman at the sawmill.

"My Lord, he's grown," Harriet said, clucking her
tongue and pressing a kiss into Cody's downy blond curls.
"Why, you're just getting to be Grandma's big boy, aren't
you?" With a smile at her daughter, she said, "Come on
inside. I've got coffee brewing, or if you'd prefer a soda,
there's a six-pack in the fridge. I've got beer, too, and oh,
why don't we open a bottle of wine? It's been so long
since you've been here! We've got to celebrate, don't we,
pumpkin?" She pressed another kiss to Cody's forehead
and breezed into the kitchen, where Cody wiggled until
Harriet set him on his slightly unsteady feet.

"I don't think I should have anything to drink," Beth
said, reminding herself of her mission. Her palms turned
sweaty at the thought of finally facing Jenner with the
truth.

"Just a glass..." Harriet opened a drawer and searched
for a corkscrew. A bottle of chilled rosé was sweating on
the counter near the sink.

Beth hesitated, then decided she'd better get the worst
over with. She didn't want to chance losing her nerve.

"No, Mom, really. I've got to drive out to the ranch
and visit Jenner McKee."

Immediately her mother's sunny disposition faded.
"Oh, God. You're going to tell him," she said stonily as
she gripped the open drawer for support. The age lines
that hadn't been apparent before seemed to suddenly appear at the mention of Jenner's name.

"I have to."

"Do you?" Harriet cast a glance at Cody, who was
already exploring the open pantry. She began to chew on
her lower lip and shook her head as if she was having a

silent argument with herself. "They'll want Cody, you know. And whatever the McKees want, they get. It's kind of the law of the land, or code of the West, or whatever you want to call it." Cody reached for a can of peaches. "Oh, dear, I've got mousetraps in there." Harriet scurried after her grandson and hauled him out of the pantry.

"I think it's only right that Jenner should learn the truth from me rather than his grandmother. It's something I have to do, my duty. Besides, I think it's time to close that chapter of my life."

"You're not closing a chapter, you're opening a can of worms and mark my words, those McKees will want Cody."

"They can't have him," Beth said.

"It's not that simple."

Cody was already wriggling to get back to the floor.

"What's Jenner going to do—try to buy him from me?" Beth laughed, but even to her own ears the sound was hollow and lifeless. She'd thought about it a million times—what Jenner would do if he ever found out he had a son, a baby boy. Each time the thought had crept into her mind, she felt a chill as cold as death course through her blood. She was in no position to fight the McKees, but she shouldn't have to. Cody was hers, and though Jenner had inadvertently fathered the boy, he had no claim to him. Of course the courts would see it differently, especially if the courts were run by judges whose election coffers had been filled with McKee money.

"You don't know what Jenner might do," Harriet said, kicking the door to the pantry shut and reaching into the cookie jar. "He's a McKee, isn't he? And even if he didn't get along with Jonah, Jenner's as ruthless and self-righteous as the rest of the clan. Look how the family won't give up on the fact that they think Jonah was murdered. *Murdered!* In a town the size of Rimrock. That's the craziest notion I've ever heard." She handed Cody a peanut butter cookie.

"Jonah made his share of enemies," Beth said.

"Haven't we all?"

Beth held her tongue. Her mother's face was suddenly crossed with an expression of extreme sadness and pain. Beth didn't have to be reminded of the rumors that had surrounded the older woman. For as long as Beth could remember, she'd heard the harsh whispers, noticed the raised eyebrows, witnessed the good, churchgoing women of Rimrock turn their backs on Harriet Winward Crandall Lambert Jones Forrester. Tongues had wagged about Rimrock's most flamboyant divorcée. Between marriages to her four husbands, Harriet had dated many of the locals, though, as far as Beth knew, she'd drawn the line at married men. Harriet's view of marriage was that it was binding and monogamous as long as both parties were happy, but at the first sign of rough going, it was over. Harriet was a free spirit who didn't believe in relationships that were too difficult. When either party was dissatisfied, it was time to call it quits and move on.

Beth, on the other hand, had a romantic, fairy-tale belief that marriage should last a lifetime; that despite the ups and downs, a couple should cling to each other, give to each other, help each other through any crisis. Even though, considering her ill-fated relationship with Jenner, she'd been proved wrong already.

"What does Stan think of all this?" Harriet asked.

Beth sighed. She hadn't confided in Stan, the man she'd been dating and thought she might marry one day. "I haven't told him. I thought I should tell Jenner first."

Harriet clucked her tongue and poured them each a glass of wine. "You may not know it, honey, but you need this." Harriet handed her daughter a long-stemmed glass, then sipped from her own.

"How's he doing?" Beth asked, taking a swallow of wine.

"Jenner?" Harriet shrugged and settled into a worn kitchen chair. "Ornery as ever, I've heard. He's not paralyzed like they first thought, but one of his legs isn't working right. Mandy Crawford—she knows Kiki, the McKees' cook—says Jenner's as mean as a nest of yellow jackets in October. Always angry. Kiki has to walk on eggshells around him.''

''But he is walking?''

''I haven't seen him myself, but that's what I hear.''

Relieved to hear that he wasn't going to be confined to a wheelchair, Beth took another sip of wine, then set the glass on the counter. She couldn't put off the inevitable. ''I hope you don't mind watching Cody while I go break the news,'' she said.

One of Harriet's arched brows lifted a fraction. ''Aren't you going to take him with you?''

''Not yet. I think I should do this one step at a time.''

Harriet smiled at her grandson who was covered in cookie crumbs. ''Well, that's just fine with me. How about you, pumpkin? How would you like to stay with Grandma and fix supper for Grandpa Zeke?'' She took a long swallow from her glass. ''Of course, we won't start for awhile. He doesn't get home from the swing shift till later.''

Cody's eyes clouded a little, but Harriet didn't seem to notice. ''Now if Jenner gives you any trouble, you just leave him to stew in his own juices. And don't let him intimidate you just because he's got McKee attached to his first name. We may not have as much clout in this valley as the McKees do, but we're family just the same. I'm here for you, and you know that Zeke will be, too.''

''Thanks, Mom,'' Beth said, ''but I'll be fine.'' She let the remark about Zeke slide. So far, her mother's marriage seemed to be holding together, but Beth didn't kid herself. Zeke didn't give two cents what happened to his wife's daughter. He had enough children and grandchildren of his own to worry about. Beth and Zeke weren't close and never would be. After her own father had left, Beth knew better than to expect anything more than cordiality from any one of her mother's husbands.

This included Zeke Forrester, a silent man who had barely glanced up from his newspaper on the night Beth had left town after making the announcement that she was pregnant and was moving away from Rimrock forever.

Harriet finished her glass of wine. "He thinks of you as his, honey."

Beth didn't believe it, but she held her tongue. Let her mother spin her little fantasies. When Harriet was in love, she adored her spouse. When the love faded, Harriet didn't believe in holding on to old baggage and she divorced the man promptly. No hard feelings. No badmouthing. No alimony. And no children. Except for Beth, Harriet had always made a clean break. Beth had often wondered if her conception had been a mistake, but she supposed it didn't matter. Throughout all the pain of growing up, she'd never doubted her mother's love. "I'll see you later then."

"Okay, but before you go, I want to give you a little advice." She lifted the bottle and filled up her glass again. "I know that Jenner hurt you and I don't want it to happen again."

"He didn't mean to—"

"Don't go protecting him, okay? Look, Beth, I've known a lot of men in my life and not one of them—well, aside from Zeke maybe—is worth a broken heart. If you think you've got to tell Jenner about Cody, so be it. I won't interfere, but don't let yourself get all brokenhearted again."

"I wasn't ever—"

"Shh. Just remember. Jenner McKee's no saint."

With her mother's words still nagging at her, Beth drove to the McKee ranch. A blanket of darkness had settled over the valley, and the Blue Mountains, rising like sentinels in the distance, seemed to blend into the sky.

She'd forgotten how black the nights were here, outside of the lights of the city. With only a quarter moon and a few stars winking behind a thin veil of clouds, the night seemed vast and endless.

Her stomach was in knots, her hands sweating at the thought of seeing Jenner again. Did he know? Had his grandmother warned him that she would be returning? Would he remember her? It wasn't as if they'd had a long affair.

Oh, Lord, how had it come to this?

The beams of her headlights splashed upon the row of trees lining the drive of the Rocking M Ranch. Her heart began to drum wildly as she turned off the highway.

What would she say? What could she?

Her stomach cramped with fear, the numbing fear that Jenner might demand custody of his son. Well, it wouldn't happen. She wouldn't let it happen. She'd never, *never* give up her child.

The ranch house was nearly dark, light shining from only one window as she parked near the garage and sent up a quick little prayer for strength.

Crossing her fingers, she climbed out of the old Chevy and stopped dead in her tracks when she noticed the charred ruins of the stables—ashes blowing in the wind, blackened beams and pipes, a pile of useless, burned rubble.

She imagined the horror that Jenner had lived through and felt a stab of guilt for her own selfish interests. How would it feel to survive a raging inferno wild enough to consume a huge building? In her fervor to keep her son, she'd thought of little else, not even the sheer terror and pain that Jenner must have experienced. Hadn't that been why his grandmother had written her in the first place?

A breeze, cool with the breath of autumn, whipped her hair and brought the smell of ash and burned wood to her nostrils. She hiked the collar of her jacket up around her neck as she walked on wooden legs across the asphalt lot

to the path leading to the front door. There was no time
for turning back or second-guessing herself. As she
stepped onto the porch, a low growl rolled through the
air. The hair on the back of her neck rose as she spied a
dog lying under a decrepit rocker, his eyes glowing with
the reflection of the security lights. "It's okay," she heard
herself saying. "Good boy."

The animal's tail gave a short thump. Determination
mingled with fear as she pushed the doorbell and waited,
hearing the chimes peal softly.

But then there was nothing. Not even the sound of a
footstep on the floor.

Again she rang the bell and waited, the seconds ticking
by slowly in contrast to her rapid heartbeat.

Not a sound.

"Come on, come on," she muttered, pounding loudly
on the doorframe. This time the dog let out a sharp bark.

"It's open!" a male voice roared and she suddenly
could barely breathe.

She would recognize that voice even if she hadn't seen
Jenner McKee in fifty years. It was a voice that still
haunted her dreams and belonged to a man she'd never
forget. Cody's father.

The screen door creaked as she opened it and her hands
were clammy. She wiped them on her jacket and walked
slowly through the darkened hall and toward a sliver of
light shining through a partially opened door.

"God help me," she whispered as she stepped into a
den and found Jenner, propped up in an old recliner, a
glass in his hand. He looked just as she remembered him,
ranch tough and cynical, his eyes slitting a little. Faded
work shirt, worn jeans, scuffed cowboy boots, unshaven
jaw—the image of the cowboy still intact. "Hello, Jenner," she said, forcing a smile so brittle she thought it
might crack.

His gaze raked up and down her body and he rolled his

empty glass in his hand before his eyes found hers again. With a look of undisguised disgust he asked, ''Who the hell are you?''

Chapter Two

Beth didn't move a muscle. "You don't remember me." It wasn't a question, just a simple statement of fact that shattered all her silly dreams. What had been so special to her had meant nothing to him. Nothing!

"Should I?" he said, glowering at her. She noticed crutches propped against the end of the couch, a wheelchair tucked into a corner near the bookcase and a half-filled bottle of some kind of whiskey on the table.

She managed a thin smile. "It would make things easier."

"Things? What things?"

"I'll get to them, but for now I think you should know that I'm Beth Crandall." Was there just the flicker of memory in his blue eyes? "Until I finished college, I lived here most of my life with my mother."

"And I knew you?"

"Not really." She remembered silently adoring him from afar. A real cowboy who won awards riding in rodeos all over the country. A man who had shunned his inherited wealth and given his father nothing but grief. A rebel. She'd been only sixteen when she'd first seen him in a local rodeo and since that time she'd fantasized about what it would be like to be the woman who might tame his wild spirit.

What a fool.

"You and I saw each other briefly about three years ago."

His eyebrows knit. "I've seen a lot of women briefly," he said, suddenly wary. The lines near the corners of his mouth deepened. "So why're you here?"

Oh, God, he's not making this any easier. Her throat felt hot and tight. "Actually, we spent a night together."

"Just one?"

"Yes."

"Too bad." He snorted, but didn't comment further, and Beth realized he didn't remember their lovemaking at all. For nearly three years, she'd dreamed of it, remembered the passion, the soul-jarring explosion of desire, the afterglow that was just long enough for rest before he kissed her again, his arms wrapped possessively around her…. Blushing foolishly, she realized that her fingers had curled into tight fists. Slowly she straightened each one as she walked all the way into the den until she was standing in front of him.

"This isn't easy for me," she admitted, staring down at him sprawled haphazardly in the recliner. Even unshaven and wearing clothes that hadn't seen a washer for quite a while, he was sexier than any man had the right to be.

"So get on with it. Oh, hell, I forgot all about my manners," he said with undisguised sarcasm. "How about a drink?" He reached for the bottle.

Yes! "No. I think one of us should be clearheaded."

"Your choice." He raised his glass and gave her a

wicked smile that once would have melted her heart. "It ain't gonna be me."

She saw it then—the anger in his sharp gaze. Fury, dark and deep, colored his eyes to a reclusive shade of midnight. In her peripheral vision she noticed the wheelchair. Though she knew that thousands of disabled people lived productive, normal lives, she couldn't imagine Jenner unable to walk or ride or make love.... He was just too tough, too independent, too damned stubborn.

Her heart gave a little lurch and she tried to ignore it, but as she watched him pour a thin stream of liquor into his glass, she remembered the cowboy she hadn't been able to tame. He'd been as reckless and free as the northern winds sweeping down from the mountains. Tall and lanky, he'd walked with a swagger, offered women a grin guaranteed to break their hearts, and loved no one but himself. Cowboy tough, with muscles honed from years in the saddle—not just on the rodeo circuit, but on the ranch where he'd grown up as the rebellious second son of the richest man in the county—Jenner McKee would never be able to accept living his life bound to a wheelchair. He was just too damned proud.

He took a long swallow of his drink, then reached for his crutches. He eyed her again without quite so much hostility. "So what is it you're doing here? I assume you came to see me, since everyone else is gone and you haven't asked about them." With a grunt he pulled himself up right. "So, is this just a friendly little chat, or did you come to get a good look at me to see if I'm in one piece, or do you really have something to talk about?"

She screwed up her courage as he, using the crutches for support leaned on the padded braces that tucked under his arms. "I think I'd better talk to you when you're sober."

"Now's as good a time as any."

True, he didn't seem drunk, but she didn't know how long he'd been sitting alone in the dark with only a bottle for company. He took a hobbling step and was suddenly so close to her that she caught a whiff of the scent that had been his that one night long ago—soap, leather and male all tangled in a smell so distinctly Jenner it couldn't be disguised by the liquor. Her insides turned to water.

"I think I should remember you."

"That would help," she said, her voice husky. He was so close. Too close. But at least one of his legs worked and his back seemed to support him. He almost seemed as virile as before.

"Beth...that was it, right?"

She was dying inside. This was the father of her child and he had trouble remembering her name. "Yes."

"What'd you come here for?" His smile was devastating, but his voice bitter. "Don't tell me. You're lonely, remembered that we'd been together and wondered if I could still get it up."

Her fantasy shattered, and shock must have registered on her face.

"No?" Swaying a little, he reached for his drink. "Then maybe you've come here to read to me from the Bible, just to let me know about the joy in life and the fact that God has a plan for everyone even a heathen like me and the reason he decided to have a beam fall down and crush my back was to make me look into my real self, find my soul. If that's why you're here, sister, forget it. I've already talked to Reverend Jacobson and I don't think he'll be back." He snorted with some kind of grim satisfaction, and when she didn't respond, he lifted a finger as if a sudden light had flicked on in his mind. "Or, if it's not a personal reason, or a calling from the Almighty Himself, maybe you want me to do a little work for you. Got some steers you want branded? Or maybe a wild colt that needs breakin' or—"

"Stop it!" she screamed, suddenly angry. She couldn't believe how hard and cruel and jaded he'd become. Where was the laughter she remembered, the look of irreverence she'd found so endearing, the knowing smile? "Look, Jenner, I don't want you to work for me, I don't care what religion you profess to not believe in, and I certainly didn't come all the way over here to ask you to sleep with me!"

"Then I guess we don't have anything to talk about."

"Just your son!"

The words seemed to echo from the beams and walls of the old ranch house. Jenner reacted as if he'd been slapped, stepping back quickly, nearly falling over, then recovering to stare at her long and hard, not saying a word. His face turned stark as granite, the set of his mouth unforgiving, as if she'd crossed some invisible moral line.

Seconds ticked by, measured by the rapid thudding of her heart.

"My son?" he finally hissed, though no trace of emotion registered on his face.

"Yes."

"And yours, I assume."

"Of course."

"Of course." Slowly he reached for his drink. "So you're claiming that you and I slept together, what, a few years ago—?"

"Nearly three, when you were in Dawson City for the rodeo. You won the—"

"I remember *that,* but I sure as hell don't remember you." His nostrils flared slightly. "But you're trying to tell me that you and I met somewhere, ended up in bed, and the result of this *one night* of passion is your—wait a minute, *our*—son. Am I following so far?"

"That's right," Beth said firmly, though she saw the doubt in his eyes, the skepticism carved in the hard line of his jaw. "His name's Cody."

"But you didn't bother telling me until now be-cause...why?" She could almost see the wheels turning in his mind. "Oh, no, don't tell me. Let me guess. I was just a dirt-poor rodeo jock, right? But now that my rich daddy's passed on, you think I might be worth a small fortune and because of this accident I wouldn't be able to scare up a sperm sample, so if the blood types are close enough, you could pawn your kid off on me. Is that what this is all about? A shakedown?''

She was flabbergasted. ''A *shakedown?* You think I'm here for your *money?* Are you serious?''

''Are you?''

''About your money? Oh, God, no!''

''Then what—why show up here?''

''Because it was time!'' she snapped, her temper escalating with all his outlandish insults. ''If you want to know the truth—''

''That would help.''

''—I didn't want to come here in the first place, but I felt it was my duty.'' She thought about showing him his grandmother's letter, but decided that that was between him and the older woman. The letter might cloud the issue. All she needed to do was explain about Cody—nothing else.

''So now you're duty is done.''

That was all he could say? After learning that he had a child? Well, that's what she wanted, wasn't it? She didn't really expect him to smile, throw his arms around her and tell her that she'd changed his life, did she? She should be pleased that he wasn't interested in Cody, that she wouldn't have to give up her son on weekends or vacations. ''Okay, so now that I've said my piece, there's really no reason for me to stay.''

''You're going to give up?'' he mocked. ''Just like that—turn tail and run? Hell, if you're in this for the money, you'd better get a little more backbone, be ready to stick up for your lies—''

''It's not a lie!'' she hissed, stepping so close to him that she had to angle her face up to glare at him. ''It's the God's honest truth. You have a son, Jenner McKee, a wonderful little two-year-old boy that I'd just as soon never met you. I don't want a red cent of your money and I don't need your sick attitude. I made a mistake when I slept with you, but I don't regret it, because I've got a child that I wouldn't give up for the world. So now that I've had my say and you've had yours, let's just call it even!'' Fury pulsed through her blood as she turned on her heel, started for the door, then felt fingers as strong as steel wrap over her forearm and jerk her around again.

She nearly slammed up against him and noticed his face had changed. No longer merely mocking, his features had turned harsh with disdain and disbelief. The slashes of cheekbone and rigid angle of jaw revealed a deeper emotion, a hatred so intense it burned in his eyes. "I don't know what you're game is, lady, but don't think for a minute that just because I can't walk on my own yet, or that I might never be able to, that I'll let any woman walk in and stomp all over me.''

"Wouldn't dream of it," she said icily.

"Good. 'Cause if I hear that you've been spreading your lies around town, believe me, I'll make your life a living hell. My family's been through enough grief and scandal in the past few months—they don't need any more.''

"Don't worry about it, Jenner," she said, attempting to yank her arm away. "As far as I'm concerned, we never met!''

His nostrils flared as he studied the lines of her face. "You'd better not be lying," he growled, his fingers still painfully gripping her arm. "'Cause you'll live to regret it.''

She wondered why she'd ever been so naive as to dream about falling in love with him. "You know, that's the trouble with you McKees. Every last one of you. Always making threats to get your way. You think that all your money gives you the right to run people off their land, force them to sell their businesses, give up whatever it is they think is valuable, and then tell them what to do in the bargain, but you're wrong, Jenner. All of you are dead wrong. You're no better than the rest of us!'' She wrenched her arm away and stormed out of the house.

The nerve of the man! To think that she'd fantasized about him!

Outside, the air was cool against her hot cheeks, and the dog let out a bark as she ran down the steps and across the asphalt to her car. Rage burned through her body as she climbed into her little Nova. Pumping the gas, she switched on the ignition and wondered at the tender little spot of disappointment and hurt beneath her blind fury. What had she expected? That he would tell her that he'd been searching for her, that he loved her, that he was thrilled to know that he'd fathered her son? Did she really think that he'd want to know about Cody, that he might even want a family? ''Damn it, Beth, you are a fool!'' she told herself as the car's engine coughed and died. ''Come on, come on, not now!'' Again she pumped the gas and twisted her key in the ignition. With a bang, the engine fired. She threw the car into reverse, pulled a U-turn, then slammed the gears into drive and sped out, her tires screeching a little. She snapped on the radio. Garth Brooks was wailing a country tune with some kind of love-gone-wrong lyrics and she changed the station to hear on old Rolling Stones tune about getting no satisfaction.

''You and me both, Mick,'' she grumbled, twisting the steering wheel and roaring away from the Rocking M Ranch and Jenner McKee. Now she could go forward with her life, close the chapter containing her silly dreams about a lonesome cowboy, and think about her future. There was Stan to consider. Stan who wanted to marry her, Stan who swore he loved her, Stan who accepted Cody, even though he had grown kids of his own.

Unlike Jenner.

Her throat tightened over a sob and she forced it back; she refused to give in to tears. She was too mature to cry over a lover who couldn't even recall her name. She sniffed loudly, turned up the volume, and told herself that she'd visit her mother for another day or so. Then she'd make hasty tracks back to the Willamette Valley and begin her life with Stan, a life she'd been putting off for reasons she'd never been able to name. On Monday she'd start looking in earnest for a new job.

She should be on cloud nine. Obviously Jenner would never be a stumbling block in her life—she'd have her son all to herself.

Why then did she feel so miserable?

Jenner watched the Nova's taillights disappear down the lane. He took another sip of his whiskey, but felt no pleasure from the drink.

Who was that woman? She was pretty enough, he supposed, and only a few inches shorter than his own six feet. Long red-brown curls had cascaded down her back, and her eyes, a shade somewhere between green and gray had blazed with defiance, almost as if she had been challenging him not to believe her. Determination had been chiseled into the set of her jaw and her cheeks had been flushed.

A woman to reckon with. A beautiful woman. A smart woman.

But the mother of his child? No way!

He hobbled over to the bar and splashed the remainder of his aged Kentucky whiskey down the sink. He wasn't drunk, just felt a little fuzzy around the edges and wished that he'd been stone-cold sober when he'd faced her. Then maybe he could make some sense of her visit.

He caught a glimpse of himself in the mirror and snorted. What would she want with him? An unshaven, broken-down cowboy with a bad attitude and a taste for expensive whiskey. What was she really asking for?

Money. Women always wanted money.

Then why hadn't she started making demands right then

and there? Maybe he should have offered to write her a
check, forced her hand, made her show her true colors.
Or maybe she wasn't sure she could pawn the kid off as
his. Maybe his remark about blood types had scared her.
But surely if she'd had the nerve to show up here, she
would've covered her bases. She seemed too bright not to
have taken care that her story would hold up.

He wondered if he *had* slept with her. Probably.
Though he wasn't proud of it, he'd slept with a lot of
women, had a lot of one-night stands three or four years
ago, in a vain attempt to erase Nora Bateman from his
mind. Funny, he hadn't thought of Nora in months, and
yet at one time he'd thought she was the love of his life.
Well, he'd been a fool. There was no such thing. He knew
that now. Nora was married to a stockbroker and living
in Denver, spending the man's money faster than he could
earn it.

Good riddance, Jenner thought. The pretty daughter of
a neighboring rancher, Nora had shown her true colors
before Jenner had been stupid enough to ask her to marry
him. He was lucky to be rid of her.

So what about Beth? He tried to remember her. Could
he really have spent a night alone with her, made love to
her, then completely forgotten about her? Or was she just
trying to get at him and the McKee fortune? It had happened before and would certainly happen again—as long
as his family had money.

Wasn't that the reason there was so much speculation
about his father's death and concern that he'd been murdered? A man as wealthy and ruthless as Jonah P. McKee
was certain to make more than his share of enemies. At
first, everyone had thought that Jonah had downed one
too many at the Black Anvil Saloon and had lost control
of his Jeep in the foothills, but now the sheriff's department along with a private investigator the family had re-
tained were certain that Jonah had been intentionally
killed—run off the road somehow so that his Jeep plunged

over the guardrail rimming the highway on Elkhorn Ridge, then nose-dived into the bottom of Stardust Canyon.

Lately, more and more townspeople seemed to have come to the conclusion that Jonah had been murdered. Even Jenner's older brother, Max, believed it. Jenner didn't know what to think.

The fire at the stables where Jenner had been injured had been set by an unknown arsonist, and now the authorities believed that the two incidents—Jonah's death and the devastating fire at the ranch—were connected. Max had seen a suspicious figure near the stables just before the blaze had been set, but no one knew who the culprit was.

In Jenner's opinion, it was a helluva mess and complicated by his own circumstances. Whoever had set the fire had been the cause of his injuries, and if Jenner ever got five minutes alone with the guy, he'd strangle the bastard with his bare hands. He shoved the hair out of his eyes and hobbled back to his father's chair. He needed time to rest and think. Beth Crandall, whoever the hell she was, had dropped a bomb that was sure to explode if he didn't do something fast.

He closed his eyes and the image of Beth's face floated through his mind. It seemed as if he almost remembered her, as if a likeness of her teased the corners of his mind. Her name wasn't completely unfamiliar, and he felt, if he really concentrated, that he could recall a night of lovemaking in a hotel in Portland with a beautiful woman with green eyes and an easy smile.

But he'd always been careful. Never trusted a woman to keep herself from getting pregnant. Even when a woman had sworn to have taken care of birth control, he'd used condoms. He didn't want any disease nor did he want to inadvertently spawn a child.

Another hole in the woman's story.

He thought back to the woman in the Portland hotel. It

had been soon after he'd won first place riding bareback in Dawson City and he'd ended up in the Willamette Valley, still celebrating his victory. She'd been pretty enough and her name had been Beth or Bess or something similar, but he didn't remember her as being so determined or so stubborn…or so damned alluring.

Maybe he'd been without a woman for too long. Ever since his affair with Nora Bateman had ended badly, he'd made it a point never to get too involved with a woman. He hadn't had any trouble keeping that vow.

As far as he could see, nothing had changed.

Jenner's grandmother and his mother returned less than an hour later. Though Mavis and Virginia had never been close while Jonah was alive, his death seemed to have given them a common purpose. Mavis had doted on her only son and accepted Virginia as her daughter-in-law, but Virginia had resented the older woman's intrusion into their lives. Now that he was gone, they found solace and comfort in each other, their shared grief bonding them when even the birth of Jonah's children had not.

Jenner heard them prattling on, talking loudly as they entered the back door and snapped on lights from one end of the house to the other. They found Jenner sprawled in his father's favorite chair. They didn't believe he had his own plans or that he'd made a vow to himself. Come hell or high water, he was going to leave the Rocking M and make a life for himself.

Mavis, her black cane more decorative than functional, walked quickly into the den. Though she was pushing ninety, she was still spry enough to get around without much help and she kept herself up. Her white hair was rinsed with blue to set off her eyes and she had it done faithfully every week at the Cut and Curl Beauty Shop on Elm Street. Though slightly stooped in the shoulders, she didn't look her age. No cataracts marred her shrewd vision, no arthritis dared flare up in her joints. Mavis McKee was still a strong woman, one to be reckoned with.

"I don't completely trust that man," Mavis was saying. "Too...oily. He doesn't tell you everything he knows."

"You don't have to trust him. Rex Stone is the best private investigator for miles around," her daughter-in-law disagreed. "Without him, the Sheriff's Department would have closed the investigation and Jonah's murderer would have walked free."

"He still may," Mavis insisted. "Hammond Polk is an idiot."

Virginia sighed loudly. "I know, but at least until the next election, he's the only sheriff we've got. That's why we have to be thankful for Mr. Stone."

"Not much better, if ya ask me." Mavis made a sound of disgust deep in her throat, but managed a smile for Jenner who had only listened to their discussion with half an ear.

"Still up?" Virginia asked her son and Jenner felt the urge to bolt again. His mother bounced from one end of the emotional scale to the other. Her smile was always bright and cheery for him, but at other times, when she thought he didn't see, her expression turned bleak and sometimes her bottom lip trembled as she struggled with her new role as widow. She slid a glance at the opened bottle of whiskey on the table, but held her tongue. "I thought the doctor said you should rest."

"All I can do," Jenner said sullenly. Hell, he hated dealing with this. He tried not to snap, but he resented having to be cared for and treated as if he were a child. "I've had enough rest to last me the rest of my life. Besides, I had company." He might as well tell them what had happened here before Beth decided to contact the family herself.

"Company?" his mother asked, and Mavis's gaze seemed to sharpen on him. "Who?"

"A woman. Said her name was Beth Crandall."

"Harriet Forrester's girl," his mother said, the corners of her mouth tightening with disapproval.

Tucking her cane beneath her legs, Mavis took a seat on the edge of the couch and tried to act disinterested, but Jenner caught the glimmer of fascination behind her glasses. "What did she want?"

Jenner's smile was humorless. "She had some cockamamy story about her kid. Claims I'm the father."

"Father? Oh, Lord." Virginia's back stiffened slightly, the way it always did when she felt the need to defend herself or one of her brood. "But that's impossible...isn't it?"

"I think so."

"Don't you know?"

"Nothing's ever certain."

"But Harriet Forrester's daughter...did you ever...I mean..." A scarlet flush bloomed from her neck, coloring her cheeks. "How old is the child, anyway?"

"Two. His name is Cody."

"Well, there you go. You were involved with Nora Bateman three years ago." Relief threaded through her voice and she managed a smile, which Jenner didn't answer.

"That's about the time Nora and I parted ways." From the corner of his eye, Jenner saw a movement of his grandmother's head. As if she was nodding.

"Certainly you weren't so foolish as to get involved with her while you were seeing Nora."

"Not during, but maybe after." Jenner closed his eyes. "I don't remember her."

"Not at all?" Mavis asked.

Jenner shrugged his shoulders and wished he hadn't brought up the subject. The less his mother knew about his personal life, the better. As for his grandmother, she seemed more interested than he would have expected.

"She's as callous as her mother. Imagine, after all this time, coming here and demanding—"

"She didn't demand anything." Jenner cut Virginia off. His eyelids flew open.

"But she must want something. Money, I suppose."

"She said she didn't," Jenner said irritably. Why was he defending Beth Crandall? Didn't he have the same suspicions his mother was voicing?

Crossing the room, Virginia rubbed her arms as if experiencing a sudden chill, then turned on the gas and struck a match to light the chunks of oak resting on the grate in the fireplace.

"So you're telling me there's a chance she could be telling the truth."

"As I said, I don't know."

"What do you mean—?" The fire caught, blue jets sizzling upward as the gas-fed flames sought new fuel and licked hungrily at the mossy logs.

"I mean there was a time in my life when...when I didn't really pay much attention."

"That's vulgar!" Virginia said. "How could you?"

"I'm not saying it was right. It just happened, okay? I'd see a pretty woman, we'd start talking, have a few drinks, and next thing I knew...oh, hell, what does it matter now?" He didn't have to explain himself to his mother, for God's sake. The time of one-night stands, of loving 'em and leaving 'em had only been a short period in his life—the time after Nora. He'd been a fool. He didn't need his mother or his grandmother reminding him about it.

"Jenner—" Virginia began to reproach her son.

"I'm not in the mood for a sermon."

Mavis waved her hand in the air as if to dissipate the argument simmering between mother and son. "Right. What's done is done. Water under the bridge and all that. Maybe we all just need to calm down. I don't know about you, but I could use a cup of coffee and some of Kiki's berry pie if there's any left."

Virginia didn't like being dismissed, but she cast her son a look that indicated the argument wasn't over and headed off to the kitchen at the far end of the house. As the click of her heels on the hardwood floor faded, Mavis's smile disappeared. "I think you should know about Beth," she said in a whisper, "but there's no reason to upset your mother."

"I should know what about Beth?" Jenner said, feeling the hairs prickle at the back of his scalp, the way they always did when he smelled trouble.

"I'm the reason she's here." Mavis seemed almost proud of herself.

"I don't understand—"

"I wrote to her. Told her to come and visit you."

"You did *what?*" Jenner thundered, anger surging through his veins as he glared at his grandmother. "Damn it, Mavis, tell me this is some kind of sick joke." But he could read the single-minded glint of determination in her eyes as she met his furious gaze.

"No joke, Jenner."

His hands clenched the arms of his father's recliner, and for the first time in his life, he wanted to strangle the feisty little woman who he had heretofore adored. She'd actually written to some woman to come and visit him— some small-town girl he barely remembered. To do what—claim that her son was his? Was Mavis crazy?

"I don't get it. This girl...woman...she's nothing to me. Or you—" He stopped suddenly, understanding his grandmother's motivation. She had to think that the kid was his! But why? How had that Beth woman gotten to her? In the past hour or so since she'd left, he'd begun to wonder about her. She'd seemed so straightforward, so sure of herself. But to trick an old lady...

"What's she told you?"

"Nothing. As I said, I contacted her."

This wasn't making sense and yet Jenner was beginning to get that same feeling in his gut that he'd experienced more than once years ago when his old man had tried to pull his strings. "What did you say in the letter?" he growled.

She hesitated a second, then glanced down at the age spots on her hands as her fingers curled over the smooth handle of her black cane. "That she should come visit you."

"Why?"

"Because of the boy."

"Her son."

"*Your* son, Jenner."

"Mine? How do you know? Hell, Mavis, I don't even remember the woman and now she's got you believing that the kid's got McKee blood running through his veins. Don't you see this is all a setup? For the love of God, when will you learn to keep your nose in your own business?"

"Just as soon as you learn to walk again!" Mavis inched her chin up a notch, then picked up her cane and nudged the crutches lying by the chair. "Without those!"

Jenner ground his teeth together in frustration and stared at the flames hungrily licking the logs. As he gazed into the fire, he felt his skin crawl with the gut-wrenching fear that interrupted his sleep and had been with him ever since the stables had burned.

"That boy is yours!" Mavis insisted stubbornly.

"Unless I'm mistaken," he said slowly, "you weren't there when it happened, so how the hell do you know?" Furious with the woman, he climbed to his feet, grabbed the crutches that his grandmother so disdained and moved toward the window to stare out at the charred rubble of the stables. He still remembered the blinding heat, the smell of scorched horsehair, the squeals of the terrified animals. Miraculously none of the livestock had been killed, only a few horses singed by falling embers, but all in all, no lives, either human or animal, had been lost. A fireman had sustained minor burns and two others had suffered smoke inhalation, but only Jenner had been permanently damaged.

Bulldozers were scheduled to scrape up the remains

now that the fire department and insurance adjusters were finished with their jobs. The fire chief was convinced the burning of the stables was arson; the insurance company was balking at paying because they suspected that one of the McKees had intentionally set the blaze to collect on the policy.

Jenner snorted in disgust. Fools. The whole lot of them. No one at the ranch would risk injury to millions of dollars worth of horseflesh for the price of the building. He suspected the insurance company was stalling.

His grandmother cleared her throat. "I wrote Beth a letter telling her how you were doing," she maintained calmly.

"How'd you even know about her?" Jenner itched to shake some sense into Mavis.

"Your father didn't keep any secrets from me."

"My father?"

"He told me about the boy."

"Jonah knew?" Again Jenner felt that prickle at the back of his scalp, the signal that things weren't as they seemed. "How?"

"He made it his business to know everything about his children. You may have forgotten Beth Crandall, but Jonah didn't, and when he found out she was pregnant—"

"*How,* Mavis?" Jenner demanded. "How could he know? Hell, isn't anything sacred?"

"Ralph Fletcher was one of his closest friends. They did business together."

"And Doc Fletcher didn't mind that he was breaking a confidence with his patient by gossiping with Jonah?"

"I don't think he saw it that way. Ralph was just being loyal to his friend."

"Bullsh—" Jenner grabbed a crutch, lifted it and pointed the rubber tip squarely at his grandmother's chest. "This is just crazy! That kid can't be mine! How does Ralph Fletcher or anyone else know who I was with?"

Mavis cleared her throat. "Your father knew—well,

guessed really. He was in Portland on business that weekend and he saw you with Beth. He always stayed in the Armitage Hotel. You should have thought of that before you registered.''

''The Armitage?'' Vaguely, Jenner remembered. ''That's quite a leap, isn't it?''

''He just put two and two together.''

''He couldn't have seen me.''

''But you can't remember, can you? So how do you know?''

Jenner dropped the crutch as he realized that he was trying to destroy his grandmother's dream. While his older brother, Max, had been Jonah's favorite, Mavis had always been partial to Jenner and his rebellious ways. And she wanted a McKee grandson. Max's daughter, Hillary, was fine, but Mavis wanted a boy to carry on her own son's name, especially since Skye couldn't have children. So she'd found herself one. Sick at the thought, Jenner shook his head. ''I can't remember, but I'll tell you this. I'm careful, Mavis. Damned careful. I've never trusted a woman who told me she was taking care of birth control. I don't take those kinds of chances.''

''Every time?'' she asked.

Thunder seemed to roll in his head. ''I don't think this is the kind of conversation I should be having with my grandmother.''

''It is when we're talking about my great-grandson.''

''There is no great-grandson!''

''Well, it's a good thing your father had more sense than you. He checked things out. The timing's right, the boy's blood type is right and Beth wasn't involved with anyone else. Cody's yours, Jenner, and it's time you were responsible for him.''

Jenner snorted in disbelief and gnashed his back teeth together. His father, Jonah P. McKee, had been a first-class bastard.

''You had no right to contact her,'' he growled, angry

at his grandmother, the world and God for letting him survive the fire. The damned fire.

"I had every right."

"I don't want to see her again." Jenner's voice brooked no argument, but the old lady wouldn't back down.

"You might not have a choice. If you want your son."

"He's not my—"

"At least look at him. My guess is that he'll look like a McKee. There's a family resemblance that goes on for generation after generation. If that's not good enough, have a blood test or one of those newfangled paternity tests where they match your genes...."

She really believed it. Always a stubborn woman, Mavis was getting downright ornery in her old age. But she wasn't foolish and she wasn't one to kid herself. If she believed the boy was really his...oh, hell. His insides cramped at the thought of it. A child? By a woman he couldn't remember? A woman who would just as soon shoot him as talk to him? His throat was suddenly sandpaper rough and Mavis was prattling on.

"You may have given up on yourself, Jenner, but I haven't. And the doctors might be satisfied that you're not paralyzed, that your legs, well, at least one of them, seems to be healing, but that's not good enough for me and it certainly shouldn't be good enough for you! Keep in mind you're a McKee, and we never give up." Two high spots of color darkened her cheeks, and she thrust her chin upward a fraction as if she expected him to understand that McKees were considered royalty in the small town of Rimrock, Oregon. In Jenner's estimation, her pretensions were worth about as much as a pile of manure.

He forced the words over his tongue. "So you've suspected for some time now that I have a son and you didn't say a word."

"Because of your father."

"What did he have to do with it?" Damn the old man. Even dead, Jonah was still pulling Jenner's strings.

She sighed wearily. "Jonah had such high hopes for you, Jenner, but you were always thwarting him, fighting him every step of the way. Sometimes he thought you rebelled just to get his goat."

"So he hid the fact that I had a son?" Jenner was incredulous. He'd known his father played dirty, but he never expected this. Without another word, Jenner hobbled across the room, snagged his keys from the mantel and headed toward the front door.

"What do you think you're doing?" Mavis demanded.

"Finding out the truth."

"But how—?"

Jenner nearly collided with his mother, who was carrying a tray laden with coffeepot and cups and thick pieces of berry pie oozing purple juice. She took one look at his face and the keys dangling from his fingers and her skin turned the color of chalk. "Jenner? What's going on?"

"Ask her," he said, cocking his head toward the den where his grandmother was watching him with a satisfied smile playing upon her thin lips.

"But you can't leave. You're not supposed to drive—"

"Don't wait up for me."

"Stop! You can't—"

"I might not be back."

"You can't just leave."

"Watch me." He shoved past Virginia and threw open the front door. A cool autumn breeze cut through his open shirt, but he hardly noticed. He plunged the crutches in front of him and moved as quickly as possible to his old pickup parked by the garage.

"Jenner!" His mother's voice trailed after him. "Jenner McKee, you come back here right now!"

"You can reach me at the apartment!" he yelled back.

"But you can't possibly climb the stairs.... You can't just take off...oh, my God."

Jenner tossed the damned crutches into the pickup bed

and hoisted himself into the cab. Slamming the door, he ignored his mother and grandmother standing on the porch, pumped the throttle, switched on the ignition, and shoved the truck into reverse.

The old Dodge lurched before he managed to work the clutch as well as the gas and brakes with his right leg. The left leg was useless, but he wasn't going to let that stop him.

Not until he'd hunted down Beth Crandall and figured out just exactly what kind of game she was playing.

Chapter Three

"I take it things didn't go all that well."

"That's the understatement of the year." Beth threw her purse onto an old rocker and tried to quiet the anger that screamed through her brain. She'd been a fool to try to talk to Jenner McKee, and in her heart of hearts she'd known it. But she'd let Mavis's letter convince her that telling Jenner he had a son was the noble, right thing to do. Well, it was done and it was a far cry from anything noble or right.

"That bad?" Harriet, curled in a corner of the couch, dog-eared a page of the mystery novel she'd been reading and kicked off the afghan that had covered her feet. A thin black cigarette smoldered unattended in a glass ashtray on an end table.

"He didn't remember me and he didn't want to believe that he had a son."

"Oh. Well, you want to talk about it?"

"Not really. It's over and done with. Something I won't

have to worry about ever again.'' She should have felt relieved, but the undercurrent of rage that had been with her ever since she'd left the Rocking M still lingered, simmering in her blood, ready to ignite.

"Maybe you'd like that glass of wine now.'' Harriet took a final drag from her cigarette and rolled onto her feet.

"I don't think so, Mom. How was Cody?''

"An absolute angel.'' Through the haze of exhaled smoke, Harriet jabbed out her cigarette. Her face brightened at the mention of her grandson. "We had a ball. Any man who doesn't want to claim that child for a son should have his head examined. Oh, by the way, Stan called. Said he'd be up until eleven if you wanted to call him back.''

Beth felt a little niggle of guilt when she remembered the message she'd left for Stan on his answering machine. He'd been out of town and she hadn't wanted to call him at his hotel in Buffalo, so she'd just left a quick recording telling him that she'd gone to visit her mother for a few days and would call when she returned.

She should have been elated that he'd phoned her, but all the doubts that had been with her since she'd started dating him assailed her. She told herself that Jenner had upset her, that seeing him made Stan all the more attractive, but she couldn't convince herself.

In the kitchen, she dialed Stan's number from memory and felt a slight disappointment when the call began ringing through. What could she tell him? That she'd met with Cody's father? That now she was free from the past? That an unfinished chapter of her life had now been completed?

"Hello?'' Stan's voice sounded distant.

"Hi.''

"Beth!''

She cringed when she heard the joy in his voice and felt a pang of remorse that she didn't love him with the wild abandon that he deserved. At fifty-eight, Stan Cole was twice her age, had been married for fifteen years and divorced for eighteen. His children were grown and he had two grandchildren already with a third on the way. An insurance salesman, he would retire before he reached sixty-five. He loved to ski and camp and he was kind to Cody.

"What're you doing in Rimrock? I thought you hated it over there." Was it her imagination or was there a trace of irritation in his usually calm voice?

Hating herself, she hedged. "You know my job ended and I thought Cody and I should spend a little time with my mom before I started the old eight-to-five grind again."

"Oh...so when are you coming home?"

"I'm not sure...."

"Monday?"

"Probably not," she said.

"Tuesday then. I'll meet you—"

"Stan, let me give you a call later. When my plans are set."

"Oh, well, of course. I just thought we could get together. I could take you out to dinner. Tuesday is two-for-one night at The Countryside—"

"I know, but I can't promise Tuesday or even Wednesday, for that matter. Mom and I have a lot of catching up to do." As she wound the telephone cord around her fingers, she tried not to hear the wheedling tone of his voice or the disappointment in his sigh.

"Well, all right. Do whatever it is you have to. I just miss you, you know. I've been out of town over a week.... Well, how is your mother?"

Why don't you ask about Cody?

Beth shot a glance at Harriet, who had taken her position in the corner of the couch again. She'd turned on the television, probably so that she wouldn't have to eavesdrop. "She's fine. Happy to see us."

"Good, good. I guess I'll just catch up on my work and when you get home we can go out."

"I'd like that."

"I'll put in a word with Lela, see if she can watch Cody."

"No. I'll talk to her when I get home," Beth said, leaning against the wall and staring out the window into the night. Street lamps washed the yards and sidewalks in a thin blue light and a neighborhood cat slunk through the shadows.

"Come home soon, honey."

"I will," she promised and hung up with an empty feeling in the pit of her stomach. He hadn't even inquired about Cody; only brought up the boy because he was anxious to find a sitter for him. The uneasy feeling that Stan would be happier if Cody didn't exist settled over her heart. Not that Stan was ever cruel or callous toward her son. But he just seemed to accept and tolerate Cody.

"Trouble?" her mother asked when she walked back into the living room.

"No. Things are fine." No need to worry Harriet any more than she already was. Fine lines crossed Harriet's usually smooth forehead.

"You're sure?"

"Everything's just a little unsettled right now—"

The roar of a truck's engine drowned the rest of what Beth was saying. Tires screeched as the vehicle swung wide at the corner and braked to a stop in front of the house.

"What the devil?" Harriet said, twisting on the couch to peer through the venetian blinds. "Oh, my God—"

A door slammed.

"Brace yourself, honey," Harriet said as she hastily closed the blinds. "It's Jenner McKee and he looks mad enough to spit nails."

Now what? Beth's stomach cramped as she heard the sound of Jenner's uneven footsteps on the front porch, and she steeled herself for another emotion-wrenching confrontation. The bell rang insistently as she opened the door and found Jenner leaning on the tops of his crutches, his eyes blazing with fury. "Son of a—" He caught her stare. "You and I have unfinished business."

"I don't think so." She stood her ground, not moving an inch, but he shoved his way through, maneuvering his crutches so that she was forced to step aside.

"Where is he?"

"Who?"

"The kid who's supposed to be my son!" he growled, glaring at her. Beneath the anger and rage, there were questions in his eyes as if he didn't quite believe everything he'd heard tonight.

"I thought you were convinced I was trying to fleece you."

"You might be."

"So why're you here?"

His face twisted with frustration. "Because you've managed to convince my grandmother that the boy's mine."

"I've never met your grandmother."

"But you wrote to her—"

"*She* wrote to me," Beth clarified. "In fact, she threatened me."

"You're trying to make me believe an eighty-seven-year-old woman scared you?" He snorted at the absurdity.

Beth's patience snapped. "You have no right to barge in here and start making accusations."

"You started this."

"No way. Your grandmother did." She crossed the room, snatched her purse from the seat of the rocker and dug through the contents until she came to Mavis's letter. Holding it out like a shield, she walked back to the door and handed him the envelope. "Read it. You might find it interesting." She flicked on the lights and crossed her arms over her chest as if protecting her heart.

Jenner tore the letter from the envelope, scanned the contents, and let out a long, low whistle. His face drained of color, but the line of his jaw was still rock hard and defiant. "Jesus," he whispered, and it sounded like a prayer.

"I didn't drive across the state to lie to you, Jenner. Why would I? Believe me, my life was much simpler without you."

A quiet cough caught her attention, and for the first time since Jenner had stormed into the house, Beth remembered her mother. Great. Just what she needed. "Listen," she said stiffly, "why don't you come in and meet my mother, Harriet Forrester."

Jenner lifted his head and his gaze touched Harriet's for just a second. "Excuse us," he said and drew Beth out onto the porch. "I don't think we need an audience."

"My mother knows the whole story."

"Well, then she's one step ahead of me, isn't she?" His lips barely moved but his nostrils flared with a single-minded fury. "I think you'd better tell me all of your little story, starting at the beginning."

"I tried to earlier."

"I know. I wasn't in the mood."

"And now you are?"

The fingers around her arm tightened just a fraction as if he wanted to shake the living daylights out of her. "Now I am," he said so slowly the words seemed pulled from his lips. "Start."

Beth yanked her arm away and rested her back against the door. She'd been humiliated and infuriated by this man already tonight, so she didn't have much to lose. *Except Cody!* Alarm bells sounded in her head, but she decided it was time to come clean. This was it—her one shot.

"You may not remember me, cowboy, but I remember you. From the time I was eleven or twelve you were already something of a legend in town. You know, in trou-

ble with the law, giving your rich father fits, breaking all
the girls' hearts. I remember when you rode your first
rodeo, right over in Dawson City. I was there and I saw
you win first prize riding a wild bull or some such nonsense.

"It's embarrassing to admit it, but I had one helluva
crush on you, Jenner McKee, and it stayed with me for a
long, long time. Of course, I thought I was long over it,
but then, a few years ago, at the Independence Day cel-
ebration in the park, I saw you again. You were still the
same cowboy I'd adored from afar, but now I wasn't a
scrawny little kid anymore." Beth choked on the sudden
gush of memories that teased at her mind—memories
she'd tried for years to hide—even from herself. Rather
than dwell on them now, she cleared her throat. "Anyway, the next time I saw you it was at the roundup in
Dawson City, then we happened to run into each other in
Portland the next week, bumped into each other in a restaurant downtown. I mentioned that I saw you win, you
bought me a drink, and even though I was old enough to
know better, one thing led to another. To make a long
story short, we spent the night together and…in the morning you were gone. No note. No loose ends. No promises
to be broken. End of story."

"Except that you claim you got pregnant."

"I did get pregnant."

His teeth gnashed together as he stared at her so intently
she thought she might crumble right in front of his eyes.
It seemed as if he thought he could tell if she was lying
or not simply by studying her with a gaze meant to cut
through steel. "Maybe I should see the boy."

Her heart nearly quit beating. She'd considered this moment a thousand times, and though she accepted that it
was bound to happen someday, she didn't know if she
had the constitution to witness father and son meeting.
What should be a joyful experience was certain to be agony. Gathering up her courage, she said, "He's asleep."

"Doesn't matter. Not if he's my kid."

She notched her chin up a bit and met his gaze boldly. "First, I think we should get a couple of things straight. Yes, Cody is biologically your son, but he's my child not only by blood but because of my emotional commitment to him. In that respect, he only has one parent. You mean nothing to him and so I won't have you saying or doing anything that might upset or scare him."

Jenner considered this, his blue eyes narrowing in the darkness. "Fair enough," he finally agreed.

"And I'm not going to wake him up. If he happens to open his eyes, okay. But other than that, he sleeps."

Jenner's lips curved in grim amusement. "What're you afraid of, Beth?"

"Nothing."

"Think I might get all caught up in some latent fatherly feelings and try to swipe the kid from you?"

"I don't know what you'll do, Jenner," she said, reaching behind her and opening the door. "But if I thought you'd do anything to hurt Cody—and that includes 'swiping' him from me—I wouldn't have come to see you, and you might have spent the rest of your life not knowing your son." She shoved open the door with her back and he hobbled inside.

"Just show me the kid."

Back ramrod stiff, Beth led Jenner past the open archway to the living room and down a short hallway past the kitchen. She didn't bother glancing at her mother, though she was certain Harriet had overheard most of the conversation and was apt to come to her own conclusions.

The door to her old bedroom was ajar and Beth leaned against it, allowing light from the hall to slice into the room and spill over the playpen shoved up next to a small closet. Cody rustled around a little and snorted but didn't wake.

The strings on Beth's heart tugged as usual when she saw the curly blond down of his hair, his pink cheeks and

the soft motion of his lips as he sighed. Gold-tipped eyelashes curved against his smooth skin and he slept with
his legs tucked under him, his tiny rear end high in the
air.

Sneaking a glance at Jenner, she wished she could read
his mind. Without expression, he leaned forward and
squinted at the boy under the faded blue blanket.

Jenner was determined to prove her a fake. One look
at the kid and he was certain he'd know the boy didn't
belong to him. But standing in the hallway, he'd begun
to second-guess himself.

*Could she be telling the truth? Could that little bit of
a human be my son, for God's sake?* For the first time
since Beth had charged into his father's den at the ranch,
Jenner began to doubt his own convictions. Not that there
was any resemblance that he could determine—the fact
that the kid was white and had pale hair didn't mean a
thing—but there was something about the woman, her
aura of determination and hostility, that bothered him.

Unwillingly he admitted that he admired her grit. He'd
insulted her, tried to reject her, and she'd given as well
as she got. But to think that this two-year-old... He
glanced at her. While gazing at her son, her expression
had softened. It was obvious she adored the child, so why
would she put him at risk and claim he was Jenner's?

For money?

Because she still harbored some feelings for him?

For revenge?

She had to know that the McKee wealth could bring
her—along with her child—to her knees. She risked being
exposed as a fraud, an unwed mother trying to scam a
rich man, a woman with no moral standards who didn't
deserve the child she'd borne. The McKee team of lawyers were merciless and would tear her story and reputation to shreds if they were ever unleashed. She wasn't

stupid; surely she must realize how tenuous her position was.

Disgusted at the turn of his thoughts, Jenner stepped aside as she quietly closed the door. He didn't move from the hallway. "You know, you never answered my question earlier."

"What question?"

"I asked you what you wanted from me."

Her gaze, which had been rock steady, slid away. "I came back because your grandmother thought you'd want to meet your son. Now that it's done—"

"It's not done. I haven't met him yet." He rubbed a hand impatiently around the back of his neck. "I want you to bring him to see me tomorrow."

"I don't know—"

He couldn't stop himself from reaching forward and gripping her arm. He felt the involuntary tightening of her muscles and saw a spark in her gray-green eyes. "You started this," he reminded her in a harsh whisper.

"Did I?" She tossed her hair away from her face. "It started three years ago, Jenner. And I wasn't alone."

"Well, it's time to finish it then, isn't it?"

"Finish it?"

Was it his imagination or did she tremble a little? "Bring the boy to my apartment."

"I thought you were living at the ranch."

"Not anymore. I've got an apartment in Doc Fletcher's old clinic on Pine and—"

"I know where it is," Beth said. "And I remember the doctor. He took out my tonsils right before I entered kindergarten and set my broken arm after I fell off my friend Mary's old horse when I was twelve. And, if I'm not mistaken, he's probably the one who informed your father that he was about to become a granddaddy."

Again the fire in her eyes, and Jenner wondered how it was possible that he'd made love to this woman and barely remembered her. "Just come around, okay?" he asked, his voice more gentle than it had been. "I should meet him."

"And then what?"

"I wish I knew," he admitted as the shape of his future seemed to change before his eyes. Not only was he a cripple, but he might have fathered a child...or had he? What if this woman, this seemingly sincere woman, was just a common con artist, a user who fed off men and their mistakes?

Or, God forbid, what if she was telling the truth?

Sagging against the front door, Beth waited until she heard the sound of Jenner's truck fade into the night. She'd seen the change come over him and realized that finally he might believe her.

And then what?

Shuddering at the thought that he might change his mind, might decide he wanted to be more than a blank space on a birth certificate, she slowly forced her legs to move back to the living room where her mother was shaking a long cigarette out of a nearly empty pack.

"He's not father material," Harriet said as she found her lighter on the table. "Not that many men are. From my experience, it seems that most of 'em would rather be little boys themselves than help raise a child right." She clicked her lighter to the end of her cigarette and inhaled deeply. "I guess I can understand how you were attracted to him. Like all the McKees, he's a handsome devil. But he's so damned irresponsible...." She glanced through the window and watched as a car crawled down the street. "Same with your father, you know. Probably the best-looking of all the men I ever dated and oh, what a charmer he was. I knew I'd marry him the first time I laid eyes on him, but I didn't expect that he would leave at the first hint of trouble. He sure wasn't father material, but I guess you know that."

Beth couldn't disagree. Growing up, she'd seen little of

her father. He always made a half-hearted attempt to visit her around her birthday, though the demands of his job and new family often interrupted his plans. And Charlie Crandall had been content to let Harriet's string of husbands help raise his firstborn daughter.

A little pang of doubt entered her heart. Cody, too, would grow up not really knowing his father.

"You're better off marrying Stan," Harriet said, gazing thoughtfully at her daughter through the smoke curling from her cigarette. "He's stable and trustworthy, won't be running around on you chasing other women or elusive dreams. You should count yourself lucky."

"I wish I could be sure about that," Beth said, feeling that ever since coming face-to-face with Jenner again, her luck wasn't getting any better.

Cursing under his breath, Jenner slowly climbed the front steps to the apartment house where he'd once planned to live in a unit on the second floor. Since the fire and his accident, the owner of the house, Skye Donahue, had hastened to make some efforts to fix up the basement apartment for him. It had a ramp as well as a short flight of exterior concrete stairs. Skye was a doctor in the clinic next door; she'd bought out Ralph Fletcher when he'd retired. Skye was also engaged to Jenner's brother, Max.

Sweating by the time he'd negotiated the five steps, Jenner plowed through the open door to the foyer and rapped loudly on the door to Skye's apartment. "Come on, come on," he growled under his breath.

An upstairs door opened at the racket he was making, and Mrs. Newby, a short, elderly woman with apricot-tinged hair poking out from a nightcap, peeked through the opening. "Oh, Mr. McKee, it's you," she said, obviously relieved as she bustled into the upper hallway and leaned over the rail. "My goodness, I thought you were supposed to be recuperating."

"I am." Jenner was in no mood for small talk.

"You're a hero around here, you know. Saving Max's daughter and those horses and all."

Funny, he didn't feel like a hero. In fact, in light of the past few hours after meeting Beth and that kid of hers, he was beginning to feel like a first-class jerk.

"I'm looking for Skye."

Behind thick, rimless glasses, Mrs. Newby's eyebrows lifted. "And good luck finding her. Between the clinic and your brother, Dr. Donahue doesn't have much time for this place, let me tell you. Why, half the things I requested to be done to my apartment haven't even been started! Just last week I spoke to her about the carpet—"

The door on the opposite side of the landing opened and Tina Evans, Skye's other tenant, stepped onto the landing. Her smile stretched wide at the sight of him. "Well, look who's come home," she said.

Jenner gritted his teeth and forced a smile. "I'm trying to track down Skye so I can get into the basement."

"It's not finished yet."

"No? I bet it's close enough."

Tina's smile faltered a little. "She's probably with your brother, but I've got a key so that I can show prospective tenants the vacant apartments."

Mrs. Newby snorted. "I don't know why she'd want more occupants seein' as she can't take care of the ones she has."

Tina tried and failed to suppress a grin. "Give me a minute to get the keys and I'll meet you downstairs."

Tina disappeared into her apartment, and Mrs. Newby, still leaning over the rail, said, "Be careful you don't trip over the cat. It's always up to no good, slinking around, carrying fleas and shedding everywhere…never giving my allergies a rest, let me tell you! I've talked to Skye. But does she listen? Of course not—"

Jenner didn't hear the rest of her complaint. He headed out the front door and down the steps to the concrete path leading to the side entrance that once had led to Doc Fletcher's clinic. There was enough light from a security lamp so that he didn't stumble, and true to her word, Tina used the interior staircase, cut through the basement, and opened the door for him.

"See," she said, snapping on the overhead lights, "it's a long way from being finished."

"It'll do," Jenner said as he crossed the threshold and looked around. Fresh Sheetrock had been nailed to the walls, taped together and mudded, but only half the apartment had been painted. The cabinets were up, but the doors hadn't yet been hung and the tile floor was bare. Appliances were still packed in boxes, but he turned on the kitchen sink and was relieved to find that the plumbing was working.

"The painters are due to finish up this week and the carpet's coming next Wednesday. Skye didn't expect you to be moving in so soon."

"Neither did I," he admitted as he crossed the room to a closet where all of his worldly possessions—a bedroll, duffel bag and a few odds and ends—had been stashed.

"If there's anything you need...?" she said, offering him the keys, and Jenner flashed her a smile he didn't feel.

"I'll let you know."

She glanced at his crutches and bit the corner of her lip before shrugging and waving goodbye. He listened as her footsteps clomped up the interior stairs, then he shut the door and threw the bolt.

"Home sweet home," he said to himself as he tossed down the bedroll. The apartment didn't have the comforts of the ranch, but at least here he was his own man. It had been a long time since he'd felt this free.

Slowly easing himself onto the faded sleeping bag, he thought of Beth and her son. A pain shot up his leg, reminding him that he was no longer a complete man, that he might forever be chained to crutches or a wheelchair.

He could no longer support a family by riding the rodeo circuit or training horses or hiring on as a hand at one of the neighboring ranches.

But he wasn't foolish enough to think that he was poor.

Max would probably let him run the Rocking M. Jenner could handle the paperwork and supervise the work in the fields from a truck. Chester, the ranch foreman, could run interference with the rest of the hands.

Max had already given him three hundred acres that old Jonah hadn't included in his will. Wildcat Creek slashed through one corner and the old cabin built by a great-grandfather needed some work, but was sound. A little bit of elbow grease and it would do just fine. For one.

But could he really just give up the life he'd known?

He wondered what kind of a father he would be. He'd never be able to play baseball, shoot baskets or teach the kid how to rope a calf. Swimming would be tricky and…oh, hell, what was the matter with him? He wasn't cut out to be a father or a husband. Seeing Beth and her kid had played havoc with his mind. Not that it mattered. He probably wasn't the kid's father, anyway.

Chapter Four

Max wanted to strangle his brother. Of all the low-life, stupid, selfish stunts Jenner had ever pulled, this was the worst. He leaned against the wall of his farmhouse, cradling the phone to his ear, imagining his mother wringing her hands.

"...so he didn't come home and heaven knows he shouldn't be driving," Virginia was saying. "I hate to bother you, Max, but I... Oh, Lord, I don't know what I'd do if anything happened to him."

Max shoved a hand through his hair and stared through the window as the first rays of sun began to spill over the horizon. His dog, Atlas, a half-grown Border collie, flushed a flock of quail from the brush bordering a thicket of pine trees. "If Jenner had been in an accident, he would have been taken to Dawson Memorial," Max said, glancing at the clock and scowling. It was only ten after six— way too early to be dealing with Jenner and his bad moods. "Skye's working in the emergency room. She would've called."

"Maybe he was life-flighted somewhere else." Virginia's voice quavered and Max silently cursed his brother again.

"Why did he leave?" Max asked as he propped the receiver between his shoulder and ear and began measuring coffee into the maker. Hell, what was Jenner up to now?

"He...he got into an argument with me. And Mavis."

"With Grandma?" That surprised Max. Jenner and the old woman had always been close. "Why?"

There was a hesitation on the other end, and Max experienced the first hazy sensation that there was more going on than Virginia was willing to say.

"Why'd he leave?" he repeated.

"You...you'll have to ask him. He just lost his temper—you know what a short fuse he has—and stormed out, claimed he might not be back. I'm afraid...well, I'm afraid he's gone for good."

"Gone where?"

"If I knew that, I wouldn't be calling you now, would I?" she snapped, then, as if hearing the anger in her tone, let out a long worried sigh. "I just don't know what to do. He...he said something about going back to his apartment."

"That's crazy."

"Tell him. I tried to call, but the phone was disconnected, and I couldn't imagine him negotiating the stairs to the second floor. I did leave a message on Skye's answering machine. Oh, Lord, Max, what if he had an accident and he's trapped in his truck. Or...or what if it wasn't an accident? Your father was forced off the road and the same thing could have happened to Jenner. Oh, God, Max—"

"Don't worry. I'll find him," Max cut in before Virginia's fertile imagination had Jenner murdered by the same madman who supposedly had killed Jonah and started the blaze in the stables. "Go to bed. Get some sleep." He hung up knowing she was about to break down into a crying jag and he felt rotten inside. His mother had always been a pillar of strength. For years, she'd held her head high, pretending she hadn't known about Jonah's reckless affairs or his shady business practices. She'd been his partner for life and had supported him throughout every ordeal, ignoring the calls from women, refusing to believe that the civil lawsuits against him and his company were anything more than sour grapes. Loyal should have been her middle name.

Within fifteen minutes, Max had showered, shaved, dressed and poured himself a cup of coffee. He shook some dry dog food into a dish for Atlas, who greeted him by jumping and barking and leaving dusty pawprints on his jeans.

"Slow down. Eat some breakfast," Max insisted, but the pup ignored his full dish and loped after him to the garage where his pickup was parked. Atlas hopped into the cab of the truck and Max didn't have the heart to shove him out. "Just this once," he said as he backed out and drove along the tree-lined lane leading to the edge of the McKee property and the county road.

He turned on the radio, listened to the sports scores and then a report that predicted cooler weather, but his mind was on his stubborn brother. It seemed that Jenner, born restless, had developed a bad case of impatience since nearly being killed in the fire.

Not that Max really blamed him. Though Jenner had improved to the point where he could walk with crutches, the outlook wasn't all that great. Most of Jenner's doctors had confided to Skye that Jenner would probably always walk with a limp, maybe even be forced to use a cane, and that his passion for riding wild rodeo broncs and Brahman bulls was now a pipe dream.

Jenner didn't have to work, of course. He owned about

three hundred acres, and if that wasn't enough, there was plenty of money in the old man's estate to go around. Since Max was not only a lawyer but the executor, he could find a way to set up a trust fund for Jenner so that he would be comfortable for life. But he doubted that Jenner would accept the money. Ever since the fire, Jenner had been hell-bent not to accept charity or pity or anything that hinted at compassion for his plight.

"Idiot," Max growled as he pushed the speed limit. By the time he reached the outskirts of Rimrock, the streetlights had turned off and morning sunlight chased away a tiny hint of fog that lingered near the river. Max barreled over to the rooming house that Skye owned and felt a good measure of relief when he spied his brother's pickup, dent free, parked at the curb in front of the house. Leaving a whining Atlas in the cab, he wondered what the hell Jenner thought he was doing. He opened the front door with his key, climbed up the flight of stairs to the second-floor landing and banged on the door of Jenner's apartment.

There was no answer, but Max wasn't simply going to go away. He didn't care if Jenner was drunk, hung over or just plain dog tired. His brother had a lot of explaining to do. "Open up!" he yelled between bangs.

A door near the staircase opened and Mrs. Newby, in chenille robe and nightcap peered through the crack. "He's not in there," she said with the authority of a busybody used to checking up on her neighbors.

Max hooked his thumb toward the front door. "His truck is parked outside."

"He's in the basement."

"But it's not finished."

"I know," Mrs. Newby said, warming to her subject. "And I told Tina she was making a mistake by letting him stay down there, but he wouldn't take no for an answer and Tina, well, she just about melts every time she sees him. Sweet on him, she is and so…he ended up in the basement.''

Max was already halfway down the stairs.

"When you see Skye," Mrs. Newby called after him, "would you be a dear and remind her about the security system I want installed?''

Max waved and hurried through the front door. In all his life he'd never been nor would he ever become anything closely resembling ''a dear.''

He took the outside steps two at a time and, once he was at the bottom of the stairwell, pounded on the door. It opened immediately and Jenner stood blocking the entry. Hair uncombed, jaw dark with stubble, shoulders hunched defensively as if he'd expected this fight, he balanced on his crutches.

"Don't tell me," Jenner growled with a sarcastic bite, "you've missed me.''

"Mom's worried.''

"I told her I wouldn't be home.''

Max pushed past his bullheaded brother and into the unfinished room. His hands curled into fists of frustration. "She was up half the night worried sick. You know, Jenner, she doesn't need any more grief from you. She's got enough problems dealing with Dad's death and the murder investigation.''

"Did she tell you why I left?''

"We didn't get into that.''

Jenner's blue eyes sparked. "I didn't think so.''

Max was suddenly wary. He sensed that something wasn't quite as it seemed. Just as he had during the telephone conversation with his mother. "Okay, I give up. Why did you drive off in one of your black rages?''

Jenner slammed the door shut. "Because I can't stand being a hypocrite for starters and I don't like anyone waiting on me hand and foot, watching my every move, hovering over me like a mother hen.''

"She *is* a mother hen and you're supposed to be recuperating. Doctor's orders. 'No straining yourself, plenty of rest, exercise with a physical therapist, and—'''

"'—and it's all a bunch of bull. You know it and I know it. The doctors aren't being straight with me. They don't think I'll ever be the same."

"No one really knows. A lot depends on you."

"More bull!" He glowered at his crutches. "Anyway, I've decided to recuperate on my own." Scowling fiercely, he rubbed his chin, and lines formed across his forehead as if he was thinking hard. Muttering a curse under his breath, he finally looked back at Max. "I don't suppose Mom told you what went on at the ranch last night."

"Just that you took off in some kind of blind rage."

"But not why."

Max couldn't help but smile. "I didn't think you needed a reason."

"I didn't. But I had one. A helluva reason," Jenner admitted. He hobbled over to the other side of the room where a hot plate, balanced on an old television tray, was plugged into the wall. An enamel coffeepot was warming on one of the burners, and the scent of brewing coffee overpowered the combined odors of Sheetrock, dust and varnish. Jenner found two chipped mugs, poured coffee, and motioned for Max to help himself. As they drank the bitter brew, Jenner settled into a folding chair and told Max some wild tale about Harriet Forrester's daughter, Beth Crandall, and Beth's contention that she'd borne Jenner a son. He also mentioned that somehow good ol' Jonah had found out about the kid, hushed it up, and managed to keep Beth from telling Jenner about the boy. Jenner didn't have all the details, but he was convinced that Mavis was behind Beth returning. What he didn't seem sure of was the paternity of the kid.

"…so the damned thing of it is, I don't really remember her, and believe me, she's a woman no one would forget in a hurry."

Max swirled the dregs of his coffee in thought. The story was incredible, but there was enough truth sprinkled into it to keep a person guessing. Max knew from personal experience that Jonah McKee was capable of manipulating his children's lives. Hadn't he forced Skye out of Rimrock years ago? Recently Max had gotten back with the woman he loved, and he and Skye were planning to marry in early December. Still, Beth Crandall's story seemed too pat. "You still think she's trying to scam you?"

"Don't know," Jenner admitted, his gaze clouding, "but if she is, she's good...damned good."

"You're buying into it and you don't even remember being with her?" Actually, Max liked the idea of Jenner being a father; it didn't even really matter if he'd sired the boy or not. Jenner needed some roots to tie him down, a reason to keep on living, and a kid would be just the ticket. Considering Jenner's accident, Max had some concern about his brother's ability to father children in the future, though no one had said anything aloud.

Max was lucky enough to have a five-year-old daughter from his first marriage. Hillary with her stubborn jaw and thick curls, was precocious, bullheaded and as cute as a bug's ear. He loved her more than he'd ever thought possible. Jenner could use a little of the joy and heartache that comes with being a parent. The feeling was like none other on earth. Since Skye would be unable to bear him any children, Max understood how precious each and every child was.

"I'm not buying into it," Jenner protested. "I'm just not sure. But I'll get to the bottom of it."

"How?" Max asked, setting his cup on the floor. "Are you going to go through blood tests? You know that would mean spending time at the hospital again—something you've stubbornly avoided."

Jenner snorted. "Before having any tests, I think I'll talk to our old friend, Rex Stone—see what he thinks."

"You're going to hire a private investigator to check her out?"

"Seems the logical thing to do." Jenner finished his coffee and set the cup on an old television tray.

"But you hate the guy, don't you?"

"Stone's a sleazeball, but I think he's good at what he does." Jenner's expression turned dark. "And I don't know anything about Miss Crandall." He concentrated on the middle distance past Max's shoulder. His jaw hardened defiantly as if he could see the woman in the room. "Before this is over," he vowed, "I'm going to know her better than she knows herself."

"What if you find out she's lying?"

"I'll make sure she regrets ever coming back to Rimrock."

"And if she's telling the truth?"

"I don't know," he admitted. "But I guess I'll cross that bridge when I come to it."

"You know there's always a need for medical help right here around Rimrock. I'm sure you could find a job if you looked. That way you could stay here, closer to me. And I could watch my grandson grow up." Harriet picked up the breakfast dishes as Beth wiped Cody's hands and face. Seated in an old high chair that Harriet had used when Beth was a toddler, Cody wriggled and protested, shaking his head vigorously.

"No!" Cody wailed. "Noooo!"

"He doesn't believe in the old connection between cleanliness and godliness," Beth said as she unsnapped the tray and placed Cody on the floor. Wiping her hands, she added, "I don't think a job this close to Jenner is such a good idea."

"I know, I know." Harriet rinsed the plates before putting them into the portable dishwasher. She looked about to say something, but thought better of it, and for the first time, Beth wondered if something was wrong. Before she could ask about it, Harriet said, "I don't trust those McKees, so don't get me wrong. But you can't run away forever, and even if you tried, there's no place on earth far enough away. If Jenner wants to be a father to his son, he will."

"I don't think we have to worry about that." Beth wiped the table, then hung the dish towel over a metal bar near the sink. "But it would be difficult for Cody to grow up here and know that his father lived in town and didn't want him...." She shook her head, her own painful memories assailing her.

"It's because of me, isn't it?" Harriet asked, her voice barely a whisper as she reached into a drawer for her carton of cigarettes. "It was hard on you growing up and you don't want your son to have to deal with all the questions and gossip you did." She flipped open the carton, extracted a new pack and tapped it against the counter. "You know, Beth, I was the best mother I knew how to be."

"I know," Beth said, a lump forming in her throat.

"And I realize that I was something of an embarrassment. I've heard the rumors, too. But most of it's just gossip. Idle tongues wagging and trying to stir up trouble." She unwound the cellophane wrapper, shook out a cigarette and struck a match. "It bothered me, of course, but the worst part was that the gossip, aimed to hurt me, probably cut you more deeply." She lit up and smoke filtered from her mouth as she sighed.

"I survived," Beth said.

"But I can't help feeling responsible."

"Mom, don't. It's over. Kids can be cruel, yes, and I hope Cody doesn't have to suffer the same things I did, but God knows I'm not the perfect parent and I don't know anyone who is. I'll make my share of mistakes." She winked at her mother, trying to jolly her out of her sadness. "Besides, all those teases and taunts made me tough—tougher than I would've been."

Harriet hesitated, then drew on her cigarette. "I hope that everything that happens here with Jenner won't make you think that you don't have any options, that you should just run off and marry the first man who asks you."

Beth stiffened. Her mother usually wasn't one to pry. "Are you talking about Stan? Don't you like him?"

"Of course I do. He's a wonderful man. I thought you should marry him, but..." She hesitated. "But he's closer to my age than to yours." Folding her arms across her chest, Harriet ignored her cigarette and let the smoke curl in a wavering line to the ceiling. "I know what I said before but I guess I'm having second thoughts. Even if you do marry him and have a wonderful life together, who knows how long he'll be around. If you want Cody to have a father—"

"Stan's only fifty-eight. That's not ancient, Mom."

"No, but when Cody's fifteen and a hellion, which, judging by his genes, he probably will be, Stan will be over seventy. He might need some special care of his own—"

"I can manage. I'm a nurse, remember."

"A *young* nurse," Harriet reminded her. As if suddenly weary, she pulled out a kitchen chair and sat on the faded cushion.

"So what do you think I should do?" Beth asked as her mother smoked silently. "Try to find a way to make Jenner marry me?"

"Oh, God, no."

"Stay single? Let Cody grow up without a father?"

Harriet ground out her cigarette. "No," she said, "but if I were you, I certainly wouldn't marry a man just to give Cody a daddy. You might find this hard to believe, Beth, but every man I ever married, I married for love. And when I stood at the altar I really believed in till death do us part. That only happened once, thank God. Will was a special man, but cancer took him and...oh, Lord, it was hard to watch him die." Her throat clogged and tears shimmered unshed in her eyes. "Do you remember him?"

"Not much, Mom," Beth admitted, placing her arm around her mother's shoulders. William Jones was little more than a hazy memory to her. "But I know he was a good man."

"The best," Harriet said as she wiped her eyes with her fingers and sniffed. "Until Zeke, he was the best." She blinked rapidly, and suddenly a smile stretched across her face. "Well, speak of the devil."

Zeke Forrester walked into the room in a gray-striped bathrobe and his slippers. A V-necked T-shirt was visible beneath the robe. Only five foot six, he had a blocky build and, before two cups of coffee in the morning, a sour disposition. "How ya doin'?" he said, pausing to buss his wife on the cheek.

Harriet scrambled out of her chair to pour him a cup of coffee, then went to open the refrigerator. "French toast?" she asked brightly.

"It's Saturday. You know I like bacon and eggs on Saturday." He shot Beth a dark look and took a quick gulp of the coffee. "Doctor won't let me eat eggs but twice a week," he said as some kind of explanation, then searched the tabletop and counters. "Where's the paper? Don't tell me the carrier didn't deliver it again!"

"I'll get it in a second," Harriet said. "And stop being so grumpy. Good Lord, you're a grouch in the morning."

"Cody and I will go out and get the paper." Glad for an excuse to escape, Beth carried Cody outside. She was still smarting from her mother's remarks about Stan, though she knew that Harriet's concerns only echoed her own. In the past few weeks, even before seeing Jenner again, she'd reconsidered her relationship with Stan. He was a good man. But he really wasn't interested in starting over with a young family.

Outside, the air was fresh, the sky a clear shade of blue. Beth breathed in a blend of fragrances from Harriet's flower garden and she watched birds flutter around a rusted feeder swinging from a low branch of an ornamental plum tree no longer in bloom.

"Well," she said, as she picked up the paper from the front porch, "how do you feel about meeting someone today?" Cody turned his blue eyes up to her.

"Who I meet?" Cody asked.

"Your fath—a man I knew a few years ago," she said, deciding it was better not to confuse her son. Not yet. Not until she knew how Jenner would react.

"A friend?" Cody asked innocently.

Beth rumpled her son's dark blond hair. "Well now, I don't know that I'd call him a friend," she admitted as she scanned the headlines. "But he's someone who wants to meet you." She winked at her boy and hurried back inside.

The phone jangled as Beth tossed Zeke's paper onto the table. Harriet grabbed the receiver on the second ring, then stretched the cord as she kept pronging pieces of bacon that were beginning to sizzle in a skillet on the stove.

"Oh, hello. Yes, she's here…no, don't worry about that. We're up with the chickens around here." Harriet's eyebrows rose as she handed the phone to Beth and mouthed, "It's Stan."

Beth's stomach clenched suddenly. She felt a jab of guilt and didn't know why, but she took the receiver from her mother's hand and tried to remain calm. After all, she'd done nothing wrong. Yet.

"Hello?" she said brightly as Zeke snapped his paper open and Harriet turned back to the stove. Cody investigated the back porch.

"Hi! Thought I might catch you." Stan's voice was friendly, and for an inexplicable reason Beth thought of her Uncle Jim with his pleasant smile and graying beard. Oh, Lord, this would never do.

"Hi! How are you, Stan? Didn't expect another call

from you so soon,'' she said, easing around the corner for some privacy and drawing the coiled cord tight as a piano wire.

"I know, but I've been thinking.'' Then as an after-thought, he added, "You know, I really miss you.''

"Oh, well—''

"I really do. It gets lonely here without you,'' he said, and she suddenly felt uncomfortable, as if a noose was tightening around her neck. "Listen, I had an idea. Maybe you could leave Cody with your mom for an extra few days and you and I could do something together.''

"Without Cody,'' she said, her heart nearly dropping to the floor.

"Right. We need time alone. To be adults.''

That was the problem. Always the problem. The noose tightened a little bit more.

"It's not that I don't love the little tyke, you know I do, but, well, frankly, Beth, he wears me out sometimes and I need a break. Besides, we never see each other without him. So...since you're there already, I thought leaving him for a few more days wouldn't be a big deal.''

"I don't think that's possible, Stan,'' she said.

"Why not? It's not like your mother sees the kid all that often. She's his grandmother, for Pete's sake. You think she'd be thrilled to have him to herself for a few days.''

"She works, Stan, and so does Zeke and...well, to tell you the truth, I don't want to leave him here alone.''

"Why not? Don't you trust your mother?''

"Of course I do.''

"Then I don't see why you couldn't spend a couple of days alone with me,'' he said in a tone that bordered on whining. Sighing patiently, he added, "You know, it wouldn't kill you to forget you're a mother once in a while.''

"Never,'' she said, and then it occurred to her how far she and Stan were apart, at least on this issue. Stan was a kind, decent, loving man, but no matter how she tried to kid herself, she had to face the fact that he wasn't willing to be a father a second time around. He'd had his kids; he really didn't want hers.

"Beth, you know I think Cody's the greatest, but—"

"But you like him best when he's not around."

"That's not true!"

"Sure it is, Stan, and something else is true, as well. This—our relationship—isn't working. Not for me or for you." She waited and heard only stunned silence. "I've been thinking and—"

"You're seeing him again, aren't you?" Stan charged, his voice an angry whisper. "Cody's father. That's the problem." Stan jumped to the same conclusion he always did, whenever they argued—that Beth was still in love with the man who had sired Cody.

"I'm not seeing him. Not like you mean."

"But you'd like to. You're thinking that the three of you could be a cute little family unit, aren't you?"

"No, I—"

"Just remember how he reacted when you told him you were pregnant, will ya?"

"I never told him," Beth said, then held her tongue. This was a subject she and Stan had avoided in the year they'd been seeing each other. It only came up when they argued. He didn't know who Cody's father was and didn't really seem to care. She'd never confided the truth to him, only told him that her relationship with Cody's father hadn't worked out and that she'd wanted a baby and had moved away. It hadn't been a lie—not really—but she'd never felt close enough to Stan to share her most private secret. There had been a part of her that had always held back. Maybe it was because he didn't seem as close to Cody as she'd hoped he'd be or maybe it was because she didn't trust him. Not completely.

"Jeez, Beth, what do you want from me?" Stan asked, unable to hide a ring of anger in his words.

"Nothing." And that was the truth. "I don't want anything, Stan."

"So this is it? You're telling me it's over?"

She tried to swallow the lump in her throat. "I think it has to be, Stan, because Cody and I, we're a package deal. You don't get one of us without the other."

"For the love of God, Beth, listen to you! Have I ever said I don't want him? Have I?"

"Yeah, Stan, you did. Just a couple of minutes ago." Tears burned behind her eyes as she said a quick goodbye. She didn't need any more emotional turmoil in her life right now, didn't want to make any abrupt changes in her life. Yet she knew deep in her heart that Stan would never love Cody as his son. She'd rather never marry than put her own son through the hell of rejection that she'd felt because of her own father. Brushing aside her tears, she cleared her throat, walked back to the kitchen and hung up the phone.

As she speared crisp strips of bacon onto a plate, Harriet slid her a glance. "Oh, honey—"

"It's all right, Mom," she said.

Zeke didn't bother looking up from the sports page.

"You sure?"

"Positive."

As her mother cracked eggs into the skillet, Beth scooped up her son and held him as if she were afraid he might disappear. To think that she had contemplated marrying a man who didn't realize how wonderful Cody was. Again she fought tears. "Come on, kiddo," she said, forcing a smile as she kissed Cody's crown. "I think it's time we got outta here."

The apartment house wasn't as huge as Beth remembered, nor as imposing. For years she'd come to this old Victorian home on Pine Street with the basement clinic where Dr. Fletcher had had his practice before he'd moved to the modern facility on the next lot. Beth had always been intimidated by the size of the house, three full stories, and detested walking down the outside stairs to a small reception area. It had smelled of antiseptic and was guarded by a no-nonsense nurse with gray hair. She'd insisted that all the children who were patients of Doc Fletcher call her Nurse Hazel. A fleshy woman, she'd lied and told Beth that the shots wouldn't hurt, then handed out balloons when the ordeal of the examination was over. With kinky hair and big eyes magnified by the thick lenses of her glasses, she'd scared the life out of Beth.

It was a wonder she'd taken up nursing, she thought now, as she parked on the street and unbuckled Cody from his car seat.

So this was where Jenner lived. It didn't seem right somehow. She could see him in the sprawling ranch house at the Rocking M or imagine him throwing down a bedroll in a bunkhouse or under the stars. But an apartment in town? No way.

Carrying Cody, she walked up the front steps, opened the door to the foyer, and knocked on the door of the first-floor unit where she supposed the new owner lived.

The door swung open to reveal a tall blond woman who looked bone weary. Her hair was damp from a recent shower and she was wearing a pink-and-gray sweat suit. Without a trace of makeup, she was still beautiful. "Can I help you?"

"I—I'm looking for Jenner McKee."

The woman's eyes moved from Beth's face to Cody's and she managed a smile that didn't quite touch her eyes. "You must be Beth Crandall. I'm Skye Donahue." She extended her hand.

Juggling Cody, Beth took the long fingers in her own. "Should I know you?"

"I'm engaged to Max and—" She yawned and placed her hand over her mouth. "Forgive me, I spent the last twenty-four hours on my feet at the clinic and then worked the emergency room at Dawson Memorial Hospital. Jenner's downstairs in the basement. He doesn't know it yet, but I intend to evict him, at least until the place is finished. I think the board of health and the city wouldn't much like it if they knew he took up residence in a half-finished set of rooms." She let her eyes stray to Cody again. "So this is Jenner's boy?"

"You already know?" Beth asked, and something akin to fear stole through her heart.

Her concern must have registered on her face because Skye said, "Don't worry, it's not common knowledge—not yet. Except for the McKees. I don't think the rest of the town knows anything. But it will. It's just a matter of time. I only know because Max and Jenner spoke earlier today, and I talked to Max on the phone when I went off duty." She stretched and sighed, her gaze lingering on Cody, and a sadness seemed to come over her. "Go on downstairs—the door's over there on the other side of the foyer. I think Jenner's expecting you."

With Cody still in her arms, Beth steeled herself for another confrontation with Jenner and hurried down the stairs. Before she could knock, the door at the base of the steps was thrown open. Jenner stood in front of her, leaning against the wall. She watched his throat tighten when he gazed upon his son.

"So you're Cody," he said as she walked into the room. She felt Cody cling to her a little more tightly.

"He's a little…nervous about being here," Beth said. The apartment wasn't small, as it had once housed a reception area, an office and three examining rooms. But it had been gutted and now was one room devoid of any kind of flooring except old tile that showed the outlines of the former rooms.

"Don't blame you, Cody," Jenner said. "Makes me nervous, too."

"Who are you?" Cody asked, his face a mask of concentration, as if he, though only two, could feel the tension between his mother and this stranger. Jenner's eyes held Beth's an instant.

"A friend of your ma's. You can call me…" His brows drew over his eyes. "Just call me Jenner."

"Funny name."

Jenner's lips twisted into a smile. "That it is. Actually, my name's General, can you beat that? My dad…" He lost his train of thought again, but cleared his throat. "He gave me that god-awful handle, but Mom, she changed it to Jenner. Not much better, but I can live with it."

"General's in the army."

Jenner snorted. "What do you know about the army?"

"Television," Beth supplied as Cody, relaxing a little, wiggled to be let down.

"Don't watch too much of that," Jenner warned. "It'll rot your brain. A boy like you…well, you need to be out playing in the creek, building forts, riding ponies—"

"He's only two." Beth bristled a little. Jenner had no right whatsoever to insinuate that she was depriving her boy.

"Yeah, but he should start young."

"Cody and I live in an apartment, Jenner, not even as big as this one." She glanced around. "It does have more than one room and it is finished, but there's no yard or barn or creek. The nearest water is the Willamette River, where the water rushes over the falls in Oregon City, and when he needs to go outside we go to the park or over to his baby-sitter's house. She's got a fenced yard and—"

"Puppies!" Cody supplied. "Lots! A new one. Barney."

"Is that right?" Jenner's smile suddenly seemed tight. "You ever ridden a horse?"

Cody shook his head.

"Ever caught a tadpole?"

"I told you he's too young," Beth insisted, exasperated now.

"You know what a crawdad is?"

Cody's little lips pursed together in concentration. "No."

This was worse than Beth had expected. Jenner didn't bother to hide the censure in his gaze. "We live in the city," she explained.

"That's a problem."

"I don't think so. And it looks to me like you're in town now, too."

"It's only temporary."

"That's what I tell myself." She felt her blood begin to boil. Jenner McKee could be the most maddening man in the world. She knew that much about him. He lived by his own code, threw convention to the wind, and didn't give a damn about what anyone else thought about him. Including her.

His jaw muscles tightened and he shoved a hand into his back pocket. "You had breakfast?"

"Pancakes at Grandma's!"

"Well then, how about I buy you two some lunch? It's nearly noon."

"I don't know—"

"Hell, Beth, that's why you're here, isn't it? For us to get to know each other?"

"I'm here because I was threatened," she said, her voice barely a whisper.

"Oh, yeah, I forgot. My eighty-seven-year-old grandma scared the living hell out of you and you hightailed it right over here."

"No say hell," Cody said, and Jenner's gaze narrowed on his son.

"Seems your boy has himself some manners."

"I hope so."

"Maybe I can change that. Come on, Cody, let's have a hamburger and French fries and a milk shake, then we'll go out to the ranch and you can ride a horse."

"A what? No way!" Beth said.

Jenner turned and his eyes sparked with determination. "You gonna fight me on this, Beth?" he drawled.

"He's too little."

"Bullsh—" He caught Cody staring at him and bit off the rest of his curse. "I was in the saddle at his age."

"He's not you!"

Jenner's expression turned to granite. "Isn't he? Well, well, Ms. Crandall. You'd better make up your mind." He reached for his Stetson, which hung from a nail near one of the ground-level windows offering only a rodent's view of shrubbery. With a cold smile he added, "Either this here boy *is* mine, or he ain't, but I'm damn sure he isn't both. So, Lady, you'd better decide which it is and get your story straight."

Chapter Five

Beth couldn't decide whether to hate the man or love him.

From her side of the booth at the Shady Grove Café, she slid a glance in his direction. His hair was mussed, his hat hung on the post at the end of the bench seat. He still looked as hard and dangerous as the outcropping of red rock that rimmed the mountains surrounding the town.

She decided that hating him was a whole lot easier and safer than loving him. Ever since she'd shown up at the Rocking M, he'd berated and degraded her and she was getting fed up. She didn't need or want the abuse.

As for loving him—it was a fool's dream, an old, silly notion that she kept rekindling because of the stupid reason that he was Cody's father. Big deal. So he'd sired her boy; that was no reason for childish fantasies about him.

An ancient air-conditioning unit rattled and wheezed, losing the battle with the smoke and heat that wafted from the kitchen. Beth swirled a straw in her diet soda and watched as Cody, his little face beaming with delight, wiggled happily in a booster seat set on the worn Naugahyde. He alternately sipped from his strawberry milk shake and dunked French fries in a glob of catsup Jenner had plopped onto his plate.

For Cody's sake, Beth managed a tight smile, but her nerves were stretched as tight as newly strung barbed wire. Jenner, one long leg stretched into the aisle, regarded his son with an amicable enough expression, outwardly seeming to enjoy himself. But his cold blue eyes betrayed him. He regarded the boy carefully as if looking for flaws, and studied Cody's facial features as if trying to find clues to the boy's parentage.

Only when Jenner glanced at Beth, when his gaze pierced hers, did she see the anger, the accusations, the repressed fury that boiled inside.

Beth ignored the hostile glare even though Jenner seemed to be silently warning her that if Cody did prove to be his son, she was in for the battle of her life. Playing idly with her straw, she worried that it was a battle she might lose. Her heart shredded a little when she noticed how easily Cody responded to this man he'd never met before.

Jenner taught Cody how to blow the paper off his straw and make a foam mustache by drinking the milk shake right from the glass. He even let Cody wear his cowboy hat.

"That's right, Cody," Jenner said, his eyes moving from the boy to Beth. "Maybe I'll take you riding, and someday we can even go camping out by the stream at the ranch."

"Don't," Beth said under her breath as Cody picked up his child-size burger. "There are no maybes when you're two years old. Either you make a promise you intend to keep or you hold your tongue."

"I keep all my promises." His voice was low and

steady, his eyes so intense that her stomach seemed to be suddenly filled with a swarm of restless butterflies.

"Do you?" she asked.

"Every last one." His jaw was set, his lips a thin line of determination, and Beth was swept away as the memory of making love to him flashed into her mind.

She remembered the heat, the raw passion that seemed to surge through his blood, the way he'd made their mating an urgent, savage event that still, even three years later, sucked the breath from her lungs. She glanced away and cleared her throat. "Then I guess that makes you a hero," she said sarcastically.

His eyes narrowed and he reached across the table, knocking over the catsup bottle as he grabbed her arm. "Let's get one thing straight, okay? I am *not* a hero. Got it?"

"Oh, that's not what I heard," Sarah, the heavyset waitress with a crown of frizzy curls, interrupted as she refilled Jenner's coffee cup. "The way I heard it, you saved your brother's little kid, and if it wasn't for you, the Rocking M would've lost all its livestock. Without you, Dani Stewart might not have made it. That girl has had a string of bad luck, let me tell you—not like her sister at all—but she lucked out this time."

Irritation pinched the corners of Jenner's mouth and the fingers of steel that had tightened over Beth's arm loosened their grip. "You've been talking to Max," he said as he let go.

"No way. Heard it from the fire chief, himself. Fred has breakfast here every morning and he thinks you saved lives. Course he's cussin' you, too, 'cause you and Max got in the way. Max wouldn't do what he was told, and you, you nearly ended up dyin' just to save some horses."

Jenner glowered up at the waitress. "It wasn't a big deal."

Sarah shrugged a hefty shoulder. "Whatever you say." She righted the bottle of catsup as she eyed Cody. "This your boy?'' Beth's heart nearly stopped until she realized the woman was speaking to her.

"Uh, yes. Cody.'' She whispered in her son's ear, "Say hello."

"'Lo,'' Cody replied, staring warily at the friendly waitress.

"He's sure a looker.'' Sarah grinned at him and reached into her pocket. She found a mint and set in on the table in front of Cody. "You're gonna break your share of hearts, son, believe you me.''

"Thank you,'' Beth said, feeling a lump form in her throat. Jenner hadn't said a word, just leaned back against the seat and watched the exchange.

"Is there anything else I can get you?''

"Not for me,'' Beth said.

"Thanks, anyway, Sarah,'' Jenner drawled.

Sarah's gaze sharpened just a tad. "Is it true what I've been hearin' around here—that your pa might've been murdered?''

"Looks that way,'' Jenner admitted with a scowl.

"Good Lord A'mighty. Why, no one's been murdered in Rimrock before—I mean, unless you count Elvin Green runnin' down Indian Joe ten years ago, but that was just an accident, I guess.''

"That's the way I heard it.''

"Anyway, I don't s'pose they have any idea who's behind it.''

"Not that I know,'' Jenner said, wishing the nosy waitress would just disappear and leave him alone. He wasn't going to confide that Rex Stone had at first come up with the brainstorm that someone in the family might be responsible. He seemed to have given up on that ludicrous assumption, and if he had any other suspects, he hadn't shared his suspicions with Jenner.

Sarah moved closer to the table and whispered, "I hear your family's offering a reward.''

"A what?" Jenner's head snapped up and he saw a gleam of greed in the waitress's gaze.

"Twenty-five thousand dollars for information leading to the arrest of the person responsible for your dad's death and the fire at the ranch."

"I don't know a thing about it."

"Heard it this mornin'. Two deputies were talkin' about it while eatin' breakfast."

"This is the first I've heard of it," Jenner said, hoping to hide the fact that he was furious. It was all he could do to remain at the table. Why hadn't anyone told him? Then he remembered. Mavis and Virginia had been at a meeting with Rex Stone last night. They must've made the decision at that time and never bothered to tell him— not that they had the chance, really, considering the conversation. But Max hadn't said a word this morning. It looked as if his family was still trying to protect him— keep him calm so that he could heal—or they were holding out on him. Either way, he was going to find out the truth. His jaw clamped so hard it hurt.

"Hey, how about a refill, Sarah?" At a table on the other side of the entrance, Cyrus Kellogg held up his empty coffee cup. He caught Jenner's attention and gave a sketchy wave. "Glad to see ya up and around, McKee. Helluva thing, that fire."

Jenner nodded to the weathered rancher who owned the spread just north of the Rocking M. Cyrus, smoking a cigarette, was seated with three other men from around the area. One was Ned Jansen, who once owned the old copper mine in the hills surrounding the town. Jenner's father, Jonah, had bought the mine for a song a few years back when Ned had needed the cash to pay back alimony to his two ex-wives. The mine was rumored to be worthless, but Jonah had taken a chance and eventually found a mother lode. Wouldn't you know? The old man had been blessed—or cursed—with the Midas touch.

Len Marchant sat with his back to Jenner. A short,

lively man, Len, too, had done business with Jonah. Once the town baker, Len had sold out at a loss to Jonah, who had remodeled and converted the old bakery into a mini-mall that now supported five small shops. The third man was Otis Purcell, a rancher with a mean streak whose single claim to fame was that he raised wolf pups and, to Jenner's knowledge, had never been swindled by Jonah McKee. That alone was some kind of record.

"Come on, let's go," Jenner said. He realized that he'd run out of conversation with Beth and didn't like the side-long glances cast in his direction from the other patrons. The Shady Grove was half-filled with customers looking for a simple, cheap meal. Most of the people tucked into the booths and seated at the tables were ranchers and townspeople Jenner had known most of his life. But there were a few strangers, as well. His gut clutched into a tight knot as his thoughts ran in a new and frightening path. What if Rex Stone was right? What if Jonah had been murdered? And what if whoever was behind the murder *and* the arson at the stables wasn't satisfied? What if he wanted to do more damage? What if, instead of holding a grudge against Jonah, the psycho behind the crimes wanted to get back at Max...or Jenner?

He sliced a look at Cody innocently sipping his shake. Beth was dabbing at the corners of his little face with a cloth, completely unaware of any danger.

Using the crutches for support, Jenner climbed to his feet just as Beth gathered Cody into her arms. What if the kid really was his and whoever was gunning for the McKees found out about him? Jenner's throat turned to dust. Cody could unwittingly become a target—as could Beth.

Cold sweat beaded on his forehead, and for the first time in his life, Jenner McKee felt vulnerable.

Beth expected Jenner to take her back to his apartment where she'd parked her car. When he'd insisted on driving his truck earlier, she'd argued, remembering how his pickup had careered down the street the night before. Eventually, after extracting a promise from Jenner that he'd be careful, she'd given in, and they'd survived, though the ride to the Shady Grove had been a little harrowing as Jenner had been forced to work gas, clutch and brake with his right leg. She hadn't complained, only held on to the armrest in a death grip with her other arm tightly wrapped around Cody. The toddler had only laughed when the truck had lurched into slow-moving traffic.

"I thought you might want to meet my grandmother," Jenner explained as he drove north and passed the city limits.

"That's not necessary."

"Sure it is, Beth," he said, looking over Cody's head to capture her in his cynical gaze before turning his attention back to the road. "You started this, so you're going to play it out."

"*We* started this," she said, unable to hold her tongue a minute longer. "You and I both. I'm sick of women always having to take the blame as well as the responsibility for their kids." She wanted to add that without men there would be no children, but she managed to swallow her words for Cody's sake. She never wanted him to hear anything that might suggest that he was unwanted or that she considered him a mistake. Because that wasn't true. She loved him more than life itself, and if given the choice again, she would gladly go through the pregnancy alone and accept the hard choices that followed. Smiling, she grabbed one of his chubby hands in hers.

"We go to Grandma's?" Cody asked, all innocence and smiles.

That was a tough one. "Not to Grandma Harriet's, honey. We're going to Mr. McKee's—"

"Jenner."

"Jenner's ranch."

"I see horses?"

"You bet you will," Jenner said.

"I ride one?"

Beth cleared her throat. "I don't think that would be such a good idea—"

"Of course you can. Got a little pony that would be perfect."

Beth shot Jenner a warning glance silently telling him to back off, but if he noticed her aggravation, he ignored it and reached into the glove compartment for a pair of aviator sunglasses. He slipped them over his nose and now he seemed more remote than ever, the dark shades hiding his eyes, his mouth set in a harsh, uncompromising line.

He seemed to be getting the hang of driving with only one leg. He managed to work the clutch smoothly enough and the old Dodge hummed over the county road that rose along the contour of the hill, but always followed the winding path of Wildcat Creek as it slashed through the land a hundred feet below. Beth rolled down the window, smelled the dust and dry grass and felt the sun warm her shoulder as the wind streamed through her hair.

How many times had she ridden this very road, listening to the radio, laughing and thinking of Jenner McKee? All those years ago, she'd never met him, but he'd been a local legend, a rebel son rebuffing his father by turning his nose up at the old man's money and striking out on his own.

She ran her fingers along the edge of the window that peaked up from the door. Yes, she'd dreamed about him, never daring to guess that someday she'd run into him, that she'd let him buy her a couple of glasses of wine and she'd end up sleeping with him and bearing his son. She chanced a look at her boy, but he'd fallen asleep in the warm cab of the truck and was blissfully unaware of the reasons she'd been forced back to Rimrock.

Jenner pulled off at a narrow spot in the road where the old guardrail had been hit and given way completely. A new piece had been fitted between two posts right at a sharp curve, nearly a hundred feet above the canyon. Beth didn't have to be told that this was where Jonah McKee had lost his life.

He stopped the truck and killed the engine. Cody stirred but didn't open his eyes, not even when Jenner opened the cab door and hopped to the ground. Using the pickup for support, he edged around the truck, leaned a jean-clad hip against the fender and gazed down the cliff face to the swift waters of the creek.

Beth eased out of the truck and joined him. The sun was warm against her crown, the hood of the old Dodge hot and grimy with dust and dead insects.

"I haven't been here," Jenner said, "not since it happened." He rubbed the back of his neck impatiently and his brow furrowed above the frames of his sunglasses. "You know, I was never close to the old man. In fact, I professed to hate his guts. I did everything I could to irritate the hell out of him." He kicked at some loose gravel and the stones rolled off the shoulder and past a few dry blades of grass to tumble freely into the canyon. "I didn't like the way he treated people, especially me and my sister. Max—" Jenner shrugged "—he was Dad's favorite, and for years Max turned a blind eye on what the old man was doing. But he found out. Damn, did he find out." Jenner turned his gaze up to the cloudless sky as if he could discover the answers to his questions in the vast heavens. "Even though my father was a liar and a cheat, even though he manipulated people, he didn't deserve to die. Not like this."

She didn't know what to say. Did he want comfort? Or was he talking not so much to her as to himself? She reached forward, her fingers touching his bare arm where he'd rolled up his sleeve.

He didn't move, just glanced down at her small white hand resting against the bronzed skin and gold hair of his forearm. He lifted his head, and from behind his dark glasses, he stared straight at her, causing the pulse at her throat to throb. For a second, she thought he might draw her into his arms, might kiss her until the breath left her body, might hold her so close she could feel every hard contour of his muscles.

Her throat worked. His lips flattened and he turned away. "Come on. We're wastin' time."

By the time they reached the ranch it was early afternoon. Trucks and cars, most covered in a haze of dust, were parked in the yard, and ranch hands could be seen working with the livestock.

Jenner guided his pickup into a vacant spot near the ga-rage. As he climbed out of the cab, he waved to a few of the men and stared at the rubble and ash still piled where Beth assumed the stables had once stood. Yellow tape, announcing a crime scene, was stretched around the charred concrete and blackened debris, while the odors of dust and ash mingled in the breeze with those of cattle and bleached grass.

Hundreds of heads of cattle had been herded into a series of pens surrounding a large barn. Calves bawled and men shouted as the animals were inoculated, their ears notched and tagged, before they were forced into a chute leading to another field.

"Cow," Cody said, blinking and yawning as he woke up. Beth got out first, then set him on the ground.

"Many cows," Beth corrected.

"Many cows, bulls, steers and calves. You want to see?" Jenner asked, starting to hobble toward the nearest fence.

"I don't know…" she said, regarding the beasts with their dusty red, black, gray and ocher hides. Most of the animals were huge, some had humps at their shoulders and wicked-looking horns sprouting from their heads. Flies swarmed and the smell of manure permeated the air.

"Lighten up, Beth," Jenner called out as he limped

swiftly toward the melee and left Beth in the shade of a solitary pine tree. "The boy's not made of glass."

"I know, but—" *But he's all I've got, and if anything happened to him...* She released Cody's hand and he ran to keep up with the man on crutches. Beth felt something inside her die as she watched her son run so confidently to Jenner and reach for his hand.

Maybe Cody wasn't made of glass, but it seemed as if her heart was.

Grasshoppers flew out of his path and flies buzzed over his head and his sneakers were dustier than they'd ever been in his short life, but there was a joy about him that brought tears to her eyes. She was losing something by introducing Cody to Jenner. Until now, she'd been everything to her son—provider, mother, friend, the sun, the moon and the stars. But Cody was gaining something— something precious—if Jenner would accept him as his son.

Something inside her seemed to tear. She blinked hard and told herself she was being a fool. Didn't she want Cody to know his father? Didn't she want him to feel the warmth of a father's love—that special warmth she'd never known? Her throat was so thick she could barely breathe as she watched Jenner, balancing precariously on his crutches, lift Cody onto the third rail of the fence so he could rest his arms on the top rail and gain a better view. His little feet shifted, but Jenner's hand, tanned and weathered, was splayed firmly against the child's back, and Beth knew Jenner would fall himself before allowing any harm to come to Cody.

"Oh, God," Beth whispered, "please let him be all right."

As if in answer, Cody let out a whoop when a rangy calf drew close enough so that he could bend over the fence and pat the animal's head.

Beth bit back a warning for him to be careful when she saw Jenner's arm surround his son's waist. Her heart twisted at the sight. Father and son. Together. A picture she thought she'd never witness.

Jenner said something and Cody laughed so loud the calf started and backed away. A few men came over and Jenner talked to them, keeping his hand on Cody all the while. More than one interested glance was cast in her direction, but she couldn't hear their conversation over the noise of the herd.

Eventually the men went back to work and Jenner peeled a reluctant Cody from the fence. Together they walked back to the truck.

"I seen lots of cows!" Cody announced, obviously pleased with himself as he climbed into her arms and managed to smudge dirt all over her blouse.

"Did you?"

"Millions of 'em."

Jenner chuckled, and together they headed toward the front door. "Brace yourself," Jenner whispered to her as they reached the porch. "I'm not in good graces with my mother just now."

"Oh, great."

"Nor with my grandmother."

"What are we doing here then?"

He slid her a glance. "Not getting cold feet, are ya? After all, this is your party." He shoved open the door and stepped inside.

Sharp footsteps echoed through the rooms as Casey half ran down the hallway. "Where the hell have you been?" she said, her hazel eyes spitting fire. "Mom and Grandma are both fit to be tied..." Her voice trailed off as she realized that she wasn't alone with her brother. "Uh... well...I didn't mean... Damn it, I don't care, Jenner, you're—"

"Irresponsible and going to roast in hell. I know. Now, maybe you'd like to simmer down and meet these people. This is Beth Crandall and her son, Cody. My sister, Casey.

As you probably noticed, she's the calm one in the family.''

"Very funny," Casey muttered, her eyebrows drawing angrily together. Somehow she managed a smile when she shook Beth's hand. "I remember you. You were in the class ahead of me in school."

"That's right."

"And this is your little boy?" Casey grinned widely at Cody.

"Yes," Beth said, her insides beginning to twist. "Cody."

"Isn't he a doll?" All of Casey's anger with her brother seemed to fade as she reached out and grabbed Cody into her arms. "Well, what're you doin', big fella? Did you come out to the ranch to rope some steers or ride some broncs bareback?"

Cody didn't say a word, but his eyes rounded in wonder.

"Beth's here because Grandma wrote to her," Jenner explained, his gaze locking with Beth's. She narrowed her eyes at him to warn him, but one side of his mouth twisted upward in a sarcastic smile.

"Grandma?" Casey repeated.

"Mmm. Seems she and Beth have quite a correspondence going."

"Is that so? How do you know our grandmother?"

Bristling, Beth said, "She wrote and asked me to come back to Rimrock because she thought it would do Jenner a world of good to see me and Cody. We've known each other a few years."

Storm clouds gathered in Casey's usually clear eyes. "Oh." She slid a glance at Cody and her face suddenly paled.

"Beth's here to clear up a few things."

Casey's throat worked and Beth felt her cheeks grow hot as embarrassment stole over her face. "That's right,"

she admitted, wondering how much Jenner intended to
confide in his sister.

"Jenner? Is that you?" Over the staccato tap of heels
on hardwood, Virginia McKee's voice carried through the
hall. She appeared suddenly through an archway and
stopped dead in her tracks when her gaze landed on Beth.
"Oh…well, I see you've brought a guest." Her practiced
smile fell perfectly into place, though she didn't seem
pleased and her eyes remained frosty, even when she
looked at her grandson for the first time. "Come in.
Please." She led them into a spacious sunken living room
decorated with pine walls, rock fireplace and heavy furniture in shades of forest green and tan. Along the back
wall, windows offered a view of a ridge of mountains
reflecting in the clear waters of a lake. "Please, sit," Virginia invited.

Jenner propped his crutches against the fireplace and
settled onto the raised hearth. "I'd hoped Mavis would
be around."

"She's resting."

"I am not!" Mavis's voice rang clearly through the
living room as she entered. "What's going on— Oh!"
Her gaze landed on Cody and Beth. "Well, it's about time
you showed up around here." Using her cane, she crossed
the room and smiled at Cody. "So this is the boy. I believe it. Just look at him, Virginia. He's the spitting image
of—"

"Mavis!" Virginia hissed. "I don't think this is the
time or the place—"

"Sure it is. We all know what's going on here."

"Not all of us," Beth said quickly, holding on to her
boy. "Cody—"

"Won't really understand what's going on, but it's time
he did. That's what you want, isn't it, Mavis? You're
lookin' to find yourself a great-grandson." Jenner's words
were harsh and cut to the quick.

The old lady took a seat in an armchair and sighed. "I

told you why I wrote to Beth, Jenner, but it was only part of the truth. I thought that seeing the boy would be good for you, yes, and good for the entire family, but I also thought that it was time to right a wrong. Lord knows I loved Jonah. He was my only child and I adored him, but…I'm afraid his father and I spoiled him and let him believe that he could take everything he wanted from life. He was a good man. I believe that with all of my heart, but sometimes he made mistakes and he…'' She sighed again and looked down at her hands, where age spots mottled the once-clear skin. ''Well, I didn't think it was right when he broke up Max and Skye, twisting the truth as he did, but I didn't interfere.

''As for you and Beth, things were different. You weren't in love like Max and Skye, but you became involved and you fathered a child, a child you never knew about. Jonah thought it was for the best and I disagreed with him, but I couldn't dissuade him. Once again, I let him have his way. But now he's gone and I can't help thinking he made a terrible mistake.''

''That bastard!'' Casey said.

Virginia's face turned the color of chalk. ''He was your father and a good father and I won't have you speak ill of him, Casey Maureen McKee!''

''Enough, Mom,'' Jenner cut in. ''Casey's just surprised. We all know what kind of a man Jonah was.''

Mavis wound her fingers nervously over the handle of her cane. ''He only did what he thought was best.''

''Best!'' Jenner snorted disdainfully, but held his tongue. Leaning back against the smooth stones of the fireplace, his arms crossed over his chest, his jean-clad legs stretched out in front of him, he watched Beth through eyes opened at half mast, as if expecting her to say something, anything, that might somehow prove she was lying.

''This is all just conjecture,'' Virginia said pointedly to Mavis, ''and I don't think you should go around maligning your own son. Jonah, rest his soul, may have made mistakes in his life, but we all do, and we have no proof that the boy is Jenner's.''

"Beth is here because I insisted she come," Mavis said, her mouth pursing.

"Why didn't she ever contact Jenner?" Virginia turned her attention to the woman who dared challenge her son.

Beth raised her chin up a notch. "He was already gone when I found out. Back on the rodeo circuit. He'd never tried to contact me since…since we were together, and afterward I heard rumors that he was engaged to Nora Bateman.''

"That was over," Jenner said sharply.

"Not according to your father."

Jenner swore roundly.

"I'll not have you speak that way about your father," Virginia admonished, her eyes narrowing. "He was a good—''

"Stop kidding yourself, Mom! Open your eyes. Jonah P. McKee did whatever he wanted, whenever he wanted, to whomever he damn well pleased.''

"Jenner—''

"Jonah McKee was a lousy husband. Why you pretend that you didn't know that he ran around on you is beyond me." Mavis gasped and Casey shook her head vigorously, trying silently to stop her brother's tirade, but Jenner wasn't finished. He was just beginning to warm to his subject. Pushing himself upright, he said, "As for his being a good father, Mom, he was a complete failure.''

Mavis let out a small groan of protest but didn't attempt to stop her grandson.

"You and I and Casey and Max and even you, Mavis, we all know the kind of man he was. Jonah's kids weren't people—at least not to him. They were just things, possessions like everything else around here. Trophies when they were good, embarrassments when they were bad. I guess I win the award for being the worst." Shoving himself forward, Jenner refused to use his crutches and half stumbled over to the couch where Virginia was sitting, clutching her hands over her heart, her eyes brimming with tears. "It's time to stop deluding ourselves. All of us."

"You didn't even know him," Virginia whispered.

Jenner snorted. "We all knew him, but we just made excuses. Mavis here, she blamed herself for spoiling him. You...I guess you figured you were lucky to catch the richest man in the county and turned a blind eye to his faults. Max believed in Dad to the point where he was almost corrupted himself, and I... Well, I spent a lot of time trying to prove that I didn't want or need him, just the way he treated me."

"He loved you!" Mavis interjected.

"He loved himself."

Beth couldn't stand any more. Gathering Cody into her arms, she said, "I think I'd better go."

"What?" Jenner turned too quickly, nearly fell over, but caught himself. "Already? Just when things are getting interesting?"

"I did what I had to do. Now I think it would be best if—"

"If what?" he roared. "We all went back to our same little lives? If we all acted as if you hadn't appeared with your son and your claims about his heritage? Is that what you expect?"

Her spine stiffened and she stared him straight in the eye. "What I expect, Jenner, is respect. That's all I want from anyone, including you!"

"Don't go!" Mavis pleaded, her lips quivering. "Jenner will apologize."

"Like hell!"

"Why did you bring me here?" she demanded, and Jenner's grin was as cold as a blue norther raging through the mountains.

"I wanted you to see what it was like to be a McKee.

You know, a lot of people in town envy us, think we've got the perfect lives, but they aren't privileged enough to see deeper than the surface into the flaws.''

"What Jenner is trying to say," Casey cut in, "is that he's being a class-A jerk to scare you off because he's afraid of what you and your son represent."

"Which is?" Jenner asked.

"Responsibility and stability."

"One psych course in college and now you know all about me."

"You're classic, Jenner."

"And you all wonder why I moved out."

"No, we all know why," Casey snapped back, her temper rising along with his. "It's because you can't face yourself in the mirror, brother. It's because you're scared to death that you're never going to be able to do the things you love. It's because you're…you're…"

"Go ahead and say it," Jenner snarled, his face flushing an angry shade of red. "A cripple. That's the word you were looking for."

"I was going to say a coward."

Virginia shook her head. "That's not true! He saved Hillary's life and Dani Stewart's, as well."

"Oh, hell, let's not forget the horses, shall we?" Jenner said sarcastically. "Don't you know, Casey? Haven't you heard? I'm some kind of hero. A goddamned, crippled hero!"

That was enough. Holding Cody close, Beth headed for the front door. "Thanks…thanks for the hospitality," she blurted out, though, considering the situation, it hardly seemed sincere. She walked through the door and headed for Jenner's pickup. Oh, Lord, why hadn't she brought her own car? She could call her mother, she supposed, but Harriet was working the afternoon shift at the Pancake Hutt and Zeke was probably getting ready to head out for the swing shift at the mill. Short of walking the nearly ten miles back to town, she had no recourse but to wait for Jenner.

"Damn! Damn! Damn!" she said, rolling her eyes to the blue sky and wishing she hadn't been such a fool. Coming back to Rimrock had been a mistake of the highest order. The more she was around the McKees, the more certain she was that she'd made an irrevocable error, one that would affect her son for the rest of his life.

"You mad?" Cody asked, his eyes round with worry.

"No...well, yes."

"At me?"

"Oh, no, pumpkin." She wrapped her arms around her son more tightly and wondered how much of the conversation in the ranch house he'd understood. She should never have subjected him to such a horrid and painful scene.

She heard the front door open and listened for Jenner's uneven gait. "Jenner's coming!" Cody obviously spied Jenner over her shoulder. Wriggling to the ground, he raced up to the cowboy who had sired him.

Jenner managed to balance on his good leg and hoist the boy into the air. Cody giggled in sheer joy and Beth's heart tore a little with the sound.

"I ride horse now!"

"Well, pardner, not right now."

"When?" Cody demanded as Jenner set him on his feet.

"Maybe later."

"When?"

"Tomorrow."

"I told you—don't make promises you can't keep," Beth warned as Cody, intrigued with the old crossbred retriever lying in the shade of an old apple tree, ran eagerly to the dog.

"Be careful," Beth warned.

Jenner snorted a laugh. "Careful of old Reuben? He

wouldn't hurt a flea. Isn't much of a watchdog for that matter.''

"Look, would you just give me a ride back into town?" she asked, not wanting to share any small talk with him. It was better when she hated him, when she didn't trust him, when her heart was hard where he was concerned.

"You don't want to stay at the Rocking M—even with the red-carpet treatment?"

"I need to get back."

Casey, half-running, hurried out of the house. "Oh, Beth, I'm glad I caught you," she said, crossing the yard. "I just wanted to apologize for my brother. He can be one helluva bastard when he wants to be."

"Now wait a minute—" Jenner cut in.

"Rude, obnoxious, self-indulgent, arrogant, a real jerk."

"Thanks," Jenner muttered.

"I'm not telling Beth anything she hasn't already figured out." Casey shot her brother a furious glare. "I don't really understand everything that went on in the house, but I heard enough to put two and two together, and it looks like I've got myself a nephew." She smiled as she cast Cody a loving glance. "I can't tell you how thrilled I am, and if...well, this sounds really hokey I know, but if you ever need anything, especially a baby-sitter, I'm available."

"Hey, hold your horses!" Jenner objected. "We don't even know—"

"Know what? That the kid's yours?" Casey whirled on him. "I heard the whole story from Grandma just now. Of course Cody's yours. Look at him, for crying out loud. He's got McKee stamped all over him."

Despite the tension straining the air, Beth almost laughed.

"How can you tell? He's just a kid!" Jenner said.

"Ever see any pictures of you as a toddler? Go look in Mom and Dad's bedroom. Cody's a dead ringer for you."

She shook her head and met Beth's amused gaze. "I'd better warn you of something. All the men in this family are muleheaded. Maybe there's still time with Cody, but the rest of them are beyond help."

"Thank you, Dr. Freud," Jenner muttered.

"I'll send you a bill," Casey quipped back, then rolled her eyes at Beth. "I'm serious," she affirmed. "Anytime you need anything."

"How about a ride into town?"

Jenner stepped between the two women. "Wait a minute. I'll give you a ride home."

"Don't bother. If Casey would—"

"I said I'd do it." He grabbed her arm possessively.

"Don't you understand, Jenner?" she said, angling her face to his. "I'm giving you an out."

"Well maybe I'm not asking for one."

Casey lifted both palms skyward. "Hey, I'm not going to get in the middle of this. I'm outta here. You two work it out and you—" she pointed a finger at Jenner "—be smart for once in your life!" Flipping her hair away from her face, Casey climbed into an imported sports car of some kind and roared down the lane.

"My sister neglected to mention that the women in the family have some of the same unique and endearing traits as the men." Jenner's fingers still surrounded Beth's wrist. He blew out a sigh and watched Reuben lick Cody's chubby little hands. "About what happened in the house—"

"Let's just forget it, shall we?" A dry gust of wind caught her hair, blowing the dark strands over her face. Just as she was brushing them aside, Jenner touched the edge of her cheek with a callused finger.

"I just wanted you to see what you were getting yourself into. What kind of family we are."

"It doesn't alter the facts, does it? Or were you just trying to test my mettle and scare me off?"

His fingers traced the line of her jaw, his gaze suddenly

warm, and the harsh edges of his face seemed to soften a little. "You've given me a shock. I just want you to realize all the ramifications of what you're doing." His hand dropped back to his side and he leaned a hip against the fender of the truck.

"I can't turn back now," she said, and he watched the breeze play with her hair again. Sunlight glinted off the red-brown curls and her cheeks were high with color, probably from embarrassment.

Suddenly Jenner felt like a heel. "Do you want to… turn back?"

"I don't know," she admitted, her jaw jutting forward in defiance. "I thought this was the perfect opportunity for Cody to meet his father. Maybe I was wrong." Before he could answer, she called to her son. "Come on, Cody. It's time to go."

"Dog come, too?" Cody asked.

"No, but—"

"Sure. Come on, Reuben." Jenner whistled to the old retriever who loped over to the truck, then upon command leaped into the bed.

"I ride with him."

Beth was horrified. "No way."

"You're up in the cab, pardner," Jenner said.

"But I want doggy."

"Who's gonna steer the truck?"

Beth let out a little squeak of protest.

"I drive?"

"You bet." He winked broadly at Beth as he yanked on the door of the old Dodge.

"God help us," Beth whispered as Cody, with Jenner's help, scrambled into the driver's side. She was climbing into an ancient pickup that was going to be driven by a man with the use of one leg and a two-year-old. "Crazy, that's what this is," she muttered under her breath.

Jenner shoved the truck into reverse, and Cody, sitting next to him in the car seat reached over and honked the horn loudly. From the bed, the dog let out a sharp bark and they were off, leaving a plume of dust in their wake.

Beth glanced at father and son, both grinning widely as if they were having the time of their lives. She couldn't help but wonder just how long it would last.

Chapter Six

Jenner smelled trouble. The kind of trouble that reeked of problems and clung to a guy for the rest of his life. Not only was that little imp of a kid getting to him, but the mother, as well.

They'd spent the rest of the day together. Though Beth had come up with a hundred reasons to return to her mother's house, he'd managed to convince her to stick around. They'd gone to the park, a dippy kid's movie in Dawson City and out to dinner at an Italian restaurant. Eventually, with Reuben still in the back of the truck and Cody falling asleep leaning against his mother, Jenner had taken her home to the cottage on Buckskin Drive. The house was nearly dark, soft light coming from only one window near the back and a single bulb burning on the front porch.

He pulled into the driveway and cut the engine. Tapping his fingers against the wheel, he squinted through the grimy windshield. "You're not what I expected," he admitted.

"I hope not. You thought I was some kind of con artist, I think."

"That about sums it up."

"Not quite. You thought I'd do anything, even jeopardize my child's emotional well-being and security, to get at a few McKee dollars."

He rubbed the stubble on his chin. "You make it sound like Monopoly money."

"You're the one who suggested I was playing a game."

He leaned back against the seat and studied this woman who just twenty-four hours ago he hadn't known existed. Resting against the door, her son sleeping in the car seat, illumination from the porch lamp highlighting her features, she kissed the top of Cody's head by instinct, and Jenner watched the movement, his gut tightening at the familiarity and warmth of this simple act. For a split second, he considered kissing her, just as he had earlier today when they were overlooking Stardust Canyon and she'd touched his arm.

Her lips were pliant and now devoid of lipstick, her arms protectively wrapped around her child. Her hair was mussed, thick mahogany curls tangled from the wind as they'd pushed Cody on a swing, or balanced together on a teeter-totter, or spun slowly on a merry-go-round. Beth had raced her son to a slide, then slid down with him when the child had protested that the contraption was too high.

"It's supposed to be high, silly," she'd explained with a gentle nudge. "Otherwise it would be flat and we would have to push ourselves along. Let me hold you first and see if you like it, okay?"

"'Kay," Cody had said reluctantly, but had soon been whooping in glorious excitement as they'd slipped down the slick piece of equipment. "Do again! Do again!" he'd insisted when they'd landed.

Beth's generous smiles and laughter had touched a dark part of Jenner's soul that was better left locked away.

Cody's little feet hadn't been able to race fast enough back to the ladder, and the second time he'd needed no prodding from his mother. "You do, too!" he'd cried, pointing at Jenner, who had been forced to decline rather than stumble up the metal steps with his one good leg.

His back teeth ground together as he thought of a lifetime of missed opportunities. A lifetime that, despite the encouraging words from surgeons, would never be the same. He stared at her long and hard. "You've never said what it is that you want from me."

"I wish I knew," she admitted, a line forming between her arched eyebrows. "I...well, when I first found out I was pregnant, I had this silly fantasy that you and I would...oh, well, you know..." Her voice trailed off in embarrassment.

"What? Get married?"

He noticed the dark stain that washed up the front of her neck. "Something like that," she admitted, her voice rough. "I knew it was out of the question, that we really didn't know each other, but I had this Norman Rockwell vision of what a family should be."

He snorted. "Not my family."

"Nor mine," she said, shifting a sighing Cody in her arms. "Anyway, I made the mistake of trying to locate you and instead I ran into a brick wall named—"

"Let me guess. Jonah McKee."

"Right. I don't know how he found out, but I suspect it was through Ralph Fletcher. They had some business dealings, I believe. Anyway, your father set me straight right away. Told me that you weren't the marrying kind and when you were you'd probably settle down with Nora Bateman. He acted as if she was the typical girl-next-door and said you two had been involved in some kind of on-and-off-again romance since high school."

Jenner scowled. "It was off when I met you."

"Was it?" She let her chin rest on the top of her son's head.

"Been off ever since."

"Then I guess Jonah didn't like me or the thought of a bastard grandchild."

Jenner's gaze skated down Cody's dozing face. A bastard? Would someone—his own father—actually look upon this dynamo of short legs, curly hair and bright eyes as a bastard? The thought brought a vile taste up the back of his throat and he realized with sudden clarity that no matter how much he protested the fact that he'd sired this boy, the kid was really getting under his skin. He experienced a strange sense of caring for this little two-year-old scamp. Funny, he'd never liked kids much. Except for Hillary, his niece, he didn't have much use for children and thought most of them were brats. He sure as hell had been one.

"I can't explain Jonah," Jenner finally said. "I don't think anyone can."

"Anyway, I think I was telling you all about my stupid fantasies." She stared through the windshield and into the night. "Once your father shattered my illusions, I left Rimrock and finished nursing school. I decided that neither Cody nor I needed you, that we could get along just fine. And we have. Until your grandmother wrote me."

Jenner still wasn't absolutely convinced. Though Beth looked as if she was telling the God's honest truth, he didn't know her. She could be the world's most accomplished liar for all he knew. "So now what do you expect of me?"

"I don't know. Recognition maybe. I, um, grew up not knowing my dad and it would've been nice to put a face with a name occasionally."

"You never saw him."

"Not much. Once in a while he'd show up, or he'd call, but it was pretty much hit-or-miss."

"And that bothered you?"

She opened her mouth as if to give a quick answer, a lie maybe, then shut it quickly. "Yeah," she admitted, "it bothered me a lot."

His gut tightened when he saw the tip of her tongue skim her lips nervously. He didn't want to feel any empathy for her, didn't want to feel anything. So she had a rotten childhood. Lots of people did and they survived.

"Well, look, it's late. Cody's already asleep and I'd better get going." She reached for the handle of the door, but he grabbed her shoulder, surprising himself.

"Wait—" His body just seemed to react on its own as he dragged her close, boy and all, and let his lips touch the wet trail her tongue had left only moments before. Her mouth was soft, pliant and brought back dusty memories as she sighed softly. She smelled and tasted familiar, but that could have been his imagination playing tricks on him. The way her body seemed to melt into his... Warmth, hot and urgent, invaded his limbs, caused his heartbeat to thunder in his ears.

Cody, caught between them, moved and made sucking noises with his mouth, but Jenner didn't mind. In fact, as his arms drew her closer, the child was wedged between them and it felt right somehow.

His heart was still pounding when Beth lifted her head to gaze at him for a second. "Stop," she said, her voice breathless. "This isn't necessary—"

"Has nothing to do with necessity."

"You don't need to prove that... Damn it all, just because you and I... Just forget it, okay?" She pushed away quickly as if suddenly afraid. Her fingers scrabbled for the handle of the door.

The latch opened. A rush of cool air swept into the cab, dispersing some of the condensation that had collected on the windows. But Jenner wasn't quite finished. He reached for her again and tightened his fingers into a firm, angry grip. "There's something you'd better understand about me," he said unevenly. "I don't *have* to do anything and I know it."

"Of course not. You're a McKee, aren't you?"

Growling a curse, he yanked her close to him again and his lips were no longer gentle, but came down with a punishing anger that was hot and wild and way out of control. She took a swift intake of breath and he pressed his advantage, his tongue delving deep into the warm, sweet recesses of her mouth.

Cody let out a squeal and Jenner let go, suddenly realizing what he was doing. Shooting a hard glare in his direction, Beth held Cody more tightly and slid from the seat of the cab. As her feet touched the pavement, she sent him a scathing look. "You made your point, Jenner," she said, taking deep gulps of air between words. "I've done my duty by coming here and you've done yours by meeting Cody. You don't owe him or me anything." Tossing her hair out of her face, she said, "Let's call it even."

"Even?"

Back stiff as sun-dried leather, she marched up the walk and disappeared inside.

"Hell," Jenner muttered. He reached across the seat and grabbed the door. A jolt of pain shot up his leg, raging like a prairie fire as it raced from his knee to his hip. Slamming the door, he straightened, ignored the throbbing and tore away from the curb.

Who was that woman? And why the hell did she get to him?

"It's pointless to stay any longer," Beth said as she eyed the small bedroom where she'd laid Cody in his playpen. Snuggled under a blanket, thumb firmly in his mouth, he'd barely awakened when Jenner had squeezed him during their kiss. She turned off the light and, with her mother following her, headed back to the kitchen. She needed a drink. Something stronger than coffee. Oh, for

God's sake, who was she kidding? She reached the kitchen, grabbed a wineglass, then shoved it back into the cupboard. Instead, she paused at the sink and splashed some water on her face. Her lips still felt the warm impressions of Jenner's mouth and her blood was still running hot. Too hot.

"But you just got here. Just because things didn't go so great with Jenner McKee is no reason to turn tail and run." Harriet reached for a pack of cigarettes on the counter.

"I'm *not* running!" Good Lord, she was protesting much too loudly.

"I thought you were staying for a week."

"I was, but—"

"But now, just like that—" Harriet snapped her fingers loudly "—you're heading back to the city."

"I belong in the city."

With a flick of her lighter, Harriet lit up and drew in a lungful of smoke. "If you say so." Her eyes darkened a second as if with a private pain, then she sighed.

"Mom…I only came back because of Mavis's letter. I felt coerced into seeing Jenner again."

"Did you?" Harriet leaned a hip against the counter, crossed her arms over her waist, and let her cigarette burn between her fingers as she studied her daughter. "I wasn't going to say anything. Lord knows I hate a meddling mother. But I feel it's only right to speak my mind.

"You've got your life all neatly planned out. Get another job working at a hospital, marry Stan and hope that he'll be the father to Cody that he doesn't have now. You'd like to pretend that Jenner McKee doesn't exist, that you don't give two cents about him, but the truth of the matter is that you're not over him. Probably never will be."

Beth dried her face on a towel hanging near the window. "I thought you didn't like the McKees."

"I don't. Don't trust 'em, neither."

"But—"

"But you'd better listen to your heart, girl, or you're going to end up in a whole lot more trouble than you're already in. Marrying Stan because he's stable, because he's nice, because he's financially secure won't make you forget Jenner."

"I already broke up with Stan and I don't know what you're—"

"You're too smart not to know. Face it, Beth. I see the way your eyes light up at the mention of Jenner. He stirs your blood, and don't tell me he doesn't. I've known enough men to recognize when one's got hold of my daughter's heart. I hoped that you'd forget him, that when you saw him again you'd see that he's not the man for you, but unless I miss my guess, that little plan backfired."

Harriet's words echoed Beth's own worrisome suspicions, but she wouldn't acknowledge them. "Jenner and I have a history, that's all."

"Not quite," Harriet reminded her. "The two of you have a son."

"Let's not talk about it now." Beth glanced out the window. "I left my car at the apartment. How about helping me retrieve it?"

Harriet grabbed her keys and purse. "All right, but just remember Jenner McKee has done nothing but hurt you."

The Black Anvil was one cut up from a dive. The bar had seen better years, the floor was made of worn oak slats polished by spilled beers, broken glass, dirt from unwiped boots and even occasional drops of blood from nosebleeds, the result of infrequent but angry fistfights.

Several of the regulars had bellied up to the bar. Jenner recognized Jeb Peterson, a big bear of a man who owned a sawmill in Dawson City and whose affinity for ale bulged over his belt. Slim Purcell was perched on the end stool and Jimmy Rickert was shooting pool. A cigarette hung limply from the corner of Jimmy's mouth as he concentrated on his game against Barry White who was somehow related to Ned Jansen. Rimrock was a small town—lots of people related to each other, everyone knowing everyone else's business.

Maybe it was time to move on.

But where? Sure as hell not back to the rodeo circuit, and he could never again hire on as a hand at a ranch. The owner would take one look at his leg and… Damn it all, he needed a drink. A stiff one.

Forcing his bad leg up to the bar, Jenner settled on a stool. "The usual," he said to the bartender.

Swiping the bar with a wet towel, Jake glanced down at Jenner's leg. "Actin' up again?"

"It's a pain in the butt. Literally."

Within seconds, a frosty mug and an open bottle sat in front of him. "Maybe you'd better get a second opinion on that knee and hip." Jake poured the brew into the mug.

"For what?"

"See if a little surgery will fix 'er up. Maybe then you could join the circuit again."

Jenner shook his head. "That's over for me," he said.

"Doesn't have to be."

"I've had enough surgeries. More'n my share."

The beer was cold and wet. Jenner sipped slowly and saw his reflection in the mirror—a broken-down, crippled cowboy who liked liquor a little too much.

His attention was drawn to the end of the bar where Wanda Tully, the waitress, was waiting for an order. Her pale blond hair looked silver in the dim light and she flashed Jenner her thousand-watt smile. Returning it with a sketchy wave, he wondered why he had no interest in Wanda. Twice divorced and working two jobs, she was a good woman who flirted with him just about every time he came through the door. Her legs were long, her breasts high, and though she was a little worn around the edges, she was still pretty. Wanda was a simple woman, one who would never place any demands on him, and right now he didn't need complications the likes of which he felt every time he was with Beth.

Yet, even here, nursing his beer, feeling Wanda's interested gaze sliding in his direction, he couldn't shake Beth's image from his mind. Her hair, a rich shade somewhere between dark brown and red, was long and full, and her cheekbones flared becomingly above hollow cheeks and full lips able to ease into a wide, sincere smile that seemed meant only for him.

"Son of a bitch," he growled, reaching for a handful of salty peanuts. Things weren't going as he'd planned. The pain in his leg was a constant reminder that his life had changed, and Beth, now that she was here, made it worse.

"Yep," Jake said, pouring a drink for a kid who looked barely twenty at the end of the bar, "if I were you, Jenner, I wouldn't give up working with the rodeo stock."

Jenner didn't argue. Gritting his teeth, he told himself that he could handle every stumbling block fate cast his way. He'd always believed that a man had to accept the cards that lady luck dealt him and make the best of any situation. Even though Jenner had been born to wealth, he'd shunned the old man's money as well as the trappings and responsibilities that came with a huge bank account.

From years riding rodeo, he'd broken more bones than he could count, been thrown, trampled and dragged by more horses than he cared to remember. Each time he'd climbed on the back of a range-tough rodeo bronc, he'd taken his life in his hands. There had always been the chance that he could have been killed or severely injured, so this…this useless leg shouldn't come as any big shock. He'd either get better or he wouldn't. But, deep down, it scared him. It scared the living hell out of him.

"Say, McKee—" a harsh voice broke into his thoughts "—I hear your family's offerin' a reward for information on the guy who started the fire in your stables and maybe had somethin' to do with your old man's accident.''

Jenner bristled. He twisted on his stool and saw three men huddled around a nearby table.

Fred Donner sniffed, then rubbed the edge of his sleeve under his nose. He'd posed the question. ''Is that right?''

''I don't know anything about it.''

The men exchanged glances. ''I heard it was ten thousand dollars.''

''Twenty-five,'' Ned Jansen said. He crushed out his cigarette. ''That's what I heard. Ain't that what you heard, Steve?'' he yelled at his son who was one of the men playing pool near the back room.

''Yep.'' Tall and rangy, Steve nodded but didn't break his concentration on the game. Money was riding on his ability to slam the next few balls into the pockets, and Steve Jansen had a reputation for knowing the value of a buck—even if his father didn't.

''Wasn't it thirty grand?'' the third man at the table, Cyrus Kellogg, asked. ''That's one helluva pile of money.'' Cyrus finished his drink and eyed Jenner. Near sixty, Cyrus owned the property on the other side of a stand of timber owned by the McKees.

''Could be just a rumor.'' Ned scowled.

''Nope,'' Fred insisted, his weathered face looking grim.

Years ago, he'd lost the water rights to his ranch because of dealing with Jonah and he'd never gotten over the sting of the loss. Fred had been one of the men living around Rimrock who'd counted Jonah as a friend. And he'd been stabbed in the back, Jenner thought. By the master of backstabbing, good ol' Jonah Phineas McKee.

''I heard it from Ada Patterson, and she knows everything that goes on 'round here.''

''Sometimes before it happens,'' Jenner agreed with a half smile. Besides being a gossiping busybody, Ada owned and was the editor of *The Rimrock Review*. Jenner finished his beer and set the mug back on the counter. A trace of foam settled back inside. "But, as I said, I don't know anything about it." Which wasn't all that surprising. It seemed that everything going on in the family these days was happening behind his back. He hadn't known about Mavis and her damned letter to Beth; nor had he been privy to some of the conversations with doctors about his...condition. Max and Skye had handled that while he was recuperating in the hospital. The insurance investigation was an ongoing battle that Max was handling while his mother was dealing with Rex Stone concerning his father's death.

Well, that's the way he'd always said he wanted it. He'd never shouldered any responsibility for McKee Enterprises while his father had been alive and he certainly wasn't going to take on any more obligations now.

Except maybe for Beth. Mavis might have started the business with Beth Crandall, but he sure as hell would be expected to finish it.

"Jeez, Jenner, you've always been a straight shooter. Jonah, well, he was one to talk in circles, tryin' to make things sound good for you when they were really good for him, and Max, hell, he's too much like your old man to do much better. But you—"

"I said I don't know anything and I don't. The rest of the family doesn't always tell me what's going on. Matter of fact, that's the way I like it!" Jenner stood. The men at the table turned back to their drinks, but he felt the weight of more than one interested gaze following him as he grabbed his crutches with jerky movements and made his way out of the building.

He didn't feel any better than he had when he'd swung into the bar and had been determined to drive Beth out of his mind. But the country music, clink of glasses and murmur of conversation hadn't stopped his thoughts from returning to her. The smoky atmosphere and thin odor of grease from a deep fryer hadn't overridden the fragrance of her perfume that still lingered in his nostrils. Nor had the malty flavor of his favorite brew washed away the taste of her lips.

"Damn it all, anyway." He tossed his crutches into the cab and whistled to Reuben. "You can ride up front," he told the old dog, who gladly bounded out of the truck bed and hopped through the open door.

Dogs were just so much easier to deal with than women.

"What the hell does this mean?" Jenner wagged the morning edition of *The Rimrock Review* under his brother's nose. Upon seeing the first edition and the story about the reward offered for the arrest and conviction of the culprit involved in Jonah's murder and/or the fire at the stables, Jenner had driven to the ranch and found his mother and brother in the kitchen, drinking coffee and sampling Kiki's sourdough biscuits as if they had nothing better to do. Jenner slapped the newspaper onto the top of the table where he'd eaten for a good part of his life.

"Want some coffee?" Kiki asked. A gray-haired, skinny woman with a sour disposition that didn't quite hide her heart of gold, she stared at Jenner as she always had, with steady disapproval.

"No, I don't want any coffee! I want answers."

"Kiki, please," Virginia said. "Jenner could use a cup."

"Maybe it should be decaf," Max suggested.

"Very funny!" Jenner pinned his brother with a hard glare. "You're all just full of surprises, aren't you?"

Max leaned back in his chair. "I take it you disapprove of the reward."

"Hell, yes, I disapprove. It's the single most foolhardy thing you've done yet. You're going to get every piece of slime in the county crawling out from under his rock to come out and try to collect."

"And we just might find the killer," his mother said

HOW TO GET YOUR
2 FREE BOOKS AND FREE GIFT

1. Peel off the 2 FREE BOOKS seal from the front cover. Place it in the space provided at right. This automatically entitles you to receive two free books and an exciting mystery gift.

2. Send back this card and you'll get 2 "The Best of the Best™" novels. These books have a combined cover price of $11.00 or more in the U.S. and $13.00 or more in Canada, but they are yours to keep absolutely FREE!

3. There's <u>no</u> catch. You're under <u>no</u> obligation to buy anything. We charge nothing – ZERO – for your first shipment. And you don't have to make any minimum number of purchases – not even one!

4. We call this line "The Best of the Best" because each month you'll receive the best books by the world's hottest authors. These authors show up time and time again on all the major bestseller lists and their books sell out as soon as they hit the stores. You'll like the convenience of getting them delivered to your home at our discount prices...and you'll love your subscriber newsletter featuring author news, horoscopes, recipes, book reviews and much more!

5. We hope that after receiving your free books you'll want to remain a subscriber. But the choice is yours – to continue or cancel, anytime at all! So why not take us up on our invitation, with no risk of any kind. You'll be glad you did!

6. And remember...we'll send you a mystery gift ABSOLUTELY FREE just for giving "The Best of the Best" a try!

MIRA ®

Visit us at
www.mirabooks.com

SPECIAL FREE GIFT!

We'll send you a fabulous mystery gift, absolutely FREE, simply for accepting our no-risk offer!

Books FREE!

DETACH AND MAIL CARD TODAY!

HURRY! Return this card promptly to get 2 FREE Books and a FREE Gift!

The Best of the Best ™

YES! Please send me the 2 FREE "The Best of the Best" novels and FREE gift for which I qualify. I understand that I am under no obligation to purchase anything further, as explained on the opposite page.

Affix peel-off 2 FREE BOOKS sticker here.

P-BB1-00
385 MDL CY2W

185 MDL CY2X

NAME (PLEASE PRINT CLEARLY)

ADDRESS

APT.# CITY

STATE/PROV. ZIP/POSTAL CODE

Offer limited to one per household and not valid to current subscribers of "The Best of the Best." All orders subject to approval. Books received may vary.

The Best of the Best™—Here's How it Works

If offer card is missing write to: The Best of the Best, 3010 Walden Ave., P.O. Box 1867, Buffalo, NY 14240-1867

BUSINESS REPLY MAIL
FIRST-CLASS MAIL   PERMIT NO. 717   BUFFALO NY

POSTAGE WILL BE PAID BY ADDRESSEE

THE BEST OF THE BEST
3010 WALDEN AVE
PO BOX 1867
BUFFALO NY   14240-9952

NO POSTAGE
NECESSARY
IF MAILED
IN THE
UNITED STATES

as Kiki set a cup of black coffee in front of an empty chair. "Come on, Jenner, sit down and—"

"For the love of Mike, Mom, don't you see what you've done?"

Virginia's gaze hardened. "Why don't you enlighten me?"

"You've drawn attention, Mom. Attention to the Rocking M. Attention to the family."

"And attention to you," Max said, pouring a thin stream of cream into his cup.

"That's right."

"And you don't like it."

"Damned straight." Placated somewhat, he shoved his crutches up against the wall near the bay window and dropped into one of the old kitchen chairs, which had the audacity to creak against his weight.

"You know, Jenner, this is a surprise. For years, you've worked hard to be in the limelight—riding rodeo and all, rebelling against Dad, getting your butt thrown in jail." His eyes narrowed as he took a gulp and watched his brother over the rim of his cup. "Seems to me, you've had a change of heart."

"I'm a cripple, or don't you remember?"

His mother gasped, but Max didn't so much as flinch. "But that's not it, is it?" Max guessed. "This has something to do with Beth Crandall and the boy."

Jenner hated it when Max could read his mind. He wanted to reach across the table and wrestle Max to the ground as he had when they were boys. He also wanted to lie. To say that Beth and her impish son meant nothing to him. But Jenner was through with lies. "I don't want them dragged into this."

"Because of the scandal," Virginia said.

"That's not it," Max said, and one side of his mouth lifted. "Jenner cares about them, doesn't want them hurt." His smile stretched even wider. "Hell, you think that boy is really yours, don't you?"

Virginia shook her head. "Oh, no—"

"Could be." Jenner grabbed a biscuit and slathered it with butter and blackberry jelly. "Whether he is or isn't, I don't want anyone from the *Review* or any damned news reporters from any other paper or magazine botherin' 'em."

"Or putting them in danger," Max surmised.

Jenner felt every muscle in his body tense with the thought of Cody or Beth being in jeopardy because of him. "That's right," he said, realizing that if anyone was going to protect them, it had to be him. From the corner of his eye, he caught a glimpse of his crutches. Some bodyguard he'd be. He couldn't even walk normally. His fingers clenched the handle of the cup. "I need to talk to Rex Stone."

"So you don't trust her."

"Do you?"

Max didn't say a word, but it was Virginia's turn to read his mind. "You'd use Rex to find out if Beth's telling the truth about the boy?" Clearing her throat, she set down her cup to stare at her second son. "Don't tell me you're falling for her story...or for her?"

"Course not," he said quickly, maybe too quickly, because Max, damn him, barked out a short laugh that called him a liar. Changing the subject, Jenner said, "There's something else we need to discuss."

"Shoot," Max said.

"I need to get back to work."

"You're not ready."

"I may never be ready." Jenner glared across the table. "I'm tired of being a hard-luck case."

"Jenner, you're not anything of the kind," Virginia whispered. "You're injured."

"And I can't stay cooped up another minute. Either I get my old job back helping Chester manage this place, or I go hunting for another."

There was silence. Aside from the click of a timer on

the stove and the swish of Kiki's broom across the floor, no one dared breathe a word.

"Don't you think it would be better if you gave yourself a rest and came back when you're a hundred percent?" Max asked.

"That may never happen." Jenner drained his cup. "You know it and I know it."

"Skye seems to think it's just a matter of time and maybe another surgery or two."

"I'm done being under the knife and recuperating!" Jenner growled, banging his fist on the table and making the spoons jump and cups rattle. Even fastidious Kiki gave up pushing her broom. "I need to get on with my life!"

Virginia tried to lay placating fingers on his, but he jerked back his hand as if her touch had burned him. "For the love of God, Mother, quit treating me like I'm a kid with a terminal illness!" He managed to pull himself to his feet with every bit of dignity he could muster and braced his hands on the tall back of the caned chair. "I'll be back tomorrow," he said to Max. "I either still have a job or I don't. You figure it out!"

Snatching his crutches savagely, he shoved them under his arms and plunged through the kitchen door.

"It's that Beth woman!" his mother whispered to Max. Jenner kept right on going as if he couldn't hear. "She's making him crazy, trying to pawn off that kid—"

"Cody could be his, Ma."

"Max, really! Don't even say it. Jenner would never get involved with Harriet Forrester's daughter!"

"Like hell," Jenner mumbled under his breath as he reached the front door and yanked it open. Fresh, cool autumn air, swept into the house. The door banged shut behind him.

It didn't really matter what Max or his mother thought, but one way or another, Jenner was going to get to the bottom of Beth's story and sort out truth from fiction. While he was at it, he'd have to make sure that the press—

and the damned culprit whoever he was—didn't discover that Cody might have McKee blood running through his veins.

"Right here—look for yourself!" Harriet wagged the morning edition of the *Review* under Beth's nose.

"What's so important it can't wait until after Cody's bath?" Beth glanced at the section of newspaper Harriet held out and caught sight of a bold headline for the want ads.

"'Wanted for full- or part-time position: Registered Nurse. Inquire at Post Office Box 762 in care of *The Rimrock Review.*' Didn't I tell you? I'll bet it's a job at the clinic or maybe over at Dawson Memorial Hospital."

"Great," Beth said, wrinkling her nose as Cody, his blue eyes gleaming mischievously, splashed water over the front of her blouse. "Then I could work with Dr. Donahue, who's supposed to soon become Dr. McKee. Max's fiancée." She grabbed a thick, rose-colored towel and pulled Cody, kicking and protesting loudly, out of the old tub. "Why don't I just find someone to torture me slowly? You know, sticks under my fingernails, or water dripped on my forehead, or—"

"Why you say that?" Cody asked, and Beth sighed.

"I'm just making jokes. I was trying to be funny."

Cody looked puzzled.

"It wasn't funny," Harriet assured her grandson. "Sometimes your mother has a very sick sense of humor."

Beth laughed and fluffed her son's hair with the towel. "So does your grandmother," she said with a wink.

"I don't know why it would be so bad to live here close to us—"

"Mom, we've been over this a hundred times on the phone."

Harriet threw up her hands and let the newspaper drop onto the floor. "Fine, then there's no use arguing, is there?'' she said and huffed out of the tiny bathroom. Beth's gaze fell to the front page of the *Review,* which had slid away from the classified advertising section. Her heart jolted as she read the headline: MCKEE FAMILY OF-FERS REWARD

A picture of Jonah McKee, dressed in a western-cut business suit and shaking hands with the mayor a few years back, graced one side of the column. Beth couldn't help feeling a tiny speck of anger at the man who had rejected his grandson and bilked the citizens of Rimrock of their hard-earned cash and property. She didn't wish him dead, but she wouldn't miss him, and only felt a stab of guilt when she realized that her son would never know his grandfather, nor would Jenner ever see his father again.

Skimming the article, she learned that Virginia McKee was offering twenty-five thousand dollars for information leading to the arrest and conviction of a suspect involved in the arson at the ranch or connected with Jonah's death. There were quotes from the sheriff's department and a private investigator named Rex Stone, all sounding overly confident, all assuring the community that justice eventually would be served.

''Splash Mommy 'gain,'' Cody said, reaching into the tub and thrusting another small handful of water at her.

''No more splashing.'' She dropped the paper. ''Come on, sport, let's get you out of here.'' She tried to wrap Cody in the towel, but he squealed and ran down the hall.

''I naked!'' he proclaimed, his damp little feet slapping against the bare floors. ''Can't catch Cody!''

Harriet poked her head into the bathroom. ''What in heaven's name—?''

''It's a game we play,'' Beth said, giving chase. Cody was already in the living room and opening the front door.

''No, Cody, not outside!''

''Outside!'' he insisted with glee. Shoving the door open, he hurtled through.

"Stop!" Beth commanded just as Cody laughed at her sorry attempt to catch him and his slippery little body collided with the long, jean-clad legs of his father.

Chapter Seven

"What's this?" Jenner asked, trying to keep his balance while he picked up the kid, who was as naked as a jaybird. "You're in your birthday suit!"

"I not!" Cody insisted. He wriggled to get away from Jenner's arms, but Jenner wouldn't let go. "I naked," he asserted, thrusting out his little chin.

"You sure are." Warm and wet and smelling of soap, the boy had a way of wedging himself into Jenner's heart, and for a second he wondered if it really mattered whether his blood was flowing in this kid's veins or not.

"I want down!" Cody said, squirming.

Beth came to the doorway and offered him a tentative smile. "Sorry. One of the convicts escaped."

"By boat, it looks like." Jenner couldn't help noticing the water on her blouse, which made the fabric more sheer and gave him a view of the edge of her bra and a tantalizing glimpse of the darker disk of her nipple. A strange knot began to unravel in his gut and he drew his eyes upward again.

She let out a soft laugh. "It's true. A person could drown trying to get this guy clean." She wrapped the towel around her son's wriggling, slick body and lifted him from Jenner's arms. "Bathing Cody is aerobic exercise. It's how I get my daily workout, isn't it?" she asked, sticking her nose into his damp hair.

The kid had left a wet impression on Jenner's shirt, and the scents of baby shampoo, soap and a fragrance he was beginning to associate with Beth lingered in his nostrils for a fleeting second.

"So what are you doing here?"

"I thought we should talk."

She hesitated a second, then smiled, "Come on in," she invited, holding the door open with her backside as Cody squirmed in her arms. Her hair was pulled into a ponytail that fell in wild curls past her shoulders and seemed to catch fire in the morning light.

Grabbing his damned crutches, he hoisted himself through the doorway and into the house. The furniture was worn but clean, the pictures on the walls colorful reproductions. Plants in bright pots were placed near the windows, and hand-crocheted afghans were tossed haphazardly over cushions that had seen better days.

Harriet Forrester was brushing away a speck of dust on an old Formica tabletop near the fireplace and trying to hide a surprised grin that bugged the hell out of Jenner. Dealing with Beth was difficult enough; he didn't want to have to face her mother.

"I think you know Mom."

He inclined his head. "We've met."

Harriet's lips twitched with undisguised pride. "Well, Jenner, what do you think of our boy?"

"Mom!"

Jenner bristled inside. Why did she want to put him on

the spot? With a shrug, he said, "Seems like an okay kid."

"Oh, he's way beyond okay. He's downright phenomenal, aren't you, baby?" she said, her gaze resting on her grandson for a second before her expression changed and her smile faded. Her lips pinched a little at the corners and she cleared her throat. "You know, I was wondering what it was that you and your grandmother want."

"Excuse me?"

"Mom, I don't think this is the time or place—" Beth interjected.

"What *I* want," he clarified.

"Mmm. And Mavis. She's in on this, too."

"Mom, don't—"

"We're talking about my grandson, Beth, my *only* grandson and we're in my house, so I think I'm entitled to a few answers. Now, Mavis wrote you, asking about Cody, demanding you come here and let Jenner meet him, on the excuse of his accident, but I want to know where we all stand." She lifted her chin a notch and looked over at Jenner again. "My family and yours run in different social circles and I've never hidden the fact that I'm not fond of anyone named McKee, but I'm willing to put the past aside for the sake of the child. However, I don't expect to be run over roughshod just because—"

"Please, Mom, for God's sake—"

"It's all right." Jenner held up a hand to stop Beth's protest, then turned his attention back to Harriet. "I don't blame you for wanting to know what's up. I didn't know anything about my grandmother's letter, just like I didn't know anything about Cody until Beth showed up at the Rocking M a few days ago. To be honest, I'm not even sure what's truth and what's fiction around here. I'm trying to sort it out."

"You still think I'm lying," Beth accused, her green eyes snapping with fury.

He didn't bother answering.

Harriet snorted, and Beth, holding a swaddled Cody, said coldly, "I don't need to be a part of this. You two, with all your built-in predjudices about each other, work this out. You can inform me later. Right now, I'm going to get my son dressed before he freezes to death."

"Or escapes again," Jenner said.

Beth turned on her heel, and walking smartly through an archway that led down a hall to the bedroom, she disappeared. He itched to follow her, to have it out with her once and for all, to hold her in his arms and...oh, hell, what was he thinking?

"You have a lotta nerve," Harriet said quietly. She hardly looked old enough to be Beth's mother.

"So I've been told."

"Do you honestly think Beth would come back here and put her heart and pride and child on the line all for the sake of a lie? Think about it!"

"Depends on how much money is involved, I suspect."

She reached for a partially smoked pack of cigarettes and shook one out. Her fingers seemed to tremble slightly as she placed the fliter tip into her mouth. "Money! Always money with you people."

"With most people."

Harriet struck a match and held the flame to the tip of her cigarette. "You sure think you can run things, don't you? Just like your father." A shadow crossed her eyes as she waved out her match and drew on her cigarette. "He took the cake, that one. You know, I have half a mind to call up Mavis and tell her to back off."

Despite his anger, Jenner felt the corner of his mouth lift a little as he thought about Harriet and Mavis squaring off. Kind of a battle of the grandmothers. "I've already tried. It didn't work."

Harriet didn't see an ounce of humor in the situation. "You be careful, Jenner McKee," she advised as she shot an angry plume of smoke from the corner of her mouth.

"Don't think you can do the kind of fast shuffle your dad was so good at."

"I'm not like my dad," he said evenly, and Harriet, through a haze of smoke, gave him the once-over.

"Aren't you?"

"No way." His eyes narrowed as he studied the woman whom he'd heard rumors about all his life. Rumors that linked her to just about every available male in Rimrock. Harriet Winward Crandall Something-or-other Forrester. There had been other names he'd heard, too. Floozy. Whore. Bimbo. You name it and Harriet had been called it. Though she'd never been linked to any married men, Jenner couldn't help but wonder if she'd been involved with his father. Maybe it was the way she'd nearly sneered when she'd brought Jonah up, as if she'd been familiar with him. That thought made him uneasy as he watched her take a seat on a worn couch and motion for him to sit, as well.

"So what're your plans?"

"Haven't got any."

"McKees always have plans."

He'd been polite long enough. "Let's be straight with each other, Mrs. Forrester—"

"Harriet. Just call me Harriet."

"Okay. Ever since I walked through the door you've been using me for a punching bag." Wielding his crutches, he moved so that he was standing directly over her. "So why don't you give me your best shot and tell me what it is you don't like about me?"

"You mean other than the fact that you used my daughter—got her pregnant—then left without a backward glance? Or if that's not good enough, let's take ridiculing her when she gathered the nerve to come and tell you about Cody."

"*After* the letter from Mavis."

"Whatever." She waved impatiently, and smoke

swirled around the hand holding her cigarette. "The point is, it took guts to come back here and face you."

"It would've taken more a couple of years ago."

"Back then she came up against Jonah. You do remember your father, don't you? How he tried to manipulate everyone in this town?" With a final drag, she shook her head, then jabbed out her cigarette in a glass ashtray. "He didn't want you tied down to my daughter and he wouldn't accept the fact that Cody was his grandson. Prince of a fella, your old man."

"She should have talked to me."

"You should've stuck around. Loving 'em and leaving 'em isn't exactly admirable."

"I think that's enough, Mom," Beth said, her cheeks flushed slightly, as if she'd heard more than she should have when she walked back into the room.

Jenner offered a lazy smile. "Your mother was only expressing her opinon about my family. No harm done."

Cody ran pell-mell into the living room, his feet in new sneakers pounding loudly. His hair was combed and he was wearing a pair of stiff new Levi's. Grabbing a book from a basket near the fireplace, he crawled onto the couch and smiled up at his grandmother. "You read?" he asked her, his eyes glinting as if he knew how adorable he was.

"Of course I will."

"I think you and I should talk," Beth said to Jenner, then shot her mother a meaningful glance. "Alone."

"Fine with me," Harriet said. "I was hoping to take Cody into town later anyway."

"That would probably be a good idea."

This was gonna be trouble. If Jenner stuck around, Beth was going to mess up his mind, sure as shootin'. But he couldn't very well just walk out on her. Besides, a part of him was curious to know what she had up her sleeve this time.

"All right," he drawled.

"Then you and I," Harriet said, giving her grandson a wink, "will go down to the Pancake Hutt where Grandma works. Since it's my day off, we'll splurge on lunch and I'll show you off to some of my friends. I'll buy you a Belgian waffle with strawberry jam and whipped cream. How would you like that?"

"Mommy come?" Cody said, and his brow furrowed.

"Not this time."

"Mommy come!" This time it was a command.

"I'll be back soon, sweetheart," Beth promised.

"Noo!" He started to wail and Beth picked him up. He let his picture book fall to the floor. "You stay! Mommy, you stay!"

Beth bit her lip, obviously torn. "We'll be back soon," she said to the boy, and Cody, clinging even more tenaciously to his mother, glared up at Jenner.

"No!"

"It'll be all right, honey," Beth whispered, holding the boy close. "I'll bring you a surprise."

"You stay with me!"

"I can't, honey, really."

"Let me take him. You two run along." Harriet peeled her distraught grandson from Beth. "We'll be fine. The minute you leave this'll be over."

Beth didn't look convinced as she grabbed a jean jacket from the coat tree standing guard near the front door. "I can drive—"

"No!" he snapped quickly as he pushed his crutches out in front of him and concentrated on limping as little as possible. "I'll drive." Cody's wails followed them to the front porch and Beth cast a guilty look behind her as she crawled into the cab of his truck and he threw his damned crutches in the back. Now what?

Trying to ignore the sounds of her son's cries, Beth eyed Jenner and wished she didn't care for him. Not at all. It wasn't as if she was in love with him or anything, but there was still a part of her that found him fascinating—on a purely sensual level. She tried to convince herself that her feelings existed simply because he was the father of her child, that of course she should care for him, but deep inside she worried that she still might harbor a little seed of the old crush she'd had on him. It was silly, really, but there it was, buried deep in the back of her mind, ready to sprout if given the least bit of encouragement.

Which she wouldn't get from Jenner, so she was safe. Out of habit, she checked her watch.

"You have to be somewhere?" he asked, braking for a red light.

"It's just that Cody...he doesn't like it when I leave him. I really shouldn't be away a long time."

"What about when you work?"

She shrugged a shoulder. "He adjusts. I've got a wonderful baby-sitter who treats him like he's one of her own grandkids."

"You mean she spoils him."

"You can't spoil a two-year-old," she said defensively. She felt her maternal talons beginning to show.

"You spoil him, too."

"As I said—"

"Yeah, yeah, I heard. 'You can't spoil a two-year-old.' Well, that's a pile of B.S. and we both know it." He slid her a glance that could cut through steel, then shifted into first gear as the light changed.

"So now you're the expert on child rearing?" she asked, arching a dubious eyebrow as he worked gas, brake and clutch with relative ease.

"Nope, just an expert on being spoiled rotten. My father thought you could buy a kid's affection and my mother always worked under the assumption that being a slave to your husband and your kids would assure you a place in heaven or some such crap. Sometimes she played the martyr so well I was certain she'd be cannonized." He snorted and his hands seemed to grip the wheel a little tighter. "It doesn't take a genius to see where my folks screwed up."

"You all seemed to survive."

"If that's what you want to call it." He was driving north where the highway cut through the foothills of the mountains. The sun was shining, but thin clouds had appeared on the horizon. "Max did everything he could to please Dad. Became a damned yes-man for a while. And Mom, hell, she knew Dad cheated on her, but she pretended that it didn't happen, that he was faithful. She still goes around acting as if he were some kind of saint. Casey's a hothead, always runnin' off at the mouth and getting herself in trouble. Doesn't seem to know what she wants out of life. Like I said, I know spoiled."

"And what about you?" Beth asked as he drove past the tree-lined lane leading to the ranch house.

"Spoiled rotten." His smile turned cynical. "I did everything I could to be a pain in the old man's backside. It seemed to work, too," he admitted, though he didn't seem pleased with himself.

Giving the wheel a sharp turn, he drove off the main road and onto an overgrown gravel drive that was barely more than two ruts cutting through a stand of pine. A gate with a No Trespassing sign nailed to the top rail warned them off the property, but Jenner ignored the faded red lettering as he climbed out of the truck, grabbed his crutches and hobbled to the fence. After extracting a ring of keys from his pocket, he tried several in the rusted lock before the latch gave way and the chain fell to the ground.

"Drive through," he yelled, pushing the gate. It opened with a squeal of seldom-used hinges.

Beth slid behind the wheel and shoved the pickup into first. Barely able to reach the pedals, she eased the truck through the opening and Jenner closed the gate. A second later, he was back in the truck and she was sliding across the seat. "Mind telling me where we're going?"

"To my place."

"Your place," she repeated. "But I thought you lived in the apartment."

"Temporary accommodations." He angled the nose of the pickup up a steep slope. The truck bucked as it hit unseen rocks, and long, dry grass and thistles scraped the undercarriage. "I wanted you to see something."

"What?"

He cast her a glance that nearly melted her bones. Her breath stalled somewhere above her lungs and her heart began to beat more quickly.

They were nearly at the crest of a hill when the road seemed to give out altogether. Jenner didn't even slow down, just kept driving through the openings in the trees until the pines gave way to a meadow. He cut the engine, then climbed out of the cab. Cursing his crutches, he managed to climb the short distance to the crest of the hill with its view of the valley below.

"What is this place?" She saw the John Day River, little more than a blue-green thread weaving along the bottom of the canyon, and the ridges of red rock that she'd always viewed from the valley floor were now huge bolders that felt the sun's warming rays.

The town of Rimrock was visible, a webbing of streets and buildings spreading around the bend in the river.

"This was the original homestead of the McKee family." He pointed to a cabin standing near the edge of the clearing. It was small, barely more than one room from the looks of it, the porch sagging, the roof caved in. Other nearby buildings, sunbleached and tumbling down, were covered in brambles. Farther away was a graveyard, fenced and overgrown, the last resting place of McKee pioneers, Beth guessed.

"Over there—" Jenner motioned beyond the edge of a cliff "—is a parcel that used to be Ned Jansen's copper mine—well, at least the back of it. The main entrance is half a mile west of here." He leaned against one of the boulders and set his crutches beside him. With one hand shading his eyes against the sunlight, he pointed to the south. "That bit over there is still part of the Rocking M. It's kept separate from the homestead, but I guess this could all be considered part of it because McKee Enterprises owns the old copper mine."

"The mine is abandoned, though, isn't it?" Beth asked. She was standing so close to him she could see the small creases in his skin caused by hours of squinting against the sun. His scent drifted on the breeze. All male and clean, it made her insides shiver in anticipation.

"*Was* abandoned. Jansen had just about given up on it—thought he'd mined all the copper out of it. His team of geologists agreed."

"So why did your father buy it?" she asked, dreading the question, dreading the answer more.

"Well, Ned got himself into some trouble. He's been married a couple of times and divorced. The divorces were expensive. When the mine seemed worthless, he had to borrow money somewhere and the banks turned him down." He leaned back and studied her, his gaze lingering on her face. "But he was in luck. Good ol' Jonah P. McKee was more than willing to help bail an old friend out of trouble. He loaned Ned enough money to get his wives off his back and pay off some overdue child support and alimony. Took the mine as collateral. Ned could never repay him, of course, and Jonah ended up with the mine. And lo and behold, guess what?"

A knot of tension had been tightening in Beth's stomach. She hardly dared breathe because she knew the answer. "The mine was valuable."

"Give the lady a prize!" Jenner mocked. "It was valuable, all right, probably worth millions in copper and silver."

"But why would Ned's own team of geologists lie to him?"

Shrugging his shoulders, Jenner stared into the distance. "I don't have any proof, but my guess is that they were bought off—paid more money than they would ever see in their lives—to fudge their reports.''

"You're saying that your father had his eye on the mine all along?"

"Of course he did! Don't you understand? Haven't you figured the old man out yet? Jonah never got involved in any deal unless it would make him money. That was the bottom line. Always. No exceptions.'' Pain seemed to flicker in his blue gaze.

"What did Ned do?"

"When he found out?" Jenner shrugged. "Nothin'. He couldn't do a thing. Jonah hadn't done anything illegal.''

"Except bribe the experts.''

"But that couldn't be proven, could it? And Ned tried to sue everyone involved, but his geologists had moved out of state, dissolved their partnership. Ned had no recourse because he couldn't prove criminal intent. Even geologists make mistakes now and again.''

The wind crept up the hillside and goose bumps rose on Beth's skin. She rubbed her arms and wondered about the man Jenner had called father, the man who had rejected her son as his grandchild. She remembered him as imposing, with thick white hair that ruffled in the breeze. She'd gone to the ranch to find Jenner, and instead had come face-to-face with his father. Jonah had just dismounted. A cigar had been clamped between his teeth, a rifle clenched firmly in his hands. Seven or eight squirrel carcasses were tethered to his saddle, little, bloody scraps of brown fur that were his trophies for the day.

"You're here lookin' for Jenner, unless I miss my guess.'' His smile had almost seemed sincere as he'd closed the gate behind him and motioned for one of the hands to deal with his horse. "You just missed him. He took off two days ago for some rodeo in Canada, I think. Alberta or British Columbia, I b'lieve.''

"I need to talk to him.''

"Because of the baby." She'd been stunned, had felt

her skin go white. "This is a small town—bad news travels fast."

"But no one knows. Just me and Dr.—" Her words had nearly strangled in her throat when she'd seen the flicker in Jonah's eyes.

"Oh, hell, there's plenty of people who work in the clinic. Word's bound to get out."

"But not about the father."

Jonah had shrugged, struck a match against the fence post, and puffed on his cigar. "Doesn't matter. Jenner'll never claim the kid and Doc Fletcher can arrange to have the whole business dealt with. There's a physician in Dawson City who'll—"

"No!" she wrapped her arms protectively around her middle. Jonah's eyes had narrowed; he wasn't used to people disagreeing with him. "I'm not going to get rid of this baby."

"It's not a child yet."

"It's your grandchild, Mr. McKee."

His face had turned to stone. "It's a bastard—nothing more. Things would be different if you and Jenner were dating seriously, but you aren't. He's about to become engaged to Nora Bateman and I won't have you ruining his life, or hers."

"I just want to talk to him."

"Why?" He rolled the cigar between his teeth. "Do you think he even remembers you? He and Nora, they broke up a few months back and Jenner decided to sow a few wild oats, kick up his heels, but now he and Nora are planning to get married and you're just one of a dozen or so women he's had a fling with."

She swallowed hard and felt like being sick.

"What?" Jonah asked, smoke sailing into the sky. "You didn't think you were special to him, did ya?" He barked out a laugh that rattled her to the bone. "Jenner's not the settlin' down kind. If it wasn't that he's been in love with Nora since he was sixteen, I wouldn't believe he'd ever get married. But he loves that gal. Always has. Always will.''

There was more than a trace of truth in Jonah's words. Beth had seen Jenner and Nora together years before. They'd dated in high school and even later when he was on the road. Then Nora had gone off to college and Beth had assumed they'd broken up. It had been a long time ago.

"It just took Jenner a long time to grow up, but now he's ready to take a wife." His smile was brittle. "Nora, now she's a good girl, comes from a good family in town. The Batemans have been in Rimrock nearly as long as the McKees. Nora's parents have been married nearly thirty years and they're strong, upstanding citizens who've worked hard and increased their land." He chuckled and puffed on the cigar. "Nora, she's just the girl for Jenner."

Beth had eventually believed him and, she realized now with a guilty conscience, accepted his bribe—money to help her start a new life far away from Rimrock and his son. Jonah had convinced her that Jenner didn't want her or her child in his life, and she'd turned heel and ran, never trying to contact Jenner again.

"Are you all right?"

Jenner's voice brought her crashing back to the present, and she shoved the image of Jonah from her mind. "Fine," she lied. "But you didn't bring me up here to tell me about your father's business dealings."

"That's true," he admitted, rubbing his hand around the back of his neck. "We should have that talk you wanted and I thought we should get some things straight about Cody."

Here it comes, she thought, bracing herself. "Something other than the fact that I'm spoiling him?"

He studied her so intently she wanted to step back. Instead, she held her ground and wrapped her arms around her middle. "You *are* spoiling him, but I'm not too worried about that—"

"You shouldn't be."

"But I am concerned about his safety."

"Safety?" she repeated. "Look, Jenner, I take good care of him! You're the one who's talking about letting him catch crawdads and ride horses and—oh!" Suddenly Jenner reached out, curled his fingers over her arm and yanked her hard against him—so hard he nearly fell over.

"This isn't about keeping little fingers away from hot stoves," he said through lips that barely moved.

"Then...what?" She tried to keep her mind on the conversation because he was telling her something important, but she couldn't ignore the feel of his hands, rough and possessive, surrounding her wrist, nor could she force her gaze away from the blue depths of his. She licked her lips and thought she heard him groan, but it could have been the soft sigh of the wind rushing through the canyon.

"All this business with my father—his supposed murder."

"That has nothing to do with Cody." Fear, stark and piercing, drove a stake into her heart.

"Maybe, maybe not. There was also the fire in the stables. The fire chief is calling it arson. People seem to think that the same person was probably involved—someone with an ax to grind against the McKees."

"But—"

"Some sicko's got it in for my family. A maniac with a helluva grudge. No one seems to know which way he'll turn, but the sheriff doesn't think he's gonna stop—not until he gets his vengeance, whatever the hell that is."

"I still don't understand."

"If this sleazeball heard you claiming that Cody's my boy," he said, his skin stretched tight over his face, "you could be placing your son in danger."

"*What?*" Beth shook her head. She refused to hear any of this craziness. But a chill as cold as death crept through her blood. "I can't believe—"

"You'd better," he insisted, his fingers digging more

deeply into her flesh. "Max's worried about Hillary. He never lets her out of his sight when she's visiting him and he's warned Hillary's mother, but Colleen has her hands full with twin girls about Cody's age and doesn't always have time."

"But no one knows about Cody."

"Except you and me and everyone at the ranch and whoever else your mother or my grandmother wants to know! Look, I'm not trying to scare you, Beth—"

"But you are!"

"I just want you to be careful."

She swallowed with difficulty. If anything ever happened to her son... "Maybe we should get back," she said, her voice the barest of whispers.

"That's a good idea." But he didn't make any move to release her. He studied her mouth for a heartbeat before lowering his head and brushing his lips slowly across her own. Beth told herself to pull away from him, to fight this stupid attraction she felt for him, but instead she opened her mouth to him and felt his tongue slide easily between her teeth.

Don't! For God's sake, Beth, don't do this! her mind was screaming, but her body was all too willing.

The voice in her head was silenced as his arms surrounded her, dragging her roughly against the straining contours of his body. Whether he planned to tumble to the ground or whether Jenner simply lost his balance, she never knew, but soon they fell onto the dry grass, kissing hungrily, hearts beating a savage rhythm. His mouth was warm and anxious, his fingers strong, as he pressed against the small of her back, forcing her against him with an urgency that caused her blood to heat as it had only once before—with Jenner on the night that Cody had been conceived.

His hands tangled in her hair and he kissed her as if he would never stop, his lips hard and demanding, his tongue supple, his body straining for release. Somewhere in the back of her mind, she knew she should stop him, that kissing him was dangerous, that she would never recover from the mistake of making love with him. Yet she couldn't force the words of denial over her tongue.

Her skin was on fire, and she felt the bulge beneath his jeans, the rough denim straining against the seams. Slowly, as if giving her time to tell him to stop, he reached beneath her jacket, found the hem of her sweater, and inched his fingers up her ribs. She gasped as his hand shoved the cup of her bra aside to grasp her breast. His thumb moved restlessly over her nipple and she arched beneath him.

"That's it," he whispered, kissing her hungrily as he shoved the jacket from her shoulders and pulled the sweater over her head. Then she was nearly naked, her bra twisted beneath one breast. While looking deep into her eyes, he traced the edge of her nipple with a finger and watched as her abdomen sucked in. "God, you're incredible," he said, then held her breast and slowly lowered his head to brush the tip with his lips.

A jolt shot through her the moment his tongue traced the path his finger had taken earlier. Grabbing the back of his head, she held him close to her, and he eagerly took her breast in his mouth, sucking as if thirsty for all of her.

Heat swirled deep in her innermost core. Wet and hot and dark, the want uncurled through her blood. She felt him shift, knew that he'd unhooked her bra and dropped it somewhere in the grass as he'd rolled her on top of him so that he could bury his face in her breasts, tasting of one succulent nipple before turning to the other.

When he finally looked up at her, his face was flushed, his eyes a deep, dangerous blue. Without a word, he slipped his hand beneath the waistband of her jeans, popping the top button. Her throat turned to sand. He moved his hand. Fingers grazed her skin and another button popped, the sound seeming to ricochet off the surrounding

hills. Pop. Pop. Pop. His hand was beneath her under-
pants, parting the nest of curls, delving deep inside her.

"Is this what you want?"

Breaking through the haze of their lovemaking, his
voice shocked her.

Yes! She tried to clear her mind, but his hands were
still tantalizing her, and he breathed hotly across her nipple, causing it to grow harder still. The hollow ache within
her begged to be filled. "I..."

"What, Beth? Tell me." His fingers moved and she
moaned, tossing back her head, letting her hair fall down
her back.

"Jenner," she whispered hoarsely.

"Is this what you want? Is this why you came to me?"

"Yes. No. I don't know."

He froze and his eyes focused. "Damn it all." Angrily,
he rolled away from her, apparently disgusted with himself as well as her. "Look, let's get out of here before we
do something we'll both regret later." He saw her
sweater, picked it up and tossed it to her. Then he hitched
himself over to where his crutches lay and hauled himself
onto his feet.

Beth felt like she'd been slapped in the face. He'd
wanted her; she'd responded to his desire, noticed the
swelling in his jeans. And yet he'd rejected her, acted as
if she'd planned to seduce him. Mortified, Beth struggled
into her clothes, fastening her bra and pulling her sweater
over her head with lightning speed. She felt the heat in
her cheeks, knew she was blushing, and wondered what
in the world she'd been doing kissing Jenner, holding Jenner, letting him touch her in the most intimate of places.
"I didn't mean to—"

"Neither did I."

"But—"

"Let's just go, okay? No need to talk about it." He
planted his crutches firmly in front of him and, with jerk-

ing movements, plunged toward the truck. "I should never have brought you here."

"Don't blame yourself."

"Oh, and who should I blame?"

Anger and frustration building in her blood, she shook the grass from her hair and started after him. "Don't blame anyone, okay? There's no reason to try to lay blame."

"Hell," he muttered.

"We both just made a mistake. No big deal," she said, feeling the lie trip on her tongue. It was a big deal and she should never have let it happen. But it was over...or was it? How could she have been so stupid? Hadn't she already learned her lesson where Jenner McKee was concerned?

Stomping after him, she saw his crutch slip just before he reached the pickup. He swore and fell to the ground with a thud. As his bad leg crumpled beneath him, he let out a cry.

"Jenner!" Beth quickly ran to his aid and dropped to her knees next to him.

"Leave me alone!"

"Let me see."

He grabbed her then and his eyes flared in pain. "I said leave me alone, for God's sake. It'll be fine!"

"Let me be the judge of that."

"You can't judge anything." He tried to move, his face paled, and his breath hissed between his teeth. "Son of a—!"

"Come on, let me help you—" She tried to touch his arm, but he yanked it away.

His nostrils flared. "I said—"

"I heard you. Loud and clear. But I'm just trying to help. I'm a nurse, for crying out loud."

"Big deal. I don't want or need any help!" he asserted as he found one crutch that had fallen into a clump of sagebrush. Gritting his teeth, he hauled himself upright.

The second crutch was farther down the hillside, and though he grumbled at her, Beth retrieved it. "You could let people help you, you know. It's not a sign of weakness."

"I said I don't want any help. Hell, you're as bad as my family!" His face was a ghastly shade of white and he winced as he plunged the crutches ahead of him and tried to walk, but he didn't say another word, only hobbled to the driver's side of the truck and slammed his crutches into the bed. "You gettin' in?" he demanded, shooting her a glance that was so hostile she nearly backed up a step. "I'd hold the door for you, but—"

"Don't!" Her temper ignited. His head snapped up and she held his gaze. "Don't you ever patronize me, and for God's sake, don't act like I'm pitying you just because I want to help you! I'm a medical professional and I think we should immobilize your leg, stretch you out in the back, and run you into the nearest emergency room."

"No way."

"But—"

"I said I'm fine, Beth. Just get in the damned truck."

"Only if you let me drive."

"Forget it."

"You're hurt, for crying out loud!"

"And I'm not gettin' any better waitin' on you!"

With renewed determination, she stalked to the driver's side and waited. "For once in your life, Jenner McKee, let someone do you a favor. Quit being so damned bullheaded and let me drive so that you don't kill us both."

"I said no."

She crossed her arms firmly under her breasts and shot him an authoritative glare that she'd practiced on her most recalcitrant patients. "I'm not about to risk my neck just because you're reckless with yours. I'm a mother and Cody's counting on me coming home in one piece, which I fully intend to do, even if his father is a muleheaded, stubborn jerk who doesn't know a helping hand or an olive branch when he sees one!''

"Oh, hell." Grumbling all the way, he climbed into the cab and slid over to the passenger side. Beth noticed the way he winced as he dragged his bad leg across the seat, swung it under the dash, then slumped against the door. She climbed behind the wheel and managed to start the old truck. She caught a glimpse of the weathered cabin and the grass that had been flattened during their love-making and she felt like a fool all over again.

Why had she let him kiss her? Why couldn't she resist him?

From the corner of her eye, she caught him watching her, his eyelids at half-mast, and she felt an uneasy fluttering in her stomach, the way she always did when he stared at her intently.

She drove slowly down the hillside, paused and let the truck idle on the far side of the gate, then swung it shut and climbed back in. Jenner didn't say a word. In fact, he spent the entire ride back to town in brooding silence.

When she turned onto the street where his apartment house was located, he roused. "You can take me to your place."

"I'll walk," she insisted. "It's less than a mile."

"I'll drive you."

"I *want* to walk, Jenner," she insisted and parked the truck near the curb.

"For the love of God, woman," he grumbled, but didn't protest any further. She let him get out of the truck by himself, but he had no choice but to accept her help getting downstairs. He slung his arm over her shoulders and used a single crutch. By the time he was unlocking the door to his apartment, he was sweating and gritting his teeth against the pain.

"Let me get Skye—"

"Don't even think about it, Beth." He yanked out the key and shouldered open the door. Once inside, she frowned. There wasn't a bed to stretch him out on, only a bedroll on the cracked tile floor. "Maybe I'd better take you to the Rocking M."

He let out a humorless laugh. "Not on your life."

"But you need a bed. And how're you going to get to the bathroom?"

"I'll manage," he said as he settled onto the bedroll and groaned.

She wasn't convinced and decided that she couldn't leave him to fend for himself. She knew he wasn't going to like what she planned, but she had an obligation to him, didn't she? She couldn't just leave him lying on the floor in agony. "Okay, Jenner, I want to look at your leg, so I'm going to ask you to take off your boots and jeans. I'll help—"

"Like hell!"

"It's either that or I call your mother or the clinic."

His fists clenched. "For God's sake, woman, just leave me alone."

"Can't do it," she said, determined to win this battle. "Now, are you going to help me, or am I going to have to strip you myself?"

"You really don't know when to quit, do you?" Jenner glared up at her as she knelt next to him. "Or is it that you just want a peek at what I've got in my pants?"

"Don't try to intimidate me." Beth was already kneeling at the end of the bedroll, ready to help remove his boots.

"This is—"

"Necessary," she supplied crisply and reached for the heel of his boot. She thought he might wrest his foot away, but he didn't.

"Damn it all, anyway," he growled but slid out of first one, then the other.

"Good. Now the jeans."

"My God," he muttered, but undid his belt. She looked away, but her back stiffened as she heard the buttons of his fly pop in rapid succession—like her own had done only an hour before.

Cursing under his breath, he tried to struggle out of his jeans, and Beth, telling herself that he was now just a patient, helped him squirm away from the denim. Her breath caught as she saw his legs, white from lack of sun, sprinkled with dark hair and firmly muscled, though his left leg was thinner than the right. A bruise and swelling had already formed at his ankle and she examined it carefully, fingers probing gently against the discolored flesh. ''Can you move it?''

''Couldn't much before.''

''Tell me if this hurts.'' Gently rotating his foot, she watched him and saw the pain flare in his eyes.

His breath whistled over his teeth. ''Hell, yes, it hurts,'' he said.

''Looks like you've sprained it…maybe more.'' Carefully she let go of his foot and tried not to notice that the front of his Jockey shorts was straining over a large swelling. ''I think you should see a doctor.''

''Why doesn't that surprise me?'' He was lying faceup, his hands beneath his head so that he could study her. ''The thing is that doctors can't do anything for me. They've already tried, or can't you see the scars?''

She'd noticed them, of course.

''I've got more plastic and metal in that leg than I've got bone and muscle.''

''I doubt that. But it's all the more reason for you to see a—''

''Come here,'' he said in a voice so low she could barely hear him.

''What?'' she said, then caught his gaze. Cloudy like blue smoke, filled with desire.

''Come here, Beth.''

''I'm here.…''

''Closer.''

''Jenner, I don't think that—''

"Don't think, Beth," he said, lowering his hands and reaching for her. Strong arms surrounded her and he pulled her steadily closer, so that she was lying half on top of him. He dragged her head to his, and hard, anxious lips claimed hers with a hunger that touched a forbidden spot in her heart. "You want to make me feel better, don't you?"

She'd told herself that she wouldn't get involved with him, that she wouldn't touch him, that she wouldn't fall for him, and yet here she was kissing him and feeling the strength of his body in hers.

His tongue pressed against her teeth and she opened her mouth to him like a flower to the sun, with no resistance. His hands slid beneath her sweater and pressed warmly against her back.

Thoughts of denial seeped from her mind as he touched her, his fingers drawing lines along her spine, his lips warm and wet as he kissed her lips, her eyes, her throat. A low moan escaped her throat as he unhooked her bra and his fingers found her breasts.

"Damn," he whispered hoarsely. "I know that I said we should stop, but I can't." His hands kneaded her breasts and she seemed to melt into him. The same deep, moist warmth that she'd felt before uncoiled inside her. Desire, forbidden and dark, slid through her blood.

He pushed the sweater and bra over her head, then pressed moist kisses to her throat and collarbone. She cradled his head as he touched her, teasing her nipples with his fingers before tasting them with his lips.

Beth sighed as he held her close and suckled and she didn't stop him when he found the waistband of her jeans and quickly removed them from her. Anxious fingers pushed her legs apart to delve into her. She quivered, for it had been so long, but his probing was gentle, at first slowly exploring, then touching that most vital spot in faster and faster strokes until she gasped his name and convulsed before falling atop him.

He kissed her again and gazed into her eyes, silently asking. Without words, begging.

Still drenched in her own sweat, she swallowed against a suddenly dry throat and kissed him. Hard. Without a trace of guilt. Her fingers found the buttons of his shirt and she pushed the soft flannel over his shoulders and down his arms. The smell of fresh air and grass still clung to him and he tasted of salt as she kissed his neck, his shoulders, and then slid down to press her mouth against his flat nipples.

"Oh, baby," he whispered, his fingers tangling in her hair as she teased him and felt him strain upward. "Beth, please..."

Her fingers found the waistband of his shorts and he groaned, whether in agony or pleasure she couldn't tell. "Whatever you want," she whispered against his skin and licked his abdomen.

He shuddered. "I don't know—I'm not sure that I can..."

Stripping him quickly, she lay beside him, naked body next to naked body. "Just lie there," she whispered, her fingers reaching forward to touch him and bring him to a release. "I'll do all the work."

His fingers twined in her hair as he dragged her head closer and his lips found hers. With slow, firm strokes she found a way to ease his pain.

Chapter Eight

Good Lord, what had she done? Nearly made love to Jenner McKee—just like before. As she lay in his arms, listening to his gentle breathing, she wanted to snuggle against him, pretend that everything was right with the world, but she couldn't. She had a son to think about, a life to live. A life that didn't include Jenner.

She reached for her clothes and the strong arm surrounding her tightened. Hand clasped firmly over her breast, Jenner cradled her close.

"I think I'd better go," she said, rolling over to gaze into slumberous blue eyes.

He managed a crooked smile. "So soon?" He shoved a strand of hair from her eyes. "I can think of other things we could do."

She blushed at the turn of her thoughts. "Any more things you come up with, cowboy, can only spell trouble."

"What's wrong with trouble?" He shifted, half-rolling

atop her and wincing a little as he moved. His skin was tight over well-defined muscles and his scars from battles with onery rodeo broncs and bulls were barely visible.

"Jenner..."

He dipped his head and, still looking at her, touched the tip of his tongue to her nipple. It hardened immediately, puckering as he gently sawed his teeth against her flesh.

"Please..."

"Please what, love?" he asked, and the endearment tore her apart inside. He didn't love her; never had. In fact, he hadn't even remembered her. Love was just a word he used when he was in bed with a woman. Any woman.

"I have to get back to Cody. You mentioned that there might be danger." She really didn't believe it, but she couldn't take any chances and she needed an excuse to get away.

At the mention of the boy, his muscles flexed and he lifted his head. "I've been thinking about him."

Her heart started to gallop. "And...?"

"I want to see more of him."

Where was this going? She didn't know whether to be elated or worried sick. "Why?"

He snorted. "*If* he is my son—"

"We've been through this before."

"Then I think he and I should spend more time together. What do they call it? Quality time. Yeah, that's it."

She glanced around the unfinished room. "You want me to bring him here?"

"Or the Rocking M." He gazed at her and his smile slid off his face. Hostility flickered in his expression as he, too, took in the bare floor and meager furnishings. "What? This isn't good enough for you?"

"I didn't say that."

"But you thought it."

She reached for her clothes again, but he ripped the sweater from her hands and threw it across the room. "What is it, Beth? Not what you planned? What did you expect—that after Jonah died, I'd be rich?"

"I didn't expect anything. Your grandmother threatened—"

"Yeah, yeah, I know. But still, when you decided to return, you thought you'd be visiting a wealthy man with a big house and bank account instead of a broken-down, crippled rodeo rider."

"That's not true!" she said angrily as she slipped her arms through the straps of her bra and clasped it into place. "I knew what you were and who you were, Jenner. I had no expectations, not after I talked to your father and found out that you'd just used me for the weekend." She pulled on her sweater, tugging her hair through the boat neck.

"I didn't use you."

"You were still hung up on Nora Bateman, intended to marry her, the way I heard it."

"From Jonah."

"He tipped me off, yeah," she said as she walked to the corner and retrieved her jacket. "But afterward, I listened to the town gossip and discovered that you'd been dating her off and on for years."

"At the time I met you, if in fact we did meet—"

"You still doubt me?" she whispered, flabbergasted. After what they'd just shared, he still didn't believe her?

His brows slammed together and he looked suddenly savage as he reached for his faded Levi's. "To tell you the truth, I don't know what to think. It seems damned convenient that after one weekend together that I can't remember, you end up pregnant, don't bother to tell me because of Jonah, and then once the old man's gone, show up, whether my grandmother wrote you or not." Some of his hostility seemed to fade a little as he wrestled with his jeans. Every time he moved his bad leg, he sucked in his breath and swore roundly. Beads of sweat dotted his brow and his face contorted with the effort.

"Let me help you," she offered, but he sent her a look that could have sliced through granite.

"I can handle it."

"So I've heard. Over and over again. You're so damned set on being independent that you don't care about injuring yourself again."

"Last I checked, it was *my* body. And *my* problem."

"I was only trying to help, Jenner, but obviously you don't want it, so I'll leave." She glanced around the room and shook her head as she reached for the door. "If you want to see Cody again, call."

Heart pounding with anger and some other emotion she didn't dare name, Beth marched outside, pulled the door shut and took several long, deep breaths. She knew she shouldn't leave him—he was in no condition to take care of himself—but she couldn't take any more of his verbal abuse.

Though she'd seen his kind of frustration in patients before, none of those she'd been caring for had been endowed with the ability to wound her as Jenner was doing. She'd been able to fend off their hostility and bad manners and harsh language with a smile or a fast quip. But Jenner was different.

She'd climbed the stairs and started for home, thinking the long walk would do her good, when she decided that there was another option. Turning abruptly, she hurried along a path at the side of the house that turned past a laurel hedge near the back porch and led to the clinic.

A bell sounded as she entered, and a stern-looking receptionist with a name tag reading Madge Bateman looked up from a computer. At the sight of the woman's last name, Beth nearly stumbled. This woman was Nora's aunt.

"You have an appointment?" Madge asked.

"No, but I'd like to see Dr. Donahue."

Madge's no-nonsense expression didn't change. "It'll be awhile. We got patients stacked up for nearly an hour."

"That'll be fine. Tell her Beth Crandall would like to see her."

"Crandall?" Madge's eyes narrowed and she pulled on the glasses that held by a glittery cord were resting against her ample bosom.

"It's personal."

"Personal." Madge, ever unflappable, wrote the message on a pink slip of paper, and with lips pinched a little at the corners, she waved Beth into one of the worn chairs in the waiting area. "I'll let Doctor know you're here."

"Good. Could I use your phone? It's a local call."

With a put-upon expression, Madge turned her phone around. "Dial nine first," she said. Once she connected with Harriet and found out that everything was all right and Cody was napping, Beth felt relieved. Jenner's conversation about danger to her son had worried Beth. Harriet said she had a few errands to run when Cody woke up, but that everything was fine.

After she hung up the phone, Beth thanked Madge, then settled into a chair near a planter and, while trying to stem thoughts of Jenner lying on the floor of his apartment, thumbed through some old newsmagazines.

In less than fifteen minutes, Beth was called to Skye's office. "Come in, come in," the doctor said, waving from her seat behind the desk. A smile stretched across her face. "What's going on?"

Madge closed the door and Beth dropped into a chair. "It's about Jenner."

"Oh." Skye leaned back in her chair and worried a pencil between her fingers. "What's he done?"

"It's what he won't do, which is seek medical attention. He reinjured his leg today and I think you or an orthopedic specialist should have a look at his ankle—maybe his knee—again. I don't know what the ankle looked like before, but, well, I examined it this afternoon and it's definitely swollen and black-and-blue. He's in a lot of pain that he won't own up to and he refuses to have anyone fussing over him."

"Sounds like Jenner." Skye rubbed her jaw thoughtfully. "*You* examined him?"

"I'm a nurse, Dr. Donahue—"

"Call me Skye."

"Okay. I've seen my share of wrenched knees, sprains, torn ligaments and broken bones. Without X rays or an MRI, I wouldn't even hazard a guess as to how bad it is. The leg still supports him—barely—but something's not right. I thought maybe you could take a look at him."

"If he lets me." She chewed on the end of her pencil. "But don't worry about that right now. I'm sure I can find a way to convince him."

"Thanks." Beth stood. "I appreciate it."

"Not at all. Someone's got to take that hardheaded cowboy and tell him what's good for him." She flashed Beth a smile. "It may as well be me!"

Jenner felt like hell. His leg was so stiff, he could barely move, his head throbbed, and he couldn't get Beth out of his mind. She'd left him feeling empty and disgusted with himself. Because of his damned leg, he hadn't been able to get her on her back and make love to her as he'd wanted to. Well, maybe this was better. Maybe now he didn't have to feel so guilty because they hadn't made love. Damned close, but they hadn't really done the deed, though the memory of her caused a tingling deep inside and a want for more. Much more.

It was dark now and he looked around his austere apartment with new eyes. He realized what she saw when she came here. A large, unfinished room in the basement of an old house. No carpet. Not much in the way of appliances or furniture. Hell, he didn't even have a bed he could take her to.

He ran his tongue around his teeth and decided he

needed a drink. A stiff one. Because he had to make some decisions. He struggled to his feet, then flipped on the light and saw the telephone. Well, it was now or never.

He reached for the receiver and punched out the numbers for one Mr. Rex Stone, private investigator. Though it bothered him more than he wanted to admit, Jenner knew he had to check out Beth—discover what her plans were, who she was. For all he knew, she could have a husband or a boyfriend back in Portland or Oregon City or wherever the hell it was she called home.

Head throbbing, he waited until the phone was answered and Rex Stone's too-smooth voice came over the line. But it wasn't the man himself. Jenner was listening to a damned tape recorder. He had just left his message and hung up when he heard light footsteps on the stairs and his stupid heart kicked a little at the thought that Beth had returned. A jab of guilt cut through him when he remembered his message to Rex Stone, but he ignored the pangs.

"It's open," he yelled at the sound of knuckles banging on the door. Bracing himself against the far wall, he felt a wave of disappointment when Skye, dressed in her lab coat, walked into the room.

"Well, well, well," she said. "Rumor has it you reinjured yourself."

"I'm fine."

"Prove it. Walk over here." She stood in the doorway, her arms crossed, defiance in her eyes.

"What is this?"

"Concern, Jenner. I got a call from Beth. She says you might need medical attention."

He let out a string of cusswords guaranteed to turn a sailor's face red, but Skye didn't budge.

"Max is on his way. Either you let us help you into the clinic where I can examine you, or we'll do it the hard way and call an ambulance, but let me tell you, you're going to get the help you need."

"I don't need—"

"Stop it! I'm tired of you telling me how to treat you. I'm the doctor here, remember?"

"What I don't remember is calling for one."

"You're as stubborn as your brother. Probably worse." She eyed him up and down, her gaze landing squarely on the leg he favored. "Now, Jenner, it's either my way or the hard way. What's it going to be?"

"All right, Skye, you can get a thrill and look me over, but I'm *not* going back to any damned hospital, so you'd better be ready to give me a brace and some pills for the pain. I can't be laid up right now."

"You might not have a choice."

"That's where you're wrong," he said, planting his crutches and dragging himself closer to her although his leg hurt like hell. "I'm still calling the shots when it comes to my body!"

No one was home when Beth returned to her mother's house, and Beth couldn't sit in the living room alone with her thoughts of Jenner and how easily she could have made love to him. When she remembered their intimacy, how passionate their lovemaking had been, she felt herself blush.

Ever since her weekend with Jenner three years ago, she'd told herself that she'd imagined the heat they'd shared, that the force of their lovemaking had been something she'd created in her mind. But she'd been wrong. Dead wrong.

Even now, at the thought of his hands and mouth touching her, she quivered inside, and a deep longing brought erotic images to her mind. Their hunger and desire three years ago had been real. The lust had been strong. But they hadn't loved each other, just as they didn't love each other now. And that was the root of Beth's problem, for she found it impossible to believe in passion without love.

Oh, sure, she knew it existed. All the time. But not fo
her.

Rather than watch the day settle into night, she foun
her purse and keys and climbed into her car. She'd driv
around Rimrock, reacquaint herself with some of her ol
haunts, and try like hell to force Jenner McKee from he
head.

"You need to see an orthopedist." Skye continued t
cluck over him like an old mother hen. In some way
because of her medical license, she was as bad as h
family, always telling him what to do. "Your ankle
probably just sprained, but the knee isn't good."

"That much I know."

"Do something about it, Jenner, or it won't get an
better. Call Dr.—"

"Yeah, yeah, I know. Kendrick. The man with all th
answers."

"Has anyone ever mentioned that you've got a ba
attitude?"

"A few times."

"Okay, so set up an appointment with Kendrick."

"I will," he said with a cocky grin, making a promi
that neither one of them believed.

A new leg brace had been fitted over his bum knee a
well as another one for his ankle. Although Skye thoug
both joints were only sprained, that the X rays showed r
sign of bone breakage, and that it didn't seem as if an
of his ligaments had been torn, she wasn't complete
convinced. "The pain pills won't last forever," sl
warned.

Jenner scowled. "I don't plan to get hooked on an
medication, Doc."

"Good. Because if you don't go see Dr. Kendrick
his clinic in Dawson City, I won't give you any more."

"Kendrick's a stuffed shirt."

Skye shook her head and rolled her eyes skywar

"Ron Kendrick's one of the best. Okay, I'll admit his bedside manner isn't particularly kind—"

"It stinks," Jenner said flatly. "The guy's got no sense of humor."

"The important thing is he knows his stuff. You can't find a more capable surgeon anywhere around."

"Thanks, but I'm not looking." Jenner turned toward the door, the edge of his pain dulled by one of the sample tablets Skye had given him. He'd started into the hallway when her voice arrested him.

"Jenner, for your family's sake, take care of yourself."

His jaw tightened as he made his way out of the clinic on the crutches. Damn, he hated anything to do with medicine. Hospitals and clinics, they were too sterile, too cold, too unfeeling. He couldn't imagine Beth working in that kind of environment.

Beth. He couldn't shake her image from his mind—the way she'd gently caressed him, the feel of her tongue against his nipple, the smell of her hair as she'd found a way to pleasure him. He'd wondered over the past few months if he'd ever be able to make love again. She'd shown him that his manhood seemed to be functioning normally. In fact, ever since she'd returned to Rimrock, his hormones had been on overload.

Once outside, he determined to see Beth again and pin her down.

He couldn't leave things the way they were.

The last thing Beth needed was to see Stan's Chrysler parked in the driveway, but there it was, big as life, sitting in the shade of a spruce tree and blocking the view of her mother's flower bed.

A weight settled over her shoulders as she edged her trusty Nova next to the curb, twisted the key in the ignition, and felt the little car's engine shudder to a stop. "I don't think I'm ready for this," Beth said with a frown. She really didn't want to deal with Stan, not after chang-

ing the course of her life forever by becoming intimate
with Jenner.

In a few short days, she had let Jenner touch her where
Stan had never dared; he was too much a gentleman. The
opposite of Jenner McKee. "Come on, Crandall," she
told herself. "You can't put this off." With a new sense
of determination, she tossed her keys into her purse and
headed out.

Inside the house, Harriet sat cross-legged on the floor
working a puzzle with Cody. Stan was leaning back in
the rocker, one leg propped on a footstool, reading glasses
perched on the end of his nose as he perused the local
paper. Beth didn't bother closing the door.

Scrambling to his feet, Cody spied her first and cried,
"Mommy! Mommy!" He hurled his sturdy little body
into her arms. "I ate a waffle this—" he held his arms as
wide as they would stretch "—big!"

"Good for you," she said, holding him tightly, her
throat suddenly clogged as she remembered Jenner's worries about his safety. Surely there was no reason to think
her son was in danger.

Carrying Cody on her hip, she walked into the living
room and offered a smile to Stan, who was watching her
over the top of his reading glasses. "Hi," she said. "I
was surprised to see your car outside."

"I know. I probably should have called but, well, for
once I thought what the hell and just took off."

"I couldn't eat it all," Cody said, casting Stan a dark
glare.

"What? Oh, the waffle. Well, that's all right. Hey, tell
me, did you meet some of Grandma's friends?" she whispered into her son's ear.

"Lots and lots!"

"They thought he was absolutely adorable," Harriet
boasted. "Oh, look, here's the duck's beak."

"Me do!" Cody squirmed out of Beth's arms and

dashed back to squat near the puzzle and shove the yellow piece firmly into place. "All done!"

"And well done," Harriet said.

"Do 'gain!"

A furrow deepened between Stan's eyesbrows. "Now, Cody, your grandmother's already helped you with it three times since I've been here. Maybe you can think of something else to do."

Harriet laughed as Cody, ignoring Stan, dumped the pieces onto the floor.

"Do 'gain, Gramma."

"Why not?"

"Cody—" Stan began to reproach him in a gentle but firm tone.

"It's all right, Stan." Beth tossed her purse into a corner of the couch and hung her jacket on the coat tree. She wondered how she looked, if she showed any signs that she'd spent the better part of the day with Jenner, most of which was involved in lovemaking.

"You know, Beth, I was worried about you. After the phone call the other morning, I thought I'd better drive over here and see what was wrong."

"Nothing's wrong."

"Nothing? But—" He stopped and cast a glance at Harriet and Cody.

"I guess that's our cue to leave, sport," Harriet said. "Besides, we've got work to do. There's some apples that need to be picked before dark if we're gonna make that pie."

Cody was on his feet in an instant. "Like pie," he said.

"Then come on, we'd better get shakin'." Harriet took his hand and, leaving the puzzle pieces in the middle of the floor, headed through the kitchen and out the back door.

Beth waited to hear the door slam before she let out her breath. This wasn't going to be easy, but she knew, as she'd suspected for a long time, that Stan wasn't the man for her.

And Jenner McKee is?

No! Maybe there was never going to be a man for her.

"Come here," Stan said, and when she didn't move, he walked across the room and took her into his strong arms. Though he was nearing sixty, he kept himself in good shape and could have passed for forty-five. "You scared me, Beth. When you said it was over."

Her heart softened a little. "It scared me, too, Stan," she admitted, carefully sliding out of his arms. "But I think it's for the best."

"The best? Are you out of your mind? I'm crazy about you." He ran a hand through his graying hair. "I...I can't imagine what it would be like living without you."

"You did it before."

"And it was hell."

She told herself to be strong, that though she cared for Stan, it wasn't enough. She didn't love him, not as he wanted or needed or ought to be loved. Then there was his problem with Cody. "I'm sorry, Stan," she said, her throat clogging, "but I've thought about it and I can't keep seeing you."

"Why not? Don't you hear me, Beth? Aren't you listening? I love you, I want to marry you, to take care of you and your son."

At one time those words would have been music to her ears, but she'd learned that she could stand on her own, take care of herself, be both mother and father to Cody. She could juggle a job and single motherhood; in fact, she was damned good at it. Her mother was right. She couldn't settle. "I—I've been doing a lot of thinking since I got here, Stan, and it's not working, not for me. And I don't think it's working for you, either."

"You're wrong," he protested, but she noticed the doubt in his eyes.

"What you and I want are worlds apart."

"How can you say that?"

"Please," she said, steeling herself, "let me finish. I want more kids, Stan."

"Good Lord, *why?*"

"It's just the way I feel. Cody needs a sister or a brother and I...I would like to be a mother again."

The corners of Stan's mouth pinched, the way they did when Cody made too much noise or demanded too much attention or got in the way when Stan wanted to take her to a movie or a ball game or a restaurant alone. "There's more, isn't there?" he said, his voice suddenly cold, his nostrils twitching as if encountering a bad smell. "You're trying to take up with Cody's father again, aren't you?"

She wanted to lie, to tell him that she didn't care for the man who had sired Cody, that she was willing to turn her back on him. But the truth of the matter was that, if she examined her feelings for Jenner more closely, they were a lot more complicated than she would ever admit. To Stan. Or to herself.

"Oh, God, Beth. Do you know what you're throwing away? All for a man who didn't want you and didn't want his boy."

Beth didn't have time to respond because at that moment she heard the distinctive roar of an old pickup's engine and knew that Jenner had just rounded the corner of the street. Her stomach clenched when she heard the engine die, the slam of a heavy door and the uneven tread of boots hitching up the front walk. Her throat worked for a second. "I'm sorry, Stan," she said with more than a little regret. She had pinned so many hopes on this man, probably been blind to his flaws because she wanted the security of a stable, rock-solid man's love.

A father figure. Not for Cody—but for myself!

Deep inside her, something broke free.

A heavy hand knocked boldly on the frame of the door. "It's open," she called over her shoulder, and Jenner, crutches thrust out ahead of him, a thunderous expression as dark as the mountains in winter, filled the doorway.

"I didn't think we were finished..." Jenner's voice trailed off and his gaze collided with Stan's for a second, and then, as if he thought the older man was a friend of Harriet's, he forced a grin. "Jenner McKee," he said, hobbling up and extending a hand, even though he was balancing on his crutches.

Stan's eyes narrowed and his gaze slid from the tips of Jenner's dusty boots, up his worn jeans, past his flannel shirt and shadow of a beard, to his eyes—blue as the Oregon sky in June. Stan's nostrils flared as if he smelled something unpleasant, but he extended his hand. "Stanley Cole. I'm a friend of Beth's."

One of Jenner's eyebrows arched. "Of Beth's."

Stan slipped his wallet out of his back pocket and withdrew one of his business cards. "That's right." He handed the embossed card to Jenner. "I'm with the National Insurance Company."

Jenner glanced at Beth as if to ask if this guy was for real.

She didn't move a muscle, just prayed that this whole thing would soon be over. Her palms began to sweat as Jenner flipped the card over once, then lifted his eyes to meet Stan's again. This time his gaze was dark and serious. "I'm a friend of Beth's, too."

"Just a friend?"

"A close friend."

"Jenner, don't—"

"Why not?" Jenner demanded. "Who is this guy?"

"Before she came back here to see you—I assume this is the guy—" he hooked his thumb in Jenner's direction and glanced at Beth who nodded "—Beth and I were planning to get married."

Jenner's mouth flattened into a harsh line.

"That's not true, Stan," Beth interjected. "We'd discussed it, yes, but it wasn't as if we'd even gotten engaged.''

''Because of *him*,'' Stan accused, his furious gaze raking down Jenner again, one finger jabbing the air near Jenner's chest. ''Because you never got over him, even though the only thing he did was get you pregnant and dump you.''

Jenner moved fast, too fast for a man on crutches, but he kept his balance and swung himself closer to Stan. His eyes were mere slits. ''You don't know anything about what happened,'' he said, his lips barely moving, his eyes bright with anger.

''I know she ended up in Oregon City—*alone*. Had a kid there. And I know that before she came here to see you, she was different.''

That much was true. In the days she'd been in Rimrock, she'd changed, become more independent, realized more fully what she wanted out of life. She'd thought once that she could be content with Stan, that she shouldn't expect more out of life than contentment and security. But then she'd met Jenner again and realized there was more. If nothing else, she owed Jenner McKee for making her face up to her own needs and wants as a woman.

''You mixed her up, McKee,'' Stan charged.

''I'm not mixed up,'' Beth interjected.

''Maybe you never really knew her,'' Jenner drawled.

''I think I know her better than some punk cowboy who's...''

''Who's what?'' Jenner demanded. ''Go ahead and say it. A cripple. That's what you were thinking.''

Stan had the decency to close his mouth.

Jenner swung around and faced Beth. ''You want this guy?'' he asked, pointing a crutch at Stan.

''Jenner I—he's my friend.''

''Sure. Well, lady, it's your choice. If you want to marry the insurance man, no one's going to stop you.''

His eyes narrowed on her, but the blue flames of anger were still visible.

"I'm not marrying anyone," she said firmly. "I don't need a man—"

"Then why'd you come back here?" Jenner asked, cutting her off.

"For God's sake, Beth, he can't talk to you like that."

"Maybe it would be better," she said, more calmly than she felt as her insides were quivering in rage, "if you both left."

The back door squeaked, and Cody, an apple with a tiny bite out of it in one hand, streaked into the room. He saw Jenner and slid to a stop. "You here 'gain?"

Stan stiffened. Beth, sending both men a glare meant to keep them quiet, bent down on one knee. "It's polite to say hello," she said, her heart thudding wildly.

"'Lo."

"He doesn't know?" Stan asked. This time Jenner's harsh glare shut him up.

"Know what?" Cody asked innocently.

"That Stan's leaving, honey." Beth picked her son off the floor and tried to paste a composed, friendly smile on her face, though she seethed inside. "Say goodbye."

"Bye-bye." Cody moved the fingers of his free hand up and down in a wave.

Stan sent Beth a withering look. "All right. You've made your decision. But when it doesn't work out with the local yokel and you fall into a million pieces, don't expect me to pick them up again."

"I won't," she answered quietly and flinched as Stan stormed out of the house, the door banging shut behind him.

"He mad," Cody observed.

"Very."

Jenner hooked an insolent thumb in the direction Stan had taken. "*That's* the kind of man you've been dating?"

"The only man," she said, still holding Cody so tightly

that her son squirmed in her arms. Every other man who'd shown interest in her hadn't accepted Cody and looked upon her son as extra baggage. She hadn't expected the same from Stan.

"Sheesh." He watched through the window as Stan slid into a shiny new Chrysler, started the engine and pulled a U-turn on his way out of town. "That guy's old enough to be—"

"Don't say it," she snapped. "He's a good man. This wasn't one of his better days."

"I hope not." Jenner's gaze lingered on Beth's face for a second longer than necessary before sliding over to Cody's. "How ya doin', sport?" he asked. Cody tilted up his face to stare at Jenner.

"Why you got those?" He pointed at the crutches. "You hurt?"

"A little bit."

"And that." Cody eyed the brace quizzically, dropping the apple in his curiosity. He poked at the straps and padding. "I wear."

Jenner snorted a humorless laugh. "Believe me, you wouldn't want to."

"It wouldn't fit, anyway," Beth said as she stood and straightened her sweater—the same sweater that Jenner had pulled over her head and tossed into the corner of his apartment. At that particular thought, her throat turned to sand and she couldn't find her tongue for a second.

Jenner turned his intense gaze on her again and she hazarded a quick glance at his face. What she saw there caught her breath, for the look he sent her was all male and sensuous, as if what had happened between them this afternoon was just a sample of what would happen, if she let it. She cleared her throat and said, "Well, since you didn't take my advice and leave, I guess I could offer you something cold to drink."

Cody, oblivious to the silent message between his mother and his new friend, said, "We ride horses?"

"Wh-what?" Beth said.

"Horses," Cody repeated, his brows knitting in frustration. "Ride."

"Oh, I don't think—"

"Sure," Jenner cut in. "How about tomorrow?"

"Jenner, it's not a good idea. He's too young."

"I was riding by myself by the time I was three."

"Yeah, but he's only two and you're certifiable, remember?"

"Come on, Beth. This is what you wanted, wasn't it?" he asked, the mockery in his face undisguised.

She couldn't answer. For the first time in a long while, Beth Crandall wasn't sure what she wanted.

Chapter Nine

"I didn't expect anything so soon," Jenner said as Rex Stone slid a manila envelope across the polished mahogany top of his desk. They were seated in the private investigator's office in Dawson City. His back to the only window, Rex was wedged into a tufted leather chair positioned behind the desk. Jenner was on the far side, in a smaller, less-imposing chair. He picked up the envelope and fingered the corners, feeling an unexpected ton of guilt settle squarely on his shoulders.

"It's just preliminary. A little background on Ms. Crandall. I can dig deeper, but I thought we'd start here and you could tell me if you wanted more. Didn't want to waste your money."

Jenner doubted that. He was certain that Rex had no qualms whatsoever of spending anyone else's cash. Nonetheless, he ripped open the envelope with his finger and slipped out the contents: copies of report cards from Rimrock High School, transcripts from Eastern Oregon College, several pictures of Beth as a student and later as she recieved her R.N. degree at the University of Oregon Nursing School. He also saw copies of her birth certificate, driver's license, social security card and a résumé of her employment record. But the document that fascinated him most was Cody Crandall's birth certificate. Beth's name was listed in full, but the space for his father's name was blank, as if the man had never existed.

Jenner's fist closed over the papers. He felt like a goddamned Peeping Tom, peering into Beth's private life behind her back. He might as well be standing on the dark side of a window, peering through the blinds, watching her undress.

"The thing that I found interesting," Rex said as he picked up a letter opener and began cleaning his thumbnail, "is that the blood type fits. The kid could be your son. But unless you want to go through all that DNA garbage, you only have her word." He flicked off a bit of smut that he'd dislodged from his nail. "So…what do you want me to do? I also did a little checking to see if she was involved with any man three years ago, just in case there was an obvious boyfriend that we could pin the kid's paternity on. No such luck."

"Good." Jenner's gut twisted.

Was Cody really his son? Did it even matter?

Jenner rubbed the new growth of beard shading his jaw.

"Good? You want the kid to be yours?"

Good question. "I don't know," he said, but deep down he knew the truth. He wanted to claim that fairhaired piece of mischief as his own, and the thought of Beth being with any other man disgusted him.

Rex leaned forward, placing his elbows on the desk. "I can keep digging, you know. It's fascinating how some people appear so ordinary and normal on the surface, but underneath they're entirely different people. I followed one woman—a schoolteacher, no less. Came from a good family, had a loving husband, two kids, even a dog. Ended up she'd been having not one affair but *two* for years. Just to spice up her life. The husband was the last to know.''

Jenner thought he might be sick. ''This is enough,'' he said, pushing himself upright and balancing on his good leg. He shoved the papers back into the envelope, folded the packet and tucked it into an inner pocket of his jacket.

''Have you talked to your brother lately?'' Rex asked.

Jenner pinned the P.I. with his intense stare. The only conversation he'd had with Max was about him going to the hospital. It hadn't ended well. ''Why? What's up?''

Rex smiled, his pudgy face stretching like kid's clay. ''That reward we offered is generating a lot of interest.''

''I'll bet. Every two-bit con artist in the state is probably coming up with stories just to get his hands on it.''

''We'll have to weed through the fakes. That's not so hard, but we might just get ourselves a concrete lead or two.'' He rubbed his fleshy hands together in anticipation. ''Even Hammond Polk thinks we might flush out a suspect or two.''

''Sure he does—he's up for reelection soon and doesn't want to lose his cushy sheriff's job.''

Nodding goodbye to the P.I., Jenner left the tiny suite of offices on the third floor. The entire conversation with Stone settled like lead in his gut. First there was the matter of the reward; Jenner was against it. The last thing his family or the Rocking M needed was a crowd of near criminals trying to find ways to get to the reward money. His mother, grandmother and Casey were alone in the ranch house every night, miles from town, with only Jonah's old Winchester and an ancient dog for protection—not that those women usually needed any.

Then there was the matter with Beth. Rex Stone, because of Jenner's request to find out the truth about Beth had just assumed Jenner wanted to prove that she was a self-serving gold digger willing to use her child to get a little fast cash from the McKee bank. But Jenner, who had once assumed the same wasn't so certain now. She

seemed to love that kid so much; it couldn't be an act. Or
could it? Or could she love the kid enough to do anything,
including pawning him off on some unsuspecting cowboy,
to assure the kid a secure future?

Hadn't the old man—Stan Whatever—said that he and
Beth had planned to be married? He seemed to believe it
even if Beth had denied it up and down. Would she have
sold herself to a man more than twice her age just to
provide for her little boy? The thought of Stan and Beth
together made Jenner's blood run cold, but, if he was
honest with himself, it wasn't so much Stan or his age
that got to him, it was the fact that Beth had been involved
with another man. Any man. "You're an ass, McKee,"
he grumbled, and a slim woman standing next to him in
the elevator glanced his way.

"Pardon me?" she asked, her perfume hanging on the
air, her blond hair sweeping her shoulders.

"Sorry. Talkin' to myself."

She favored him with a smile that would have, at one
time, ignited something within him. "I do it, too. More
often than I'd like to admit."

He shrugged and turned away. The attractive woman
held no interest for him—not like she would have a few
weeks ago. Not like she would have before Beth Crandall
had marched into the den of the Rocking M and announced they'd had a brief, hot, one-night stand and now
were the parents of a two-year-old scamp named Cody.

Could the kid really be his? He was starting to believe
it. Otherwise, Beth was taking a helluva risk, including
scandal, because these days it was pretty easy to prove
paternity. Hell, what a mess. What a goddamned, no-easy-
way-out, gut-churning mess!

The elevator stopped and he maneuvered his way
through a crowd who'd been waiting for the car. Most
people gave him the right-of-way because of his crutches,
and he didn't know which he minded worse, the do-
gooders who stepped aside and offered tentative, pitying

smiles, or the hard-nosed, self-important jerks who took no heed of his...his what? *Disability?*

His stomach soured. Surely he wouldn't be disabled for life. His blood congealed at the thought and he shoved it aside. Maybe Skye and Beth and his whole damned family was right. Maybe he should go back to that orthopedic snob and sign himself up for the physical therapy he'd signed himself out of.

"Here you go." An old lady walking a dog no bigger than a rat held the door for him and he cringed inside.

He wanted to shout out that he could damned well handle the door himself, but instead he forced a cold grin and tipped his head. "Thanks."

"No trouble. Come along, Felix," she said with a winning seventy-year-old's grin as she tugged on the rat's leash. With a yip it headed into the building.

Outside, the day had turned cloudy with gusts of wind blowing down from the north. Any hint of summer seemed to have fled with the dry leaves scurrying across the street and the smell of rain in the air. Jenner climbed into his truck and glanced up at the offices of Rex Stone. The guy gave him the creeps. Stone seemed to *enjoy* digging into the dirt surrounding a person. But he wasn't just interested. No his fascination stemmed from some kind of deep need to prove that other people had failings—big-time failings.

Jabbing the key into the ignition and pumping the gas pedal, Jenner glanced in the rearview mirror and caught a glimpse of himself. Unshaven and weathered, squinting hard, he wasn't a pretty sight, and not much better than Rex Stone. Hadn't he ordered the investigation of Beth Crandall?

"Damn it all, anyway," he muttered as he eased the truck into the uneven flow of traffic in downtown Dawson City. Shrugging his shoulders—as if he could shake the feeling of being akin to a snake like Stone—didn't help, and the investigator's report felt like a dead weight in his pocket. He'd never liked this slimy little P.I., but Rex was necessary it seemed to find out who was behind his father's death.

He pushed the speed limit and chewed on his lower lip. What if this mess about the murder was true? What if someone was really after the McKees? What if they'd stop at nothing to get their revenge or whatever it was they wanted? What if Cody and Beth were in danger?

"You promised!" Cody insisted, his lower lip protruding petulantly.

"I said I'd think about it. That's not a promise."

"But I want horse ride!"

Beth gritted her teeth. Sometimes her boy could be so stubborn. *Just like his father!* The father who was definitely to blame in this case for offering to teach Cody to ride. A two-year-old! While the orthopedist was checking out his leg, Jenner McKee should have a neurosurgeon examine his head. "Look, I said we'd go out to the ranch this afternoon and I'll take you, but it's not time yet."

"When?"

"In a couple of hours."

"Now!" Cody protested. Beth decided he needed a nap. It was barely noon, but he was showing all the classic signs of being overly tired. He rubbed his eyes and stuck out his lower lip, looking more like Jenner than ever.

Jenner. Beth's heart seemed to clench each time she thought of him. He was the reason she was sticking around. By all rights, she should be returning to Oregon City and starting to look seriously for a new job. The little bit of savings she'd put away wouldn't last forever and she needed to get on with her life. She'd done her duty by the McKees; now it was time to start over.

Except she couldn't. Not until things were settled with Jenner and Cody. She carried her son into the back bedroom but when he saw the playpen, he balked. "Nooo!" he wailed, sounding like a siren. "No. No. No!"

"Come on, sweetheart," she cajoled, grateful that they were alone in the house. Her mother, bless her, had infinite patience with her headstrong grandson, but Zeke wasn't as understanding. He'd made a couple of comments and glared at Cody enough times to let Beth know they were about to wear out their welcome.

"Nonsense," her mother had insisted when Beth had mentioned it, but her smile hadn't been quite as wide as usual and Beth knew that Harriet, though she protested, was feeling the strain, as well. Yep, soon it would be time to go home.

Home. And where was that? The tiny apartment overlooking the Willamette River, where the sound of traffic was steady all night long? Or here in Rimrock, where the sky seemed to stretch forever and the moutains loomed like craggy sentinels and she knew many of the townspeople on a first-name basis.

Was home Oregon City, where she was anonymous and her son would grow up without a father, without many questions being asked, where many of his friends would also have single mothers?

Or here. Where everyone would know that he was Jenner McKee's bastard son? That his mother had been unmarried when she'd given birth? Would he grow up knowing that his mother and father had never really been in love and that his conception was just a mistake of white-hot lovemaking for a single weekend? What if Jenner married and had other children?

"Read!" Cody demanded, and Beth was grateful to turn her thoughts away from Jenner and concentrate on the worn pages of a collection of fairy tales, the same book that her mother had read to her. The pages were smudged, the cloth-bound cover ripped, crayon marks scattered throughout and corners of the most loved passages torn. She'd grown up with these fairy tales, believing her mother's soothing voice as she'd read about castles and princesses and enchanted frogs who, with a single kiss, could be changed into the handsome, rich son of a king.

They were silly, childish stories and still they rested deep in her heart. Didn't she, a grown woman, still believe? Wouldn't she always?

Jenner parked his truck near the garage and glanced past the barn to the dry fields where the horses turned their noses to the wind, ears flicking, as they smelled the approach of the storm. A few anxious nickers rippled on the breeze and the younger colts, tails aloft, raced along the fence line, bucking and rearing and feeling the energy in the air.

He felt the storm approaching, too. The wind was picking up, tossing the branches of a pine tree near the garage and shifting the old weather vane on the roof of the barn. He'd always liked the excitement a thunderstorm brought with it and he anticipated the sizzle of lightning streaking across the sky, looked forward to the crack of thunder rolling over the valley.

Hired hands on horseback sorted through paddocks of cattle, separating the heifers from the young bulls. A couple of other men were amoung the hands—new cowboys he didn't recognize. One sat atop the fence, another leaned against the barn. Both seemed vigilant, but not all that interested in working with the stock.

He felt a drip of apprehension in his spine. Something wasn't right and it wasn't just the approaching storm that caused the hairs on the back of his neck to raise.

In the near paddock, Dani Stewart, Skye's younger sister, was working with Max's daughter. The fiesty five-year-old was astride a docile gelding named Cambridge. Over the protests of his ex-wife, Colleen, Max had presented the palomino to Hillary on her fifth birthday. The stirrups were so high they looked comical, but Hillary was serious about riding. Even though she'd had a terrorizing experience during the fire, when she'd been trapped in the stables with Dani as they'd brushed Cambridge after a lesson, Hillary was persistent and claimed that she wanted to be a trick rider someday, just as Dani had once been.

Jenner climbed out of his truck, smelled the scent of ash and charred wood that still lingered after the fire, and pocketed his keys.

Dani's voice carried on the wind. "That's it, Hillary. Show him who's boss." With a quick little kick, the girl urged the horse into a trot. "Take control. There ya go."

Again Hillary gave a nudge of her heels. Flicking his tail, the horse broke into a slow gallop much to Hillary's delight. "Faster!" she cried, her brown curls bouncing in the brisk breeze. "Come on, faster!"

"I don't think so." Dani watched her small charge carefully. "Come on, slow him down. Pull back on the reins easy now. Don't hurt him. I swear, Hillary, someday you're going to be the best cowgirl in the county!"

Hillary giggled at the praise, then reluctantly obeyed and slowed Cambridge into a trot, then a walk.

"That's about it," Dani said, and Hillary's face fell.

"One more time," she begged. "Please."

Dani checked her watch and shook her head. "I can't, hon, really. I'm supposed to be at the Purcell place in fifteen minutes and it'll take me twenty to get there. So come on, you help me with the saddle and bridle." She looked up as Jenner hobbled to the fence. At the sight of his crutches, she winced. She, too, had nearly lost her life in the fire.

"Jeez, are you still on those?" she asked as she uncinched the saddle.

"For a while yet. Here, let me help you—"

Her gaze stopped him cold. "I can handle it," she assured him as she swung the saddle from the horse's back and plopped it onto the top rail of the fence. "I do this for a living, y'know."

"So I've heard," he drawled.

"Just because I'm a woman—"

"It has nothing to do with that, Dani. Okay? Give it a rest. I only wanted to help."

She lifted a shoulder. "Well, I don't need it, but thanks, anyway." She yanked the blanket from Cambridge's back and told Hillary to run into the barn and fetch a curry-comb.

A pretty woman with curly red-blond hair and eyes the color of whiskey, she had a temper that was legendary. Years before, there had been rumors about her. She'd been wild. A party girl. Someone you could call for a good time. Or so the town gossip mill had insisted, though Jenner didn't know anyone who'd actually taken her out.

Now, she was a strong woman who, in Jenner's opinion, married the wrong man. Jeff Stewart was one year younger than Jenner and seemed to spend more than his share of time on a bar stool at the Black Anvil flirting with the single women who happened in.

Jenner knew. He'd been there himself.

Hillary returned with brush and comb and both she and Dani started working on the gelding. "That's it," Dani encouraged as Hillary, tongue angled out of her mouth, tried her best to groom the horse. Jenner leaned against the top rail of the fence, watching his niece wrestle with a knot in Cambridge's tail.

"Be careful," Dani said. "He's even-tempered, but even the best horses have been known to kick."

The knot gave way and Hillary dropped her brush onto the ground. "All done," she announced.

"Good job." Dani was still brushing the palomino's hide. She glanced up at Jenner. "I don't know if I ever really thanked you for—"

Jenner waved off her words. "It was nothing."

She rolled her eyes to the darkening heavens. "Hear that, Hillary? He thinks saving our lives was nothing."

"That's because Uncle Jenner's full of B.S."

"Says who?" Jenner asked, and reached over the fence to swing the little girl into the air. She gave out a whoop of delight while he tried to ignore the shaft of pain that sliced down his leg. The screen door banged, and from the corner of his eye, Jenner watched Max stride across the parking lot. His face was stern and set, his mouth an angry line.

"Mommy says."

It figured. These days Colleen Smith didn't have anything good to day about the McKee family. "Well, tell your mommy that I think—"

"Don't say anything," Max warned his brother as he approached. He winked at his daughter. "When you go back to Mommy's, you tell her that you had a nice time and that you were safe, okay?" Max shot his brother a look that warned him not to argue.

Jenner wasn't having any of it. He gave Hillary a hug. "You tell your mom that you're a brave girl and that you can handle a horse as good as the best of 'em. And you tell her Uncle Jenner said so."

"I will," Hillary pronounced with a mischievous grin cast in her father's direction.

Jenner couldn't let it go. "And let her know she's right. I am full of B.S."

"He means hot air," Max said quickly, "but since you're relaying messages, Hillary, tell Mommy that Uncle Jenner's a troublemaker who doesn't know when to keep his big mouth shut... No, on second thought, just tell her you had a great time while you were here at the ranch. She doesn't need to know all the details." Max lifted Hillary from his brother's arms and squeezed her in a gentle hug. "So, how'd the lesson go?"

"Great. Hillary's a natural," Dani said as she unbuckled the bridle, and Cambridge, glad to be rid of the straps of leather, snorted, tossed his head, and took off, bucking and running to the far side of the corral. Hanging the bridle on a fence post, Dani sighed. "I guess he's glad the lesson's over."

"How about you?" Max asked.

"Me? Naw. I could do this all day." Dani climbed over the fence, dusted her hands on her jeans, and pulled a set of keys from her pocket. "I'll be back next week." She managed a smile for her enthusiastic student. "Practice if you can and when you're done, you put Cambridge away. Make sure that he's taken care of. Cooled off and brushed. Don't let your dad do it for you." With a wave she climbed into her dusty Bronco.

As Dani drove off, Max set Hillary on the ground and rumpled her wild curls. "Why don't you see if you can wangle a piece of Kiki's pie from her?"

"She made pie?"

"Apple and blackberry."

"I want both."

"Good luck," Max said, and Jenner smothered a smile. Kiki was outwardly gruff, complaining about kids these days being spoiled, but the old cook had a soft spot in her heart for all the McKee children and grandchildren— she'd even done her share of the spoiling. Jenner guessed that with one sly little look, Hillary would have all the pie she wanted.

Hillary took off in a cloud of dust, her tiny red boots pounding the dry earth, her hair streaming behind her, Max followed her with his eyes, his grin suddenly wide and proud, and Jenner understood, really understood, the bond between father and child for the first time in his life.

Because he might just have a child of his own.

He shoved his hands into the front pockets of his jeans. "I'm here about work," he said.

Max eyed his crutches, and the smile that he'd had on his face for Hillary, disappeared. "You can't—"

"I damned well can, Max. I told you I'm tired of being a charity case." That much was true. He wanted to work, needed to feel his hands doing something, anything, to get rid of the restless energy in his blood. There was another problem, as well. He wanted to be closer to the Rocking M, to the investigation into his father's murder because

of the worries that gnawed at the back of his brain—
worries about Beth and Cody's safety. "Just because I'm
on crutches doesn't mean I'm useless."

"I know, but you should take your doctor's advice
and—"

"To hell with my doctors! I want to work, and I'm
gonna do it. Either here or someplace else." That was
stretching the truth a bit, but he didn't care. "I already
told you—"

"Okay," Max said, his eyes narrowing. "You can have
your old job at the ranch back. You know it's waiting for
you, anyway, but you've got to agree to keep seeing the
physical therapist and the doctor."

"You can't tell me—"

"I can and I will. As long as you work for the Rocking
M—" Max bit back the words. "Oh, hell, Jenner, just use
your head for something other than a spot to hang your
hat." He ran stiff fingers through his hair and cast a wary
glance toward the dark-bellied clouds moving slowly
across the sky. "Besides, I need you around. We got problems."

"That much I know."

"All of a sudden we've got more witnesses than we
can handle—witnesses who claim they know who killed
Dad and started the fire."

Jenner's muscles tensed. "You believe 'em?"

"None so far. All just fortune hunters."

"Big surprise."

"But we're generating a helluva lot of interest."

Jenner's mouth curved into a cynical smile. "Ain't it
amazing what a few dollars can do?"

"I'm not taking any chances. I hired a couple of security guards to keep an eye on things. Chester's not too
happy about it, but I think they'll work out."

Jenner glanced back at the two cowboys who didn't
quite fit in, undoubtedly the men who were supposed to

guard the ranch. From whom? Who was out to get the McKees?

So Max was concerned enough to take some extra precautions. That worried Jenner. It worried him a lot.

The first drops of rain plopped against the Nova's windshield as Beth parked her car next to Jenner's truck. The sky was slate gray, the clouds shifting in the rain. Any plans for Cody to go riding would have to be postponed now. She didn't like thinking about arguing with her two-year-old, who wouldn't understand that sometimes promises had to be altered. No, she thought as she glanced at her son asleep in the car seat, Cody would give her a hard time when she tried to explain about the weather.

Great.

He barely roused as she unbuckled his seat belt, pulled up the hood on his sweatshirt and dashed through the raindrops to the front porch. With her free hand, she rang the bell as Cody yawned and settled against her shoulder.

The door opened and Jenner stood framed in the doorway. Backlit by the lights in the hall, he seemed as rugged as the rocky gorge of Wildcat Creek. For a brief second, they stared at each other, gazes touching, Beth remembering what it was like for his work-roughened hands to caress her skin. Her throat was suddenly dry and she licked her lips nervously as he stood aside.

"Come on in." He held the door for her and she walked into the fortress of the Rocking M. "Great day for a ride, eh?"

"You explain it to him."

"Thanks a lot," he said sarcastically. "Everyone's in the den."

Beth wasn't sure she was ready for 'everyone,' but she took a deep breath and walked into the room. A fire crackled against pitchy wood and gave the room warmth against the coming storm. Beth's spine stiffened when she saw Virginia, huddled in a corner of the couch, her face without a trace of warmth. Max was seated behind the desk and Mavis rocked in a chair near the fire. At the sight of Cody, the little old lady found her cane, stood stiffly, and made her way across the room. "Well, here he is," she said as Cody's eyes blinked against the soft lights. "Been sleeping, haven't you?"

"He's usually a little grouchy when he wakes up," Beth cautioned.

"Am not!" Cody's expression was dark and mistrusting. "Not grouchy!" He clung to her.

"It's all right." But she felt as if she was lying because the hostility in the room fairly sizzled.

Mavis knew when to retreat. "Well, when you wake up, dumpling, come on over and see me. I think we have a book to read or—"

"No!"

"It'll just be a few minutes," Beth apologized, embarrassed at Cody's behavior. He was only two, but she wanted him to show his best side, to be the adorable little boy she loved, to prove to the whole McKee family that he was as special and bright as she thought he was.

But why? So they would accept him? Part of her heart squeezed as she saw the censure in Virginia's features. She would never love this boy, nor would she ever believe that he was her grandson. And Beth would never put Cody in a position where he was judged by a bitter woman who couldn't face the truth.

"He just needs some time to wake up," she explained to Mavis, who, diametrically opposed to her daughter-in-law, seemed anxious to welcome the boy into her family.

Mavis crackled a laugh. "Don't we all? Sometimes I'm a little grumpy when I first wake up. So was that son of mine, rest his soul."

The room turned suddenly quiet at the mention of Jonah, as if his ghost had entered the room.

"Oh, Lord," Virginia whispered.

Jenner, shifting his body so that he stood between Beth

and his mother, ruffled Cody's head. "I think I promised you a horseback ride."

Beth's stomach clenched. "But it's raining."

"Never stopped a good cowboy."

Cody managed a shy smile. "I ride?"

"Right now, if you want to."

Beth felt everyone's gaze rest on her. "I don't—"

Jenner grabbed her arm and turned her toward the door. "We'll discuss it in the barn." With a glance over his shoulder, he said to his brother. "We'll be back in a little while. Beth and Cody are staying for dinner."

"Oh, no—" Beth protested.

"Of course you are." Resting both hands on her cane, Mavis beamed while Virginia's eyes slid away to stare out the window at the darkening countryside.

"Glad to have you," Max said, though his smile seemed a little forced.

Outside, Jenner moved quickly, and Beth, protecting Cody's face with her body, dashed across the parking lot. Rain splattered against the pavement and pounded on her head as she ducked into the barn. Jenner switched on the lights and the fresh scent of rainwater was overcome by the odors of horses, dung and dust.

"We used to let the cattle in here, but until the new stables are built, Max keeps only the most valuable horses inside." Where there had once been a large area for the cattle to mingle and feed, there were now new stalls constructed out of fresh lumber, individual boxes that broke up the large space. Horses snorted and hooves rustled in the straw.

"Lots of horses!" Cody said, his eyes round with wonder.

Jenner paused near a small box with a palomino gelding. "This guy—" he hooked a thumb at the horse "—isn't worth all that much, but he belongs to Hillary, Max's daughter. Docile as a lamb. Come on, fella, let's give you a thrill."

Rather than protest, Beth relinquished her baby to the strong arms of his father and watched as Jenner, without his crutches, opened the stall gate, braced himself on the rails and limped through. He placed a beaming Cody on the palomino's bare back and was rewarded with a grin that stretched across Cody's face.

"Hang on...and be careful." Jenner kept a firm grip on his son's back. "Now, don't kick old Cambridge."

"I ride, Mommy!" Cody announced proudly.

"You sure are."

"Take a handful of his mane—this stuff—so you won't fall off. There ya go."

"I not fall!"

"I've said that before and been wrong. Got the scars to prove it."

All of Beth's apprehensions fell away. Jenner's hands were always on the boy, and the horse was calmer than any she'd ever seen. Cambridge's eyelids nearly drooped and one back leg cocked as Cody sat, short legs barely able to straddle the gelding.

"What you need is a pony," Jenner said.

"And a puppy!"

"That, too."

"Wait a minute," Beth said, though she couldn't help the warm feeling in her heart as she watched Jenner smile at his boy. "My apartment barely holds the two of us. I don't think it could handle a dog or a horse. Besides, the manager might object."

"I want!"

"I should strangle you right here and now, Jenner McKee," she said, but she couldn't keep the corners of her mouth from twitching into an unwanted smile.

"Like to see you try," Jenner drawled, his gaze suddenly intense enough that she could barely breathe and the large barn seemed to close in. "The results could be interesting, but you might get caught," he warned.

"Caught?"

"Mmm. By the law."

She couldn't stop the pulse at her throat from fluttering. "Justifiable homicide," she said quickly. "Any mother on the jury would agree with me."

His lips curved into a sexy smile.

"Ride outside!" Cody said.

"Not now. It's raining."

"Ride outside!"

"Tell ya what." Jenner's attention was focused on his boy and Beth thought her heart might break as she watched father and son communicate. "You come back here tomorrow, and if the sun's out, I'll see that you ride outside."

"Now!"

"Can't happen now, cowboy," Jenner said. "This here horse's tired, gonna take himself a nap. But when he wakes up tomorrow, he'll be roarin' to go. Then you can ride him."

Cody might have argued his case longer but the door to the barn swung open, and Casey, along with Hillary, hurried in. Wind whipped through the building, scattering loose hay and dust.

"Hey! That's *my* horse," the five-year-old proclaimed, her face knotting into an angry scowl. "Cambridge is mine. My daddy gave him to me."

One of Jenner's eyebrows rose. "And now you're sharin' him for a few minutes."

"I don't wanna share him!"

"Hey, Hillary, is that any way to act?" Casey said with a mock frown. "You're a big girl. You can share."

"Not Cambridge!" she said stubbornly as she crossed her arms over her chest and glared at the usurper astride her horse.

Jenner lifted Cody from the gelding's back. "Haven't I shared my horse with you?"

"Yes, but—"

"We've been riding and I never complained, did I?"

"It's not the same!" Hillary said, her little lips tightening over her teeth, her eyes sparking with fire. "He should have asked."

"That's right and it's my fault. I apologize," Jenner said. "Next time I'll ask."

"Hey, come on, let's not get into a tiff." Casey smiled at Beth and rolled her eyes. "Hillary and I thought that Cody might want to see the new kittens."

"Kitties?" Cody asked.

"Yup. Five of 'em. On the back porch."

"I see!"

"But you have to promise not to touch them, okay?" Casey said gently. "The mama cat, she can be mean when she wants to and she won't want you to disturb them. They're only a few weeks old."

Cody squirmed out of Jenner's arms, much to Hillary's obvious relief. She stopped glaring at her uncle as Cody's feet touched the floor and he raced out of the barn.

"Hey, wait up!" Casey took hold of Hillary's hand and they ran from the barn together. Beth started after them, but Jenner clamped a hand over her arm, forcing her to spin up against him.

"Wha—" she said as his head lowered quickly and his lips captured hers in a kiss that seemed to draw the breath from her lungs. When she lifted her head, her heart was knocking and her bones felt weak. Jenner, as he braced himself against the wall, pulled her closer still, so that her legs fit between his. "But Cody—" she said, motioning toward the door.

"Will be fine. Casey's got a way with kids."

"He doesn't know her very well."

"Won't matter." He looked at her long and hard. Her insides seemed to melt under his direct gaze and she licked her lips. With a groan, he kissed her again, his arms wrapping around her, his mouth branding hers with his own unique taste. The floor seemed to shift beneath her feet and she sagged against him.

Don't do this, Beth. Don't get involved with him again.

But she was already involved. As much as she wanted to deny what she felt for him, it was impossible. His lips were hungry and hard, his hands flat against her back. The outside of her legs rubbed against the inside of his, denim moving against denim, creating friction, creating heat.

Beth closed her eyes as he drew her shirt from the waistband of her jeans, and his fingers crawled up her ribs, searching and exploring. In frustration, he worked at the buttons of her shirt, parting the soft flannel and reaching inside to cup both breasts in his palms, pushing them upward so that they nearly spilled out of her bra. Groaning, he buried his face in the deep cleft he'd created and his breath was hot and wet against her skin, causing a tingle to race through her nerves. Her insides turned to molten wax.

He kissed the top of each mound while his thumbs, through the lacy fabric of her bra, teased her nipples. Inside she was burning, and when he touched a nipple with his tongue, her back bowed, her fingers twined in his hair, and she drew his head closer still, cradling him against her, feeling his tongue and mouth suckling through the lace.

"Beth," he growled, "sweet, sweet Beth." He found the clasp of her bra, unhooked it, and let her breasts swing free. With eager haste, he pulled off her shirt and the flimsy scrap of lace, then began his ministrations again. This time he kissed her, flesh against flesh, wet tongue on anxious nipple, hands splayed over her spine, one between her shoulder blades, the other at the small of her back, his fingertips brushing under the waistband of her jeans.

A sensual, moist heat swirled inside her and she rubbed against him, wanting more, needing to feel all of him. Her fingers worked at the buttons of his shirt and soon she'd discarded it onto the hay-strewn floor with her blouse. His hands burrowed lower, past her waistband, to her buttocks, and she gasped when he reached into her panties, delving to the moist cleft that awaited him.

"Beth..." His finger plunged deep into her and she was on her toes, bracing herself with her hands on his shoulders. "Make love to me."

"Here?" she whispered, vaguely aware that it was dangerous, that anybody could come along and open the door.

"Anywhere." His mouth found hers and cut off further protest as his fingers delved and retreated and delved again, and she moved against him, wanting more, images of their sweaty, naked bodies swimming in her mind. He touched her in that oh so sensitive spot and she bucked, arched against him, rubbed her jeans against the bulge in his. Her fingers dug into his shoulders as her body, like a tightly coiled spring, suddenly found release in a burst of ecstasy that brought beads of perspiration to her face. Her mouth found his and she kissed him hard with a fierce abandon that she couldn't deny.

She reached for his zipper, but he grabbed her wrist. "This...isn't enough," he said, his eyes mirroring her own feelings. "I want more."

"I—"

"I want all of you, Beth." His voice was a raspy whisper that seemed to echo in her soul. "I want to make love to you. All night long. Over and over again until we see the morning together."

She sagged against him and pressed her lips to his neck. "I want it, too." Though she knew she was playing with fire, that she most certainly would be burned, she couldn't resist.

"Soon," he promised, kissing her crown. "Very soon."

"You know, I'm looking for another nurse at the clinic," Skye said, her smile infectious as she stared across the table at Beth. The entire McKee family was seated around the long dining-room table, which was laden with roast pork, potatoes, squash, beans, fruit salad and fresh hot rolls. Max sat between Skye and Hillary, across from Jenner, Cody and Beth. Virginia and Mavis were seated at opposite ends of the table and Casey was wedged between Hillary and Kiki, who, as Beth understood it, was considered part of the family. Reaching for her water glass, Skye continued, ''I thought you might be interested in the job.''

Conversation and the ever-present sound of flatware scraping against plates seemed to stop. Beth felt Jenner's gaze move toward her. ''I don't know how long I'll be in Rimrock,'' she managed to say. ''I've got a place in Oregon City.''

Skye lifted a shoulder. ''No law says you can't move. I pay the same scale as the city, but the cost of living is cheaper out here.'' She winked at Beth. ''You might want to apply.''

From the corner of her eye, Beth saw one of Jenner's eyebrows rise in expectation. ''I'll think about it,'' she said, ''but Cody and I are pretty settled.''

She couldn't read Jenner's expression, but she felt his hand slide over to grip her thigh.

Virginia seemed to breathe a sigh of relief.

''Rimrock's a good place to raise a family,'' Mavis interjected. ''A nice, quiet little town where everyone knows everyone else by their first name. Not like the city all full of strangers, where you really don't even know your neighbors. And there's so much less crime.''

''Unless you want to talk about murder and arson,'' Virginia countered. Her eyes never warmed as she glanced at Beth and Cody. ''And sometimes small-town gossip can be cruel.''

Beth didn't need to be reminded; she'd grown up knowing about the ravages of gossip and she'd promised herself that she would never put Cody through the same agony she'd experienced as a child. Suddenly her appetite waned, and the home-cooked meal, which had smelled so wonderful, seemed to congeal on her plate.

"More 'tatoes!" Cody demanded, and though she was a little embarrassed by his outburst, Beth was grateful for an interruption in the conversation.

"You like them, do you?" Mavis asked the little boy propped on two pillows in his chair.

"Like 'tatoes!"

"Well, come on, Virginia, pass them along, will you?"

Grudgingly Virginia grabbed the bowl of mashed potatoes and handed them to Jenner, who scooped a dollop onto Cody's plate.

"My guess is you'll need this, too," Skye said, picking up the gravy boat as her eyes lingered wistfully on the boy.

Somewhere Beth had heard that Skye, though she adored children, could have none of her own. Beth didn't remember where she'd heard the rumor, and now, as she drizzled gravy over Cody's potaotes, she chalked the information up to small-town gossips with wagging tongues. No, Rimrock wasn't the place for a boy whose rich family wouldn't recognize him, who would be considered a joke, a bastard, Jenner McKee's mistake, for all the years he attended school.

Cody deserved better. As for her relationship with Jenner, she had to face the fact that it would always be just what it was—lust. Even now, with his hand resting on her thigh, she felt it—that slow-burning ember that could ignite into a hot flame with just a look, a movement, a touch.

Somehow she finished the meal, then packed Cody up and said her goodbyes. Jenner walked her onto the porch and she knew by the look in his eye that there was unfinished business between them. There always would be. She'd never been a slave to her passions except where Jenner McKee was involved and whenever he was around, she seemed to lose touch with what was important.

"You don't have to go," he said, his fingers curving possessively over her arm.

She offered him a sad smile. "What's the alternative? I spend the night here?"

"We could go somewhere."

"Where?"

"There're hotels—"

"With Cody."

"Leave him with your mother. She probably wouldn't mind."

"No, Jenner," she said with honest regret. "I don't think that would work. I'm not sure any of this is working."

He dropped a crutch and it clattered to the porch as he wrapped a strong arm around her and kissed her hard on the lips. Her head began to spin and only Cody's laugh brought her up short.

"He kiss you, Mommy!" Cody said, pointing a chubby little finger at Jenner. "He kiss you."

"He sure did," Beth agreed.

"Soon," Jenner said softly into her ear. "Remember."

A thrill whispered down her spine as she turned toward her car, but she caught a glimpse of the window to the den and a figure parting the blinds. Her insides froze when her gaze touched Virginia McKee's just before the blinds snapped back into place.

Dashing across the yard, she heard Jenner's voice with its erotic promise. "Soon...very soon." But she couldn't shake the image of Virginia glaring through the slats, condemning her silently with a gaze as frigid as the bottom of a well.

Chapter Ten

"Tell me exactly what Stone's got." Jenner couldn't hide the irritation in his voice as he leaned against the window and stared out at the dark night. Beth had been gone for hours and he still wanted to chase after her. As if he was obsessed or something. As if he needed a woman complicating his life. No, not just any woman. Only Beth.

He took a long swallow from his glass and felt the whiskey hit the back of his throat, but the liquor didn't drive away his thoughts. Of the kid. Of Beth. Of making love to her. His brain burned with the image of lying with her in an open field, arms and legs entwined, bodies glistening with sweat, mouths anxious.

"Stone's got ideas…leads, he thinks. I'm not so sure." Max picked up a poker and began jabbing at the fire.

Virginia and Mavis had retired. Skye had been called to an emergency at the clinic and Casey wasn't back from Dawson City where she'd gone to a movie with an old high school friend. So Max and Jenner were alone, drinking the old man's expensive whiskey. And worrying.

"Stone's got a list of suspects as long as my arm. Some of 'em make sense, others…" He shook his head as the fire, just a few glowing embers, sparked and caused golden shadows to deepen the lines on his face. "Others are too farfetched to count."

"Tell me about the ones that make sense."

"All right." Hanging the poker back on its peg, Max leaned against the stones and folded his arms across his chest. "A couple come to mind right off the bat."

"People Dad swindled," Jenner guessed.

"Right." Max reached for his drink on the mantel and took a swallow.

Though some of the people in Rimrock considered Jonah McKee a god, others thought that he was Satan incarnate. Jenner knew the man was somewhere in between, although, in Jenner's opinion, Jonah definitely favored the devil.

"Most of the people Dad dealt with—"

"You mean cheated," Jenner corrected.

"He didn't cheat them all," Max said, automatically defending Jonah as he had for years. Then, seeing Jenner's disbelieving stare, Max lifted a shoulder. "Okay, so we both know that Dad made more than his share of enemies. Some threatened him, some took a swing or two at him when they were drunk, and others sued him."

"Fred Donner," Jenner surmised.

"Yep. He's on the top of the list. Dad and Fred exchanged money for water rights, then diverted most of the water from Wildcat Creek to the Rocking M. Donner was left with only a trickle."

"Then there was a drought."

"Yep." Max stretched and his back cracked. "Several years of it. The Donner homestead nearly dried up. Things got worse for Fred. His wife nearly divorced him, the bank was on his tail. Dad had to bail him out."

"By buying his place and incorporating it into the Rocking M."

"Fred never forgave him."

"Do you blame him?" Jenner tossed back a swallow of whiskey and felt its warmth work its way down his throat. His fingers clenched hard around the glass as he considered the crook that had been his father. The homestead had been in the Donner family for over a century before Jonah found a way to incorporate the dry acres into part of the ever-growing Rocking M. And why had he wanted the extra land? Why did he need the extra fields? Because of the damned water rights. The way they'd originally been worded, hadn't proved convenient for the McKee spread, so Jonah had made it his mission to strip the Donners of their family land.

"I'm trying to help Fred out—offered him the homestead and the water rights back," Max said, shaking his head. "All he has to do is repay the original note to Dad, which isn't a whole lot, and I'm willing to let him work it off here at the ranch. Hell, I'd probably forgive most of it."

"What'd he say?"

"I think the quote was something like, 'You can keep your goddamned charity and shove it where the sun don't shine.'"

"So he blames you—or us—for what Dad did." Jenner rubbed his chin. "I've never really liked Donner, but I don't think he's a killer. Or an arsonist."

"Maybe he's never been this desperate before."

"Okay, Donner's on the list. Who else?"

"Randy Calhoun. Dad fired Randy less than a month before he died."

"Yeah, I remember," Jenner said. Randy had been a loyal employee of the Rocking M for nearly fifteen years, but, for reasons no one quite understood, Jonah had humiliated Randy and handed him his walking papers. Randy had always had a little trouble with liquor, but

Jonah had put up with it in the past because Randy had been so loyal and good with the stock. But suddenly Jonah had ordered the man off the ranch, fired him in front of the rest of the hands. Made him a laughingstock.

It had been early summer, toward evening, and the sun was just beginning to dip below the horizon. Jenner had been part of a tired group that had spent the day setting fence posts on the line bordering the Bateman place, but Randy hadn't been part of that crew. He and a couple of other hands had worked in the paddocks surrounding the barn, sorting and castrating calves.

Jenner remembered being dog tired as he parked his truck by the garage. Some of the ranch hands had clustered near the door to the machine shed. They'd been smoking, talking and getting ready to go home for the day, but had stopped and were watching Jonah give Randy the ax.

Randy was braced against the wall of the barn, smelling of whiskey and looking as scared as a rabbit staring down the barrel of a shotgun.

"That's it, Calhoun, you're out!" Jonah roared, his face flushed with anger, one hand firmly around the barrel of his rifle.

"But Mr. McKee, you can't fire me."

"I can and I will."

"Wait a minute." Jenner vaulted over the fence and strode up to his father. "What's going on?"

"Butt out!"

"Give it a rest, Dad. Randy's one of the best—"

His father had whirled on him, and his face, mottled with rage, was set in furious determination. "Don't you ever tell me how to run my business, boy," he said, his lips curling in disgust.

"I'm just pointing out that Randy—"

"Back off!" Jonah lunged at him. Jenner grabbed the gun and ripped it out of his father's hands.

"What're ya gonna do, Dad? Shoot him?"

Eyes narrowing, Jonah barked, "If I thought it'd do any good." He whirled on Randy again. "Get out now!"

"Jonah," Chester Wilcox, the ranch foreman, said, stepping in, "I think—"

"Well, don't, or you'll be out of job, too! This is still my ranch, last I heard."

Jenner didn't back down. "What happened?" he demanded. But Chester shook his head, obviously not wanting the story to come out in front of the rest of the hands. "Randy's been with us for—"

"I don't give a rat's ass how long he's been here!" Jonah, snatching his rifle away from his son, spun around, his eyes moving from one ranch hand to the next before landing on Chester. "Make sure he packs up all his gear and gets out."

Randy, nearly sixty, straightened to his full five feet six inches. "I want an explanation, Jonah."

"You really want it? Here in front of God and the rest of the men?"

"Yes." Randy's skin turned the color of bones that had been bleached in the son.

"Fine." Jonah's voice shook with rage. "Aside from being a useless drunk who can barely throw a lasso, you've been cheating me, Calhoun. I know about some of the calves we lost last winter. What really happened to them."

Randy's Adam's apple bobbed nervously. "What's that?"

"You culled 'em out. Sold 'em. That's why we never found any carcasses."

"I didn't—"

"Like hell!" Jonah thundered. "You're out, Calhoun, and unless you want me to call Hammond Polk and have the sheriff's deputies poke around, you'd best get in that damned bucket of bolts you call a pickup and leave. You can pick up your check at the office."

Randy's hands shook, but Jonah wasn't finished with

him. He pointed his rifle at Randy, then at each of the hands standing on the far side of the fence. "Let this be a lesson to the rest of you. No one. *No one* screws around with Jonah McKee!"

Jenner had nearly quit right then and there. His father had always been a bastard, but he'd never seen him in action before, and though he'd followed Jonah into the den and pleaded Randy's case, Jonah had turned a deaf ear.

"Whatever happened to innocent until proven guilty?" Jenner had demanded.

"Give it up, Jenner. I know that slimy little drunk's been cheating me for years. I turned a blind eye, 'cause he had a way with the stock and the rest of the men seemed to look up to him. But he was stealin' from me and I won't have it."

As Jonah poured three fingers of whiskey into a crystal tumbler, Jenner had glanced around the room. A man's domain with Indian prints on the walls, an old flintlock mounted over the fireplace, a globe in a mahogany stand sitting near the desk. Leather couch, old rocker, crystal glasses and polished floors completed the picture. Casual, yes, but obviously the office of a wealthy man. What did he care about a couple of calves? Randy Calhoun was nearly Jonah's age and had nothing but a broken-down Chevy pickup, a saddle and a room he rented by the week at the Lucky Star Motel.

Randy hadn't been able to get decent work since. His drinking had made him a regular at the Black Anvil. Yep, Randy had motive and opportunity.

"Randy wouldn't do it," Jenner said, remembering how beaten the man had appeared as he'd driven away from the ranch where he'd spent so many years. "Who else?"

"Corey Stills."

Jenner didn't need an explanation for that one. For years, it had been rumored that Jonah had kept Corey's young wife, Grace, as his mistress. The gossip had been floating around like a bad smell, but somehow Virginia McKee had ignored it, explaining to her children that powerful men were always the target for vicious lies involving their moral character. Why, just look at the politicians in Salem and Washington D.C., always being accused of this liaison or that liaison.

Jonah had been linked with a lot of women ranging from Wanda Tully, the blond waitress who worked at the Black Anvil, to Carol Larkin, once his secretary and eventually vice president of J.P. Limited, one of the corporations owned by McKee Enterprises.

"Dad was involved with a lot of women."

"But they didn't all have jealous husbands who adored them."

That much was true, and Jenner just recently had learned about jealousy. The thought of another man making love to Beth brought a bitter taste to his mouth and his fingers tightened over his glass. "Okay, I'll buy it. Corey hated Dad enough to kill him. But once Dad was dead, why the arson?"

"Who knows? Maybe Stills's hatred has been building for years and he wanted to get back at everything and everyone associated with his old enemy."

"But why not do that while Dad was alive—let him see the destruction, let the old man twist in the wind?"

"'Cause Dad was too powerful. Corey would've been found out and God only knows what might've happened if Dad got the sheriff's department and Judge Rayburn and Rex Stone on his side. Think about it."

"I don't know. Anyone else?"

"Mmm. Ned Jansen's near the top of the list. Dad did a number on him with the copper mine. I tried to talk to him about it, work out some kind of deal, but he wasn't interested, said he'd just as soon spit on a McKee as do business with one."

"Nice attitude."

"Not uncommon around here."

"And Ned did have an old axe to grind with Dad," Jenner thought aloud. "If you can believe the rumors."

Max frowned and rubbed the back of his neck. "You mean because he was supposed to have been involved with Mom years ago?"

"Well, that's just what they say. None of us were around."

"Come on, Jenner. That's old news. Over thirty years ago."

"Okay, so there are other people who have more recent grudges, right?"

"Yep. Even Slim Purcell has a reason to hate us."

Jenner snorted. "Maybe we should move."

"I wouldn't go that far, but..." Max hesitated, then shoved his hands into the back pockets of his jeans. The worry lines over his eyes deepened. "You know I've started taking precautions, not just around here, but at Colleen's place, too."

"You think someone might actually hurt Hillary?"

Max's eyes flared with fury. "I'd kill the bastard who tried," he said, his face suddenly harsh, his jaw thrust in a challenge. "I don't think it'll come to that. Hell, I hope not, but if I were you—"

"You think Cody might be in danger?"

"Or Beth." Jenner's muscles tightened. "Anyone close to you. I've even got someone watching the clinic and apartment house, though Skye doesn't have a clue. If she did, she'd probably kill me herself."

"Okay, you've convinced me," Jenner said, his thoughts already racing ahead. He couldn't let anything happen to Beth or Cody, and if it meant their going into hiding, well, so be it. Slinging his jacket over his back, he limped over to the desk and opened the top drawer. He sorted through key rings until he found the one he wanted.

One corner of Max's mouth lifted in a smile. "This is one helluva time to take a vacation."

Jenner pocketed the keys. "It's *not* a vacation."

"I guess you won't be showing up for work tomorrow."

"I'll call," he said, reaching into another drawer for a cellular phone and batteries.

"Don't bother."

Jenner grabbed his crutches, hitched his way to the door and shouldered it open. Hearing thunder rumble across the hills, he hiked the collar of his jacket up around his neck and considered his next move.

Beth wouldn't like it, but that was just too bad. If, as she so adamantly insisted, he was the father of her kid, then he owed that boy a decent, safe life and he was going to start giving it to him right now.

For the first time in his life, he was worrying about someone other than himself. His own hide was pretty much useless, but Beth and the boy, they were important.

He drove with a purpose, pushing the speed limit, forgetting that some of his leg movements were limited, and being damned if anyone was going to hurt Beth or Cody. The town of Rimrock hadn't changed in the past few hours; it was the same little town Jenner had lived in most of his life. But now he was looking over his shoulder for a sinister presence, jumping at shadows, afraid that some criminal might be planning to do bodily harm to a woman and child he'd met recently but who had already woven themselves so deeply into his heart that he couldn't imagine them ever leaving.

That thought jolted him and he nearly swerved into the oncoming lane. A horn blasted loudly from a station wagon traveling in the opposite direction, but Jenner hardly noticed. He'd spent his life cultivating the art of being a loner, making sure that he put down only the shallowest of roots, and here he was, thinking in terms of the future with a woman he didn't even trust and a boy who might or might not be his.

He turned off the main road and stopped at an all-night market for a few essentials, then drove straight to Beth's mother's house. A soft light shone through the front window and Jenner cut the engine. It seemed he was forever chasing this woman, insisting she be a part of his life, then pushing her away.

Telling himself he was the worst kind of fool, he hitched himself up the steps and knocked softly on the door. She answered quickly, as if she'd been expecting him.

"What are you doing here?" she said. "Everyone's asleep."

"Good." He reached for her arm, pulled her onto the porch and kissed her as long and as hard as he wanted. Her lips were soft and yielding against his, her body as hungry and anxious as his own. Fire swept through his blood. "Come with me."

"Where?"

"I'd rather not say."

Her smile was tentative. "What is this—twenty questions?"

"Please."

She stopped short and he realized he'd never used that word with her before. "Look, Jenner, I just can't leave Cody here—"

"Tonight, Beth. Now. It's important. Bring Cody with you."

"You want him, too?" she asked.

He hesitated for just a heartbeat. "Yeah," he admitted, surprised at his own emotions. "I want him."

Blinking hard against a sudden rush of tears, she swallowed. "Let me just tell Mom that we're leaving."

"And won't be back for a while."

"Wait a minute."

"A few days."

"I don't know—"

He grabbed her arm more tightly. "Pack a bag, Beth. Now!"

"But why—"

"Just do it," he said, and the tenor of his voice must have convinced her.

"I don't usually let bullheaded cowboys push me around," she grumbled as she pulled away from him. "You have some explaining to do."

"I will. Later," he promised, jangling his keys nervously.

She ducked back into the house. Through the open door, he heard conversation as Beth explained the situation to her mother. Harriet's words were muffled through her bedroom door, but their import was perfectly clear. She wasn't happy that her daughter was taking her grandson and leaving in the middle of the night with the no-good McKee rebel who had knocked her up and left her without a backward glance three years ago. Jenner didn't have to hear the words to get the gist of the conversation.

Within minutes, Beth was back on the porch, carrying Cody and a huge bag. She handed him the sleeping baby and Jenner smelled the soap, baby powder and shampoo that he remembered from his niece, Hillary a few years back. Except this was his son. Well, maybe.

Cody was a dead weight, barely moving as Jenner held him and Beth hurried to the truck to stow the bag in the back.

Jenner couldn't move. He didn't dare try to negotiate the steps with his crutches and carry the boy, so he had to wait until Beth, breathless, returned and retrieved her son, blanket and all. Some bodyguard he'd be, trapped on crutches, unable to carry the boy and run if need be, unable to protect them. He cursed under his breath.

Pathetic, that's what he was. But not much longer. He wouldn't just accept the fact that he couldn't take care of people who might rely on him. If he had to go back to the damned doctor, so be it. If he was forced to spend hours in physical therapy, he'd give it a shot. But he wasn't going to be useless any longer.

Damn it, Mavis had been right. This woman and his kid seemed to be all the motivation he needed to try again. And if he failed? If his leg refused to mend? If, after surgery and therapy and acupuncture and voodoo and whatever else it took, he still couldn't walk, then he'd accept the damned wheelchair and make the best of a bad situation. Somehow.

He didn't really have much choice.

Beth told herself she was nuts—certifiably crazy. What was she thinking, taking off in the middle of the night with Jenner McKee? Her mother's protests echoed in her ears.

"You're making a big mistake, Beth. Think about it.

"It's not that I don't like him, but he's got a reputation! The family's got a reputation! They're users, every last one of them. If you aren't thinking about yourself, consider Cody. He's just a baby.

"I hate to say it, Beth, but Jenner could be using you again. He'll break your heart and never look back. Just like before!"

Those final words kept reverberating in her heart, and she silently vowed that it wouldn't happen, that it couldn't; she mustn't lose her heart again.

Jenner didn't say much and the radio played a steady stream of country music, songs of broken hearts, missed opportunities and regrets, but Beth refused to think of them in terms of her relationship with Jenner. She was content to stare out the window at the night-darkened countryside while Cody slept soundly in the seat between them—his father and mother.

"You haven't said where we're going."

"Does it matter?" His voice was a rough whisper.

"I suppose not."

"Didn't think so." They drove through Dawson City and further east until eventually they turned off the main road and wound upward through the mountains, past stands of timber and along steep cliffs.

Though she had no idea where they were, Jenner drove as if he knew where he was going, turning easily at each fork in the road as if by instinct. Finally a gap appeared in the trees and he parked near a three-story lodge that had seen better days, a huge summer home from the looks of it. It was built on the shores of a placid lake, which seemed to shimmer under the stars.

"What is this place?"

"A retreat, I guess. Dad ended up with it in one of his business deals. I think it belonged to some civic group for a while, but it was originally built as a hunting lodge. We used to come up here as kids, whenever Mom couldn't stand another minute of the old man's B.S. Here...use this." He reached across her, the back of his arm brushing her breasts as he opened the glove compartment and extracted a flashlight.

Beth carried Cody inside and Jenner grabbed a couple of sacks from the back of the truck, which he managed to balance while using his crutches.

The steps were covered with dirt and leaves, and rodents had gnawed through some of the boards, but Beth closed her eyes to the state of disrepair and waited while Jenner fitted an old key into the lock. The door creaked open.

The interior smelled musty and dry, as if no one had stepped over the threshold in years. A haunted house, like something out of a horror movie, she thought. The flashlight's beam seemed small against the dark hallways and shadowed corners. A wide staircase with hand-carved railing and posts curved upward, but Jenner walked straight ahead, through a wide arch into a room as large as a ballroom in a Portland hotel.

"Over there," he said, pointing across the room to a

huge rock fireplace. She shone the beam on a massive mantel where hurricane lanterns stood under a cloak of dust. ''That's it. Hold it right there.'' He crossed the room, struck a match against the hearth, and lit each of the three lanterns. The room began to come alive as the lantern light was reflected in the mullioned windows and made shadows play upon the old plank floor. Jenner stripped sheets off a couple of pieces of furniture and found bedding smelling of cedar in a back closet. ''We'll put him here,'' he directed as he opened up a sofa bed in the corner, covered it with blankets and waited as Beth laid Cody gently on an old hand-pieced quilt. The little boy snuggled deep in the bedding, sighed and didn't even open his eyes.

''Why did you bring us here?'' she asked.

''A couple of reasons. I'll explain it all later. First I want to see if I can turn on the water and build a fire.'' He snagged a lantern from the mantel. ''Wait here.''

''I'm tired of waiting,'' she said as he hitched himself out of the room, but there wasn't much else she could do because she didn't want Cody to wake up frightened in the unfamiliar surroundings. She shone the beam of the flashlight to the ceiling, three stories above the main floor. Two sets of balconies, one above the other, skirted the huge room on three sides while windows filled the fourth wall. Through the dusty glass, the lake was visible, a breeze raising ripples to gleam in the soft light of the stars and a crescent moon.

She pulled off several more sheets and discovered Victorian furniture, antiques, she supposed, that included gateleg tables, brass lamps, club chairs and sofas, even an old player piano. The walls were decorated with heads of animals—bison, deer, antelope, elk, a mountain lion and even a moose. Rifles, spears, snowshoes and a variety of bows and arrows were interspersed between the furry faces with glass eyes that stared down at her.

What kind of man owned a hunting lodge?

The same kind who owned a ranch, a real estate company, racehorse and a copper mine. A man who had thought that the more he owned, the more important he was. A man who ended up getting himself killed.

Goose bumps rose on her arms and she shivered as she thought of Jonah and wondered who could have hated him enough to force his Jeep off the road. She glanced at Cody anxiously, but her baby was sleeping undisturbed, as if everything was right with the world. He didn't understand about his relationship to Jenner, had never even asked why he didn't have a father, and certainly had no clue that his ruthless grandfather had been killed.

Jenner's uneven gait announced his return. He was dragging pieces of firewood stacked on a sheet.

"Oh, for heaven's sake, I would have gotten that," she said, crossing the room quickly.

"I didn't want your help." He was sweating profusely, though it was cold up here in the mountains. "I didn't need it, did I?"

"It would have been simpler if—"

"Would it have?" he said, his voice rising. "Not for me. I'm not going to ask for help for every little thing."

"This wasn't a little thing."

"It's done, all right?" He made his way to the fireplace, opened the flue, laid down kindling, then stacked chunks of oak and fir over handmade andirons shaped to look like wolves baring their teeth. He struck a match and touched it several times to the tinder-dry wood. "That's better," he said, dusting off his hands.

And it was. Flames began to lick at the logs, casting the room in shadows of gold and causing the sweat sheening his forehead to glow. The cavernous room seemed suddenly cozy and warm. Aside from the quiet hiss of the fire and Cody's soft breathing, the lodge was hushed, and she was suddenly aware of being alone—really alone—with Jenner and his son.

Beth warmed her hands by the fire. "So now you're going to tell me why you brought me here, right?"

His smile was wicked. "I'll give you one reason."

"Just one?" She couldn't help the teasing lilt of her voice.

"The most important," he said slowly as he walked closer to her and ran a long finger down the side of her jaw. "I wanted to be alone with you."

Her heart pumped wildly as his finger slid lower to the pulse point at the base of her throat. It lingered there, drawing lazy, sensual circles.

"We—we didn't have to come this far."

"I didn't want to be interrupted." He let his finger catch on the neckline of her sweater and she hardly dared breathe. He pulled gently, the knitted fabric stretching before she moved her head. He kissed her softly, his lips brushing hers in a chaste, yet sensual movement. "Come on," he whispered. "I'd carry you, but considering the circumstances, I guess you'll have to make it on your own. Bring a lantern." Cocking his head toward a short hallway, he grabbed the flashlight and hobbled ahead, following the uneven beam.

Beth knew that Cody was fast asleep and wouldn't awaken, so she grabbed the light and followed Jenner. Her heart was racing as he led her into a room as large as her apartment. A canopied bed stood on a dais, though the bedding had long since been stripped from it. Another fireplace rose to the beamed ceiling and Jenner drew the curtains to show off a view of the lake.

"Who used this room?" she asked, sweeping her arm around the room.

"The owner's private quarters," he explained. "Complete with bath, kitchen, sitting area and a bed fit for a king."

Logs had been left in the grate and Jenner started another fire. Carpets had been rolled up against the wall and a chandelier covered with cobwebs swung from the ceiling.

Jenner reached into a cedar cupboard, found some quilts and tossed them onto the bed. Beth smiled as she walked up to him. "Why, Mr. McKee, you didn't bring me all the way up here just to seduce me?" she teased.

"That was the general idea," he admitted, watching her close the gap.

"Good." She let her coat fall to the floor and heard his breath rush over his teeth.

He dropped his crutches as she approached and climbed up the short steps of the dais. When she reached him, he grabbed her roughly around the waist. "I've been waiting for this for a long time," he said, and his lips came crashing down on hers in a kiss that was hot and hungry and wet.

Wrapping her arms around his neck, she kissed him back, and when his tongue sought entrance to her mouth, she opened it willingly to him, feeling him plunge and taste, plunder and explore. He cupped her buttocks, drawing her close to the swelling in his jeans, pulling her against him so that she felt his heat.

The fire crackled and popped as they tumbled to the bed. Still kissing her, Jenner reached beneath her sweater boldly, as if he expected no protests. His hands were rough against her flesh as he delved into her bra, his fingers cupping her breasts, and rubbing her nipples anxiously. "Beth, oh, Beth," he groaned, stripping her of her sweater, then shedding his jacket.

He couldn't get enough of her. He kissed the tops of her breasts, his tongue outlining the sculpted lace of her bra, and she arched her back, moving closer, silently begging him to take more. Through the sheer lace, his tongue laved her nipples, moistening the fabric, teasing each little peak until she moaned with desire and pushed her pelvis closer to his. A warmth swirled deep within her, growing more intense, pulsing with need.

He kissed first one nipple, then the next, and little goose bumps of pleasure rippled along her skin. She was with Jenner, and her heart opened to him, though she'd sworn long ago that she'd never let him touch her, never trust him again. She cradled his head against her, feeling him suckle her breasts, thrilling as his hands slid along her spine, his fingers dipping past her jeans to touch the dimples in her bottom.

"Make love to me," he whispered, and she couldn't deny him.

Slowly she unbuttoned his shirt, touching the stiff hair on his chest, outlining his flat nipples, watching in fascination the play of muscles in his abdomen. He sucked in his breath and she kissed his navel. His fingers dug into her hair and he held her there, feeling her tongue wet and filled with promise as it explored that little dimple of flesh.

He smelled of soap and tasted of salt and he groaned in pleasure as she moved her hand up his torso and let her fingers explore the sinewy muscles of his shoulders and arms while her mouth left moist impressions on his chest. He bucked when she kissed his nipple and cried out as if he could stand the frustration no longer.

His hands moved quickly. Stripping off her jeans, he touched her everywhere, his hands eager, his lips quick to sear a kiss against her bare skin. He kicked off his own Levi's, and if he experienced any pain while undressing, he hid it well. Reaching into a pocket, he found a packet, opened it with his teeth and handed it to her.

As sweat broke out to slick his skin, she fitted the condom on him. He moaned at the feel of her fingers against his shaft. "Oh, Beth," he whispered. Then as the firelight bronzed his skin, he kissed her roughly again, his mouth molding to hers as he pulled her atop him. He didn't wait for her to settle; instead, while gazing hotly up at her, he lifted his buttocks and impaled her.

She gasped as he started to move and she closed her eyes and threw back her head.

"Watch me," he commanded.

"Wha—"

"I don't want either of us to forget this happened. Not ever." His eyes locked with hers, he rocked up and down, his hands kneading her breasts, his breathing ragged. Slowly he rocked, drawing in and out as her blood heated and her body seemed to fuse with his.

A storm built inside her, hot and savage and wild and she began moving of her own accord, to her own rhythm, a furious pace that caused his eyes to darken as he gazed up at her.

"I can't stop...Beth—"

She let out a scream as the world seemed to collide with some unseen heavenly body. He arched up and cried out her name like a litany. "Beth, oh, Beth... Ahhh!" His voice was hoarse and she was jolted again when he grabbed her around the waist and pulled her down to the bed with him where they tangled together, arms and legs entwined, smelling of sweat and lovemaking.

Jenner's fingers tangled in her hair and he breathed hard against her ear. She listened to his heartbeat and cuddled up to him, noticing the scars on different parts of his body and the way his muscles coiled beneath his skin.

For minutes they were silent, their heartbeats slowing.

"Why *did* you bring me here?" she asked again when she could finally talk. She kissed his chest. "Besides the obvious reason, I mean."

He pushed a strand of hair from her eyes so tenderly she thought her heart might break right then and there. "I thought it would be safer up here."

"Safer?" She laughed, then her smile faded when she remembered another conversation they'd had. "You still think there may be a nut out there somewhere, planning to hurt us?"

"I don't know for sure," he admitted. "But I can't take a chance." He kissed the top of her head and told her everything he and Max had discussed.

Beth held him and listened, but she couldn't help the smile that teased her lips. For no matter what else he said, no matter what theories Max or the private investigator or the police could come up with, one thing was certain: Jenner McKee cared. About her and about his son. There was no other reason he would go to such lengths to hide them. Slowly, whether he liked it or not, Jenner was beginning to accept the fact that he was a father.

She didn't know where that realization would lead, but had to believe a major stumbling block was out of the way. So she listened. As Jenner stroked her hair and kissed her crown and explained just how many people in Rimrock had reason to hate his father, Beth smiled and wondered what the morning would bring.

Chapter Eleven

Beth never wanted to leave. Sighing contentedly, she stretched on the rumpled bedding. She and Jenner had made love most of the night and she had no regrets. Though he didn't love her, she knew that he cared, and caring was a start—a large step in the right direction.

She pulled on her clothes and gazed through the dusty panes of the window to the lake where the rays of morning sun glinted on the ripples. Geese flew overhead in wavering V formations and ducks skimmed the surface of the water.

From the corner of her eye, she saw Jenner walking with his crutches near the lake's edge, and with him, dragging a stick, was Cody. Beth's heart nearly melted when she saw Jenner pause and point to a squirrel racing in the branches of an ancient pine tree.

Rather than disturb father and son, she decided to go and explore the old lodge. On the second floor were bedrooms, some single, some double, some with several sets of bunks, which shared communal baths branching off the balcony. The third was filled with complete and odd-shaped suites tucked under the eaves. The place was dusty and there was evidence of mice in some of the bedding, but she found only one spot where the roof leaked. All the old lodge needed was some solvent, polish and lots of elbow grease.

On the first floor there were meeting rooms, a dining room, a sun porch, kitchen and baths, as well as the main hall and master suite. In the basement, there was a recreation room with an old pool table, the furnace room, laundry, a wine cellar and larders, now empty. Coal and wood chutes were strategically placed near the back of the lodge and a dumbwaiter connected the floors.

The lodge was a mansion out of one of the stories Beth had read as a child. She climbed back up to the first floor and went to the kitchen, where Jenner had a pot of coffee heating on a huge wood stove. Beth rinsed a cup under a groaning faucet, which delivered only cold water, then poured herself some of the strong brew.

With a feeling of contentment she hadn't experienced in years, she carried her cup to the wide back porch and sat in an old cushioned swing. She rocked slowly as she watched Jenner and Cody by the lake. Jenner's voice was muffled, but he spoke to the boy often, and when he did, Cody tipped his face up, his eyes round with wonder.

This was how it was supposed to be—father and son discovering the world together. Tears burned the back of her eyes as she realized how desperately she wanted this for Cody, how much she'd missed by not knowing her own father. Could she ever deny her son the right to know the man who had helped create his life? Even if things didn't work out between Jenner and her, she couldn't break this fragile bond that existed between these two.

As if he'd read her mind, Jenner turned. She felt her heart close in on itself as her gaze locked with his. She was aware of the breeze that tickled her neck and bent the grass near the water's edge, but time seemed to stand still in that one instant. Cody, turning to follow Jenner's gaze, saw her. He threw back his head and laughed, the joyful sound rising into the sky.

"Mommy! Mommy!" he cried in pure delight. "We find squirrels and birds and snakes!" His little legs started churning as he ran along the bank, then found the weed-choked brick path that led to the porch.

"Snakes?" she echoed as she placed her coffee on the floor and reached out to scoop him into her arms.

"Yeah! Rattlesnakes this—" he held his arms out wide "—big!"

"Rattlesnakes!" she gasped, her heart faltering.

But Jenner only laughed as he joined them. "No rattlers."

"They were! I seen 'em."

"If you say so, pardner," Jenner agreed with a wink at Beth, and she relaxed. "Come on now, I'll make you both some breakfast."

Cody scrambled to the ground and tore into the lodge. His little feet pounded loudly on the floors, and Beth, still outside, could hear him running from room to room. "You've got yourself a good kid," Jenner admitted when they were alone.

"So do you."

"Do I?" His eyes held hers and he drew her into the circle of his arms, kissing her lightly on her forehead, her eyelids and her cheeks before his lips settled over hers and she sighed into his open mouth. Everything seemed so right up here—away from the rest of the world, just man, woman and child. No worries, no gossip, nothing but this tiny little family.

She broke the embrace suddenly at that thought. *Family?* They weren't a family. She was a single mother with a two-year-old son, and Jenner was a die-hard bachelor content to be single. How could she ever think of them as a family? How could she delude herself?

Jenner, feeling her tense, held her even more tightly.
"It's all right," he said against her ear. "It'll be all right.
I promise."

"You do?"

"Mmm." He kissed her crown again and she leaned
against him, feeling his strong arms surround her.

It'll be all right.

If only she could believe him.

They had so far spent three days at the lodge. Jenner
had driven them into a small town where the post office,
general store and hardware store shared one building.
Beth called her mother and explained that they were together and getting to know each other. Jenner called Max,
asking about the investigation and checking on the rest of
his family.

During the day, Beth cleaned and cooked and spent
hours with her son and Jenner. They explored the lake
and the woods, startled owls and spied a fawn lying still
in the undergrowth. A family of raccoons scavenged near
the kitchen at night and it was all she could do to keep
Cody from chasing after them, intent on catching one of
the smaller masked beasts.

Jenner enthralled them both with the history of the
lodge, though Beth suspected his stories of colorful past
figures spending time here were embellished a little. Each
night as they sat near the fire and Cody listened raptly to
this stranger who was his father, Jenner seemed to thaw
a little more toward his son. The brackets around the corners of his mouth disappeared and a kinder side of him
emerged as Cody tagged after him all day long, his short
legs keeping up with Jenner's without any trouble since
Jenner was slowed by his crutches.

"You may as well know that I promised Max I'd go
back to the doctor and physical therapist," Jenner admitted one night as they sat huddled together on a couch near
the fire, stockinged feet propped on the broad hearth,

Cody snoring softly as he lay in the crook of Jenner's arm.

"What changed your mind?"

Jenner stared at the bright embers and scowled. "You did. You and Cody." He turned to look at her and his eyes were as clear and blue as the lake outside the back door. "You know, I hate like hell to admit it when someone is right and I'm proved wrong, but when Mavis wrote to you, she knew what she was doing." His eyebrows drew together forming one thick line. "I guess I'd given up, decided that if I couldn't ride and rope and brand and all that nonsense that seemed so important—" he waved his hand as if he was brushing aside an inconsequential fly "—that I'd just give up. Then you showed up with this little dynamo and bang! My whole world was turned upside down. Everything I'd ever believed in..."

Her heart nearly stopped beating and she realized there in the shadowy room how much she'd come to love this rugged loner of a man, not with the silly schoolgirl fantasies she'd harbored all those years before, but with a love based on trust and understanding and the knowledge that he could stir her blood as well as her soul. Jenner was a hard man, a distant man at times, but he was honest and strong.

"Anyway." He slapped his thighs and Cody shifted. "I guess I wanted to pour myself into a bottle and drown." He slid her a glance. "Not a very practical plan, but it seemed to keep the demons at bay."

"Did it?" she teased as he slung an arm over her shoulder and his breath whispered across her hair.

"Not very well. I never could seem to get enough booze. Kinda the same way I feel about you." He kissed her hard enough to start her heart pumping with wild abandon. Her arms curved around his neck and she moved closer still, her breasts brushing his ribs through their shirts.

With a groan of frustration, he released her. "You're going to get yourself into big trouble, lady," he warned.

She winked at him. "I'm counting on it."

"Are you?" A devilish light flamed in his eyes and he hauled Cody into his arms and helped the boy into his bed. Once satisfied that Cody wouldn't wake up, he linked his fingers through Beth's and they moved to the bedroom without his crutches, Jenner leaning on her, she supporting him, until they fell on the bed together and he wrested the shirt from her body. Slowly, eyes locked with hers, he made love to her as passionately as they had the night Cody was conceived, as savagely as their first night alone in the lodge together.

The next morning Jenner announced they had to get back. He'd called Max. Things were stable at the ranch and he was needed. Jenner grinned at that. "Yep. Max seems to think I can actually be of some help. One of the men quit last night and the Rocking M's shorthanded. Can you believe it?"

"Yes," she said, her voice catching. Of course he was needed. Didn't she need him? Didn't Cody?

Her heart was heavy as she packed to leave this mountain retreat, but she managed to hide her disappointment. Truth to tell, she, too, had to start thinking about the rest of her life as well as the rest of Cody's. She needed to return to Oregon City and start hunting for another job, but that thought brought a lump to her throat.

Life without Jenner.

Shuttling Cody from the Willamette Valley to Rimrock where, as he grew older, he'd eventually hear the gossip and have to live with the rumors. *Bastard. Unwanted. Mistake.*

But at least he'd have a father's love.

Certainly that was worth the risk and the heartache of facing the taunts leveled at him by other children and the gossips in town. Or was it? Instead of becoming simpler, her life was getting more complicated by the minute. Because of Jenner and the horrid fact that she loved him.

Cody chattered incessantly as they drove back to Rimrock, and with each mile that passed, Beth felt the tension in the cab increase. Her stomach clenched as they turned off the main road and into the lane leading to the Rocking M. The trees lining the drive seemed to bend in the wind and dry leaves scattered as the truck bounced over potholes. Dark clouds clustered in the sky.

"Home sweet home," Jenner said sarcastically as he stopped near the garage.

Max stood in the doorway of the barn talking with Chester Wilcox. Hillary was riding Cambridge in one of the enclosures, her curls catching the late afternoon sunlight as Dani, holding the lead rope, coached her young charge. Cattle milled in nearby pens and the horses grazed in the dry fields.

"Maybe you should take me home first—"

"This'll just take a minute." He slanted her a glance and private little smile. "We McKees don't bite...well, unless it's in the middle of the night when things get a little rough and—"

"Enough. I get the picture," she said, her blood swirling through her veins.

Cody, spying Hillary on her horse, clamored to get out. "Me ride!" he insisted.

"Oh, honey, not now—"

"It's all right," Jenner assured her, glancing at the heavy bellied clouds.

"I don't think Hillary's going to like it."

"He doesn't have to ride Cambridge. We can find him another mount. Come on, pardner." And the two of them were off—father limping on crutches, son scampering through the dust as fast as his short legs would carry him. The dog, Reuben, was sleeping in a patch of weeds near the garage and he let out a quiet woof as Cody raced past.

Beth followed her son and leaned against the rails of

the fence. She watched Dani and Hillary while Jenner
stopped to talk with his brother and the ranch foreman.
Cody was hopping up and down, demanding his attention,
and Jenner, after a sharp word to the boy, picked him up
and held him as naturally as if he'd done it all his life.

A natural father. She smiled to herself. Wouldn't he
die to think of himself, the rugged, lone wolf of a cowboy,
now able to read a bedtime story, change a night diaper
and kiss scratches and "owies" as naturally as if he'd
been born to do it?

So caught up in her fantasy, she didn't hear the sound
of footsteps behind her until she felt a breath of chill air
against the back of her neck. "So...you decided to come
back, did you?" Virginia's voice was cold.

"Pardon me?" Beth turned to face the censure that was
Virginia McKee.

"I know what you were doing, don't think I don't. You
think you've got your hooks in my boy but you're
wrong."

"I don't understand—"

"Sure you do," Virginia insisted in a harsh whisper.
"You thought by luring him away with sex and the boy
you could make him change his ways, even marry you,
but you haven't got a chance. Jenner's only interested in
himself—he'll never be tied to a family. And if you think
you can pass off your boy as his—"

"Don't even say it," Beth warned, her temper snapping. "Jenner is Cody's father and that's the way it is,
even if you've got a problem with it." She stepped closer
to the woman who seemed determined to hate her. "I
don't know what it is you have against me, and I really
don't care. You can think what you want. But when it
comes to my son, you'd better be careful, because I won't
let anyone—not even you—hurt him."

"Then why did you bring him here?"

"Because I had no choice."

Virginia's mouth twisted into a thin, wicked little smile.

Behind her, Casey had come out of the house and was approaching, but Virginia didn't stop. "You may as well know something about me. I'm a lot stronger than I look and I don't back down easily. I was the one who insisted that my husband was murdered when the police were ready to give up and write the whole episode off as a nasty accident. But I proved them wrong.

"I know you came here because of Mavis—that old woman would do anything to convince herself that the McKee name isn't going to die. She and I both know that Skye can't give Max any sons, and Casey, well, that girl doesn't know what she wants, but if and when she does get around to marrying, the children won't carry the McKee name. So Jenner is Mavis's last hope and she pinned that hope on you, as well."

"Because it's the truth." Beth leaned closer to the older woman and held her gaze. "If you have a problem with me—a bone to pick—why don't you just tell me about it?"

"You really want to know?"

"Yes."

"All right," Virginia said, clearing her throat and straightening to her full height. "Isn't it obvious? You bore a child out of wedlock."

"Jenner's child."

"So you say."

"He was involved, too, and I refuse to accept your double standard."

"And now you're back, trying to drag his name—our name—through the mud. The whole town will be buzzing."

"Is that what's bothering you?" Beth asked. "After all the scandal you've endured?" She couldn't believe it. "There's something more, isn't there? Something else that's bothering you."

Beth saw the hint of a shadow in Virginia's eyes—the flicker of a secret—but it quickly disappeared. "I just don't want my son—a McKee—involved with poor white trash," Virginia said and turned on her heel, nearly running into Casey.

"How could you?" Casey said as Virginia stopped short.

"This family's name has been dragged through the mud too many times. I won't allow it to happen again."

"Is that it, or are you afraid that we'll all finally come to terms with the kind of man our father really was?" Casey asked.

Virginia's throat worked. "He was a good, decent, hardworking—"

"He was a crook, Mom. He deceived people and cheated them out of their money, then he tried his best to ruin his children's lives. If you face facts, you'll even realize that he tried to ruin yours, as well. It's just that you turned a blind eye to all of his affairs and mistresses."

"I won't hear this…this blasphemy!"

"Maybe it's time you faced the truth, Mom, and quit deluding yourself."

"I don't—"

"Of course you do! You always have. Oh, God, I've got to leave this place before I go out of my mind!"

"Don't even talk that way. You tried leaving once before—"

"I was just a kid then, didn't know what I wanted."

"And you still don't!" Virginia said, then stared straight at Beth. "Jenner doesn't believe you, you know. He thinks you're nothing but a fortune hunter, and though you've turned his head for a while, it won't last. Because, deep down, he knows the truth and he'll find a way to prove it." Virginia whirled on her heel and walked swiftly toward the ranch house.

"Don't listen to her," Casey advised. "She's been a basket case since Dad died. Maybe even before."

"She hates me."

"She hates the world." Casey sighed. "Things didn't

turn out the way she'd planned. People showed their true colors. Her husband didn't turn out to be Prince Charming and her kids weren't perfect little angels.'' Casey cast a glance back at her mother, who was making her way into the house. ''But none of us should pay her any mind. Especially you. I've seen the way Jenner looks at you, Beth, and he's never, *ever* looked at a woman the way he looks at you. Not even Nora Bateman. As for Mom, she's just going through this thing…what with Dad's death and all. She'll accept you. Eventually.''

''I'm not so sure about that,'' Beth replied, not really certain if she wanted to be condoned by Jenner's mother.

''Give it time. Believe me, anyone who can put up with Jenner is a saint in my book.''

''You think he's that bad?''

''Are you kidding?'' Casey's eyes twinkled. ''He's the worst!''

''I heard that,'' Jenner said as he came from the barn. He was leading an old gray horse with Cody perched atop.

''Good. Then maybe you'll straighten up.''

He darted a quick, sexy glance at Beth. ''Never.''

''Hopeless,'' Casey said under her breath. ''Hey, Hillary!'' Casey waved an arm wildly at her niece. ''Looks like you've got yourself some competition.''

''I ride, Mommy!'' Cody yelled excitedly.

''Big deal.'' Hillary wasn't impressed.

''It is a big deal,'' Dani assured her.

''He's just a baby.'' Hillary tossed her hair and nudged her palomino's sides.

''Am not! Big boy!'' Cody replied, then ignored his cousin completely. So wrapped up in riding the gray horse, he didn't catch one of the dozen superior looks cast in his direction.

''Dani's good with kids,'' Beth said to Casey as the horses slowed. Both children protested loudly and refused to climb off their mounts.

''Yeah. She seems to have a thing about 'em.'' Casey

frowned a little. "She once said something to me about her husband, Jeff, not wanting any. At least not right away, but I think she'd have a dozen of 'em."

"A dozen's a lot," Beth said, but understood Dani's feelings. Wasn't her own biological clock ticking? Wouldn't she love a sibling for Cody—a new baby for her to cuddle? She watched Dani as she helped Hillary from the saddle. Dani had been wild in her youth. There had been stories about her and talk of a child she'd given up for adoption. No one but Dani knew the truth, and Beth hadn't listened too much to the town gossip as she'd experienced her share of it over the years.

"Come on, pardner, you need to meet Gary. He's one of the hands and he'll show you how to brush a horse," Jenner said, leading the old gray toward the barn.

"It's amazing," Casey said. "He's so good with Cody."

"Yes." Beth's heart swelled.

"Who would've guessed?"

Not me. Not in a thousand years.

"The next thing you know he'll want to settle down and have another one."

Beth's heart caught.

With a sigh, Casey slapped the top rail of the fence. "It must be nice, knowing what you want." Raking her fingers through her hair, she gazed across the paddock. "Mom was right about that, though I hate to admit it. I never have been able to figure out what I should be doing with the rest of my life."

Little footsteps sounded in the dust. "You see me ride, Mommy?" Cody asked as he approached.

"I sure did."

"I want a horse."

"Of your own?" She glared up at Jenner, certain the idea had sprouted with him, but he lifted his hands off his crutches to express his perplexity, as if this was news to him.

"Cody's idea," Jenner said.

"We're still debating on a puppy."

"Want a puppy, too. And kitties. You got kitties." He looked eagerly at Casey.

"Hey, slow down," Beth admonished. "One at a time." She checked her watch. "I think we should go. He missed his nap."

"No!" Cody cried.

"Right after a hamburger and French fries!" Jenner promised as he swung the boy off his feet and plopped him onto the top rail of the fence. He held him steady while Cody whooped and squirmed in delight.

"Now who's spoiling him?" Beth said, and Casey chuckled.

"I wish I had a picture. My brother—the father." She winked at Beth. "Take my advice. Run now while you still can. He can't catch you now, but once he gets off those sticks, he'll be hell on wheels again."

"Thanks a lot." Jenner's voice dripped sarcasm, but he flashed his off-center smile at his sister as he covered their bags with a tarp and glanced at the dark sky. "Okay, let's go. Can't keep Grandma waiting."

"See Grandma!" Cody said, running to the truck, and Beth couldn't help thinking of Virginia McKee and her dislike—no, hatred—of her grandson.

As they drove into town, the first raindrops splattered against the windshield, and by the time they'd finished a quick dinner at the Shady Grove Café and Jenner had pulled into the driveway of Harriet's little cottage, the storm was in full force, wind blowing, rain peppering the ground. Cody had fallen asleep in the seat between them, and when Beth reached over to take hold of him, Jenner's hand caught her wrist.

She looked up and found herself staring into blue eyes that were dark with confusion. "What do we do now?" he asked.

Love bloomed in her heart. "I guess we take it one step at a time."

His jaw tightened. "To what end?"

"Whatever we want."

"Then maybe I should make something clear," he said, releasing her and letting out his breath. He held on to the steering wheel in a death grip and stared through the water sheeting on the windshield.

Beth could barely breathe. Something was wrong—horribly wrong. The carefree and loving Jenner she'd known at the lodge was gone and the hard man, the lone cowboy, had returned.

His voice was solemn. "I don't think I'm what you're hoping for," he said, weighing his words carefully. "I'm nothing more than what I look like—a broken-down, washed-up cowboy who owns nothing. I've got a little bit of land, not a whole lot, and probably less than two thousand dollars in the bank. My family is always there to help me out, of course, but I've never taken and will never take their charity. Even though I'm going to work for Max and see a few doctors, there's no guarantee that I'll ever walk again without a wheelchair or crutches or something." His knuckles showed white over the steering wheel. "I've never wanted a wife or a kid or anything that would tie me down. And maybe if things were different…" He scowled. "If I was independent—hell, if I could walk again—I'd feel differently, but right now…"

Her throat clogged, and as he turned his eyes to her, she saw the pain in their blue depths. She couldn't help but reach forward and place her hand against his cheek. He grabbed it and held it against his warm flesh, then turned his head and kissed her palm, leaving a warm impression. "I can't stand the idea of being half a man."

"You're not!"

"And I can't stand the thought of anyone pitying me—especially not the woman I'm involved with."

She couldn't help the edge of anger in her voice. "Do

you think I'm sticking around because I *pity* you? Because I *feel sorry* for you?'' she asked, astounded. After the past three days together, how could he even begin to believe such nonsense?

''Why *are* you sticking around?''

''Because—'' *Because I love you!* ''—because of Cody. I—I don't want him to grow up always wondering. Not knowing his father...like me.''

''I knew mine. It was no picnic.''

''Maybe not, but...'' Finally she understood. He was telling her as gently as possible that it was over, that they'd had their fun, that yes, he did care a little, but it was over. For her. For Cody. Oh, God! Her heart squeezed painfully and she swallowed against the lump suddenly forming in her throat. ''I—I'd better go....'' Condensation had begun to cloud the windows as the rain continued to fall.

''Would you stay here?''

''Pardon?''

''In Rimrock. You could get a job. Skye needs help at the clinic. I could see Cody. We could try—''

''I don't think so,'' she said quickly when she heard the doubt in his voice. She wouldn't live the life her mother had lived, the subject of small-town gossip. Without another thought, she lifted her son onto her lap. This wasn't the time for goodbyes or making plans. Not after all the emotional ups and downs she'd experienced since returning to Rimrock. She knew that Jenner felt something for her and she didn't doubt that he would come to love his son, but the argument with Virginia and the chip on Jenner's shoulder about the use of his legs were too much to deal with right now. She needed time alone to think. To sort out what she really wanted and what would be best for Cody.

''You don't have to go—''

''I think it would be best. Mom's expecting me and—''

''I mean you don't have to leave Rimrock.''

"You want me to stay?"

He didn't answer, just stared at her long and hard, as if he couldn't decide whether to trust her or not. Although he'd seemed to believe in her at the lodge, now that he was back in Rimrock, things had changed. He'd changed. "I want you to do what's best for the boy."

The boy. Not *our son,* just *the boy.* "I—I'll think about it," she whispered as she reached for the door handle. Jenner glanced at the rain and struggled out of his jacket. "Here, you can cover him with this. I'll get your bag."

"It's no trouble. I can manage—"

"I said I'll handle it." Jenner's voice was firm, his eyes narrowed, and she didn't argue with him.

Let him carry the damn bag if it made him feel whole. How could he believe that she cared if he ever walked without the use of crutches? After all they'd shared, why would he think that she pitied him, that he couldn't be a husband or father or— That thought caught her up short. *Husband?* As if they'd ever discussed marriage. Jenner McKee wasn't the marrying kind and she was foolish to think that he would ever change. If she was to stay in Rimrock, she would have to settle for a little part of him, for having an affair, for being one name among many in a little black book. And Cody would know the truth, learn that the man who had sired him didn't care enough about his mother to marry her, that he had other women, maybe even other children. Oh, Lord. She blinked hard, then opened the door. With a firm hold on Cody, she stepped out into the rain. Cody cried out as the rain hit him and the jacket slipped down to the ground.

"Oh, Lord…"

"I'll get it," Jenner said, but he slipped a little as his crutch caught the edge of a pothole. Still holding Cody, Beth bent down and retrieved the jacket by the lining. A manila envelope slid out of the inside pocket.

She heard Jenner's sharp intake of breath as she grabbed the dripping packet and the contents fell out onto the wet driveway. "Oh, I'm sorry. I didn't mean—" Her name swam before her eyes, and for a second she didn't realize what it was that she was reading. But as she picked up the soggy pages and recognized copies of her birth certificate, her report cards, credit reports, various other typed documents and Cody's birth certificate, she froze.

"You—you had me investigated?" she stammered, turning to face him as rain ran down the back of her neck and Cody, blinking against the drops in his face, began to cry.

Jenner's face was stony, his eyes without emotion. "I asked Rex Stone to look into your background."

"Why?"

"Because I thought you were a fake."

"Even though your grandmother..." she began, then words failed her. They would never trust each other, she realized, and he would always have trouble believing that Cody was his. Even if all the tests pointed to him, Cody would still be his bastard, his mistake, the reason he had to keep seeing Beth.

"I told Stone to back off," he said.

"But not until you got what you wanted."

Tossing the offensive documents back into the mud, she held her son close to her breast, protecting his head from the rain just as she wished she could protect his innocent heart. "I think you'd better leave."

"I can't."

"Like hell. You didn't want us involved in your life and that's just fine with me. You and all your family can go to hell!" She turned but he caught her arm, spinning her back against him.

"Beth—"

"Don't, okay? Just don't."

He kissed her then. His wet lips captured hers in a kiss that threatened to draw the life from her body. She felt the passion, the raw desire that he inspired, and her heart shattered into a million pieces. With all the strength she

could muster, she broke away, and her hand drew back
as if to slap him.

"Mommy!" Cody cried and Beth let her hand drop to
her side.

Jenner's expression was harsh. "Listen, I don't want
you to think, I mean, I'll take care of you and Cody. I—"

"What? You feel *obligated?* You feel *responsible?*"

"Hell, yes!"

"Too late, Jenner. Cody and I, we don't need you!"
That was a lie. Both she and her son needed him on the
most basic of levels. "Just leave us alone."

"I can't."

"Well, you'll have to."

"No way!" His fingers tightened over her forearm.
"That boy's mine, too, and—"

"Oh, so you finally believe me."

"I want to be a part of his life."

"What life?" she demanded, her voice catching. "I
won't allow him to be ridiculed by the people of this
town, nor will I have your mother treating him like something that should be swept under the rug. He's my son,
Jenner. *Mine!*" She hooked her thumb at her chest. "You
made your noble gesture, but now you can just bow out."
Balancing Cody, she reached into the back of the truck
and yanked out her bags, tossing them onto the soggy
ground.

"I'm not going anywhere," he insisted, the rain slash-
ing down his face. "You can't take my son away."

"Watch me!" Grabbing one bag she spun around and
ran up the steps to the front porch. Water washed down
her face and she didn't know if it was raindrops falling
from the dark sky or her own tears flowing down her
cheeks.

Chapter Twelve

The Black Anvil with its smoky atmosphere and loud patrons didn't lift his spirits. Jenner had downed one beer and was nursing his second. After the fight with Beth, he'd driven back to the Rocking M and, keeping silent about his problems, worked with Max on blueprints for the new stables. Max, sensing something was wrong, but smart enough not to pry, had told him that the investigation into the arson and Jonah's murder was still progressing. The list of suspects was narrowing, even though the leads offered by would-be snitches for their share of the reward had heretofore been busts. Max was still keeping security tight on the ranch, but nothing out of the ordinary had happened.

Jenner hadn't stayed at the Rocking M for dinner and instead had wound up at the saloon with the regulars. Slim Purcell was shooting pool with Fred Donner. Elvin Green occupied his usual stool, and Cyrus Kellogg, Jeff Stewart and a few others clustered at a couple of tables and griped about hunting restrictions.

Jenner wondered where Beth was and if she'd already taken off for the Willamette Valley. The thought depressed him and he tried to think of his life without her—the life he'd found so appealing before she'd shaken up his world. And what about the boy? How could he go on from day to day knowing that there was a kid out there—*his* kid—who needed to be raised properly, with a father? He couldn't help but smile when he thought of the little blond scamp and hoped old Jonah was roasting in hell for trying to screw up his grandson's life.

He saw a movement in the mirror over the bar. Jake was drawing another beer for Jimmy Rickert's glass and Jimmy glanced at Jenner before looking quickly away.

"Think that's about it," Jake said as he slid the mug over to Jimmy. "This is your last."

"You cuttin' me off?" Jimmy's speech was already slurred, but that was a normal state. "Hell, I'm one of your best customers."

"That's why your next drink is coffee. And you might want to settle up your tab."

"Shiii—" He bit off his curse as his eyes met Jenner's in the mirror again. This time he didn't look away. "Well, McKee, surprise, surprise. I thought you gave up hangin' out here."

"I have," Jenner said, startled at his admission. The Black Anvil held no appeal for him anymore and he was sorry he'd shown up. Ignoring the rest of his beer, he left some bills on the bar as Jake fiddled with the knobs on the television mounted near the ceiling.

"Too good for the rest of us since your woman blew back into town?"

Every muscle in Jenner's body tensed.

Jimmy, seeing Jenner's reaction, cackled. "Didn't think we knew, did ya? Hear ya got yourself a son." Another cackle of malicious laughter. "Pr'bly got seven or eight strung out along the ol' rodeo circuit, eh?"

"You're listening to gossip, Jimmy. Never a good idea."

"Yeah, well, I hear a lot. Keep my ears open." His grin was wide. Sly. Teasing. He knew something, all right, and he was enjoying having one over on Jenner. Jimmy reached into his breast pocket for a crumpled pack of cigarettes and lit up. Plucking a piece of tobacco from his tongue, he blew smoke to the ceiling. "Learn more'n I should sometimes, if ya get my drift." Puffing out a smoke ring, he slid Jenner another knowing glance. "Anyone collect on that reward yet?"

"You tell me. You seem to have all the answers," Jenner said, his eyes narrowing thoughtfully on this barfly. If anyone would know what was happening in the Rimrock underground, it would be Jimmy. He knew who hunted without a license, who was sleeping with another man's wife, who'd been in a fight and who was driving with a suspended license. Nickel-and-dime stuff, but the gleam in his eye promised something more.

"I don't know nothin'."

Jenner doubted it. Jimmy had always been a snitch, but the sheriff's department had questioned him repeatedly and Jimmy had come up with an alibi for the night Jonah was killed as well as for the time of the fire. "Twenty-five grand isn't anything to sneeze at," Jenner drawled.

"Petty cash to you McKees."

"Could set a man up, though." Jenner rubbed his chin. "Someone could put a down payment on a ranch or buy a new truck or bet the ponies.... Hell, I dunno, a guy could even take a vacation."

Rickert's smile faded and his nose twitched a little—like a rat sniffing cheese. He was hooked. All Jenner had to do was reel him in and the drunk would spill his guts.

"G'night, Jake." Jenner slid a glance at Jimmy. "You, too, Rickert."

He walked outside and smelled the rain that still lingered in the air. The storm had passed, but water filled the potholes in the parking lot. How had Jimmy learned about Beth and Cody? That thought chilled him as much as the wind ripping down from the north, reminding him that winter was just around the corner. Snow had already been predicted for the weekend.

He'd started for his old Dodge when he saw Jimmy stagger out and head toward a battered four-wheel-drive rig that had already tangled with a ditch or two. Both front fenders were crumpled, and where there had once been a headlight, there was now only a black hole.

"Let me drive you, Rickert."

"You?" Jimmy spit his cigarette into one of the puddles. "You're a goddamned cripple. I'll take care of myself."

Jenner's muscles tightened. "You're drunk."

"I hope so…the amount of money I spent in there." He swayed a little as he tried to shove his key into the lock. Jenner didn't believe in being holier-than-thou, but he didn't like the idea of Jimmy's truck weaving through the streets of Rimrock, streets where Beth might be driving or into which Cody might inadvertently dash.

"Hard up?"

"I do all right," Jimmy said, still unable to locate the lock. "Son of a—"

"Your truck could use some work. Here, let me help you." Before Jimmy knew what hit him, Jenner had reached forward and snagged Jimmy's key ring.

"Hey, what d'ya think yer doin'?" Jimmy shouted.

"Probably saving your useless neck."

"Don't do me no favors." With that, Jimmy took a swing at Jenner and it was all the incentive he needed. Balancing on his good leg, he slammed Jimmy up against the side of the truck and forced a crutch beneath the sorry little snake of a man's chin.

"Don't even think about it," Jenner snarled as he saw Jimmy's fingers curl into a fist.

"What the hell's goin' on?" Jimmy rasped, his eyes bulging a little.

"You tell me everything you know about the fire and my dad's murder."

"What?"

"You heard me. Were you in on it?"

"Hell, no. Are you crazy? I was with Maryellen Inman, I swear."

"Do you swear?" Jenner pushed the crutch a little harder and Rickert began to cough.

"You bastard. Just you wait. You McKees will get yours!" Jimmy's face was turning an ugly shade of red.

"That's more like it, Jimmy. Lay your cards on the table. Maybe you'll get lucky and get twenty-five grand, or maybe you'll end up in jail."

"Damn it, let me up!" the drunk sputtered. "Okay, okay. I know a little, but I wasn't involved. Swear to God."

Jenner pocketed Jimmy's keys and eased up a little, just enough so the snake could breathe but still applying enough pressure to keep Rickert's spine curved over the hood of his truck and his mind on the business at hand.

"Hey, what's going on here?" Jake was peering from the doorway and some of the other patrons were staring through the windows.

"Call Hammond Polk," Jenner growled. "Jimmy here has a story he wants to tell the sheriff."

"So you're leaving? Just like that?" Harriet snapped her fingers, then threw her hands in the air as her daughter stripped clothes from the closet and threw them into suitcases. Her wet bags were drying over a heat vent and Cody, in his playpen, was crying to be let out.

"You knew this wasn't permanent!"

"I know, but I'd hoped." Harriet walked over to the

wailing child and picked him up. "What's wrong, darlin'?" she whispered against Cody's curls.

The little boy sniffed. "Want a horse."

"He's been this way ever since Jenner left."

"Well, if you want one, surely you can have one."

"Mom!"

"I'm talking about a stick horse or a stuffed animal or a figurine or—"

"Want a horse! A big horse!"

Give me strength, Beth silently prayed. She should never have come back here; she'd been a fool to think that returning to Rimrock would solve anything and she'd let an old woman's letter get in the way of her common sense. Why? Because, deep down in the darkest recesses of her heart, the place where she'd hidden all her feelings, she'd *wanted* to face Jenner again, she'd *wanted* to show him his son, she'd *wanted* to try to win his heart. Oh, she'd told herself differently, bravely facing him and pretending that she didn't care, but the entire situation had blown up in her face. Now Cody was involved, caring for a man who would never claim him. She zipped up the bag and remembered doing the very same thing—packing her things—at the lodge with Jenner after three blissful days of falling in love with him.

God, she was a fool!

"Stay one more night," her mother said softly.

"Why?"

"Because I need you and I don't want you driving over the mountains at night in this storm. It's raining here and snowing in the mountains. Beth, please." She laid a hand on her daughter's arm. "What will one more night hurt?"

Beth looked at her son, his cheeks red from crying as he clung to his grandmother's neck. She was still too angry to drive safely, and in the morning the mountain passes would be blocked with snow. "All right," she agreed, "but bright and early, first thing, we're out of here."

"Fair enough. We'll eat dinner, then we'll go out to the McKee ranch."

"*What?* That wasn't part of the deal."

"I know, Beth, but I have unfinished business out there and I want you to go along."

"No way. It's over."

Her mother's fingers dug deep into Beth's arm. "Do this for me, Beth. It's important. To me. To you. And to him." She looked at her grandson and Beth felt a quiver of apprehension at the thought of facing Jenner one last time.

Jenner, along with Max and Rex Stone, listened to Rickert's nonconfession to Hammond Polk.

The punk admitted seeing Jonah on the night he died—everyone who'd been at the Black Anvil knew that Jonah had been drinking. But Jimmy, rather than going straight to Maryellen Inman's as he'd first said, had staggered out the back door, slipped near the garbage cans and nearly knocked himself out. He'd seen Jonah arguing with someone, but it was dark, the other man's voice was muffled, and Jonah, after telling the man to go to hell, had gotten into his Jeep and roared away. The other guy had climbed into his rig—a dark blue or black pickup—and hightailed it after Jonah.

But Jimmy was short on details. The suspect had been a man nearly as large as Jonah and he wore a light-colored Stetson and cowboy boots. The description could have fit half the ranchers in the county. Jimmy claimed that he hadn't come forward before because the man had recognized him and had shouted out the window as he'd driven off, "Careful, Rickert. I know where you live. If you squeal, I'll kill you and that woman you're livin' with."

Jimmy had been too drunk to recognize the man, but the words had screamed through his head. Even after the McKees had posted the reward, he'd been too scared to say what he knew. But now he figured that he was owed the money.

As for the arson at the ranch, Jimmy could provide no insight. If the two events were related, he suspected that the same man was behind the fire. Hammond Polk found no reason to hold him and Jimmy was released.

And Jenner was scared to death. Now, it seemed, his mother's crazy theory was dead on and everyone who was involved with the Rocking M was a potential target to some psycho. Including Beth and Cody. And he'd let them get away. Despite the fact that he loved them and couldn't live without that mule-headed woman and her sprite of a son, he'd let them slip through his fingers.

He *loved* them? The thought stopped him cold. For years he'd told himself he didn't love anyone. No member of his family. Not even himself. Yet here he was thinking about a woman and her child and he didn't give a damn whose blood flowed in the kid's veins; he just wanted to be a part of that life. And come hell or high water, he intended to do just that.

"Just tell me what's going on," Beth demanded as she drove past the outskirts of town and headed north toward the McKee ranch. Her mother was in the passenger seat and Cody was buckled in his car seat in the back. A pickup was following them at a distance, headlights bright in the rearview mirror.

"I guess you could say that I have a score to settle."

"With?"

"Virginia."

"Jenner's mother? Why? What kind of score?"

Harriet frowned. "You'll hear soon enough."

"Look, Mom, I'm not into high drama. Why don't you just tell me—" She noticed the pickup gaining speed, though there was no place to pass as they wound past Elkhorn Lake and into the foothills. "Damn it all."

"What?"

"A truck's been following us. Ever since we left town."

"Whose?"

Beth shrugged and told herself she was imagining things. "You tell me."

Craning her neck, Harriet took a look through the back window, then at her sideview mirror. "Can't see anything but his headlights. It's too dark."

Beth bit her lower lip and told herself to keep cool, that nothing was wrong, that she'd seen too many movies and television shows with car chases and that Jenner's worries about security at the ranch had gotten to her.

"Slow down," Harriet advised. "Maybe he'll pass. I hate it when someone tailgates you on these winding roads."

Beth's heart began to knock. She glanced in the mirror and saw only the glare of headlights. Her fingers were wet with sweat. She eased off the throttle.

"When did you notice him?" Harriet asked.

"In town, at the last light. I didn't think much about it." She slowed a little more, but the truck didn't alter position even though they were on a fairly straight part of the road. "Probably some rancher who lives out this way," Beth said, but she didn't believe it. Her stomach knotted.

"The least he could do is dim his lights."

Clamping her hands firmly over the wheel, Beth stepped on the accelerator. Her little Nova took off, but the truck didn't falter. Within a split second, he was nearly on her bumper.

Keep going. Just keep going! She had no choice and the ranch was only a few miles ahead. Certainly Max with all his security or Jenner would be there to help them. Oh, God, Jenner. Beth's throat closed up and she tried not to let her imagination run wild, but she thought for just a moment that she might never see him again, that he might never hold Cody's little body close to his.

She took a corner too fast and the Nova's front wheel slid off the road and onto the shoulder. Gravel sprayed. The car shimmied and Beth tried not to think about the fact that they were in the mountains, that the road was cut against the cliffs. She braked. The Nova skidded.

"Oh, God!" Harriet screamed.

Cody began to cry. "I scared. Mommy, I scared!"

I'm scared, too! Gritting her teeth, Beth yanked on the wheel and the car careered away from the shoulder and into the oncoming lane.

"For God's sake, watch out!"

The truck bore down on them.

She managed to straighten the Nova into the right lane, and stepped on the gas again.

Bang! The truck rammed her car, sending it onto the shoulder again. Harriet screamed. The guardrail caught the fender.

"Oh, God, oh, God, oh, God!"

Metal screamed against metal. Sparks flared. The Nova shuddered. Windows rattled, but the car hung together. Beth wrestled with the wheel.

A second set of headlights appeared in the mirror.

Horns honked and sirens wailed in the distance as the Nova slowed. "Hold on!" Beth cried, bracing herself for the impact of the larger vehicle, but the truck raced past them and Beth stood on the brakes. "Come on, come on," she said, her fingers clenched around the wheel.

The car skidded to a stop as the second truck pulled over.

Beth was shaking as she watched the driver. Jenner! Tears flooded her eyes as she watched him running, limping, throwing himself toward her. He yanked open the car door and dragged her into his arms. "Are you all right?" he whispered hoarsely, his hands tangling in her hair. "Cody...Cody!"

"Out!" Cody cried between broken sobs. "Me scared! Mommy! Want out!"

Jenner reached into the back seat.

"Me, too! I think I twisted my ankle!" Harriet said, her voice shaking badly, and Beth sent up a prayer of thanks that everyone was alive and well enough to complain.

A siren shrieked closer and the lights of a cruiser from the sheriff's department flashed red and blue in the night. Beth hardly knew what was happening. She felt Jenner's arms surround her, felt Cody's little body pressed against her own and knew that her mother was being freed from the car by deputies.

"I followed you out of town, saw what was happening, and used my cellular phone to call the police," Jenner explained. "Oh, God, Beth, I thought—" His throat seized up, and standing in the glare of his headlights, he kissed her and held her as if he never intended to let her go again. "I love you," she thought she heard him say. "I love you and Cody and thank God—"

"I love you, too," she whispered, tears raining from her eyes. He kissed her again until Cody, caught between them, protested.

"It's all right," Jenner assured him as his strong arms folded over his son. "I'm gonna marry your mother."

"You what?"

"I'm gonna marry her. A wedding, you know. That is, if she agrees."

Beth blinked against her tears. Jenner was proposing? Here, on the edge of Stardust Canyon, by her wrecked little car? "Marry a broken-down, useless cowboy like you?" she said, then laughed and sniffed and wiped away her tears. "Get the preacher. I can't wait." She threw her arms around him and kissed him soundly before the quiet cough of a deputy caught her attention.

"I really hate to break this up, but I think someone should tell us what's going on."

"Didn't you hear?" Harriet quipped as she was pulled

from what had once been the Nova. ''There's gonna be a wedding!''

It was hours later before they finally reached the ranch after enduring questioning by Hammond Polk and several of his deputies. The department was now on the lookout for a dark-colored, late-model, American-made truck with Oregon plates and a dented bumper.

The ranch house was ablaze with lights since Jenner had telephoned Max with the news, and his entire family, including Skye, was waiting. In the den, Jenner was re-telling the story. ''…and so, now that we're all safe, I've asked Beth to marry me and she's agreed.''

''Oh, no,'' Virginia gasped, but Mavis climbed to her feet and grinned widely.

''Let me be the first to congratulate you!'' the old lady said.

''Maybe we should make it a double ceremony,'' Skye offered, as her wedding to Max was scarcely a month away.

''No.'' Jenner shook his head. ''I want ours just for us.''

''But…'' Virginia said weakly, then turned her eyes on Harriet, who was seated in the room.

''The kids are getting married,'' Harriet said, ''and it's high time they should. Whatever bad blood there is be-tween us has got to stop.''

''I don't think this is the place—''

''It's time to clear the air,'' Harriet said, her lips pursed. ''I know this is hard for you, Virginia, but you may as well hear the truth. There was a time, years ago, when I worked for Jonah. He and I—''

''I can't hear this!''

''—were never lovers. I don't know why you believe otherwise, but it's not true! Whatever you may think of me, the simple truth is this. I was never in my life involved with a married man. Not your husband and no one else's, for that matter.''

Tears began to form in Virginia's eyes.

"Now, listen, I don't believe in sugarcoatin' the truth. He approached me, offered to set me up in my own place, but I turned him down and quit working for him right then and there. I'm not saying he wasn't an attractive man, and if he'd been single, I would have thought long and hard about it, but he wasn't, so I didn't. That's the God's honest truth, and I would hope you're a big enough person not to let some old lie stand between you and your grandson, because if you aren't, you're a bigger fool than I take you for.''

Mavis's smile had faded. "She makes sense, Virginia.''

"Well, I've said my piece.'' Harriet stood proudly. "Now, if someone would kindly drive me home—''

"No!'' Virginia's lips trembled and she drew in a long, steadying breath. "Stay, Harriet. I, um, I think you're right and if I've misjudged you, I apologize. Whether I like it or not, we have a wedding to plan.''

"Another wedding!'' Mavis said, winking at Skye and Max. "If only Jonah were alive to see it.''

"He's probably rolling over in his grave,'' Jenner said. "He worked hard to break up Max and Skye and keep me from knowing about Cody.''

"He would've changed his mind,'' Virginia said.

Casey shook her head. "I don't think so. But he'd bit off more than he could chew. Looks to me, at least for you four—'' she motioned to Jenner, Beth, Max and Skye "—love really does conquer all.''

Jenner linked his fingers through Beth's and led her to the back porch. The sky was dark, the wind chilly, but with Jenner's arms around her, Beth was warm inside. "We could live in Rimrock, rebuild the cabin at the old homestead if you want,'' he said, "and you could work for Skye, or…''

"Or?''

"We could get the old lodge going again. Hire a skeleton staff and turn it into a kind of hotel and dude ranch."

"Would you be happy with that?" she asked.

His smile, crooked and cocksure, gleamed white in the darkness. "I'm happy with you. Doesn't matter where we are or what we do. As long as we're together. What do you say?"

She sighed and shook her head. "It's about time, cowboy."

"Mommy? Mommy, where are you?"

"Out here. With Daddy."

Cody poked his head out the door. "No, you're not. You're with Jenner."

He hurried over and Jenner lifted him off his feet. "From now on you can call me Dad."

Cody grinned. "Okay, but I can have a horse?"

"A dozen of 'em."

"And a puppy?"

"As many as you want."

"Wait a minute," Beth said, and Jenner's smile faded. "No way, lady," he said, his eyes turning an erotic shade of blue. "I've waited too long already." With that he kissed her, and Beth leaned happily against the man she loved, knowing that they would be together forever.

Dear Beth,

I've always been a solitary man. Never wanted anyone else around much. Until you and Cody showed up on my doorstep and gave me back a reason to get up in the morning, to walk again, to live, I really didn't give a damn.

You changed all that and made my life complete.

I don't think there are the right words (at least I don't know them if they exist) to tell you how I feel, but each morning when I get up and you're in my arms, I'm glad it's a brand-new day, and each night when I lie down beside you, I'm thankful to be alive.

You and Cody are the reason.

All I can say is that I love you and I'll never stop loving you.

Forever,
Jenner

* * * * *

A Letter from the Author

Fall 1994

Dear Reader,

I hope you enjoyed Beth and Jenner's story. Jenner is one of my favorite heroes and Beth is just the woman to tame him. I can assure you they, along with their son, Cody, will have a wonderful future together.

The next book in the *Love Letters* series is *C Is for Cowboy,* the story of Casey McKee and Sloan Redwing.

As you know, Casey is the stubborn daughter of Jonah McKee. She's a woman who, upon seeing her brothers find happiness with the women in their lives, is dissatisfied with her own fate. For years she's spent her life as the spoiled daughter of a rich man, but now she wants to strike out on her own and find out who she really is—not as Jonah McKee's daughter or Max and Jenner's sister, but as an independent woman in her own right.

However, her plans are shattered when she's kidnapped.

When the McKee family receives the ransom note, Jenner won't trust the police or the feds to save her. He contacts an old friend, Sloan Redwing—a rodeo cowboy who's half Nez Percé Native American. Sloan is a strong, silent and proud man whose very presence makes some people nervous. His eyes are dark and menacing and along with his rodeo prowess, he's inherited the hunting skills of his Native American ancestors.

Against his better judgment, Sloan accepts the job and tracks down Casey's abductors to rescue her.

Sloan doesn't want or need the complications of a woman in his life, and he tells himself that Casey McKee is definitely not the kind of woman for him.

Casey wants to be her own woman and doesn't need a man telling her what to do, yet she can't stop her unsettling feelings every time Sloan is near.

In *C Is for Cowboy* the murder of Jonah McKee is finally solved, but the book is really a love story between two very different people trying to discover themselves. I think it's a story that's as explosive as it is endearing. I hope you agree.

If you'd like to write to me, I'd love to hear from you.

Regards,

Lisa Jackson
333 S. State St., Suite 308
Lake Oswego, OR 97034

C IS FOR COWBOY

Prologue

Sloan,

I never thought it would come to this, but it's time to call in my marker. I hate to do it, but you're the best damned detective in the country and we—my family and I—need all the help we can get.

As you can see from the enclosed ransom letter, my sister, Casey, has been kidnapped. I'm afraid the bastards who abducted her seem bent on revenge as they are interested in money. There's no telling what they might do.

The local sheriff's department and FBI have been called in but you know that I don't put much stock in the law. Then there's Rex Stone, a P.I. my mother hired when she suspected Dad was murdered. Stone's an oily bastard and I don't trust him. Not with Casey's life. Even though we've offered a twenty-five-thousand-dollar reward for convictions of the culprits, no one's taken the bait.

So, I'm asking. I managed to convince my brother Max that you could find Casey and find her fast.

The family will pay you one hundred thousand dollars if you locate Casey, bring her home alive and nail the creeps behind this. If something's happened to her and she doesn't return home, I want you to track down the bastards and I'll personally show them my own kind of justice.

To save time, I'll fax you a copy of this letter and the ransom note we received earlier today.

Jenner McKee

McKee Bastards:

We've got Casey. Just to prove it, we're sending along her ring and a lock of her hair. She's unharmed and will be returned to you if you pay one million dollars in cash. All bills are to be in denominations of twenty dollars or less.

We'll send instructions on how to deliver the money later.

If you don't do as we say, believe that you'll never see your sister alive again.

Chapter One

"**S**on of a bitch," Sloan muttered under his breath as he read the pages that whirred from his fax machine. His jaw tightened until it ached and he narrowed his eyes at the ugly words. Who the hell would've had the guts to kidnap Casey McKee, youngest child and only daughter of the richest man in eastern Oregon?

Sloan had no use for sneaks and cowards. In his opinion, anyone who would steal away a girl had to be a chickenshit. He'd love to take the bastards down.

Besides, he owed Jenner and he could really use the cash.

He cranked open the window and considered the money—even though, if push came to shove, he wanted to take the case whether he was paid or not.

But a hundred thousand dollars wasn't something to sniff at. A man could change his life with a hundred grand. Sloan looked around his office—two small rooms equipped with a computer, printer, fax machine and copier. He'd picked all the equipment up at a liquidation sale. His battle-scarred desk and the three chairs had been handed down. The couch in the waiting room had been purchased new fifteen years before—the first piece of furniture that he and Jane had bought together. He should've sold it before now, but he hung on to it for sentimental reasons, just as he kept pictures of Jane and Tony to remind him that there was—or at least there had been a long time ago—some good in the world.

As a cool breath of winter breeze fanned into the room, bringing the scents of lemon trees and the faint aroma of exhaust from the Santa Monica Freeway, Sloan picked up a picture fading in an old frame. It was his favorite snapshot—a picture of Jane with her hair blowing in the wind. She was standing on the ridge over a desert canyon with the blue sky and dusty hills as a backdrop and holding Tony, scarcely two, on one hip. Her feet were bare, and a beaded bracelet circled her ankle, just below the hem of her long skirt. While Tony squinted, Jane smiled into the camera as if she didn't have a care in the world.

Sloan's insides seemed to turn to sand and he moved his gaze to the top of a file cabinet where all of his rodeo trophies were beginning to gather dust. Riding rodeo— his catharsis—was how he'd met Jenner McKee and now the crazy son of a bitch was in trouble. Big trouble. Not that trouble didn't chase after Jenner. Or was it the other way around? But this was different—not just a barroom brawl or argument over a card game. This was the big time.

One side of Sloan's mouth curved into a smile. He'd always liked Jenner and appreciated his irreverent and rather crooked sense of humor, so he was half-inclined to take the offer, money or no money. A favor for a friend. The problem was that he had a personal code of ethics— one he'd never yet broken. He drew the line at working for people he cared about. He didn't bug their phones or take pictures of their spouses cheating on them. Sloan was content to leave that kind of work to someone who didn't care who was doing what to whom. Taking on a case from a friend violated one of Sloan's basic rules to himself.

But this was different.

And he owed Jenner his life.

Son of a bitch.

Casey was missing and there had been a ransom note. His brows drew together as he read the words a second time. Casey McKee was a headstrong girl. Rich and spoiled. Sloan had never met her. He only knew what Jenner had told him and had seen a faded picture of her that Jenner kept in his wallet. If he remembered right, Casey was pretty, blessed with the McKee good looks that ran in the family.

Sloan scratched the stubble on his chin, trying to remember what he knew about the McKee family. Casey was the youngest child and only daughter of Jonah McKee, one of the richest men in all of eastern Oregon, if the rumors he'd heard were true. Sloan had met the man a couple of times and hated him on sight. Jonah, while trying to rein in his wayward second son, had shown up at two rodeos and each time he'd looked down his patrician nose, his blue eyes condescending. Sloan had read Jonah's unspoken thoughts. From years of interpreting the slightest of sneers, the discomfort masked by curiosity at his decidedly Native American features, Sloan Redhawk could smell prejudice a mile away.

It hadn't mattered to Jenner. He and his old man had always been at opposite ends of any argument. Jenner had had no respect for his father, but Jonah McKee had tried to bend his son's incredible will to his.

As for the rest of the kids, Max seemed to be the least rebellious, but Casey was supposed to be a firecracker. Jenner, after a few beers that loosened his tongue, had seemed proud of his temperamental little sister. According to Jenner, Casey could rope a calf, brand a steer, shoot a .22 straight as an arrow, and was pretty and feminine to boot. Jenner also seemed to think that Casey was more stubborn than he and his brother rolled into one, though she'd been doted on all of her life.

He knew about rich women. They and their families were nothing but trouble. With a capital *T*. The kind of trouble Sloan usually avoided.

Except she needed help.

And Jenner wouldn't have asked unless he was desperate.

Swearing under his breath, he reached for the phone. So he'd help out an old friend and make himself enough money to buy a ranch, a place of his own in the country where he'd lived as a small boy and young man—the high desert of his ancestors. He was getting too old to ride rough-and-tumble rodeo stock, he was tired of chasing after men who cheated on their wives, and he'd had it with the snarl of L.A. traffic, which had only gotten worse since the earthquake. He wasn't cut out for the city, but he'd never completely been able to move on, not permanently, because of the memories that still lingered here—ghosts that seemed to be a part of his life.

But it was time to leave California. He'd called this part of the country home for nearly twenty years and he was beginning to feel penned in.

Besides, he owed Jenner a favor. A big one. It was time to pay up. He read the two notes again and his gut clenched. There was a chance, a very good chance, that Casey McKee was already dead.

"You keep your filthy hands off me!" Casey glared at her abductor, a man she'd known all her life, a man she'd been forced to trust when her car had broken down, a man who'd bound and gagged her and dragged her to this ramshackle cabin in the middle of God-only-knew where. Barry White.

"I was just tryin' to make you comfortable." He spat

a stream of tobacco juice into the fire of the wood stove and the flames sizzled in protest.

"If you were concerned about that, you'd untie me." Casey struggled against the rope that cut into her wrists and made her hands feel numb.

"I'd untie you if I trusted you, which I don't." Barry grinned, his lips curving in a week's growth of red beard stubble. He wasn't a handsome man to begin with, and now that he'd been stuck in this cabin in the middle of the wilderness, he looked worse than ever. His hair receded past a bony ridge in his skull and his pale blue eyes were small and set deep in his head. His nose was large with little red lines crawling across the tip—proof of his love of the bottle.

Casey knew that if she had any chance for escape it was to lull Barry into believing that her spirit was broken and that she was too scared or numb to do anything as rash as try to break out of the cabin and start hiking through the snow and woods in search of civilization. She looked through the grimy window and watched as the snow fell steadily. The tiny flakes were driven by a wind that howled through the rafters of the one-room cabin.

"My brothers will hunt you down like the dog you are," she said, and he seemed to pale a bit as he reached for the bottle of whiskey he kept on the single table in the room.

"Yeah, yeah. So you keep telling me. So let 'em. They'll never find me." He sat with cocky confidence, straddling a corner of his chair, glowering at Casey, who was sitting on a sleeping bag wedged between the old wood stove and the wall.

"I wouldn't count on it," Casey said, pressing her advantage. Barry was a coward and certainly not the brains behind this operation, though in the five days since she'd been abducted, he hadn't given a clue as to who his partner in crime was. "You know how determined Jenner can be."

"Jenner's a cripple." Barry sniffed noisily and a little tic developed beneath his eye. He took a swig from the bottle as if to calm his nerves.

"Not anymore. He's off crutches and onto a cane—getting stronger every day. With all the physical therapy he's been through, he's tough as nails again and I bet he could take you with one hand tied behind his back. I think he did a while back, didn't he? At the Black Anvil? Broke a pool cue over your head when you wouldn't stop insulting Wanda." Casey remembered the story well. Wanda Tully, a blond waitress at the Black Anvil, had always had a soft spot for Jenner. That night, Barry, who'd been three sheets to the wind, had insisted on getting another drink but the bartender had cut him off. Wanda had delivered a cup of coffee with the news, and Barry had snarled invectives at her, called her a cheap dime-store whore as well as a bitch. Jenner had told Barry to knock it off and Barry had turned on Jenner, intent on pounding him. Even though Jenner had been on crutches at the time, he sidestepped the blow and cracked a pool cue over Barry's slightly misshapen head. That was all it had taken; Barry had passed out on the spot.

Now, Barry let loose with another stream of tobacco juice, spitting it out with a look of disgust. Again the fire crackled.

"Jenner's got a mean temper," Casey reminded her abductor. "And then there's Max."

"Shut up."

"You know about Max, don't you?"

"Only way I couldn't is if I was deaf. All you been talkin' 'bout since I took out your gag was your brothers. But that's all it is—just talk. They ain't come to save you yet, have they?"

"But they will. You and I both know it. They won't give up," Casey said bravely. She had absolute faith in the McKee men.

Barry's eyes shifted. His tongue rimmed his lips. "Max don't scare me."

"Then you're stupid, Barry. Just 'cause he's got a law degree and runs a business doesn't mean he isn't tough as nails."

"If I'm so stupid, why're you tied up while I'm sittin' pretty drinkin' my whiskey and playin' cards, hmm?" He picked up a ratty old deck of cards and started laying them out on the table, snapping the edges so loudly that Casey wanted to scream.

Where were her brothers? Why hadn't they found her? A small insidious fear wormed its way into her heart, but she ignored it. She wasn't about to back down; she knew she was getting to him, putting him on edge. Antsy and uptight, Barry would soon make a mistake, and when he did, she'd take advantage of it. "You just better hope your partner doesn't sell you out," she said, using a different, but well-worn tack. "What's to prevent him from keeping the ransom money and leaving you up here to rot?"

"He'd never do that," Barry said with conviction, but his eyes shifted to the window and the near blizzard outside. He sniffed loudly, his reddish brown eyebrows forming a solitary line as he considered her words.

"Men'll do anything for money," she persisted, forcing herself to sit taller. "Even sell out their partners."

"Yeah, well, then I'll go to the sheriff and make a deal."

"If you're alive."

"Shut up!" he roared suddenly, his nostrils flaring. "You talk too much! You're like a goddamned broken record, playing the same old sorry song over and over. My partner won't sell me out. Not ever!" But a muscle twitched just below one of his eyes.

Fine. Let him think it over. Casey was dirty and tired. Her skin itched and she could use a bath. Worse than that, she was scared to death, though she'd never let Barry see her fear. She only hoped that somehow Barry and his accomplice had tripped up, that even now Jenner and Max were on their way, or if not them, then the police or the FBI or *someone* who would come bursting through the door intent on helping her. Where was the cavalry when you needed it?

She rested her head against the wall and noticed the dead insects and dust trapped in spiderwebs that stretched from the ceiling to the window. How had she gotten herself into this mess? Scowling at the lantern set square in the middle of the table, she wondered at her chances of escape. Without help, she wouldn't get far. The temperature had plunged far below freezing; at least it seemed that it had from the times she'd had to hike to the outhouse. She'd managed a look at her surroundings, seen the dense forest, eyed the steep hills and deep ravines and listened for any sound of civilization. There had been none. No rumble of a train on distant tracks, no hum of electric wires, no thrum of an engine, no barking of a dog, no whisper of traffic anywhere. No sound of someone chopping wood, no muttered words of frustration from hunters, no smell of a campfire. Nothing.

It was as if the rest of the world didn't exist. Somehow, some way, she had to escape.

Barry had a pickup—an old Ford parked in a lean-to, which had probably been a shed for cows or horses decades ago. If she could break her bonds, snag the keys and somehow start the damned thing, she could drive to the nearest town and get help.

If only someone would find her. Certainly her family was worried. They couldn't possibly guess where she was. She knew only that Barry had traveled continuously northeast, crossed the state line from Oregon to Idaho, and at one point driven into Montana, but she wasn't certain that they hadn't strayed back into Idaho.

Less than a week ago, she'd been at the McKee ranch, living with her mother and grandmother, feeling restless because her life seemed to be at a standstill. Both of her brothers were busy planning their futures. Max, her older brother, and his fiancée, Skye Donahue, were busy planning a Christmas wedding. And Jenner, once the self-proclaimed bachelor, would probably wait until around Valentine's Day to marry Beth Crandall, the woman who had borne him a son he hadn't known about until just a few weeks ago. Max was running the company, McKee Enterprises, Skye had her medical practice at the clinic, where Beth had started working as a nurse, and Jenner had been helping out around the ranch. Once he was on his feet again, he planned to open up the old hunting lodge and make it into some kind of dude ranch, where he, his new wife and two-year-old son, Cody, would live.

Her heart was suddenly heavy. Max had his daughter, Hillary, from a previous marriage, and Jenner's son was an adorable scamp who had captured his aunt's heart immediately the first time she'd met him.

But Casey had no plans for the future, no man in her life, no children. She probably would have left Rimrock and started a life of her own somewhere, but her father had recently died—been murdered, it seemed—and there had been a fire in the stables, which had been started by an unknown arsonist. As she stared at her kidnapper, though, Casey knew that Barry had been involved in Jonah's death as well as the fire. But he wasn't the man who had planned the crimes; she was certain of it. He just didn't have the mental capability. He was only a flunky.

He tricked you, didn't he?

She bit her lip at her own stupidity. She should never have trusted him, even though she'd felt she had no other choice. She should have declined his ride and tried to walk through the snow back to Rimrock in hopes that someone else would come along and help her.

For a split second, she wondered if Clarisse was in on the plot to kidnap her, but couldn't believe her friend would turn on her or lure her into such a vile trap. No,

Clarisse's phone call hadn't been a setup—just a coincidence.

Casey had taken the call in her room, and Clarisse's voice on the other end of the phone line had sounded too broken, too desperate for her to have made up her story. "Casey...I didn't know who else to call. I'm...I'm in trouble," Clarisse had admitted, and her voice had sounded strangled, as if she was on the verge of tears.

"What kind of trouble?" Casey had asked. Clarisse was one of her best friends. They'd known each other since college, but had drifted apart after Clarisse's marriage a few years back.

"I—I left Ray."

"You did?" Casey couldn't believe her ears. Though she'd never much liked Raymond James, Clarisse had adored him. They'd met in college, and Ray hadn't only been handsome, he'd also had money and charm. Casey was wary of men who seemed too slick and polished. Men like Ray James. Clarisse had been married in a lavish ceremony and Casey had been her maid of honor. Since that time, however, Clarisse and Ray had moved back to his hometown of Spokane, Washington. Clarisse's phone calls had all but stopped and the monthly letters had dribbled down to a Christmas card with the name of the family embossed in gold letters and a brief note that really revealed nothing. Casey had assumed Clarisse was too busy with her two sons and successful husband to have much time to keep up old friendships. "What happened?" she'd asked Clarisse as she stared out the window of the bedroom, watching the black clouds and dreading Clarisse's answer.

"Oh, God, Casey..."

"You can tell me." Casey's heart was thrumming and a sour taste rose up the back of her throat. She sensed what was coming, before the words were out of Clarisse's mouth.

"He, uh, he hit me."

"Clarisse, no..."

Sniffles. "It's...well, it's not the first time, but he never took it out on the kids before. This time he was in such a rage he hit Charlie, slapped him so hard he left a red mark that turned into a bruise."

Casey's stomach seemed to drop to the floor and she thought she might get sick. Charlie was barely five. "Oh, God, Clarisse, where are you?"

"In a women's shelter in Seattle, but I'm broke and...I need someone to talk to and I don't know what I'm going to do." She was struggling not to sob, but her voice cracked, and Casey imagined her face bruised, tears raining from her eyes.

"Give me the address and I'll be there tomorrow," Casey promised. "I'll wire you some money—"

"You don't have to."

"I *want* to."

"But I can't pay you back. Ray has all the money in his name—his and his mother's—and—"

"Doesn't matter," Casey said quickly, rage roaring through her blood. She couldn't understand how a man could hit the woman he loved, or his child, though she'd seen her father backhand his own two boys more times than she could count.

"But—"

"Really, Clarisse, don't worry. Just take care of yourself and your boys. Stay at the shelter—don't let him or his mother know where you are. When you get back on your feet, you'll get a job. It's not a big deal. Haven't you heard, I'm a rich heiress these days?" Casey joked, though that was stretching the truth a little. Her portion of her father's estate was still tied up in land and company holdings and the like, but she had a savings account that she didn't really need. As far as she was concerned, Clarisse and her boys could have it all. "I'll be there by morning."

After scribbling down the address of the shelter and

Clarisse's new bank in Seattle, Casey had driven into town, transferred some money to Clarisse and returned to the house, where she'd begun packing.

"Where are you going?" her mother had asked as she'd walked into Casey's room and found her folding some jeans and sweaters before tossing them into an open suitcase on the bed.

"To Seattle. Clarisse is in trouble."

"I thought Clarisse lived in Spokane."

"She does, but she's moved."

"Why? What kind of trouble?" Virginia sat on the corner of the bed, holding firmly to the post.

Casey bit her lip. She didn't really want to discuss her friend's private life with anyone. "Look, it's kind of personal. She's splitting up with her husband—"

Virginia's frown deepened into a grave, disapproving scowl.

"—and she needs some support."

"Money?"

"Yeah, some."

Virginia clucked her tongue. "That's the problem with your generation—ready to throw in the towel at the littlest bump in a marriage."

Casey couldn't stand the condemnation in her mother's eyes. "Mom, he hit her, okay? Hard. And he didn't stop there. He slapped Charlie, too. Left a welt on his face."

"Oh."

"So she needs a friend and I'm going to be it."

Virginia's fingers twisted together. Virginia had suffered an abusive marriage in her own way, Casey had thought, though she'd never spoken her mind on the subject. Jonah McKee had never struck his wife, but he'd often belittled her, and his string of mistresses had been legendary in the town. Casey had heard the snickering behind her mother's back, seen Virginia's friends cover their mouths and smile at the knowledge that *their* husbands had been faithful, while Jonah McKee had strayed.

Virginia, ever the loyal wife, had turned a blind eye to her husband's marital lapses and raised her children without ever saying a word against her philandering husband. But they'd all known.

"How long will you be gone?" she asked as she plucked at a piece of lint on the quilt her mother-in-law, Mavis, had pieced together.

"I'm not sure," Casey replied. "I've been thinking it's time that I—"

"That you what?"

"I wish I knew. But I really can't stay here and tread water. I need to do *something*. I need a purpose, Mom."

"Don't tell me this is some kind of mission to find yourself—your real identity—or something as trite as that."

Casey snapped the suitcase closed. "Right now this is a mission to help Clarisse. After that, who knows? I'll call," she promised as she swung her bag off the bed.

"Be careful."

"Always am, Mom," Casey had said with a wave. She'd driven away from the ranch feeling free, not even really paying attention to her mother's warning, the same one Virginia repeated every time any of her children left the ranch.

Just a few miles out of Dawson City, Casey's car had given out. Cursing the miserable piece of junk, she'd started walking through the snow. Barry, in his beat-up old pickup had stopped and offered her a lift, and she'd been grateful that she wouldn't have to battle the wind and snow and a potential case of frostbite. What she hadn't known was that he had a gun in the truck, and as soon as she was settled in, he'd grabbed her, forced a pair of handcuffs on her and cuffed her to a handhold in the armrest. Then he'd tromped on the accelerator, kept the pistol pointed squarely at her chest and warned her to stay put. She'd screamed, yelled and cursed him, all to no avail. He'd seemed delighted to have captured her and she'd prayed it was all just a prank.

Now, of course, she knew differently.

She had to escape, but she couldn't, not with her hands tied. For the most part, she was allowed to be unbound, unless Barry was sleeping or whenever he left to drive into town for supplies or to call his partner. Otherwise he seemed to think he could stop her if she tried to bolt. He wasn't in the best of shape, but he was heavy and strong, and though she was certain she could outrun him if all things were equal, she couldn't slog through eighteen inches of snow and leave him in her dust. Besides, where would she go?

Today, as if he sensed she was plotting a way to get out, he'd tied her up again, using rope instead of the handcuffs, which he'd rendered useless when he'd clumsily dropped the key down a hole in the floor the last time he'd released her.

She mentally kicked herself for the thousandth time for getting into his truck, then decided she'd had no choice as she couldn't have argued with the barrel of a gun. She just had to make the best of it and find some way to escape. "Just what is it you want?" she asked as Barry took a long tug on his bottle, then belched. They'd been over this before, but she hoped each time she asked, she'd get to the bottom of her abduction and learn the identity of Barry's silent partner.

"A million big ones."

"I know that, but why?"

He yawned and stretched an arm over his head. "'Cause you McKees are all too big fer your britches, that's why." He slanted her an evil smile. "It's time you got yours."

Sloan scanned the two pieces of paper he'd received four days before, searching for some clue that had escaped him. The letter and ransom note revealed nothing new, nor did the silver-and-turquoise ring or lock of dark hair—proof that the kidnappers did indeed have Casey. He clenched his fingers over the ring and turned his attention to the glossy eight-by-ten color photograph of Jenner's sister.

She was a looker, he'd give her that much. Spoiled, but beautiful. Straight, coffee brown hair framed a face that would make a man look twice. High cheekbones, stubborn McKee chin, arched eyebrows and hazel eyes. It was her eyes that got to him. Greenish brown shot with silver, they stared past curling black lashes and seemed to look straight into his soul. Jenner's old snapshot had hinted at her looks, but Sloan wouldn't have guessed she would turn out to be so intensely beautiful.

Disgusted with himself, he shoved the letters, lock of hair and picture into a manila envelope and locked the package in the glove compartment of his battle-scarred pickup, then slipped the ring into the front pocket of his faded jeans.

As he climbed out of his rig, he was pleased that his old truck seemed to fit into the landscape of Rimrock. A small town in a rural Oregon where most of the townspeople worked on ranches, in the woods, in sawmills or in the copper mine just outside of town. Dusty pickups and four-wheel-drive rigs in all shapes and sizes were parked along the streets.

After arriving in Rimrock, he'd had one meeting with the McKee men and then pretended to be an out-of-town drifter looking for work and hanging out at the Black Anvil Saloon. There were several watering holes in town, but the Black Anvil seemed to be where all the action was. Besides, it was the last place Jonah McKee had frequented before he'd been killed.

Inside the Black Anvil, the smoke was thick, the conversation loud, the click of billiard balls ever present. Talk of Casey McKee's kidnapping was still floating around. Sloan ordered a beer and settled at a table in the middle of the room where he could appear to be watching a hockey game on television while he nursed his drink and listened to the gossip.

Casey's name peppered several conversations, less now than a few days ago, but people were still interested. "Can't believe it," one woman was saying. "In a town the size of Rimrock?"

"Has nothin' to do with Rimrock. It's those uppity McKees. Someone finally decided to take them down a peg," her companion, a buxom redhead, said as she poured beer into a frosty glass.

"But murder? And kidnapping? And arson?"

"Someone's real ticked off, let me tell you. You heard that Beth Crandall, the girl who's snagged Jenner McKee, she was nearly run off the road. Had her mother with her. You know who she is…" She snapped her fingers. "Her name was Jones. Now she's married to Zeke Forrester. That's it—Forrester! Anyway, nearly scared the devil out of Harriet because her grandson was with her."

"Makes you wonder what the world's coming to," the first woman said, scanning the room with nervous eyes. "Seems as if you can't trust anyone these days."

"Not if your name is McKee." The redhead barked out a short laugh and reached into her purse for a pack of cigarettes.

"I just hope Casey's okay."

"Oh, she will be. One thing about that gal, she always lands on her feet."

Sloan hoped so. He didn't know Casey and wasn't sure that if he did he would have liked her, but he worried about her. No one should have to go through whatever it was she was enduring. He only hoped that he could save her. In time.

A cold fear cut through his soul. *But you couldn't save Jane, could you? Or Tony. Where were you when the ones you loved needed you most?* He slammed his mind shut from those ugly thoughts and turned his attention to the matter at hand.

He caught the McKee name in several conversations, but heard nothing that really helped. He waved to a few of the locals. For the most part they were a friendly, hard-working lot who just needed a beer and a little downtime when they got off work.

One of the good old boys was Cyrus Kellogg, a rancher whose spread was just north of the McKees'. He'd given Sloan a day's worth of work chopping wood. The physical labor had felt good and accepting the job had completed his cover. People had begun to trust him after Cyrus had spread the word that Sloan was a hard worker.

Near as Sloan could tell, Casey had been kidnapped as part of a revenge scheme against the McKee family. In the past few months the McKees had suffered more than their share of grief, presumably at the hands of someone holding a grudge against one or more members of the richest family in the county. First, Jonah's Jeep had been forced off the road to land in the swift waters of Wildcat Creek at the bottom of Stardust Canyon. Then, the McKee stables had been set on fire, and Jenner McKee had been badly injured as he tried to save his niece and the live-stock. Now Casey was missing.

It all added up, and Sloan was laying odds that the thug behind the kidnapping was in the crowd at the bar, or would be within the week. Even if the culprit decided to lie low and avoid frequenting the Black Anvil for a while, he was sure to turn up again—like the proverbial bad penny. Besides, most lowlifes were creatures of habit, and if one of the regulars began staying away, people would start asking questions. There was also the pride factor to consider; Sloan bet that whoever had killed Jonah would love to brag about it. But right now, he was just running scared.

Sloan believed, as did the authorities, that whoever had

kidnapped Casey was the one who had murdered Jonah and burned down the McKee stables.

He'd spent the past few nights chatting with the locals, keeping an ear tuned toward the gossip while he pretended interest in the television mounted over the bar, where complimentary sports programs were offered free of charge to the patrons, just like the salty pretzels and popcorn.

During the day—when he wasn't doing odd jobs for some of the ranchers to gain their trust—Sloan sifted through her personal papers, interviewed the family and asked Jenner to check on places where Casey had gone to school and been employed so that his cover wasn't blown. He probably knew more about Casey McKee than she did herself. He'd checked telephone records to the McKee ranch, then flown to Seattle, interviewed Clarisse James, the friend who'd called Casey the day she was kidnapped. Before meeting Clarisse, he'd thought that she was in on the abduction, but the distressed woman was worried sick about Casey, her fear evident in her eyes. A battered woman who was trying to get back on her feet and survive with her two children, Clarisse convinced him that she didn't have a clue as to what had happened to her friend.

The FBI seemed to be concentrating on Clarisse James, thinking her desperate, a young mother who'd run away from her rich husband, but Sloan's gut instinct told him that she was clean. Clarisse had her own problems, and the money suddenly appearing in her account had been given to her by Casey, no strings attached. Virginia McKee had confirmed it.

So Jenner's hothead of a sister had gotten herself into big-time trouble. Sloan Redhawk wasn't surprised. It seemed to be a McKee trait. Sloan had known Jenner McKee for years. They'd spent a lot of time riding rodeo together, and Jenner was always getting himself into one scrape or another.

Jenner's older brother, Max, tended to keep his nose clean, but most of the people he'd talked to agreed that Casey was a stubborn, spoiled, headstrong girl. Flirting with danger seemed to be a family tradition. Even Jenner's old man, Jonah, had courted trouble, skirting the law with his business deals, but coming out of each scrape without a scratch because he had enough cash to buy off the judges, deputies, competition and local politicians.

Yep, Jonah McKee was as crooked as a dog's hind leg. He'd made his share of enemies by cheating men out of their businesses or sleeping with their wives. And his enemies seemed to hate anyone named McKee. Sloan only hoped that whoever had taken Casey wasn't desperate enough in his thirst for revenge to kill Jonah's only daughter.

He listened to the gossip surrounding him, but the conversation wasn't all that interesting, even when he sauntered over to the pool tables in the corner and then to the men's room. He picked up snatches of grumbling about the coming winter, a problem with water rights, hunting restrictions and property taxes, but aside from the gossip of the two women, he didn't learn too much more of the McKees and their troubles.

By the time Sloan sat back down at his table, he decided to call it a night. He had a couple of leads to work on. Randy Calhoun was a disgruntled ex-employee of the ranch and Fred Donner felt that Jonah had swindled him out of his water rights. Corey Stills held a grudge because his wife had been Jonah's mistress, and Ned Jansen and Slim Purcell had both lost valuable property—a copper mine and a racehorse—to Jonah McKee. All reasons to hate the family.

"Hey, how's it goin'?" Don Bateman, a rancher who lived near the Rocking M, clapped Sloan on the back.

"It's goin'."

"Mind if I join you?"

Sloan kicked out a chair. "Be my guest."

After ordering a drink and checking out the score of the hockey game, Don settled in. "You know, this place isn't the same without old Jonah McKee," he observed.

"How's that?"

"You'd have to know the man to appreciate it, I guess, but McKee had a presence about him. Oh, don't get me wrong, he was as twisted as the Snake River, but he wasn't all bad and people kinda looked up to him. Pr'bly 'cause of all his money."

"He was a regular?"

"Oh, yeah, like clockwork. Well—" he shrugged "—most of us are."

Sloan scratched his chin and gazed around the room. "Yep," he agreed. He saw one of the Purcell boys, Ned Jansen, Cyrus Kellogg and Jimmy Rickert, the snitch who had told Jenner McKee that on the night he was murdered Jonah had argued with a man in a dark pickup. Rickert didn't know or wouldn't say who the culprit was, but, according to Jenner, the truck would have a crumpled bumper from nearly running Beth's little Nova off the road a few weeks ago.

Sloan had checked the pickups in the parking lot every night. He hadn't found any trace of a dark blue or black pickup with a creased bumper.

Don started complaining about the cost of feed for his cattle and horses while Sloan finished his beer. A few more men stopped by and the conversation slipped to concerns about a new virus that was affecting some of the stock. Sloan, usually a patient man, was beginning to feel frustrated. So far there were no new clues to Casey's disappearance. He reached for his hat as the door swung open, and a man he recognized as Steve Jansen made his way inside. Long and lanky, Steve ordered a beer, greeted a few friends and set a couple of bucks on the glossy mahogany.

Steve had a wife and two kids, a small ranch and an auto-body shop in town. If anyone in Rimrock wanted work done on his car or truck, say to pound out and fix a dented bumper, Steve would be the man to ask. Sloan had already poked around a bit, and Rex Stone, the McKees' P.I. who was investigating Jonah's murder, had talked to Steve and his partner, George Patterson, soon after they'd been questioned by one of Sheriff Polk's deputies. Nothing had turned up.

"How about a game?" Jimmy Rickert, making eye contact with Steve, thrust his chin toward the pool table.

"All right," Steve drawled. He grabbed his beer.

"Hey, Steve, where's Barry? Poker game's kinda dull without him."

"Don't know," Steve replied with a lift of his shoulder. "Just up and left. He does that sometimes."

"Yeah, but never for this long. Not this time of year."

Barry White was Steve's half brother. Though Don Bateman was rattling on about a short growing season, Sloan was only half listening to the conversation. His eyes narrowed on Steve and he considered.

"He'll be back. That's the trouble with Barry," Steve said with a cocksure grin. "You're never able to get rid of him for long."

Sloan smiled to himself, but he turned his attention back to Don. "Barry White a regular around here?"

Don signaled for another beer. "Frankly I'm surprised the Black Anvil's stayed in business without him." He snorted a laugh and poured a little more from his bottle into a frosted glass. "No one knows what Barry does for a living. Works for his dad a little, well, his stepdad, really. Ned Jansen. Ever since he lost the copper mine, Ned's been scrambling to make ends meet—not easy when you've got two ex-wives and a passel of kids. Now he owns a small logging operation, and most of the time Barry works for him—as long as there's work." Don grabbed a handful of popcorn and plopped a salty kernel into his mouth.

"What kind of truck does Barry drive?"

"A beat-up old four-wheel-drive rig, I think. Seems to always have a headlight out or a dent in the side." Don chuckled again. "I guess he could keep Steve in business if he wanted to."

"I guess. Is he friends with most of the guys around here?"

"I s'pose so. He plays cards with Slim Purcell and Corey Stills and hung around with Randy Calhoun while Randy was still around—before Jonah gave him the boot. Never understood that one," Don admitted. "Randy had been with the McKees for years, one of Jonah's best men. Real good with the stock, but then, all of a sudden, Jonah accuses Randy of stealing from him—cullin' out the best calves or some such nonsense. Fires him on the spot in front of the rest of his hands. Stripped the man of his dignity, if ya ask me." Don shook his head as the waitress, Wanda, picked up his empty bottle and deposited a fresh one in front of him. "Sometimes Jonah McKee could be one mean son of a bitch. Me, I liked him, been his neighbor for years. We got along, but then he didn't cut off my water like he did with Fred Donner and he didn't mess around with my wife, Donna, like he did with Corey Stills." He poured a thin stream of beer into his glass. "If ya ask me, Jonah McKee had it comin'."

"But why would anyone want to burn down the stables or kidnap his daughter after he was dead?" Sloan hooked the heel of his boot on an empty chair.

"Beats me," Don replied, squinting at the television screen over the bar. "Maybe everyone's barking up the wrong tree. Maybe no one's out for revenge against Jonah. Maybe the problem is one of the boys—or Casey herself." He gave a long, low whistle. "She's a hothead, that one." Don reached into his pocket and drew out a pair of glasses, then settled back to watch a basketball game that was just starting.

So as not to arouse any suspicions, Sloan sat around for the next thirty minutes letting the information sink in, then he left. Barry White had just become the number one suspect in his case. It would take a little time and digging, but Sloan would find the bastard, and when he did, Casey had damned well better be alive and unharmed. Otherwise there would be hell to pay.

Chapter Two

Barry checked his watch for the tenth time in less than that many minutes. Casey knew that the solitude was getting to him, that his nerves were strung as tight as piano wire. Obviously he hadn't expected to be cooped up so long. He'd run out of chewing tobacco this morning and all day long he'd been jumpy.

"Trouble?" she asked him as he walked to the window and glared out at the continuing snowfall.

"I don't know what you're talkin' about."

"Sure you do. Either negotiations between your partner and my family have fallen through or your friend, whoever he is, has taken the money and flown the coop."

"No way," he said, but his lips flattened over his teeth. No doubt he was thinking about the fact that he might have been double-crossed—and thinking hard. Casey tried to swallow back her panic because, if Barry's partner had turned on him, then there was no reason to keep her alive.

Barry couldn't trust her not to name him as one of the kidnappers.

So why would he even let her live at all? As long as she was alive, she could point her finger and identify him. Her throat turned to dust and she eyed the shotgun he'd propped in the corner. It was loaded—she'd seen him check the chamber several times. Then there was the sheathed, long-bladed knife that was strapped to his belt and stayed with him while he paced the cabin.

She'd been working for days on her plan to escape because she'd given up on her brothers and the law. Obviously Barry had hidden her so far away that she'd never be found. She'd listened for the sound of whirring helicopter blades, or the deep rumble of a truck's engine, hoping that someone was on his way to free her. But as each day had passed, her hopes had begun to fade and she knew that she could depend on no one but herself.

Well, fine. She wasn't one to worry a situation to death and she wasn't about to let some dim-witted thug like Barry White take advantage of her. Even if he did have a wicked knife and a no-nonsense shotgun.

Fortunately, Barry, preoccupied with his own problems, was getting sloppy and trusting her too much. He'd taken off her gag and kept her untied most of the time. He'd even bragged that he didn't have to keep her shackled because there was no place she could run. The nearest civilization was over fifty miles by road—if she was even able to find a road.

She'd tried to pretend total acquiescence because all she had to do was bide her time and wait for Barry to go back into town, where he picked up his meager supplies and made his calls to his accomplice. She thought about the man without a face and wondered for the thousandth time who was pulling Barry's rotten strings.

"I'm goin' out," he growled, eyeing her. He reached for the rope, seemed to hesitate, but bound her hands, anyway. "The storm might trap us here and I'm damn near out of booze."

"Why do you bother with tying me?" she asked, flinging her hair from her eyes as she tried to squirm away. He was big and brawny and smelled foul. "It's not like I can go anywhere."

"So?" He squinted at her warily. "But it'd be just like you to try and get away."

"To where?"

"Don't matter. It'd be a pain in the butt if I was to come back here and find you gone." He hitched the rope a little tighter and she winced. "My partner, he don't like screwups."

"Your partner's going to leave you to take the fall, Barry. You know it. Why else hasn't he shown up to let you know that the money's been paid, hmm? You really think my family won't come through?"

"It takes a while to scrounge up a million bucks. Even for you McKees."

"Is that the line he's been feeding you?"

"Oh, just shut up!" He gave the rope a final tug, checking the knot. Then, satisfied that she wouldn't be able to escape, he yanked his jacket from a rusty nail by the door, shoved his arms through the sleeves and shouldered open the door, letting in a blast of raw, icy wind and a swirl of snow. The door banged shut behind him.

"Bastard," she muttered between her teeth, hardly daring to breathe, hoping that she had the nerve to go through with her plan. Straining to listen, she heard the door to his truck open, then shut and the old engine cough and grind before it finally caught. She sent up a prayer of gratitude as she heard the shifting of gears, the roar of the engine as Barry tromped on the accelerator and the spin of tires on packed snow. A few seconds later, there was silence—peaceful and frightening silence.

Casey steeled herself. It was now or never. Though her chances of finding help in the mountains in winter were slim, she couldn't sit around and wait for Barry's accomplice to insist that she be killed before she could finger Barry to the law. Whoever was behind the plot was probably smart enough to realize that Barry was a sniveling coward who would spill his guts and hang his partner rather than take the rap alone.

Barry had tied her wrists in front of her rather than behind her this time. Frantically, knowing that it would take hours and Barry wouldn't be gone forever, she began working at the knot with her teeth and wiggling her fingers until her skin was raw. Pain seared her flesh, and though she worked herself into a sweat, she couldn't loosen the damned knot.

There was no knife; Barry had taken the only knife with him and there wasn't any piece of metal sharp enough to work through the strong hemp. Then her gaze settled on the lantern and the flame flickering on the wick. Her heart hammered. Her only hope was to burn through the rope. No doubt she'd singe herself, as well, but she could suffer a few burns to save her life.

Then she saw it. An easier way. If she could break the glass on the lantern and wedge a jagged edge between the boards of the table, she could saw through the tough cord and risk only a cut or two rather than char her flesh or have her clothes and hair catch fire.

No sooner had she come up with the plan than she blew out the flame. The cabin was suddenly immersed in darkness, with only the orange glow from the window in the door of the wood stove giving off any kind of illumination. Casey didn't care. Heart thudding, she slammed the lantern onto the floor, near the door, far away from the stove where the drizzling kerosene might be set ablaze. Then, carefully, she picked through the glass, cutting her fingers twice before she found two large pieces and carried them back to the table. She worked quickly, for the sooner she escaped, the farther she could flee from the cabin before Barry returned. She had no watch, couldn't judge the time, but each minute she stayed was one minute closer to Barry's returning, seeing what she'd done and wreaking his own kind of vengeance.

She cut her fingers again as she tried to force the glass between the slats of the table, but the boards were too close together, the space between each one too small, and she had to waste valuable time cutting at the old wood, creating a space, before at last she had a makeshift saw. Her hands were sticky with blood as she worked, back and forth, moving her wrists over the fragile blade, feeling the hemp slowly begin to loosen.

She worked for what seemed hours but might have only been minutes, her shoulder muscles bunching in pain as she kept on, sawing steadily in the darkness, silently praying that she would be able to break free.

"Come on, come on," she whispered, sweat trickling from her brow. She felt the rope give a bit. Hope soared in her heart. Just a little longer. She shoved the hemp closer to the glass.

How long had Barry been gone? An hour? Two? How long would he stay away? She only hoped that he'd spend some time in the local bar, drinking and laughing and flirting with the waitress and losing all track of time. But what if he didn't? What if, even now, he was on his way back, with express instructions to kill her?

Frantically she worked over the piece of glass. The rope pulled and burned at her wrists before there was a sudden wrench, the hemp unraveled and she was free.

She couldn't believe it. With a gasp of joy, she jerked her jacket off the nail near the door and wished she had a pair of warm boots as well as a thick sheepskin coat. Her jean jacket and sneakers wouldn't stop frostbite, but she had no other options.

She had just slipped her arms through the jacket when she heard a scrape outside—the sound of footsteps. She swallowed back a scream as she heard the latch click. Her heart catapulted and she scrambled to the table to search

for her piece of glass, a futile weapon against a shotgun
and knife, but she'd be damned if she was going to be
tied up like an animal again—just waiting to die.

Suddenly the door burst open, banging hard against the
wall. Casey nearly jumped out of her skin. The wind raced
through the room, causing the embers in the stove to glow
red, and in the shadows she saw a man—a huge man—
in the doorway.

"Casey?" The voice was deep and male, but didn't
belong to Barry. "Casey McKee, you in here?"

Her heart pounded, thudding in her brain. *Stay calm,*
she silently told herself though her insides were frozen in
fear, *Just try to keep your wits about you.* The intruder
snapped the door shut. Casey slid behind the wood stove
and ducked down, fearing an assassin had been sent.
Maybe Barry didn't have the guts to kill her himself. Or
maybe it was someone here to save her. She almost spoke,
but bit down hard to quell the cry that sprang from her
lips.

"Casey? You here? Jenner sent me."

Jenner? Oh, God! If only she could trust this stranger!
But she couldn't. This could all be a ruse.

The thin beam of a flashlight swept the room and she
cowered deeper into her hiding spot. In the soft orange
half-light she saw that the man was taller than she'd first
thought. He stood well over six foot, she guessed, and his
shoulders were massive.

"The name's Redhawk. Sloan Redhawk. We've never
met, but I know your brother. Jenner and I go way back.
Rode rodeo together, got drunk in Pendleton and landed
in jail and—" The beam washed over the floor, then
stopped on the broken glass and spilled kerosene. "For
the love of God, what happened here?"

She couldn't see his features in the gloom, but remembered Jenner talking about the man. According to her
brother, Redhawk was a strong man whose actions spoke
louder than words. Half Native American, Sloan was as

tough as nails and as harsh as the desert that spawned
him. His gaze was dark, nearly malevolent, and a lot of
people were uncomfortable around him. His mere presence had been intimidating even to the toughest cowboy.
He didn't smile often and stared out at the world through
eyes that looked as if they'd seen enough pain and suffering to last a lifetime. Or so Jenner had painted him.

"Look, we don't have much time...." Again the beam
swept across the room and this time it landed squarely on
Casey's face. She gasped, blinked at the harsh light directed into her eyes and held on to her wedge of glass as
if it was a prize. "Holy Mother of God, look at you. What
happened? Your hands—"

"Stay away!" she growled when he approached. The
wicked wedge of glass glinted in the beam of the flashlight as she inched back farther into the corner.

"We've got to go. There's not much time. I heard
White leave but he could come back."

"How do you know? How did you find me?"

"We'll discuss it later. Right now, let's get out of
here."

"How do I know you're not one of them?"

"Hell," he muttered, then shone the flashlight upward
on his own face and the black Stetson on his head.

"Oh, God," she said, recognizing the angular features
of Jenner's friend. She'd seen a few snapshots of him, and
remembered the slash of his cheekbones, sharp nose and
dark, intense eyes. Tears suddenly clogged her throat, but
she didn't give in to the urge to cry in relief. She scrambled to her feet as the sound of a truck's engine rumbled
through the hills. Headlights flashed against the window.
"Oh, no!" Her heart plummeted. Barry was back!

Sloan grabbed her hand in his gloved fingers. "Does
he have a weapon?" he asked in a rough whisper.

"Yes, a shotgun, and maybe a pistol in the glove compartment of the truck, I'm not sure...but I know that he
does have a knife, a long hunting knife."

"You hide where you were before, behind the stove." Firmly Sloan guided her back into her hiding spot, then slid stealthily behind the door.

The truck's engine roared and its tires whined up the slippery slope before grinding to a stop. Casey's heart beat wildly and still she clutched her pathetic piece of glass as if the tiny useless weapon could somehow save her. Footsteps crunched in the snow and a swinging beam of light flashed against the window. Casey's heart flew into her throat as the door swung open.

"What in the…? Casey…?" Barry yelled, and the room turned instantly cold from the snow and wind and smelled of liquor. "Where are you? For cryin' out loud, this is no time to play stupid ga—"

Sloan sprang. Like a savage cat, he threw himself at Barry. They both landed on the floor, rolling and kicking, swearing and breathing hard. A fist connected with flesh; there was a sickening crunch of bone. Glass crunched.

Casey leapt to her feet. She wasn't going to sit around and wait for the outcome. Somehow she had to help Sloan.

A shotgun blast roared through the cabin. Sparks sprayed, and Casey jumped as the window shattered. A man screamed in pain. Oh, God! Not Sloan. Casey could barely breathe, didn't dare say a word as her eyes adjusted to the dark after the blinding explosion from the gun.

"You okay? Case?"

"Y-yes." Thank God.

A flashlight switched on, the harsh beam raining down on Barry, who lay writhing on the floor, clutching his arm. "Get up," Sloan growled. In one hand he held the flashlight, in the other the shotgun.

"Who the hell are you?" Barry demanded.

"Your worst nightmare. Get up."

Barry winced as he climbed to his feet. Sloan kicked out a chair. "You an Indian or what?"

"Sit."

"Some kind of goddamned Indian tracker—is that it?"

Sloan didn't answer. The temperature in the cabin dropped and the wind whistled, causing the embers in the stove to glow more brightly. "I said sit down." Sloan's voice brooked no argument.

"Why?"

"Sit down, you bastard, before I shoot you."

Barry's knees seemed to wobble and spittle collected at the corner of his mouth. The wind howled through the trees before racing through the broken panes. Barry stepped away from the chair. "Hey, man, I don't know who you are or who sent you, but if this is a double cross, I swear I'll keep my mouth shut."

"Good. Sit."

Barry stumbled backward, falling into the chair.

"You should pick more trustworthy partners," Sloan advised, still training both gun and flashlight on the coward. "Now, you, Casey, take his knife and tie him up."

"No, you can't," Barry said, eyeing the window. "It's freezing in here."

"Should have thought of that before you blew the window."

He slid a glance at the corner where Casey had been hiding. "Tie him or cuff him, whatever it takes."

Casey, her nerves strung tight, her insides shaking, fumbled in Barry's pack until she found the handcuffs.

"Hey, no...the key's lost," Barry whined, his eyes in the glow of the flashlight round with fear.

"Too bad." There was pleasure in Sloan's voice.

Casey pulled Barry's knife from its sheath, handed it to Sloan, then forced the coward's hands behind his back. Barry struggled and Sloan shoved the shotgun against Barry's chest, so that the barrel rested over his heart. Barry stopped moving instantly. Fingers sticky with her own blood, Casey clicked the cuffs around his wrists.

Barry was suddenly desperate. "For the love of God, man, you can't leave me here—"

"Like you left her?" Sloan thrust his chin in Casey's direction. "Somehow I think it's fitting."

"No way, man, please..."

Casey's stomach curled at the way Barry begged. She understood his helplessness. Hadn't she wanted to get down on her own knees and plead with him to set her free? Only her pride had prevented her from groveling as Barry was now.

"You know," Sloan said, "he's not gonna like this."

"He? Who?"

"You know who I mean."

Barry seemed to catch on that they were talking about his accomplice. "He'll help me. Count on it."

"Humph. He's not too happy with you."

"Why not? Hell, I took all the risks while he sat on his fat—" Barry suddenly clamped his mouth shut, his eyes narrowing angrily as he finally seemed to realize that this wasn't a double cross. "You lyin' son of a bitch," he said, glowering up at Sloan.

"That's right, you yellow bastard, I'm with the good guys."

"You don't know a damned thing, do ya? You don't know anything about what's goin' on."

"I know you're goin' down, White. And unless you spill your pathetic guts, you're goin' down alone." His voice was low and chilling. "If you're smart, you'll save both of us a whole lot of trouble and tell me the name of your partner."

"You'd like that, wouldn't you? Come in here as if you know all about it, when you don't know one god-damned thing. Well, I ain't a rat."

"Fine." Sloan shoved the flashlight into Casey's hands. "Hold this on him. Keep the beam right there, in his eyes."

Barry's tongue rimmed his lips nervously. "What're you gonna do?"

Casually, as the snow continued to blow into the cabin,

Sloan straddled Barry's chair and legs, then calmly placed his hands on each end of the long barrel of the shotgun and shoved it under Barry's bearded chin.

"Hey!"

Sloan pushed a bit. "What I'm goin' to do is break your damned windpipe if you don't tell me who you're working with."

Barry shook his head, and though it was way below freezing, sweat dripped down the sides of his face. Casey thought she might be sick.

Sloan shoved a little harder and Barry gasped, trying to breathe. "Stop it, you're killin' me."

"That's the general idea."

"You can't murder me!"

"Better than you deserve for what you did to a woman who trusted you for a ride. Now, White, who's the brains behind this seedy little operation? Cooperate and tell me now, and you might not have to spend the rest of your miserable life in jail. On the other hand, if you hold out…"

Barry snarled and spit at Sloan. "Go ahead, Injun," he dared, "kill me. Then you'll never find out, will ya?"

In the shadowy orange light, Casey saw Sloan's lips curve into a cruel smile. "Whatever you want, White."

Casey's heart was thudding. She hated Barry but she couldn't watch Sloan murder him. "You can't—"

"Hush!"

"But he's our only lead to his partner."

"She's got a point, Injun."

Sloan pressed a little harder on the barrel of the gun and Barry choked. "I guess she does. So you'll just have to wait up here and hope that the bastard you're tryin' to protect finds you before you freeze altogether."

"That's murder, Injun," Barry croaked. "You won't let it happen. If you do, she'll be an accomplice." Barry smiled boldly as if he'd won. Sloan yanked back the shotgun, stood and glowered down at him.

"You're lucky, White. If it was up to me, I'd kill you, gut you right here and hide your body so it'd never be found, but I guess I can't." With one eye on Barry, he strode to the wood stove, opened the door and added a couple thick chunks of oak, then slammed the door so hard Casey jumped. "Well, you've made your choice. You can just wait here for your buddy. Kind of guy he is, you shouldn't have to wait more than a day or two, a week on the outside. Maybe you can give some thought about what it was like for Casey." In disgust, he glanced down Barry's form, as if assessing his thick ski jacket, then slid Barry's knife under his belt. With one hand on the shotgun, he grabbed Casey and propelled her to the door.

"Hey, wait! I'm bleedin' here!"

"We can't just leave him," Casey protested over Barry's curses and angry shouts.

"Like hell. Come on." He found his hat, which had fallen to the floor in the struggle and plopped it onto his head. As he shepherded her outside, she heard Barry yelling loudly, shouting invectives over the keening wind.

Sloan didn't seem to care. He stopped by Barry's truck, opened the door and reached into the glove compartment. He found the pistol, stuffed it into his pocket, grabbed a mackinaw blanket and eyed Casey. Peeling off his jacket, he ignored Casey's protests and forced her to put it on over her jean jacket, then placed his huge hat over her head before tossing the mackinaw over his broad shoulders. His black hair caught in the wind and he looked more savage than before. His dark eyes held hers for a second before he opened the hood of the truck, rummaged around and pulled off the coil wire, which he stuffed into a pocket. "Just in case he manages to get lucky," he explained. "I want to make sure that he doesn't go anywhere."

"Aren't we going to use it?" she asked. His jacket was

heavy and smelled of horses and worn leather. Somehow it felt safe.

"The truck?" He shook his head. "Nope."

"But why…?" She looked frantically around for another vehicle.

"His partner might recognize it."

"You think he's close by?" Fear put a stranglehold on her throat.

"Don't know, but we can't take a chance. Come on." He helped her trudge through the knee-deep snow away from the lane leading to the cabin. "It won't take long, but this way we won't meet up with any of White's buddies, whoever the hell they are."

Casey's teeth were chattering, her hands felt as if they were freezing and she couldn't feel her feet. Ducking her head against the wind and snow, she knew she had to keep moving, plowing through the drifts. She didn't know how Sloan could tell where he was going as they walked steadily down the hillside through the trees, snow blowing in their eyes. He kept plodding forward, following a path he'd broken earlier, and eventually they came to some kind of utility shed where a horse—a huge draft animal—was waiting. Her rescuer didn't say a word, just opened a bag slung over the horse's haunches and handed her a pair of gloves. He helped her put them on, then shoved a pair of boots her way. Her fingers were too stiff to untie her shoes, so he took over the task, holding his gloves in his mouth as he worked at the frozen laces. After he took off her shoes, he stripped her of her socks. "Hey, wait—"

"I have another pair. Insulated. We can't risk frostbite." He rubbed her bare feet, making them sting when the warmth from his hands pierced her flesh. It felt as if he were pricking her with dozens of needles. His hands were big and rough but surprisingly gentle as he helped her into the thick socks and fleece-lined boots that reached to her knees. "We'll take this along just in case," he said. He shrugged off the mackinaw and handed her a down coat with a hood. He helped her with the zipper, then offered her a leg up on the horse.

"You expect me to ride him?" she asked.

"If you want to get away." He dressed in his own jacket again and rammed the Stetson onto his head. For the first time, she noticed the silver hatband and feathers surrounding the black crown.

"But a horse—"

"Snowmobiles make too much noise," he said without a smile. "Besides, it's only for a couple of miles. Come on."

He handed her a scarf and helped her onto the heavy-boned animal, then took the reins and started down the hillside. She wrapped the scarf around her face, but the frigid air still burned her lungs. So cold she could barely speak, she held on to the saddle horn and rocked with the gelding's swaying gait.

At the bottom of the hill, Sloan stopped the horse. A creek, the banks frozen, a swirl of water in the center, rushed through a steep ravine. Sloan hesitated, then, frowning, looked up at Casey. "This is gonna be a little tight," he said and swung up into the saddle with her.

Casey stiffened as she felt his legs surround her own, his crotch pressing her rump since they were wedged together so closely. She told herself she was being a ninny, that of course he didn't want to slog through the water and risk frostbite, but when he wrapped one strong arm around her waist to keep his balance and clucked his tongue at the horse, she bit down on her frozen lip and tried to ignore the intimacy of the situation. They were running for their lives, for God's sake; she couldn't worry about anything else.

As they rode, the heat of his body seemed to seep into her skin and she couldn't help feeling intense relief that someone was taking care of her. Though she'd always been a strong-willed woman and often proclaimed her independence from a domineering father, worried mother and overprotective older brothers, she now wanted to do nothing more than collapse and let someone else worry about keeping her safe and warm. Sloan seemed the answer to her prayers—a strong, silent man, her knight in slightly tarnished armor.

She was being silly, of course. Her thoughts were running away with her, dragging her along a ridiculous course because she wasn't thinking clearly, probably the result of the numbing cold, for one thing and the ordeal of the past week for another. She would perk up once she was rested. After a week of tension, fear for her life, angry arguments with Barry and sleepless nights filled with nightmares and plots to escape, she just wanted to shut down—to turn her brain off and fall into bed and sleep for days. If she'd been the kind of woman prone to tears, she was certain they'd be freezing on her cheeks right now. As it was, she simply wanted to go home—to the ranch she'd so recently wanted to leave.

All her wishes for independence seemed so petty at this point. She thought vaguely of Clarisse, but her mind was too cloudy to concentrate, and instead she closed her eyes and leaned back against Sloan's strong chest. Through her jeans she felt the muscles of his thighs grip hers, and his breath was warm against her head. She smelled the scent of him hanging on the bitter-cold air as the horse followed the course of the creek, plodding through the icy water until they reached a bend.

Sloan sucked in the cold through his teeth. He pulled on the reins and wished to God that he didn't feel the curve of Casey's rump rubbing intimately against his crotch. Hell, he didn't need this. She was Jenner's sister, for crying out loud, a rich girl who had just been through the trauma of her life and the last thing he needed was to think of her in any way the least bit sexual—especially out here in an Arctic storm blowing straight down the mountains from Canada.

At a jog in the creek, he urged the bay to the bank and

climbed off. Half-dozing and taken by surprise, Casey nearly toppled, but she caught herself and kept her balance. "You all right?" Sloan asked in concern.

"Fine." Snowflakes sprinkled her eyelashes. "Come on. Let's go."

Blowing on his gloved hands, Sloan led the horse along a twisty, snow-encrusted path that snaked through a thicket of pine. The trail widened into an old mining road with just enough space to park his rented truck and horse trailer. He'd made the arrangements by phone once he'd figured out where Barry was hiding. Unfortunately he'd had two false starts before he'd located the old cabin, which was owned by Barry's half brother, Steve Jansen.

Sloan had cursed himself for following the other leads—one to a fishing cabin on the Deshutes River outside of Bend owned by a buddy of Barry's and the other to an old house outside of Boise, which Barry had rented from a distant cousin.

Now, the problem was getting Casey home before the worst of the Arctic storm predicted for the past two days by the weather service hit.

"Come on, get inside," he said to Casey as he helped her to the ground. Good Lord, she was a tiny thing—couldn't weigh much more than a hundred pounds and barely five-three unless he missed his guess. He opened the passenger door of the old Chevy truck, gave her a boost inside, then climbed behind the steering wheel and started the engine.

While the cab warmed, he took care of the horse, a gelding he'd borrowed from Wes Duncan, a man he'd known for years, an ex-rodeo rider who lived about forty miles from here. Sloan had rented the trailer, as well, leaving a healthy deposit with Wes. So far, his plan had worked. He was certain no one had followed him and he hadn't had to deal with a surprise visit from Barry's accomplice, whoever the hell he was.

He unsaddled the horse, offered him a quick drink of

water, then quickly wiped down the gelding's coat, including his legs, dried the big animal, then tethered him in the trailer. After snapping the back gate closed, he climbed into the pickup again.

Heat from the radiator fogged the windows, and Casey, huddled in the corner, gazed at him with eyes the color of a forest at dawn. "Why you?" she asked as he revved the engine and rammed the truck into gear. "Why not deputies from the sheriff's department or Rex Stone or the FBI?"

"Jenner doesn't trust them."

"He doesn't trust anyone." Her gaze was thoughtful as she stared at him and he felt something inside of him crumble—an old wall that he'd so valiantly built. "He doesn't have many friends, I mean real friends, so why you?"

Sloan lifted a shoulder as he stared through the frosty windshield. The wipers were having trouble keeping up with the snow falling on the glass, and even with the headlights on, visibility was poor. From the corner of his eye, he noticed that she was still staring at him, her brow furrowed in concentration, her eyebrows pulled into a single line, as if she couldn't quite figure him out. "You okay?" he finally asked.

"Yeah."

"Let me see your hands."

"What?"

"They were bleeding."

"Oh." She seemed embarrassed. "I, um, cut them on the lantern. I'd decided that I had to escape, that if I didn't, Barry or one of his accomplices would probably kill me."

"One of?" he repeated, digesting this new piece of news. Not just one other criminal. "How many people *were* involved?"

"I—I don't know," she admitted, her lips pursing into a scowl. "I wish I did."

"But you think more than just one partner?"

She shook her head. "He never said, but he was always calling someone, and I got the feeling that he was talking about more than one man."

"But you don't know who?"

"I haven't got a clue."

"He didn't say a name or—"

"Look, I said he didn't," Casey snapped as if tired of a conversation she'd had with herself over and over again for the past week. "I don't know who he was working with, okay? I tried to pry it out of him, but he wouldn't slip up. It was a game with him, I think, and he felt smug about it. Like he had one more thing over me." Shuddering, she added, "It was like he hated me just because I was named McKee."

"Why does he hate the McKees?"

Again she shook her head and stared out at the white forest, and he wondered if she even noticed the trees, so deceptively peaceful and serene, their branches laden with snow, as the truck sped down the hill. "I asked him why about twenty times, and like I said, he seemed proud of himself and his secret. He *liked* me to ask him, at least at first he did. Acted as if it was some big joke on me and my brothers." She worried her lower lip as she thought about it. "You know, it seemed as if he thought this was all a game, one that he could finally win."

"You ever have any run-in with him before?"

"No." Her eyes shadowed as she shook her head once more. "He's older than I am, went to school with Max, but that was years ago. He's always been around Rimrock, even worked for Dad for a while."

"Did Jonah fire him?"

Casey shrugged. "I didn't keep up with Dad's business."

"But there has to be some reason he hates you, right?"

"Beats me," she said, then turned to the window again, her breath fogging the glass. "I spent the past week trying to figure out who he was working with, trying to trip him up, but I didn't get a clue. All I know is that whoever it is controls Barry.''

Sloan's jaw tightened. ''This won't be over until we find out who's in charge.''

The tone of his voice made Casey shiver. She'd never been a shrinking violet, or a fearful woman who jumped at shadows. But she'd never had a reason to be. As Jonah McKee's daughter, she'd been treated as a princess in Rimrock, and when she'd gone off to college she'd taken with her enough confidence to win people's respect and make friends easily.

''So let's take a look at your fingers.''

''What?''

''Your hands.'' A look of annoyance flashed in his eyes when she didn't immediately respond, as if he was a man who was used to his orders being obeyed. ''They were bleeding. I want to make sure they're not infected.''

''I just cut them a little while ago,'' she argued, but yanked off the gloves carefully since her blood had dried to the lining.

He flipped on the overhead light and took one hand in his. Though big and callused, the fingers that probed hers were gentle. His scowl deepened when he noticed the dark stains below her nails and the blood that had coagulated over her scratches.

''Hurt?'' he asked, touching her fingertips and examining them as he kept one eye on the road.

She winced a little when he touched the tender skin of her fingertips. ''I'll live,'' she predicted, then thought of the irony of that statement. Without Sloan Redhawk, she wondered about her chances of seeing tomorrow. Whether she wanted to admit it or not, he'd probably saved her life.

''We'll clean 'em up as soon as we stop.'' His gaze slid down her body and he sighed with dismay. ''Your jeans are soaking wet.''

"If you remember, I've been trudging through snow."

"Here." He reached behind the seat of the truck and pulled out a nylon bag she recognized. "There's a change of clothes in there. You'd better put on something dry."

"Now?" she said, staring at him as if he'd lost his mind.

"Now."

"I can't—"

"If your fingers are too sore, I'll pull over and do it, but—"

"No way!" She couldn't imagine him tugging down her wet jeans, baring her cold legs and trying to yank on a dry pair of pants. Cold as she was, she still had some pride left.

"Then do it." He snapped off the overhead light and turned his attention back to the road.

"I'm not going to change here. Not now."

He sent her a look that was all business. His features were set and grim, and impatience etched the corners of his mouth.

"You can't bully me into this."

"It's for your own good."

"Is it?"

"Look, lady, I just risked my neck to save you. The least you could do is put on a dry pair of pants and make sure you don't catch pneumonia until after we get back to the ranch."

"I'll wait till we stop."

"Could be hours."

She considered this. She didn't like him ordering her around, but the truth of the matter was that her jeans were wet and dirty and cold. If she had any brains at all, she'd do what he suggested and forget the fact that he was treating her as if he was a drill sergeant and she an underling. "I just don't like to be told what to do, okay?" she said, opening the bag and wincing at the pain in her fingers.

"I've been ordered to do this, do that, go here, stay there, all week long, and I'm sick of it."

A muscle knotted in his jaw and he stared straight ahead. "Okay. Have it your own way," he said calmly. "Would you *please* change your clothes so that you live to see tomorrow and I'm not dragging a corpse back to Oregon with me?"

"Very funny," she muttered under her breath, but started unzipping her jeans. She cast a wary glance in his direction, but if he wanted to sneak a peek at her, he didn't, and she felt foolish even to think that he was trying to see her without her clothes. For God's sake, she looked like a street urchin or worse. Using the Indian blanket as a screen, she worked off her boots and peeled off her wet pants.

"There's a towel in the bag, too," he said, and she glanced up quickly, expecting to find his dark eyes assessing her, but his gaze never left the road. Heat rose on the back of her neck and she felt a childish urge to fling the wet jeans at him. Instead she left them crumpled on the floor of the truck as she wiggled into her favorite pair of faded Levi's. Zipping the fly was no problem; she'd probably lost over five pounds in her week of captivity. "Better?" he asked, and she sent him a glare.

"Yeah." She even managed a smile.

"Thought so. You should find some underthings in there and a couple of sweaters, I think. Other stuff, too. Makeup, soap and shampoo, that kind of thing."

"You went to the ranch and got my clothes?" she said when the realization finally struck her. He'd been prepared, she'd give him that much.

"I asked your mother to pack what you needed."

"So you were pretty sure you'd find me, weren't you?"

He turned, his eyes meeting hers in the darkness. Her stomach did a slow roll. "If the money's good enough," he said, "I always find what I'm looking for."

Chapter Three

She let out her breath slowly. "So this is about money."

"Everything's always about money."

"You sound like Jenner."

He lifted a shoulder and the truck rumbled through the dark hills while snow collected on the ever-moving windshield wipers.

"How much are they paying you to bring me home?" she asked, wondering why it hurt a little to know that her rescue had been bought. She wasn't stupid; she knew he wouldn't work for free. Yet a part of her wanted to think of this dark, dangerous-looking man as her hero, a man who would lay down his life for her, a cowboy who lived by his own strict moral code. God, she was a fool. Or delirious. Or maybe a little of both. When he didn't answer, she prodded, "How much?"

"Does it matter?"

"Just curious. I'll find out later, anyway, so you may as well tell me now."

"A hundred grand."

She sucked in her breath. "A hundred thousand dollars?"

He sent her a cynical smile. "Cheaper than a million, isn't it?"

"My family would've paid the ransom," she snapped, suddenly defensive.

"No doubt." He said it as if the thought was distasteful.

"You don't approve."

"I don't like giving in to extortion."

"Nobody does, but wouldn't you if it were your child?"

His hands tightened over the wheel and a muscle came alive in the corner of his jaw. He shifted down for a bend in the road.

"Well?"

"No."

"Oh, come on—"

"It only encourages more criminals to commit a similar crime and most of the time the victim doesn't survive, anyway. That way no one can identify them later."

"Well, if it was my kid, I'd beg, borrow or steal the money just to get him back. I wouldn't take any chances."

"Do you have a kid?" he asked, but she guessed he already knew the answer. Just as she knew about him from Jenner, no doubt he'd learned a few things about her, as well.

"No, but—"

"Then you don't know how you'd react."

"Oh, yes, I do. Because I'm an aunt and I know that I'd walk through hell and back for Hillary and Cody. I think those feelings would only be stronger with a child of my own."

Amen, he thought, his throat tightening at the thought of Tony. Casey was glowering at him, her anger radiating like heat waves. Good. Anger was a good sign. And he'd rather have her angry with him than thinking he was some kind of damned hero. Or a pervert. He'd seen the changes of emotion on her face, one of grateful adoration when he'd rescued her and one of confusion and fear when he'd insisted she change into a dry pair of pants. Truth to tell, he had watched her from the corner of his eye, and though she was more trouble than she was worth—a spoiled rich girl used to getting anything she damned well pleased— he couldn't help his natural urge to try to glimpse a little of her bare legs.

Stupid. That's what he was. The girl was trouble, no doubt about it, and it was his responsibility to get her back safely, so he'd better make sure his gaze was glued to the road and keep reminding himself that she was Casey McKee, Jenner's little sister, and she'd just gone through the worst trauma of her life. She was probably vulnerable, if that word could be applied to anyone so damned hot- headed and self-confident, so he'd better keep their rela- tionship strictly professional.

Relationship? As if they had one! Inside his gloves, his hands began to sweat. What the devil was wrong with him? She was his charge, he was her guardian, her body- guard until he dropped her off on her rich little behind on the front porch of the Rocking M.

He glanced at his watch, frowned, but decided enough time had passed and he'd managed to scare the hell out of Barry White. He reached into his coat pocket, took out a cellular phone and punched out the number of the local sheriff's department.

"You have a phone?" she asked, amazed. She stared at the black instrument as if it were heaven-sent.

"Looks that way," he drawled as the call connected.

"Then let me call my mother. She's got to be worried sick—"

"Shh!" he responded harshly as an operator for the department answered. "I'd like to talk to the sheriff or the deputy in charge. I have a crime to report." He waited until a deputy—a young guy by the name of Eddington—answered.

"What's this I hear about a crime?"

"There's been a shooting up above Blue Hollow, in a cabin owned by Steve Jansen, I think. You'll find a man there, Barry White. He's Jansen's half brother and he's cuffed to a chair and gettin' colder by the minute. He—"

"Has he been shot?"

Sloan paused. "Well, grazed a little, I think, but not really shot. Not seriously. He'll survive, but he's wanted by the FBI."

"Is this some kind of joke?"

"Of course not." He shot a glance at Casey who was listening to his conversation with the ghost of a smile playing on her lips. "You go on up there on your snowmobiles and you find him and call Agent Sam Revere of the FBI. Revere's at the Rocking M Ranch near Rimrock, Oregon. The number is—"

"The FBI? Hey, who is this?"

Sloan hesitated. "That doesn't matter," he finally said, deciding that he didn't want the authorities breathing down his neck, not just yet. It was bad enough that he had to call at all; he didn't want someone picking him up because, when it came right down to it, he, like Jenner, had a problem with the law. At least in this case. "I just rescued a woman—Casey McKee—from the cabin."

"Right." The deputy's voice dripped sarcasm.

"Who'd make up a story like this in the middle of a blizzard?"

"You'd be surprised."

"Well, check it out. Call Revere. And send someone up to the Jansen cabin. If that man escapes it'll be on your record. He's wanted for questioning about the murder of Jonah McKee, arson at the McKee ranch and this damned kidnapping. I'm telling you, either you call Revere, or I do."

"We'll check it out," the deputy said after a moment's

hesitation, "but we don't have any time for wild-goose chases, mister. This storm's a son of a bitch. We got highway crews stuck in the mountains, stranded vehicles all over the roads and some spots in the county have lost electricity. If this turns out to be a prank, you'll be in a helluva lot of hot water."

"It won't. Just call Revere." Disgusted, he clicked off. "Damned fool."

"I need to call my mother." He hesitated. "Please...just to ease her mind."

A muscle worked in the side of his jaw, but he handed her the telephone, and though her fingers burned from the scratches, Casey punched out the number.

It rang twice. "Rocking M."

"Max?" The sound of her brother's voice brought tears to her eyes. "Oh, Max..."

"My God, Casey, is that you?" His voice was suddenly muffled as he said, "It's Casey!" Other voices chimed in, but Max shushed them. Casey pictured her family, concerned for her safety, seated in the den. Her mother and grandmother, who lived at the Rocking M and probably Beth Crandall, Jenner's fiancée who helped them manage Skye's apartment building, Skye if not on duty at the clinic or hospital, would be there, too. "Are you all right?"

"Fine."

"You're sure?" he asked, and the voices in the background stilled as his voice became deadly serious.

"Yes, Max, really, I'm fine. I—I'm with Sloan."

"Thank God." Relief echoed in his voice.

"We're in the truck. I don't know where—"

"Who kidnapped you?"

"Barry White—"

Sloan snatched the phone from her fingers. "I don't think it would be wise to talk too much over the telephone," he said gruffly. "The kidnapper should be in custody within the hour, but he has at least one accomplice, maybe more, we're not sure. We just wanted to let everyone know she's fine and—'' he glowered through the windshield at the dark heavens ''—weather permitting, we'll be home by tomorrow.''

She didn't get the chance to hear her brother's response as Sloan cut the call short. ''Hey, I wanted to talk to my mother.''

''You will.''

She couldn't help the anger that seeped into her words. ''I don't understand why you're being so damned rude. All I wanted to do—''

''Has it ever occurred to you that there might be a leak?''

''A leak? What're you talking about?''

''At the Rocking M, or in the sheriff's department, or through McKee Enterprises.''

''That's ridiculous,'' she said, but a shred of apprehension shot through her and she leaned her head against the window of the passenger door.

''Is it? Why is the law always one step behind the culprit? Why wasn't Jonah's death investigated as a murder in the first place? Why was Beth Crandall's car carrying Jenner's son nearly run off the road? How did someone know where she'd be? And what about the arson? Who could get to the stables, set the fire and slip away without being noticed?'' His face had turned grim, almost menacing, in the shadowy cab of the truck. ''And how did Barry know where to find you? Coincidence?''

''I don't know.''

''Of course not. One time, maybe. But not every time. Unless I miss my guess, someone's talking too much, maybe not on purpose, but just shooting the breeze with the wrong crowd.''

''I don't think that—''

''Come on, Casey. Use your head. Someone's letting the cat out of the bag. Whether intentionally or not, I don't know. But this time, we're gonna have the jump on him, and I'm sure as hell not going to make it easy by announcing where we are. Once Barry's arrest hits the news, or he gets in touch with his accomplice, you're in more danger than ever before.''

''Why?''

''Because whoever the other person is, he can't be certain you don't know his identity. White didn't impress me as a genius, so unless his partner is as stupid as he is, he'll be pretty concerned that good ol' Barry let something slip. Next time, you won't be kidnapped, Casey, you'll be killed.''

She shivered. ''If you're trying to scare me—''

''Damned straight. I hope I scared the living hell right out of you!''

He scowled through the windshield and saw from the corner of his eye that Casey wanted to argue with him. Her chin was set at a stubborn angle and her eyes were narrowed in anger. Fine. Let her be angry. He wasn't going to let her get herself into trouble again—not until he had her safely back at the McKee ranch and had pocketed the money. A hundred thousand dollars. Enough money to change the course of his life.

If he could just hang on to her. Right now, things weren't going well. The snow was coming down hard. Millions of tiny flakes swirled with the wind and piled in heavy drifts. Several times the truck and trailer had skidded on the narrow, winding road, and Casey's hands looked like hell. The cuts needed to be cleaned and smeared with an antibiotic ointment and he hadn't ruled out her seeing a doctor. Worse yet, she was staring at him as if trying to figure out what made him tick.

''Why don't you try to get some sleep?''

''I can't. Too keyed up.''

He slid a glance at her and tried not to notice the sweep of her lashes or her eyes, a mix of green, brown and gray. She reached into the nylon bag, found a small zippered pouch and pulled out a comb. Turning the rearview mirror

in her direction, she gritted her teeth as she tried to untangle the knots from her hair. "Where are we going?"

"North first."

"Oregon's southwest—ouch! I mean, I think it is.
Weren't we in Montana?" Tugging, she dragged the
comb through her tangled strands and made a face. "God,
what a mess."

"Yeah, we're in Montana, but we've got to make sure
that we don't run into Barry's accomplice, and most likely
he'd come up from the south." He didn't add that there
was a major flaw in his plan; he'd heard over the crackle
of static on the radio that he was driving toward the blizzard instead of trying to outrun it. The weather service
had been reporting all day that a storm, straight out of
Canada, was moving toward the northern United States.
This part of Montana was smack-dab in its path, and he
felt as if he were driving into the maw of a great Arctic
beast. But there was no other option if he wanted to keep
Casey alive. He supposed he should be completely honest
with her, but right now she didn't need any more worries.
She'd been through enough in one week to last a lifetime.

Sliding a glance in her direction and watching as she
finally slid the comb freely through her dark hair, he fiddled with the radio, but they were still too deep in the
mountains, too far away from any signal towers to receive
anything more than static. He used the phone again to dial
the weather service, but the line was busy.

Nearly an hour later, he pulled onto the main road. Five
inches of snow greeted him; the road hadn't been plowed
or sanded. Swearing under his breath, he continued heading north to return the horse and trailer rig.

"Why did you do it?" she asked as she tucked the
small pouch back into the bag. Apparently finished with
grooming, she twisted the mirror back in his direction and
he adjusted it.

"Do what?"

"Come and get me. Was it just the money?"

''What else?''

''That's what I'd like to know.''

He shrugged idly, as if it didn't really matter, then hated himself when he saw her face crumple a little. She tossed her hair over her shoulders, turned to look out the window instead of at him and her shoulders stiffened.

Son of a bitch! Usually a man of few words, he couldn't control his urge to explain. ''The money's the big issue, yeah, but I owed Jenner a favor. A big one.''

''Why? I can't imagine owing Jenner anything.''

Damn but she was a persistent thing. ''He saved my life.''

She made a sound of disbelief and he didn't elaborate, didn't want to think about it. Sloan didn't like owing any man, even Jenner McKee. He was glad that once Casey had been deposited on the doorstep of the Rocking M and he'd tracked down Barry White's partner in crime, he'd be free of that particular debt.

But he didn't like their chances of beating the storm back to Oregon. Snow had been falling steadily for hours on end, the drifts on the side of the road were deep enough to cause the pickup's wheels to spin and they had hundreds of miles to drive before he could leave Casey at the McKee ranch, find the other bastard or bastards involved in the attacks against the McKees, collect his reward and start a new life, a solitary life far away from L.A. He was tired of the inadequate web of freeways, the smog and the paralyzed traffic. He'd put up with earthquakes, mud slides and fires that raged out of control for too many years.

There had been a time when he'd embraced the city, when he'd felt at home in the sunshine and walked on the sand near the ocean. The vast Pacific had been calming, the rugged hillsides had risen in stark contrast to the bustle of the city and he'd loved his job with the police department. It hadn't been glamorous, but it had been steady and filled with excitement. When the long hours of the night were finally over, he'd return to his little two-bedroom cottage and find Jane, cozy and warm, snuggled under thin blankets and smiling up at him.

But that had been long ago, in a distant time that had been his youth. Things had changed; his life had been ripped apart into jagged pieces, which never seemed to quite fit together again, as if the one vital and integral part of him was missing. He wondered if he'd ever be whole again or if there would always be a tear in him, a black void that he kept hidden and denied, but that kept him awake at nights when he was lying alone in his empty double bed, staring at the slowly rotating paddle fan and examining his life.

So now he'd have a hundred thousand dollars. That thought should have warmed him from the inside out, but it didn't. Even the idea of purchasing his own ranch didn't lift his spirits. Besides, they weren't home free. Not yet.

Casey closed her eyes, but she didn't sleep. Not even the warm cab and the steady drone of the engine could make her relax. She was still too anxious, her nerves strung tight like new fence wire, and she needed time to unwind.

The more distance they put between them and the horrid cabin where she'd been held hostage, the better she felt, and yet she couldn't help wondering if Sloan was driving them into some kind of trap. Sloan's concerns about the telephone call made sense but she didn't want to think that anyone close to her or the investigation had given away any information that someone might have used for his own vile means. The same old questions that had plagued her for a week ran in circles through her brain.

Who was Barry's partner in crime? Just one man? Or two? Maybe more? Why had they killed her father? Why had they tried to burn down the stables, crippling Jenner and nearly killing Hillary and Dani? Why had they run

Beth off the road? And why for God's sake did they feel the need to kidnap her? For money? Hatred of the McKee family? Who were these people and what did they want? Would their thirst for revenge never end? Jonah was dead, but they still weren't satisfied—probably never would be.

A familiar rage burned through her blood and she felt violated all over again. Was it possible that someone, probably someone she knew and trusted, was laughing at her family's pain, was, at this very moment, scheming more ways to torture them? Whoever the culprit was, she silently swore, he would pay.

Sloan turned onto a highway that intersected the road they were following and the terrain flattened a little. They met a snowplow heading in the opposite direction and eventually came upon pavement that had been cleared at one time but was already becoming thick with snow again.

Once the truck was rolling along a fairly clear stretch of road, Sloan reached under the seat and found a thermos. "Coffee. If you want it. There's an extra cup in the glove compartment. Wait—" he glanced at her fingers and frowned "—I'll get it."

"I can do it." She reached in and withdrew a blue enameled cup.

But she couldn't open the lid of the thermos. Her fingers, hot with pain, refused to grip. Frustrated, she handed the thermos back to him, and he somehow managed to uncap the jug. He handed her its plastic cup and poured a thin stream of coffee into it. She held out the enameled cup and he poured again. "I wish I had remembered this earlier," he said, capping the thermos. "Guess I had too much on my mind."

Taking a long gulp from the enameled cup, he settled lower on his back as he drove. Long and lean, his body folded neatly behind the wheel. Faded jeans, sheepskin jacket, flannel shirt—marks of a cowboy. The black felt hat, with its feather band and touch of silver added to his appeal. Earthy, sexy and charged with a raw energy, he was exactly the kind of man she'd always found fascinating but had told herself to avoid.

Tearing her eyes from him, she stared out at the night. The boughs of the pines bowed under the weight of the snow and still it just kept falling, piling up on the road, dancing in front of the headlights. They met no cars or trucks, and to Casey it felt as if she and this silent, brooding man were the only people in the universe. She sipped her coffee. It was hot and scalded the back of her throat, but warmed her from the inside out.

"How is my family—I mean, you were at the ranch. How did they deal with the kidnapping?" she finally asked.

"As well as could be expected." He forced a smile. "But Jenner, he couldn't stand waiting around. Faxed me a letter the day they got word from the kidnappers."

She imagined her mother and grandmother nearly frantic with concern, and her brothers—both well-known hotheads—would probably want to strangle Barry White with their bare hands. Sighing, she leaned against the window and pictured her mother. Two months ago, Casey had been convinced that Virginia McKee was losing her mind because of her wild theories about her husband's supposedly accidental death. Virginia was convinced from the beginning that Jonah had been murdered. Turned out her mother had been right all along.

Swallowing another long sip of coffee, she slid a glance at the man who had saved her. "I guess I should thank you."

"Just doing my job."

"I thought this was a favor."

"That, too." He looked at her for a second and her breath seemed to stop somewhere between her throat and lungs. His features seemed harsh in the reflection of the dash lights and his countenance grim. A dangerous man, she thought, one who shoved rifle barrels under men's chins and blasted out windows with a shotgun. A man to reckon with.

As he drove, he drank from his cup, stared straight ahead and did his job. Period. She wondered what he thought of her and decided it didn't matter. "Jenner said you were married," she said to break the silence.

"I was."

"But not any longer?"

His lips tightened just a little, his eyes narrowed a fraction. "Jane died," he said quietly.

The cab seemed suddenly small, filled with unspoken emotions. She saw the pain in his eyes and how quickly he disguised it. Her throat tight, Casey reached out to touch his arm. "I'm sorry—I didn't know."

"How could you?" His jaw was set in stone, his gaze dark, his lips flat over his teeth.

"Look, I didn't mean to pry."

He glanced pointedly down at the fingers still resting on his sleeve. "You didn't."

"But—"

"Just forget it."

The wheels of the truck whined as he veered off the road and the trailer swung wide before gripping the icy pavement. Casey started, nearly spilling her coffee, but the truck plunged through six inches of new snow that covered a lane of some kind, a road that parted the forest.

"Where are we?" she asked, squinting into the night.

"Wes Duncan's place. He's the guy who loaned me the horse and trailer."

The pines gave way to a clearing, where a small cabin and barn were illuminated by a single security lamp that flooded the snow-covered paddock and yard with watery blue illumination. Icicles hung from the eaves of the house and patches of warm light glowed from the windows. Smoke curled from a single stone chimney that climbed up one wall.

"This'll just take a minute." Sloan let the engine idle

and hopped down from the cab of the truck just as the front door flew open. A wiry man in earmuffs, work boots, overalls and ski jacket appeared in the doorway.

"Well, whaddya know," the man said, his breath fogging in the frigid air. "Hell, Redhawk, I'd just about given up on you. Molly said you'd be back tonight, but I figured with the blizzard and all it wouldn't be till morning or later."

"A little snow doesn't scare me." Sloan closed the door of the pickup. Casey strained to hear their conversation over the rumble of the truck's engine and the gusting of the wind.

"I heard on the radio that they're closin' down the main road. Plows can't keep up with this damned stuff. So I figured I wouldn't see you until this all passed over, which, from the looks of it, will be a while."

"Hell," Sloan growled.

Wes cast a quick glance in Casey's direction as he plodded through knee-deep snow to the back of the truck. "Maybe you two had better bunk here for the night. We got a couch and a recliner and the electricity hasn't kicked off yet. If it does, we've got the wood stove and the fireplace and enough kerosene lanterns to last a week or two. Might be best if you stayed here till morning."

No way! She had to get home. It had been so long. She wasn't going to stay here in the middle of nowhere and... Her heart sank as she realized she didn't have much choice in what happened. She was completely at Sloan Redhawk's mercy, and while she was indebted to him and grateful that he'd rescued her, she wouldn't sit still and let him run her life. Without really thinking about what she was doing, she set the empty thermos lid on the dash and flung open the door.

An icy blast of wind cut through her jacket and brushed frozen grains of snow against her face. She dropped into six inches of powder just as Sloan was unhitching the trailer and Wes was leading the packhorse toward the barn. The wind howled and cut through her jacket as if she were naked.

"What're you doing?" Sloan demanded. "Get back in the truck. You'll freeze—"

"I just want to know what's going on."

"Oh, for God's sake!" He swung the coupler head of the trailer away from the hitch.

"If the roads are closed—"

"Don't worry about it."

"Are you crazy? Don't worry? I heard Wes telling you—"

"I know what he said." Sloan yanked open the door.

"But—"

"Are you going to get into the truck or am I going to have to push you?"

"If the roads—"

So quickly she nearly lost her breath, he spun her around to look at him. Snow fell around his head and shoulders, clinging to his eyelashes and running down the hard planes of his face. "I've gotten you this far, haven't I?"

When she didn't answer, he let out another oath. "For the love of God, Casey, have a little faith, will you? Just get into the damned truck and let me worry about the rest!"

Deciding she had no other choice, she hauled herself into the cab and jumped as he slammed the door behind her. Head ducked against the wind, he dashed to the driver's side, sketched a wave to Wes and climbed behind the wheel.

Shoving the truck into gear, he guided the truck along the tracks he'd laid down only a few minutes before, ruts that were already filling with snow. Casey, still fuming, huddled in the corner, but she couldn't control her tongue.

"Listen, Redhawk, I've thanked you for rescuing me and I meant it. If it wasn't for you, I don't know if I would have lived or died, but just because you saved my life doesn't give you the right to tell me what to do.''

''Like hell.''

''Now, wait a minute—''

''You wait a minute.'' He cranked on the wheel and the truck skidded through the soft snow to the main road. Casey braced herself by planting her feet on the floor as the truck straightened. He wasn't finished. ''Until you're back at the Rocking M, safe and sound, you're my responsibility.''

''Just as long as we both understand I'm *not* your captive.''

He flashed her a sidelong glance that was meant to cut her to the quick, but she tilted her chin up a fraction and didn't flinch. ''For the past week I've had an idiot tell me what to do—when to eat, when to sleep, when to get up, even when to go to the bathroom. It was the most degrading, dehumanizing experience of my life and so I'm a little touchy about men I don't know and don't really trust barking out orders and telling me what to do.''

''You don't trust me?''

''I don't *know* you.''

''Don't you trust Jenner? His judgment?''

She snorted. ''Jenner doesn't have a great track record, you know. For a lot of years he spent his time between the rodeo arena, the local bars and cheap motels. The people he met weren't always trustworthy.''

''I am.''

''How do I know that?''

One side of his mouth lifted in a humorless grin. ''Well, you don't, do you? I guess you'll just have to find out the hard way.''

''Which is?''

''Just have enough patience to wait until I prove it to you. However, my guess is, Miss McKee, you're not a woman long on patience.''

The understatement of the year, Casey thought as he drove through the blinding blizzard.

How did she come to this—being caught in the middle of a snowstorm in the middle of the night with a stranger, a man who had saved her life?

Just hang in there, Casey. Things are bound to get better. But as she cast a furtive glance in Sloan Redhawk's direction, she wasn't so sure.

Chapter Four

The pickup jolted and Casey's eyes flew open. She must've dozed off, mesmerized by the steady rumble of the truck's engine and the hypnotic effect of watching the snow fall. Sloan was pulling into some kind of restaurant. Neon lights in red and blue winked through the ever-falling flakes and a sorry strand of Christmas lights with only a few winking bulbs outlined the doorway.

Christmas! She'd nearly forgotten the season.

"What're we doing here?" she asked, stretching and feeling her cramped muscles come to life.

"Can't go any farther. Signs say the road's closed at Stillwater."

Rubbing her eyes, she tried and failed to stifle a yawn. "Stillwater?"

"The next town."

She studied the rustic building. Long and low, it ran parallel to the road. A pitched roof was covered in snow, and icicles clung to the eaves. A fluorescent sign adver-

tised a steak-and-shrimp special as well as the fact that
there was at least one vacancy in the adjacent motel.
Trucks and cars, parked haphazardly, littered the snow-
encrusted parking lot.

"So this is home?"

"At least for a couple of hours."

She sent him a smile. "It sure beats the last place I
stayed."

"I'll bet." Sloan cut the engine while she grabbed the
nylon bag.

Pushing open the door, she braced herself as the frigid
wind blew inside, instantly draining the cab of any
warmth. She hopped to the ground and dashed through
calf-deep snow to the restaurant entrance. From the corner
of her eye, she saw Sloan settle his hat on his head, lock
the truck and half run to catch up with her.

Inside, the restaurant was warm and the smells of cigarette smoke and oil from a deep-fat fryer mingled with
the scents of after-shave, coffee and warm bodies.
Through an archway leading to the bar came the sounds
of laughter and clinking glasses, as if the patrons didn't
have a care in the world and were glad of any excuse to
hole up with a frosty glass of beer and cable television.
In concession to the season, silver letters spelling out
Merry Christmas & Happy New Year had been strung
from the ceiling.

Casey sighed. It sure didn't seem like Christmas, at
least not the Christmases she remembered.

On the restaurant side of the building, a cooler behind
the counter displayed home-baked pies and cakes. Casey
was suddenly starved; her stomach growled and she realized that she'd lived for a week on a diet of canned stew
and white bread with peanut butter.

A slim waitress with frizzy hair and a world-weary
smile set aside her cigarette and showed them to a booth.
Her name tag read Therese, and she waved to a couple of

regulars as she plopped plastic-coated menus on the chipped Formica. "Anything to drink?"

"Coffee," Sloan said.

"For you?" Therese asked, her glance moving to Casey.

"The same. With cream."

"You got it."

Spying the rest rooms, Casey said, "I'm going to clean up, but you can order for me. I'll have a hamburger and french fries and some of that apple pie."

"Is that all?" he said, and for the first time she saw a glint of humor in his black eyes.

She was already on her way down a short hallway but called back, "Just add a little ice cream. Apple pie à la mode."

In the rest room, she surveyed her reflection and groaned. Her hair, though combed, was oily and lank, her face smudged with dirt. Her sweater, which she'd worn for nearly a week, was wrinkled and smelling of smoke from the wood stove.

Using the towel Sloan had brought, she scrubbed her hands gently, cleaning her wounds as best as she could, then worked on her face with the wetted towel and dispenser soap. The results weren't that great, even after she finger combed her hair and applied a little bit of makeup. Lipstick, blush and mascara couldn't hide the pale color of her skin or the lack of spark in her usually clear eyes.

"Just hang in there," she told her reflection because she knew she'd be home soon—a day or two at the most. Then she'd sink into a hot bubble bath and wash her hair with lilac-scented shampoo and sleep in her own bed for a week. But until then, she still had to get through the next few hours which, if the storm didn't let up, could stretch into a couple of days. With Sloan. At the thought of the brooding cowboy, she glanced again in the mirror and frowned. She was beyond unappealing, which usually didn't bother her.

She'd grown up on the ranch, was used to dust, dirt, flies, manure and sweat. She'd mucked out the stables, groomed horses and even branded calves. She'd been plenty dirty in her life and more often than not had supported a bruise or two from trying to ride a half-broken colt. Jonah McKee's only daughter, though spoiled, was no porcelain princess.

During her growing-up years, lots of ranch hands had seen her grimy, tired and cross, and it hadn't disturbed her a bit. But the idea of Sloan finding her bound and helpless and filthy bothered her. It bothered her a lot.

"You'll get over it," she said to her image as she shook her hands dry, glad that her scratches hadn't started bleeding again. Fortunately none of the cuts looked deep, and if she was lucky and took care of herself, they wouldn't get infected. The raw spots on her wrists where the rope had cut into her skin looked worse, but there wasn't much she could do but keep them clean for now.

By the time she made her way back to the booth, Therese was setting two paper-lined baskets filled with steaming French fries and thick hamburgers on the table. "I'll bring that pie when you're finished with these," she promised as she snagged a bottle of catsup from another table and plopped it in front of Sloan. "You need anything else, just holler."

"Will do." As she turned away, he said, "Wait a minute," and offered her a smile of white teeth guaranteed to melt a woman's heart. "Is everyone else here stranded?" Sloan asked.

"Whatddya mean?" Therese grinned back.

His gaze swept the interior where a few men and women sat in booths. "Travelers caught by the storm."

She frowned. "Nah. Most everybody but you is a regular." She scratched her chin thoughtfully, then nodded at a small family—a man, woman and child of about three. "'Cept them, I s'ppose."

"Thanks."

"No problem."

"What was that all about?" Casey asked.

"Just making sure we weren't followed."

"Of course we weren't followed. We were the only truck on the road for miles."

The smile he'd donned for Therese's benefit faded and his eyes glinted with determination. "It doesn't hurt to make sure," he said. "We're not out of the woods yet, y'know. Now—eat." Again his gaze swept the interior.

"What about the bar?"

"Checked it out when you were in the rest room."

"No murderers holed up, waiting for a chance to jump me?" She couldn't help bantering. Though she'd been frightened for her life at the cabin, she couldn't believe this rustic roadside café and bar was anything but safe. Barry was tied up or more likely in custody, and his partner—or partners—probably hundreds of miles away. "You're paranoid, Redhawk."

"I get paid to be paranoid." He picked up half of his burger. "And I don't want to spend any more time than I have to here, so dig in."

Casey had never been so hungry in her life. She wasn't going to let his case of nerves get to her because the farther they were from the cabin, the safer she felt. Ignoring the fact that he continued to watch the door, she dipped the hot fries in a glob of catsup and savored each and every calorie. The burger was hot and juicy and undoubtedly loaded with cholesterol, but she hardly gave that a second thought.

They ate in silence and Casey tried not to stare at the man who had rescued her. Taller than most of the men in the dining room, Sloan sat high in the booth. His hat rested on a post at the end of his seat, and under the bright lights, she finally got her first good look at him. His hair was straight, black and slightly longer than the current fashion, his eyebrows dark and fierce-looking. She saw now that his skin was bronze-toned, even in the winter, and his face was sculpted with sharp angles and planes that clearly hinted at his Native American heritage. Good-looking in a rough-and-tumble way, he would stand out in almost any crowd, but there was an air of menace about him that he seemed to encourage by speaking seldom and smiling even less. Unless he wanted to pour on the charm to get something, as he had with Therese only minutes before, then the danger faded with the appearance of his heart-stopping smile.

Therese brought two thick wedges of hot apple pie with vanilla ice cream melting on the crust and set them on the table. "Anything else?" she asked, pouring them each a fresh cup of coffee.

"This should do it," Sloan said, then glanced at Casey, "unless there's something more for you."

Eyeing the huge slice of pastry, Casey shook her head. "I think this is enough."

"Just holler if you change your mind," Therese said as a roar of approval came from the bar. "Big ball game on cable," she explained as she tore off the bill and set it facedown on the table.

Casey had barely started on her pie when she topped out. Her stomach was stretched to the bursting point by the time she'd taken three bites of the spicy apples and flaky crust. With a groan, she shoved the plate aside.

"Too much?" Sloan asked, one side of his mouth lifting into a semblance of a smile.

"Way too much."

"Just don't make yourself sick."

"I'm not."

"Good." He finished his pie. "So you're feeling better?"

"Than yesterday?" she asked, her gaze meeting the dark questions in his. "Are you kidding? Yesterday I was convinced that I'd never see anything but that cabin's walls." She sighed and shook her head, refusing to dwell on the fear and uncertainty that had been her constant companions during the past week. She shuddered inwardly to think that she'd been so weak, so totally dependent, on a piece of scum like Barry White. She'd always prided herself on her ability to take care of herself, to handle any situation, to stand on her own. Barry White had undermined her self-confidence in a big way. She was determined to get it back. "This—" she gestured expansively at the interior of the restaurant and bar "—is heaven."

He snorted and wadded his napkin. "You could've fooled me."

"Heaven, I tell you," she insisted. "You want the rest of this?" She offered him the remains of her pie, but he shook his head and settled back in the booth with his cup of coffee.

"How about you? Want anything else?"

She groaned. "I couldn't eat another thing if you paid me."

"Then I guess we'd better find ourselves a room."

"A room?" The thought stopped her cold. She'd suspected that they'd have to spend the night on the road, of course, but when actually faced with a night alone in a strange hotel room with Sloan Redhawk, her insides quivered slightly and she balked. She'd seen how strong he was, how he could take charge of any situation and she knew she could depend on him, but there was another side to him, one that was disturbing. Not only was he a dangerous man, a man who probably lived by his own rules, he was incredibly sexy, and though the last thing she wanted was male attention, she couldn't ignore the fact that he was just the kind of man who attracted her—the kind of man she'd told herself to avoid at all costs.

Now she'd be stuck with him. Alone.

But it had to be safer than the past week she'd been with Barry White.

She licked her lips nervously, then patted them with the corner of her napkin.

"If we're lucky, it'll just be for one night," he was saying, obviously unhappy with the set of circumstances that had forced them into immobility. "Until the road crews get a handle on the situation."

"And if we're not lucky?"

His mouth flattened into a straight line. "Then we'll decide what to do when the time comes."

She didn't like that possibility, wanted to argue about the arrangements, but knew she was being ridiculous. There was no choice.

"Believe me," he said, and his voice was suddenly kind, his dark eyes sincere, "I know you've been through a lot, maybe more than you're willing to admit, and want to get home. I'll do everything I can to get you there safely, as quickly as I can. Trust me."

Her throat closed and unwanted tears threatened her eyes. "Thank you," she said, her voice a little raspy with emotion.

"Don't thank me yet. We aren't there yet."

From speakers mounted over the cigarette machine, the strains of an old Tammy Wynette song began to warble over the dining area.

"Wait here," Sloan said, glancing quickly at the other tables. "I'll be right back."

He walked swiftly to the door, said something to Therese and then disappeared into the night. Casey remained in the booth, sipping coffee and telling herself there was no reason to be nervous. She could see his pickup through the window, but Sloan passed it by and hurried across the snow-covered parking lot to the motel office.

Her stomach twisted and she turned her attention to her coffee. So what if she was spending the night alone with him—it certainly couldn't be any worse than a week with Barry White. She shuddered inwardly at the thought. Barry hadn't physically abused her, but she'd caught him staring at her often enough when he'd had too much to drink and she'd seen a flicker of lust in his pale eyes.

She'd thought she might have to fight him off, but he'd never made any attempt to take advantage of the situation. For that, she supposed, she should be thankful.

She glanced up when the bell over the door tinkled. Sloan stomped snow off his boots, and when he looked at her, she felt her heart lighten a little. Silly. Just because he'd freed her, she needn't feel so dependent upon him. Just a week ago she was an independent woman used to making her own decisions, and though she'd reached a crossroads in her life about her future, no one who knew her would ever have dared accuse her of relying on anyone.

"Let's go," he said as he approached the table. He picked up the bill and paid at the cash register as Casey grabbed the nylon bag and followed him.

Outside, the storm was raging. The wind raged through the trees surrounding the buildings and sliced through her jacket as she dashed across the parking lot to the U-shaped building with the flashing neon sign announcing cable TV and vacancies. Snow turned to ice pellets stung her face. "What about the truck?" she asked as he unlocked the door and flipped on the lights of a small unit.

"I asked the owner of the restaurant if we could leave it over there."

"Why?"

"So that it doesn't give away what room we're in."

"To whom?"

"Whoever might have followed us."

"That's crazy. No one's chasing me in this blizzard." She stomped the snow from her shoes.

He fiddled with the thermostat. "How can you be so sure? You're the million-dollar heiress, remember?"

"But Barry's truck is disabled, he's tied up, freezing his behind in the cabin, or maybe by now he's behind bars."

"That would be my guess."

"Then what do we have to worry about?"

He looked at her then, his dark gaze piercing hers, and her throat suddenly seemed to close and throb under the intensity of his stare. "His friends, for starters. As we discussed, we don't know how many accomplices he has and where they are. So for now, we'll take all the precautions we can." Hooking his thumb toward the window, he added, "I've got some things in the truck. I'll be right back." But he didn't move. He stared at her another few seconds and her heart knocked painfully. "And don't make any calls, okay? Not yet."

Breaking away from his gaze, she glanced at the phone. "Not even my mother?"

"Especially not. No calls to the Rocking M. We'll work something out tomorrow, okay?"

"I don't see why—"

He grabbed her, his fingers digging through her jacket to find her shoulders. "We're going to do things my way. You may not like it, but that's too damned bad. Until you're back where you belong, I'm in charge."

"And what am I supposed to do?" she demanded, her temper rising again. "Meekly agree and bend over and kiss your boots?"

One side of his hard mouth lifted in a sardonic smile. "Now that would be a start."

"In your dreams."

His grin widened just a fraction. "You wouldn't want to guess about my dreams, lady," he said, and for a fraction of a second, she thought he might kiss her. His eyes held hers and the breath stopped somewhere deep in her lungs. She swallowed and his smile faded. Time seemed to stand still. He reached upward as if to trace the edge of her jaw, thought better of it and dropped his hand. "I'll be right back. Lock the door behind me."

"You're joking, right?"

His eyes flashed. "Just do it, okay?"

He disappeared through the door and slammed it behind him. Feeling foolish, Casey shoved the bolt into place and waited, checking out her surroundings. The motel room had seen better days. A dingy floral spread on the only bed matched the faded yellow curtains covering a single window. She wondered about the sleeping arrangements, but didn't let her mind wander too far. The rug was a faded brown that didn't quite hide the stains near the door. A small pedestal table with two sagging chairs had been shoved under a swag lamp in the corner. There was a tiny bathroom, an alcove that sufficed for a closet and a color TV propped on a low bureau that was marred by cigarette burns.

"The Ritz it's not," she thought aloud, but decided central heating, television, phone service and freedom beat her accommodations of the prior week.

Sloan let himself in with his key and tossed his hat onto the table. He carried a small duffel bag as well as Barry's shotgun, knife and pistol. "Armed and dangerous," he joked, and Casey felt a smile tug the corners of her mouth. So he did have a sense of humor.

"Is there a reason we ended up with a room with only one bed?" she asked. The heater had kicked in and she took off her jacket.

He sent her a look that turned her knees to water. "A good one. It's all they had. Two units available, each with one double bed." She lifted a skeptical eyebrow. "What? You think I'm cheap?"

"I didn't say that."

"Maybe you think I planned to seduce you."

She didn't move for a second, then tossed her head. "I just wanted to know, that's all."

"You can have the bed. I'll camp out by the door."

"Are you serious? You don't have to—"

"I would, anyway," he said, his voice firm.

She let it drop. She knew arguing with him wouldn't do any good. "Fine." Running her hands through her hair, she felt suddenly grimy and tired. "Look, if you don't mind, I think I'll clean up."

"Fair enough."

She grabbed the nylon tote bag before heading into the bathroom. It was cramped, the linoleum cracked, the single bulb bare, the shower stained by years of rust. She turned on the water and thought of the bubble bath she'd envisioned at the cabin. With a half smile, she decided that she'd have to wait for that kind of luxury.

Silently Sloan cursed the fates that seemed against him. The storm wasn't letting up; the weather service predicted another six inches by morning and highway crews weren't able to keep up with the cold white powder that wouldn't stop falling. Great. Just great.

He checked the chamber of the old shotgun, then unloaded it. He didn't like guns, had seen his share of destruction and death caused by handguns and semiautomatic rifles. He'd only been with the Los Angeles Police Department a few years—six to be exact—but in that time, he'd witnessed the ease of killing by gunshots.

Even Jane. And Tony. Hot pain seared through his soul and he closed his eyes. He had to quit thinking of them. For years he'd buried their memories deep in a private part of him and rarely let them surface, but ever since chasing down Casey, thoughts of his wife and son had preyed on his mind. He didn't understand why these long-suppressed images were troubling him now or why Casey McKee made him remember the happiest years of his life as a husband and father. He was just tired and worried. That was it. Thoughts of family life had nothing to do with Casey.

He heard the water start to run in the shower and he imagined her stripping off her clothes and stepping into the steamy spray. In his mind's eye he saw the hot water running through her hair, past her shoulders and along the cleft of her spine. Drops clung to her chin and drizzled over her breasts... "Quit it!" he growled, furious at the direction of his thoughts.

He'd never been a ladies' man, never dated more than one woman at a time, and when he'd married Jane, he'd intended to be her husband for the rest of his life. He'd never wanted another woman, couldn't imagine ever cheating on her. Then suddenly, senselessly, she was gone, and he'd been left with his vows of forever still etched into his heart.

He wasn't a foolish man and knew that he couldn't live without a woman indefinitely, but he'd promised himself never to become emotionally attached to a woman again. Every time one got a little too close, he backed off.

And no one had ever touched him the way Jane had. With her, their physical relationship had been more than sex. A playful kiss, a secret laugh, a soft touch... Hell, he still missed that.

For years he'd been convinced no other woman would ever break through the emotional barrier he'd so carefully built, but now, as he cast a look at the peeling paint of the bathroom door, he wondered if the feisty little woman standing naked in the hot shower could break through his defenses.

But that was crazy. He barely knew her. She was a spoiled, rich brat who didn't have enough brains to figure out that Barry White was the enemy before jumping into his truck.

He double-checked the locks and windows, though he didn't really believe that anyone could have tracked them here. He'd been careful, and most likely, Barry White's accomplice, whoever the hell he was, was in Rimrock, waiting to hear from him.

He heard the squeal of ancient pipes, then silence as the water quit running. He glanced at the bed and wondered how many days he'd be forced to spend alone with her. "Get a grip, Redhawk," he muttered under his breath. He couldn't allow himself to think of her as a woman. She was Jenner McKee's baby sister. She was a wealthy woman who could buy and sell him countless times over. And she was a job—his ticket to a hundred thousand dollars. He could think of her as any of these—but not as a woman.

Casey finally felt warm. In a soft flannel shirt, sweater and jeans, her hair still damp but clean, every crevice in her body washed for the first time in a week, she stepped out of the bathroom and found Sloan sitting in a chair by the door, his boots propped on another chair, the shotgun angled across his legs.

He glanced up at her as she folded a knee beneath her and sat on the edge of the bed. Self-conscious, she leaned against one of the pillows, then tossed the other to him. "You don't have to stay over there," she said. "If you want to sleep in the bed—"

"Don't worry about it." He didn't crack a smile. "Go to sleep."

"But—"

"I'm getting paid for this, remember. When I get tired, I'll roll out the sleeping bag."

"You're sure?"

"Wouldn't have it any other way," he said, but the twist of his lips suggested differently. Sighing, she climbed gratefully under the covers and watched as he set down the shotgun and reached into his duffel bag. "I think you'd better use this," he said as he withdrew a tube of antiseptic cream and tossed it onto the bed.

"I think I'm okay—"

"Let me be the judge of that." He stepped into the bathroom, ran the water for a while and came back into the room, drying his hands.

"Really, Sloan..." she protested, though she had no sound reasoning to argue with. He was just being safe and she was defying him because she was tired of being told what to do.

But he wasn't about to be discouraged. He sat on the edge of the bed and uncapped the tube. Reluctantly she showed him her hands, which he took in his and surveyed with the cool professionalism of a doctor. Gently he applied the cream to her cuts and the burns on her wrists. "Doesn't look like any infection," he said gruffly, though still examining her fingers.

"I told you."

While still holding her hand, he stared straight into her eyes and her heart did a strange little flip. His gaze was black and intense as he reached into the front pocket of his jeans and extracted a ring. The room seemed suddenly close. "I think this is yours." He placed the turquoise-and-silver ring in her hand. "White sent it to your family."

"Oh…thanks."

"I wouldn't wear it yet. Not until you're completely healed."

"No…I won't."

With one last look at her fingers and wrists, he seemed satisfied and walked back to his chair by the door. She told herself that he was just being thorough, that nothing had happened between them, but she couldn't stop her heart from pounding in double time.

"So tell me about your friend in Spokane."

"Clarisse?" she said around a yawn.

He nodded.

"We were best friends in college when she started going out with Ray. She thought he was wonderful, but I didn't like him right off the bat. He seemed too stuck on himself. Kind of a dandy. A rich dandy. And critical. Jeez, he was critical. Of Clarisse's hair, her clothes, her grades, even her car. He seemed to enjoy picking on her, though he kept telling her it was just to help her, you know, that whole self-improvement thing through constructive criticism. B.S., if you ask me." She shook her head. "Anyway, Clarisse thought he was perfect and she tried to please him. I quit trying to change her mind about him when they got engaged because it was too late. I was in her wedding party, and then they ended up moving back to Spokane, where they had a couple of kids and I kind of lost touch with her. She quit calling and answering my letters and it got to where we were only jotting a quick note on the bottom of Christmas cards.''

"But she called you,'' he prodded as she sank back on the pillows, ''when she was in trouble.''

"Yeah.''

"And you wired her a lot of money.''

"She needed help,'' Casey said a little defensively.

"What about her family?''

"I didn't ask. They don't have a lot of money, though, and they also thought Ray was a great catch.'' She snorted in disgust, then yawned as weariness settled over her.

"The FBI thinks she was in on the kidnapping.''

"No way.'' She bit her lip thoughtfully. "I had a lot of time to think this past week, but I decided Clarisse doesn't know a thing about it. Barry bragged about tampering with my car—''

"He did. We found scratches on your distributor cap.''

"Scratches? That's it? Just scratches?''

"Looks that way. So the car ran for a while and then just stopped, right?''

"Yeah. I braked for a curve and everything went dead.''

"So Barry, he follows you and offers you a ride and you think he'll take you back to the Rocking M.''

Casey nodded, her insides growing cold as she remembered the numbing fear when she realized that she'd been trapped. "I didn't see the gun until I got inside. He pulled it from behind the seat, then handcuffed me inside the car. Nothing I could say or threaten would change his mind. He drove for hours. I tried to trick him and tell him I had to go to the bathroom or that someone was expecting me, but he just laughed and told me to go in the truck and whoever was waiting for me was going to wait a long time.''

She saw Sloan's expression turn hard and his hands curl over the stock of the shotgun in a death grip. "Sounds like I should have let him freeze up there."

"Then you'd be charged with murder and we'd never find who he was working with."

"Bastard." Sloan's eyes narrowed. "Let's just hope he's the coward I think he is and cuts a deal with the D.A. and spills his guts."

"He won't."

"Why not?"

"He's too scared," she said, remembering Barry's nervous twitch just under his eye and the way he would jump every time there was a noise outside the cabin. "And it wasn't only being afraid of being caught. Whoever he's working with scares him spitless."

Sloan smiled. "Maybe we can work that to our advantage."

"How?"

"I'm not sure yet. Go on, go to sleep and I'll think about it." He settled a little farther onto the small of his back and crossed his ankles, the leather of his boots creaking in protest. Casey snapped off the bedside lamp. She knew she couldn't sleep a wink, not with Sloan in the room, yet she closed her eyes, let out a sigh and drifted away.

Sloan, satisfied that she was asleep, turned on the television and kept the sound down low. The news was depressing as hell and the weather report set his teeth on edge. Though this blizzard would soon end, there would only be a short break—a day at the most—and then the next storm, an Arctic blast racing down from Canada, would take up where this one left off. More snow. More subzero temperatures. More treacherous roads.

More nights trapped alone with the most intriguing woman he'd met in a long, long while. The next few days were going to be torture. He glanced over his shoulder and saw her sleeping, her hair spread around her face in a mahogany cloud, her lips parted in unknowing invitation.

Yep, sheer torture.

Chapter Five

She knew she was making a mistake. Kissing this man, this stranger, could only spell trouble, but then she was in trouble already, running from some danger, some inner fear that she couldn't quite name. He took her into his arms and his mouth settled eagerly over hers, dispelling the cool touch of snowflakes on her skin. His hands were big and broad, his skin bronzed as if he had a tan. Impervious to the cold, he stood bare chested, his black hair touching the back of his neck, his eyes as dark as obsidian.

Inside she melted. Despite the snow that drifted beneath her feet and clung to her hair, she was white-hot, burning with an inner fever, and she wanted him to touch her in the most forbidden of places. Her breasts began to ache and when he reached beneath her sweater—

"Wake up!"

Casey started and the dream began to fade quickly. She was in bed—a strange bed. She blinked and found herself staring into the same intense black eyes she'd seen in her dream. "Wha...?" she asked, then remembered yesterday. Her face flushed with color as her dream still lingered in her mind's eye and her skin still tingled with the imagined feel of his touch. "Is something wrong?"

He paced from the bed to the window and she noticed the way the faded denim of his jeans stretched tightly over his buttocks. Quickly she drew her gaze to the other side of the room. "There's a break in the weather and the road's being plowed and sanded," Sloan said. "But it won't last long. Another storm's due in a few hours, so we'd better get moving if we want to get closer to Rimrock."

That was all the incentive she needed. She threw off the bed covers and headed to the bathroom. "Just give me a minute." She splashed cold water over her face, combed her hair and added just a touch of makeup.

Within minutes they'd loaded the truck and were on the highway, snow crunching beneath the pickup's tires. There were patches of blue in the sky, but clouds, dark and threatening, were beginning to roll in from the north. While she'd been sleeping, Sloan had gone to the restaurant, where he'd bought a bag of doughnuts for the trip and had the thermos filled with coffee.

As he drove, Casey poured the coffee and handed him a glazed doughnut, which he somehow managed to eat while concentrating on the road ahead. She wasn't really hungry and picked at a maple bar while she sipped her drink.

Later, when the road finally straightened, he pointed to the cellular phone with his chin. "Maybe you want to call home."

"I thought you were worried about being found out."

"I think we're safe."

She didn't wait, but dialed quickly and drummed her fingers impatiently on the window ledge until Jenner picked up the phone far away at the ranch in Oregon.

"Hi."

"Casey! Where are you?"

"Heading home—I don't know exactly where…" She cast a quick glance at Sloan, who shook his head sharply. "Did they arrest Barry White?"

Jenner let fly a string of blue words that made Casey wince. "…that low-life bastard, if I ever get my hands around his fat neck, I swear I'll kill him myself."

Casey couldn't help but grin at the thought. God, how she missed her hotheaded brothers. "Don't kill him before you find out who he's working with."

"Yeah, well, when I find out who that guy is—"

"I know, I know. He's dead meat."

"Beyond dead meat."

"Maybe I should talk to Mom."

"Okay, but first, just tell me this. White didn't hurt you did he? 'Cause if I find out that slimebucket so much as touched you, I'll cut off his— Well, I'll take care of him."

"I'm fine and don't worry, Barry didn't hurt me." That was a little bit of a lie. Barry, though he hadn't been horribly cruel, had probably scarred her psychologically for life. Except that she wouldn't let him. Barry wouldn't win.

"Thank God. Look, Mom's climbing the walls to talk to you."

"Then put her on."

There was a slight hesitation, then Jenner .said, "Case?"

"Yeah."

"I'm glad you're okay." Her throat was suddenly thick and she blinked hard. Jenner wasn't a compassionate man or a particularly kind man. His emotions usually ranged from stony silence to rage with not a whole lot in between.

"Me, too. I miss you."

He cleared his throat. "Yeah, well, here's Mom."

"Thank God you're safe!" Virginia McKee's voice sounded strained. "I've been so frightened, I can't tell you. And your grandmother, Lord, I thought she might have a stroke.''

''I'm fine!'' Grandma's voice was distant, but strong and filled with McKee conviction. Casey smiled. Her grandmother, Mavis, had never really gotten along with her daughter-in-law, but they always banded together when facing a family crisis. ''Virginia, you tell her I'm just fine.''

''Grandma says she's okay.''

''I heard.''

''Anyway, you get home as quickly as you can.''

Casey slid a glance at Sloan. ''We're working on it.''

''Well, where are you?''

''In the mountains.''

''*What* mountains? There're ranges all the way from here to Alaska.''

''I don't know, but Sloan thinks we shouldn't discuss it.''

''Why not? I'm your mother, for crying out loud.''

''I know, I know. Look, Mom, we'll be home as soon as we can.'' She caught Sloan motioning toward the phone with one hand. ''I think Sloan wants to talk to Jenner. Would you put him on again?''

''Yes, well, all right.'' Reluctance hung heavy in her words. ''But you take care now, y'hear.''

''Promise.''

''Good. Here's Jenner.''

Reluctantly Casey handed the phone to Sloan. He asked questions about Barry's arrest, and the conversation became one-sided as Jenner explained how slowly the wheels of justice were turning in Rimrock.

Sloan finally cut the connection and glared at the road, once white but now sprinkled with gravel. ''White's still in Montana,'' he said, frowning thoughtfully. ''The FBI agent, Revere, flew up to Montana but hasn't reported back to your family about White's story. Good ol' Barry will probably be extradited, but it might take a while.''

"Is that bad?"

Lifting a shoulder, Sloan shifted down for a sharp curve in the road. "Maybe, maybe not. At least he's behind bars. I doubt if his partner will dare show his face up here, for fear he'll be found out. But he'll be plenty worried that Barry will rat on him. Jenner, he wants Barry back in Rimrock. He thinks he can somehow help intimidate the guy into confessing, but that's not how it works. The Feds will break him if he's gonna be broken. If not, Jenner might as well save his breath."

Casey curled up on her side of the truck and stared out the window. They were heading west now and had crossed the Idaho border. Closer to Oregon. Closer to home. And what then? Could she pick up her old life and forget about the kidnapping, or would it forever be a part of her, a dark fear that kept her awake nights and forced her into being cautious, even skittery.

She'd been ready to leave the ranch and the life she'd known there a week ago. So what about now?

As if he could read her thoughts, Sloan said, "Jenner told me you weren't very happy at the ranch."

She wasn't certain she wanted to share too much of herself with him and yet she supposed it really didn't matter. They'd be cooped up together for a day—maybe two—if the storm hit, then he'd drop her off at the Rocking M and she probably wouldn't see him again until Jenner's wedding, if then. He might show up for the ceremony, which was scheduled for sometime in February, and he might not. Chances were he'd disappear from her life completely. That thought was unsettling and she didn't want to examine her feelings about it too closely. He was a stranger, for God's sake, a man paid to find her. That was all. And he was waiting for her answer.

"I thought it was time I got my life together," she admitted as she watched the sky turn the color of slate. "It seemed to me that I'd never really proved myself. I'd gone away to college and had a job in L.A. for a while—

landed a job as an assistant in a production company. My father didn't approve of my choice of careers, but I didn't really care. I liked L.A. and needed a change of pace from Rimrock.''

"But you didn't stay."

"For a few years, then the company I worked for went under. I scrambled around looking for another job, but in the end I went home, just to kind of rethink what I wanted to do. Dad tried to talk me into working for him, but I still didn't want to be tied to Rimrock. I thought about going to graduate school, but hadn't really made up my mind when Dad was killed. Then everything changed. For a while, Mom was a basket case. I thought she was going to break down completely. Then there was one thing after another. The fire, Jenner's recuperation, Beth coming back to town with Jenner's little boy…well, you know the rest.'' She drew into herself at that point and watched as the first few flakes fell from the leaden sky. There was more to the story, of course.

There was Peter.

But Peter belonged to a different world, a different time, a different city. During her rebellious period in Southern California, she'd wanted to fall in love with Peter Zeller; but she'd learned that Peter was in love with someone else: himself. He didn't have time or room for her kind of woman in his life and they'd parted ways as soon as she was out of a job.

Peter was everything Sloan wasn't. Lanky, with curly blond hair streaked by the sun and eyes the color of the Pacific Ocean, he was a smart dresser, seemed like a shrewd businessman and ran with a very fast crowd.

He'd spotted Casey at a trendy restaurant and asked for her phone number, and though he really wasn't her type, she'd started dating him. She saw past the flashy exterior to a man who'd been raised dirt-poor, had helped support his alcoholic mother and made something of himself. The trouble was, she really didn't like the something he'd become. He hid his past as best he could and made up stories about his childhood. He seemed to have regretted confiding in Casey and soon they grew apart. Their relationship lasted all of three months, and even during that time he'd been with other women, women who were easier to deal with as they looked no deeper than his expensive suits, flashy cars, famous friends and healthy bank account.

Now, Casey didn't know what she'd seen in him. He'd appealed to her rebellious nature because she knew that her father disapproved of L.A., the film industry and slick record producers. But deep down, she'd known her interest in him had been only skin-deep. Just as his had been for her.

The snow had started coming down in earnest and was piling up on the road again, sticking on the windshield until the wipers slapped the stubborn flakes away.

It was late afternoon by the time they crossed the Idaho border and drove into Spokane, Washington where they stopped for a late lunch at a roadside diner. Sloan didn't say much, but watched each of the patrons come and go, his eyes shifting from the doorway to the booths and back again as he ate a sandwich and bowl of soup.

"You really think we're being followed, don't you?" she said, smiling and shaking her head as she set down her fork and pushed her plate of half-eaten salad aside.

"Just being careful." A bell tinkled over the door and he glanced up sharply at the sound.

Casey looked over her shoulder and swallowed a smile. A woman with a toddler bundled in a snowsuit entered. Her face was red from the cold, her smile wide, the little boy running to an empty booth and announcing to everyone in the restaurant that he wanted hot chocolate. "I don't think she's a hired assassin," Casey said dryly.

"You never know."

"Oh, for Pete's sake, Sloan, relax."

"Relax?" His gaze narrowed on her and he studied the contours of her face with such intensity that she swallowed hard and had to fight the urge to lick her lips nervously. "Do you really believe that your family's enemies will give up? That just because you've escaped, they'll just roll over?"

"But Barry's in jail."

"We think."

He wasn't sure?

"And he has a partner, maybe more than one. A guy who just about now is getting pretty nervous."

"Then why not call the FBI?"

Sloan's mouth flattened. "You don't get it, do you?"

"Get what?"

"I don't trust anyone."

"Not even the government?"

His smile was cold. "Especially not the government."

"Who could have found us?"

"Anyone."

"We were in the middle of nowhere, in a blizzard."

He grimaced. "Someone besides Barry White knew where you were. Maybe more than one guy. We don't know if his accomplice was in Rimrock. Maybe someone else in the nearest town to that cabin was in on the deal."

"I don't think so. Barry would have said something."

"You think."

"Yes."

"But you're not sure." He finished his sandwich and reached for the bill the waitress had slipped onto the edge of the table.

"You're paranoid," she accused, not for the first time.

"Worse than paranoid."

"I think we're safe."

She saw the shoulders beneath his shirt bunch as the door opened again and a solitary man entered. Long and lean, a cowboy type, with hair that had been tied back in a ponytail and a Stetson that had seen better days, the man sauntered into a booth on the other side of the diner, stretched his legs beneath him and reached into the breast pocket of his jacket for a pack of cigarettes. His face was weathered and lined, and as he lit up he glanced casually in Casey's direction before shooting a stream of smoke from one side of his mouth and looking away.

"Know that guy?" Sloan asked.

"Never seen him before in my life."

"Let's go." Sloan grabbed his jacket, which he'd slung over the back of the booth.

"You're jumping at shadows."

"Maybe."

She shivered inside, but followed his lead and slid her arms through the sleeves of her coat. Sloan left a tip on the corner of the table, then paused at the register to pay the bill. Though he didn't stare, Casey sensed that he watched every move of the stranger, from the way he let his cigarette burn unnoticed in the little tin ashtray to the way he flirted with the slim red-haired waitress who took his order.

The man didn't look evil or malevolent or the least bit interested in Sloan or Casey. In fact, he paid them little attention and, after ordering his meal, headed into the rest room.

Once they were outside and in the truck, Sloan glanced in the rearview mirror. "You're sure you didn't know him?"

"No."

"Positive?"

"Look," she said angrily, "I've already told you. Sure, he looks and dresses like most of the men in Rimrock, but I swear to you, Sloan, I've never seen him or anyone else in that restaurant in my life before."

"He looked familiar to me."

"To you? Where'd you see him? In L.A.? Riding rodeo?"

The corners of his mouth tightened a fraction. "In the Black Anvil," he said, slowly as if he finally remembered.

"Something about his boots—did you notice them?—the silver chains on the heels."

Casey's heart seemed to turn to stone. "In Rimrock? You're sure?"

"That's right. Now I remember. He was shooting pool with Jimmy Rickert."

"Jimmy?" she repeated, and her stomach turned over. Jimmy, the town snitch, had been in more than his share of scrapes with the law. "But why? How?"

"I wish I knew," Sloan said, his hands gripping the wheel until his knuckles showed white. "I wish to bloody hell that I knew. Let's go."

Sloan didn't like leaving anything to chance. If Casey hadn't been with him, he would have accosted the man in the diner, forced him to show his hand, but he couldn't risk it—the man could be armed or have an accomplice lurking about.

All Sloan had to do was keep Casey safe until he got her back to the McKee ranch, which wouldn't have been that big of a deal, if he didn't have to fight the worst storm in the history of eastern Washington.

He drove as fast as he could, considering the conditions, and tried to remember the name of the guy with the boots. Mike? Michael? Miles? The name eluded him, but he was certain he'd seen the face, as well as the boots, before.

"What the devil?" He eased on the brakes as he saw a line of traffic forming, taillights glowing scarlet.

"Looks like an accident," Casey said, craning her neck to look past a minivan filled with skiers.

Sloan's back teeth ground together. They were south of Spokane, eighty miles away from the diner where he'd spied the cowboy. During the drive, Sloan had checked his rearview mirror every ten seconds, expecting the man from the diner to have followed and caught up with them. He'd been just about to relax when this accident—a jackknifed semi from what he could see—had blocked the road. Cars piled up behind their pickup while a tow truck, fire fighters and police tried to get the disabled rig off the road. It seemed to take forever. "Nothin' to do but wait," he said.

She looked through the windshield to the sky. "And it looks like more snow."

"Great." He climbed out of the truck, eyeing the crowd gathering as other motorists stretched their legs, smoked and talked among themselves while climbing on bumpers or hoods to get a better view of the accident. He didn't see a face he recognized, and the man he'd spotted back in the diner, if he was tailing them, was lost in the serpentine of cars that stretched around the curves of the mountain pass or was hidden by the veil of snow now starting to fall.

Casey joined him and they sipped coffee and joked with a couple in a red car. The woman was eight months pregnant and her husband wanted nothing but to get her home safely. Sloan knew the feeling as there was talk among the stranded drivers that the road might be closed again.

The wind picked up as the police finally cleared one lane and everyone climbed back into their vehicles. The snow was thick and the fierce wind seemed to bring the temperature down below zero.

Maybe Casey was right, Sloan thought as he started the engine. Maybe he was just paranoid, but he didn't want to take any unnecessary risks. Not when her life was at stake.

Night was falling by the time the state trooper waved them on with his flashlight. Sloan eased his truck around the crippled semi and followed the steady stream of taillights that wound along the road through the mountains. They drove for several miles and the traffic thinned, but still the snow fell, silent and dangerous, gorgeous to watch, deadly if someone became stranded.

"Looks like we might have to put up for the night again," he said, frowning to himself.

"Why?"

"The storm."

"There are always storms."

"Not like this one." Sloan squinted into the darkness. "One of the guys I talked to—a trucker—has a CB radio. He's been talkin' to rigs all over this part of the state. A couple of them said this road's shut down for the night. Trees have fallen across it, power lines are down and the road crews can't keep up with the weather."

He saw her shoulders slump and knew she wanted desperately to get back to her family. He didn't blame her. He, too, needed to see that she was safely home, and the prospect of spending another night alone with her set his nerves on edge. It had been all he could do to keep his hands off her last night. Damn it, he'd nearly kissed her, and the thought of another eight hours listening to her soft breathing, hearing her murmur in her sleep, watching her turn her head against the fan of dark hair on her pillow would be pure hell.

"Something's wrong." Casey's voice snapped him out of his reverie. She was staring at him, her hazel eyes wide and curious. "Something more than the storm."

If you only knew. He felt guilty about his thoughts; she was frightened, running for her life, and he was fantasizing about her.

"What is it?"

He didn't bother responding, and she smiled, one side of her mouth lifting to show her dimple. "More bad guys chasing us?"

"Don't know." He glanced in the rearview mirror and saw headlights trailing at a distance. The muscles at the base of his skull knotted, but he told himself it wasn't unusual to be followed, especially since the traffic had been backed up so far. But it still bothered him and his gut tightened in warning, the way it always did when he sensed danger. They'd just have to wait and see what the night brought.

"It looks like our friends with the CBs were right," Sloan said as he put down the cellular phone and cursed under his breath.

"The road's out."

"For the next few hours. Until the crews can clear up the fallen trees and downed wires."

"And snow."

"Amen."

"Where's the problem?" she asked, straining to see.

"Twenty miles ahead." He cranked the wheel for a curve in the road and the pickup's tires locked on the ice. They spun, Casey gasped, and he eased up on the gas before the truck finally straightened. "Damn," he growled. Four-wheel drive, so reliable in deep snow, wasn't much good on ice, and now that the roads were busy and the temperature had plunged with the descent of darkness, the snow-covered road was deceptive. Patches of ice had formed when the snow had melted from the heat of exhaust and friction of tires, then refrozen as the traffic had thinned and the temperature plummeted. "So, we have two choices—turn back and hope that we can find another way to Rimrock, or find a place to stay."

Her stomach nose-dived, but she didn't argue. There really wasn't much choice. Turning back would mean hours wasted and who knew how far they would get. Sloan had tried to listen to the radio, but the reception in the mountains had been spotty, the static so harsh it was hard to hear. However, there were storm warnings posted, travel in the mountains was restricted, roads blocked and closed.

He stopped at the next town and Casey smiled as she saw Christmas lights strung along the porch of the general store. With a pang, she thought of her family and wondered what they were doing. Were Skye and Max busy planning their wedding? Was Jenner shopping for the perfect gift for the son he'd only recently met? Was her mother coping with the fact that this was her first holiday season as a widow? Was Kiki, the cook, elbow-deep in Christmas-cookie dough? Or were they all just sitting around the phone, waiting for news, sick with worry over her?

She tried not to think of what was happening on the Rocking M. This was usually a time of merrymaking when the hands would hitch up the old sleigh to some of the horses, and even dour-faced Kiki indulged in a little cup of Christmas cheer. Since he was twelve, Jenner had always kept a sprig of mistletoe in his back pocket. This year he'd reserve it for Beth. She sighed. This Christmas was certainly different, and soon, if things went well, she'd be home in time to share it with the rest of the McKees.

Rather than dwell on her family, she concentrated on the tiny little town that looked as if it had been built during the heyday of gold and silver mining. A smattering of false-fronted buildings lined the street; many were empty, their siding bleached gray, the doors bolted and windows boarded over as if they'd been abandoned for years. There was one hotel in town, which looked as if it had been built around the turn of the century. With a western facade and even a hitching post still in evidence near the front porch, the building was lit by kerosene lanterns placed on tables near the windows.

Inside, the main floor was divided into a registration area for the hotel and a dining room. A huge fir tree, strung with tiny white lights and tinsel, stood guard near the staircase, and clusters of mistletoe had been hung from the brass chandeliers with red bows. The clerk was wearing a Santa hat that jingled as she registered Mr. and Mrs. Sloan Redhawk. Casey slid him a glance when she saw the registration card, but knew that he was just being careful.

Mrs. Sloan Redhawk, she thought, turning the name over in her mind. She couldn't imagine being married to this rugged man, and yet a part of her found the idea appealing. She wondered how many other women had posed as his wife in the lobby of some out-of-the-way motel, then decided it wasn't worth considering. He was her bodyguard for all practical purposes, just doing a job the best way he knew how. There was nothing more between them.

In a few days, well, maybe even after tomorrow, she wouldn't see him again, except perhaps at Jenner's wedding. For some reason she couldn't name, that prospect was sobering and she considered her future, stretching out before her in a haze of uncertainty. She'd forget him, she told herself, as she'd managed to get over Peter.

After registering, they walked into the dining area and seated themselves at a table near the back, which offered Sloan a view of the front door as well as the main desk.

"You still think we're being followed," Casey said when Sloan's gaze moved restlessly around the room.

"I'm just careful."

"Always?" she asked as she smoothed her napkin. His gaze centered on her face and she felt her heart begin to pound, pulsing hot against her throat. The reflection from the flame of the lantern glinted in his dark eyes.

"Always."

Her stomach tightened and she could barely breathe. The air was suddenly charged with an urgency she didn't understand and didn't want to consider. "I don't think so." She knew she was goading him, but couldn't stop herself. "Anyone who does what you do for a living— what you did—likes danger."

"What I did?"

"Riding rodeo broncs and Brahman bulls." She paused while the waitress set glasses of water on the table and took their drink orders. "Besides, didn't I hear Jenner say you were a policeman or something?"

"Or something."

"What?"

He hesitated, then shrugged. "Detective. In L.A."

She wasn't surprised. "And from that you became a cowboy?"

"That's right," he said, avoiding her eyes. The blond waitress set a long-necked bottle of beer in front of him and a glass of white wine near Casey.

"Figured out what you want yet?" the girl, barely twenty-one from the looks of her, asked as she clicked her pen and held her notepad ready.

"I'll have the trout special," Casey replied.

"And you?" The waitress rained a smile on Sloan.

"Grilled steak. Rare. Baked potato with the works and coleslaw."

"And another beer?"

Sloan lifted his bottle. "In a minute."

"Coming right up." The blonde disappeared behind the swinging saloon-style doors to the kitchen.

Casey sipped her wine. "You were telling me about being a policeman."

"No," he said. "You were asking."

"So why'd you quit the force?"

A shadow passed behind his eyes. "It was time."

"After what—five years?"

"Almost seven." He drained his bottle and picked at the label. All the while, his black gaze moved from Casey's face to the front door and back to the surrounding tables. Obviously he didn't want to discuss his past, but Casey wondered what made a man quit his job to become a drifter of sorts, a man who gave up his life in the city to follow the rodeo circuit, riding wild horses and roping calves.

She suspected it had something to do with his wife's death. What kind of a woman was Jane Redhawk? What had happened to her? She wanted to ask, but knew her questions would be met with the same stony silence that surrounded him whenever the conversation turned too personal.

Were there other women in Sloan's life? He'd never mentioned any, but she had to remind herself she'd been with him little more than a day. It seemed like longer—like she'd known him for years—but the truth of the matter was that she knew *of* him but not *about* him. Jenner had never elaborated about his friend and she'd never asked.

Now, she had trouble picturing him living in Southern California, in the sprawling city that was L.A. He looked as if he'd be more at home riding alone on the barren range than driving along the webbing of clogged freeways, or perhaps going under cover on city streets. No, he seemed more suited to playing the part of the cowboy, with his unruly black hair, piercing eyes, rugged features and faded jeans.

"Can I get you folks anything else?" the waitress asked, startling Casey out of her reverie. She hadn't been aware that she'd been staring. At Sloan.

"This...this'll be fine," Casey said as she eyed the platter of fresh trout, rice and broccoli that was placed in front of her.

"We'll let you know if we need anything," Sloan added. "Thanks." When the waitress drifted to another table, Sloan turned his attention to his steak. "What is it you want to know?"

"What?"

"About me."

"You think I'm interested in you?" She pronged a piece of broccoli and feigned nonchalance.

"I think you're curious."

She wanted to lie, but didn't. Why bother? It seemed as if he could nearly read her mind as it was. "I just wondered what it is that makes you tick," she said.

He sawed off a piece of steak. "Meaning?"

"Why you do what you do."

Chewing thoughtfully, he glanced over her shoulder as the front door opened and a rush of cold air swept through the lobby to ruffle the back of Casey's hair. "You want my life story, is that it?"

She grinned. "Well, at least a couple of chapters."

He considered, swallowed some beer and kept eating. Whoever had entered the lobby didn't keep his interest. "What do you want to know?"

She smiled. "Where did you come from?"

"Grew up around the Warm Springs Reservation."

"On the reservation?"

He shook his head. "Nah. My mom and dad had a house in town, not far from the sawmill where my father worked. We went to the reservation, sure, but I spent my growing years in town."

"So how did you get this affinity for horses?"

"My grandfather had a ranch. Not much of one, really, but I didn't know it at the time. About twenty acres of dusty land with a creek slicing through it. I remember going over there on weekends. I wanted to spend all my time over there because my grandfather used to teach me how to track, hunt, fish and ride. At night, he'd smoke on the back porch and tell me stories about my heritage, something my father never talked about."

"Why not?"

Sloan set down his fork and looked past her shoulder to the middle distance where memories of his youth seemed to pass before his eyes. "My mother's family didn't approve of her marrying a Native American, or Indian as we were called back then, so my father did his best to deny his background. He worked in the mill, bought a house in town, avoided the reservation and didn't spend any time with my grandfather."

Casey felt sick inside. "His own father?"

"They didn't get along, which I don't suppose is all that uncommon. Look at your family."

At the mention of Jonah, she felt a great sadness settle

over her shoulders. It was true; her family would probably be what psychologists now called dysfunctional, though she hadn't heard the term except in recent years and likely wouldn't have cared while growing up. Her brother, Max, had always tried to please their demanding father, Jenner had outwardly rebelled and Casey had been frustrated in the role of Jonah McKee's special daughter. Her mother, Virginia, had held her head high despite the rumors of her husband's numerous affairs, and her grandmother, Mavis, still considered her son nearly perfect. They'd lied to each other, wounded each other and ended up not trusting each other.

"We weren't talking about my family," she reminded him as she sliced a bite of fish and plopped it into her mouth.

"Well, there's not much more to tell about mine." He frowned as if discussion of his parents brought back an onslaught of unwanted thoughts. "My dad worked in the sawmill in town during the day and drank too much at quitting time." He shoved his plate aside. "It wasn't that unusual. Everyone in town stopped off for a beer after work, just like they do in Rimrock at the Black Anvil."

"Do you have any brothers or sisters?"

He snorted a laugh. "A kid sister in Seattle. Works for a news station."

"But you don't see her often," Casey guessed.

"Nope."

"Are your parents still in Warm Springs?"

He shook his head. "Dad died early. Cancer. Mom moved in with her widowed sister. She lives in Hood River. Never remarried."

"And your grandfather?"

His smile was cold. "Dead, too. Had to sell his ranch to pay for the nursing-home bills." He reached into his wallet and tossed a few bills onto the table. "I think that's about it for twenty questions," he said. "Come on."

A swarm of butterflies erupted in her stomach at the

thought of spending another night alone with Sloan. Tonight they would have separate beds, though Sloan had insisted they stay in the same room as he wasn't convinced that even being a connecting door away was close enough to keep her safe.

They headed upstairs with their meager luggage, and Casey's mouth felt dry as he unlocked the hotel-room door. They entered without saying a word. Were circumstances different, Casey would have been thrilled with the antique beds and mirrors filling the old room. Completeing the picture, braided rugs were tossed over the polished wood planks of the floor.

Reflected in the windowpanes, the colored Christmas lights of the general store shone red, green and blue. Casey could easily imagine this room as an ideal spot for a romantic tryst. Except that she was here alone with Sloan and he was certain someone was following them.

She tossed her bag into the little closet, then nearly jumped out of her skin when she heard him turn the lock, cutting them off from the rest of the world.

Just the two of them. Alone. In the middle of the mountains with a blizzard raging around them and a killer stalking them.

Merry Christmas.

Chapter Six

Lying across his bed, Sloan fingered the barrel of the shotgun and tried not to stare at Casey. She was restless, tossing and turning, messing up the covers, and he was dead tired. He hadn't slept for the better part of three days and he couldn't help fantasizing how it would feel to curl up next to her, her small body pressed tightly to his. He imagined falling asleep, breathing in the scent of her hair while listening to the steady drum of her heart.

He hadn't wanted to sleep with a woman since Jane. There had been times when he'd wanted sex, but never had he wanted that emotional commitment of spending the night with another person, waking up to see a new day begin together. With Casey, he felt differently. The urge for sex was there and he imagined that it would be hot and wild, a fevered and emotional joining unlike anything he'd ever felt before. But there would be more to the fusing of their bodies than the physical; there would be a bonding at a deeper level, a level he wasn't certain he could accept—a level that he wanted to avoid.

She made a whimpering sound and he looked up sharply, staring at her and wondering if her nightmares were of Barry White. If only he'd found her sooner, if only he hadn't followed so many false leads before he'd discovered the cabin owned by Steve Jansen, Barry's half brother. Did Steve know that White was using the cabin as his hideout? Was Steve part of the plot, White's accomplice? Or was the connection to Jansen just one of convenience?

No doubt the FBI, Rex Stone, Virginia McKee's private investigator, and Sheriff Hammond Polk were looking into Steve Jansen's relationship with his half brother.

He closed his eyes. Tomorrow. Weather permitting, he'd be rid of this mess. Not that he could just walk away. He'd already promised Jenner that he'd bring Casey back and stay on the case until all the culprits were safely behind bars. But at least she wouldn't be his sole responsibility any longer.

He glanced at her and felt an unnatural twist to his heart, almost as if he *wanted* her to be his charge. But that was crazy. Rolling off the bed, he decided to stretch his legs, and just as he'd done every hour, he walked to the door, checked the peephole, then opened the latch and surveyed the corridor. It was short; only eight doors opened off the hallway. The stairs curled up one story to the third floor and down one to the main floor. The elevator, a new addition since the old hotel was originally built, was silent. Everything was silent. Except for the wind moaning outside and the blower for the heating system wheezing, there was no noise.

He ducked back into the room and locked the door, then checked the windows, pushing aside the shade and peering through the icy glass to the street below. The snow was still falling, but seemed to have slowed a little. He checked the highway but there was no sign of a road crew. Nor did he see any would-be assassin huddled against the wind, lurking in the shadows, his malevolent gaze glued to the hotel.

Maybe Casey was right. Maybe he was paranoid: No one could have followed them through this blizzard.

She made another cry and this time it was louder. Sloan dropped the shade and turned as she flung her body from one side of the bed to the other. ''No!'' she yelled in a broken sob. ''No! No! No!''

''Casey,'' he said sharply, but she cried out again. He walked to the bed, grabbed her by the shoulders and felt her cringe beneath his touch.

''Noooo!''

''Wake up, you're dreaming.'' Giving her a little shake, he saw tears flow from her eyes.

''Let me go! I want to go home!''

''Casey!'' Her eyes flew open, and even in the half-light from the reflection of the snow, he saw her fear. ''It's me. Sloan. You're all right. Just having a bad dream.''

Trying to pull away, she looked frantically around the room, the terror of her dream still not fading.

''You're okay,'' he assured her and felt the rigid muscles in her arms relax slightly.

''Oh, God.'' She buried her face in her hands. ''I'm sorry…it was so real…''

''Shh. It's all right,'' he said, feeling her shudder as he wrapped his arms around her and she buried her face in his neck.

''It was so awful.''

''But just your imagination,'' he whispered against her hair. The fragrance of lilacs tickled his nostrils. She felt so small and vulnerable, her body, usually strung as tight as a bowstring, slumped against his. She was only wearing a T-shirt and panties, and through the thin wall of his clothes he felt the tips of her breasts brush against him. Again she shuddered and he couldn't help himself; to calm her, he kissed her crown. "You're all right," he said. "I won't let anything happen to you."

She was warm in his arms, that snugly warmth from being under the covers, and she let out a trembling sigh. She lifted her head to look at him.

His diaphragm slammed up against his lungs, and staring into those frightened hazel eyes, he could barely breathe. Swallowing, she shoved a handful of hair away from her face and licked her lips.

It was his undoing. Without thinking of his actions or what the recriminations might be, he drew her close to him again and kissed her. Her lips were warm and soft and pliant and she let out a little moan as their mouths met.

A thousand warnings flashed through his mind.

Don't do this, Redhawk.

She's half-asleep, for crying out loud.

She'll hate you for taking advantage of her.

She just woke up from one helluva nightmare, and she doesn't need some randy man who's supposed to be protecting her coming on to her!

She'll hate you forever and you'll scar her.

She's Jenner's sister, you idiot!

Still, he couldn't stop himself. His arms pulled her tight against him and he kissed her with a passion he'd thought was long dead. Her body fitted perfectly against his, her bare legs brushing his jeans, her abdomen flat against his, her breasts crushed against his chest.

"No," he said, but she still clung to him. The pounding beat of his heart was thundering through his brain; fire raced through his blood.

He pressed his tongue against her teeth and felt her open to him. Easily. Willingly. Trustingly. Her tongue mated anxiously with his, touching, exploring, causing sparks of liquid fire to spray through his blood.

His heart was pumping fast, and the rest of the world—

the storm, the danger, the reward—seemed to fade. All he could do was smell her, taste her, touch her.

Her fingers were light against his back, and through his sweater he felt their soft exploration. She didn't flinch when he found the hem of her T-shirt, went under and touched her skin. Instead she moaned softly and pressed more urgently to him. His fingers inched up her ribs to cup the underside of her breast.

Still she kissed him, rubbing against him as he found her nipple and gently rolled it between his thumb and finger.

Don't do this! She doesn't know what she's doing! She's reacting, damn it, still half-asleep! She'll hate you in the morning and you'll regret what you're about to do for the rest of your life!

But he didn't take heed. His body was aflame with long-banked desire, his pants suddenly too tight, her body soft and willing. He yanked the T-shirt over her head and gazed down at the soft mounds of her breasts. They were small, with red-brown areolas and nipples that pointed eagerly upward. He kissed one of those rosy peaks and she bucked, yearning to be closer to him. He held her close, his fingers splaying over her spine, his fingertips feeling the ridge of bones beneath her skin and he kissed her. Leisurely, as if he were drinking his fill, he teased and suckled at her nipples, tasting of their sweetness, ignoring the fire in his loins as he laved all of her. She was anxious and hot, more than willing, and wearing only a pair of bikini briefs.

He wanted her. Desire thundered through his brain, racing in electric currents through his blood. She arched against him and he slid lower, letting his tongue trace a path from her breasts to her navel, feeling her hard, flat abdomen against his face.

"Sloan," she cried as his hand slipped beneath the waistband of her panties and surrounded a firm buttock. "Please...oh..." He stripped the panties from her and kissed her so intimately that her hips rose from the bed, inviting more of his touch, of his kisses, of him.

He didn't know what he was doing, didn't think about the consequences. Still tasting her, he unsnapped his fly, kicked off his jeans and fumbled hastily for the foil packet he kept in his wallet buried deep in his pocket. His brain was burning and he didn't want to delay a second's pleasure.

His fingers delved into her moistness and she groaned, her hips thrusting upward, anticipating. She clung to him, wanting more, nearly begging him to take her. Closing his mind against any more recriminations, he climbed over her, pried her knees farther open with his own. Then, staring down into the most beautiful eyes he'd ever seen, he pushed forward and entered her swiftly, feeling only the slightest resistance, watching as her face twisted in pain and she cried out, her fingernails digging into his shoulders. He withdrew, pushed again, and she gasped.

"Casey—"

"Don't stop!" she cried, and he thrust forward, letting his animal urges take over, feeling her warm and wet and willing as she met each of his strokes with her own.

It had been so long.

He tried to wait, but couldn't, and within a few more short strokes, he poured himself into her, collapsing against her, holding her close. "Casey, Casey, Casey," he whispered into the sweat-dampened strands of her hair. "What have you done to me?"

Casey heard the words and blinked back tears. *What have you done to me?* she asked silently, for her world had changed this night. Forever. And he didn't even know. Hadn't even bothered to take off his sweater. Rolling to one side, he held her close, one arm draped over her breasts, the other around her abdomen, pulling her spoon fashion against him.

She felt cheap and told herself it didn't matter. This wasn't the nineteenth century and she was in her late twenties—which must be some kind of record these days. She'd decided over a week ago to change her life, to become a woman and shake off the shackles of being Jonah McKee's little girl, so she wasn't going to cry, not when everything was going her way.

Exhausted, she closed her eyes. Like Scarlett, she'd worry about everything tomorrow.

She awoke later in the night and felt him kissing her back, his fingers teasing her nipples. Her entire body tingled and she didn't resist as he licked her spine, but rolled over to face him. His eyes were at half-mast as he kissed her, his moans low and primal.

His sweater was gone and his naked skin surrounded her. Flesh upon flesh. She kissed his shoulders and neck and eyes, then slid lower to press her tongue wetly against the nipples buried in the swirling hairs of his chest. Sweat dampened his skin as it dampened hers. His abdomen retracted as she traced an imaginary line with her tongue to his belly button.

"Casey, wait," he groaned, hands twining in her hair. Pulling her upward, he kissed her and the hands caressing her explored her back, her breasts, her rump. He rolled her onto her back, and slowly, while staring at her with eyes as dark as obsidian, he parted her with his fingers, delving deep, causing a deep rumble in the back of her throat.

She arched upward, moist and hot and wanting, and he didn't deny her. This time he spread her legs, kissed her, and then he eased into her and moved slowly, back and forth, deeper and deeper. She felt the world begin to tilt and spin and she called out his name, her voice rough as she moved against him in a timeless dance. His rhythm increased and the stars behind her eyes collided in a fiery shower of sparks. Her body convulsed, and he cried out and fell atop her, spent and loving, kissing her temple and holding her close. "Casey…" He murmured her name as if it were a caress. "Oh, Casey." Snuggling against him, she wished the night would last forever.

"You were a virgin?" Sloan stared at her in disbelief and she saw the condemnation in his eyes as he looked from her to the sheet.

"Does it matter?"

He ran an impatient hand through his hair. "Of course it matters."

"Not to me."

"Damn it, Casey, why didn't you say something?"

"Like what?" she countered, picking up her clothes and feeling a stain of embarrassment wash up her cheeks. "Excuse me, Sloan, could you stop so I can give you my complete sexual history?"

"No, but—"

"It's not that big of a deal." She'd decided that much during the night when she'd slept nestled soundly in the warm protection of his arms, and now he was acting as if she was some kind of criminal.

"Not a big deal. Then why—"

"I never met the right man, okay?" she said quickly, then when his black eyes flashed with regret, she bit her tongue. "I—"

"Damn it all to hell!"

"Look, just forget it, okay? Pretend it didn't happen."

"Can you?" His eyes bored into hers.

"If I have to."

"I don't do casual sex."

She smiled cynically. "Neither do I, and I guess I can prove it."

"That's not what I—"

"Let's not argue about it. It's too late to change anything, anyway. I'm going to clean up."

She tried to walk away, but he grabbed her arm, spinning her so quickly that she dropped her sweater and stood naked in front of him. He, on the other hand, had the advantage of having stepped into his jeans.

"We can't just shrug this off."

"I'm not trying to." She angled her chin up defiantly. His eyes, still flashing angrily, moved from her face to her breasts and lower still to the dark curls at the apex of her legs. He swallowed as he lifted his gaze, his fingers digging deep into her arm, and for a second she thought he might kiss her.

"This was a mistake." But desire flamed in his eyes.

"Then we won't make another one, will we?" Yanking her arm away, she strode to the bathroom not bothering to lock the door behind her. She was disappointed in his reaction, but what had she expected? Not that she was going to tell him she'd never been with a man, of course, but the telltale signs on the bed had been her undoing. She hadn't been able to lie and say that she'd cut herself shaving or something.

She twisted on the hot water, waited while rusted, ancient pipes groaned, then stepped under the spray. She washed her body and tingled a little when she touched herself between her legs. Smiling as the water cascaded over her head and shoulders, she felt a small triumph. True, she'd always thought she'd save herself for the man she loved, but she didn't regret making love to Sloan. In fact, standing here in the hot spray, she imagined the touch and feel of his hands and mouth all over again. Maybe it hadn't been a well-planned, romantic act, but it had happened, and she was a firm believer in dealing with reality.

It wasn't the end of the world.

In fact, a silly little part of her thought it might be just the beginning. She lathered her body and imagined an affair with Sloan. He was exciting and mysterious and sexy, and while he wasn't perfect husband material, she wasn't looking for a husband.

So what is it you are looking for?

What about love?

Well, what about it? She had always wanted to believe in love, though her parents' marriage was proof enough that either love didn't exist at all, or didn't endure. Lots of her friends were already divorced and working on their second marriages. But deep down, true love must exist. Max and Skye, Beth and Jenner seemed proof enough, though both couples had suffered through hell before they'd found heaven and true love.

She had to believe that love endured, but not for everyone, and certainly, from her limited track record, not for her. Her few dates in college and short-term relationship with Peter didn't give her much perspective. As for Sloan...she bit her lip. He'd already had his taste of love; she knew that from the look of adoration that came to his eyes whenever he spoke of his deceased wife. Now *that* was love, the kind a person only finds once in a lifetime, and only if he's lucky.

Rinsing her hair, she decided to be pragmatic. She'd made love with Sloan and enjoyed it, and though she really didn't believe in affairs, she saw no other option with Sloan. So she'd have to be content to be with him today and perhaps tomorrow and then, once they were back in Rimrock, she'd have to steel herself to say goodbye. Lucky for her she wasn't in love.

Her throat clogged at the thought and she leaned against the wall of the shower stall. Her knees were suddenly weak when she thought about how easily she'd given herself to him, how much she'd wanted him, how easy it would be to fall in love with him. *Don't be silly,* she told herself. *It was just sex, nothing more.* But it felt like more. A lot more.

She took in a bracing breath and squared her shoulders. She couldn't hide in the bathroom forever. Sooner or later she had to face him. She was about to step out of the shower when she saw him through the hot mist. Naked, his jaw set, he stepped into the shower.

"Hey!"

"You want me to leave?" he asked as the water splashed and cascaded over him.

She wanted to lie, but couldn't. She shook her head and he came to her, took her face between his hands and kissed her until her knees were weak. His slick body pressed hard against hers and his mouth was everywhere.

His hands tangled in her hair and he kissed her hard. "Tell me no," he said.

"I can't."

"Oh, hell, I should be shot for this." His fingers found her rump. Lifting her off her feet, pressing her back up against the shower stall, he entered her. Gasping, she grabbed his shoulders and held on as he moved upward, groaning and straining, his body filling hers. Closing her eyes, feeling the water wash over them, she wrapped her legs around his waist and hung on as he pressed her ever upward until the world seemed to splinter. She collapsed against him, her head bowed against his shoulder.

"Casey," he gasped. "Sweet, sweet Casey." He held her tightly and brushed soft kisses against her wet skin.

When she finally lifted her head, she managed a smile. "I guess you don't call this casual sex."

"With you, nothing's casual."

"Mmm. But still a mistake."

His grin was positively wicked. "Of the highest order," he admitted before kissing her again and making her lose all concept of time and place.

Sloan mentally kicked himself over and over again. He'd seduced Casey McKee. Jenner's little sister. No, Jenner's *virgin* little sister. Not once, not twice, but three times within twelve hours. How could he have been so stupid? He'd always been cool when it came to women. Only Jane had turned him inside out.

And now Casey. He ran a hand through his hair and listened to her humming—*humming,* for Pete's sake—in the bathroom. The sheet mocked him. *Idiot!* What was the matter with him? He was supposed to protect her, for crying out loud, not steal her virtue, not climb into the shower like a lusty beast. He threw the covers over the evidence that reminded him of how he'd put himself and his needs above hers.

This was crazy. Yet he couldn't blame only himself. She was responsible, too. And she had been more than willing. But that didn't make it right. He kicked his duffel bag and sent it flying across the room. Even now, when he knew better, when the proof of his mistake was right under the crumpled bedclothes, he imagined kissing her again, touching her and making love to her until they were both exhausted.

He remembered the texture of her slick skin, how it looked in the shower, rosy from the hot water. How easy it had been to strip, press her against the tile walls and enter her sweet moistness. He grew hard just thinking about her. He closed his eyes, cursed and was thankful that the sanding crews were out. He'd heard them early this morning, working on the roads, making it possible for him to return Casey to her home and family.

His guts twisted at that thought. If Jenner ever got wind of what had happened, he'd come at Sloan fists flying. Sloan didn't blame him; he'd do the same. Even in these days of equal rights, women's open sexuality and guilt-free sex, he believed that a man should live by a strict moral code, as should a woman. As he'd told Casey, he didn't believe in casual sex, and though he wasn't old-fashioned enough to think that a person had to be married to have sex, he thought it was probably best to love a person before knowing them physically. As he had with Jane.

Although—and he felt guilty for acknowledging the fact—his lovemaking with Casey had been every bit as satisfying as sleeping with Jane. Maybe more so. Before last night, he wouldn't have believed that he could be so emotionally attached to a woman, but Casey had changed all that.

Damn her.

Still being in love with Jane had been safe, and it had helped assuage the guilt he felt whenever he thought of her and little Tony. "Forgive me," he said. He reached into his back pocket, withdrew his wallet and flipped it open to a picture of Jane and Tony taken years ago. Their images had faded with time. Behind the photograph, in a secret pocket, was his wedding ring—a wide gold band. What a sentimental fool he was. And a hypocrite. The same wallet that held his gold band also held a small supply of condoms—just in case.

"Son of a bitch," he muttered just as the door to the bathroom opened. Casey, her hair still damp, her face flushed, her gorgeous body covered with wrinkled clothes, stepped into the room. He closed the wallet and slapped it into his back pocket. "We'd better go."

"Yes, well..." She picked up her belongings and seemed embarrassed.

"The roads are clear."

"That's good."

"We might make it home today."

Her shoulders hunched a bit. "Great."

"Yeah." He rubbed the stubble of beard on his jaw. "Look, I don't want you to think that I'm some kind of Neanderthal, that I go around bed hopping and jumping in showers and—"

"Don't apologize." Her head snapped up and there was a trace of sadness in her eyes. "Why do you always think you have to apologize?"

"Because whether you admit it or not, this was a big deal to you."

"Male ego talking," she quipped.

"Male ego? After you've waited for twenty-odd years to—"

"Let's not talk about it. Not yet. It was just sex, okay?

And it was time I got my feet wet—or whatever other body part was involved.''

"Jeez, Casey, I'm just trying to say that—''

"What?''

Her eyes beseeched him and he wanted to tell her that she was special, that whenever he was around her he got a little crazy, he did become a Neanderthal, an overprotective, sex-starved Neanderthal, who wanted to hold her all night long, to touch her hair, to kiss her lips, to whisper his most intimate secrets. Instead he cleared his throat. "It won't happen again.''

One of her dark eyebrows arched. "Not even if I try my best to seduce you?''

He sucked in a swift breath. "You're something else.''

"I certainly hope so. Shouldn't we be leaving?''

"Fine.'' He checked his watch, though he didn't know why. "Right.'' She had a way of turning his thoughts around. "Let's go.'' Slinging the strap of his bag over his shoulder, he reached for White's shotgun and took a final look around the room. He'd remember this place. For a lot of reasons. Some of which he'd rather not examine too closely.

Again Sloan stopped by the restaurant, had his thermos filled with coffee and ordered a bag of hot corn bread and scones, then hauled it all to his truck.

Outside, the air was crisp, and dawn was creeping over the mountains, allowing sunlight to slide into the town. Casey stepped off the front porch and reached for the door handle of the truck.

CRACK!

The report of a rifle blasted through the still morning air.

Casey's heart froze. The bullet whizzed past her head and bored into the fender.

"Oh, hell!'' Sloan, on the other side of the truck, vaulted the vehicle, grabbed Casey and dragged her around to the driver's side. "Stay down," he growled, scanning the surrounding hills.

Casey was shaking as Sloan threw open the pickup's door. "Wh-what was that?"

"What do you think it was?"

"Oh, God, someone's shooting at us."

"Looks that way." He pressed her body against the truck, using his as protection. "Wait here," he whispered against her ear.

"But—"

He'd already slid along the seat of the truck. He reached forward and started the engine. With a roar and a plume of exhaust, the pickup came to life. Casey trembled.

"Can you drive this thing?"

"Yes, but—"

"Good. Do it." Tucked low, he shifted across the seat to the passenger side. People peered through the windows of the hotel. "Get in and keep your head down!"

"Are you sure?"

"Now!" He was crouched on the floor of the truck, the shotgun at the window, and Casey climbed in behind the wheel, hunching down. She slammed the door, stretched to find the pedals, shoved the truck into gear and tromped on the accelerator. The wheels spun. Snow flew.

Another blast from the rifle. Snow in front of the truck sprayed onto the windshield.

"Go!"

With a silent prayer, Casey, ducked so low that she could barely see over the dash, drove like a maniac down the main street of the little village. Her heart pounding, she watched as Sloan stared through the open window, the shotgun poised.

"There's a turn at the far end of town. Take it and drive over the bridge. Whoever he is, he won't be able to get a clean shot at us there."

"Where is he?" she cried.

"On the ridge above town. Somewhere." Frustration sliced through his words.

By this time, people were peering out the windows of the few cabins that lined the road. With Sloan tensed beside her, looking out the window, shotgun propped against his shoulder, she cranked the wheel. The truck swung wide, tires spinning wildly before the body straightened just as they reached the bridge. The truck shimmied over the icy surface, skidding sideways. Casey sucked in her breath, eased up on the gas and they slid over the crossing.

"Just keep going," Sloan ordered, and Casey did exactly as she was told, hitting the accelerator as the tires gripped the road again. The snow was deep, but the truck plowed through the drifts and eventually she saw the turn to the main road.

"Go north."

"But Rimrock's—"

"I know, but we've got to lose this stupid jackass."

She was shaking, her insides turned to jelly, her palms sweating on the wheel, even though, with the window open, the temperature had fallen below freezing.

"You okay?" he called over his shoulder.

"Yeah."

"You sure?"

"Yes! It's just that I'm not used to people shooting at me." She heard her voice break and clamped her mouth shut. She would not fall apart like some simpering fool woman. She would not! "I'm fine, really."

"Well, I'm not," he muttered. "I don't like people taking potshots at me. Makes me angry."

"What about scared?"

"That, too. One of the reasons I hated working as a cop. I just didn't like someone deciding to use me for a target."

"Did that happen?"

Silence. Only the whine of the truck's engine made any noise. A few seconds later, she thought she heard him say, "It happened once," but his voice was so low, she wasn't certain.

Their conversation died and she concentrated on keeping the old pickup on the slippery road. Sloan kept a lookout, never giving up his grip on the shotgun, his mouth flat over his teeth, his eyes, when he slid a glance over his shoulder to check on her, dark with a need for vengeance.

The miles sped behind them as the road, plowed and sanded, was finally passable. Except that they were going away from Rimrock, away from home. She didn't care. Now, she was scared. Really scared. She'd never really believed that Barry White would hurt her, but this man— this unknown assassin—seemed to want her dead. At that thought the marrow of her bones turned to ice. Who was he and why the need for such violence?

They passed trucks and cars and Sloan watched each with a wary eye, seemingly convinced that the entire population of eastern Oregon was hell-bent on killing her. Her heart began to slow a little as they put distance between the small town and the truck, but Sloan never let down his guard. She then drove west for miles, leaving the mountains to drive over flat high-desert terrain.

Sloan never relaxed, not even when they had to stop for gas in a small town near the Columbia River. He bought a six-pack of soda, a bag of potato chips and two prewrapped sandwiches at a deli in the grocery store. Once the tank was full and he was behind the wheel, he never let his eyes stay in one spot. He was forever glancing in the rearview mirror, at the oncoming lane, down a side road, or over the snow-covered countryside as they took roads leading in varied directions.

They ate in silence but Casey could barely swallow; her stomach tied in painful knots when Sloan decided they could double back. Sloan kept their direction south and west for two hours, then altered his course once they'd crossed enough roads to keep whoever it was that was shooting at them guessing.

By nightfall they were only a couple of hundred miles from Rimrock and the sky was clear. Sloan stopped in a town large enough to house several motels and a car dealership that advertised Rent-A-Wreck. He registered and paid for a room, left the truck outside, then had Casey climb into an old station wagon he'd rented for the night.

"Just in case," he told her as they drove out of town and headed home. "I'll pick the truck up tomorrow, once I know that you're where you belong."

"And then what?" she asked, her hands around a cup of cooling coffee.

"And then I tell our story to the law. So will you. After that shooting spree up north, I'm sure we'll have to go through one helluva grilling."

"I'm not talking about just the next day or two," she said, hardly believing that the words crossed her lips.

"Oh." His hands tightened over the wheel. "I guess I'll hang around town until we nail the bastard." His jaw had turned to granite and Casey realized that finding the culprit was more than a job for Sloan; it had become a personal quest.

"And once all the bad guys are locked up and they've thrown away the key, where will you go?" She tried to sound nonchalant, as if what happened to him wasn't of the slightest interest to her, when, in fact, her nerves were strung as tight as new barbed wire. "Back to L.A.?"

He shook his head and her heart fluttered with the silly little hope that he'd be close by. *Why? He means nothing to you. So he saved your life. It was his job. So he slept with you. It was a mistake and you both know it.* She took another swallow of bitter coffee.

"I'll probably settle down somewhere around Warm Springs. Maybe buy my grandfather's ranch if the owner's interested in getting rid of it. Raise horses, sell livestock."

"The good life," she said with more than a trace of sarcasm.

"What about you?"

"I guess I'll pick up where I left off."

"Which was?"

I wish I knew. I wish to God I knew. "Once things settle down, I might move to Portland or Seattle."

"You want the big-city life?" He frowned as a few flakes of snow drifted from the dark sky to land on the windshield.

"I can't live with my mom in Rimrock forever."

He slid a curious glance in her direction. "What is it you do when you're not being kidnapped?"

"Good question." She managed a small smile. "Believe it or not, my degree is in education. Physical education."

"You teach kids to play baseball?"

Her lips twitched. "There's a little more to it than that."

"So why the move to L.A. to sign on with some production company?"

She leaned against the seat and thought back. "It was probably to rebel against my father. He wanted me to be a corporate lawyer, kind of like Max. Then he expected me to move back to Rimrock and work at McKee Enterprises. I wasn't interested. So, I went to school, and since I was pretty athletic, it only seemed natural to go for a physical education degree. I also took a lot of drama and fun courses. But when I got out, teaching jobs were scarce and I really wanted to get away from my father." She took a drink of coffee, and after she swallowed the tepid brew, she looked quizzically at him and asked, "Did you ever happen to meet him?"

Sloan nodded. "Only briefly, a couple of times, but I've talked to a lot of men—including Jenner—who knew him well. He didn't make many friends."

"He was a stubborn, self-centered bastard," she admitted, staring out the window and remembering Jonah McKee. "He doted on me, though. Told me I could be anything I wanted, that I had the world by the tail. But, that if I used the brains that God had given me, I would take up law, come back to Rimrock, marry a local boy— one with money, preferably—and work for Daddy. He already had a couple of potential husbands picked out for me."

Sloan snorted. "I can't see you on the family payroll."

"Neither could I."

"What about the hometown boy?"

"As I said, Dad had a couple in mind. Judge Rayburn has a son, Billy, but I thought he was a jerk, so Doc Fletcher's boy, Sam, was next in line. Trouble was, Sam was fifteen years older than I was. Besides, I wasn't into letting my dad pick out my dates or my husband."

Sloan set his empty cup on the dash. "Who were your choices?"

"No one who lived around Rimrock. All the boys in town were interested, but I wasn't fooled. It was because of Dad and his money—no one seemed to look beyond that. I dated a few guys in college, but no one seriously. We all hung out as a group mainly, and then Clarisse started seeing Raymond James—getting serious about him—and that didn't look so good. Besides, I was always attracted to the wrong type."

"What type is that?"

She bit her lower lip. "Not the kind who wants to settle down in a house with a white picket fence and drive a station wagon with cruise control."

"Is that the kind you want?"

She glanced at him. "I thought so."

His eyes narrowed a fraction. "So you avoided getting too close to anyone."

"I guess. My parents' marriage was a sham. Max's first marriage to Colleen Wheeler was on the rocks from the beginning. Clarisse was my best friend and it wasn't long

after the wedding that I suspected she was miserable, so
I didn't see any reason to tie myself down. When I went
to L.A., a lot of the men I saw were only interested in
one-night stands and that isn't my style…'' Her voice
drifted off as she thought about the night before and a
huge lump filled her throat. ''Well, it wasn't.'' She slid a
glance his way and found him glaring through the glass
of the windshield, his jaw tight, his fingers clamping the
steering wheel in a death grip.

''I think we should talk about last night.''

''No—''

''And this morning.''

''Why?''

''It happened, Case. Whether you want to think about
it or not.'' Her stomach nose-dived. ''I didn't mean to—''

''I know.''

''As I said, it was a mistake. You were having a nightmare and I wanted to calm you down. I shouldn't have
touched you or kissed you or let things get so out of
hand.''

''What about this morning in the shower?'' she demanded.

To her amazement, he blushed. ''I couldn't help myself.'' He muttered something under his breath. ''Believe
it or not, I usually have a lot of self-control, but this morning, just hearing the water running and knowing you were
there… Damn it all, anyway. Look, I'm trying my best to
apologize here.''

''It wasn't your fault, okay?'' she snapped. ''I was
there, too. I wasn't some whimpering female who couldn't
say no.''

''I took advantage of you.''

''You didn't.''

''I should never have—''

''Right, maybe so, but you did and I did and it's not
that big of a deal, okay? We had sex. It was good and
I'm not sorry, are you?''

"Yes," he said without a second's hesitation, and her heart seemed to close around itself.

She turned her head and stared out the window, determined not to let him see the tears of frustration in her eyes. She blinked hard, forced herself not to sob and wished she had more self-control, but she'd always been a person who wore her heart on her sleeve, whose emotions were always just under the surface of her skin, ready to rise up at any moment. Whether it be anger, love, worry or fear, her feelings were evident in her eyes.

"Casey." He touched her arm then and she jerked it away.

"Just forget it," she forced out as she looked ahead and saw the winking lights of Rimrock glowing in the valley in the distance. "I already have."

Chapter Seven

The Rocking M had never looked better. With snow crystallizing on the roof of the barns, and golden lamplight reflecting on the icicles hanging from the eaves of the house, the ranch was a welcome sight. Snow had drifted against the fence line, and horses, tails to the wind, dotted the hillside. A handful of stars threw down enough light to sparkle on the ground, and as the rental car slid to a stop, Casey, anxious to see her family, was already reaching for the door handle.

Sloan didn't try to stop her and she slogged through the drifts just as the outside lights flashed on. The door opened, and her mother, silhouetted against the bright backdrop, paused for a second before running onto the porch.

"Casey!" Virginia McKee cried as Casey ran into her mother's outstretched arms. Tears shimmered on the older woman's cheeks. "Thank God you're all right! I was so worried. Why didn't you call? We heard there was a shooting up north and...oh, dear Lord, I was so upset.''

"I'm fine, Mom. Really."

"I've prayed every night—'' Her voice cracked.

"Me, too." Casey's throat clogged with emotion and her eyes gleamed in relief as Reuben, the family's cross-bred Lab, barked excitedly.

"Well, let's not stand out here and freeze like a couple of ninnies. Come on in." Still holding each other, they walked inside. Casey drank in the scent of Virginia's perfume, the same fragrance she remembered from her childhood, while memories filled with love and warmth flooded through her. For the past few weeks, before her abduction, she'd been so hell-bent on leaving that she'd pushed aside the good times that now whispered through her mind. "I didn't know you'd miss me so badly," she teased, then heard Sloan's boots against the hardwood floor as he entered and softly closed the door behind him.

She glanced in his direction, but he didn't come forward, just leaned against the door as if he was unwilling to break into the family reunion.

"We've been worried sick." Mavis, Casey's grandmother, walked stiffly from the den, and she seemed to rely on her cane more than Casey remembered. "I tell you, the whole world seems to have gone to hell in a hand basket. Even little old Rimrock's not the same as it used to be." She shook her gray head and frowned at the unpleasant turn of her thoughts. "But at least you're safe now. That's all that matters."

Casey dashed the tears from her face and forced a smile. "Well, you're right about that," she said, trying to lighten the mood. She kissed her mother on the temple and peered into the living room. "So where's the Christmas tree?" she demanded. "The one you usually put up the first of December. And the house lights. This is the first year they haven't been lit the day after Thanksgiving. Hillary will be so disappointed. Jeez, Mom, I'm gone for a little over a week and it looks like the whole place has gone to seed.''

Mavis chuckled, then pointed with her cane to Sloan. "Seems like we owe you a big thank-you,'' she said, her eyes bright. "For bringing our girl back.''

Sloan lifted a shoulder. "All in a day's work.''

"Like holy hell, pardon my French. I heard how you tackled and hog-tied that Barry White. I only wished you'd done more. Needed to be castrated, he did.''

"Mavis!'' Virginia said.

"Well, he did!'' Mavis insisted, thrusting out her chin. "Think about what he did to Casey. Prison time isn't enough. Even if he is convicted, he'll probably be off on parole in a few years.'' Using her cane, she hitched back to the den. "I've half a mind to find out where he is and take care of him myself!''

"Grandma!'' But Casey smothered a smile.

"Done it before, to calves and lambs, you know. Even a horse a couple of times.''

Virginia's back stiffened. "Mavis, please, we have a guest.''

"Oh, all right. I guess I'll have to call the boys instead. Maybe they'll do the job for me.''

"Please, don't pay her any mind,'' Virginia said to Sloan, whose lips were twitching upward in amusement. "She's getting on in years and sometimes—''

"I heard that,'' Mavis called from the den. "Nothin' wrong with my hearing!''

"For the love of Mike.'' Virginia, dabbing at her eyes, started toward the back of the house. "Come on into the kitchen. Kiki's still here and I'm sure we can rustle up some coffee and food. You must be hungry.''

"Starved,'' Casey said as she and Sloan followed Virginia along the familiar hallway, where pictures of her family were hung on the wall. A portrait of her as a baby, a picture of Max looking stern as he posed with his football helmet, a glossy black and white of Jenner roping a calf in his first rodeo, a snapshot of Casey going to the prom with a freckle-faced boy she'd lost touch with long ago. Other pictures were there, as well—memories of the good times but none of the bad.

In the kitchen, Kiki was working feverishly. As she mopped the floor, she had the radio on full blast to some talk show discussing gun-control laws. She glanced up as the small party approached, caught sight of Casey and nearly dropped the mop. "Well, look who finally decided to come home," she said with a look of mild reproof. But her old eyes glistened and she gave Casey a hug with her bony arms. "We've missed you around here."

Again, Casey's throat swelled shut. "Glad to be home."

"I thought maybe there was something we could heat up," Virginia offered.

"Always is." Kiki pointed to the table with her chin. "Set yourselves down." She stuffed the mop in a pail on the back porch, then, ignoring the damp floor, went to work. Within minutes, there were cups of steaming coffee, reheated chicken and dumplings and thick slabs of carrot cake with whipped cream. She buzzed around the room, refilling the cups, offering slices of home-baked bread with boysenberry jam and insisting that Casey should eat more as she appeared to have lost weight.

By the time they'd finished, and Casey, over Kiki's strenuous arguments, had pushed her plate aside, headlights flashed through the windows. Two trucks, traveling much too fast, pulled into the drive almost in unison. Brakes squealed and doors slammed shut.

"Looks like those no-good brothers of yours are here," Kiki said as she peered through the lace curtains. Light from a third vehicle splashed through the window as the front door opened. "And they're not alone. Hammond Polk and that idiot from the FBI seem to have caught wind of the news."

"Casey!" Jenner roared, his voice reverberating through the house.

"We're in here," Virginia responded.

Boots rang down the hall. Max appeared first, his dark blond hair mussed, his eyes shadowed with worry. One look at Casey and he grinned. He yanked her out of the chair and twirled her off her feet. "Thank God."

Jenner's uneven gait followed and he was swearing a blue streak about having to depend upon a cane as he entered the kitchen and offered the group a crooked smile. His gaze landed on Casey, still embracing Max, then skated to Sloan who was seated at the table finishing the last of his coffee. "Well, Redhawk, I guess I lose my bet."

"How's that?" Sloan asked.

"I figured that being cooped up with Casey for more than a day would drive any sane man crazy. You don't look ready for an institution."

"And I love you, too," Casey said as she released Max and one of Jenner's arms surrounded her waist.

"Hey, I'm complimenting the man. I expected that by this time he would be ready to wring your neck."

"Not yet," Sloan agreed and slid Casey a glance that fairly sizzled. She felt a stain of heat wash up her neck. "But I came close a couple of times."

"Thanks a lot."

"I'm just glad you're in one piece," Max said, running his hands through his hair and declining a piece of cake that Kiki seemed determined to thrust into his hands. "Hell, Case, you gave us a scare. What were you thinking of, getting into a car with Barry White?"

Here it comes—the third degree. "It was a truck, and considering the situation, I didn't have a whole lot of choices," she said, bristling.

"I told you to get a cellular phone."

Ever the responsible older brother. "I know, I just hadn't gotten around to it yet."

"No reason to belabor the point," Sloan said. "She didn't mean to get herself abducted."

"That's right," Virginia agreed, quick to come to Casey's defense.

Casey gave Sloan a grateful smile, surprised that he would stand up to her brothers when she knew that he thought she'd been a fool to climb into Barry's truck, too.

A harsh pounding echoed through the house.

"The law—always the last to know," Kiki mumbled as she untied her apron and headed down the hall to answer the front door.

"So where the hell did he take you?" Jenner demanded.

Sloan scooted his chair back. "Let's hold off on the questions," he said, his face serious. "I think we'll have a lot to answer for the authorities and there's no reason to repeat everything."

He was right. Hammond Polk, the thick-waisted sheriff, and Sam Revere, the wiry, sandy blond agent for the FBI asked hours' worth of questions. They spoke with Casey and Sloan in the den, allowing the rest of the family to listen in and add anything they knew. Everyone found a place to sit, even on the hearth. Sloan found a spot on the window ledge.

Casey went through her ordeal day by day, from the time she received the call from Clarisse and the breakdown of her car, to the abduction by Barry White and the following days when she nearly went out of her mind with anxiety, trying to escape and praying that someone would save her. Taking turns, she and Sloan filled in the rest, including the shooting incident near the hotel where they'd spent the night.

Over and over the information they went.

"Just one more thing…"

"Can you tell me who White was working with? Any idea?"

"Why'd you trust him in the first place?"

"Did he mention any names?"

"Why would someone want to do this to you?"

"You got any personal enemies?"

"Did he say why he decided to kidnap you?"

"Did he admit to damaging your car?"

"How did he treat you?"

"Did he sexually molest you?"

Casey felt as if her entire life was on exhibition for everyone in the family to view. "No," she said, answering the final question. "He didn't touch me."

She saw her brothers' shoulders slump in relief, noticed that her mother seemed to whisper a prayer but Mavis didn't flinch, her expression staying the same throughout the ordeal.

Sloan, his eyes as restless as they had been for the past week, leaned against the window ledge, his long, jean-encased legs stretched out before him, his gaze moving from the den to the dark night. He answered questions concisely and never seemed ruffled, even when Hammond Polk told him Barry White was considering pressing charges against him for assault.

"Let him try," Sloan said, a slow smile stretching across his face.

"He claims that you nearly killed him."

"He survived."

"I'm just passin' on what he said."

"Then give him a message from me. Tell him if he doesn't start talking and soon, I'll find a way to get to him and this time I won't go so easy on him."

"Now, Mr. Redhawk, you know I can't do that," Hammond Polk protested, but Revere didn't say a word, though his eyes glinted a little, as if he liked the idea.

Sloan's black eyebrows drew together. "I'd be glad to deliver it in person."

"We get the picture," Revere said, his gaze meeting Sloan's in silent understanding. "I'm still in charge here

and there will be no intimidating the witness. He'll talk—
it'll just take time."

"Time we don't have," Sloan noted. "Whoever it is
has already taken a couple of potshots, nearly hit Casey.
We can't take any chances." His gaze locked with hers
for an instant and she realized suddenly how safe she felt
with him—this big stranger she barely knew, the man to
whom she had so willingly given herself.

"Don't worry about White," Revere insisted. "We'll
handle him. Now, let's go over a few points that aren't
really clear to me, all right? You've known Barry White
for how long?" The questions started all over again.

Casey tried her best to answer quickly and concisely,
but she felt as if she'd done something wrong, something
to provoke Barry White, that she was looked upon as the
criminal. Whenever she snapped crossly at a question she
felt she'd already answered, she glanced over at Sloan,
whose frown increased as the minutes ticked by. The interrogation lasted hours, and when the questions finally
slowed, midnight had come and gone and Casey was exhausted. Tired to her bones, she watched as the sheriff
and Sam Revere took their leave.

"You go on to bed," Mavis insisted. "Now that you're
back, maybe things'll get back to normal around here."

"Not until Jonah's killer is found," Virginia said
firmly, then sighed. She rubbed the back of her neck and
stared out the window. She suddenly looked older than
her years; the months of strain were beginning to show in
the drawn set of her mouth and the tired lines near the
corners of her eyes. "When will it ever end?"

"Soon," Jenner said, obviously impatient. "It has to."

Casey yawned, then caught Sloan's eye. His gaze was
thoughtful and dark as if he might be thinking of their
last night alone together. How good it would feel to sleep
with him, to have his strong arms wrap around her, to feel
the hard wall of his chest and powerful beat of his heart
against her back. A blush stole up her neck and she man-

aged a tiny smile at him before she trudged to her bedroom. It was a little girl's room, really. Pink curtains adorned the windows and the top shelf of her bookcase still held old high school memorabilia. The double bed was covered with a quilt Mavis had patched for her when she'd turned twelve. White furniture, soft pastel colors, pictures of horses and riding trophies, faded flowers from the senior prom. No wonder she'd bolted, and yet she was glad to be home, happy to feel as if she belonged somewhere. She barely had time to untie her shoes, nudge them off and drop back against the pillows before she fell instantly asleep.

The women had retired and Max closed the door of the den. He and Jenner had been comparing notes with Sloan for over an hour, drinking expensive whiskey and cursing the faceless bastards who were hell-bent on causing grief to the McKee family.

"There must be some new leads," Sloan said as he finished his drink and shook his head when Max offered him a refill. "Someone who tops off the suspect list."

Frustration etched the features of Max's face. "So far, all we've been able to do is eliminate some. We're down to a few central suspects, but not sure about any one of them."

"Let me hear what you've got."

Max stood by the cold fireplace, leaning his hip against the blackened stones. "Okay, the list of suspects could be just about anyone in town, but if we narrow it down to people Barry White would be in cahoots with we come up with several. The first is his half brother, Steve Jansen. After all, he owns the property and cabin where Barry hid out. But the only beef he had with Dad was over some sale of a used truck years ago."

Sloan, too, considered anyone related to Barry a prime suspect. He set his empty glass on a table and listened.

"The trouble is motive. There isn't much of one," Max

elaborated. "But Steve is in the auto-body business and that keeps him high on the list. According to Jimmy Rickert, Dad had words with a guy in a blue or black American-made pickup in the parking lot of the Black Anvil. Less than half an hour later, Dad was forced off the road. Then Beth's car was rammed by a dark-colored pickup just a few weeks ago, probably the same vehicle. Now, if anyone wanted to replace the bumper or get a little auto-body work done, he'd probably go to Steve."

"Is Rickert reliable—as a source?"

Jenner and Max exchanged glances. "He usually knows what's going on in town," Jenner said.

"But he was nearly passed-out drunk when he saw the argument and he couldn't name the guy. Jimmy? Reliable? Not really," Max said.

Sloan sighed. "Great. Okay, Steve's on the list."

"Then there's his father—Barry's stepfather. Ned Jansen. Ned has a thing for women. I think he was even going out with Mom before Dad came into the picture. Anyway, Ned got himself into trouble by chasing after one while married to another. Anyway, his divorces cost him a lot, he had to borrow money, and in the end, he used the copper mine as collateral. He figured it wasn't worth much, that all the copper had been mined from it. Even a geological team told him as much. Dad ended up buying the place, and lo and behold, he discovers that the geologists were wrong. There is still copper on the property—not exactly where the old mine was, but close enough to the original one. Boy, was Ned burned. He claimed that Dad had set up the whole deal, paid off the geological firm and everything."

"He probably did," Jenner interjected. "It was just like the old man."

"So why, if his beef was with your father who's now dead, would he take after Beth and Casey?" So far, the choice of suspects seemed weak to Sloan.

"Who knows?" Jenner shrugged. "Ned always did have a screw loose, if you ask me."

"Any more?" Sloan asked, rubbing his chin thoughtfully.

"A whole list. There was a water rights dispute between Dad and Fred Donner. Fred lost not only the dispute but the family homestead, as well."

Sloan let out a long, low whistle. "Any way these guys could have been in on it together?"

"I wish I knew," Jenner said, tossing his cane onto the floor and dropping into a recliner. He rubbed his eyes as if suddenly tired. "Betty Landsburg lost her rooming house. Jonah turned it into kind of a minimall. Slim Purcell lost his prize quarter horse in a bet."

"Corey Stills blames Dad for the breakup of his marriage because his wife, Grace, had an affair with Dad," Max said.

Sloan's brows quirked.

"Dad was a ladies' man," Jenner admitted.

"Like Ned Jansen."

Jenner lifted a shoulder and finished his drink. "Then there was Randy Calhoun."

"The hired hand?" Sloan asked.

"I was there the day Dad fired him—not only fired him but humiliated him in front of all the other hands. The man had been a loyal employee for years, but Dad was certain that Randy had started stealing cattle from him." Jenner's blue eyes darkened with the memory. "That day, Randy was drunk, which didn't happen very often. He had a drinking problem, but usually kept it under control. Dad had his old Winchester with him—I think he'd been hunting squirrels—and he told Randy that he was out. Chester, the ranch foreman, was supposed to watch over him, make sure he packed and cleared out. I tried to stand up for Randy, nearly quit myself, but Dad wouldn't listen."

"How long was that before your dad was killed?"

"About a month."

"Did Randy have any connection with Barry White?"

"They were friends, drinking buddies. Spent time together at the Black Anvil."

Sloan rubbed his jaw and stared at his friend. "If you stood up for him, why would he want to hurt you or your son by running Beth off the road? Or why burn down the stables?" Crossing one booted foot onto his knee, he thought aloud, "Maybe everyone's been barking up the wrong tree—assuming that whoever's behind the attacks was seeking revenge against Jonah. But unless the culprit's a mental case, he would've stopped when Jonah died." He glanced at the two brothers. "Have you ever considered that whoever's behind this isn't an enemy of your father's, but an enemy of yours?"

Jenner's jaw clenched tight and Max's lips thinned with worry.

"Even Casey or your mother could have made enemies."

"Damn, but this is gettin' complicated," Jenner said under his breath, but Sloan suspected this wasn't new territory. Max's shoulders slumped.

"It's possible, I suppose."

"More than possible," Jenner agreed.

Sloan didn't like the idea; in fact it scared the hell out of him. Somehow it felt safer to blame the culprit's motives on a hatred of Jonah McKee. A man who was hellbent against one of the living members of the family seemed more deadly because his mission wasn't yet finished. Who knew how far he would go?

Although Jonah's accident had been the only fatality, that was just sheer luck. Jenner and Dani Stewart had nearly died in the fire and Casey had been the target of the rifle attack.

Whoever was behind the plot against the McKees was intent on killing and wouldn't give up.

"I'll want a list of anyone the family might distrust. Dig deep. Start with your grandmother and work through your mother and the rest of you. Think hard and don't pull any punches. Concentrate on any grudges that might exist with you and someone associated, even remotely, with Barry White.''

''That could take a while,'' Max said.

''I'll need the beginning of the list tomorrow morning.''

''You don't ask for much, do you?'' Jenner said with a grin.

''Just doin' my job and tryin' to get paid.''

Jenner stood and stretched, but the lines of worry didn't leave his face. ''You think anyone will attack the ranch again?''

''I don't know,'' Sloan admitted.

''Hell—''

''Or they could attack anything owned by a McKee. Anyone close to you.''

Jenner's nostrils flared and he kicked the chair in frustration. ''We'd better hire extra security.''

''Already have,'' Max reminded him.

''Maybe it's not enough.'' His gaze centered on Sloan. ''I expect that you'll stay here at the ranch—be a bodyguard to Casey, Mom and Mavis.''

Sloan nodded; he'd already decided that he wasn't going to let Casey very far out of his sight. Not until the madman was captured.

''Make sure that Casey doesn't do anything stupid again and that Mom and Mavis are safe. I'll be in the apartment in town with Beth and Cody, and Max will be at his place. Both phone numbers are on a list by the phone in the kitchen. Come on, you can bunk down in my old room. It's right next to Casey's.''

''I'm not one for sitting around,'' Sloan reminded him as he thought ahead; being this close to Casey and having to keep his hands off her would be torture. He followed Jenner down the paneled hallway.

''I know, I know, but we could use another good hand around here. Bateman's bull tore down the fence between

his place and ours a few days ago and we were just waiting for the weather to clear in order to fix it. Right now
it's patched. And the stock need to be fed, the pipes
warmed and ice chipped out of the troughs. A couple of
mares are due to foal, and if that isn't enough to keep you
busy, there's always firewood that needs to be chopped.''

"All this and watch over your family?"

"Should be simple for an all-around cowboy-detective
Native American tracker like you."

"Piece of cake."

Jenner grinned over his shoulder. "I thought so.
This—'' he hooked a thumb at a closed door on the right
side of the corridor ''—is Casey's room. Mine was here.''
Shoving open the door, he walked through and snapped
on the lights. Sloan eyed the surroundings. Queen-size oak
bed, thick quilt, built-in bookshelves stacked with trophies
of roping and riding, weight bench shoved into a corner,
television mounted on the wall near the window, and private bath. A rich boy's room. He thought back to his room
in Warm Springs. It had been added on to the house, a
lean-to barely big enough to stand in, with a single bare
bulb, hand-me-down chest of drawers, small mirror and
comic books stashed under a secondhand twin bed. But it
had been home and warm when the winter wind had
blasted through the town.

"This'll do," he drawled, and Jenner seemed embarrassed. Sloan knew why. Ever since he'd left the Rocking
M to make it on his own, Jenner had lived a simple life,
moving from place to place, all of his life's possessions
packed in a single duffel bag and bedroll.

"Good. I'll see ya in the morning."

"Wait a minute." Sloan's voice halted Jenner. "You
know any cowboy, long and lean, weathered face with a
broken nose, brown hair long and in a ponytail, wears
black and has boots with silver chains on the heels."

Jenner thought for a minute, then shook his head.

"I think he hangs out at the Black Anvil," Sloan added.

"What'd he do?"

"Don't know, but like I told Revere and the sheriff, I saw him at a roadside diner in Spokane the day before we were attacked. Seems too coincidental. Could be he somehow followed us to the hotel. Maybe someone on the staff would recognize him, but if he did register, my guess is he'd use an alias. I keep trying to remember his name... Mike, Miles...something like that."

"I'll think on it," Jenner said, his lips thinning thoughtfully.

After Jenner and Max left, Sloan unloaded the truck. He went inside to Casey's room, opened the door and found her lying on the bed, asleep, her hair billowing around her peaceful face. Beautiful. Intriguing. A woman of fire and ice, strength and determination. A woman who touched him in ways he'd forgotten existed.

Frowning at his thoughts, he reminded himself that she was a rich girl and had been, in her own way, pampered. Just as Jane had been. Jaw tight, he left her nylon bag near the door, closed the blinds to her room and gently yanked the patchwork quilt and drew it over her body. She felt warm, smelled of lavender, and it was all he could do not to linger. Brushing a strand of hair from her eyes, he kissed her temple, then ignoring the swelling that had begun beneath his jeans, walked softly out of the room.

He acquainted himself with the house, locked all the doors, made sure the windows were secure, then made his way back to Jenner's room. Dog tired, he kicked off his boots and stripped down to his shorts. He'd rest, but only for a few hours, because whoever was out there stalking the McKee family wasn't going to give up.

It was nearly noon before Casey was finally up, showered and changed into fresh clothes. She should be thrilled, she told herself as she brushed out her hair; she was home again. She was safe. She was *alive!*

But she and Sloan were no longer alone, and waking

up in bed without him brought a lingering sadness she couldn't quite understand. Instinctively she realized that it wasn't just because they'd made love, at least she hoped not, but the melancholy clung to her like her shadow. Somehow she'd have to get rid of the sense of depression. Sloan would be leaving in a few days or as soon as his job here was finished. That was all there was to it. He wouldn't look back and neither should she.

Setting the brush on the bureau, she decided it was time to get on with the rest of her life. She'd had a lot of hours to think while being bound and sometimes gagged and she'd come to terms with her future. She didn't want to live at the ranch the rest of her life; she needed some sense of independence, but she couldn't be too far away, either. She'd tried the life of the big city. The bright lights of L.A. had been dazzling at first; the exciting city had pulsed with a life all its own. But the allure had faded with the everyday problems of commuting, smog, crowds and her own unfulfilled ambitions.

So, even though she'd told Sloan she was considering moving to Portland or Seattle, she realized that she had to be closer to home. She'd find an apartment in Dawson City, where she would try to substitute teach for the remainder of the year, and hope to eventually find a full-time job working with kids. *And what about Sloan? Are you just going to forget him? Chalk him up as an interesting experience?* She glowered at her reflection, shook her head and decided that she'd simply have to find a way to get over him. That thought caused her to stop as she reached for the handle of the door. Get over *what?* It wasn't as if they were in love or anything. It was just circumstances, physical chemistry and a moment of weakness. That was all.

But you've never been weak before, have you? Never let a man touch you too intimately, much less let him talk you into his bed. No, Casey McKee, weakness isn't a part of your nature. You made love to Sloan Redhawk because

*you wanted to and it didn't have anything to do with grat-
itude for his saving your life, either. You wanted to make
love and you wanted to make love to him. No one else.
In all your grown-up life, only him.*

Swallowing hard, she squared her shoulders and told
herself to forget him; she was better off without a silent,
brooding man complicating her life.

She headed straight to the kitchen where Kiki was busy
peeling carrots and potatoes. Beef broth was simmering
on the stove, lending the air a warm, spicy odor. "'Bout
time you woke up," Kiki teased. "I thought you might
sleep 'round the clock."

"Almost."

"There's coffee warming, if you're interested."

"What, no espresso? No cappuccino?"

Kiki chuckled. "No, city gal, there ain't. Just dark, bitter, gut-rotting ranch coffee around here. You missed
breakfast, but I could scramble some eggs and there's left-
over biscuits and—"

"I'm really not that hungry, but the coffee sounds
great." Casey grabbed a mug from the cupboard and
poured herself a cup of the strong brew, then sat at the
table. She glanced out the window to the barn, and her
insides lurched as she spied Sloan standing in the paddock, ankle-deep in snow, talking with Chester Wilcox,
the ranch foreman. As if he'd been a part of the Rocking
M for years.

She couldn't help the expectant little beat of her heart
and chastised herself for being such a fool.

"I wasn't sure how long he'd still be here—Sloan, I
mean. I thought he was paid to bring me back here and
then he'd leave..." Or had he said something about hanging around until the criminals were caught?

"Him leave without botherin' to say goodbye?" One
of Kiki's steely eyebrows elevated a fraction.

"I didn't think it was necessary."

"Didn't ya now?" Kiki dried her hands, then sliced off

two thick slabs of homemade bread, which she popped into the toaster. "Nope, the way I hear it, he's stayin' on as a ranch hand and a kind of security guard for the Rocking M. At least until the culprit who's been causin' all this trouble is caught." She reached for another potato from a ten-pound bag lying open on the counter.

Casey's stomach tightened. "Oh."

"He's takin' over Jenner's room for the time being."

"Is he?" She warmed her hands around her mug and didn't say more. The thought of Sloan being at the ranch was comforting in one way, disconcerting in another. She knew he'd do his level best to keep everyone in the family safe, but then there was her heart to consider.... She was attracted to him, dangerously so, and if she ever did fall in love she would probably fall for a man like him. She'd tried to convince herself for years that she wanted the button-down type. Sharp suits, good job, easy smile, educated to the hilt and yet... She'd always been more attracted to the rough-and-tumble men of the range—not that she'd been involved with any. At least not until Sloan. She'd been smarter than that.

Kiki plopped a plate of toast and a jar of raspberry jam on the table in front of her, but Casey's eyes strayed through the window and past the curtain of falling snow to Sloan, his Stetson firmly in place, only a fringe of black hair visible near the sheepskin collar of his jacket.

What was she going to do about him?

Nothing. There was nothing she could do.

In the privacy of her bedroom, she dialed the long-distance number of the women's shelter in Seattle. On the third ring, a woman answered and Casey explained who she was. "I'm looking for Clarisse James," she said.

"Ms. James is no longer here," was the abrupt reply.

"But a week ago—"

"I'm sorry. If you want to leave a message I'll see that it's passed along to her."

"I need to talk to her."

"Is that what you want to say?"

Frustrated, Casey gritted her teeth. "Please tell her that Casey McKee called. I'm all right and back in Rimrock. She can reach me at the number for the ranch." After rattling off the telephone number, Casey hung up and wished she knew that her friend was okay.

She saw her ring—the silver band set with turquoise that she'd fished out of her pocket earlier. She'd always loved the ring. Jenner had bought it for her when he'd been on the rodeo circuit and had stopped somewhere in New Mexico. Now it reminded her of the day Barry White had demanded she take it off to send to her family. Her stomach turned at the memory, but she was determined not to let her abductors win. She slipped the ring over her finger and didn't even wince; her hands had nearly healed. "There," she said, glancing at her reflection. All of her was beginning to heal.

She heard the front door burst open. "Aunt Casey! Aunt Casey!" Hillary's voice, punctuated by the sharp, fast tap of the child's boots against the floor, carried through the house.

Casey dashed out of her room just as her five-year-old niece came charging down the hall. With a squeal of delight, Hillary hurtled her little body into Casey's eager embrace. Chubby arms circled her neck. "Did your daddy bring you?"

"Daddy and Skye," Hillary said. "They got to make plans about the wedding. I get to be a flower girl!"

"Do you?"

"And wear a fancy dress and shoes!" Hillary beamed, her cheeks bright from the cold, her eyes glowing at the prospect of a wedding. "They said some bad guy took you away and hid you in a cabin in the mountains."

"True, unfortunately," Casey said as she transferred Hillary to her hip and carried her back toward the sound of excited voices.

"But Uncle Jenner's friend rescued you."

"That he did." Her heart warmed at the mention of Sloan.

"Were you scared?" Hillary asked.

"Nah!" Casey said, then, deciding that she should be a little more honest with her niece, sighed. "Well, yeah, I was a little. But I knew your daddy wouldn't let me stay up there forever."

Skye was hanging her coat on a clothes tree near the front door. Her blond hair fell around her shoulders and a smile crossed her face when she spied Casey. "Thank God you're safe!" she said. "I was so worried..." She let her voice trail off when Hillary's eyebrows drew together. "I mean, it just wasn't the same here without you."

"Are you gonna ask her?" Hillary demanded.

"Ask me what?"

Skye winked at the curly-headed girl before meeting Casey's curious gaze. "If you'll be in the wedding. Dani's going to be my matron of honor...at least I think she is," she said as a shadow passed over her gaze, "but I'd like you to stand up for me, as well."

"You get to be in the wedding, too!" Hillary enthused.

"Of course I will," Casey said with a grin. "I think a wedding's just what we need to lift some spirits around here."

"Well, there's going to be one. We didn't want to send out any invitations until we were sure you were all right, but they're going out in the mail today. The wedding's scheduled for the weekend of Christmas. That cuts it kind of close—only two and a half weeks away—but we figured no one would mind, what with the extenuating circumstances. It's going to be small, anyway, here in the house, with only about fifty guests."

"Small or not, you've got a lot of work cut out for you."

Skye blew her bangs from her eyes. "I think we can handle it."

Hillary, impatient with the conversation, wiggled out of Casey's arms and announced she was going outside to ride her horse.

"It's snowing," Skye said gently. "Maybe another time."

Hillary shook her head. "Daddy will let me."

"He usually lets you ride when Dani's here to instruct you, but she's not coming by today."

"Doesn't matter. Uncle Jenner can teach me or that guy who saved Aunt Casey. He's a cowboy, isn't he?"

"Yes, but—"

Hillary didn't stop to listen. She yanked open the door.

"Hey, wait. Let me zip your jacket...." Skye's voice trailed after the girl who would become her stepdaughter. Embarrassment staining her cheeks, Skye closed the door behind Hillary, who raced across the porch and through the snow to the paddock. "I'm afraid she inherited her father's stubborn streak."

"It's a McKee family trait."

"Don't I know?" Skye said with a laugh, and Casey was reminded of the pride and lies that had caused Skye and Max to break up years ago. Only this past summer had they found that their love was strong enough to enable them to endure the pain of the past and face the future. Oh, if only she could find a love like that.

"But you came back, didn't you?" Casey observed as they walked to the kitchen, where the scents of a spicy stew mingled with the aroma of carrot cake. "Despite everything."

"Yeah," Skye agreed, gazing through the window to the barn where Max was talking with Jenner, Chester and Sloan. As Hillary approached them, he leaned down and, in one swift motion threw her into the air, caught her and slung her over his broad shoulders. "Max was a hard act to follow."

"You never got over him."

"No," Skye admitted as Casey poured them each a cup of coffee from the pot still warming. "I told myself I did, but it was a lie."

"Same with Beth and Jenner."

"I suppose." Skye sat in a chair next to the window. Snow collected in the corners of the panes and the warm air of the kitchen caused steam to fog the glass. "I guess when you fall in love, I mean, really fall in love with the right man, you never fall out of it—not completely. I've never considered myself particularly romantic, but when it came to Max...well, it's hard to explain. Nothing like it had ever happened to me before." She took a sip of her coffee, but her gaze remained fixed on the man she loved, while Casey slid into a chair on the opposite side of the table. Kiki, in a rare moment of sensitivity as if she knew the conversation was private, turned up the volume of the radio. A Garth Brooks song was echoing through the room when Kiki headed out to do the laundry.

Skye's relationship with Max hadn't been smooth. They'd been lovers but had a falling-out, mostly instigated by Jonah, who knew of Skye's apparent inability to have children and felt that his firstborn son should marry another woman, Colleen Wheeler. Jonah had lied about Skye to Max and even created some incriminating evidence that seemed to prove that she was just using him, that she wanted only to further her career as a doctor and wasn't interested in a husband, only dating him because of his money. Skye had left town, and Max, brokenhearted and believing that she had betrayed him, had taken his father's advice and married Colleen. The result of their short, unhappy union was Hillary, the apple of Max's eye.

As if reading Casey's thoughts, Skye said, "Everything worked out for the best, I think." She didn't elaborate, but Casey understood. If it hadn't been for Max's marriage to Colleen, he never would have become a father.

Skye had been told her chances of bearing children were nearly zero.

"So, tell me what can I do to help with the wedding plans," Casey said.

"I wish I knew where to start. What I need is more time. Even though Jenner and Beth have helped out a lot by managing the apartment house, I still have a million things to do. Beth's been a dream—she helps out at the clinic, too. We needed a nurse of her caliber. I don't know what we'll do once she and Jenner get married and move into the lodge next summer. Oh, well, I guess we'll cross that bridge when we come to it."

Casey couldn't imagine the ranch without Jenner. Though he'd been away for a period of years, off chasing his dreams of becoming a rodeo star while he rebelled against their father, the Rocking M had never been the same without him.

But then, things were changing. Quickly.

Skye set her cup on the table and folded her hands under her chin. Skewering the woman who would become her sister-in-law with a searching look, she said, "Why don't you tell me all about Sloan Redhawk."

"What's to tell?"

Skye's lips twitched upward. "Lots, unless I miss my guess," she said, glancing out the window to the paddock. Max was leading a horse through the heavy snow while Jenner, Chester and Sloan looked on. "That man is one sexy cowboy. And don't tell me you haven't noticed, because I won't believe you. I just saw the way you looked at him, and believe me, Casey, I know that look. You're in love with him, aren't you?"

Chapter Eight

Sloan hated inactivity. Worse yet, he hated the feeling that while he was doing nothing other than trying to protect Casey, she was a sitting duck. Oh, he was busy enough, he supposed, as he sat astride a gray gelding and blinked against the snow, searching the drifts and brush for signs of any cattle that might have strayed from the herd. But this work, the kind he usually enjoyed, was little more than irritating for him now because he wanted to do something, *anything* to find the bastard behind Casey's abduction.

He'd started his search with Jimmy Rickert, but the little snitch hadn't revealed anything. He'd checked Steve Jansen's work orders—the ones the sheriff's department had already subpoenaed. He'd even started a computer check of boot companies that sold black leather boots with chains on the heels. But it wasn't enough. Even background searches—on top of the ones he'd already conducted—of the suspects hadn't gained him any more insight.

His nerves were stretched as tight as a newly strung bow, his gut feeling telling him that Casey wasn't safe. Even though Jenner and Max were somewhere on the ranch today, Sloan didn't like being separated from her. If he had his way, he'd steal her away himself and hide her far from Rimrock until he was convinced that all the culprits involved in the plot against the McKees had been put behind bars.

He found a small herd of five cows huddled against a windbreak of spindly pines. Shaggy red coats stood out against the stark, snow-covered ground. As he had since he was a kid on his grandfather's ranch, he used his horse and voice to move the lethargic animals, urging them to follow the lead cow, who plodded through the drifts back to the central area of the ranch. Within half an hour, they were in sight of the herd, and with a loud bawl, the lead cow picked up the pace, lumbering toward the other disinterested animals. Knowing that the animals would now return safely to the herd, Sloan rode along the fence line, found the break and repaired it as best he could, restretching the broken, rusted wire and staking it together with a branch from a pine tree. His efforts were only temporary; once the weather had improved, this whole stretch of fence would have to be replaced.

But it wasn't his problem. He'd be gone long before spring began to thaw the frozen ground; hopefully he'd be on his own ranch, with his own herds of range cattle and quarter horses. He climbed into the saddle, clucked his tongue, and the gray responded, trotting after the cattle.

Sloan had talked things over with Max and Jenner, the FBI, Sheriff Hammond Polk and even Rex Stone, the private investigator whom Virginia McKee had refused to kick off the case. In Sloan's opinion, Stone was a slimy bastard, an unprincipled man who would do whatever he had to—including breaking the law—to get what he wanted.

A lot like you, my friend, an inner voice taunted, and he couldn't really argue. Hadn't he, like Rex Stone, accepted the case because of the lure of dollar signs? Wouldn't he bend the law as far as possible to put the right man behind bars? Wouldn't he damn near kill to protect Casey? And really, how noble were his intentions when he was anticipating accepting the reward money and then leaving?

His jaw clenched painfully at the thought of putting distance between himself and Casey. Though he'd known her less than a week, he'd grown attached to her, looked forward to being with her, enjoyed her quick wit and sharp tongue. And then there was the matter of sleeping with her. He couldn't quite forget the feel of her body pressed willingly against him, her soft, feminine curves molding to the harder male angles of his body.

He'd kept his distance, sleeping restlessly in the room next to hers, never giving in to the urge to go to her. He couldn't. Making love to her had been a mistake—a huge error in judgment. He'd let his body rule his mind and he wouldn't let it happen again.

He squared his hat on his head and growled a curse at himself as he clucked to his horse and headed back to the house. Overhead, the sky was the color of gunmetal. More snow had been predicted though the intense storms seemed to have passed through.

Within minutes, the buildings of the Rocking M were in sight. His horse trotted toward the barn and pulled up short near a water trough where a thin stream of water was visible in the ice. Sloan climbed out of the saddle. A young hand by the name of Hank Something-or-other, who'd been chipping ice off the trough, offered to take his horse. Sloan didn't argue, just handed the kid his reins. Turning, he spied her and the air froze in his lungs and seemed to stay there indefinitely.

Casey was standing on a ladder, stringing Christmas lights along the eaves of the house. She glanced up at the sound of his boots breaking through the snow, and the smile she threw him was enough to melt the ice surrounding his heart. Her head was uncovered and snowflakes caught in her dark hair and melted against the flush of her cheeks.

"Need help?" he asked.

"Maybe a little. Hillary was working with me, but she bailed out when Kiki offered her some hot cocoa." Casey plugged one strand of lights into another. "Ever done this before?"

"Nope." Not even in L.A. while Jane was alive. Funny, he hadn't thought much about Jane in the past twenty-four hours.

"Okay, novice, you untangle the cords and hand them up to me and I'll do the rest."

His gloves felt awkward as he straightened the strings of colored bulbs, plugged them into each other when instructed to do so and watched as she diligently wove the wires around icicles and up the few gables of the old ranch house. At one point he thought they were done, but she only laughed at him and insisted that he loop strings of smaller lights through the shrubbery and into a solitary dwarf apple tree in the corner of the front yard. By the time they were finished, the afternoon sky had darkened.

"Okay, stand here," she ordered as she dashed back to the front door and flipped a switch. Hundreds of lights blazed in a rainbow of colors, flashing scarlet, gold, green and blue against the snow. The lights in the leafless apple tree were clear and winked slowly. "What do you think?" Casey was at his side again, surveying her work with a critical eye.

"That the electric company might run out of juice."

"No, seriously."

"Seriously?" he repeated, and she turned to find him staring at her, his black eyes somber, his face ruddy with the cold. He reached up a gloved hand and brushed a snowflake from her hair. "I think you might be the most incredible woman I've ever met."

Stunned by the compliment, she couldn't speak, and when his hands slid to her shoulders, she felt a jolt of anticipation, a rush of adrenaline that caused her heart to pump just a little faster. As their gazes touched and held fast, she knew he was going to kiss her. Her mouth turned dry and she tilted her head just as his cold lips brushed across her mouth.

Her eyelids fluttered down and his fingers tightened over her shoulders. "Casey," he breathed into her mouth before his lips caught fire and the cool kiss heated in the snow-dusted night. She wrapped her arms around his waist, and through thick layers of clothing, she felt his heat, the urgency of his body. His tongue pressed against her teeth and her mouth opened easily, inviting him in, wanting to taste and touch him.

With a groan, he yanked her against him, and his breathing came hot and shallow against her ear. Her blood thundered through her veins, pulsing at her temples, pounding in her throat. His smell—horses, leather and musk—invaded her nostrils and brought images of making love to him into the forefront of her mind.

Her legs were suddenly weak, and when he lifted his head to stare into her eyes, she saw the hot intensity, the fires of desire flaming bright in their coal black depths.

She'd told Skye that there was nothing between Sloan and her and that Skye's suddenly romantic imagination was running wild. Sloan had helped her, true, saved her life, but she wasn't involved with him. No way, no how.

But now, clinging to him beneath the thin veil of clouds blotting the moon, she doubted her own convictions. Yes, she was involved with Sloan. Yes, they were in the middle of a relationship, even an affair. But no, she didn't love him. She couldn't. He wasn't the loving kind. Whatever he'd once shared with his deceased wife, he wasn't about to share it again with any woman.

"This will never work," he said, voicing her own doubts. The words hung in the air like tiny cold shards of ice and pierced deep into her heart. Though she was thinking the very same thoughts, to hear them spoken hurt to the quick.

"I know."

"We can't—"

"I know!" She pulled out of his embrace and cleared her throat. Pretending that she felt nothing, she tossed her hair off her face and checked her watch. "Come on. It's cold and late. Kiki will be fit to be tied if we hold up dinner." She started back to the house.

"Casey..." The sound of her name caught her off guard, but she steeled her heart.

"What is it you want from me, Redhawk?" she demanded, whirling to face him again. Planting her fists on her hips, she glared at him and felt the heat of her temper rise in her cheeks.

His jaw tightened. "I wish I knew."

"The way I see it, you're here because you have a job to do. Nothing more, nothing less."

"That's the way you see it?" He lifted a skeptical brow.

"Can't be any other."

Frowning, he squared his hat on his head. "You're more to me than a job, Casey."

She felt a jolt in her heart and ignored it. "Then you're a fool."

His sudden smile caught her by surprise. "No doubt about it." Grabbing her elbow, he spun her to face him, held her close enough that she felt the warm fog of his breath and hesitated. She expected him to kiss her, felt that special little thrill whenever he was so close as he slowly tipped up her chin with one gloved finger and stared straight into her eyes. "And you're a liar, Casey McKee. A damned sweet liar, but a liar nonetheless."

"I *don't* lie."

"Right." His lips settled over hers and she wanted to pull back, to shove him away and prove that he meant nothing to her, but she didn't. Instead, a small moan escaped from her lips, and as he pressed closer, her spine bowed so that her head was angled upward to him. Heat swirled in her blood, her senses dimmed and snow fell around them in soft white flakes that seemed to curtain them from the rest of the world. When he lifted his head, he stared at her with an intensity that caused her heart to pound. "You're the last person I should be involved with."

"We're not involved," she said, angry with herself for lying just as he'd accused her.

"Yeah, that's what I try to tell myself, too. It doesn't work." He kissed her again, lightly this time, then slowly released her. "Don't want to keep Kiki waiting now, do we?" Shoving his hands into his pockets, he headed toward the house and the magic of the moment before was broken.

Casey trudged after him and wondered what in the world she was going to do.

Sloan's cover was blown. Everyone in Rimrock knew that Casey had been rescued by the ex-rodeo rider turned investigator. He could no longer expect any loose tongues to confide in him at the Black Anvil. The culprits, whoever they were, would be more tight-lipped than ever when he was around.

But there was nothing he could do about it.

After four days at the ranch, with the snow deep enough to keep him close to the house—close to Casey—he was going stir-crazy, thinking that someone out there was plotting against them. The nights were worse. Just knowing that she was only one room away burned through his mind and kept him tossing and turning and spending more time than he wanted beneath the stinging spray of a cold shower.

Still, he wanted her. Plain and simple. He wanted her as he'd never wanted another woman.

He'd taken to staring out the window and watching the snowy terrain, while his mind spun with erotic thoughts of making love to her. Though he'd only slept with her that one night on the road back to Rimrock, he couldn't stop thinking about it.

He rubbed the kinks from his neck and watched as a night owl swooped beneath the blue glow of a security light near the barn, its shadow passing over the silver ground. He couldn't sleep, his nerves jangled, and he decided that he could use a cup of coffee. He was familiar with the house and could walk barefoot across the cool plank floors without making a sound.

The ranch house itself wasn't all that assuming, not for the richest man in the county. But Jonah had seemed to have a sense of loyalty to his family's original homestead, and over the years the old home had been updated and added to so that it was a single sweeping story with an incredible view of the acreage that was now part of the Rocking M. But it wasn't a grand mansion—it was a livable house.

In the kitchen, he snapped on the lights, heated water in the microwave and waited. Two spoons of bitter-tasting, freeze-dried coffee later, he was on his way back to Jenner's room, wondering what his next step would be. He couldn't just sit and wait for someone else to make a move.

He'd planned on seeing Barry White, who was being extradited to Oregon, the minute the bastard landed in the county jail. So far, the FBI hadn't been able to bully a story from him. Even though they'd offered him a good deal with a shortened prison sentence if he cooperated and named his partner or partners, he'd kept his silence. He'd hired an attorney, a slick guy from Dawson City by the name of Reggie Camp.

Camp seemed to be working for free because White didn't have a dime to his name. Either Reggie thought the notoriety of this case would bring him bigger cases in the future and make the value of his services go up, or someone was paying Barry's bills for him. Sloan smiled in the darkness. That was an interesting angle. Who? Steve Jansen had a little money and maybe Ned did, as well. But Randy Calhoun was supposed to be broke—almost destitute. The Purcell family had a few bucks between them. Otis had quite a bit of land, some of it timber rich. Fred Donner wasn't supposed to have much cash, not since Jonah had laid claim to his water rights and eventually his ranch.

Max was trying to right some wrongs from the past, including working a deal with Fred to give him back what was rightfully his. But Fred wasn't interested, had nearly spit on Max when he'd made the offer. Yep, there were a lot of people who hated the McKees. None of them rich men, yet someone was able to finance Reggie Camp.

Not for the first time, Sloan wondered about a conspiracy. Maybe all the citizens of the town who'd been ripped off by Jonah McKee had banded together and formed an evil coalition determined to ruin everyone and everything associated with the McKee name.

So who the hell was it?

He rounded the corner and trod silently down the hallway, his mind working.

Max was a lawyer. Maybe he could make a few inquiries, find out about Reggie Camp—who his clients were, if he could be bought, just how far he'd bend the law. Or did Camp, too, have a personal ax to grind against the McKees?

He opened the door to Jenner's room and slipped inside.

"Sloan?" Casey's voice caught him unawares and he nearly dropped his cup.

"What're you doing here?" he demanded, spying her on the window ledge, one leg tucked up beneath her as she leaned against the casing.

"Couldn't sleep."

"You shouldn't be here."

She didn't argue, just stared up at him with those round hazel eyes. Even with only the pale light from the white snow filtering into the room, he could see her clearly. A soft white robe had been cinched around her waist and her hair was dark against the thick terry-cloth fabric.

Sloan closed the door quietly behind him. "Is there something you want?"

"Just to know where I stand." When he didn't answer, she added, "With you."

"I thought I made that clear." His heart was pounding and he kept his distance, certain that if he walked any closer to her, he wouldn't be able to resist the fragrance of her hair, the feel of her skin, the throaty sound of her voice as she whispered. "You knew I was staying here long enough to put whoever is behind Jonah's murder and your kidnapping behind bars."

"What if you don't find him?"

"I will."

"You've never failed?"

"I said I'll find the bastard." He leaned a shoulder against the wall and sipped from his cup. The coffee was beginning to cool and tasted flat. He didn't care. "You want coffee? I made a cup—"

"I want to know what your plans are."

Fair enough. He'd give it to her with both barrels. No matter what else, he had to scare her off. Though his body screamed to touch her, to hold her, to tell her no woman fired his blood the way she did, he couldn't let his emotions and his damned lust interfere with their lives—hers or his. He hadn't kissed her since that day they'd strung the Christmas lights and he'd managed to keep his distance by sheer force of will. But she was tempting, damned tempting. He couldn't afford to give her any false signals. It wouldn't be fair—to either of them. "Okay. I plan to find the son of a bitch, just like I told you. I don't know how, when or where, but somehow I'll flush him out, and after I do, I'll collect my money, take off and buy a ranch northwest of here."

"In Warm Springs."

She remembered that? Hell, she was beginning to know a little too much about him. "Maybe."

"Your grandfather's ranch."

He stiffened. "Don't know if it's for sale."

"But you'll find out," she countered, turning her gaze from his face to stare out the window again. There was a sadness about her that he'd never seen before, a loneliness he'd rather not witness. It was easier to think of Casey as a hothead—a passionate woman who was always on the verge of losing her temper. He knew differently, of course, had seen her frightened and courageous, worried and relaxed. He'd laughed with her and held her when she'd been scared out of her mind. Hell, he'd made love to her and, at least for a few hours, forgotten all his own pain and suffering, had seen a sunnier side of life that he'd thought had disappeared, just because she was near.

"Tell me about Jane," she said, turning again to face him, her hair tumbling to rest on her collarbone. The front of her robe gaped a bit and he caught a glimpse of her skin and some kind of lace from a nightgown.

"I don't talk about her."

"Why not?"

"No point."

Tucking her feet closer to her body, she clasped her arms around her legs. "You loved her very much."

"Too much." He cleared his throat and stared at her, hoping that in so doing she would get the message and leave—not that he really wanted her to go. It would just be better. Safer. For both of them.

"How did you meet her?"

"I really don't think you should be here—"

"Do you have any children? I don't recall Jenner mentioning it."

The question seemed to bounce off the walls and ricochet through his heart. *Oh, my son. My little Tony.* "Tony. I don't think I told you about him," he admitted, his voice wooden because he couldn't allow any emotion to color his words. "He died."

"With Jane?"

"Yes." His throat worked and he took another long swallow from his cup. His hands were unsteady as the painful memories began to spin through his mind.

"Tell me about her."

"If I do, will you leave?"

She hitched her chin up a notch and waited. Why she'd decided that she had to know about the wife he adored, she didn't really understand. She'd come to this room, not to discuss Jane, but because she couldn't sleep, and knowing Sloan was so close had made it impossible not to want to be with him. She wasn't planning to try to seduce him, of course, but...if he'd just hold her again....

He set his cup on the top of the television and closed his eyes for a minute, as if gathering thoughts that ran in a painful jumble through his brain. "Jane was a student at UCLA when I met her. I was new on the police force and we met through a common friend. Jane was... different from anyone I'd ever met before—she seemed more vital somehow. Anyway, we hit it off right away, began seeing each other and one thing led to another and we got married. A simple ceremony." His voice lowered. "At a justice of the peace. Her parents didn't approve. Thought she should finish school and find someone...different." An edge of anger flavored his words.

"Different?"

"Different from a half-breed Indian boy who'd managed to get himself through school and become a cop."

"Oh," she said as if she understood. She didn't. Any parents should have been pleased to have Sloan for a son-in-law, but then parents rarely were satisfied with their children's choices—she only had to look at her two brothers and her father to prove that point.

"Jane's folks were from San Francisco. Old money. Had big plans for their only daughter. Thought she should marry a doctor or a lawyer or at least someone with money and background. But Jane was a stubborn thing, told her parents she was going to live her own life. Once she married me, they cut her off, never called or wrote, not even when our son was born." His voice had lowered to a grim whisper. "I only saw them at the funeral. Even then they didn't speak to me—stood apart with their own circle of friends." His gaze became dull and he couldn't manage to hide the pain in his voice.

"I'm sorry," she whispered.

"You don't even know what happened."

"I know you lost a family you loved." She ached to hold him, to say she understood, but she didn't dare.

Shoving his hands into the back pockets of his jeans, he scowled. His face turned suddenly savage and a quiet fury burned in his eyes. "Lost them," he repeated with a snort. "That's a nice way of putting it." He crossed the room and stopped bare inches from her, close enough that she could feel the angry jets of his breath. "Don't you want to know what happened?"

"Only if you want to tell me," she said, suddenly feeling as if she was prying into a very private part of his soul, a part he wanted to keep hidden away from her and the rest of the world. A part no one should dare question.

"Well, it turns out her folks were right—being married to me was a big mistake. One of the punks I'd put in jail got himself paroled and he came lookin' for me, planned on killing me with an explosion in my truck."

Her stomach turned over and she could scarcely breathe. "Sloan, if you don't want to—"

"You asked, damn it."

"But—"

His nostrils quivered slightly. "Jane's car was acting up—sometimes it wouldn't start, so she decided to use the pickup. Just strapped Tony into his car seat, climbed in herself, started the engine and BAM!" He rubbed his eyes with his hands as if to wipe out the memory.

"Oh, God," Casey whispered.

"So, in a way, they're dead because of me." His voice was so low she could hardly hear it, the ravages of sorrow carving deep grooves in his face.

"You couldn't have known."

His eyes slitted. "But I should have suspected, been more careful." His hand clenched and the veins stood out on his arm. She saw him relive his anguish.

"You can't blame yourself." She reached forward, touching the side of his face.

"Who, then?" He grabbed her hand and squeezed. "Who, Casey?"

"The guy who did it! You said they knew who it was. He was caught, wasn't he?"

"Yep."

A chill swept down her spine.

"You—"

"I didn't kill him. But only because my partner broke it up. I had my hands around that punk's neck and I wanted to squeeze until he stopped kicking, but my partner convinced me to back off, that if I did the bastard bodily harm, my hide would have been nailed to the wall and the guy might walk. After killing my wife and son. So we hauled the creep off to jail and I turned in my badge."

"Just like that?"

He dropped her hand. "I only went back to testify, then I split. Took up riding rodeo. Wasn't much good at first, but it all came back and pretty soon I was scratching out a living and keeping mobile. Didn't want the grass to grow under my feet."

Or get involved with another woman. He didn't have to say it, but Casey could read between the lines. He was still blaming himself for something that happened years before. Time hadn't healed his wounds; the scars were still fresh and bleeding.

Unable to help herself, she slowly stood, reached up and touched his face again, her palms pressed gently to his beard-rough cheeks. He stiffened, but didn't move, and she let her hands slide down his strong, inflexible shoulder muscles as she leaned her head into the crook of his neck. "I'm so sorry," she murmured.

"It's over."

"Is it?" She tilted her head up to his and brushed her lips against his.

Groaning, he wrapped his arms around her. "Casey, please..."

"Please what?" She kissed him again and this time he didn't protest. His lips crashed against hers in repressed fury and he dragged her close, one hand on the lower curve of her back, the other twining in her hair.

"Don't tease me," he growled.

"I'm not."

Swearing under his breath, he tried visibly to get control of himself. "We can't. Not here. Not now."

"When?" she demanded, refusing to let go.

"Maybe never."

"I won't believe that."

"Casey, it won't work."

"Why not?"

He closed his eyes as if waging a silent battle with himself. His muscles grew taut; his jaw tight. "You and I...we want different things in life." His rejection stung. "You want to settle down, have a family, drive a station wagon, join the PTA. You're used to a life-style that I can't provide—''

''I didn't ask you to marry me,'' she said, hurting inside. ''Did you think I came in here, planned to seduce you and then what…expect to walk down the aisle?'' He didn't say a word, just looked at her with hot black eyes. ''I just wanted to talk to you, Sloan.''

Silently he called her a liar, but took a step backward, leaned against the wall, crossed his muscular arms over his chest and waited. ''So talk.''

''I thought we should get to know each other.''

''Why?''

Her insides began to shred. ''Because…because…''

''Because we made love,'' he said, finishing for her.

''Yes!''

''Casey—'' his voice was suddenly soft ''—don't do this.''

''Do what?''

''Make something more of it than it was.''

''Damn it, Sloan,'' she said, her temper exploding. ''You want me! Right now you want me!''

''Yes.'' His honesty shocked her. ''I've wanted you from the first time I saw you in that damned cabin in Montana,'' he admitted. ''All cut and scraped and scared to death—and I wanted you! Hell, that doesn't make it right.''

''We're two adults.''

''And you were a victim. I was supposed to save you, Casey, not sleep with you.''

''I wanted—''

''You were grateful. You saw me as some kind of hero on his white horse, but that's not the way it is. Don't try to make me into something I'm not, Case, because it won't work. What I am is a broken-down, out-of-work cowboy who snoops into other people's business just to pay the rent and keep enough beer in the fridge so that it's there when I need it. I don't like to be tied down and

I don't want a woman in my life.'' He shifted. ''I think you'd better leave, Case.''

''I don't believe you.''

His smile was cold. ''Don't you?''

''No, you were married once and—''

''Once is enough. I'll never go through that again.''

''You loved your wife!''

''And look what happened,'' he said as he walked across the room and threw open the door. ''Now, are you going to go quietly?'' he asked, his voice steely with determination, ''or am I going to have to wake up the whole damned house?''

Chapter Nine

Sloan was gone. Casey didn't have to ask anyone; she could just tell by the feel of the house. With a sinking sensation, she knocked on the door of Jenner's old room and, when there was no response, opened the door a crack. The bed was made and the room was cold.

She forced herself through the shower and paid more attention to her makeup than usual, hoping to hide the dark circles under her eyes—the result of another sleepless night. "Fool," she told her reflection as she thought about her confrontation with him. She should never have gone into his room uninvited, never kissed him, never played the part of a seductress.

Her cheeks burned at the memory. What was it about Sloan that brought out the worst in her? Without an answer, she dressed and dragged herself into the kitchen, where she found Jenner and Max seated at the table, arguing as they had since they were kids.

"I say we beat the living daylights out of him and find out what he knows!" Jenner asserted.

"We have to wait and see. Hammond might have some ideas."

"Hammond Polk? Are you out of your mind? He's the poorest excuse for a sheriff I've ever seen—" Jenner looked up, saw Casey and fell silent.

"What's going on?" she asked, pouring herself a cup of coffee and leaning a hip against the counter. The men exchanged glances. "Where're Mom and Grandma?"

"Both getting ready for a meeting with Rex Stone," Jenner said, shaking his head. He'd never trusted the detective and hadn't bothered hiding the fact from anyone, including Rex himself. "Then they're gonna talk to the florist and the caterer about the wedding. They're meeting Skye around noon."

The wedding. She'd nearly forgotten.

"What about Kiki?" she asked, suddenly realizing that the cook wasn't around. The kitchen seemed foreign without the staccato tap of her footsteps or the smell of baking bread or the gentle noise of her radio tuned in to a talk show or a country-and-western station.

"Car trouble—nothing serious. She's down at the garage having it worked on and she'll be here a little later. So you can cook breakfast yourself or settle for corn-flakes." Max winked at her.

Casey wasn't hungry for either. "So what were you talking about when I came into the room?" Jenner rubbed his jaw and Max avoided her eyes. "Come on, guys, give it up. I'll find out soon enough."

Max scowled, but glanced at Jenner, then turned his attention to his sister. "Okay, it's really nothing—at least not yet. But last night, Randy Calhoun and Slim Purcell got into it down at the Black Anvil. They'd both been drinking quite a bit and they never have liked each other much. Randy started insulting Purcell, and Slim took the first swing, which was just what Randy wanted. They started really going at it and Randy ended up with a busted nose. Slim lost a few teeth.''

''So?'' Fistfights at the Black Anvil weren't uncommon.

Jenner picked up the story. ''It turns out that before they started swinging and were just in the insulting stage, Randy accused Slim of being involved in your kidnapping.''

Casey's insides froze. Slim Purcell? She hardly knew the man.

''Jake, who was tending bar at the time, told the guys to take the fight outside, then called the sheriff. Hammond hauled both men to the jail, and now he and Revere are talking to both of them—trying to sort truth from fiction.''

The muscles at the base of Casey's skull knotted, bringing on a headache. ''I'm surprised you two aren't beating down the door of the jail.''

Max winked at her. ''We tried and were politely told to wait until the proper authorities had handled the interrogation their way.''

''It's a bunch of crap,'' Jenner muttered under his breath.

''What about Sloan?'' she asked, glancing through the window to the empty space where Sloan's truck had been parked. Thick ruts in the snow reaffirmed what she already knew—that he was gone. Her heart gave a little lurch, but she managed an indifferent smile.

Jenner stared at her long and hard. ''What about him?''

''I thought part of his bargain with you was that he find the culprit. Looks like he took off.''

''He's already down there, but I don't think they'll let him in on the interview,'' Max said. ''The one who's really fit to be tied is old Rex Stone. He's not happy that Redhawk's around, anyway, tried to talk Mom and Grandma into firing him.''

Jenner grinned. ''Then Redhawk had the gall to show up with you, and Stone, who hasn't found out diddly-squat, had to eat crow. Mom straightened him out and told him that he was hired to find out who killed Dad. Period.''

Casey smiled. ''I bet that went over well.''

''About as well as the proverbial lead balloon,'' Max agreed as he held up his cup, waiting for a refill.

Casey, shooting him an I'm-not-your-slave glance, grabbed the coffeepot and poured a thin stream of coffee into Max's empty mug. Truth to tell, she was glad to be back on the ranch with her brothers, relieved to be in familiar surroundings. She felt safe here, even if there was a maniac on the loose. The Rocking M was a haven, though oftentimes while growing up, she'd viewed it as a gilded prison. But she wished Sloan hadn't left. ''He'll be back then?''

''Who? Sloan?'' Max asked.

Jenner's eyes slitted. ''You two get into some kind of a row?''

Casey shrugged. ''We never see eye to eye. Why?''

'''Cause he was on the warpath this morning. About as friendly as a hungry bear. Nearly snapped my head off when I mentioned your name.'' He drained his cup. ''He's usually quiet and calm, but he sure had a bee in his shorts this morning.''

''Maybe he didn't sleep well.''

One side of Jenner's mouth lifted, but no humor sparked in his eyes. ''Funny. That's exactly what he said.'' Eyeing his sister thoughtfully, he finally answered her question. ''Yeah, he'll be back. He won't leave until he's done what he's being paid to do.''

She felt a jab of pain at the reminder that Sloan was only staying with her because of the reward money, but she didn't even flinch and wished Jenner would stop staring at her as if he was trying to figure out an intricate puzzle.

Max finished his coffee and pushed his chair from the table. ''Duty calls,'' he said as he left his mug in the sink.

"I'll be at the office if you need me. Looks like the insurance company is finally coming through. As soon as the weather breaks, we'll be able to start construction on the stables."

"Good. Well, I guess I'll stick around here for a while." Jenner checked his watch. "I told Beth I'd meet her for lunch before I had to go back to the torture chamber again."

"Physical therapy isn't torture," Casey reminded him.

"Remind me of that when I get back." Again, Max and Jenner exchanged glances. "I'll check on the stock," Jenner said, but Casey read the silent messages between her brothers.

"You're staying here for me, aren't you?"

Jenner didn't answer, but Max reached for his hat. "We're just being careful. With Dad gone, there's no man around—"

"That's what this is all about? A *man?*" She could hardly believe her ears. "This is the nineties, Max. I don't need some man to—"

"It's not just you," Jenner reminded her. "There's Mom and Mavis—"

"Oh, for God's sake, I—we—don't need a babysitter!" she snapped. "This is the Rocking M, for crying out loud! If we're not safe here, we're not safe anywhere."

"Exactly!"

"You're crazy, Jenner. Always have been, always will be."

Max reached for his leather jacket on a hook by the back door, then said, "Look, Casey, after what happened—"

"I don't care what happened. Okay, I was stupid to get into the truck with Barry, but I didn't have much choice, did I? No one's going to be crazy enough to come to the ranch and—"

Max slid his arms through the jacket. "Someone already did. They burned the stables, remember?"

"But I can't live my life like some frightened little mouse," she protested. "You've hired extra security guards for the ranch." She pinned her older brother with a furious stare. "Aren't they enough?"

Max's jaw turned to granite. "I wish I knew."

"I'm not going to be treated like some glass doll that could break at any given moment and I won't let you two bully me into staying here like a recluse or some kind of prisoner—"

"You're not a prisoner, Casey! If you want to go into town, you can go. But just wait for Sloan and he'll take you," Jenner said.

"So now he's my baby-sitter."

"Bodyguard."

"I don't need one."

Jenner flew out of his chair, but nearly stumbled as he reeled toward her and only caught himself by bracing a hand against the refrigerator. "Don't forget what happened to you," he growled. "Weren't you scared out of your mind?"

She didn't answer. Her throat was suddenly as dry as sand.

"And, am I wrong, or did someone try to shoot you?"

"But—"

Jenner's face was livid, his eyes flashing fire. "This isn't a game, Casey. Some bastard's playing for keeps. So, for now, you stay close to home, with someone— preferably Sloan—nearby."

"You're as paranoid as he is," she accused.

"I don't think so."

"Jenner, hey, slow down a little," Max, ever the voice of reason, said. "Come on, Casey, just go along with us for a little while, okay?"

Jenner snagged his cane and, with a harsh glance over

his shoulder, announced that he was going to the barns to check on the brood mares.

Max placed a comforting hand on Casey's shoulder. "Maybe this fight at the Black Anvil was the break we needed. At least maybe now we'll know who the enemy is. Just trust us. Stick with Sloan."

Stick with Sloan. Oh, Max, if you only knew.

Sloan glanced up from his uncomfortable seat in the reception area of the sheriff's office. He'd been there for hours and had heard the noon whistle in town blast just twenty minutes earlier. Alone in the small room with the cracked linoleum floor and yellowed woodwork, he could see through a glassed-in counter to a larger room partitioned into offices. One deputy sat at his desk, phone headset cradled against his shoulder, and at another, a secretary was busily typing into a computer terminal. Over the rapid clicking of the keys, the sound of piped-in music floated through air that smelled of stale cigarette smoke and disinfectant.

Hammond Polk, sweating profusely and mopping his forehead, finally emerged from behind the closed door to his office. "Thought you might be here," he said as he spied Sloan sitting in a chair, leafing through a two-year-old copy of a fly fishing magazine. Opening the gate through the counter, he shook his head. "Another dead end."

"Is that right?" Sloan sounded skeptical.

"Yep. What we got in there—" he hooked a thumb toward the interrogation room "—is just a couple of busted-up locals who had a little too much to drink. Neither one of 'em knows anything about the kidnapping," the sheriff assured him.

"Then there's no reason I can't talk to them." Stretching his full height out of his chair, Sloan looked down at the shorter man.

"Later. Right now I have to sort out who did what to whom and who's gonna press charges."

"Why would Calhoun accuse Purcell of being involved in Casey McKee's abduction?"

"Who knows? Drunks say lots of things, most of which don't make much sense. Calhoun's been a suspect since day one, so he's probably trying to put the heat on someone else. As for Purcell, well, that whole family's crazy. Old Otis, Slim's dad, is still raisin' wolf pups even though years ago one bit his daughter and made a helluva mess of her face. She just got it fixed a few weeks ago—some plastic surgeon recommended by Skye Donahue—well, anyway, that's neither here nor there, I suppose. Back to the boys, believe me, if either of their stories changes, I'll let you know."

Hammond clapped him on the shoulder as he held open the door. Sloan left but not before he decided that he'd find a way to speak with both Purcell and Calhoun before the day was out.

He spent the day downtown, eating lunch at the Shady Grove Café, listening to the local gossip, drinking coffee and talking with a few men who'd seen the fight firsthand. He checked out Steve Jansen's operation again and wondered if he should go so far as to break into the office to get a closer look at the books, perhaps a second set not meant for public inspection—not just those subpoenaed by the D.A.—and see for himself if there had been any bodywork done to a black or dark blue pickup, the one that had forced Jonah McKee's Jeep over the edge of the canyon.

Steve Jansen's was the only auto-body shop in town and he was related to Barry White. After all, Steve, though he protested his innocence and swore he had nothing to do with the kidnapping, owned the cabin where Casey had been held.

According to Hammond Polk and the FBI, Steve was a suspect, but came out clean. His books had been gone through with a fine-tooth comb and his phone records studied. His story that Barry had a key to the cabin and used it at his leisure, usually during hunting season, seemed to hold water.

But Sloan wasn't convinced. Steve's name cropped up too often to be just a coincidence. It wouldn't help to talk to Steve; his story was down pat. But what about Jimmy Rickert? Maybe it was time to talk to him again.

He had to do something and soon. Time was running out and he needed to get away from this mess and away from Casey. He was still waiting to hear from a couple of boot companies, but hadn't seen the lanky stranger whom he suspected was part of the conspiracy. He had to move fast before he became even more entangled in a relationship with Casey. She'd almost been his undoing last night. He remembered the scent of her perfume, the warmth of her skin, the sweet taste of her lips...oh, hell, he couldn't think like this! It was getting in his way.

Never before had he been so torn. On the one hand he wanted to be with Casey day and night, make sure she was safe, be with her every minute; on the other hand he knew that being with her was an emotional trap. He'd sworn to himself long ago not to get involved with another woman, and before he'd met Casey, he'd kept his vow. Since Jane's death, there had been no woman who had touched his heart, and he planned to keep it that way. All he had to do was find out who was terrorizing the Mc-Kees, put the bastard behind bars, collect his money and run.

But first, he had to find a killer. He started walking to McKee Enterprises where Max had given him temporary use of an office complete with telephone, fax machine and computer. Somehow, someway, and sometime soon, he'd flush out the creep. A grim smile caused his lips to curve. When he did, he hoped that he didn't kill the son of a bitch himself.

* * *

Kiki arrived in a bad mood. "Anything worse than car trouble, I'd like to know what it is," she groused. "And me with everything I've got to do for the wedding and Christmas. Lord, that car better not break down on me again." She kicked off her boots on the back porch, bustled into the kitchen and tossed her coat over a peg near the door. "Good thing I got a start on dinner yesterday," she said.

"You need help?" Casey asked.

Wrapping an apron around her thin waist, she shook her head. "Don't think so, but thanks for offering just the same."

The doorbell rang, Reuben barked and Kiki's scowl deepened. "Now who the devil is that?" she wondered aloud.

"I'll get it." Casey hurried to the front door, flung it open and found herself staring face-to-face with her friend. "Clarisse!"

"Hi, Casey."

Casey hugged the other woman fiercely. "I've been so worried about you."

"Are you kidding? I've been the one who was worried. The police and FBI told me what happened and…" Tears starred her eyes. "Oh, God, Casey, I was so upset. Then someone from the shelter called and said you'd been looking for me and I hauled the kids into the car and just started driving. I guess I had to see that you're all right."

"Well, come in." Casey looked around. "Your boys, where are they?"

"They both fell asleep in the car and I left them there until I knew…well, the police seemed to think that I had something to do with your disappearance—" Her throat caught and she avoided Casey's eyes.

"Don't be silly. They know better now. They were just checking every possibility. Come on, let's get the kids and bring them inside." They trudged through the snow together and found Charlie, Clarisse's five-year-old, strapped into the passenger seat, his head lolling to one side. Brian, the two-year-old, was holding his blanket and blinking as he awoke. "They're adorable," Casey said, and a pang of longing swept through her.

She wanted children someday, but in her mind's eye she didn't picture two blond boys with startling blue eyes. No, she saw herself as the mother of dark-haired children with tanned skin and brown eyes, who bore a striking resemblance to Sloan. But that was crazy. Sloan didn't want a wife or kids; he'd told her so himself. And she wasn't in the market for a husband. But as she opened the side door and helped a groggy Brian out of his car seat, she experienced a longing so intense it nearly hurt.

Charlie was beginning to wake up. "Can't we play out here?" he asked, eyeing the snow-laden barns and out-buildings. "Where are we...who's she?" He pointed a condemning finger at Casey and his lower lip protruded.

"That's the lady I told you about. My friend, Casey."

"Hi, Charlie."

Rubbing his eyes, Charlie said, "Don't like her."

"Oh, honey, sure you do. She's your friend, too," Clarisse said placatingly. "Casey, I'm sorry—"

"Don't worry about it. Let's take these two guys inside and see if Kiki can rustle 'em up some hot cocoa."

"With marshmallows?" Brian asked around a yawn.

"If you want 'em."

They lugged the boys into the kitchen, where Kiki muttered about being behind schedule, yet managed to scrounge up hot chocolate, marshmallows and cookies. Charlie was enticed from his grumpy mood, and Clarisse managed to balance Brian in her lap and help him keep his hot drink from spilling while she talked and sipped coffee.

"Outside!" Charlie announced when he'd had his fill. "Let's make a snowman."

"Snowman." Brian wriggled down from his mother's lap, but Clarisse wouldn't release him until his jacket was zipped to the chin, his mittens were in place and a stocking cap had been pulled over his ears. His brother got the same treatment, and soon they were both outside trying to roll snowballs and build snowmen.

Casey and Clarisse carried refilled mugs into the living room where they could keep an eye on the boys through the windows. Tucking a leg beneath her, Casey settled into the deep cushions in a corner of the couch and sighed as she watched the siblings argue, then work together. "You know, they're about the same age as my niece and nephew."

"Nephew?" Clarisse said. "I thought Max was divorced and he only had a daughter—Hillary, wasn't it?"

"Yes, well, I guess you're not up-to-date." Quickly Casey explained about Jenner and the son he'd only met recently. "Cody's a dynamo," she said proudly. "The spitting image of his father. Even though I've only known of him for a little while, I can't imagine him not being around. And what a change it's brought to Jenner. All of a sudden, he's gone from a touch-me-not type of cowboy to father of the year." Chuckling, she shook her head, then caught the pain in her friend's eyes. "Oh, God, Clarisse, did I say something wrong?"

"No, of course not." Clarisse dashed her tears aside. "I was just thinking of Ray. Father of the year, he wasn't." She sounded bitter as she stared through the window at her sons.

"Or husband of the year, either," Casey added sympathetically.

A muscle worked in Clarisse's jaw and she fought valiantly against an onslaught of tears. "That I could have dealt with," she said.

"You shouldn't have to."

"I'm divorcing him," she said, biting her lip as she struggled to find the right words. "It's been hard. I mean, I was taught that love was supposed to last forever, that when you said your vows, it was for a lifetime. And there's the kids to consider.'' She smiled faintly as she watched her older boy try to heave one large snowball on top of the other. ''I wanted us to stay together, to be a family, you know, the all-American dream—successful, good-looking husband, two children, nice house—and I convinced myself that we had it all, that if Ray didn't drink, but then—'' her voice wobbled ''—then he hit Charlie. Afterward he was apologetic, promising that it would never happen again, but I'd heard the words a hundred times before with me. I couldn't let him start with the boys. That's when I woke up from my all-American dream and knew that I'd only been fooling myself. Ray would never change.'' Her eyes, filled with tears, lifted to meet her friend's. ''Oh, Casey, I can't tell you…when I saw him hit Charlie…oh, God…'' Her voice failed her and she shook her head, slowly regaining her strength. ''Well, that's all in the past now. I'm through crying tears for Ray James.''

Tears stung the back of Casey's eyes. ''Good for you, Clarisse. He's just not worth it.''

''I know that now.'' Clarisse reached into her purse, took out a tissue and dabbed at her eyes. ''And now that I know that, I've decided to make a new start. Here. In Rimrock.''

''You're kidding!'' Casey cried. ''But why here?''

''Because of you mainly, I guess,'' Clarisse admitted. She unfolded her wallet and withdrew a cashier's check. ''Here's the money you loaned me. I don't know what I would have done without it.'' She tried to hand the check to Casey.

''No, Clarisse, you don't have to—''

''Please, take it back. I've got a little money of my own now. My grandmother came to my rescue, and so the boys and I are fine. We just need to find a place to stay and then I'll look for a job. Eventually Ray will pay child support, so—'' she shoved the check into Casey's hand

"—don't argue with me. I'm a new woman these days. A woman who's in control of her own life."

"Without a job or a roof over her head."

"Temporary setbacks," Clarisse said firmly. She forced a smile. "Things will work out."

"Of course they will."

"Uh-oh." Clarisse was on her feet in an instant and running to the door. Casey looked over her shoulder and spied Brian, face red, tears streaming from his eyes, his mouth open long before he let out a wail loud enough to wake the dead. Just as he began to scream, Clarisse was out the door and across the yard. Snatching him up from the ground, she held him close to her. Casey couldn't hear the exchange, but understood from the devilish look in Charlie's eye that he had either shoved some snow inside Brian's jacket or washed his face with it. Either way, Charlie didn't seem the least bit penitent even though his mother was obviously scolding him while trying to calm his little brother.

Casey glanced down at the check and smiled. Ten thousand dollars plus a little extra for interest. She didn't really want the money. As far as she was concerned, Clarisse could keep it until she got back on her feet, but she didn't want to argue with her friend or her newfound pride.

With Brian propped on one hip and Charlie in tow, Clarisse returned to the open door. "I think we've overstayed our welcome," she said, her breath fogging the air.

"Nonsense. You just got here. Come on in."

"Later, maybe. We're all wet, and besides, I really need to get into town and try to find a motel for the night. I want to start looking for an apartment or a house in the morning."

"I think I can solve that problem," Casey said, her mind already spinning ahead with an idea that would work so well she couldn't believe the family's good luck.

"Don't even suggest we stay here. I wouldn't impose

on your family, especially not with everything else that's
been happening.''

''You won't have to. And come on in, for goodness'
sake. A little melting snow won't hurt this place,'' Casey
insisted, hurrying through the den and snagging her coat
from the clothes tree near the door. The small family
tagged after her. ''Drive me into town. I want you to meet
my soon-to-be sister-in-law. I think you and she can solve
each other's problems.''

''You're scheming,'' Clarisse guessed as they walked
outside again and followed a path broken through the
snow to the parking area. ''I've seen that look before.''

''It's not a scheme. Come on.''

They strapped the boys in the back seat and climbed
into Clarisse's car.

Jenner was talking with Chester in the doorway of the
barn. He spied his sister, and when she ducked into the
car, he started hobbling in her direction, but Casey only
smiled and waved. She was not going to be held prisoner
in her own home, for Pete's sake, and if Jenner didn't like
it, he could follow her into town.

As they drove down the lane, Casey checked the sideview mirror and swallowed a smile when she saw Jenner
rip his hat from his head and throw it into the snow in
frustration. Served him right. He could talk a good story,
but if the situation was reversed and she was bossing him
around and telling him that he had to stay housebound
until God-only-knew when, he wouldn't take it lying
down.

As for Sloan, she was tired of hanging around the house
wondering what he was doing. She'd never been one to
sit idle and she wasn't going to do it a minute longer. Not
for Jenner. Not for Max. And especially not for Sloan
Redhawk.

''I'll buy you a beer when we get into town,'' she said,
winking at Clarisse.

''A beer?''

"Well, a soda, if you prefer. But I think we should celebrate."

"Okay, fine." Clarisse gave her a cautious smile. "Celebrate what?"

"Freedom."

With a laugh, Clarisse said, "You're on!"

They spent the afternoon in town and shared French fries and soft drinks at the Shady Grove Café. Casey felt like a tour guide as she described some of the businesses that had been in Rimrock for over a hundred years and fielded questions from Clarisse about the kidnapping.

"I couldn't believe they thought you were involved," Casey said. "Oh, turn here." She pointed to Pine Street, and Clarisse took the corner. The streets were almost clear, with only a light dusting of snow powdering the pavement.

"I guess my timing wasn't so great," Clarisse admitted. "It's not really a surprise that everyone thought I might be involved. But why would I ever—"

"You wouldn't. Pull in here." Casey indicated a small parking lot near the old Victorian home that Skye had purchased from Doc Fletcher this past summer. The house was huge and rambling and had once housed Fletcher's medical practice in the basement. After his family had moved out, Fletcher had carved the house into apartments and moved his medical practice into a new clinic on an adjacent lot. "This is Skye's place. She bought it before she decided to marry Max and now she's looking for someone to manage it. I thought you might be interested."

Clarisse stared up at the magnificent old building with its wide porch and snow-covered roof. "Surely she must know someone who wants the job."

"Well, there was Jenner, but he wasn't interested. Too tame, you know, and then when Beth showed up, he decided that he needed a place of his own. He's still living in the basement unit, but he and Beth are going to get married around Valentine's Day and move out to an old lodge they plan to turn into a working dude ranch. So if you and the boys can bunk in a one-bedroom unit until Jenner moves out, then you could have the basement. It's not huge, but it does have two bedrooms—an adjustment Jenner made after he found out he was a father—and it would help you get on your feet.''

Clarisse's eyes shone and she swallowed hard. "I don't know what to say."

"Well, whatever it is, save it for Skye. And keep your fingers crossed that she hasn't found someone else."

"I'm sorry, I only have a minute," Skye apologized as she bustled up the laurel-lined walk linking the clinic with the apartment house. "There's a little lull now and I should be doing some paperwork, but my next appointment is in—" she checked her watch and sighed "—twenty minutes."

"This'll only take a little while." Walking briskly up the back steps, Casey made hasty introductions, explaining quickly about Clarisse's predicament without going into the reasons why she and Ray were splitting up.

"It's true I do need a manager," Skye admitted. "Tina Evans, who lives upstairs with her daughter, has been helping me out, but she's changing jobs and doesn't really have the time, and since Jenner's going to move and I'm hardly ever here anymore...well, come on in and let me show you around." She gave Clarisse and the two boys a quick once-over, glanced at Casey and seemed to make up her mind as she snapped on the lights of her kitchen and guided them through her own unit. They had to walk around boxes in the process of being packed. "Excuse the mess, if you can. You could have this place and use the sun-room as the second bedroom," she said, "and then when Jenner moves out downstairs, you can either stay here or move into his place."

Skye's apartment on the main floor was the most

charming. Old woodwork, a fireplace, the sun porch and a large kitchen with a breakfast nook, along with a bedroom, gave the apartment a homey feel. Fresh paint and wallpaper, a new kitchen counter and polished wood floors added to the overall appeal. Jenner's apartment in the basement was more utilitarian with two small bedrooms, a kitchen alcove and living area. Sparsely furnished, it would serve the purpose of providing living space but had none of the ambience of the upper suite.

While the women discussed arrangements, Clarisse's sons ran wild, charging up and down the stairs, shouting and laughing. "I'm not so sure you'd want these two living here," Clarisse said, catching Brian as he raced by.

"Don't be silly. They're wonderful." A wistful look came into her eyes, and Casey felt a pang of regret for her soon-to-be sister-in-law. She knew Skye would love to have a houseful of children but would have to settle for being a part-time mother to Hillary.

"I'll send you a résumé," Clarisse promised as Brian slithered out of her grasp and ran up the carpeted steps leading from the basement to the main floor, "but I haven't worked in years and—"

"You don't need one." Skye's smile was kind as they walked outside and climbed the concrete steps to the backyard. "I need help and you're here. I was hoping that my sister, Dani, might move back here since she and her husband are separating, but she's determined to keep leasing that ranch and training horses." Skye's eyes clouded. "I hope she knows what she's doing."

"If anyone knows her own mind, it's Dani," Casey observed, though she worried a little about Dani, too. She'd always been impulsive, charging through life, and her marriage to Jeff Stewart had been stormy. Casey put a hand on Skye's shoulder. "Quit being an older sister. She'll do fine and she's probably better off without Jeff."

"That's what she says," Skye admitted, "but I don't know if I believe her. Oh, well—" she cleared her throat and extended her hand to Clarisse "—we can write up a contract later and you can move into my apartment next week. When Jenner moves out—"

"Your apartment is perfect," Clarisse said quickly. "It's bigger and we can work out the bedroom arrangement. I can sleep in the sun-room and the boys can double up in the bedroom. It'll be wonderful."

"Good." Skye smiled, then glanced at her watch. "Look, I've got to run. I've got two more hours of patients before I have to meet with the seamstress for a fitting of my dress." She blew a strand of blond hair from her eyes. "This getting married is no picnic."

"You should have just run off to Lake Tahoe and tied the knot," Casey said.

"Tell that to your brother!" With a wave, she was off, hurrying back to the clinic.

"She's wonderful," Clarisse declared as they climbed into her car.

"Yeah," Casey agreed. "She and Max have had their ups and downs, but it's finally working out. Same with Beth and Jenner. It's kind of weird, if you think about it. They've been single so long, and now, within months, they're both getting married."

Jabbing her key into the ignition, Clarisse glanced in the rearview mirror at her two sons. "I don't think I'll ever get married again."

"Never?" Casey was surprised. For as long as she'd known her, Clarisse had been a woman who had only wanted to be married. Even when they had been in college, Clarisse hadn't been interested in a career; she'd only been in school to pass the time until she could marry and raise children.

"I've got the boys," Clarisse said philosophically. She turned the key and the engine caught. "Why do I need a man?"

"I don't know. Won't it be hard, raising your sons alone? Won't you get lonely?"

Clarisse's smile was grim as she eased the car into the slow-moving traffic of Rimrock. "Believe it or not, Casey, I like being by myself. It's just safer."

Casey's heart constricted for her friend and she felt the sting of tears against her eyes. How many times had Clarisse been the victim of Ray's violence? How many times had she feared for her life? For her sons' lives?

Casey wished she could make Clarisse understand that all men weren't like Ray James. But it would take time. A lot of time. "Well, you're starting a new life now," she said, hoping to sound encouraging. "All that's behind you."

Clarisse's jaw clenched. "That's right. A new beginning. Now, what about you? What are your plans?"

An image of Sloan floated through Casey's mind, but of course he wasn't in her future. "I'm not sure," she admitted. "I think I'll stay around Rimrock, too. I've considered substitute teaching, finally using that degree in education. But first I've got to check to see that my credentials are up-to-date."

"You—a teacher? I thought you wanted to be involved with films. Weren't you a producer or something?"

"An assistant to an assistant, but I got tired of L.A."

"So you're back in Rimrock."

"Yeah. Who would have thought it?"

"Not me," Clarisse said, "but, you know, it's not a bad little town. Maybe you'll meet some nice hometown boy."

"This from you—the woman who's never going to walk down the aisle again?"

They sped through the city limits and headed north out of town, past the turnoff to the old copper mine. "Yeah, but you haven't even been down once. So tell me, aside from being kidnapped, what've you been up to? Who's the man in your life?"

Chapter Ten

Sloan was waiting for her. Looking as if he could spit nails, he stood in the parking area as Clarisse stepped on the brakes and slid to a stop.

"Looks like you're in trouble," she whispered.

"Me? No way." But Casey's heart was thudding and Sloan's stern expression didn't change. He strode to the passenger side as Casey opened the door.

"Where've you been?" he demanded, his lips flat with anger.

"In town. Where were you?"

He seemed about to say something, but bit down hard and grabbed her by the arm. "We've been worried—"

"I was with my friend." Smiling despite her anger, Casey motioned to Clarisse, who had stepped out of the car. "Sloan Redhawk, Clarisse James. I think you've met before."

"That's right." Clarisse managed a smile from the other side of the car.

Sloan threw a quick glance at Clarisse as she unstrapped her boys. He tipped his hat, then tightened his grip on Casey's arm and half dragged her to the side of the house, out of Clarisse's earshot. "What do you think you're doing?" he demanded.

"Helping a friend."

"You could have been shot or killed or—"

"But I wasn't, was I? And what do you expect me to do? Sit on my hands while you *men*—you and my mule-headed brothers—decide what's right for me? Well, forget it." She curved a thumb toward the middle of her chest. "I'm my own person, Sloan, and I'm sick and tired of being treated as if I need to be protected or coddled or as though I'm any different from any one of you. As if I don't have a brain of my own. Let me tell you, if Jenner or Max had been abducted, they'd be out for blood right now and they wouldn't let everyone else go out chasing the bad guys. No way, no how. I expect the same is true for you."

A muscle throbbed at his temple. "This is different, damn it."

"Don't you dare say it's because I'm a woman!" she snapped. "Now, if you're done manhandling me and treating me like I don't have a lick of sense..." She yanked her arm back and glared up at him. "From now on, I'm either an active part of your investigation, or I'll work on my own. Either way, I won't be held a damned prisoner. I had enough of that a week ago, thank you very much." Without waiting for a response, she stormed back to a stunned Clarisse.

"What was that all about?" Clarisse asked. She hauled Brian into her arms while Charlie dashed into the snow and flung himself on the ground backward, waving his arms and making a snow angel. Reuben, acting more like a puppy than the old dog he was, romped around the boy and barked excitedly.

"I guess he's my bodyguard. Jenner hired him."

"I know that much, but why the strong-arm tactics?" Clarisse's eyes twinkled as she stared at Sloan, who was still standing near the house, glaring at Casey, his hands thrust into his jacket pockets. "Oh, I get it," Clarisse whispered. "He must be the man you wouldn't tell me about when I asked you who you were seeing."

"No, now wait just a minute—" Casey sputtered.

"You're in love with him, aren't you?" Clarisse cut in, guessing.

"In love? With Sloan?" Casey retorted, tossing her hair over her shoulder. "Are you serious? He treats me as if he's some kind of Neanderthal! He's the last person on earth—"

"Sure he is," Clarisse said, smothering a smile. "Sure he is."

She didn't bother protesting any further and silently cursed herself for wearing her heart on her sleeve. It had always been her failing, she supposed. Because of her hot temper, quick tongue and expressive face, she'd had trouble hiding her true emotions. But *love?* With *Sloan?* Impossible. He wasn't the kind of man who wanted a woman. He'd told her himself that what they each were searching for in life was vastly different—too different. Yet... Oh, Lord, could it be possible?

From the corner of her eye she watched him walk to the barn and she only hoped that he hadn't overheard Clarisse's remarks.

Sloan fed the brood mares and tried to calm down. He'd been a fool, grabbing hold of Casey's arm, treating her as if she were a child, but he'd been scared out of his mind, more frightened than he'd ever been in his life.

When he'd come back to the ranch and found out that she was gone, he'd nearly lost control. Even the fact that she was with Clarisse hadn't convinced him that she was safe, and he was nearly ready to take off after them when the nose of Clarisse's little car had come into view.

Thank God she was safe.

Pouring grain into the manger, he watched as the horses ate eagerly, tails switching, ears flicking at the slightest sound. He'd always loved being with the animals, rubbing their soft noses, scratching their bony foreheads, avoiding swift teeth and hooves. The barn was filled with odors— dust and sweat, urine and leather, grain and manure—all mixed together to bring back memories of his grandfather's ranch.

While living in the city, he'd missed the vast open spaces of the range and the feeling of oneness with beasts of all kinds. Unlike some of the ranchers who hated coyotes, wolves, rabbits and foxes, he'd enjoyed trying to outsmart the pests. Sure, they'd gotten under his skin when they'd attacked his grandfather's herds or garden, but he'd felt it was all part of the game—man against nature. In L.A. it had been man against man. The law versus the criminal. He'd only stayed in Southern California because of Jane.

Jane. Funny, her image had faded in the past few days and he felt a little jab of guilt because he knew the reason why: Casey. Whether he'd wanted to or not, he'd found a woman not to replace his wife, but to become a new part of his life. If he'd let her.

He climbed to the hayloft and kicked several bales over the side, then jumped down and slit the twine holding the bales together. Still thinking of Casey and the ever-present problem of dealing with her, he grabbed a pitchfork hanging from a nail in the wall and shook loose hay into the mangers.

Life was getting too damned complicated.

Though Casey insisted, Clarisse refused to stay at the ranch. She and the boys rented a room at the Lucky Star Motel on Lee Street in Rimrock. Casey argued that they had plenty of room at the ranch, that the Lucky Star was in a bad part of town, that she wanted Clarisse to stick around, but her friend was adamant.

"You've done enough, and besides, I'll see you every day. Just let me do this by myself," Clarisse insisted after they'd finished dinner. "I'm trying to prove myself, remember? The boys and I can't be taking too many handouts."

"It's not a handout," Casey protested, but realized Clarisse wouldn't change her mind. She was just getting ready to leave when Max strode in with Skye, bringing with them the chill winter wind.

"You missed dinner!" Mavis protested. "Kiki!" she yelled toward the kitchen, "Kiki, Max and—"

"We've already eaten," Max said. "We just dropped by because before I left the office I found this on your fax machine." He handed a sheaf of papers to Sloan. "They just came in."

Sloan fingered through the documents and let out a low whistle. "From the boot company—Hardtack," he explained. Seeing Casey's confused expression, he added, "Remember the guy with the boots in the diner?" When she nodded, he continued. "They were unique, so I did some digging, checking out every boot manufacturer who makes cowboy-style boots with silver chains on the heels. Turns out only two make the style that the guy wore and only one sells them in this part of the country. This—" he held up a sheet "—is a list of retail stores where they can be found…and guess what?"

"I couldn't," she said, her mouth suddenly dry.

"One of the outlets for Hardtack Boots just happens to be in Dawson City."

"That doesn't mean anything."

"Not yet," Sloan agreed.

"Boots with chains?" Clarisse said, only half listening as she tried to help Charlie into his jacket and hood. "Like the kind the other private investigator was wearing?"

"What other investigator?"

"Oh, what was his name? Rex Stone, I think. Let me see." She found her purse, pulled out her wallet and drew out a business card with Rex Stone's name emblazoned across it.

"What the devil?" Max muttered as the two men locked gazes.

"What did Rex Stone want with you?"

"Same as everyone else. He thought I might know where Casey was." She looked up at them both. "Wasn't he hired by the family?"

"Yeah," Max said, "but if Stone ever wore a pair of cowboy boots, I'd eat mine."

Clarisse laughed. "He looked like he wore them all the time. And he must've because they'd surely seen better days."

"He never said anything about meeting you."

"It was just the other day."

"In Seattle?" Casey stiffened. "When?"

"Let's see—the day before yesterday, I think." Satisfied that Charlie's hood was in place, she straightened.

"How'd he find you?"

"I asked him that, 'cause no one at the shelter would tell him, I know that. But I'd stopped by there and he saw me. You know, it was almost as if he was waiting for me." She finally noticed the frozen expressions surrounding her. "What?"

"He recognized you?"

"Yes." She looked from one face to another. "What's the matter? Did I do something wrong?"

"Of course not," Casey reassured her. "But two days ago, Rex Stone was here, in Rimrock. Not Seattle. Mom went to visit him in town in the middle of the day. What time did you meet him?"

Clarisse bit her lip. "About one in the afternoon."

"What did he look like?" Sloan asked before Max could say another word.

"Oh, I don't know," Clarisse said. "Like a lot of guys

from around here. Tall and lanky, western-cut suit jacket with jeans and those boots with silver chains on the heels. Three chains, I think.''

"Tall?'' Max repeated.

"Yeah, and kind of weathered-looking, you know, dark skin and too many wrinkles. Oh, yes, and he was wearing a hat and he either had short hair or—''

"A ponytail,'' Sloan guessed.

"I suppose. You don't think he was Stone, do you?''

Max rubbed the back of his neck. "Rex Stone is barely five-eight and weighs over two hundred pounds.''

"Oh, no...'' Clarisse whispered. "Then who was he?''

"That's what I'd like to find out. We saw the same guy in a diner on the way back to Rimrock. The next day we had potshots taken at us.''

Clarisse gasped.

"I'll drive her down to see the sheriff,'' Max offered. "I think he'll want you and Sloan to look at mug shots.''

"I'll do anything,'' Clarisse said, shuddering, her eyes dark with concern. "Oh, Casey, I'm sorry.''

"What did you tell him?'' Sloan asked.

Her face fell. "That I had gotten a message from you and that you were at the Rocking M. He didn't seem surprised at all. I mean, I thought he knew... Oh, God, this is terrible. I probably led him right to you.''

"He probably knew we were on our way here, anyway,'' Casey said, though her stomach was clenched.

"But now he's certain.'' Clarisse looked near tears. "Oh, Casey, what have I done? You've been so good to me and—''

"Don't worry about it, really. We're all fine,'' Casey said, hoping that her face hadn't drained of color.

"But if something happens to you—''

"Nothing's going to happen,'' Sloan said, his hands crumpling the papers he still held in his fist. His brow furrowed in thought.

"You think Stone's in on this then?'' Max asked.

"No!" Virginia said.

"I don't know what to think," Sloan admitted, "but I'm sure as hell going to find out."

Casey read Hillary's Christmas list for the third time but she could barely concentrate on the note naming a dozen different toys she'd never heard of.

Everyone staying at the ranch was seated in the den. Virginia was curled up in a corner of the couch addressing Christmas cards, while Mavis played a game of solitaire at a small table near the window. Sloan, big as life, resting on the small of his back in the desk chair, his long legs stretched out so that he could prop the heel of a boot on the hearth, was deep in a telephone conversation with Max. From Sloan's clipped remarks, she guessed they were discussing her kidnapping. Again. As if she weren't there. As if she weren't involved, for crying out loud. She was sick of it. Tired of being pampered. Anxious to get on with her life.

Her nerves were strung tight being so close to Sloan yet knowing that he was only staying at the Rocking M because it was his job. The walls seemed to be closing in on her, and at times she felt as if she were a prisoner in her own home. That wasn't entirely true, of course, but she wasn't used to having to account for every minute of her time—not even to Sloan.

He hung up the phone and settled back in the desk chair. His eyes narrowed as he stared through the window into the night. "Barry White's being extradited. Should be in Rimrock in a couple of days."

Casey stiffened at the mention of her captor. Images of the cabin flashed through her mind, and her skin crawled. She remembered the fear—the stark, naked terror—she'd felt being at his mercy. "I want to talk to him."

"It won't be that easy," Sloan said.

"I don't care." A slow-burning rage crept through her blood. "I just want to talk to him, okay?" she snapped, then dropped the Christmas list and rubbed her arms. "Because now he's not controlling me. I'm not his hostage anymore. I have a lot of questions I want to ask him."

"He won't talk to you," Sloan said. He reached for a pencil and twirled it in his fingers as if deep in thought. From the hallway, the grandfather clock ticked off the seconds.

"Stay away from that White character," Mavis warned.

"And for God's sake, don't do anything unless you talk to the lawyer." Virginia set her pen and half-written cards aside. "You don't want to jeopardize the case—"

"I don't care about the case!" Casey stood quickly and walked to the window, gazing out at the snow-flocked barn. "I just want to find out who was working with that creep and lock them both away forever. It's time to end this!" She didn't realize it, but she was shaking inside. She was tired of being the victim. Tired of trying to remain calm. Tired of controlling the anger and tamping down the fury that scorched through her veins every time she thought about her abduction.

"We all want to get it over with." Sloan's voice didn't calm her. Instead it reminded her how he wanted to collect his money and leave, end this chapter in his life—a chapter that had briefly and heart-wrenchingly included her.

"I can't stand this anymore—this sitting around. Waiting for something to happen." She stormed out of the den, down the hall and through the kitchen. At the back porch she grabbed her old suede jacket from its peg and rammed her arms into the sleeves. Searching quickly, she found gloves in the pocket and yanked them on as she headed to the barn. As a girl, every time she'd been upset, she'd gone riding, and right now she wanted to feel the wind streaming through her hair, breathe the winter-crisp air and fight back her tears as she rode through the winter night.

"Casey!" her mother yelled from the door. "Casey, what're you doing?"

"Give me a break," she muttered under her breath. Flinging open the door to the barn, she snapped on the lights, grabbed a bridle from the tack room and opened the stall of one of her favorite little mares. "Come on, Jezebel," she said, buckling the chin strap. "Let's stretch our legs."

She sensed Sloan's presence before she saw him. Taking in a deep breath, she turned and found him standing in the doorway, his huge frame silhouetted against the night. "Don't try to talk me out of this," she warned as she led the mare from her stall.

"Wouldn't dream of it."

"Sure."

"You want to go riding. Ride." Glancing up to see if he was teasing, she felt her heart skip a beat. He was staring at her intensely, his dark eyes unreadable, his chin seeming to be chiseled from stone. "I don't blame you."

"You're not going to follow me?"

"Not unless you want me to."

She felt suddenly contrite, as if she'd been acting like a wayward, spoiled child. All that her family and Sloan wanted was to keep her safe. "Look, I just need a little breathing space, all right? I feel like a horse trapped in a two-foot-square stall."

"I'm just trying to keep you alive."

"That's all?" she asked, angling her chin upward, defying him to say more.

"That's what I'm being paid to do."

Her heart seemed to wither. "Right. I forgot. You're in this for the money."

He didn't bother answering, just stared at her with eyes as black as coal. Clucking to the mare, she walked into the paddock, climbed onto the sorrel's back and leaned forward. The snow was too deep to ride fast; she had to be content with a walk, but it was enough. A full moon cast silver light over the landscape and the snow seemed to sparkle as if spangled by a million sequins. The air was frigid against her face and the mare's breath misted the air in two smoky plumes. She rode through the connecting fields and toward a stand of pine, passed the turnoff to Max's house and continued even farther, up a winding trail past the old homestead. The mountains, huge dark hills topped with the outcropping of stone for which the town of Rimrock was named, loomed above her.

The mare stopped. Chestnut ears flicked nervously. Casey's stomach knotted. She remembered the gunman taking shots at her. *Don't be silly!* Casey's heart hammered in fear. Urging Jezebel forward, she pulled on the reins. Here, in the open, she was an easy target, but if she rode into the thicket of pine trees, she'd be harder to spot.

Again the horse balked, stopping dead in her tracks and snorting. "It's all right," Casey whispered, barely able to hear her own voice over the pounding of her heart. "Come on, girl."

Jezebel tossed her head, jangling her reins, and Casey's throat went dry. The wind ripped through the hills with a sudden ferocity. Straining to see, Casey leaned forward and dug her heels into the horse's side. "Let's go," she said, and the feisty mare moved forward into the trees, where long shadows of twisted, bare limbs stretched eerily on the snowy ground.

Casey told herself she was being foolish, that the mare was just skittish about being out at night, that she knew the ranch better than anyone. She'd ridden these ridges, canyons and trails all her life. Still her heart was thundering and sweat collected along her spine. Her breathing was shallow and she urged the mare into a trot.

When the horseman appeared, she nearly screamed. The mare fidgeted, then neighed, just as Casey recognized Sloan, tall and broad shouldered in the saddle, his black Stetson firmly in place. Relief flooded through her, and for a second she wanted to fling herself into his arms.

"I thought you weren't coming," she said, embarrassed by the breathless tone of her voice.

"Changed my mind." He rode his horse close to hers.

Inwardly she warmed, hoping that he'd also had a change of heart. Then she noticed the rifle in the scabbard of the saddle and she reminded herself that he was just doing his job. "What changed it?"

"A call from Hammond Polk." His eyes were mere slits in the darkness, his brows drawn low as he scanned the countryside.

Her heart sank. "What call?" she hardly dared ask.

"A call warning us that Barry White's escaped."

"What? Oh, God." Her insides congealed and she steadied herself in the saddle. "But how—"

"During the transfer, somehow. I don't have all the details, but I gathered he was handcuffed and left alone in a cruiser. The car was idling and someone forgot to lock him in. While the Feds and the locals were discussing how to move him, he hopped into the driver's seat, grabbed the shotgun and started blasting. Injured a guard, got the key and undid his handcuffs, then took off in the car, lights flashing. They chased him, of course, and he eventually drove through a guardrail and into a river. They're busy right now trying to pull the car out of the water. He's probably dead, but we can't be sure."

Will this never end? "You think, if he survived, he might come here?"

Sloan's lips were grim, his nostrils flared. "I'm sure of it," he said, frowning into the surrounding darkness. "Dead sure."

Chapter Eleven

Sloan wasn't taking any chances. As they rode back to the heart of the ranch, he kept his horse close to Casey's little mare. With one hand on the reins, the other on the rifle, he scanned the night-darkened scenery, searching the low brush and scrub oaks, nervous that an unknown assassin was watching.

Surely Barry White was dead. No one could survive a crash like the one described by the sheriff, but until White's body was found, Sloan couldn't be certain. Nor did he have any idea where the lonesome cowboy posing as Rex Stone might be.

Casey's life was in danger, and he was certain she was still the prime target. Before, it seemed, whoever was behind the mayhem at the ranch had been choosing randomly. Certainly the culprit had deliberately planned Jonah's death, but the arson in the stables hadn't been aimed at one individual. The blaze could have wounded or killed anyone, including the livestock. As for Beth's car nearly being run off the road, Sloan suspected it could have happened to Skye or Virginia or Max or anyone connected with the McKees. But now, with Casey as a possible witness, Sloan believed Barry White's partners would be after her. She—not just any member of the McKee family or any McKee property—was the mark. That thought chilled him to the bone.

The night closed in around them and he saw death behind every boulder, felt a killer's gaze on their backs, sensed danger in the frigid air. The horses plodded through the snow, breaking a new trail down a hillside and across a frozen stream. When they were close enough to see the house, its windows bright in the night, Christmas lights strung in bold colors, he felt a sense of relief. They rode through a series of paddocks near the barn, then dismounted. He led his gelding into the barn first, flipping on the lights and making sure that no one was lying in wait.

A few soft nickers greeted them and hooves rustled in the straw. A black-and-white barn cat, on the prowl for mice, slinked past several barrels of grain.

"What? No boogeyman?" Casey quipped as she yanked off her gloves and stuffed them into her pocket. With a grin cast in his direction, she unbuckled the bridle and slid it from the mare's head.

"Not yet." He glanced up to the hayloft and his ears strained for any sound out of the ordinary—the scrape of a boot on the floor, the hiss of a match, the click of a rifle being cocked.

"I think we're safe here," she said, patting Jezebel's nose.

"Maybe." Leaning his rifle against the wall, he tugged off his gloves, uncinched the saddle and slung it over an old sawhorse. He spread the saddle blanket over the top of the stall and expertly removed the bridle, as he'd done thousands of times. The barn did seem safe and warm against the cold winter night. All too easily he could be

lulled into a false sense of security. Just as easily he could
let himself forget who he was, who Casey McKee was,
and get lost in her again. He glanced up and found her in
the empty stall next to Jezebel's staring at him with eyes
that seemed to see straight into his pitch-black soul.

He knew then that he had to kiss her. All the hours of
being with her and denying himself had taken their toll.
There was only so much temptation a man could resist.
He snapped off the lights and walked through the open
stall gate.

He heard her swift intake of breath, saw her face in the
blue light reflecting off the snow and filtering through the
window. Wrapping his arms around her, he drew her
close, his mouth finding hers, his lips hard and demanding, a fire starting deep in his loins. She didn't protest,
but kissed him back hungrily, as if she, too, had been
starved for his touch.

Don't do this, his mind warned, but he couldn't stop.
She tasted so sweet, her lips were so yielding, and desire
rolled through his blood in urgent, hot waves. He reached
for the zipper of her jacket. It slid downward with an easy,
sexy hiss. Reaching inside, he felt her breasts, full and
firm beneath her sweater. *Stop! Now. While you still can!*

Still kissing her, he inched the sweater up slowly, feeling her flesh, warm and supple against his fingertips. She
moaned deep in her throat as he scaled her ribs and
cupped her breast in his palm. "Sloan," she whispered,
"oh, Sloan." He drew down the strap of her bra, felt the
hard button of her nipple between his fingers, pressed
against her jeans with the bulge in his. His mind was on
fire and images of making love to her burned behind his
eyes.

He could think of nothing save loving her. Pressing her
back against the wall, he buried his head in the crook of
her neck and touched her, running his callused hands over
her soft skin. Passion thundered through his brain. He
shoved her jacket off and pulled the sweater over her

head, then stared down at her, watching her chest rise and
fall with her rapid breathing, seeing the cleft between her
breasts, the soft mounds rising over a pale peach-colored
bra, her nipples hard and dark beneath the lace, one strap
falling over her shoulder.

With one trembling finger, he reached forward and
traced the sculpted edge of her bra. "You're too incredibly beautiful," he murmured. "So beautiful." With a
groan he bent his head and began kissing and touching
her, suckling through the gossamer fabric, tugging on
straps, feeling her arms cradle his head even closer as
together they slid to the floor and she was writhing beneath him. He couldn't get enough of her and she arched
forward, pressing more of that sweet, supple flesh into his
mouth.

She moaned deep in her throat and the hardness between his legs burned hot and urgent. He reached for the
waistband of her jeans, heard the series of pops as the
buttons gave way and delved deep with his hand, exploring the soft curls and the hot moist cleft between her legs.
She gave a sharp cry as he touched her, penetrated deep.
"Make love to me," she pleaded, her eyes glazed, her
mouth parted in open invitation. "Oh, Sloan, make love
to me and never stop."

He intended to do just that. Quickly stripping off his
jacket and shirt, he stretched out beside her. He'd take it
slow, prolong this little bit of heaven while they still had
time together. He couldn't think about leaving her, would
push that dark thought to the farthest corner of his mind.
But he would love her tonight as he'd never loved another
woman, as he would never love again.

He stripped her of her bra, gazed at the beauty of her
breasts and kicked off his boots and jeans, then pulled
hers from her. Somewhere, as if far in the distance, he
heard the rumble of a truck's engine and the quiet nicker
of a horse. While staring deeply into her eyes, he slowly
spread her legs with his knees and waited just a heartbeat,

long enough for their gazes to connect and twine, for eternity to shine in her eyes, for him to realize that he would never feel like this with another woman.

His muscles strained and sweat slid down his spine. ''I've never wanted anyone the way I want you,'' he admitted, and she swallowed hard.

''Then take me, please,'' she breathed. ''Now.''

With an anxious thrust, he entered her, felt the liquid velvet of her body sheathing his and knew that his soul was forever fused to hers. Slowly he withdrew only to push forward again, and then he lost control, moving rapidly, thinking of nothing save loving her.

''I love you, Sloan,'' he thought he heard her say, but it might have been the whisper of the wind in the rafters or the wild beating of his heart, he wasn't sure. But the heat within him surged and built, and with a cry he poured himself into her, gathering her into his arms and holding her close, feeling the ecstasy of passion and the agony of despair. For this was the last time they would ever come together as man and woman. He knew it and she did, as well, because he felt her warm tears run down his chest.

''Shh,'' he soothed, but her shoulders trembled as she struggled not to sob. ''It's all right,'' he whispered, his breath ragged, his heart thundering as he lied to her. It wasn't all right. And it never would be. Nothing was, because they could never be together. Still he cradled her, holding her close and gently rocking, waiting for her breathing to slow, hoping that she would someday remember him fondly. When at last she relaxed, he plucked a piece of straw from her hair and murmured against her ear, ''I think we'd better go inside.''

''Not yet.'' She held him tightly, kissed his cheek. His heart ripped a little.

''Casey, just listen. Pretty soon someone will come looking for us.''

''So?''

"You don't care if your mother or your grandmother or one of the hands finds us together?"

"No," she said defiantly.

"Sure. Come on." But he didn't make a move for his clothes and only when he heard the front door of the house bang shut did he swear and grab his jeans.

"Casey? Sloan?" Jenner's voice rang with concern. Casey, startled, reached for her clothes, struggled to find them in the dark, her fingers scraping through the straw to graze the concrete floor.

"Son of a bitch," she heard Sloan growl as he zipped his jeans. "Where the hell's my shirt?"

She found her jeans and wiggled into them. Her bra was on the ground; she stuffed it into her pocket and flung her sweater over her head. Now, her jacket. She searched frantically on the floor before Sloan tossed it to her.

"Where are they?" Jenner muttered, his uneven steps stopping near the door of the barn just as Casey slid her feet into her boots.

Jenner threw open the door and snapped on the lights. "What the hell?" he said, his gaze landing on Sloan and Casey, standing together in the stall. One of Sloan's arms was flung protectively around her waist and Casey could feel the scratch of straw against her skin. She probably looked a sight. A dark scowl crossed Jenner's features as he leaned on his cane. "What's going on here?" he demanded, his eyes narrowing suspiciously on Sloan. "Oh, sh—"

"Stop it!" Casey cut in.

"The two of you? Sloan, you bastard!" His face turned an ugly shade of red.

"It's none of your business, Jenner," Casey insisted, tossing her hair and thrusting her chin forward mutinously. Who did he think he was glaring at them with his condemning stare? As if Jenner McKee had ever come close to being some kind of saint!

"Like hell it's none of my business!"

"Leave it alone," Sloan said.

"What were you thinking about?" Jenner demanded of Sloan. "You were hired to protect her, not to try and get into her pants!"

Casey gasped. "Jenner, don't—"

"She's a victim, for crying out loud! And your responsibility! You're not supposed to take advantage of her!" His nostrils flared and his hands clenched into fists.

"No one took advantage of anyone, Jenner," Casey said, stepping between the two men.

"What's that supposed to mean?"

"That I've been throwing myself at him from the day he saved me."

"Oh, give me a break!" Jenner yanked his hat from his head and slapped it against the wall.

"She's lying." Sloan's voice stopped them both short.

Casey trembled. "No, Sloan—"

"You're right, Jenner. I should have stayed away from her."

"Damned right!"

"This has nothing to do with you, Jenner." Casey whirled on Sloan. "Let's get something straight. No one took advantage of the other one, okay? I'm an adult and so are you and my brother has no right—" she turned and faced Jenner with all her wrath "—*no right* to stick his nose into my business. Got that, Jenner?"

"But Casey, you're—"

"Old enough to make up my own mind. Now, what is it you wanted to tell us?"

He opened his mouth, closed it again, then shook his head. After swearing under his breath and looking at the ceiling to compose himself, he said, "Okay, we'll play it your way, but just for the record, I don't like it."

"Fine. What's going on?"

"A couple of things, but no big surprises, I guess. Clarisse James didn't recognize Rex Stone and so she's going through mug books again, trying to identify the man who really came to see her in Seattle. And—'' he let out a tired sigh ''—they pulled the police cruiser out of the river and Barry White's body wasn't in it. Neither was the shotgun.''

''What?'' Casey's heart slammed against her ribs. ''But—''

''Damn it all to hell,'' Sloan muttered.

''He's either dead in the river or still at large.'' Casey thought she might be sick. Barry White free? Maybe armed? ''They'll dredge in the morning, but until then we'll have to act as if he's nearby and dangerous.'' Casey's legs nearly gave way, but Sloan caught her around the shoulders. Jenner saw the gesture, looked as if he was about to say something, then closed his mouth. He turned and, with the aid of the cane, limped slightly as he headed for the door. ''I'll meet you in the house,'' he said without looking back.

''We're coming.'' Sloan reached for his rifle; his face had become as hard as stone. Casey straightened her shoulders and took a deep breath. She wouldn't live in fear regardless of what had happened to Barry White. That bastard wasn't going to win and ruin her life. No way. No how.

The next day, Jenner, Max and Sloan took turns at the ranch doing odd jobs and chores, but all the while restless and watchful, their main purpose to protect the place and everyone who lived there.

Skye and Dani stopped by with the seamstress who was making the dresses for the wedding. The woman, small, spry and near fifty, was a patient of Skye's. She promised that both attendants' dresses as well as Skye's gown would be finished within two weeks, just in time for the wedding.

They spent hours on fittings, though Dani only went through the motions. As she was in the process of divorcing her husband, the marriage festivities held little interest for her. "Don't get me wrong," she said to her sister in the kitchen after the seamstress had bundled up the nearly-finished gowns and left. "I'm thrilled for you and Max, and you should have been together forever, but it's just that it's a bad time for me."

"I know," Skye said, patting Dani's shoulder. "Things'll work out for you."

"Of course they will," Dani replied, searching in her pocket for a pack of cigarettes. She'd given up smoking years before, but the stress of the divorce had driven her back to her old habit. "I'm going to remain single for the rest of my life. Men are nothing but pains in the butt— well, maybe not Max." She shook out a filter tip, lit up, then blew a stream of smoke toward the ceiling.

"He can be a pain, too," Casey said, trying to lighten the mood. Dani's life hadn't been easy. She'd been a rebel in her youth and there were rumors that she'd had a baby out of wedlock and given it up for adoption; no one really knew the true story or the name of the father. For years she'd hated the McKee family, though Jonah's death had seemed to mellow her, and she'd accepted the rest of the family, even been happy for Max and Skye. But now that her marriage to Jeff Stewart was falling apart, she was caught up in her own problems.

She scowled at her cigarette and crushed it in the ashtray Kiki had provided. "I've got to give these up again."

"You will," Skye predicted.

Surprisingly the day flew by, plans for the wedding, flowers, caterers, photographers and the minister being melded together between phone calls from Rex Stone, the sheriff's department and FBI. Both Christmas and wedding seemed surreal considering the circumstances.

Later that afternoon, the entire family gathered together for an early dinner. Jenner brought Beth and their son Cody, Hillary was with Skye and Max, Virginia and Mavis sat in their usual seats, leaving Casey and Sloan seated next to each other, as if they, too, were a couple, another part of this big family. Sloan didn't seem to mind being included and Casey's heart ached to think that he'd never belong to the McKee clan. She'd finally come to terms with the very simple and awful fact that she loved him. Despite the fact that he was a loner, a drifter, a cowboy with no intention of ever marrying again, she loved him. Blindly. Desperately. Passionately. She probably would for the rest of her life. As the others laughed and talked about the weddings or the holidays or worried over Barry White and the possibility of more treachery being leveled at the Rocking M, Casey was pensive, caught in her own quiet thoughts of ill-fated love.

When would she ever learn?

That night, Sloan couldn't sleep. He felt like a caged animal. He couldn't leave the ranch and yet sensed that he was getting close to breaking the case wide open and finding the culprit. He needed some freedom of movement, but he had to stay close to Casey. Everyone was now in bed and he walked through the house, checking the locks on the doors and windows. Security at the Rocking M had never been strong.

Rimrock was a community where no one had ever locked their doors, where leaving the windows open wide in summer was natural, where people were more concerned about drought or a cattle virus than they were about safety from their fellow man. Most of the windows did latch—those that didn't were in the process of being fixed and were jury-rigged with stakes to keep them shut. The rusty bolts on the doors had been thrown closed so the house was as secure as it could be. Still he was restless.

He didn't bother returning to the bed in Jenner's room, just stayed in Jonah McKee's old recliner in the den, near the center of the house where he could hear noises that didn't belong, see through the windows to the barn and outbuildings. Ears straining, eyes ever watching, he waited.

He heard the sound of feet coming from Casey's room, listened as her door unlatched. His stomach slammed into his diaphragm. He didn't want to see her in the middle of the night, didn't want to be tempted by her wide eyes and soft lips. He steeled himself as she padded into the den and stood before him—a little thing in her white robe and bare feet.

"You gonna stay in here all night?" she asked, yawning.

"Probably."

"Won't you sleep better in—"

"I don't plan on sleeping."

She looked at him with those eyes of hers and his determination started to seep away. Damn, she was beautiful with her hair all mussed from tossing and turning, her eyes still slumberous. "Want some company?" The white robe gaped just a bit, showing a hint of cleavage above the ruffle of her nightgown.

"I'm fine."

"I know but—"

"Casey, please," he said, his voice quiet. "What happened last night—"

"Is over. I know."

He wanted to tell her that it would never be over, that what they'd shared would last forever and could never be matched, but then he thought of Jenner and the condemnation in his friend's eyes. "You should go back to bed."

"Can't sleep." She wandered over to the couch and tucked her legs beneath her.

"Casey…"

"I just want to be out here with you, okay? It's not a crime or anything, is it?"

He snorted. "You'd be better off in bed."

"I'll decide where I'm better off," she said, yawning again, and he didn't contradict her. She stared at him awhile and he kept his vigil, gaze moving from the interior of the house to the outside where the security lights blazed blue against the blanket of snow. "Tell me how Jenner saved your life."

"It's a boring story."

"Come on."

He shifted in the chair, but didn't answer. The swelling in his jeans was commanding most of his attention. Why couldn't she just leave him alone? Even in this room filled with the smells of old, long-banked fires, cold coffee, leather furniture and tobacco from the cigars in the humidor on old Jonah's desk, the fragrance of her perfume lingered and teased his nostrils, conjuring up forbidden images. She was still watching him, waiting for an answer. "Ask Jenner sometime. Now go to sleep."

The old dog, Reuben, lying on a rug near the front door, let out a quick bark and a low growl. Sloan was out of his chair in an instant, but motioned Casey to stay still. He walked to the window and stared out, straining to hear or see whatever it was that had disturbed the retriever.

Ignoring Sloan's warning, Casey climbed to her feet. Reuben was still growling, his eyes on the door, the hairs on the back of his neck standing straight up. Casey's heart was a drum, beating with fear. The dog could have heard anything—one of the barn cats or a night bird or the rustle of a rodent in the shrubbery—but whatever it was, it was still there.

"Get down!" Sloan yelled. "Casey, duck!"

CRASH!

Shards of glass sprayed through the entry hall. She heard a scream and realized it was her own voice. Sloan hurtled forward, pushing her to the floor and holding her down as if he expected another attack. Reuben was barking and jumping at the front door. A rock, larger than a baseball, rolled across the hardwood.

Virginia raced from her room. "Oh my God," she said,

her face white, her eyes wide with fear. "What happened?"

"Shh! Don't turn on the lights, and get down, for God's sake!" Sloan ordered, then whispered into Casey's ear. "Are you all right?"

"I—I think so."

Virginia was sobbing. "Why? Oh, Lord, why?"

"Hush!" Sloan moved on his belly back to the den.

Mavis clomped down the hall. "What the devil's going on— Oh, my goodness!"

"Get down!" Sloan ordered again as he reached the den. He grabbed Barry White's shotgun, extra ammunition and pistol and, still crouching low, dashed back to Casey, who was leaning against the wall. "You know how to shoot?"

She let out a nervous laugh. "I'm Jonah McKee's daughter, aren't I?"

"Then use this if you have to," he snapped, shoving the shotgun into her hands and handing her extra shells.

"Where are you going?"

"After him."

"No, Sloan! It might be what he's waiting for. He only threw a rock through the window, and if you run outside he'll probably shoot you."

"If he was planning to shoot, he would've tried to break in."

"You can't take the chance—" She clung to him, but he peeled her hands from his shirt.

"Stay here. Call Max. And if the dog starts barking again, shoot first and ask questions later." Without thinking, he kissed her long and hard on the mouth, his fingers twining for a second in her hair. "Don't forget, call Max and the police."

He unlocked the dead bolt and threw open the door. The fool dog took off, barking and carrying on loudly enough to wake the dead. Somewhere in the lane, an engine sparked to life and tires screeched.

"Hell!" Sloan muttered as he rushed out through the open door and flattened against the wall of the porch. No crack of a rifle. No whine of a bullet. Crouching low, he raced to his old truck, flung open the door and slid quickly behind the wheel. This time he wasn't going to give up. This time he'd catch the bastard. Or die trying.

Casey's stomach was knotted with fear. She sat near the door, sweaty hands gripping the shotgun, silently praying that Sloan was safe. She'd called the sheriff's department as well as both her brothers, and now she was huddled near her grandmother and mother. Waiting. The wind whistled through the broken window of the darkened house.

The sound of a truck's engine split the night and her heart soared. He'd come back. She waited patiently, then heard the welcome sound of boots. "Casey? Mom? Grandma?" Her brother's voice boomed through the air.

Max! Casey shoved open the door. "Oh, Max!" she cried, falling into her brother's arms.

He held her fiercely. "Has Sloan come back yet?"

"No," Casey said, her lower lip trembling a little. "He's still off chasing whoever did this." Max snapped on the lights just as the Casey heard sirens wail in the distance.

"Is anyone hurt?"

"No." Casey shook her head. "They probably threw the rock just to scare us...or lure us outside."

"Why?" Max asked, his eyebrows drawing together as red and blue lights flashed in the lane, splaying over the walls, and the shriek of sirens rent the air. The temperature in the house had plummeted and Max's breath was a cloud. "Why would anyone do this?" He stared at the broken window and the black rock lying against the hallway wall, still wet from being buried in the snow.

"I wish I knew," Casey said, peering out the window as Hammond Polk and a deputy raced from their cars to the house. Why a rock through the window—a warning of some kind? Or just another way to scare them? She opened the door for the sheriff, but her thoughts were miles away. On Sloan. *Please God, keep him safe. Don't let him be hurt because of me.*

Sloan's truck slid to a stop at the first red light in town. He'd never seen a hint of the attacker, not even a glimpse of his vehicle. The bastard had either pulled onto a side road and waited until Sloan passed by, or driven like a bat out of hell without the use of his lights.

Fear congealed in his blood. What if the man had waited near the ranch, lured Sloan away, then returned? He reached for the cellular phone, punched out the number for the Rocking M and felt an immense sense of relief when Max answered. The authorities were already at the McKee ranch and Max was boarding up the window until a glass company could be called in the morning. Everyone was safe, though jittery. Max had even taken the precaution of sending Skye back to her apartment house to be with Jenner, Beth and Cody, rather than leave her alone. Hillary, too, was safe, asleep in her bed at Colleen's place in Dawson City. So everyone connected with the McKees was accounted for.

But Sloan wasn't going to give up.

It was near closing time at the Black Anvil, but a few rigs were still parked outside. Jimmy Rickert's vehicle was in its favorite spot and Sloan decided to gamble. Jimmy seemed to know everything about everyone in town and for the right amount of money he could be convinced to talk. Except during all this McKee business, Jimmy had been closemouthed. Sure, he'd told Jenner about old Jonah being in some kind of argument with a guy on the night he'd been run off the road, but the details had been spotty, the story incomplete, and Sloan was willing to bet that Jimmy, given the proper inducement, could be persuaded to spill his guts. One man wandered out of the bar, hitched up his pants and spit tobacco juice from the corner of his mouth before finding the keys to a big Chevy Suburban and driving away.

Sloan's fingers drummed on the steering wheel. Who hated the McKees—not just Jonah but the whole lot of them? He dismissed Randy Calhoun as a suspect because, even though Jonah had fired Randy, Jenner had stuck up for the hired hand. Casey seemed to like him, too, and it didn't make a lot of sense that Randy would try to take out his frustrations not only on Jonah, but on the entire family, as well.

Slim Purcell was low on the list, too. He wasn't clever enough. Though he'd been cheated out of a racehorse, he didn't seem to hold a grudge, and between him and Barry they didn't have enough brains to plot and execute Casey's kidnapping.

Fred Donner was a possibility. He'd lost his family's homestead and he might hate the rest of the McKees as well as Jonah, and also envy them their ranch. But would he kidnap Casey and put Jenner's kid's life in danger? For what? Half a million dollars—his split of the take— when Max was trying to work a deal with him to give him back his land? It didn't seem likely, but men had been known to do much worse for a lot less. Half a million wasn't anything to sneeze at. Fred was definitely a candidate, but certainly not the most likely.

Sloan rubbed his jaw impatiently. Who?

Corey Stills blamed Jonah for stealing his wife. Would he be vindictive enough to kill Jonah and torture his family? Would he gain some sick sense of satisfaction in nearly killing Jenner and scaring the bejesus out of Casey? But why? He couldn't even rub Jonah's nose in the family's terror. It would have made more sense for Corey to do the terrorizing first, make Jonah twist in the wind a little by seeing what havoc was being wreaked on his family before killing him.

Sloan bit his lip and thought. Steve Jansen didn't have

much motive, but his half brother was Barry White. Most of Steve's dealings with the McKees were through his father and Ned had a helluva motive. He'd lost a copper mine that was supposed to have been worthless. Then Jonah took over and discovered plenty of ore, proving that the original geological survey was falsified. Now that could make a man angry—but angry enough to kill? And after Jonah was dead, why keep harassing the McKees?

Unless there was another reason.

A deeper reason for hatred. But what? What would cause someone to want to hurt not only a man, but his family, as well?

The door of the Black Anvil opened again and Sloan felt a smile tug at the corners of his lips. Jimmy Rickert stopped, belched, fumbled in his pocket for his keys and found his way to his beat-up, four-wheel-drive rig. He drove out of the parking lot and Sloan slipped his truck into gear. Jimmy didn't know it, but he was going to have a surprise visitor when he got home.

Casey eyed the sheriff who looked like a beaten man. In all his years as keeper of the peace, Hammond Polk had never left a case unsolved—until now. And he was fit to be tied from the looks of him. He surveyed the mess in the hall for the fourth time and gratefully accepted a cup of coffee from Virginia. Frustrated, he'd questioned everyone in the family, determined to discover where the attacker had been standing when he'd hurled the rock through the window.

Even Rex Stone had made his way to the ranch, where he'd somewhat defensively admitted to everyone that he'd never met Clarisse James. He'd intended to pay her a visit, but had never gotten around to it because Casey had been so adamant about her friend's innocence. Obviously someone had impersonated him, but he couldn't guess who. He was given a description of the man in hopes that he would remember handing him a business card, but Rex, looking foolish, had shaken his head.

"Anyone can get one of my cards. Even when I'm not in the office, they're in a little holder on my receptionist's desk. I'll ask her in the morning, of course, but I can't imagine who the guy is."

Max scowled at the rotund investigator and Casey could read his thoughts. Though Virginia believed that Rex Stone would eventually find Jonah's killer, none of her children had any faith in the slick private detective. He'd had plenty of time, come up with a list of suspects that could be connected to the crime but had found nothing concrete. "Don't just check with your receptionist," Max advised. "Find the bastard."

"And how am I supposed to do that?"

"You tell me. You're the private detective."

Rex left the house muttering under his breath. Hammond Polk once again shook his head at the mess. "We'll find the perpetrator, Virginia. Don't you worry." But he didn't sound his usual confident self.

Mavis stomped her cane against the floor. "Well, you'd better do it fast, Hammond. 'Cause next time it might not just be a rock—maybe one of them firebombs or dynamite or heaven-only-knows what else!"

"We're trying, Mavis."

"Then try harder. I haven't voted for you for the last three terms just to hear that you try. Do something."

Casey couldn't help but smile. In true McKee fashion, Mavis believed that by simply demanding results she would get them.

Hammond finally left, and Virginia, after downing aspirin, headed back to bed. Mavis, despite Max's urging to try to get some rest, stayed up with them. "If I were younger, I'd take off after the culprits myself."

"God help us," Max growled.

"That's not all. When I found 'em, I'd wring all their scrawny necks!"

"Barry White's neck isn't scrawny," Casey said, remembering her captor and shivering.

"I already told you what I'd do to that one. String him up by his private parts, that's what. Now, anyone else for a cup of hot cocoa?"

"No thanks, Grandma," Casey said, tagging after the older woman as she headed to the kitchen. Casey's stomach was already in knots with worry for Sloan and she knew she wouldn't be able to keep anything down.

While Mavis heated milk, Casey grabbed the broom from the pantry and began sweeping up the chunks of glass in the hallway. Max secured the house again and decided he'd spend the rest of the night at the ranch or stay until Sloan returned.

Where was he? Casey wondered. She'd been relieved when he'd called, but now, as the minutes passed with no word from him, she was beginning to worry all over again.

Jimmy Rickert lived in a rented shack on an old, bone-dry piece of ground just outside of town. Sloan, parked on a side street, watched the snitch weave drunkenly up the steps and let himself in the front door. He slammed it shut and snapped off the porch light.

"Don't you know there's no rest for the wicked, Jimmy?" Sloan asked softly as he walked through the trampled snow leading to the porch and leaned on the bell.

The porch light, a single yellow bulb, lighted up again. "What the hell?" Jimmy said, opening the door in his stocking feet.

"I think we need to talk."

"No way. I'm beat." He tried to push the door shut, but Sloan was too quick and moved through the crack into a parlor with stained walls and bare floors. "Hey! Whaddya think you're doin'?"

"I'll ask the questions."

"Get out."

"Not yet."

"I'll call the police."

Sloan grinned. "Do that," he said. "I think they'd like to hear what you have to say."

"I'm not sayin' nothin'."

Sloan heard a door open behind him and looked over his shoulder to see a thin woman with mousy brown hair and pale skin standing in the doorway to a bedroom. A threadbare chenille robe was wrapped around her body and her feet were bare.

"Hey, you, Maryellen. G'wan back to bed!" Jimmy slurred, waving a finger at her. "He's leavin'."

"Maybe she wants to hear what I have to say."

Jimmy leaned against the wall and crossed bony arms over his chest. "She don't do nothing I don't tell her to do."

"Then she's not interested in twenty-five thousand dollars?"

Jimmy's eyes slitted and the woman didn't move. "That's the reward for information about Jonah McKee's killer."

"I know it," Jimmy said, nodding his head nervously. "So what?"

"I think you could probably collect."

"If I knew who the killer was, don't you think I would've claimed the money before now?"

"Not if you were too scared."

Jimmy sneered. "I ain't scared of nothin'!"

This was where Sloan gambled. He sauntered up to Jimmy and towered over the smaller man. "Not even Barry White?"

Jimmy made a sound of disgust in the back of his throat. "He's nothin' to me."

"He's escaped you know. Drove a police cruiser into the river, and guess what—they can't find his body."

Jimmy's Adam's apple bobbed nervously. "So?"

"He probably knows that you told the police about the

argument you overhead in the parking lot on the night Jonah was killed.''

"Don't bother me.''

"Maybe it should. 'Cause even if you're not afraid of Barry, you know that his partner's trouble, don't you?''

"Don't know who he is.''

"I think you do.'' Sloan slid a glance in Maryellen's direction and the woman licked her pale lips nervously. "All you have to do is name him and you've got twenty-five grand and probable immunity from prosecution.''

"I ain't done nothin' wrong!'' Jimmy protested.

"It's against the law to withhold evidence. A man…or a woman could end up spending a good amount of time in jail.''

Maryellen let out a soft moan.

"Quiet!'' Jimmy ordered.

"But the baby,'' she said, touching her slightly rounded abdomen. "Jimmy, we got to think of the baby.''

"Quiet, I said!'' Jimmy's face was flushed, his eyes wild. "We don't know nothin', y'hear. Nothin'!''

"You got a kid on the way, Jimmy?'' Sloan asked as Jimmy reached into the pocket of his T-shirt for a crumpled pack of cigarettes.

"What of it?''

"Won't help him to have his pa in jail.''

"I'm not in jail.''

"Not yet. But you will be.''

"What makes you so sure?''

"Hammond Polk's unhappy. He's up for reelection in a year or so and he wants to solve this case and look good to the voters. Best way to do that is to find Jonah's killer and lock him behind bars.''

"Jimmy—''

"Shut up!'' he yelled, striking a match then sucking in a deep lungful of smoke.

"Think about it, Jimmy. What have you got to offer

her or your kid? You want him to have the same miserable existence you had?''

"It weren't so bad.''

"No? Well, with the reward you could start over, maybe look into buying a place of your own.''

"Listen to him,'' Maryellen said, suddenly lifting her chin.

Sloan decided to gamble. "Besides, it's just a matter of time before we get the goods on Jansen—then it'll all be over and you'll be out the money.''

Maryellen gasped.

"How did you know—wait a minute.'' Jimmy's cigarette bobbed up and down in the corner of his mouth and smoke drifted from his nostrils.

"He hired a man to kill us, the cowboy with the boots who impersonated Rex Stone in Seattle. The law's on to him—it'll just be a matter of days before he's hauled in and implicates Jansen.''

"Jimmy…'' Maryellen pleaded.

"Son of a bitch,'' Jimmy said, plucking the cigarette from his mouth. "Son of a goddamned bitch.'' He smoothed back his thinning hair, looked at the woman carrying his child and sighed. "All right, Redhawk. Let's you and me make a deal with the sheriff,'' he said, studying the tip of his cigarette. "I get to walk free and collect the reward in exchange for my testimony against Ned Jansen.''

Chapter Twelve

Dawn was breaking when the telephone jangled. Casey nearly jumped out of her chair, but Max reached over his head, picked up the receiver and said, "Rocking M." Was it Sloan? Clutching her cup of coffee in a death grip, Casey was seated at the table with her mother, grandmother and Kiki. Barely daring to breathe, she watched as Max shook his head. "Ned Jansen? You're sure?" A pause. "Hell, that's been over thirty-five years."

The women exchanged glances. Ned was behind the attack? Casey's mother nearly dropped her cup.

"Yeah, well, Jimmy Rickert would say just about anything to get his hands on twenty-five grand." There was a pause while Max listened intently to the conversation. He propped a boot on the rungs of his mother's chair and swore under his breath. "Okay, okay. We'll wait. Yeah, we're all here." He hung up and his eyes were dark. "Ned Jansen's been arrested. He hasn't confessed to anything yet and wants an attorney. Guess which one."

"Reggie Camp," Casey said, remembering the name of the man who was representing Barry White.

"One and the same."

"Oh, Lord," Virginia whispered.

"Why would Ned kill Dad or burn the stables or—" Casey caught the warning look in her brother's eyes, and when she glanced at her mother she swallowed hard. Tears filled Virginia's eyes. "Mom?"

"This is because of me," Virginia replied shakily. "Not your father."

"I don't understand—"

"Oh, piffle!" Mavis muttered. "You can't believe that! Just because years ago you were dating Ned when you met Jonah."

"It was more than dating him. I...we...well, Ned and I had talked about getting married."

"Mom, it's been so long ago. This couldn't possibly have anything to do with you. Think about it. If he'd wanted some kind of revenge, why would he wait so long?"

"I think..." She hesitated and bit her lip, then drew in a shuddering breath. "I don't think it started with me. Years ago, when I broke it off with Ned and told him I was going to marry Jonah, he was livid. I'd...well, I'd never seen anyone so angry. He almost hit me, but thought better of it." Her eyes glazed over as the memories of her youth ran through her mind. "He told me that I'd get mine, that marrying Jonah would ruin my life."

"Hogwash!" Mavis said. "Marrying my son was the smartest move you ever made. Who was Ned Jansen? A nobody, that's who! And look at him. How many times has he been married and divorced? Three, the last I counted. Probably more. Nearly broke him with all that alimony and child support."

"And losing his copper mine to Dad," Max added.

"Ned Jansen never had a lick of sense." Mavis took a long swallow from her cup.

"So why go after us now?" Casey wondered aloud. "This is all ancient history."

Mavis nodded, her firm McKee chin thrust forward defiantly. "That's right."

"No one's sure yet, but the theory is that the copper-mine deal pushed Ned over the edge. He was already in trouble financially, and when Dad ended up with the mine and it was suddenly valuable, Ned decided to get even. But he couldn't stop there. Killing Dad wasn't enough. He wanted to destroy everyone and everything Dad cared about."

"Because of me." Virginia set her cup on the table. Nervously twisting her wedding ring, she shook her head, as if fighting a losing battle with her guilt.

"And because his life fell apart. He never found another woman who would stand by him the way you stood by Dad." Max scowled darkly. "Anyway, he's in custody, and once they locate Barry White's body, I guess the mystery is solved and we can get back to our normal lives again."

"Ain't nothin' ever been normal here," Kiki said, scooting back her chair and reaching for the coffeepot. She refilled everyone's cup, then went to wash her hands. "May as well start breakfast. I imagine Hammond Polk will be out here soon enough trying to get all the credit for a job well done when we all know that without Sloan Redhawk this case would still be unsolved."

Sloan. Casey's heart was suddenly heavy. He'd done his job. All he had to do now was collect his payment and move on. She hurt so badly inside, she could barely speak. What would she say to him when he showed up at the ranch to collect his things? How would she say goodbye?

Sloan was bone tired as he drove back to the ranch. It had been a long night and the satisfaction of solving the mystery still eluded him. Returning to the Rocking M, he realized how attached he'd become to these solitary, snow-covered acres. The land was vast and wide, the mountains red giants that knuckled into flat rises and plateaus. But most of all this place reminded him of Casey.

He felt an unexpected tug on his heart at the thought of her, and as he parked his truck near the barn, he wished there was some way to come to terms with her. Instinctively he knew that he'd never meet another woman like her and he only wished he'd had the sense and common decency not to have made love to her. It seemed whenever she was around, he lost his head.

So now he'd be moving on. With enough money in his pocket to start a new life. A life alone. The realization settled like lead in his stomach, but he told himself he'd get over it.

He walked to the house and nearly stopped when he saw her, standing alone on the porch, the breeze lifting her hair from her face, her arms wrapped around her middle. She looked as if she'd been waiting for him all day, the wife searching the horizon expectantly for the return of her husband.

She managed a smile, frail that it was, and he couldn't help himself. He opened his arms, and she fell into them and held him close. She smelled of lilacs and something deep inside him broke. No doubt he'd spend the rest of his life hoping for a whiff of just that scent.

"I was worried about you," she said, sniffing and fighting back the tears that threatened her eyes. "So worried."

"No need." God, it was nice to have someone care. He looked up and saw Jenner, his gaze thoughtful as he stared at them.

"I guess you earned your money, Redhawk."

"Looks like."

"Come on in. Max'll make out a check."

"Sure thing," he replied, wondering why the money didn't excite him, why the thought of buying his grandfather's old place didn't cause his heart to leap. Extricating himself from Casey's embrace, he winked and tipped his hat. "Nice knowin' ya."

"Yes," she said huskily, her eyes bright with unshed tears.

Together they walked inside to the den, where Max had already written the check. "This calls for a drink," he said, handing the payment to Sloan. Clapping him on the back, he said, "I guess my brother's faith in you was well-founded."

"I owed him one. Now we're even."

"Yeah, what was that all about?" Max asked.

Jenner poured whiskey into several glasses, and Sloan, though Jenner had made him swear never to talk about it, decided it was time to clear the air. "It happened in Wyoming, a bar in some little obscure town. I can't even remember the name."

"During a rodeo?" Max guessed.

"No reason to dredge it all up again," Jenner protested, but Sloan intended to have his say.

"It was one of those barroom things. A guy was hitting on this woman. He was all over her and she didn't like it. Told him to get lost several times, but he still kept pawing her, so I stepped in. The guy took offense and came at me with a knife." Sloan shook his head at the memory. "Jenner was with me at the time. Hell, I never saw anyone move so fast. Just as the guy lunged, swinging that blade at my throat, Jenner here stepped in. The knife slashed at my chest, cutting through my jacket, but Jenner slammed the guy against the wall and beat his fist against a table until he dropped the knife."

"No big deal," Jenner mumbled.

"Depends on what side of the blade you were on. It was a big deal to me."

"And now we're square."

"Right." He glanced at Casey. "Except that Barry White's still on the loose."

"Not for long. Polk called. Looks like they picked up

his trail north of Dawson City. Dogs are tracking him. They think he'll be in custody by nightfall."

"Good," Sloan said, then realized he had no reason to stay. He folded the check into his wallet.

Max cleared his throat. "You know, we can't thank you enough."

"No need."

"No, I mean it. If it wasn't for you, Casey might never have been found and—"

"But I was," Casey said with a toss of her head. Her eyes still bright from her fight against tears were steady with determination. Crossing the room, she extended her hand. "Thanks, Sloan. Now it's my turn to owe you."

He shook his head, but saw a glint in her gaze. "Goodbye," she said, and he'd never realized until just that moment how final that word could sound.

Hours later, it was over. Ned Jansen, breaking down completely, had confessed to everything. He even named the man he'd hired to kill Sloan and Casey—a drifter by the name of Mitchell Cox—and told Hammond Polk where he was hiding. A deputy reported back that Cox had been arrested.

The FBI had come and gone and Sheriff Polk was proud of himself, even if Sloan had broken the case. It was just a matter of time before Barry White would be hauled in and that would be that. Jonah McKee's murder, the arson, the attack on Beth's car, Casey's kidnapping—everything solved. And one neat feather for his cap. Yep, Hammond left the ranch full of himself, and Casey felt empty inside.

She was relieved that the trauma was over, but the thought of Sloan leaving caused an ache deep inside. She paused at the door to Jenner's old room and felt cold to the marrow of her bones. Then, because she couldn't stand another second of sitting in the house and pining for him, she found her jacket and boots and took off for the barn. She'd go riding. This time alone. This time with-out fear. Even though her heart was cracking.

"Come on, Jezebel," she said as she entered the barn and switched on the lights. She had just reached for the bridle when she saw him. Mud streaked and unshaven, his eyes ablaze with anger, Barry White was crouched be-neath the ladder to the hayloft. She tried to scream, but before she could utter a word, he jumped and pressed one grimy hand hard against her lips, while the other held her firmly against him.

"Now listen!" he growled. "You're my ticket out of here. I know that Ned sold me out, but I'm not goin' down, got it?"

She nodded, but her mind was spinning ahead. She knew that she would never allow him to victimize her again. "You're going to drive one of the rigs from the ranch away from here and you're going to take me with you. To Canada, just like in the original plan. Then I swear I'll let you go. I never did hurt you before now, did I, Casey?"

She wasn't even listening to his excuses because now she knew how violent he was. Hadn't he shot a state trooper or policeman, then probably crashed his car on purpose to give him time to escape?

"Okay, now remember, I got this here gun, and if I have to, I'll use it, so you go real quiet like and walk over to one of the trucks. I'll follow along and no one will be the wiser."

He turned toward the door as headlights flashed through the windows. "Damn!"

Without a second's hesitation, she rammed the heel of her boot into his shin. He let out a howl, and she spun, kneeing him in the groin as he fumbled with the gun. Horses neighed wildly. With a holler, he grabbed his crotch, and she whirled away from him and ran backward trying to reach the door.

"Stop!" He leveled the barrel of the rifle at her and

she dropped to the floor, crawling snakelike to cover behind a barrel of oats. "Stupid move, Casey," he rasped, his breathing short, anger making his words tremble. Oh, God. She couldn't just cower here, waiting for him to lunge. She looked around wildly and then reached upward, knocking the pitchfork from the wall.

"Ain't no little pitchfork gonna save you."

"Help!" she yelled, then screamed at the top of her lungs.

"Son of a bitch!" Barry kicked the oat barrel aside.

The door flew open and Sloan dived into the room, knocking Barry to the floor. The gun exploded. Horses screamed in terror. Shouts erupted from the house as the two men struggled, grunting and cursing, rolling on the floor. Casey picked up the pitchfork and forced the wicked tines into Barry's leg. He squealed, but didn't give up his hold. Barry had his hands around Sloan's neck, but Sloan was astride the other man, intent on pounding his head against the floor.

Casey saw the rifle and grabbed it, pulling it to her shoulder and aiming right at Barry's balding head. "Stop!" she commanded. "Stop it right now, or I swear, I'll kill you!"

Barry's hands dropped to his sides just as Max ran into the barn. "What the hell? Oh, God! Casey, are you all right?"

"I'm fine," she said as Sloan hauled Barry to his feet.

"Call the sheriff," he said.

Max grinned wickedly. "Should we let Grandma at him first? She has plans for this one." Casey remembered just how Mavis thought she might teach Barry a lesson.

Using baling twine, Max tied Barry's hands behind his back, then marched him back to the house. Casey started to follow, but Sloan pulled her back into the barn. "Don't you want to know why I came back to the ranch?"

She squared her shoulders and braced herself. "Why?"

"I forgot something."

Her heart squeezed a little. "What's that?"

He looked long into her eyes and then drew her closer to him. "You, Casey. I forgot you."

"You what?" she whispered, barely daring to breathe.

"I had just about reached the city limits of Rimrock when I realized that what I was leaving was more important than what I was running to—and that's what I was doing. Running. Because you scared me."

"Scared you?" she repeated, her heart thundering. "I didn't think you were scared of anything."

"Oh, there was one thing."

"Which was?" she prodded, hardly able to catch her breath.

"Love." He groaned and touched her forehead with his. "I didn't want to fall in love again. Not with anyone and especially not you. You were too alive, too stubborn, Jenner's little sister. But I couldn't help myself."

Her throat chocked up with emotion and she could barely speak.

"Casey, why I came back, why I couldn't leave is because I don't want to spend another day without you." He brushed a strand of hair from her cheek. "I want you to marry me."

"Oh, Lord—"

"And I want you to come to Warm Springs with me. Help me buy a ranch. Find the right place for us. For our children."

"Ch-children?" Her heart soared. Could this be real?

"I love you."

She couldn't believe her ears. "But—"

He placed a finger to her lips. "If you say no, I might just have to kidnap you myself." He held her so tightly she could hear the pounding of his heart, see the raw emotions in his eyes. "I came back to ask you to marry me and then I found you with Barry White and I thought I'd lose you all over again." He blinked rapidly and his dark eyes shone. "Marry me, Casey McKee, and I'll promise to make you happy for the rest of your life."

She couldn't help but smile. "You already have, Sloan," she whispered. "You already have."

Poinsettias filled every corner of the house. Holly, mistletoe and ivy were strung along the mantels and through the hallways. Millions of tiny white lights winked in garlands strung with miles of red ribbon.

Skye was in white, her simple gown touching the floor as she stood with Max in front of the preacher and exchanged vows. Casey watched the ceremony and her heart was filled to overflowing as she witnessed her brother marrying the woman he'd always loved. They shared a private secret, one that Skye had whispered to Casey just before the ceremony. Skye was pregnant. Despite the odds against it, she and Max had conceived a child. She planned to tell him tonight, on their honeymoon.

Casey couldn't help beaming. She shot a glance across the sea of guests standing in the living room and spied Sloan near the windows. Her life was so full and she loved him so much. They planned to marry soon, just after Jenner and Beth, then move to Warm Springs.

Everyone seemed blessed today. Even Dani was smiling at her sister, and Clarisse, escorted by her two boys, caught Casey's eye and winked. But Casey only had eyes for Sloan. He was staring at her so intently, she blushed. They shared a secret smile, but Sloan waited until the bride and groom had greeted all of their guests and were busy pouring champagne and cutting the cake before he pulled Casey outside.

"What are you doing?" she asked, laughing when he kissed her bare neck. She trembled, as much from his kiss as the snow-laden breeze.

"I have something for you."

"What?"

"A pledge."

She didn't know what to say as this man she loved handed her a cream-colored envelope. She opened it slowly. Inside was a diamond ring, along with a letter. She read the words and tears filled her eyes, then she turned to him and he slipped the ring over her finger.

"I love you," he whispered as the wind kicked up and lifted the hem of her skirt. Somewhere in the distance, a horse neighed.

"And I love you."

"Forever?"

"And a day."

She smiled up at him and laughed at the snow catching on his eyelashes. She would spend the rest of her life with this cowboy. Finally, after years of searching, she'd found everything she wanted in life and oh, so much more.

Dear Casey,

I'm not much for words, so I'll be brief.

I never thought I'd fall in love again, never thought I'd want to settle down with a woman and raise children, but you've brought me past my pain, made me see that there is a tomorrow.

I vow to love you and our children forever. Trust me and know that I'll always be at your side.

Until eternity,
Sloan

* * * * *

Watch for Lisa Jackson's new miniseries coming in Special Edition in late 2000, only from Silhouette Books!

Author Note

Dear Reader,

I hope you enjoyed the Love Letter Trilogy. It was an exciting project and now that the murder of Jonah McKee has been solved and the three couples happily married, I hope that I'll be able to write more stories about the citizens of Rimrock and their lives and loves.

In the future I plan to write *D Is for Destiny,* the story of Dani Stewart, Skye Donahue's sister.

Thank you for reading the Love Letters Trilogy from Silhouette Special Edition. I look forward to continuing with the series and hope you do as well.

Warmest regards,

Lisa Jackson
333 S. State St. Suite #308
Lake Oswego, OR 97034

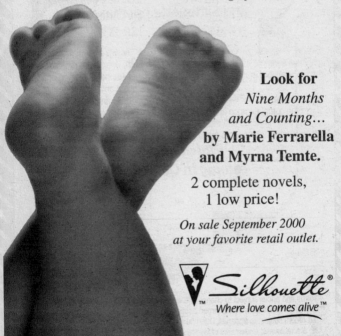

***Don't miss
an exciting opportunity
to save on the purchase of
Harlequin and Silhouette books!***

Buy any two Harlequin or
Silhouette books and save
$10.00 off future Harlequin
and Silhouette purchases

OR

buy any three
Harlequin or Silhouette books
and save **$20.00 off** future
Harlequin and Silhouette purchases.

***Watch for details
coming in October 2000!***

PHQ400